Murmurs, whis[...]
these rose from [...]
wife, Rebecca, had heard about, maybe read
about, this kind of hypnosis. The goal was to find
out who you had been in a past lifetime.

"Where are you now?" Perry asked softly.

"Nowhere."

"But you are still you, aren't you? Are you still
Harrison Wayne Thorwald?"

"No."

"Then who are you? Do you have a name?"

"I am what I am. I am myself, I am me."

"Go back further. The year is now 1915. Tell
these good folks where you are."

Hank hesitated. Then: *"Ich kämpfe in Frankreich."*

"He's speaking German," Rebecca said incredulously.

"You're fighting in France? Who are you fighting?"

"Die Franzosen."

"You're fighting the French?"

"Ja."

"Just who in the hell are you, Hank?"

*"Ich bin Gefreiter in den Gräbern des grossen
Krieges."*

"He said, 'I am a corporal in the trenches of the
great war.' "

"And what is your name, Corporal?"

A horrible, breathless silence clutched the
room. . . .

KATASTROPHE

RANDALL BOYLL

AVON BOOKS
An Imprint of HarperCollinsPublishers

This is a work of fiction. Names, characters, places, and incidents are products of the author's imagination or are used fictitiously and are not to be construed as real. Any resemblance to actual events, locales, organizations, or persons, living or dead, is entirely coincidental.

AVON BOOKS
An Imprint of HarperCollins*Publishers*
10 East 53rd Street
New York, New York 10022-5299

Copyright © 2000 by Randall Boyll
ISBN: 0-06-109750-0
www.avonbooks.com

First Avon Books paperback printing: December 2001
First HarperCollins hardcover printing: May 2000

Avon Trademark Reg. U.S. Pat. Off. and in Other Countries, Marca Registrada, Hecho en U.S.A.
HarperCollins ® is a trademark of HarperCollins Publishers Inc.

Printed in the U.S.A.

10 9 8 7 6 5 4 3 2 1

I'm dedicating this novel to the most wonderful woman I've never met. She is always there when I need her, she calls me up from out of the blue just when I think I've been forgotten, she has unflinchingly stood by my side through years of winter, years of summer. I've never seen her face, but I would recognize her anywhere.

She is my agent, Lisa Bankoff.

I'm also dedicating this novel to the most amazing man I've never met. He has shown me, through his remarkable insight, that a writer's words do not stand in the shadow of the guillotine for no reason. No one's patience has ever been so severely tested as I tested his, and I think someday, if he lives, he may forgive me.

He is my editor, Dan Conaway.

PROLOGUE

The man held a gun in one hand and a chicken in the other. Joe Riley had him cornered in the barn this rainy night, holding him prisoner with a twelve-gauge shotgun that was empty, but the man didn't know it was. He looked less scared than Joe as he stood there in the beam of the flashlight while the chicken that dangled neck-first from his fist cackled and fought, and Joe Riley was no stranger to fear. In 1961 he had been a private in the very first U.S. Marine Corps battalion sent to fight in Vietnam.

"You'll be wanting to let the chicken go," he said, gesturing with the barrel of the shotgun. "My wife's already called the sheriff."

The man's fist relaxed. The chicken hit the dirt running.

"Now how's about discarding that revolver?"

He was a strange fellow, besides being a chicken thief in an age when nobody stole chickens anymore. He was wearing only one shoe, a muddy Reebok sneaker. His face bore the bruises of a recent beating, and he was bleeding through his clothes in two or three dozen places, as if he had rolled around in barbed wire.

"Is the answer no, or are you still thinking it over?"

He hesitated for a bit, then lowered his hand, but the pistol remained. If he pulled the trigger now, Joe saw, he would shoot a hole through his own bare foot. Joe wagged the flashlight, stroking him up and down with the beam. "Who are you, anyway? I know I've seen you someplace."

He only stared. He was a young guy, tall and thin, with brown hair that the pounding rain outside had plastered across his forehead. In his eyes and the cast of his face Joe saw hunger and exhaustion. Still not an excuse for breaking into a barn and stealing a chicken, though. If he had wanted a meal, he should have knocked on the door and asked for one. In rural Ohio folks were willing to help anybody who truly needed it.

"Christ sake, you must have a name," Joe said. "When I tell my grandkids about this I don't want to call you Mr. X through the whole story, and my grandkids like long stories." He relaxed his hold on the shotgun a little. "Can you help me out here, or not?"

The young man seemed to be straining inside, arguing with himself. Joe was sure he had seen him before, maybe on TV or in the newspaper, maybe on a wanted poster at the post office in Soldiers Bend. But he said nothing.

"Fine, then. When the sheriff gets here he'll solve the mystery, and we'll just see—"

"Hank Thorwald," he said.

Joe Riley drew back and frowned, thinking, but it only took a moment. "Oh my dear God," he breathed. "You."

Hank Thorwald swung the pistol up with both hands and aimed it at Joe's face. "Don't make me waste a bullet on you. I've only got four left."

Joe smirked. "I could blow you in half with this shotgun, and you know it."

The chicken thief drew the revolver's hammer back with a thumb. It clicked into place, ready to snap forward at a single touch of the trigger. "A man tends to spasm when he's shot," he said. "You'll die with me."

Joe knew he was right—especially since the shotgun had been collecting dust for years and he had no shells for it. "Then I guess you'd better be on your way, Mr. Thorwald." He carefully lowered the shotgun to the wooden floor and backed up a step, keeping the beam of the flashlight on the pistol. "You know how to get out."

"Kick it toward me."

Joe took a step and kicked it. It bounced harmlessly across the floor. "Won't do you much good," he said as Hank Thorwald bent to retrieve it. "No ammo."

He gathered up the shotgun anyway. By the clumsy way he handled it, Joe could see that he had never used one before: if there was a shell in it he would already have blown a hole through something.

The gusting wind outside began to carry the wail of a siren that rose and fell, rose and fell, growing closer. Hank Thorwald's eyes, glistening in the light, got bigger, then narrowed. "Which is the best way to go? Any dense woods around here?"

"Any way off my property is the best way for *you* to go."

The chicken thief fired. On the wall beside Joe's head a bucket hanging from a nail jumped away and banged to the floor. In the darkness both of his cows kicked fretfully at their stalls. "You'd better get more helpful than that," Hank Thorwald snarled at him.

"Head north," Joe said, and pointed the flashlight. "Go out the same damn door you came in and keep going. The woods up that way are thick and full of brambles, if that's what you want."

He nodded. "Hand over the flashlight."

Joe turned the light on his own face. "I won't do that, not for you or anybody else. It's a Snoopy flashlight from my granddaughter on Christmas. She saved her pennies."

He turned the light back. Hank Thorwald's attention was somewhere else—his eyes seemed slightly out of focus. "Maybe you'd better keep it, then," he said with remarkable sadness, then came to himself. "Could I ask you not to tell the cops which way I headed?"

"You can ask," Joe said, and tracked him with the light as he hurried away while the chickens squawked around his feet.

At the door in the back of the barn he stopped and shuffled around. "Hey there."

Joe took a step. "Still here."

"Do you believe?"

"Believe what they're saying?" He took in a slow breath. "I'm thinking that I do, Mr. Thorwald. Seeing you in this shape, I'm thinking I do. And you?"

He leaned the empty shotgun against the warped and knot-holed boards of the back wall. The siren was close now. "I've got three bullets left," he said. "I'm thinking about saving the last one for myself."

"That's what Hitler did," Joe said.

Hank Thorwald pushed the door open and lumbered out into the rain, leaving the shotgun behind. The wind blew the door shut.

Joe Riley told the sheriff which way he went.

THE ZIGARETTEN

I

Rebecca Thorwald had smoked cigarettes since the age of eleven. In that innocent summer of her eleventh year, her boy cousin, Barney Willden (who had journeyed with his parents in a station wagon all the way from Richmond, Virginia), spent two weeks at her house in Terre Haute, Indiana. Barney was all kinds of weird, was two years older than Rebecca and cussed and spit a lot. He taught Rebecca how to smoke, how to suck up a mouthful and scoop it into her lungs, because if she just sucked air straight through the hot cigarette it hurt too much, made her cough.

A girl who smoked cigarettes at that age could be forgiven as just another victim of peer pressure, but a woman of twenty-nine had no such excuse. Especially not the mother of a little girl and the wife of a nonsmoking man, Hank Thorwald. Time and again Rebecca Thorwald had tried to quit, but time and again she had failed. At her age, grazing dangerously close to the grass at the shadow of the thirty-year milestone, she was old enough to admit that the time for horseplay with this habit was gone, it had to escalate into an all-out war, and she could not win the war alone.

This evening she was sitting at the vanity, cigarette burning at her right. Hank's head appeared in a corner of the mirror. Fresh from the shower, his hair was a weed field of brown curls, his face as rosy as a summer peach. "The countdown begins," he said, grinning, and motioned toward her cigarette. "Tell the burning bastard his days are numbered, Becky. He's about to be hip-mo-tized."

She smiled at him in the mirror and he went away. In truth,

7

she was scared. She had tried the nicotine gum and wound up sneaking cigarettes between chews. She had not yet tried the patch but it didn't seem likely to work—how could an enlarged Band-Aid make her not smoke? That left only cold turkey, which, so far, was a bird she had plucked and shucked a dozen times. So tonight then, at eight o'clock this evening, her perhaps final chance would come. The advertisement had occupied a quarter page of the *Terre Haute Tribune-Star* for two weeks running: a renowned clinical hypnotist would be in town for three evenings. A stop-smoking therapist with an astonishing success record, Roger Bevins-Clarke could accommodate one hundred and thirty persons per session at the Wabash Valley Inn, banquet room 6. The program wasn't cheap: two hundred and forty dollars for one evening's attendance.

Rebecca went for the cigarette in the ashtray, observed it a few seconds at its position between her fingertips, and pressed the filter to her lips. One deep drag just like Barney had shown her, a small backward tug of her head, then inhale. There was something about the whole procedure that brought satisfaction. If you lit a good cigarette, you could bet it would treat you right. Cigarettes were friends.

She sighed at her reflection in the mirror. Here is Rebecca Thorwald, age twenty-nine, age almost-thirty, no wrinkles yet but a lot of skin getting as thin as paper. Reddish hair with dark roots, forever doomed to the suspicion of using color. Her hand came up automatically to insert the cigarette between her lips. She watched herself, watched the tip glow bright orange, watched herself nod her head back and inhale. She had mastered the art of being sexy while she did it.

Hank popped into the room wearing his shower towel and a white shirt, already doing battle with his tie. This was a strange man, she had discovered during their marriage of twelve years, a man of unexpected shortcomings and abilities. He was a gifted man full of knowledge and good humor, but a troubling awkwardness plagued his teaching, or so he complained. His memory was almost frightening in its exactness, yet he often lost his shoes and his car keys. When it came to the practical side of life, he was nearly helpless. Hank could not be trusted to go grocery shopping. If sent to buy, say, a gallon of milk, he would return with grapes, cheese, a bottle of wine and some crackers, two quarts of motor oil, and six boxes of Cap'n Crunch. No milk. Any complaint from Rebecca seemed to destroy him completely, and most times she wound up being the one to go back to the store. Hank was gifted, but you had to look for those gifts in unusual areas, and forgive the areas where he had no gifts at all.

Tonight, though, both of them were going to the Wabash Valley Inn for this expensive stab at ending her addiction to tobacco. Sharri was old enough now to stay home alone; her last birthday cake had required eleven candles. But Rebecca would worry nonetheless because a scary world lurked outside the safety of their suburban home. Her angst in this matter would run riot if she did not squelch it, so she swapped it for simple annoyance at Hank. After all, this evening was his fault. She was not sure she could be hypnotized. Nor did she believe hypnosis could end her smoking even if this three-name hotshot Roger Bevins-Clarke could put her under. Worst of all, though, she loved smoking too dearly to give it up. She had uncles in their seventies who smoked, aunts in their eighties who burned through two packs a day without keeling over prematurely. So why be afraid of it?

Her reflection in the mirror rolled its eyes. Okay, it was also true that she had relatives who had keeled over quite young from cancer or emphysema. She took one final drag, then stamped the butt violently in the ashtray, confused and unhappy.

Hank reappeared wearing pants. The knot of his tie was located beside his left armpit and was about the size of a grapefruit. "Damn thing," he muttered, then glanced at her. "You're going to the hotel in your underwear?"

"Oh." She looked down. "What time is it?"

He lifted his wrist, where only a pale bracelet of skin resided. "Ten till something," he said. "Where's my watch gone to?"

She saw it on the bed and motioned with her eyes. "Hank?" she said quietly as he crossed the room. "Is this really going to work?"

"Sure. I put it on and it tells me the time. A very effective and precise machine."

Rebecca did not match his smile. "Not funny, Hank. We're shelling out five hundred bucks for an hour's worth of hypnosis. What if it's bogus?"

"It probably *is* bogus," he said immediately. "But Perry believes it could work for you, so I think we should at least give it a try."

She allowed herself to nod. Perry Wilson was chair of the psychology department at Indiana State University, and Hank's opponent in a million games of chess. In his pre-teaching years he had been licensed to perform hypnosis on his patients and was convinced of its powers. Perry got nearly hysterical on the subject of hypnosis when you poured a few drinks into him at a faculty party. "Okay, Perry lives and breathes it," she said. "God knows he's the crown jewel of the profession."

"Thinks he's that, and a grand champion of chess," Hank replied, and looked at his watch when it was in position. "It is now officially seven-fifteen. You have fifteen minutes to unlock the mystery of my tie, and five minutes to put yourself together. Then we must go."

"Jeepers, do your own damned tie," Rebecca blurted, and bent to work on her face. He wandered away, shaking his head, grinning a little. His belief in hypnotism, she knew full well, ranked right up there with his belief in ghosts and UFOs.

The Wabash Valley Inn was such a new addition to the Terre Haute skyline that it still reeked of the glue that held the delicious red carpeting to the floor. Lined up to register for the seminar, Rebecca was very aware that the place was lousy with no smoking signs. WE ARE A SMOKE-FREE ESTABLISHMENT, the words on the entrance doors boasted. That meant, to her, that the Wabash Valley Inn violated the civil rights of a dwindling minority. In this rarified air she could smell the tobacco smoke that permeated every single person in line. She had heard that after some weeks as a nonsmoker, the scent of smoke would become repulsive, but could not imagine that day arriving. Hank had quit cold turkey six years ago, just decided that he was done with it, and never smoked again. She secretly believed there was an ulterior motive for his being here, his taking part in this experiment. Years of chess and friendship with Perry Wilson and his hypnosis-mongering had reached a saturation point and he wanted to test the subject himself. If over a hundred smokers could be put under a spell at the same time, he wanted to see if one renegade nonsmoker could slip through the ranks and be made to squawk like a chicken at the sight of a cigarette he no longer craved at all. His spoken intent was just to be there to keep her company; his tacit intent was to keep her from hiding in the ladies' room through the entire hour.

"Thorwald," Hank said to the young woman at the desk. "Hank and Rebecca, two packs a day each." He winked at her. "We'll be needing the double whammy."

The girl smiled as she found the Thorwald name in her Wabash Valley Inn double binder and checked it off. "Mr. Bevins-Clarke will give you all the whammy you need," she said sweetly. Rebecca saw a bunch of potential ad-libs flit through her husband's eyes before he decided, with surprising sanity, on a simple thank-you.

They walked on. The hotel unfolding before her was a marvel, the finest she had seen since a trip to Chicago when Hank had attended a conference there. All four doors of the banquet room were standing open as four young ladies handed a brown folder to each passing entrant. Odd music drifted out, wooden flutes trilling slowly up and down. Hank took two folders and passed one to her as they went in. The words TAKE CONTROL! were nicely embossed on the top.

Rebecca glanced at the other people passing through the doors, wondering if they had confidence in this, wondering how they justified blowing three months' worth of cigarette money on a dubious cure. By the looks of the crowd a cross section of local society was represented here, every single person drawn, she supposed, by the same desire to quit smoking. Except, as Hank quite suddenly tugged at her hand to hurry her toward a pair of empty chairs, Rebecca herself.

"This isn't right," she whispered fiercely, trying to tug herself free. The strap of her purse slipped from her shoulder and slid down to her wrist in a series of jumps. "Not tonight," she said quietly when he looked back. "Please." Her need for a cigarette had never been stronger. Just to stand free outside, to light one more last one and smoke it until the filter was on fire. Just to—

Hank jerked hard, gave her a glare, and towed her along. Anger flared inside her, then melted into embarrassment. Finally, he stopped and swept a hand. "Will these do?"

She seated herself on a chair beside an elderly lady with thin white hair, and nodded politely to her as Hank dropped heavily onto the chair at her left. "I wonder if they show cartoons first," he murmured, and tried to cross his legs: the toe of his shoe clunked against the chair ahead. He shrugged and crossed his arms over his chest instead.

Rebecca clutched her purse to her lap, taking in the surroundings. From the most stubborn core of her being she swore to herself that after this lunacy she would stay up all night smoking, just plain chain-smoking at the kitchen table and loving it, precious Camel Light after Camel Light. At that moment the entry doors swept shut. As Rebecca turned to look, the music rose and the lights dimmed, almost to the point of a total blackout. She sought Hank's hand and found it, pressed it tight. A weird light behind the podium flickered alive, some kind of bluish neon that made the wall behind it glow in spots.

Hank leaned sideways until his head touched hers. "Black light," he whispered. "Hippie stuff from the sixties. You watch."

The music droned on, a pleasant but alien tune, something that might coax a snake out of a basket. Barely discernible behind it was the sound of ocean swells, a piping or two of birds, a distant waterfall, a beached whale groaning in the night. A figure appeared out of the darkness to the left of the podium, became a floating white-purple apparition that wafted to the right and slid to a stop behind the microphone. The apparition tapped the microphone twice with a glowing blue finger, and spoke.

"The world no longer exists around us tonight. We are an island that is protected from the world by these walls, we are sheltered by the strength of our being, we are more powerful than we know, we are more powerful than we ever have hoped. But to acknowledge this power we must surrender all of ourselves, we must put the world to rest."

Oh indeed, Rebecca thought nastily. But she had to admit that his voice was mesmerizing, the music and the black light captivating. Listening to this guy could put a body to sleep.

"Let us begin our hypnosis by sitting in a comfortable position," the glowing man said. "If you have a tendency to fall asleep, you might wish to sit in a straight-back position. Now, the reason for this unusual lighting is that I will become your focal point, a figure you can concentrate on.

"Let's begin with your first big, deep breath. Everybody inhale, slowly, feel the air, sense its effect inside your body."

Rebecca inhaled along with everybody else, aware that Hank had too.

"Good. Now exhale, sigh it out, just let the breath come out easily and gently, don't push it out, just sigh it out, okay, done. Now your second nice big, deep breath, feel your lungs expanding, growing larger, holding it in, feeling the strength of the oxygen, holding it in. Now you exhale, let all the tension go, feel it all the way down through your toes. Now another nice deep breath, feeling that expansion, expanding those lungs. This time as you exhale let your eyes close, just let yourself go instantly into your hypnosis, quieting the mind now, relaxing the body. Tonight is yours, set aside the world, there is no world outside, just you and I."

She realized that she was getting drowsy already. With a jerk she sat up straighter.

"Let us begin our relaxation process by using your imagination. I would like you to picture yourself looking at a beautiful sun, golden rays of sun, and that sun shines in and you can feel the warmth of it on your head, breathing and relaxing any tightness or tension that you might be holding onto in that area. Relaxing the mind, releasing the world, you begin to feel a floating sensation, you see yourself rising, you feel the sun and the gentle wind and are relaxing, you are relaxing, relaxing, relaxing . . ."

2

The entire incident that Friday evening remained as clear as polished glass even after Alan Weston woke up with the most catastrophic hangover ever suffered by a human being. He was a newspaper reporter by trade—in his opinion had been born to snoop and pry—and at thirty-two had gained a certain amount of notoriety at station WXRV in Indianapolis. Some of it good, most of it bad. The station boss hated him, and some of his colleagues at WXRV hated him as well. It had been said more than once that he was the Howard Stern of the Midwest. It also had been said that he was a publicity hound and a manufacturer of news stories. If this reputation bothered him, he did not show it. The fact that it *did* bother him was his own business, and he kept it private.

Except from his bartender. At the northeastern corner of the city, just a small hike from Highway 465, was a lounge called the Breeze Inn. Alan had discovered it one night after a fight with his wife, who was now his ex. Barely more than a shack, it boasted a small clientele and, best of all, no television. Alan Weston's face and upper torso appeared on Channel 8 just about every evening, *Alan Weston on Us* was the tag, a play on the initials "U.S.," a play on his reputation: Alan Weston is all over us. The ratings were good and getting slowly better, never getting worse, so no one could touch him. But most of his viewers hated him, as the mailbags proved each week.

"Life fucks," he groaned over his usual Jack and Coke.

The bartender's name was Pat. He was a tremendously fat man who had to squeeze himself painfully through the swing-up counter gate to get out from behind the bar, using both hands to pull his gut in, squinch-faced and gasping when he finally passed through. Right now he was relaxed; it was just after seven o'clock in the evening and he would stay here until closing. Alan Weston knew his schedule, preferred Pat over the lady who manned the afternoon shift. She watched too much TV at home, had too much to say about it. All Alan wanted was to not think about it. Until the camera was rolling, and that was a different story.

Pat the bartender dumped both elbows onto the wooden bar in front of Alan Weston, folded his ham-hock arms across each other, and squatted slightly to face him. "Don't you mean life sucks?"

Alan snorted. "Give me the medical definition between 'fucking' and 'sucking.'"

Pat straightened. "At this stage in your life," he said gravely, "you can no longer perform either."

Alan laughed. It tickled him again and he leaned back on his stool to laugh some more. It was so absurd. Much like himself and his career, so absurd. He was at a level other television personalities his age would give their lives for: his own spot on a network affiliate in a state capital. He had the strength of the network lawyers behind him when he ruffled feathers, had the mayor fearing him on one side and the police chief fearing him on the other. Yet he was unhappy, lost and unhappy, and angered by the fact that he had let himself become a cliché in his own business.

He was burned out. In the three years since his dramatic rise, it had gradually come to him that people weren't tuning in because they respected his disrespect for society, his voice that was full of irony and sarcasm. No, they were tuning in to see a freak show, to see who Asshole Weston would humiliate this time. The local politicians were absolutely terrified of him. At first he assumed they had something to hide, something he had to dig for, and dig he did, now and then uncovering some astonishingly juicy nugget of hypocrisy or duplicity. But mostly they feared him because he was a muckraker, Indianapolis's one-man *National Enquirer*. When had he slid from solid journalism into sordid showbiz?

"You've got that look again," Pat said, exhaling the odor of pizza-for-lunch into Alan's face. "Alan, my famous friend, why must you beat yourself up every time you come in here?"

Alan lifted his glass, took a drink. "Because I can. Cradled here in the comforting arms of anonymity, I can."

The cowbell above the tavern door announced the arrival of four or five motorcycle types, lots of black leather and tattoos, several shaved heads bobbing among the group. Pat stumped over and eyed them to check their ages, requested one ID, scanned it and handed it back. Pitchers of beer were ordered and the group headed back to the pool table while Pat went to the taps.

Alan hoisted his drink to his lips and sucked three huge swallows down to empty it. The Michelob clock on the wall indicated seven-thirty. Seven-fucking-thirty. He was halfway toward the relief of being totally drunk, but it was only seven-thirty in the evening, too damned early. Well, fine. With the divorce now as final as a bullet through the heart, it no longer mattered what time he got home. All he needed was a KFC or a taco, all day tomorrow to sleep the whiskey off, and be at the station in time to voice-over Friday's tape of the cop whose patrol car spent a lot of its time parked behind a massage parlor. Here, folks, we have a gross dereliction of duty. It didn't matter that the reporter on the scene kept his own fucking car parked behind a tavern all weekend, did it?

"Hypocrisy," he mouthed to his image in the mirror. The image regarded him silently with black holes for eyes. "Muckraking," he told it softly. "Character assassination. Libel. Slander."

The image had nothing to offer except a snapshot of himself in a cheap bar with his mental health smoldering toward ashes. "I am weary unto death," he told it, and in that moment someone sank heavily onto the barstool beside him and exhaled cigarette smoke against the side of his face. Alan turned, squinting.

It was one of the skinhead guys. "I know you," he said. Behind his lips Alan saw the blank slots of missing teeth. "You're that asshole on TV."

Alan's first thought was to deny it. It was a weekend, he was not Alan Weston as the public knew him, he was just Joe Schmoe trying to have a quiet drink in a quiet bar. "Wrong on that one," he said. "Sorry."

"Am I?" The young man hesitated, then grinned. "Alan Weston himself. You got a mole under your eye just like he does, and my mom loves you more than she loves me." He extended a hand in a leather glove that had the fingers cut off. On the inside of his forearm was an elaborate swastika tattoo. "You're a good dude, man," he said, and Alan shook his hand, bewildered. How odd, he thought, that he would shake the hand of a Nazi. Or at least a neo-Nazi. Distant relatives of his had attended the gathering at Auschwitz and not survived it. His grandmother knew their names.

The young man straightened and turned. "Yo, dudes," he called loudly to his friends. "Alan Weston in person. TV celeb. Good dude. Let's get his autograph."

Alan shut his eyes. Publicity in his secret hideaway. But did they know he had done a story not two weeks ago in which he had lambasted the rank-and-file cop for ignoring the antics of the motorcycle gangs? Apparently not, because the whole crew trooped right over and regarded him with wide eyes and smiles. Alan glanced at Pat, who gave a small shrug. These men seemed pretty tame despite their scraggly beards and all those tattoos, many of them involving things perched on a swastika, under a swastika, around a swastika, right through the damn swastika.

"It *is* him," one of them said, and pushed the others aside. He was older, halfway bald, his face pitted with acne scars. "My name's Leroy Phipps, but the guys call me Commando," he said as he picked up Alan's hand and pumped it vigorously. His breath reeked of cigar smoke and beer. "Dude, you are one mean motherfucker on TV. You tell it like it is, man, and that's what we're all about." He released Alan's hand and eyed his men. "We're buying this dude's beer all fucking night. Somebody get me a piece of paper and a fucking pen, man, 'cause next time some big bad cop rousts me I'm gonna show the autograph to him, tell him about my man here."

He hooked a meaty arm around the back of Alan's neck and pulled his head to his chest as if to knuckle his hair. The smell wafting up from his armpit nearly made Alan's eyes water. "We're bros, dude, bros to the end," he crowed as the bones of his forearm threatened to snap Alan's neck. He released him to holler at Pat. "You! Fatboy! Hustle your ass!"

Pat ambled over while Alan readjusted his hair. "The name's Pat, not fatboy," he said. "What's your pleasure?"

The man called Commando whipped his head around to look at the pool table. "Clarence! Go grab the pitchers, man! Yo, Alan!

Alan raised his eyebrows.

"The fat man wants to know what your pleasure is. What do Jews drink, anyway? Mogen-David?"

They all laughed while Alan's insides shrank. It was a setup, this was all a ghastly prelude to harassment, maybe a beating, maybe a cue stick across the face and a stapled jaw. He had not often faced prejudice, but his fame had made the issue arise before, always just behind his back or in the mailbag.

Pat leaned closer. In the shadow between the cash register and the cooler, Alan knew, resided an ax handle that had been used only twice in the last ten years. "The man," Pat said softly, his hand drifting that way, "drinks Jack Daniel's with Coca-Cola."

Alan waited for the silence of the moment to grow too long, to hear the first grunting of hate, feel the first punch. Instead, Commando slammed a fist down on the bar, which made both Alan and the ashtrays jump. "Then get him a Jack and Coke," he bellowed. "Get the man what he likes, and don't stop till he's belly-down on the floor." He looked at Alan with a gap-toothed grin. "Providing I get that autograph, though. Cop repellent."

Pat, visibly relieved, brought him a handful of Breeze Inn napkins and a felt-tip pen.

While Alan Weston was signing autographs, sunrise had already broken over Frankfurt, Germany, and the city was alive with pedestrians and Saturday morning traffic. In the *Stadtmitte*—the core of downtown where the tracks of the streetcars meshed to branch in a dozen directions—skyscrapers had been built over the wreckage of the war that had destroyed all of Germany, and the *Stadtmitte* was once again the commercial hub of the nation's banking and finance industry. But to the man gazing sourly across the skyline through the bluish glass of an air-conditioned suite on the top floor of the Euro-Bank building on Kaiserstraße, the cheery morning could not make up for the bleak night he had just endured. Karl-Luther von Wessenheim was a tall and pale son of the German system of royalty, a peerage that had lasted a thousand years before being dismantled, along with all of Germany, at the end of World War Two. But still there remained, among the elite of society, a tacit acknowledgment of the royal house of Wessenheim, and a discreet respect for its heir. But on this morning Karl-Luther von Wessenheim's concerns were not of the erasure of his heritage, but of something more pressing: he had lost a bid at the auction block last night, and he was not a man to lose easily.

Standing at the window, von Wessenheim poked an expensive Reemstma cigarette between his thin lips and lit it with a match. Europe had not yet been infected by the American antismoking fever and ashtrays were never far away, but in his mood it did not matter and he dropped the match to the stiff blue carpet. When a faint string of smoke wisped up, he crushed it under the toe of his Italian shoe.

The double doors to the suite swept open behind him. "She's agreed to a meeting," the man said, and softly shut the doors. Von Wessenheim turned; it was his lawyer, Franz Bohr. "And I would not be surprised if the price has already doubled."

"Impossible," von Wessenheim said. "Even I wouldn't pay that kind of money, and she knows it."

"That's just the point, sir. She does not want to sell outside the group."

"But she has agreed to meet with us. To me that shows a willingness, no matter how small."

His lawyer worked on the knot of his tie, loosening it. "Do you want my real opinion?" he asked.

Von Wessenheim eyed him. "Only if it agrees with mine, Franz."

"Then you might not like this. Shall I go on?"

Von Wessenheim turned his attention back to the window. "Go on."

Bohr crossed the room and settled himself on the sofa, a ghostly reflection in the dark glass before von Wessenheim's eyes. "We are talking about a hobby here. We are talking about enough money to purchase a fleet of brand-new Mercedes, all for the sake of your hobby."

Von Wessenheim nodded and took a puff of his cigarette. "That's assuming that a collection of irreplaceable items from a bygone era is only a hobby."

"I know," Bohr said, raising his hands defensively. "One man's hobby is another man's career. But *my* career, as your attorney, hinges on you having enough money left to pay me for my services. Are you really willing to spend a hundred-thousand Deutschmarks for an old hat?"

Von Wessenheim turned. "But look at who wore it."

"Only once."

"The moment was captured in a photograph."

"With the man under it looking as if his underwear was too tight."

Von Wessenheim sucked on his cigarette. "You know, I don't care if there was a lollipop sticking out of his ass. The hat was on his head and I have photographic proof and I want the hat in my collection." He stalked a few steps across the room and dropped his cigarette in the nearest ashtray. Offered for sale last night had been items from the National Socialist era of modern Germany's history: a pink granite bust of Hermann Göring, chief of the German air force; a wicker chair whose armrests were supported by wicker swastikas, once sat in by Hitler; a pair of kid gloves worn by Heinrich Himmler, head of the SS; the collar worn by Hitler's dog Blondi; a crude clay swastika made in grade school by one of propaganda minister Josef Goebbels's five children; a riding crop used by Hitler's mysterious right-hand man Martin Bormann, who had vanished in 1945 without a trace; a letter to Hitler from Josef Mengele, head of the medical department at the Auschwitz concentration camp; an autographed photo of Rudolf Hess standing beside the airplane he would later fly to England in an unauthorized attempt to negotiate peace with the duke of Hamilton. And other things from that era, things that were not known to exist but did, things steeped in history but wanted by very few.

Franz Bohr stood up. "I take that to be your final word."

"You take it right," von Wessenheim said. "I will meet with her, and the hat will be mine. That, or she'll be wishing it were."

Bohr lowered his head. "I'll pretend I didn't recognize a threat in that. But I can't pretend to be in favor of your actions. Have you ever heard the English saying about money?"

Von Wessenheim frowned. "I know enough English to get by."

"They have a saying we can't quite match in German. 'Penny wise and pound foolish.'"

He rolled his eyes. "Interpret."

Bohr nodded. "You know how much it pains you to pay for a parking slot? Know how much you resent having to tip a waiter?"

"Highway robbery," von Wessenheim agreed. "Money sifting through the cracks of the floor. But I already know your point, and I disagree."

"You grumble about Pfennigs but are ready to pay thousands of Deutschmarks for a top hat. A faded black top hat."

At this von Wessenheim smiled. "That top hat spent a few hours perched on the head of Adolf Hitler the year before he became chancellor."

"If it is the same one."

Karl-Luther von Wessenheim darkened. "The hat is genuine. If I have learned one thing since being allowed to participate, it is that those people know Hitler better than anyone ever has. They were all members of the Hitler Youth, they have nothing but fond childhood memories of their Führer."

"They do tend to worship him," Bohr said glumly.

"Correct. Thus they would not worship the hat if it were not genuine."

Bohr fidgeted. "You realize that we're dealing with sick people here, don't you? People with enough money to buy half of Frankfurt with only the change out of their pockets, yet they all get together in secret and barter for Hitler's underwear."

"I saw no evidence of underwear," von Wessenheim said. He moved to one of the overstuffed chairs and lowered himself into it. For a long moment he gnawed at a fingernail, then came to himself and paid attention to the cigarette in his other hand. "Oh. A joke. Sarcasm. Clever."

Bohr ducked his head, reddening a bit.

"So when is the meeting with the old bat?" von Wessenheim asked.

Bohr checked his watch. "Six hours from now."

Von Wessenheim stood and moved back to the row of windows with their skyscraper scenery, took in the panorama of a reborn Frankfurt slashed into chunks of light and shadow by the morning sunlight, and tried to imagine the streets below as they had been, as they had been in 1937 when Adolf Hitler's motorcade toured the city and thousands upon thousands cheered him on.

By ten o'clock Alan Weston was drunker than he had ever been in his life, even counting his teenage years when five beers was enough to earn him a crawl to the toilet. His new friend Commando had not reneged on his promise: the Jack and Cokes had come in an endless supply. He had recently lost the ability to speak in sentences and was now trying to play eight ball with one of the bikers, a long and lanky dude named Shaver who could shoot pool like you wouldn't believe. Pat's insistence that Alan call a cab was beginning to get annoying. For the first time in years Alan found himself free of his demons, and now Patman wanted to cut the program short, edit the tape, drop the star from the credits, and cancel the act.

"You did a show last year," Shaver was saying as Alan fumbled a cube of blue chalk against the tip of his cue stick.

"Killer show, dude. The show about that Reverend Jacoby dude, the religious dude who was pulling a Swaggert."

Alan refocused his eyes. The air was dim with cigarette smoke and smelled like a house on fire. "Segment," he said. "Not a show, just a segment."

"Segment." Shaver lowered his lanky self down to be at eye level with the cue ball, lined up the seven, and smacked it into the pocket in a blur of speeding red. "That Jacoby, man, what a phony. Swaggert to the bone, man, the fucking pervert."

Alan tried to condense the clouds of his thoughts into intelligent rain. Swaggert? Oh, yeah, *that* guy. Mr. Fire and Brimstone TV preacher who kept a whore on the side. The esteemed local reverend Sam Jacoby, purveyor of righteousness, had been caught in a massage parlor getting more than his parlor massaged, if you know what I mean. "I raked his ass," Alan said. "Over the coals. I raked his. His ass, the fucker. I raked it. Him."

Shaver went for the five ball, sliding the cue back and forth over the swastika tattoo that resided in the web of skin between his thumb and forefinger before zinging the orange ball into the side pocket. The cue ball spun off the rail and rotated to a quick stop behind the three. Amazing. "The local guy was worse than Swaggert, dude. Jacoby was funneling American money into the Israeli secret police. Zionism is the anti-Christ, so the dude was working for the devil."

"Interesting. Angle." Alan wiped blue chalk off his fingers onto his new slacks.

"It's like this, see. Jesus came to save the Jews but they rejected him. They formed Zionism and stole Palestine from the Arabs. Did you know that it's illegal in Israel to be a Christian missionary?"

Alan put the cube of chalk on the edge of the pool table. A second later it ticked to the floor, a victim of random gravity. He eyed the remaining balls on the table, nearly all of them his. He had once done a segment on a local pool champ who had turned out to have an extensive police record in Kentucky, as well as a wife in Indy and a wife down there. Alan's last line of the segment had been excruciatingly cute: "You gotta admit, the guy's got balls."

"It's all in the Bible," Shaver said as he lined up his shot. "Jesus cursed the Jews when he was crucified, and that ended their power until the last days, which is now."

Click! The one ball dropped into the corner pocket as if hauled there by magnets. "The year two thousand is God's breaking point, dude. He will end the reign of the Jews when Jesus returns to destroy them."

Alan took a backward step, reaching out to his right. There was a small table there with his drink on it, and an ashtray in which Shaver's cigarette was turning into a gray tube. He picked up his drink and sucked half of it down without pause. Things were becoming discordant, his demons were awakening and rubbing at their eyes, once again his spirit was being stirred by the need to investigate and report, investigate and report some more. He put the glass down with all the balance his hand could muster, aware that he was wobbling back and forth on ankles that had become treacherous. "We have a different calendar," he said. "Back in biblical times it was totally different, the Jewish calendar goes back five thousand years and more. Like the Chinese one."

Shaver was lining up on the eight ball. On the crescent of his right ear Alan could count five earrings, between the greasy twigs of his hair, two of them ruby studs. What kind of man was this, this man with his tattoos and black leather and body odor that the ceiling fan churned into a generalized gas? "The colored races inherit one half of the earth," he said out of the side of his mouth as he squinted down the line of his stick. "Satan's side gets the dark side of the world. Jesus will rule the side that is in the sun." He glanced at Alan. "Eight ball in the corner pocket, amigo."

Alan watched him smash it in. Shaver skirted the table and offered his hand for shaking. "Give me another game," he said. "I love winning against a rich and famous Jew."

Alan felt his hand pulled out of place, winced as Shaver squeezed it and jerked it up and down; a sharp slap on his shoulder clinched their friendship. He waited for his hackles to rise, waited for the surge of elemental anger that would goad him into exposing the benign sort of bigotry enjoyed by these bikers. But in truth he wanted another game with

Shaver, wanted to show him that Alan Weston was not always Asshole Weston and could muster a good shot or two without a television camera in his face, and also in truth he did not give a shit if they were bigoted or not. They liked him. They respected his work and they enjoyed his company. The same could not be said for his colleagues and his viewers.

"I'll rack'm up," he said. There was a hair stuck to his tongue. Attempts to pluck it away failed.

Shaver was grinning. "So Jews eat pussy, and will miracles never cease. So do what you do best, Mr. Alan Weston, and rack the fuckers up."

Alan racked them up, then later racked them up again. After eleven games he gave up, but only because the Breeze Inn shut its doors for the night.

The bikers made sure he got home in one piece. One of them spray-painted a swastika on his front door as they left, which caught the attention of a paperboy the next morning, then the paperboy's mother when he told her, then the police when she called them, then station WXRV, and then the whole damned city.

Alan Weston woke up with the most catastrophic hangover ever suffered by a human being, and a whole lot of shit hitting a city full of fans.

3

orning drifted over Terre Haute as a spiritless gray fog, herald of a building summer rainstorm that the city's inhabitants were never surprised to get. Hank Thorwald got out of bed and ambled to the window, scratching absently at the base of his tailbone, and pulled the curtains apart. Another wet Saturday, another reason not to tackle the lawn and the yardwork, a fine excuse for staying indoors to catch up on his reading. Earth sciences, his general field in teaching, was in a state of rapid change as new discoveries were made nearly every week. Most of what he had been taught in grade school had been junked; volcanos were no longer the last gasp of the world's overheated formation, but were the result of plate subduction. Earthquakes were not the earth adjusting its mantle as it cooled, they were the result of plate tectonics. The earth's atmosphere had not shielded it from asteroid impacts, the earth was more heavily cratered than the moon. For some this seemed as unimportant as the price of Brylcreem in 1954, for him it was a revelation. Earth was a miracle, a hellishly hot ball of nickel and iron coated with a preposterously thin skin of cooled rock. A marvelous thing, almost as marvelous as the millions of life forms that inhabited it. If religion had any impact on Hank, he honestly tended toward worship of the earth and the sky. But that kind of thinking could lead to the wearing of tie-dyed silk clothing, having long hair and hugging trees, so he preferred to keep his brand of theism quiet. Occasionally, Rebecca would drag him off to church—usually when her parents were in town—and there he suffered without complaint, finding that the Catholic traditions he was discovering were as mysterious as the universe itself.

He let the curtains fall together and headed toward the shower, thinking about the night before. He had sat patiently with Rebecca while the mystic guru tried to convince everyone to surrender themselves to the power of his suggestion. The big question for today, though, was this: Would Rebecca want a cigarette, or would she not?

In the shower he found himself humming a strange tune. Then it came to him: it was the music from last night, that eerie Made-in-India song that had lasted a full hour. Spooky, almost. He closed his eyes as he washed his hair and the scene at the hotel banquet room jumped before his mental camera, a perfect picture complete with the glowing man behind the podium. He snapped his eyes open and it was gone.

"Weird," he muttered, then got soap in his eyes and closed them again.

The banquet room: semidark, yellow walls, a glowing purple form, a brass railing that encircled the room to keep the world out. The sun shining hot on his head, the rays of the sun that were so bright, his lungs pulling in the salty scent of the beach, the sun winking on the turquoise water . . .

"Bugga-bugga," he said aloud, and scrubbed his hair with his eyes open. In seconds he was belting out a basso version of a Barbra Streisand song, one of her sad ones. As he stepped out of the shower Rebecca wandered in. She was her usual frumpy mess, disheveled but alluring, her body under the pink negligee full of all the right curves in the usual places. There was a half-finished cigarette dangling from her lips. Hank formed a quick grin as he snatched up a towel. Perry Wilson was a fool and hypnosis was a crock. About five hundred bucks spent for nothing.

"I'm a hopeless case," Rebecca groaned, and plopped down on the toilet. She took a short, angry puff and eyed him. "I knew it wouldn't do any good."

"I don't know," he said, massaging the towel through his hair. "You made it all the way back from the hotel without a cigarette."

"The hardest twenty minutes of my life."

He was drying his chest when the smoke hit him. It was a black, oily smell that made him jerk back with a grimace. "What the hell kind of cigarette is that?" he barked.

Rebecca's eyebrows drew upward. "Camel Light, same as always."

"Jesus!" He clamped the wet towel in a wad over his nose and mouth. "Smells like, smells like . . ."

Now she frowned. "Burning feathers?"

"Yeah! Or burning hair or something."

Her eyes widened. "I will be damned," she whispered slowly. "You were hypnotized last night. The guy said cigarettes would now smell and taste like burning feathers."

Muffled, from behind the towel: "Bullshit."

She leaned to the side and dropped the cigarette into the sink. Equipped with his impromptu gas mask, Hank went to it and cranked on the water. "Looks like a soggy turd," he groused.

She was standing up. "Really hypnotized, Hank. You must have been really hypnotized. I wasn't."

He felt an awkward mixture of denial and shame. "I've put up with your cigarettes for years," he said. "Now they finally got to me."

As she stripped off her nightgown she said, "Actually, you've been an angel about it. I guess from now on I have to smoke outside."

"No way." He lowered the towel to a breath of ghastly air. "This thing will wear off, it'll be gone in a few hours."

"But Perry says hypnosis lasts a lifetime."

"Yeah, but Perry also says my chessboard is rigged, which it ain't."

She went up on tiptoe to plant a kiss on his lips. "Of course it's not."

He choked back a gag of revulsion at her breath, smiled, and hurried out as soon as she stepped into the shower. After a high-speed romp down the stairway to escape the fumes, he saw that Sharri was already up. She was spooning down mouthfuls of Cap'n Crunch while staring intently at the little television beside her bowl. "Anything new on the boobus toobus?" he asked by way of conversation as he moved to the refrigerator for his morning treasure hunt, and got a grunt as an answer. Sharri was entering the age where her love of Daddy was starting to become disdain of Dad. It was with a measure of guilt that he restricted her hours of TV, screened her programs, buttoned up her time to allow mostly the things he approved of. A lot of guilt, actually. He was a college prof and a sometime believer in the idea that learning, no matter what it was or what its source, was a good thing. But not at age eleven.

He scouted the contents of the Kenmore Mark IV series, frowning. A full jug of orange juice beckoned like an oasis in the refrigerated wasteland and he hauled it out. With the first swallow—straight from the jug, since the little Frau wasn't around to see—the burning smell cleared from his sinuses. He closed his eyes as he drank and saw only the usual colors and drifting shadows, felt only a vague wish to go back to bed and start the day over in two or three hours.

"Gah, sick!" Sharri exclaimed behind him, and he turned his head.

"A guy has the sexual organs of both male and female! I think they're going to show it!"

Hank nearly sprained both ankles as he whirled around and dived for the set. "No talk shows, and you know it," he said as he fumbled for the power switch. "Dammit, Sharri, show me how to turn this sucker off."

She pushed his hand away. "It's only a commercial for tonight, Dad. Alan Weston's going to interview him. Or her."

Hank straightened, feeling foolish. "Oh. You suppose Alan Weston's going to wear the gorilla suit again? Sharri?"

He was being heavily ignored. As he pulled another long draft from the jug Rebecca appeared at the bottom of the stairway. She had replaced the negligee with a fuzzy blue robe. Bleary-eyed and with her hair hanging in wet strings, she performed a shambling beeline for the Mr. Coffee standing in its usual nook beside the stove. Moving by rote, she began the process. "Don't drink out of the jug, Hank."

"Wouldn't dare. Did you look outside? It's raining pretty heavy."

"Heavily."

"Okay, it's raining pretty heavily, Miss English Major. There's nothing to be done with the lawn, we can't go golfing, and we can't go skydiving."

She turned to frown at him. "We've never skydived."

"Damn this weather, huh? And I was so ready for my first jump."

"You dillweed." She coughed out a small semblance of a laugh. Then it became coughing for real that made her clutch the counter and bend at the waist as she tried to clear her lungs.

"Jeez, Mom." Sharri said with a scowl. "Get a grip."

Rebecca coughed so hard that it was followed by a short spell of retching. Hank put the orange juice down and came up behind her, girding her waist with his hands as she spasmed. Those goddamn cigarettes, he thought. All she had to do was quit.

"I'm okay," Rebecca said, and he released her. Wordlessly she went back to creating her morning coffee. And that was the one and only and single-most thing Hank had been forced to give up in order to quit smoking those years ago: coffee in the morning. Whoever invented the brew must have been a smoker, because there were no two things in the world so firmly coupled. Maybe Freud had been right with his oral-retentive crap. Many of life's pleasures seemed to involve not just the sense of taste, but several tastes combined, and the physical act of drinking, eating, and swallowing. It was a subject he could bring up with Perry, if he wanted his ears talked off. "Maybe the Patch," he said to the back of her neck.

"Not right now," she said. "Nothing right now."

"The track record is good, from what I've read. People who smoked for thirty years, forty years, and they conquered it."

Her shoulders sagged. "Not right now, Hank. Please."

He shuffled forward as she reached into the cupboard for a Mr. Coffee filter, and wrapped his arms around her. "The time will come," he murmured into the tickling strings of her wet hair. "You'll win the fight."

He felt her muscles tighten. In an abrupt move she shoved his arms away and spun around. "You know what, Hank?"

she said. "You know what? I am so sick of your vendetta against my smoking that I could puke. I am so sick of walking around here like a third-class citizen that I could puke again. Yabba-dabba-doo for the bigshot who quit smoking six years ago, but here we have a small shot who just doesn't possess the iron will that you do."

Her eyes were hard and sparkling with anger. Hank shrank back, raising his hands. To his left he heard Sharri scoop up her television, and glanced to see her charge out of the kitchen as if the ceiling were collapsing.

"Becky?" he said, backing up another step. "Honey?"

"I am a human being," she said, and indicated herself with a sweep of her arms, one hand clutching a coffee filter that fluttered as she moved. "I have failings, I have faults, I work part-time in a cut-rate department store because I did not finish college. Not only that, I enjoy smoking and will continue to smoke until the last gasping, wheezing, emphysematic breath leaves my body."

Emphysematic, he thought wonderingly. Thirty-two years he had lived, and in those years had never heard that word. Rebecca had a talent for language, knew by instinct how to spell well and how to speak well; he had often encouraged her to become a writer or a newspaper reporter. He raised his hands higher, offering more surrender. "I'm sorry," he bleated. "Please forgive me."

She glared at him, the small bump of her Adam's apple jumping up and down underneath the skin of her throat as she picked at words. "Just—just lay off, Hank. Please. Lay off, give me room to breathe and think." The tone of her eyes softened, and she pressed her fists under her chin, her sign of mental distress. "I know I have to quit smoking, Hank. I know I have to do it just like you did, I have to make that final decision." She shifted her eyes. He saw that they were wetter than usual, and could not imagine anyone crying over a failed attempt to quit smoking, was stunned to hear this college-degree business.

She raised her head and blinked away the tears, fussed with her hands for a moment, then dabbed the coffee filter at the inner corners of her eyes. "It wouldn't be so bad, you know, it wouldn't be so bad if I had just an ounce of willpower. One ounce. I don't ask too much from myself, just that one ounce. But do I have it? Can someone give it to me? No."

"Doesn't matter," he said, and took a step toward her, his hands still raised, ready to enfold her or jump away. "*Macht nichts*, matters not."

"You sound like my brother," she said, and emitted a liquid, miserable kind of chuckle. "Three tours of duty in Germany and he's forgotten how to speak the king's English."

Hank produced a small laugh, trying to sound genuinely amused. Her older brother Michael was a career army officer who bounced between Saudi Arabia and Germany on a permanent rotation of sorts. He didn't care much for the heat of the desert but loved the German tradition of beer and oompah music. He told of the awe-inspiring cities there, but all Hank could picture was the bombed ruins of World War Two, Berlin nothing but a black-and-white panorama of rubble printed on old newsreel film. "I've watched too many war movies," Hank said. "Picked up some of the jargon."

Rebecca offered a perfunctory shrug, then eyed him directly. "Hank, I don't think I can quit smoking now. Not now, not until I'm satisfied with myself and my life."

His heart seemed to sag a couple of painful inches inside his chest. Satisfied with herself, with her life? When had she become so unhappy?

"It's nothing serious," she said. "I'm just not at a point where I can handle more stress. My crappy little job steals more than half my time, my—"

He cut her off with his expression. "Not a crappy little job."

"Okay, a wonderful crappy little job. Whatever. I have to deal with all of your faculty functions, where I have to be the most charming little thing that ever danced the earth, I've got Sharri teetering between womanhood and infancy, she's already started menstruating and needs a training bra I haven't gotten around to buying."

Hank stared, dumbstruck. Sharri Lynn, his little girl, already having periods? It could happen at her age, he knew that, but this early, to a girl so young? Cripes, she had yet to celebrate her twelfth birthday, and this should not be so. But of course it *was* so, and it seemed he had missed a lot of things around here that he should not have missed. "So do you want to quit your job?" he asked. "Stay at home more, be a housewife?"

"Nothing that radical, Hank. And really none of this is a big deal, it's just my mood. That stupid thing last night, that Roger Bevins-Clarke guy, you know? The whole thing left me with a bad case of the creeps."

"Me too," he offered, relaxing as her anger dwindled. He stepped forward and took control of her hands, then snugged them at the sides of his waist, pressed them into place until they stayed. "How about a new rule in this household," he said gently. "Smoke 'em if you've got 'em."

She smiled. "Sounds good to me."

"Wunderbar," he said, and kissed her. The stench of tobacco nearly made him gag.

4

The meeting between Karl-Luther von Wessenheim and the woman who had outbid him at the secret auction began exactly at two o'clock in the afternoon. Von Wessenheim's lawyer had motored him from the Euro-Bank's prestigious headquarters in Frankfurt to the site the woman had specified, a small town to the north that boasted a natural mineral spring, a *Bad*. In antiquity the Germans of Bad Nauheim had erected a tremendous thirty-foot-high hedge made of supporting logs densely woven with sticks; the mineral water flowed through a trough at its crest and trickled down between the branches to filter and medicate the air. Once Teddy Roosevelt had vacationed here in an effort to heal his bronchitis, for when the wind blew through the mineral water the stench of sulfur was said to cure. And it was here, sitting at a cement picnic table near the shade cast by the giant hedge, that von Wessenheim and his lawyer met with the woman and, of course, her lawyer.

"Schmidt, Reinhart," her lawyer introduced himself, using his last name first in the German custom. He offered his hand to von Wessenheim.

"I think we know each other," Franz Bohr said nastily. "My client Herr von Wessenheim, your client Frau Dietermunde. Sit."

They sat. Immediately the woman's lawyer spoke up. "What we are dealing with here is a piece of history."

"Hardly," Bohr replied, casting a warning glance at von Wessenheim. "An ordinary hat of dubious authenticity."

Frau Dietermunde leaned close to von Wessenheim, her

earrings sparkling, her blonde hair catching glints of sunlight. Despite being two decades older than von Wessenheim himself, she was a healthy timepiece with her bright blue eyes and scarcity of wrinkles. But hidden under the tinted hair and makeup, he knew, were the scars of a plastic surgeon's knife. And in her bankbook, he also knew, more money than any woman should be allowed to have. "The price for the hat is double what I paid for it last night," she said sourly in his face. "Two hundred thousand Deutschmarks become four hundred thousand overnight. Wait another day and they become eight hundred thousand."

Von Wessenheim put both elbows on the table and dragged his hands wearily down his unshaven face. "She's drunk," he snapped at her lawyer, Schmidt. "I thought she needed six hours of sleep, not six more glasses of beer."

"What she does on her own time is no concern of yours," Schmidt retorted. "Let's get down to business."

Von Wessenheim rose up and planted both fists on the cement table where his elbows had been. "The stupid bitch is too drunk to negotiate!"

Franz Bohr spread his hands apart as if to press the opponents to neutral corners. Von Wessenheim drew back and looked around for eyes and ears, shocked at himself. The breeze pushing through the wattle of the hedge was warm and heavy with sulfur, the noise of the falling water comfortingly loud. Displays of anger in public were not welcome in the restful setting of the *Bad*, and he had fortunately not disturbed anyone. But while he had spent six hours last night pacing and smoking three packs of overpriced Reemstma cigarettes, Frau Dietermunde had been basking in booze and her own good fortune at having acquired Adolf Hitler's top hat. The galling thing was that he had hesitated to outbid her on the hat because his attitude was tainted—corrupted—by Franz Bohr's insistence that its authenticity was questionable. Who could offer two hundred thousand Marks for a hat that might have been perched on the head of a department store dummy just last week? Frau Dietermunde, that's who, and she got exactly what she wanted: the real thing.

"Please forgive me," he muttered, and busied himself lighting a cigarette.

Schmidt affected a smile. "Good." The smile got hastily swept under the rug. "Now," he said, adjusting himself, and spoke to Franz Bohr. "The price you pay will depend on how long this takes. So you must understand that in this instance, time is, quite literally, money."

Bohr was silent for a moment, then snorted. "You might wait yourself out of a sale."

"And that is exactly what Frau Dietermunde hopes."

Von Wessenheim remained quiet, glancing disgustedly at Frau Dietermunde now and again. It had often struck him as odd that their small group of like-minded purchasers of National Socialist memorabilia should be so often at each others' throats, but that was the way things stood. Each of the veterans of the Hitler Youth, in differing ways, thought they could preserve their memories of the Third Reich by enshrining the artifacts of the era in their own way. To von Wessenheim they simply picked and pecked at their treasures like vultures over a dinner of sun-baked corpse.

Schmidt was eyeing his watch. "Time is passing," he murmured as if to himself.

Franz Bohr shook his head, chuckling. "This little show is pathetic, Herr Schmidt. Our time is no less precious than yours."

Frau Dietermunde let out a huge and unexpected belch. Von Wessenheim closed his eyes and turned his head to the side, afraid to inhale, then grew tired of the entire ordeal in a sudden burst of distaste. "I offer you three hundred thousand Deutschmarks," he said, standing to look down at the old woman and all her glitter. "Absolutely no more, not one Pfennig more. Take it or leave it, take it or leave it *now*!"

His own lawyer, Franz, jumped to his feet. "His offer is not binding under the laws of the Hessian state of the Federal Republic of Germany!"

"God, would you *stop*!" von Wessenheim roared, and shoved him to the side. Bohr's thighs were wedged under the edge of the cement table and he twirled in a clumsy circle before falling to his knees on the ground. But he was up in a flash, dusting the grass from his pants, grinning idiotically while his face became engorged with red.

Frau Dietermunde glanced uncertainly up at von Wessenheim. He flipped his cigarette away and thrust a hand under her chin, gathered a quick fistful of clothing and necklaces, and jerked her to her feet. "Now you will tell me," he growled in her face. "Is the hat real?"

Her teeth were clenched, her eyes as blue as the sky above her. "The group does not dabble in fakes," she rasped. "Do you?"

He shoved her back down. "Four hundred thousand Marks, Frau Dietermunde. My lawyer will write a check for that amount as soon as he can fumble his way to his car."

Her lawyer stood. His face was dark with anger, his eyes small and shiny. "This meeting is over," he said. He looked at Frau Dietermunde. "I believe everything here is finished, is it not?"

She stood and faced von Wessenheim. "Karl-Luther, if I may use your given name, I leave you with no hat and one bit of advice."

He crossed his arms over his chest. "I have a lawyer to give me advice. Advice, and huge bills for his time."

Her lips drew up at the corners in a parody of a smile. "My advice is free, Karl-Luther, and the best advice you may ever get: leave the group to those who have paid the price of membership."

"I will not," he said immediately.

"You will not be asked back," she said. "A grave mistake was made with you."

He tried to smirk but was caught up in a study of her eyes. Behind the brighter sheen of the alcohol lurked a depth and tone he could not define. She was old enough to remember the war years, had probably been in grade school and could remember practicing bomb drills during which she hid under her desk, maybe crawled under the building with her classmates. Was that it, did von Wessenheim's relative youth exclude him?

He decided not. "Keep your hat, Frau Dietermunde," he said evenly. "The day will come when you and the others all come to *me*. Because I will have the greatest treasure of all."

She smiled, an expression that quickly widened into a chuckle, then a laugh. "It does not exist," she said, dabbing a finger at her eyes. "If it did, I would already have it." She looked at Schmidt. "Let us leave this man to his fantasy."

He nodded, and they walked away. After a few steps toward the parking area she turned back, shielding her eyes from the afternoon sunlight with her hand. "Karl-Luther," she called.

He offered her a stare.

"It really does not exist," she said. "The Russians searched, the Americans searched, and even the Germans have searched. More than fifty years have passed and he is still gone, never to return. I, the group and I, we have given up the idea. Better, perhaps, that he stays gone forever. He is a mystery, and soon will be a legend."

Von Wessenheim eyed her for a time. "Mysteries and legends don't leave bones behind," he called out.

"Nor did he," she said. "Just like Jesus, of whom we have no trace, Jesus who ascended into heaven."

Silently he watched her; after a bit she turned and walked away in the pleasant sunshine and oddly fragrant air.

Franz Bohr stepped up beside him. "Just an old hag," he said. "An old hag who would compare the Führer to Christ. We're better off without her and her associates."

Von Wessenheim said nothing. He watched her and her lawyer get into a silver Mercedes, watched them drive away. "I will always be an outsider to them," he cursed in a whisper.

"Better that way," Bohr said. "They're a dying breed."

Von Wessenheim dropped his gaze and dismally eyed the grass poking up between the soles of his oiled Italian shoes. From around him came the noise of people conversing at the other tables, of children playing and laughing not far away. In Frau Dietermunde's childhood bombs had rained down and children had died by the thousands as the war years ground on. Children everywhere across Europe and Asia, on every side. This was, he felt bitterly sure now, the reason he would forever be estranged from them. He was a German child who had been born too late to risk death. To the survivors of the Hitler Youth, he was, in effect, an *Ausländer*, as foreign to them as a Turkish laborer.

"I want to initiate an exploration," he told Bohr. "I want you to hire a staff of experts. Price is no object."

Bohr froze in place. "What kind of experts?"

Von Wessenheim gave him a glance and burrowed for a fresh cigarette. "Qualified experts on the subject of the Führer's death and the disposition of his body."

Bohr raised one hand and touched his forehead, then his nose, his chin. The skin of his neck above his collar was fleshy and pimpled like the skin of a chicken. "Herr von Wessenheim," he said, "I am a doctor of jurisprudence, by no means a historian, but it is known worldwide that the remains of Adolf Hitler were never found. In the last week of the war his corpse was doused with gasoline and burned in a bomb crater."

Von Wessenheim's eyes shifted to the horizon. The tops of the houses and spires of Bad Nauheim's churches thrust up toward the sky as they had done for centuries. The very age of Europe seemed embedded in the soil, the culture of thousands of years rooted as if to the center of the earth. "Josef Goebbels was burned in a bomb crater," he said quietly. "The Russians found his body and autopsied it. There are documents, witnesses, photos."

Bohr seemed to shrug. "But he was not the Führer."

"Indeed not, just the highest-ranking minister of government."

"I don't follow."

Von Wessenheim turned. "Hundreds, maybe thousands of Nazis fled to South America in the last days of the Reich, taken there in submarines and boats. Why toss the Führer into a crater and burn him like a dog when others were given safe passage?"

"But that was the treatment given to Goebbels, Hitler's best friend."

"Goebbels gave the world a cremated corpse to marvel at," von Wessenheim said. "The natural assumption is that Hitler met the same dismal end."

Bohr sank down on the bench vacated by Frau Dieter-munde's lawyer. "Then you're saying Hitler survived, escaped to Argentina."

"No, of course not." He sat beside him. "The Israelis would have found him like they did Eichmann. Look at Klaus Barbie, after so many years! I have no doubt that Adolf Hitler killed himself in Berlin."

"Then what is the point?"

"The point is, what really happened to his body? Perhaps it was taken a few blocks from his bunker and simply buried. Berlin was littered with corpses, maybe Hitler wound up bulldozed into a mass grave by the Russians."

"Which means," Bohr said, "that it will be impossible to locate his skeleton. I assume that it is what you goaded Frau Dietermunde with. You will uncover the greatest prize of all, the bones of Adolf Hitler."

"That's correct."

"But all of Germany is littered with the bones of millions."

"All of Germany can go to hell," von Wessenheim snapped. "It is in Berlin, the area around the bunker, perhaps even beneath the Reich's Chancellery itself. An area of maybe twelve square city blocks. That is where his bones are."

"If they weren't blasted to bits by a bomb."

Von Wessenheim stood again. "Franz, you are the most uninspired man I have ever known. You are a defeatist."

"A realist."

"I say look at the beauty of the sky, you say it will soon rain. I say the future is bright, you say that death awaits us all. I say his bones are beneath our very feet, you say they have vanished." He paced away a few steps and turned again, sucking furiously on his cigarette and blowing out clouds of smoke. "You know," he said, putting on a tremendous frown, "you have been an excellent lawyer for me, an *excellent* lawyer."

Bohr looked at him steadily. "By keeping your—enthusiasm—in check."

"By keeping me ever hesitant and always afraid."

"I don't see it that way."

"You don't see a lot of things," von Wessenheim said, smoking.

"By nature I am a cautious man."

"Fine. By nature I am a man prone to act on whims. My whim now is to fire you on the spot."

Bohr rose slowly to his feet. "Because of a hat? Is it the hat?"

Von Wessenheim nodded. "Of course because of the hat, for when I find the bones I will need a DNA sample from the skin flakes in the hat. If they match, I have won. But I will never know unless I get the hat from Frau Dietermunde."

Franz Bohr clicked his heels together and bowed slightly. "Then I consider our relationship terminated."

Von Wessenheim flipped the butt of his cigarette into the shadow of the hedgerow. "You have a fascination with the old adages of the English language, do you not?"

Bohr thought about it. "The commonsense sayings of many languages."

"'Penny wise and pound foolish,' as you told me? Remember that one?"

"I do," Bohr said.

"Would you like to hear a new one?"

He eyed von Wessenheim cautiously. "Maybe."

"'Fuck you and the horse you rode in on.'"

Bohr puzzled over it while von Wessenheim stalked away to phone a limousine service.

5

The rain clouds over Terre Haute departed at noon, chased by a lazy wind that eased them apart and casually swept the remaining tatters over the brim of the horizon. Hank had been puttering around in the garage while the rain drummed down, his two-car garage that had steadily been losing the capacity for car number two as the years and the junk piled up. The Lexus got parked in here, of course, but Rebecca's little blue Pontiac had become a victim of overcrowding and was now forced to deal with the weather outside. Piled in its space were heaps of furniture and cardboard boxes Rebecca's mom and dad had left behind: when Dad turned sixty they had bought a Country Coach the size of a city bus and driven off to tour America.

So none of their stuff could be thrown out. Hank eyed the Lexus in its roomy expanse of garage, eyed the rest. Rebecca's Pontiac had graced the cement floor with tire marks and an oily, black stain, so it was easy to imagine where the car should sit once room was made. By kicking things aside he could enlarge the passageway well enough, but the real problem lay in getting the nose of her car in far enough to close the garage door.

He took a drink from the can of half-warm Pepsi in his hand, grimaced at its flatness, and set it on the topmost box of a short stack of cardboard boxes to his right. It tipped over and chugged out a few blurts of Pepsi that surfed into the dimples in the cardboard, slid down the sides. He swatted the can away, glanced around for a rag, and settled on some paint-speckled newspaper. As he tried to sponge the Pepsi away, the brittle old tape holding the flaps together gave up the ghost and the box popped open.

Hank tossed the balled newspaper away, annoyed. There were places called storage units, people rented them by the month. Rebecca's parents, rich enough to afford a Country Coach, could not afford the luxury of stockpiling their own crap. What could it cost? Thirty dollars a month, maybe forty?

He shrugged to himself. No sense in wasting anger on people who weren't on hand to enjoy it. There was a roll of duct tape around here somewhere, probably on his tool bench. The bench had been a gift from Rebecca's dad, who had hoped to interest Hank in things carpentorial. Wrong. There weren't enough Time-Life home-repair books on the planet to interest him in the field. As a professor with barely three active years under his academic belt and tenure still a golden ring too far from the merry-go-round to be snatched, it would be handy to be a handyman. But when you grow up in a family where the dad is a union pipe fitter either laid off or on strike most of the time, and the mom bounces from convenience stores to hamburger joints and back when paychecks are scarce, you get light-headed when your new prestige and steady income earn you every credit card ever made, afford you more luxuries then you ever needed. So why bust ass, really? It was far easier to pay someone else.

He peeked inside the box and saw folded clothes. Some fat brass buttons gleamed mellowly under the garage's fluorescent lights; the unmistakable aroma of mothballs drifted out. He turned the box and read its marking, fat strokes of a black Magic Marker: *G-pa's Old Stuff.*

G-pa. That would be his own grandpa; the grudge against Rebecca's parents faded. Grandpa had died of respiratory failure ten years ago, give or take. Hank lifted the clothing out, spread it, and found himself holding a faded brown army uniform. A couple of mothballs ticked to the floor. Frowning, he examined it: World War Two era, and yes, Grandpa had fought in Italy or France or somewhere. He was shot through both lungs and spent most of the war recuperating. Hank remembered his wound as a little round scar on his side.

Two medals were pinned to the pocket—the familiar shape and color of a purple heart, and another of some kind, red and yellow and round. High on one shoulder was a triangular patch that identified itself as the insignia of the Third Armored Division, below that the single chevron of a private first class. It looked like Grandpa had been an average GI Joe who'd caught a bullet and been rewarded with a couple of medals.

He set the coat aside and dug deeper while the rain dripping from the trees blipped here and there on the roof. Wrapped in a wad of waxed paper was a square of cloth, a handkerchief. Hank flapped it out. Most of it was dark with dried blood. With a grimace he wrapped it again. It was likely the makeshift compress a medic had stuck in Grandpa's bullet hole. Hard to imagine that Grandpa would keep it.

Blut und Eisen . . .

He blinked. What the hell did that mean? Sounded like a song, a crazy voice singing nonsense in his mind. He tapped his forehead, frowning more deeply.

Cigarettes are a poison . . .

He dug into the box again, his heart beating faster. Hearing voices? Prelude to schizophrenia? Could a schizophrenic gain tenure at Indiana State University?

He withdrew a flat white box that rattled, and forced his mind to be still. The stench of mothballs was acrid and foreign. There seemed to be more shadows in the garage now, as if one of the overhead fluorescents had failed. Naturally, he thought as he forced a cocky grin onto his face. You are rummaging through a dead man's belongings, you ought to be jumpy.

He pried the box open and found more military stuff, brass insignia stamped with shields and heraldic images, an unfired bullet nearly as long as his finger, two others that were smaller. Hank didn't know much about guns, but it didn't take boot camp to know these were serious business. Underneath was a photograph of soldiers standing for a group picture. Unshaven and dirty, they wore their helmets cocked to the side, were sneering and clowning. The scene behind them was of a town or city that lay in bombed-out ruins. On the back of the picture, in pencil, he read this: "Alfred T. Thor-wald with friends in Charlie Bat 2/27th FA, 3rd Armd Div, St. Lo. France." Hank turned it over again and scrutinized the faces. Very young men, unlike the movie GIs like John Wayne and Robert Mitchum, guys well into their forties. One of the men—boys—was Grandpa.

Grandpa was standing beside a grinning young fellow. Two of the fellow's fingers were stuck up in a V formation behind Grandpa's helmet, resulting in rabbit ears. Grandpa himself had a cigarette dangling from a corner of his mouth, had an arm stuck out to prop himself against the remains of a partially collapsed wall, had one dirty boot casually crossed over the other as if to dare the wall to fall. To his right were two soldiers holding an unfurled Nazi flag, stretching it out for the camera. It was burned around the edges.

Hank put the flat box back together and set it aside. Poking again into the larger box, trying to see inside it, his hand encountered a strap. He lifted it out.

Leather belt, a wide one. Flat rectangular buckle that seemed likely to be brass, if cleaned up. He held it closer to his eyes. Inside a stamped wreath stood an eagle perched on a swastika. Curving over the eagle's head were two letters: "SA."

South America? Had Germany stationed troops in South America? Every year or so a Nazi war criminal got rounded up there, so maybe so. These were, obviously, Alfred T. Thorwald's war trophies. If he had shared them with Hank years ago, Hank had kept no memory of it. His fingers curled over a cool metal object, a length of pipe by the feel of it. When he dredged it out, his jaw dropped: a dagger in a metal scabbard, obviously very German and perhaps valuable. He held it in both hands, marveling. The hilt was black with a pearly-red swastika stamped into the middle. He slid the knife free of the scabbard, awed by the weight of it. Words in large italics had been machined into the blade: *Meine Ehre heißt Treue.*

"'My honor,'" Hank muttered, turning it over in his hands. "'My honor is called loyalty.'" The blade was still as shiny as the day it was made, still had a decent edge on it when he scraped it across his thumb. Something like this might be sold to a collector for a lot of money. Better, a museum should display a flawless piece like this. Hank wondered: Had Grandpa taken this from a dead German soldier? It was a chunk of history no matter how he'd gotten it. He shoved it into a back pocket of his jeans, anxious to get some colleagues to look at it. Scrabbling at the bottom of the box, he found the last of Grandpa's treasures, a large manila envelope. Hank snatched it out, mystified and expectant, and found that it was still sealed. More than fifty years ago, he mused in wonder as he held it, a young Grandpa had licked this envelope and closed it, shutting its contents inside for the next five decades. Now, on this morning, it would be reopened by his grandson. There was something poetic in that.

He brought it to his ear and shook it. Rustling. Nothing identifiable. He shrugged and carefully tore the envelope open. Probably some old German money, or some letters Grandma had sent to him overseas during the war. Maybe even an autographed picture of the Führer himself.

But it wasn't any of those. Hank stared, both bemused and incredulous. Inside the envelope, biding its time for five decades, was a pack of French cigarettes, another of Grandpa's souvenirs. Nothing else.

But after fifty years it still smelled enough like tobacco to make him crumple the envelope and hurl it away with a cry.

Alan Weston, investigative journalist for station WXRV in Indianapolis and the world's most hungover man, was ripped from unconsciousness about then by the hammering of his front door as the police smashed it open with a battering ram. He sat up, bleary and confused, and noticed that his telephone lay in two pieces on the floor—sometime during the night, he assumed, the damned thing had rung and he'd knocked it off the nightstand rather than face the horror of waking up. But now he *was* waking up, was actually quite awake when the door hit the floor in the foyer, became even *more* awake when six or eight SWAT-team types swarmed through his house and into his bedroom, M-16s held at the ready, wearing bulletproof vests and helmets the color of Spiderman's eyes.

Jesus God, he thought hollowly, *I finally went and murdered the ex.*

"He's alive," someone shouted, and at that point Alan noticed, through his bedroom window, that a virtual sea of humanity and news cameras heaved and tossed in his backyard, barely contained behind a police blockade. He rocked himself out of bed, groaned when his head gave a huge painful thump, and groaned again as he flopped back down seeing stars.

"He's wounded," the same someone shouted. "Get emergency response in here *now*!"

Alan closed his eyes. He had the d.t.'s, obviously, and this was a first-class hallucination complete with voices and images, though, curiously, the pink elephants were absent. Behind his closed eyes he tried to reason things out. He had gotten plowed last night on Jack and Coke over at the Breeze Inn, he had been feeling sorry for himself and had overdone it. And he had made some new friends, played some pool. They had been proud to make his acquaintance, asked for his autograph. They had even driven his drunken ass home in his own car, so nice were they. Must have been quite a cavalcade, all those bikers roaring along behind his Mercedes. Hopefully no one had *seen* the cavalcade.

Hands prodded him. Something cold and hard touched his chest, and he dragged his eyes open to see a white figure cutting his shirt down the row of buttons with a pair of surgical scissors. Crazy, man, the shirt had cost eighty bucks and it was time to get serious about sleeping this off. Then someone yanked his left eye open and shined a penlight into it.

Alan screamed. More hands pressed him hard to the bed as he jerked and twisted. "Start an IV," one of the hallucinations shouted. "Charlie, notify Union General that we're ready for transport."

"Roger."

Weird, Alan thought as the pain in his eye lessened. My hallucinations are named Charlie and Roger. He was rolled over onto his stomach. Scissors cut the legs of his slacks open. "No visible trauma."

"We might be dealing with poison here. Blunt trauma to the cranium, maybe. No telling what the bastards did to him."

"Beat me in pool," Alan croaked as they mauled him.

A head ducked close. "Say what?"

"Beat me in pool."

"Jesus." The head went up. "They beat him in the pool. Sergeant?"

A new voice: "Yeah?"

"Get forensics to the pool out back."

"Done deal."

Sergeant left. A gurney rattled into the bedroom. With a great heave he rose to his knees on the rumpled ruins of the bed. "All right, you stupid motherfuckers," he roared, batting their hands away. "*What the fuck are you doing in my house?*"

Silence dropped faster than a vaudeville stage curtain on a lousy act. One of the medics eyed the other one, and in the utter stillness Alan could fairly hear their thoughts: Is he okay, or has his cranial trauma induced dementia?

"I'm fine," Alan snarled at them, then clutched his head with both hands. "Not fine. Got any Demerol?"

"Look," one of the medics said, "you've taken a bad beating, you're confused. Lie down and let us do our work."

Alan knee-walked to the edge of the bed with his disassembled shirt drooping to his waist and his pants dragging along in tatters, swung a shoe out, and got to his feet on the floor, which pitched and rocked a little before quieting down. "You guys have got the wrong man, the wrong house. Nobody got beaten here."

The police sergeant was back in time to answer. "You're Alan J. Weston at 16674 Grand View Northeast, are you not?"

Alan squinted at him through watery, blood-red eyes. "I am."

"You've failed to answer your phone and disregarded all amount of noise on your doors and windows for the last few hours. We had to assume you were either incapacitated or dead."

"Or asleep."

"Nobody could stay asleep, not through all that."

Alan spread his hands. "I offer myself as evidence. I also offer that many people choose not to answer their phones and doors, but to this date never at such risk to their clothing."

The SWAT guys were wandering away, the medics stooping to assemble their wares. "It's like this," the sergeant said. He was beginning to look familiar; perhaps, Alan thought, Asshole Weston had once ripped him apart on TV for some trivial thing. "You're a high-profile figure in this city. You've publicly said more than once that you're Jewish, and so now you get a big swastika painted on your door and we have to assume the worst."

"Swastika? What swastika?"

"The big purple one painted on your front door, asshole."

He left the room muttering while Alan stood speechless in his expensive rags. After things grew quiet he tottered to the doorway, shambled down the hall with his heart banging sickly in his ears, and came upon the scene of the crime. His newly de hinged door lay flat on the floor, a drippy, fluorescent purple swastika touching all four corners. He sagged against the wall. The drunken bikers had left behind their signature, for whatever reason, most likely as a harmless but tasteless barb for their favorite famous Jew. Beyond the police barricade out front waited the cameras and microphones and gawkers. As he watched, the police rolled up the yellow tape that held the horde at bay and a surging tide of people broke loose, heading his way.

His brain was bruised and aching but his mind was still intact. The world could never know what had really happened, that he had spent the night whooping it up with racist bigots whose favorite tattoo was a copy of the one on his front door. The local press would plaster the front pages with the story, the Jewish community—which he historically ignored anyway would rise up against him; all his relatives, including his own mother, would demand either an explanation or a public apology. Pat the bartender would be interviewed. The very bikers themselves, Commando and Shaver and the others, *they* might be tracked down and interviewed. The truth, ugly and fatal for Alan, would arise. It would take less than two days, maybe three. He would be lucky to get a job delivering pizzas.

He touched his forehead, his thoughts racing. Come up with something fast, hotshot, think like you have never thought before. You have been in tight situations many a time and you have always come out clean, or maybe soiled but at least still in one piece.

Then it came to him. He had been at the bar doing research for an upcoming segment on racist bikers. Befriended them just to expose them. Would it work?

The horde was racing down the lawn now. Alan saw among them Phil Goodner, news editor at the *Indianapolis Star.* There with him were other familiar faces, friends from other walks of life, even his own uncle Max standing at the curb with his arms folded over his chest, his face haggard, his rabbi standing with him looking dark and ominous beneath the cup of his yarmulke. Even some of his own colleagues were in attendance: they would watch with glee while Alan Weston went straight down the tubes, the jealous bastards.

He looked down at himself. His clothes were preposterous, they looked as if they had been fed through a SaladShooter. He could envision his head as it must look, his rust-colored hair a pile of barbed wire, his face bloated and pasty, his eyes as pink as a flamingo's ass.

He had an idea. Why not tell the truth? Come completely clean. Tell of your career burnout, your embarrassment about who you've become, your animosities toward the WXRV staff, your contempt of Indianapolis, your contempt of all the pathetic hicks of Middle America in general.

The crowd was invading the porch. Microphones were jabbed at his mouth, video cameras captured him, people fought for position. It was now, or never. "I'm sore and aching but alive," he heard his voice tell them. "What I endured last night is just the small tip of an iceberg called hate, and it is an iceberg sometimes covered by the calm waters of reason but is always ready to rise to the surface once more, as it did last night for me."

He inhaled. Questions drilled him, hammered him. The lenses of the cameras were huge. He raised one shaking hand. "It is my decision not to involve the police in what I believe is a personal struggle against the forces of bigotry and hate, and therefore I have sent them away without answers. Because of the events of last night I have decided—and I hope my friends and colleagues will support me in this—I have decided to expose the gross and malignant persecution of Jews throughout the Midwest, a persecution that has, I very much hope, met its match in Alan Weston and the good and tolerant people of this city we call home, Indianapolis, Indiana."

Questions. Alan wobbled on his feet, sick and weary. The crowd threatened to drive him back into the depths of the house but suddenly a big man stood there pushing everyone back, old Uncle Max. His rabbi moved behind Alan and began to pray loudly in Hebrew. Uncle Max turned and laid his heavy hands on Alan's shoulders. "Look at you," he said in his raspy old-man's voice. He smelled strongly of his cigars, a smell akin to the smoke-filled tavern last night, and now to Alan's horror his eyes were welling up with tears as he shuffled around to face the cameras. "Look!" he brayed to the media crush. He clamped one big hand around the back of Alan's neck and jerked his head up higher. "Look at what the Nazis have done to my sister's only child!"

"I'll be fine," Alan bleated, pulling away. The smell of tobacco had awakened the memory of all those Jack and Cokes. Now nausea crawled up from his stomach to the back of his throat and perched there like a toad. He covered his mouth with a fist. Uncle Max turned and embraced him while the cameras rolled and the microphones listened. The rabbi's voice trilled up and down as he prayed the ancient prayers. The contents of Alan's stomach began to squeeze upward.

Without apology he ripped himself from his uncle's bear hug and bolted down the hallway to the bathroom and veered inside. *Bam,* the door was shut; *click,* it was locked. He stumbled to the mirror and put his hands around the cold white rim of the sink, propped most of his weight on it. His arms shook from the effort. His image stared back at him, gaunt and unshaven and slowly becoming aware of the magnitude of what he had done.

"Way to go, shit for brains," he said to his image, then bent with a groan and threw up all over the chrome pop-up drain.

6

Hank's first class on Monday was his least favorite: Intro to Earth Sciences 101, three full hours of it. Summer classes were pretty much loathed by the teachers and professors, for two good reasons. One, the freshmen were still high-schoolers in spirit and a fair number of them would drop out after the first two classes. Two, the entire university was as dead as an air-conditioned tomb and the summer students tended to be dull and unresponsive, wishing they were outside.

After surviving the class Hank decided to have lunch at the Quad, where a lot of students congregated and the excitement was always high. Hiking across the lawns with his little briefcase knocking against the side of his knee, he was struck by the scent of the summer grass—which brought his neglected golf clubs to mind—and the pods of students that had sprouted under the trees to rest in the shade. This was Ovid's dream, an idyllic place where learning and beauty met and embraced as lovers.

But at the top of the steps that led down into the boisterous Quad he spotted Perry Wilson lying in wait for him, magnetic chessboard bulging in the interior pocket of his tweed vest. Transplanted from a stuffy military academy decades before, he still could not make himself wear anything less than a vest and tie in the heat of summer, bunches of raiment and scarves and a greatcoat in the winter. He had managed to get himself a prime table in a corner of the Quad where the hot sunshine did not intrude. Hank paused, flexing his fingers under the handle of his briefcase. With an internal sigh he unlocked his knees and headed down. A game of chess right now would be like celebrating your birthday on the *Titanic*.

At the bottom he wended his way between bodies. The Quadrangle was a combination snack shop, cafeteria, and meeting place for the people who ventured here, the couple thousand students of Indiana State University who needed a breath of air before diving into their next classes. Though he was only thirty-two and likely the youngest professor on the payroll, Hank was beginning to learn that in an unfortunate way, these students were statistics. Your class starts with sixty and winds up with forty just two weeks into the semester, and the heat begins to filter down from above: attendance means tuition dollars coming in. What, Thorwald's dropout percentage is higher this term, what the hell is wrong with Thorwald? Thorwald's grade averages are falling, why is he becoming such a lousy teacher all of a sudden? Of course everyone from the president of ISU down to the short-order cooks in the Quad knew that each new year brought students both good and bad; some semesters they were sparkling young stars and some semesters they were turds. So do you coddle the underachievers in order to get their money, or do you maintain high standards to protect the reputation of the university? It was a question nobody seemed anxious to hear postulated, much less answered.

At the little two-person table Perry was already assembling the chess set, a little hinged board about the size of a decent pot holder. The plastic pieces stood less than an inch tall and came in either white or an attractive shade of red, shipped all the way around the world from exotic Taiwan. Hank seated himself and hugged his briefcase to his chest. "You're older than I am," he said by way of howdy-do. "Do you remember World War Two?"

"Let me see now," Perry said with a frown. "Us against the Germans. I believe we won."

"Were you alive then?"

"Born the year after it ended."

"Fat lot of help you are," Hank said.

Perry regarded him. "White or red. Red or white. Choose." Hank sighed. "Red."

Perry spun the board. "Your first move will unveil your second. Your second will unveil your third. You haven't a chance."

Hank smirked. "Been reading Hoyle again?"

"Yes. Make your move."

Hank pushed a pawn forward. "I found a war-vintage knife in my grandpa's stuff the other night," he said. "It's in my briefcase here."

Perry made his move, a pawn shoved one square up. "I wondered why you were making love to that thing."

Hank twitched his shoulders. "You'd hold on tight if you had a fortune in your lap, Perry."

"I see." He made motions with his fingers. "Open it up, get this over with so I can trounce you."

Hank looked around, slowly popped the little latches, and eased a hand inside. He grasped the knife but kept it out of sight, lowered the briefcase to the floor and pinned it to the wall with his foot. "Keep it kind of private, okay?" He hastily passed the knife over the table to Perry, who immediately jerked it out of its scabbard and held it up to the light. "Solingen steel," he remarked. "Good materials, excellently crafted. This is an SS ceremonial dagger, and though you're probably hoping it is a blood-spattered combat knife, it was never used in anything more severe than a parade."

"Meaning?"

Perry cocked one shoulder up in a lopsided shrug. "Meaning as in monetary value, how many thousands of dollars? I don't have a clue." He sheathed it with a click and handed it back. "Do not go to pawnshops for appraisals, Hank. Talk to Clem Manners over in European history, he probably knows somebody."

Hank nodded and put it away.

"Your move," Perry said.

Hank studied the board without really seeing it, wondering.

"We only have one hour," Perry said.

Hank perked up. "Fine, here." He slid another pawn forward.

"Mmm." Perry leaned over it. Hank waited without surprise as some minutes drifted past, as the noise and the laughter and the bubbling clitter-clatter of humanity thrummed inside the concrete walls of the Quad without bothering Perry. At his house the silence had to be absolute. It struck Hank again that this chess stuff had gotten out of control, that he was enduring the games instead of enjoying them, and not enjoying this one at all. But how could he abridge the schedule without hurting the man? Rebecca had told Hank more than once of the value of just saying no. But without the games Perry had nothing else to entertain him, he was a widower whose children had abandoned ship, the university and the chess marathons were his world. And then there was the trouble of having a seasoned and tenured professor angry with him at just about the time decisions were being made at the highest levels: tenure for Hank, or not?

"Got it," Perry said. He lifted his bishop to the edge of the board, planted it to menace Hank's knight on the diagonal. "Move it or lose it," he grunted.

"Fine," Hank muttered, and moved his knight at the other side of the board.

Perry smiled. "Kiss it good-bye, *mein Freund.*" He scooted his bishop across the magnetic board while Hank watched with a puzzled expression on his face.

"The move was too complex for you?" Perry asked after a bit.

Hank raised his eyes. "You spoke German."

He craned around with a frown. "I don't see any signs on the walls outlawing the act. What did I say?"

"You said 'my friend.'"

Perry leaned harder against the back of his seat. "You must forgive me, but I simply do not know the German words for 'my enemy.' Maybe it's *mein enema.* You think?"

Hank ignored the remark and shoved another pawn forward. "It's just that I seem to be speaking a lot of the Deutsch lately, and now you're doing it."

"And so you're wondering if you're at the center of the *Zeitgeist?*"

Hank gritted his teeth. "The point is, I don't have any background in the language. My dad liked war movies, so we watched them all, but all I learned in German was 'Vo In Der Heck Is Der Volkswagen.'"

"A solid start." Perry brought his knight into play. "Nothing we see or hear or learn is really forgotten, as I've told you. With hypnosis your mind can be called upon to remember trivial details many years old. A lifetime old. Clear back into infancy, the moment of birth."

Hank let his head drop. "Oops. Hypnosis hath reared its ugly head again."

"As well it should. But it doesn't always take hypnosis to awaken sleeping memories."

Hank raised it again. "Booze. My dad had a friend who would get smashed and cry about a dog that died forty years before, when the guy was nine."

"Your move, and in a way you're right. A strong emotion acts the same as a strong odor, it catalyzes the mind. We sit inside a new car and smell all that Detroit, it reminds us of our own car's younger days—and makes us want to buy another. We smell paint, it reminds us of the last time we painted something, maybe the very first time we painted anything at all, a paint-by-numbers kit from childhood."

Hank frowned at the board, then lifted a hand and presented his other knight. "So you're saying I either smelled something familiar, or felt an old emotion, then *ach du Lieber!*, I'm speaking a language that I never spoke before—just like now."

Hunched over the little board again, Perry glanced up at him. "You never spoke it, yet your mind can't forget the garbled phrases you learned, such as the whereabouts of that Volkswagen. It was just shoved to the deepest recesses of memory until a catalyst forced it out. Under hypnosis I could make you recite the entire dialogue of a movie you watched twenty years ago. I could make you recite *Gone With the Wind* word for word."

Hank wagged his head. "I don't believe it."

Perry's eyes sharpened with a trace of anger. "Why do you doubt every thing I say?"

"Because in this instance it is scientifically impossible."

Perry rose slightly. "How can a man who calls himself a scientist be so adamantly opposed to a proven subject? I can make you remember every word in the goddamned movie and even the day you watched it!"

"Don't blow a gasket, Perry." Hank grinned. "I've never seen *Gone With the Wind*. Read the book, though."

Perry slumped. "If not for your remarkable abilities in the game of chess, I would arrange to have you murdered, and believe me, I could arrange it quietly and well. Now shut up and let me think."

Hank kept himself silent, chuckling inwardly but a little embarrassed. Perry was becoming a downright grouch. After a bit he lifted his knight, traced his possible moves by wagging the little white horse here and there, then placed it in front of his pawns, where the tiny magnet built into the figure's base sucked it tight to the board. "Of two choices I've chosen the best," he declared unhappily.

"Perhaps you should read and memorize Hoyle," Hank said.

"I'd read and memorize *Mein Kampf* if it improved my game."

"Hitler played with toy soldiers, not chess pieces."

Perry straightened. "But chess *is* soldiers, Hank. This is a microcosm of war, this is battle to the cleverest degree. Your move."

"Fine." Hank shoved another pawn forward. A look at his watch showed him that fifteen minutes of his lunch hour was already gone. He was suddenly fed up with chess for today. "Um, Perry?" he ventured quietly.

No response. Perry had gone into a trance that might last twenty minutes. Without a checkmate Hank would have to show up at his house tonight to finish the game, be wheedled into yet another on the bigger board, get home late feeling grumpy and used, unload the frustration on Rebecca and Sharri, and wake up to a frigid household in the morning.

"Perry?" he said again. "Professor Wilson?"

He looked up. "What?"

Hank ducked his head. "I can't finish this game right now.

I've got a one o'clock sneaking up on me and I still have to get lunch."

Perry raised himself enough to look above heads. "They've got food here, you know. Sandwich, soup, burgers, the whole array. I won't make my move while you're standing in line."

"Oh." Hank craned his head. It was hard to tell if there was a line at all, just a jostling group of happy people, a lot of them dressed in the latest quasi-hippie fad, brilliantly colored tie-dyed shirts, beads and necklaces, ankle-length silk dresses you could plumb see right through when the light was right.

He rounded to face Perry again, reluctant but ready now to tell him the truth, that the games had become boring and ate up too much of his free time, but Perry had bent again over the board, leaving only the white hair at the top of his head and the pink scalp beneath it to talk to. Hank hesitated, then nudged his briefcase closer to himself with his foot. Maybe, he thought, the German knife could provide excuse enough to flee this place: gotta find a museum, gotta go. "Hey, Perry?" he said.

Perry jerked up a hand and flapped it at him. It meant shut the hell up and let me think, Hank knew. It was also a reminder, among a growing list of reminders, that Perry Wilson did not care about anything on Hank's side of the board unless it was a checkmate, or dangerously close to that. "Perry?"

Nothing. Hank lifted his briefcase from the floor and propped it upright on his lap, hugged it. As far as body language went, this was a shout in the dark.

Perry snatched up his bishop by its pointy white head and zipped it diagonally to capture another of Hank's pawns. "Kasparov employed this maneuver in 1975," he said as he pried the pawn up from the board. "Your move, but be careful. Like a good plot, the game thickens."

Hank dropped his gaze to the board. What we have here, he thought tiredly, is a fancy game. With all the time he had wasted just this month over chess he could have cleaned out a dozen garages, yet his own garage still waited for completion, was still heaped with furniture and boxes that might never go away. What a dumb mistake to have ventured to the Quad knowing Perry was on the loose. He glanced up and saw that Perry's eyes were fixed on the board and twitching back and forth as he imagined his next moves. "Say, Perry," Hank said. "I really don't have the time now to pursue this any further, I just realized I have papers in my briefcase here that have to be graded."

Perry raised his head slowly. "Is that why you're making love to your briefcase again? First we have a knife, now we have papers to grade. Are you afraid of losing this one?"

Hank took a breath. "To be honest, Perry, these games have been eating up too much of my time, really. I enjoy the hell out of them, but one and sometimes three games per day leaves me no time for anything else. You have to admit we've been going overboard."

"I will not admit that. Overboard is for water enthusiasts, chess is for mental enthusiasts."

"I'm serious," Hank said. "I can maybe line up some other people who'd play, get a regular team going."

"I see. A chess team. Chess is a two-person game only and has been since the dawn of time, but now we can make it a team sport."

"You know what I mean. Arrange some new opponents for you, give you a fresh challenge."

Perry cocked his head. "You are my fresh challenge, Hank. Not one other person in this university commands the skill you do. You have an instinct for battle, you would have made a great general."

Hank let his eyes fall shut. "I've got things to do, Perry. Can't we limit the games to twice a week? Three times?"

"A true general goes down fighting to the last man. Show your instincts, trounce me."

"No." Hank lifted his briefcase and stood. Rebecca thought it was easy to just say no, yet this was anything but easy. "We can do a game Wednesday evening, how about that?"

"So now you dictate a schedule for me?" He jerked an

arm up and slashed it across the board to sweep it clean. The small figures exploded outward to clatter and ping across the tiled floor. Heads turned, a lot of them. "You seem to have forgotten the things I've done for you, my efforts to help you achieve tenure. You seem to have forgotten what you owe me."

"Actually, I believe I have repaid you with a thousand chess games I didn't want to play."

Perry rose up and leaned on his hands, the tip of his tie crossing over the chessboard like a pendulum as he spoke. "I have power here in the politics of the university, and I am a master politician. Be careful of antagonizing me further."

Hank covered his eyes with his hand; this was suddenly like trying to talk sense with Darth Vader. "Christ, Perry, this thing is getting crazy. Staying alive just to await the next game is an addiction, a rotten way to live. You need to branch out, socialize."

"Now you are my psychologist?"

Hank lowered his voice, reddening. "Go to a party, attend a social function. Take a lady out for a *date*, for God's sake."

Perry suddenly dropped onto his chair. "Get out of here, go grade your papers." He began to snatch up the figures that had stayed on the table. "You sneer at the science of psychology, you scoff at my findings in hypnosis. I'm twice your age and yet I'm the fool here. Fine." He bent under the table, grunting as he tried to fish up the fallen soldiers. A couple of students nearby sheepishly scooped some up and spread them on the table, then moved hastily away to their own business. Hank wavered on the edge of an apology, of blaming it on fatigue or a spat with the wife. But then the endless games would resume, he would be clenched even tighter in Perry's grip.

"This is nothing personal," he said, groping for words. "I simply can't keep up the pace anymore. Can you see it in that light?"

Perry was now trying to slam the little chessboard shut. Bits and pops of plastic jumped, red shards, white speckles. He paused to glare up at Hank. "At least leave me the dignity of seeing it in whichever light I choose to see it. And so, then, good-bye."

Hank shuffled uncomfortably. "Hey, Perry, this thing—"

"Good-bye, Hank."

He turned, almost turned again, then rolled his shoulders and headed for the stairs. Rebecca had said it never hurts a body to say no once in a while, but this time it hurt like hell.

7

It was ten in the evening in Berlin, Germany. Karl-Luther von Wessenheim was pacing the rooms of his suite at the Berlinische Residenz, waiting for the arrival of two experts who should have been in town an hour ago. Since firing his attorney von Wessenheim had wallowed in the luxury of following his own instincts, charting his own future without that cackling goose Franz Bohr to squawk in his ear. He had driven himself for the first time over the alien highways of the former East Germany to reach Berlin, quite apprehensive at first, but after settling in and seeing no Russian troops the drive became pleasant enough. But here it was, ten o'clock come and gone and his experts were late. Von Wessenheim consoled himself with the knowledge that after the Berlin Wall had come down both Germanys had been tossed into a bit of chaos that hadn't ended yet.

Still, though, promptness was a German specialty. He wandered to the drapes and drew them apart, opened them more and pressed his face to the warm window. The night below was remarkably clear, the streetlights of the famous Unter den Linden arrowing left and right like runway lights, with the rest of Berlin spread beyond in miles of more streets, more lights. To the left towered the Brandenburger Tor, lighted by searchlights, Berlin's historical equal of the Champs-Elysées in Paris. Von Wessenheim tried to picture the scene as it once was, all the lights blacked out to avoid the aim of the bombers, Berlin slowly reduced to ashes and thousands upon thousands of people blown to bits as the war ground on. Somewhere down there was buried the skeleton of Adolf Hitler, waiting only to be found.

Behind him the phone trilled. Von Wessenheim pulled the drapes together and hurried to pick it up. "Yes?"

It was the front desk, an uninspired voice performing its duty.

"He's expected," he said, and dropped the receiver onto its ivory cradle. The man heading for the elevator right now was Dr. Konrad Rudiger, author of a scholarly book about Hitler's last days. Still expected was Dr. Friedl von Lütringen, a historian and renowned expert on the life of Hitler's wife, Eva Braun. This was an aspect of the disappearance that no one seemed to have investigated before. Eva Braun supposedly killed herself by drinking poison, while Hitler chose to shoot himself through the mouth. Wherever the grave of Hitler was, Eva Braun was there too, at his side to this day, he was sure of it. Many people had searched for Hitler's corpse. None had searched for hers.

There was a soft rapping on the door. Von Wessenheim strode to it excitedly and swung the doors apart. Standing before him was a man whose wild forest of gray-black locks poked up from his scalp like burned stalks of corn, a pudgy-faced man whose rumpled blue suit failed to hide his oversize belly. Dangling from one fist was a briefcase. "Herr Doktor Rudiger?" von Wessenheim asked.

"Herr von Wessenheim?"

They assessed each other, von Wessenheim using a smile to disguise his consternation at the appearance of his expert. "So good of you to come," he said, and swept an arm to usher Dr. Rudiger in. "How was your trip? Would you like to sit down?"

Dr. Rudiger answered by lumbering to the sofa and plopping his briefcase on the ornate coffee table that fronted it. After a brief look around, he sank down. "Never buy Italian shoes," he muttered, and tugged at the knot of his tie.

"I'm afraid my other guest hasn't arrived yet, Herr Doktor," von Wessenheim said. "Perhaps you and I can discuss matters in her absence."

Dr. Rudiger dug his knuckles into his eyes, yawning. Von

Wessenheim reminded himself that intelligent people often have quirks, that he had a quirk or two of his own. Even Einstein himself kept a wild hairdo, and often forgot to wear shoes in the snow. "You're exhausted from the drive," von Wessenheim said tenderly. "I'll call room service for some coffee, if you'd like."

"What I'd like," Dr. Rudiger grunted, prying a shoe off his foot, "is a good pilsner and a hot bratwurst with mustard and a roll."

"Then you shall have it." Von Wessenheim hurried to the phone; it rang with his fingers inches away and he snatched it up. "*Ja?*" Again he smiled. "Yes, yes, send the lady up." He spun around. "Frau Doktor Friedl von Lütringen has arrived. We can begin work tonight."

Dr. Rudiger was massaging his feet. "Frau Doktor von Lütringen? Biographer of Eva Braun?"

Von Wessenheim lifted his chin. "I believe we will make a good team."

Dr. Rudiger snorted. "She's insane."

"Pardon?"

He was peeling one of his socks off. "Haven't you read her book?"

"Of course I've read her book, and quite recently." Quite recently was actually two days ago, and though he had hurried through it he had at least caught the gist of the thing.

"It is her suggestion that in the final days of the Reich, Hitler was incapacitated by an enormous mental breakdown caused by his years of failing leadership and the attempt on his life by his generals. Frau Doktor von Lütringen suggests that Eva Braun herself dictated the final events of the war. That she was, in fact, the Führer of Germany as it collapsed. She utterly ignores the role of Martin Bormann, Hitler's most trusted friend. Why would he hang back and let Eva Braun take over?"

Von Wessenheim perched himself on the edge of a wing-back chair. "It's not beyond belief."

"No, but I find her research substandard, her conclusions conjectural."

Von Wessenheim cleared his throat. "The point here, though, is not to decide which of the two acted as Führer at the end. It is to find physical evidence of their remains."

Dr. Rudiger yanked his other sock off. To von Wessenheim's surprise he folded both of them neatly together and slid them into a pocket inside his coat. Then came another peck at the door. Von Wessenheim jumped up and hurried to it, planted his hands on the brass levers; he took a breath and swept the doors open.

"Herr von Wessenheim?" she asked.

A sigh of relief exited soundlessly from his lungs. Frau Doktor von Lütringen was a short woman of maybe thirty-five, wore big round glasses and a simple brown hairdo that curled neatly under the hinges of her jaw. "I believe I'm expected?" she said, eyebrows raised.

"Please come in."

She stepped inside. "I've always loved this hotel. Rich in history, yet newly built. That is one of the oddities of Berlin, buildings that are hundreds of years old yet so recently erected. Have you ever wondered about that, Herr von Wessenheim?"

He nodded, having never wondered at all.

"The war, everything demolished but newly risen, much of it sturdier than before. Did you know that construction workers find dozens of unexploded bombs each year?"

Von Wessenheim smiled an apology. "That is why I have asked for your service, Frau Doktor. I am quite ignorant of such things."

"I hope to be of good service to you." She rose up slightly on tiptoe and looked over von Wessenheim's shoulder at Dr. Rudiger. "You have a guest?"

Von Wessenheim took a step to the side. "Sorry. Frau Doktor von Lütringen, allow me to introduce Herr Doktor Konrad Rudiger."

He rose, and they shook hands. "You are a historian, aren't you?" she asked as their hands parted. "I may have read your works."

"*Hitler's Final Hours*, published by Rheinhold Presse," he grunted. "And many scholarly pieces on the subject as well."

"I believe I've read some," she said thoughtfully.

He dropped onto the sofa. "Herr von Wessenheim and I have been discussing strategy in our attempt to locate the Führer's remains. He believes that Martin Bormann might have played a role in the burial."

Frau Doktor von Lütringen chose the wing-back chair von Wessenheim had abandoned, sat primly on it, and smoothed her skirt over her knees. "Interesting idea." She tossed her head almost disdainfully. "As I told you on the phone, this is not an impossible undertaking," she said as von Wessenheim seated himself on the other end of the sofa. "The possibility exists that both Hitler's and Eva Braun's bodies were flown northwest to an area still under German control."

Dr. Rudiger straightened. "The airport had been under small-arms and artillery fire by the Russians for days. Nothing came or went."

"Not true. Hannah Reitsch was able to land through the gunfire and make her way to Hitler's bunker."

Dr. Rudiger's face began to take on a pinkish color. "Hitler's greatest fear at the time was that he would be captured, dead or alive, and be hung from a scaffold for public display, dangling upside down from a rope around his ankles, which was the fate his friend Benito Mussolini suffered when his regime in Italy collapsed. So why would his most loyal soldiers pack his body onto an airplane that probably would not get off the ground?"

Frau Doktor von Lütringen cocked her head. "I am aware of the history. I am simply exploring areas that have not been examined before."

"Then perhaps we should explore the area of kidnapping by aliens from another planet."

She glanced over at von Wessenheim. "I thought we were to have a serious discussion here."

"And we will," he responded. "Dr. Rudiger, I would ask that you put aside any professional jealousies in the interest of the project at hand."

Dr. Rudiger glared at him, then seemed to bite off whatever he was about to say. "As you wish, Herr von Wessenheim."

"Good." He turned to Frau Doktor von Lütringen again. "Please go on."

She nodded. "My point is that there are many possible solutions to this mystery. Do we believe what Hitler's closest associates attested, that Hitler shot himself, Eva Braun drank poison, and the bodies were dragged outside under intense Soviet artillery bombardment to be burned in a bomb crater?"

"Seems odd, given the circumstances," Dr. Rudiger said. "A burned corpse can be hanged by the ankles as well as an unburnt one. Also, the bodies could have been found where they lay, and both Hitler and Eva Braun, would have their skeletons on display in a museum today."

Frau Doktor von Lütringen nodded. "The Russians combed the area for years, collected corpses and autopsied them, desperately trying to find what Stalin was demanding."

"So his associates must have lied," von Wessenheim said.

"I don't believe they did," she replied. "They attested to what they knew: Hitler and Eva Braun killed themselves, and were taken outside. The solution offered for the missing bones all these years is that a bomb landed in that crater, blasting the corpses to bits."

Dr. Rudiger leaned forward and propped his forearms on his knees. "So maybe we can agree on this: that due to Hitler's dread of an end like Mussolini's, he would never have been satisfied to be hastily cremated a few feet from the door of his bunker."

Von Wessenheim frowned, tapping his lips with a finger. "But wouldn't he be reduced to ash anyway?"

Frau Doktor von Lütringen shook her head. "It takes the incredible heat of a crematorium hours to reduce flesh to dust, and even then the skeleton must be ground up a little in order to fragment. Merely torching a corpse with gasoline only makes it blacken and shrink."

"So the skeleton could exist," von Wessenheim said excitedly. "And it could be located."

Dr. Rudiger raised a hand from his lap. "We know that the Nazis were obsessed with ceremony, flashy medals, ornate daggers, and gleaming belt buckles. And the fanaticism of Hitler's SS troops is legendary." He glanced at the woman. "You see, even though the war was obviously lost, the inner cadre of the SS still adhered to their oath of allegiance to

Hitler. The SS actually started out as a protectionary wing, a troop of bodyguards that appeared in parades and marches in their black uniforms. Later their role became larger and more mysterious, until their full function was revealed at the end of the war—the horror of the concentration camps, the atrocities we all know only too well."

"Terrible," von Wessenheim muttered.

"A tragedy beyond comprehension. But we must adjust our focus back to the facts at hand. Hitler's and Eva Braun's corpses were disposed of by his most fanatically loyal troops, men who would not hesitate to die for him. I believe, personally, that these men buried the bodies at a prepared gravesite, performed a solemn ceremony, then scattered to other places and killed themselves so that they could not be tortured by the Russians into ever revealing the location."

"That's a little extreme," von Wessenheim said.

"But not without precedent. At the entrance to Hitler's bunker, young SS soldiers stood guard in full uniform. When one of them fell as the artillery rained down, another came to take his place. Picture that: standing at strict attention like the guards of the Royal Palace in London, who dare not smile or move their eyes under those huge feathered hats. The enormous Battle of Berlin is grinding furiously along around them. One SS guard is shredded by shrapnel and another immediately steps out to take his place. And on, and on, until at last the Führer was carried off to be buried. At which point, I have little doubt, they all shot themselves."

"Loyalty to the point of lunacy," von Wessenheim whispered, stunned.

"Well, they faced almost certain torture and death anyway. Better, maybe, to die with some dignity. Just like their Führer, who wanted the same."

Frau Doktor von Lütringen was nodding silently. Dr. Rudiger leaned closer to her. "Is that a sign of agreement?"

She carefully pressed her fingertips together. "Yes, I find I agree with the concept. And if Hitler's nervous collapse left him incapacitated and Eva Braun was at the helm, as my research suggests, the circumstances you describe would still have played out."

"Right. And I suggest here for the first time that even if Hitler and his bride killed themselves with no mind to the fate of their corpses, Martin Bormann assembled a team of fanatically loyal SS men who would have handled their bodies reverently. And please note that not only did Hitler and Eva Braun vanish, but Martin Bormann as well. That is the heart of the mystery."

"Then we all concur," von Wessenheim said. "With the suicide of the SS loyalists, the secret of the Führer's burial became complete. We agree that his bones may be intact to this day, buried most assuredly in the small part of Berlin that was still under German control at the moment he pulled the trigger." He smacked his palms together. "Now, how do we find them?"

The two twitched their shoulders at the same time. "Well," Frau Doktor von Lütringen said, "they found the *Titanic*, didn't they?"

"They found it indeed," von Wessenheim said with a smile. "They did indeed."

8

Hank woke sweating from a dream about a chess game against an old man, an endless game with no winners. He rolled his head from his soggy pillow with a groan, and eased out of bed. Rebecca, a rumpled shape in the grayish light, did not stir. His trip to the bathroom was mandatory; he stood there in the dimness yawning and scratching his tailbone, then fumbled his way downstairs with a hazy idea of finding some orange juice in the fridge. It was a good way to start the day, lots of vitamin C, he would live to be a hundred.

He snorted as he wandered into the kitchen. Life at thirty-two was old enough; in these years he had struggled plenty. Just a few years back he was laboring over his doctoral thesis and practicing his orals, engaged in a slow-burn nervous breakdown that might really have happened if he had had one more stinking year of college to face. Times had been lean, oh yes they had. With that kind of strain, and little Sharri to raise, his marriage to Rebecca had sometimes teetered on the edge of some invisible, yawning chasm from which it would never return. They had met in college, found an almost instant attraction to each other, and were sleeping together two days after saying hello.

Hank frowned in the semidarkness. Well, so what? Sharri had been conceived in those early days, hurrying the marriage a little, but the marriage was inevitable anyway. Planning things would have been wiser, staying childless until he graduated would have been the smart thing to do. Yet standing here this morning in his dumpy blue robe with his eyes bloated and puffy, Hank could not imagine a life without lit-

71

tle Sharri. He and Rebecca had been blessed, the whole world had been blessed by her birth, and to imagine a world without her was to imagine his own death.

He rolled his eyes. He was growing mawkish, pretty soon he would be looking through her baby book and babbling to himself about how cute she was. Instead he trundled to the front door and snatched the morning newspaper out of a slanting bar of half-hearted sunshine on the porch. The head-lines of the *Terre Haute Tribune-Star* gave evidence that not much of anything was really going on worldwide, but that some local stuff might be interesting. He turned and flipped the paper open, eased the door shut, and wandered out of the foyer lost in reading. A picture on page three caught his eye, a photo of a doorway with the door crushed on the floor and emblazoned with a misshapen swastika.

INDY TV STAR STILL SILENT
by Tim Andrews
Terre Haute Tribune-Star

For the third consecutive day, Indianapolis television channel WXRV has refused to respond to questions concerning Alan Weston, the station's controversial investigative reporter who Saturday morning revealed that he had undergone "a night of hell" at the hands of neo-Nazis who broke into his home. Wes-ton, who is Jewish, has likewise refused to cooperate with police in favor of conducting a personal investigation, warn-ing of the hate he says is still out there.

Indianapolis police spokesman Arthur Berry said that at present the department is keeping a careful watch on Wes-ton's house, but expressed frustration at Weston's lack of co-operation. "It is difficult," Berry told reporters at a Monday afternoon press conference that Weston did not attend, "very difficult to investigate a case in which the victim and only witness won't even talk to us. We have no description of the suspects other than those provided us by Mr. Weston's neigh-bors, who heard motorcycles and laughter in the middle of the night. I invite everyone here to conduct an investigation based on that information alone, and wish you a lot of luck."

Weston is renowned in the Indianapolis area as an investigative reporter who often delves into the bizarre. He once
publicly dumped 1,500 hate letters off the Oliver Street
Bridge into the White River below, for which he was arrested. He termed his many death threats "love letters" and
once aired a segment in which he randomly invited pedestrians to "punch me out."

Attempts to contact Weston at home have failed.

Hank dropped the paper onto the kitchen table, wondering,
as usual, what this world was coming to. Nazis in Indianapolis, a swastika on somebody's front door, a guy being beaten
up for being a Jew. Can't we all, to quote Rodney King, just
get along? Hank was not an arthropologist but humans
seemed a lot like ants, they took slaves and waged wars and
slaughtered each other by the pound. Wars and rumors of
wars, humankind had a bestial element that might not vanish
from the species for ten million years, if at all.

Sieg oder Todt . . .

Hank frowned. What the hell was that, anyway? It sounded
like a whisper in his left ear. "Zeeg odor tote," what had his
brain been eating lately? He shook his head in a blur,
harkened for a bit yet heard no more messages, then ambled
to the Mr. Coffee and set about making a fresh pot of the java
as a morning surprise for Rebecca.

Deutschland über alles . . .

His hands balled into fists. Okay, brain, enough of this
scary shit. He had labored too long and hard to get where he
was just to ruin it all with a bout of schizophrenia. The idea
terrified him, mental illness of any kind was ultra-bad news.
You could heal a fractured skull but not a fractured brain.

Sieg oder Todt . . .

The phone rang and Hank dived for it, jerked it apart and
slammed the receiver against his offending ear, the one
where all the voices originated. "Hello?"

"Hi, Hank, this is Perry."

"Perry?" The phone cord had somehow gotten around his
neck and was trying to kill him. He ducked and dodged while

the coily white cord swung in circles like a jump rope. "What's up?"

Perry breathed into the phone. Then: "I want to apologize about yesterday afternoon. I lost my head."

Hank muttered and cursed as he fought the cord. "Hold on a sec, Perry," he said, and whipped it into submission. "What was that again?"

"You're making this pretty damned hard. I said I'm sorry for yesterday. I blew up."

"Ah, jeez," Hank returned. "I was way out of line."

"Don't back out on my apology, Hank. I rarely make one."

"Then I consider myself honored," Hank said, and smiled. "Shall we do chess today? I can squeeze a game in, you know."

"Only if you've got time," Perry said. "I've taken to heart some of the things you told me, did a lot of soul-searching last night, and I discovered you were right."

Hank frowned, trying to remember what he had said.

"I'm a widower and the father of three grown kids who can't even lift a telephone to say 'hi' or 'go to hell.' I've become obsessed with a silly game and am wasting my golden years moving small objects around on a checkerboard."

Hank said nothing.

"Basically, you told me to get a life, and that is probably the best advice I've ever gotten."

Hank reddened. "Well, I didn't mean to, um . . ."

"Yes you did, and I'm okay with that. So this Friday I want to borrow your wife."

"Oh?"

"Yeah. This Friday evening I'm going to throw a faculty party at my house, and I can't get it ready alone."

Hank's eyes popped open wide. A party at Perry's place? The walls would cave in from the shock.

"I figure seven o'clock is the normal time for such functions. You and Rebecca have thrown bashes like this, haven't you?"

"Couple of times."

"And Rebecca rose to the challenge? Called the caterers, blew up the balloons, bought the party hats?"

"I believe we skipped the catering and the balloons and the hats. All you need is a few hors d'oeuvres, some music, and as much booze as your cabinets will hold, plus mixers and a thousand pounds of ice. Throw in some parlor games, stir well, bake at three-fifty, and voilà, you have a party."

Perry mulled it over. "All I have so far is a parlor game, which is why I need Rebecca to guide me in this thing. You think she would?"

Hank smiled. "I'll have her call you when she gets up."

"Great. I don't have a class until one, so my morning's free."

"I've got a class in an hour, then nothing until two-thirty."

"Okay then," Perry said cheerfully. "We've got time to squeeze a game in."

Hank's heart sank, but he immediately buoyed it up. One game today between classes, and then back to the sanity of playing maybe once or twice a week. "I'll swing by your place," he said.

"It's a deal."

Perry hung up. Hank pulled the receiver from his ear and regarded it with a quizzical look in his eyes, shrugged to himself, and gently put it down. He crossed the room and started up the stairs to rouse the little lady.

The voice was back, whispering but insistent: *Deutschland . . .*

"Shut up," he muttered, and stuck a finger in his ear.

At three o'clock in the afternoon Sharri Thorwald was running through four blocks of a new rainstorm with an encyclopedia clapped over her head, just to get to her friend Nandy's house without melting à la her favorite witch in the land of Oz. There were five umbrellas in the closet at home but carrying umbrellas was a thing old people did. The Bluewater Pointe subdivision in southern Terre Haute was stuck full of upscale houses that tended to look alike if you prowled its winding streets and cul-de-sacs, but Sharri had lived here a long time and knew the area by heart. When she got to Nandy's house, it was Nandy herself who opened the door.

"Be quiet," she said.

Sharri folded the encyclopedia shut as she stepped inside. "Still asleep?"

Nandy nodded. "Upstairs in bed. Has a headache. Took Tylenol PM because we're out of regular Tylenol."

Sharri eased the door shut. She winced as the bolt clicked loudly into place. "What about Joe-Bob?" she whispered.

"He went to Freddy's for a couple of hours. He'll probably eat supper there too."

Sharri gently lowered the book to the floor. "Got enough guts?"

Nandy glanced down the hallway. For no reason Sharri could think of she was wearing a pink swimsuit. "I just hope she doesn't wake up and catch us." She drew a finger across the front of her neck, tracing her throat from ear to ear. "Certain death." She glanced at Sharri. "Let's do it."

Sharri followed her, both of them practically on tiptoe. The hallway opened to the right to offer the dining room and kitchen, then to the left to offer the family room and its billiards table and monster television. They mounted the carpeted stairs three steps at a time. At the landing Nandy cut a quick left, then stopped in her tracks. Her parents' bedroom stood there guarded by the blank white slab of a closed door. "Footprint check," she whispered when Sharri had drawn close. "She might be pacing around."

Together they lowered themselves to the floor and peeked under the door. Sharri swept her hair out of her eyes with a hand but there was nothing to see except a forest of sculptured green carpet inside. Both girls raised their heads at once. "I'll open the door a crack," Nandy whispered. "You look for her."

"No way," Sharri hissed back at her. "She's your mom, so *you* look."

Nandy let her eyes fall shut, then hung her head. "Okay, let's just get the stupid thing out of the closet and get this over with."

"Okay."

Nandy rose while Sharri leaned back into a squat. The knob made a tiny metal noise above her head and the door swung inward about an inch, then another. One more push wafted it delicately open and Sharri could see the bottoms of shoes sticking up from the foot of the bed. Nandy's mother was as flat on her back as if shot and killed. The coast was about as clear as a coast can get.

"It's up on the shelf," Nandy whispered as they crept toward the closet.

"Low enough to reach?"

"Don't think so." Nandy cut to the side and slid the plush little chair from under her mom's vanity table, eased it to the floor in front of the closet, and then slid the doors apart.

Clothes in darkness. Mom had herself a lot of clothes, Sharri could see. The smell of old perfume and a forgotten mothball or two drifted out. Nandy stood on the chair, eyeballed the pile of odd boxes and paper sacks that were split open from their own weight, and hesitantly wormed a hand into them all. Papery noises rustled out like the crackling of flames. After a painful stretch of time, she worked something out of the tangle, an old brown briefcase with a zipper across the top. "This's got to be it," she whispered.

Sharri's ears were prodded by an unfamiliar noise and she twisted her head around to look at Nandy's mom, who was still blissfully comatose on the bed while blustery rain pecked hard at the windows and a tree branch scratched at the glass. When she looked back up at Nandy she was handing the briefcase down.

"Don't drop it," she hissed.

Sharri took it after a quick glance at Nandy's mom again, tucked it tightly to her chest, and was starting to turn when the phone beside the bed rang with the force of a scream. Both girls dropped into an automatic crouch, Nandy on the velvet chair and Sharri on the sculptured green carpet, their eyes wide and horrified as the entire scheme collapsed like a tent under an avalanche. Nandy's mother groaned and rolled onto her side, stuck out an arm and fished for the phone, got it and wobbled it to her ear. "Mmm?"

Time, inching along as if riding bareback on a snail.

"My house doesn't need new siding," she grumbled, and clunked the phone down. She rolled onto her back and let out an instant snore. All this without opening her eyes even once.

Several years passed before the world resumed its pace. Nandy clambered down and breathlessly carried the chair back to its place at the vanity, came breathlessly back and slid the closet doors shut, remained breathless as the two of them tiptoed out. "All the way down to the basement," she exhaled when the door was safely shut, and they charged down the stairs giddy with victory and excitement. The entry to the basement was a trapdoor in a false pantry at the side of the kitchen, as if the builders had tried to hide it from the owners. Nandy hauled it open on its springs and a metal stairway dropped down into the darkness below. The dank smell of mildew rose to stand guard a few feet above the floor.

"Me first, I know the place," Nandy said, and Sharri silently agreed. Nandy made her way safely down and found a light switch. Sharri followed. To the right stood a gigantic metal machine that sprouted fat silver pipes that jutted here and there, penetrating the house from below like an octopus wanting to pull the upper floor down. In the next room two white tanks stood side by side with copper-colored tubing sticking out from the tops. These also branched to the ceiling of the basement. Down here was an aura of mystery that made her feel, as Nandy slowed, that she needed to use the bathroom for a few minutes. Creepy yet exciting. Cool, in an unsettling way.

Nandy stopped abruptly. "This is the room my dad hides in." She clicked a light on. Sharri backed away and looked at where she was. Drab cement walls, more pipes overhead, mazes of electric wires poking through holes and slots cut into the wooden beams above. In one corner stood a lonesome folding chair that cast a stark shadow on the concrete floor. There was a slipshod pile of magazines on one side of it, and at the other side a Folgers coffee can. "Dad smokes here when he's mad at mom," Nandy said.

Sharri went to the can and looked down inside it. Nandy's dad smoked different cigarettes than Sharri's mom. Mom always left filters behind. Nandy's dad left little twists of white paper burned down to almost nothing. Even the smell wafting up was different, sweeter. Nandy lowered herself to the floor and pulled her legs in to sit cross-legged. Sharri chose to stay on her feet, wary of bugs and the shadows down here.

"Now we need to make some rules," Nandy said primly as she steadied the briefcase in front of her. She squeezed its sides, bent her head to listen for clues. "If this is full of money, we won't steal any, we'll just put it back. If it's got somebody's ashes in it, like my grandpa's or somebody else dead, then we ask my mom who it is."

Sharri clutched her arms around herself. "Yikes."

"Okay then," Nandy said, taking the tang of the zipper between her thumb and forefinger. "Let's do it." She wrestled the zipper open. Both girls scuttered backward, squinting as if expecting a firecracker to explode in a spray of noise and burning paper. But nothing like that happened, the old briefcase just keeled slowly over with the sides dimpling as it adjusted to having its mouth open. Nandy got to her feet and inched back to it, stooped over and righted it, then dared to look inside. "Just clothes," she said, and dropped to her haunches. Then she gasped. "No, wait!"

Sharri waited as ordered, her heart pulsing in her throat. Nandy began hauling things out, all of them black and very shiny, vinyl or leather stuff that squeaked as it unfolded, glistening under the naked light of the bulb overhead.

"Oh my God," Nandy squeaked, and Sharri looked. Stretched between her hands she held a pair of something like panties made of black lace, but there was nothing in the crotch area, it just kind of hung open like you could, mmm, take a pee without pulling them down. Nandy tossed them aside and pulled out more stuff: a squirming bunch of small chrome chains, more weird underwear made of leather this time, a metal-studded black hood with eyeholes, a short black stick that had long vinyl streamers sprouting out one end.

Nandy stood up. "This is sick," she whispered, and coughed into her hands.

Sharri moved closer and knelt over the briefcase. More stuff was in there, odds and ends, not all of it black or metal. She lowered her face for a better look inside, smelled plastic like new Barbie dolls fresh out of the package on Christmas morning. Tipping the briefcase helped; she grubbed inside while Nandy paced around in white-faced shock. The first thing she drew out was a red bandage of some kind, maybe a headband. It had a white circle on it with a stark black design in the middle, the Nazi sign from the movies and TV.

"They are so *sick!*" Nandy croaked as she paced.

Sharri brought out a pair of chrome handcuffs. A lot of the chrome had chipped off, revealing cream-colored plastic underneath. A reddish crust seemed to have hardened along the fracture lines. She dropped them onto the cement floor with a shiver, scared but absolutely fascinated by the first treasure hunt she had ever taken part in.

Nandy quit pacing. "I bet he whips her every night with that," she said, pointing at the thing on the floor that looked, to Sharri Thorwald, kind of like a handlebar grip with streamers, the kind they put on girls' bikes. "Or else my mom whips him. Either way it's sick. I can't live here anymore. I want to move in with my grandma Joan. This is sick. Even Grandma Helen, I could stand it, she's mean but she's got a lot of money."

Sharri saw another flash of metal and went fishing for it. When she drew her hand out, a loop of jewelry chain dangled from it. She opened her hand slowly and saw that it was a necklace with a small Nazi symbol dangling from it. This, apparently, was the preferred neckwear when wearing black clothes and a metal-studded ski mask. Inside she found another one, this one bigger, part of the man's outfit, she guessed.

Nandy was babbling on. Sharri wrapped her fingers tighter around the small necklace, enclosing it entirely in her fist. The urge to steal it was strong, the necklace was so unusual that you probably had to buy the whole outfit to get one. And after today, she knew, Nandy's mom and dad would have no further use for it, no use for *any* of this stuff. It occurred to her to advise Nandy to forget it, this would embarrass her parents for the rest of their lives, but Nandy was busy freaking out.

So Sharri stuck the necklace into a front pocket of her jeans. Her face quickly reddened and she felt hot with shame.

Never had she been a good liar, not to mention her first time as a thief.

"Sick!" Nandy cried. "They are so damned *sick!*"

Sharri made noises of apology, noises of good cheer, left unnoticed, and walked slowly home with the encyclopedia on her head to shield it from the rain, thinking.

9

Rebecca had already been at Perry's house most of the day Friday, the day of his groundbreaking faculty party. The weather had been looking iffy, and the forecaster on station WTHI predicted more rain, but now, just approaching seven o'clock in the evening, the skies were still clear and the weatherman was once again the fool. This was vital because Perry's old house was not quite big enough for a full-fledged party, yet it boasted a monstrous patio out back that was made of polished slabs of different kinds of rock, had a gas barbecue built into an outdoor fireplace made of the same slabs, had permanent holes cemented into the ground for erecting either umbrellas or kerosene torches. For tonight it would be torches when it got dark, but just to be sure Rebecca and Perry had dug all the umbrellas out of the garage and shaken the dust and cobwebs off.

Now, fifteen minutes before seven o'clock and the arrival of the guests, Rebecca was both exhausted and proud of herself as she took a cigarette break out back. The torches were erected and filled, the patio looked as fresh and polished as if just built, the backyard trees were fluttering gently in the evening breeze. She wished suddenly that she had strung Japanese lanterns, but it was far too late for changes.

Perry appeared wearing his usual summer outfit, slacks and a vest and a tie not much wider than an electrical cord. He had his hands shoved deep in his pockets, was frowning while he chewed on a dead cigar and surveyed the patio. "All set?" she asked him.

He plucked the cigar out of his mouth and grunted an answer. "On this night, history will be made."

"You bet it will." She lifted her watch into view. It was time for people to arrive. She zoomed to the bathroom to check her makeup, check her hair, check to make sure none of the hors d'oeuvres had wound up on her dress. The Rebecca in the mirror seemed well put together. She touched at her reddish hair, ducking and bobbing, checked her eyes, bared her teeth. She gave herself about a B- or a flat B, decided she could live with it, and went out. The doorbell bonged and she saw Perry dump his cigar in an ashtray and scutter toward the foyer.

It was Hank, weighted down with wet grocery bags. "Here's the ice," he panted as he hurried past her. "Soda pop's in the car, I think Perry's gone after it."

She followed him. "Did Sharri's girlfriend show up?"

He lowered the tattering bags to the countertop. "Yeah, they'll be fine, she knows the safety routine and all the doors are locked."

"Supper?"

"Giant pizza. What else?"

"Movies?"

"Two PG's, no R's. Hope they don't find our porno films."

Rebecca wrinkled her nose. "What porno films?"

"Oops." He grinned. "Wrong wife. But ain't it bigamy to tell you?"

She squealed as he rushed over and snatched her up by the waist, laughing. "You're wrinkling me," she cried, batting at him while he laid sloppy, sucking kisses on her neck. When he relented he dropped her and went for her lips, but she blocked his aim by clamping a hand over her mouth. "Lipstick," she said into it. "People coming."

"Ooh, pillow talk," he crooned.

Perry walked in freighted with two-liter jugs of soda. "Cut the heavy petting and help me out," he said. "Cars are pulling up."

"Let the festivity commence," Hank said. "Is everything ready?"

"I committed your advice to memory," Perry grunted as

Hank unloaded him. "Food and spirits, music, a parlor game."

Hank cocked his head. "What music?"

Perry drew his bushy white eyebrows together. "Forgot to wind the Victrola," he muttered, and hurried away. Soon violins were playing softly from his cracklingly old hi-fi in the living room.

"I thought Beethoven died," Hank said quizzically. "Beck, you want to go find something real before people start falling asleep halfway to the door?"

"That's all he's got."

Perry reappeared. "There, that takes care of the music, which leaves only the parlor game in abeyance, but that's for later, anyway."

Hank glanced at Rebecca as he lined up the jugs of soda. "What'd you get? Pictionary?"

She shook her head. "Actually, Perry has a game of his own in mind." She looked to him. "That's what you said, right?"

"I did."

Hank went down the line opening the big jugs one by one. The doorbell gonged and Perry flinched. He cleared his throat, touched his tie, brushed at the knees of his slacks, and straightened. "Thus does it begin," he whispered, raised his eyebrows and slid his eyes shut for a moment, then opened them and marched away wearing a grim expression.

Hank snugged his arm around Rebecca's waist as they watched him go. "You'd think he was headed for the guillotine, wouldn't you?"

She let her head fall against his shoulder. "I'm exhausted. Let's go to bed."

"Curb your hormones."

"Screw you."

"Again with the pillow talk?"

Laughter and voices invaded the house. She pushed away from Hank. "Time to be charming, Prince Charmless. And remember, Perry did all this work himself, he has always lived in a very clean house, none of this is new."

He was frowning. "Damn," he whispered, and screwed a finger into his left ear, wincing.

Rebecca stepped closer. "What's wrong?"

He jerked more erect and let his hand fall. "Nothing. Water in my ear. It's gone."

"So shall we make our grand entrance?"

"Do we have to pretend we just got here?"

She nodded. "And keep your fingers crossed that the party isn't a dud."

He took her hand. "No smoking in here unless somebody lights up first, okay? Even though Perry smokes those cigars, we don't want to offend anybody."

She felt a twinge of the old anger at such persecution, but it was their regular party routine and she was used to having to go outside to do her dirty business like a dog. "Not a problem," she said evenly, already wanting a cigarette.

"Then let's go."

Hand in hand, they went.

By ten o'clock the party was in full swing. The WTHI weatherman who had predicted showers was wrong enough to get fired, in Rebecca's opinion, but it was a welcome mistake. Under a starry black sky through which the moon effortlessly floated, surrounded by the dancing flames of the torches and the weird shadows they cast, about thirty people were busy with each other. The liquor was flowing smoothly and in no danger of running out, the hors d'oeuvres were holding up well, and even the ice in Perry's antique refrigerator was staying solid. She could see Hank engaged in hand-waving conversation with Dr. Paul Heinreid, mathematics professor and—like Hank—an astronomy buff. Perry Wilson was cruising between the knots of people like a professional party host, making sure glasses were filled, inserting himself to whip up conversation when things seemed to flag. Rebecca felt intuitively that she would remember this night fondly: the dark shapes of the trees tossing in the night breeze, the fluttering torches and the smell of them that came to her once in a while but pleasantly. She had literally created this magic moment out of dedication to duty and with her own sweat. Never had she seen Perry so animated and full of cheer. Hank's tale of their argument seemed to be very old news now, though she had been secretly glad to hear of it. All those chess games for Hank, all that time away from his family. Something had to break, and break it did, hopefully forever.

She popped an olive into her mouth to help disguise the smell of her latest cigarette, and ambled toward Dr. Hank and Dr. Heinreid. "Imagine it as it was for such a short time," Hank was saying. "Earth has two moons, is ringed by a belt of cosmic rubble while its surface cracks and heaves from all the debris raining down. Meanwhile the infant sun is shooting jets of gas from its poles that stretch a million miles in both directions."

"Cosmic chaos," Dr. Heinreid said with a nod, and tipped his glass to the area of his graying beard where his lips formed an opening. "Sort of like my intermediate trig class last year."

Rebecca joined the group by stepping up beside Hank. "Darth Vader is on the phone," she said soberly. "Needs directions."

Paul Heinreid winked at her. "Tell him to take a left at Saturn and a U-turn at Pluto. Look for the fork in the road."

"Just tell him fork you," Hank said. "Isn't this a grand party?"

"Old Perry's full of surprises," Rebecca agreed, taking Hank's hand and glancing up into his eyes. He was holding his liquor well, more interested in talking astronomy than guzzling down his drink, which was the usual Scotch on the rocks that could make him silly very fast.

"He's hopping around like a toad," Hank said. "More spry than I've ever seen him. Like a Perry I didn't know existed."

"You deserve a lot of credit for that," Paul told him. "I noticed it when he took you under his wing. A lot of us did, really. Even the gods of the administration watched and waited, when they weren't busy knifing each other in the back."

"*Dolchstoss,*" Hank said.

"Pardon?"

Hank shifted his drink to his right hand and touched his

ear, rubbed it. "Clearing my throat," he said with an off-kilter grin. "Stuffed-up ear."

"Summer colds are the worst," Paul acknowledged. His eyes wandered to his right, brightened, and he raised a hand. "Frances Hulberson is over there throwing me kisses," he said with a laugh, wagging his hand. "I've secretly loved her for the last thirty years, so excuse me while I go make a complete fool out of myself."

"Party on," Hank said.

They watched him walk away, and Hank turned. "Glorious night, my dear," he whispered. "Thank you."

She smiled and he bent to kiss her; at that point Perry Wilson appeared out of the crowd and stuck his face up close, ending it before it could happen. "Apologies," he said. "Rebecca, I need a hand, and Hank, forgive me for stealing her away from you again."

"Getting used to it," Hank said with an easy smile. "Dollface, make the man happy."

She snorted. "I'll dollface you, jerkface."

Hank snapped a kiss against her cheek and she walked with Perry back into the house, wondering what he needed a hand with this time. He led her deep inside the house to the den where he and Hank performed their legendary games of chess; she had been in here a few times, in each instance to rescue Hank from a game that had dawdled past midnight. Sometimes Hank had been so comatose as he stared down at the silver chessmen with his chin on his hand that she had to shake him into awareness.

Perry turned. "I need to know how to get us all together for the parlor game," he said in a whisper. His breath carried the scent of limes. "Everybody's having a good time, but pretty soon I need to herd them in here for the fun part. What should I do, blow a whistle? Or blow out the torches? Help me here."

Rebecca touched her forehead, commanding her thoughts to unite in spite of the drinks she'd had. "Things are still moving along at a good clip," she said. "Hold off for an hour or so." She dropped her free hand onto his shoulder. "And having a game or not won't affect this grand party at all, Perry. You've become a legend."

He lifted his wrist to catch the light. "I enjoy becoming legendary, Rebecca, but it's already a quarter after ten. People will be wanting to go to bed soon."

She had to smile. "It's a Friday night, Perry. Nobody goes to bed this early."

He scratched at his upper lip, then used both hands to fiddle with the undersized knot of his skinny necktie. The suave and debonair party host had suddenly become the hapless Perry Wilson again. Rebecca was taking a breath to comment when Hank appeared at the doorway. "Somebody's been horsing around with your barbecue and broke a knob off," he said. "Smells like gas outside."

"Christ," Perry grumbled. As he moved to follow Hank the doorbell gonged out its simple ding-dong. Rebecca was struck with visions of the police at the door in their blue-and-chrome finery, of orders to quiet things down. "Get that for me, can you?" Perry said, and hurried out. Rebecca followed, wondering just who in the heck would show up so late, then wondering as she passed into the living room if the police were searching for her with the news that Sharri had been kidnapped, had choked on a bite of pizza, had been run down by a car.

In the foyer the door had already been pushed open slightly. Under the porchlight stood a tall man wearing a baseball cap that announced his allegiance to the Seattle Seahawks. Beneath that rested a pair of sunglasses, and beneath that a face that had not encountered a razor for days. "This is the Wilson residence," she said. "Can I help you with something?"

"Looking for Perry," the tall man said, and maneuvered himself around her to get inside. His hands were shoved deep into the pockets of his jeans, his head bowed slightly as if he were afraid of scraping the door frame with the crown of his hat. "Sounds like a party," he said. "Perry didn't mention a party in his letter."

Rebecca eased the door shut. "I didn't know he sent written invitations. Maybe I should go get him."

"Not necessary," the man said. "I'll just come by some other time when he's not so busy."

"Can I tell him who came calling?"

"Just a former student of his."

"Well, then don't go," she said, trying to coax him farther inward. "He's out back with all the others, something went wrong with the barbecue grill and the gas is leaking out."

He swiveled his head, his eyes behind the sunglasses nothing but mysteries. Darth Vader after all, she thought.

"Let me fix you a drink," she said sprightly.

His mouth twitched up in a smile that came and went about as fast as she could blink. "That would be good."

"Okay." She slowly herded him into motion, resisting the urge to take his elbow to get him going. He seemed stiff and reluctant, not overly pleased at being here. "What's your favorite?" she asked him. "Beer? Wine? Harvey Wallbangers?"

"Whatever you've got is fine with me."

She steered him into the kitchen and presented the array of bottles. "You go ahead and mingle and I'll make you a screwdriver," she said, thinking that it might be the kind of drink just about everyone would like. "Should I be miserly with the vodka, or throw caution to the wind?"

He looked at her, his face a blank oval that was spookily bug-eyed because of the sunglasses. "Forget the orange juice and concentrate on the vodka," he said. "In fact, I'll borrow the whole bottle." He stepped to the counter and lifted the bottle of Absolut. As she watched he unscrewed the cap, sniffed it, then upended the bottle for five or six huge swallows measured out by the up-and-down strokes of his Adam's apple. "Woof," he grunted as he lowered it. "Like the fires of hell."

Rebecca worked up a smile. "So then, would you like me to drag you all over the patio for introductions?"

He had clapped a hand over his mouth and was breathing noisily between his fingers. After a tall pile of seconds he pulled it away and thumped the bottle down on the countertop, then turned. "I'm sorry. What was the question?"

"Introductions. Would you like to be introduced individually, or en masse?"

He pulled his sunglasses away from his face and ground his knuckles into his eyes. A huge yawn overcame him as he put them back on and he had to take a backward step to keep his balance. "Only if there are some eligible bachelorettes. Nymphomaniacs, preferably."

She forced out a laugh that sounded just as phony as it was. "Nothing like that here, as far as I know." She took a breath, fished for something to say but found herself bewildered and looking through the patio door at Hank and Perry, who were squatted in front of the barbecue looking befuddled. "Know anything about gas grills?" she asked conversationally.

He shrugged. "Knowing Perry, it was probably manufactured in the Iron Age."

"Sounds like you *do* know him."

"The strangest and most old-fashioned man I've ever known. If he were a teacher of art instead of psychology, his students would be painting reindeer and saber-toothed tigers on the walls of caves."

She smiled, but did not fully agree. "My husband says Perry is an absolute genius in the classroom. Students stand in long lines at registration, practically fight each other to snag one of his classes."

"And that is exactly what I did," he said. "Perry starts you out with an absolute bang, says read the first fifty pages of the textbook and draft a two-page typewritten rebuttal of everything it says. Boom-bang, you're in the classroom and then out, it's your first day of college, you've got the rest of the hour to kill and the last thing on your mind is this stupid rebuttal thing. Suddenly it's bedtime and you haven't even read the text yet. In a panic, you stay up half the night working on the rebuttal. Bleary-eyed, you show up for class, knowing, though, that your intelligence and wit will blast Professor Wilson off the planet. The papers are handed forward, Perry takes them and drops the whole pile into the trash can beside his desk. "Frankly, students," he says, "until you make it halfway through the semester and have not dropped out, you can keep your opinions to yourself.'"

"Ouch," Rebecca said with a grimace.

The patio door slid open slightly and Hank poked his head inside. "I used to have a wife," he informed all of creation. "Earth to Rebecca. Have Scotty beam you down." He pushed the door fully open and stepped in, nursing his glass to keep it from sloshing. "There you are, Becka." His eyes drifted over to find the tall man. "Hey, welcome to the party."

The only acknowledgment he got was a nod. Perry appeared behind Hank, frowning mightily and dusting soot off his hands. "Enough of this drinking binge," he said darkly. "The damned cooker's about ruined."

"Don't lose the party spirit," Hank warned him.

Perry was looking over to the Seahawks' fan. "Well holy Jesus, look what the cat finally dragged in." He eyed the clock above the stove. "Late for class, as always. But since the gang's all here, I think we can move on to the next phase. You men make your introductions, tend bar. Rebecca?"

She almost drew herself up for a salute. "Here."

"The time has come." He turned and heaved the door fully open. The scent of the torches blew in past him, not quite as pleasant to Rebecca as they had been before. "Give me your attention, everybody!" he shouted out. "Please refill your drinks if you need to, and assemble yourselves in my living room. Let the games commence!"

He turned and walked past Rebecca, stopping briefly to murmur something: "Your job is to keep my fuzzy blue re-cliner unoccupied, and drag a kitchen chair in beside it. Got it?"

She nodded. "Okay, got it."

"I'll be out as soon as everyone is quiet."

"Got it."

He looked around with that unfamiliar excitement growing in his eyes again, appeared to make a final decision or two, and strode away. She glanced at Hank, who could only return the mystified look in her eyes. People started drifting in, some of them pausing for a refill. Hank doled out ice while Rebecca wiped up spills and handed out fresh napkins. When the party had finally shifted into Perry's living room, both of them breathed a sigh of pure relief. "This must be Perry's revenge," Hank said as she joined him to wash her hands at the sink.

"It's something. But I keep wondering what kind of games he has in mind."

"Who knows?" He motioned at something with little bobs of his head. Rebecca frowned, looked around, then saw. "One of Perry's former students," she whispered while the noise of the water covered her voice.

"Not exactly Mr. Personality," he whispered back.

She shut the water off and shared a towel with Hank. "Well, it's dwindling down to a roar. Time for me to tap on Perry's door so we can figure out what kind of party game he's keeping such a secret."

Hank put on a big smile, and turned. "Say there, former student, you've probably known him longer than I have. Any idea what he's cooked up?"

The student in question was caught in the act of chugging directly from the bottle of Absolut. He unplugged it from his lips and pounded on his chest, coughing. "Perry," he rasped out. "Perry always has a trick up his sleeve. He walks around looking like Father Time, he's got too much hair growing in his nose and too many hairs sprouting out of his ears. He has no time for stupid or uninterested students, all the time in the world for those who excel or try very hard to. Has he ever asked you over for a game of chess?"

Hank started, then cleared his face of emotion after an apologetic glance at Rebecca. "From time to time."

"Well, don't let him suck you into it too deep. Classmate of mine, Chaim Goldberg. Born in Israel, basketball fanatic, came to ISU because Larry Bird graduated from there and became a superstar. Bright kid, Chaim, but no basketball player. He started playing chess with Perry in January. By the end of April, he was a wreck, started cutting classes."

"Oh, really?" Hank said.

"In early May he vanished, ostensibly while walking to school. Left no notice behind, left everything behind, was never heard from again. *Unsolved Mysteries* did a piece on him four years ago, got nothing for their efforts. Turns out that after the disappearance Perry spent a week in mourning, couldn't work, spent the nights tinkering around in the basement here. God knows what he was doing."

Rebecca found herself sidling toward Hank, who dropped an arm over her shoulder.

"Some say he made a chess game out of Chaim when he refused to play anymore, carved the figures from his bones and dipped them in silver, made the chessboard from plywood and squares of Chaim's flesh, the dark meat for the black squares, the white meat for the white. Mummified rectangles of meat and skin."

"I could believe it," Rebecca whispered. "But do people come with white and dark meat?"

"Indeed they do. When I played chess years ago in that dungeon he calls a den, Perry's chess set was made of heavy wooden pieces about five inches high. Is that what he uses still?"

"Silver," Hank said.

He took another swig off the bottle, whoofed, and beat himself on the chest. "The man is a menace. The man must be stopped."

"Must be stopped," Hank agreed.

"How many more senseless chess deaths do there have to be before we all wake up?"

Hank laughed in a big, sudden blurt, but Rebecca poked him in the ribs with her elbow, not amused one bit by this horror story, even if it were a joke, probably a joke only a man could appreciate. "I have to make sure nobody's in Perry's recliner," she said coolly. "And he wants a kitchen chair put in there beside it, so, Hank, you grab one."

"Aw, lighten up," Hank said, and grabbed for her, but only plucked up a twist of skirt from her fanny. He tightened his grip and tugged her backward. "No kisses from the missus?"

She pulled free and whirled around, knowing that the skirt now had a big wadded wrinkle in the back that might never get ironed back into place. As if sensing a drop in the local temperature, Perry's friend hurriedly screwed the cap onto the vodka and vacated the kitchen without a word, carrying the bottle with him.

"It was a bad joke and you laughed," she said. "Bad, maybe even racist."

"Oh, bullshit."

"Then why was the student from Israel?"

Hank shrugged. *"Bloss ein verdammter Jude."*

She took a backward step. "What?"

He blinked with raw surprise. "Just clearing my throat. Warbling, I think. Yodeling."

"No, you said 'Blose ine fairdammtuh youduh.'"

"Mumbo-jumbo," he said, screwing a finger into his left ear. "Honey, you'd better go and make sure Perry's recliner is empty."

She studied him with a frown. "Do you have an ear infection?"

He pulled his hand away and looked at it. "I dunno. Don't think so."

She rose on tiptoe to look in his ear. "You've rubbed it all flaky inside, Hank. That's the sign of an ear infection, at least with babies."

"I've been hearing noises there, kind of."

She looked inside his other ear, then gave him his head back and stepped away. "Tomorrow you see a doctor. Might even be a blockage."

He seemed to brighten. "That's probably right. An ear infection and a blockage. Should explain the funny noises I've been hearing."

"I'm surprised you're not in pain." She turned and peeked into the relative darkness of Perry's house. The transplanted guests were simmering down, people were adjusting to new comfort or, if they were stuck sitting on the floor, bad comfort. "Time to do my thing," she said to Hank, and gave him a swift peck on the cheek. "Go find us a place where we can sit."

Then she was gone. Hank snatched up his drink and poured it down his throat. The urge to clap both hands over his ears was strong. It wasn't just the left one anymore, it was the right ear too, it was like a stereo now, with the right speaker getting just a trickle of power, and it was growing. That was scary, the way things were building, that was schizophrenia served cold and lumpy in a wooden bowl chained to the bars of an asylum cell, but what was worse was his growing ability to understand all the schizophrenic mumbo-jumbo, and make it mumbo-jumbo no more.

He set the glass aside and looked down at his trembling

fingers. Less than a week ago he had captivated a classroom with his oratory, and now he was afraid to open his mouth in case another stream of alien words jumped out. How had Rebecca phrased his last one? "Blose ein fairdammtuh youduh." She had a good ear for languages, had the accent down pretty well. She had no idea what it meant, could not know what an ugly little phrase it was.

But Hank Thorwald knew. And Hank Thorwald was more frightened now than he had ever been in his life.

10

Alan Weston was only too glad to find a space on the floor in a corner by the window, shielded from casual view by the fake potted palm Perry kept there. The front door was only a few steps away and the lights were dim; his former professor was not big on lamps and bulbs, so Alan could walk out as easy as you please if someone seemed close to recognizing him. The last thing he wanted was to answer questions about the bikers, what they'd done, how he was going to exact his revenge, what the hell he was doing here at all. In truth, he was here because this was not Indianapolis and his relatives did not live here.

He let his eyes fall shut and tipped his head back onto the wall, hoisted the bottle, and drank. A hot locomotive piloted by a Russian guy named Absolut chugged down his esophagus and crashed into his stomach. Maybe it was time, he thought dismally, really time for him to crawl out of the bottle and make some decisions: leave the station, migrate eastward or westward, write a novel or a screenplay, maybe direct a cable TV show or an avant-garde film. Something that involved behind-the-scenes work, no more fame.

The guy named Hank wandered out of the kitchen and looked around for a place to sit. He seemed puzzled, distraught, lost. His wife must have reamed him good, Alan decided. Judging by his own failed marriage, that seemed to be what wives were best at.

Rebecca appeared at the mouth of the hallway with a sheet of paper in her hands. "'Good evening, my dear guests,'" she read, then waved the paper. "Perry wrote this, see, I'm just reading it." She cleared her throat and continued. "'Tonight you are invited to a very special parlor game. Just as in the Victorian days when people inhaled laughing gas or played with Nikola Tesla's electrical inventions to make their hair stand on end, I will tonight perform extraordinary feats of mesmeristic legerdemain.'"

"Quick," a voice called out, "grab me a dictionary!"

Laughter. Rebecca read on: "'For those of you who flunked English 101, get a dictionary.'"

The crowd laughed and clapped. Rebecca bobbed her head, reddening, and continued. "'I need only three things from you, my audience. The first is your attention, the second is quiet, and the third is willing volunteers.'"

This led to a shoving match as everyone volunteered everyone else. Alan spotted Hank again, sitting on the floor to his right, the only man here not wearing a smile. He had his head lowered and was fiddling with his ear.

"'In lieu of that, my lovely young assistant, Rebecca Thorwald, will choose a person at random.'" She looked up. "I added the 'lovely' part myself."

Applause was followed by hoots and boos.

"'The volunteers,'" she recited from the paper, "'may be either male or female or any combination thereof. In the case of females, proof of virginity may be required.'"

The crowd reacted with laughter, a few complaints of sexism, the mention of a dirty old man. Alan lifted his sunglasses and perched them on the bill of his hat, aware that things were warming up now and that no one could see him. This was getting fun.

"'And now, before the volunteers are selected and ejected from the crowd, allow me to introduce the man we all know and love, the man of a thousand disguises—most of them involving a spreading waistline and gray hair—our own Perry Wilson!'"

The applause was thunderous. Perry appeared dressed in a black cape of sorts, wearing a preposterous turban on his head, huge silver earrings clipped to his earlobes. Alan guffawed and began to quietly clap along with the others, watched bemusedly as Perry turned this way and that to perform a deep bow from the waist. He lost his turban—it must have been a bath towel at one time—and chased it down, molded it back onto his head.

"Ladies and gentlemen," he shouted as he raised his hands. "A little quiet please! The great Wilsoni must have quiet!"

Rebecca scurried away to join her husband, her face a bright shade of cherry. "Friends and colleagues," Perry said as the noise died down, "the great Wilsoni is a master of both the conventional and the bizarre." He fumbled his tie aside and reached into the confines of his shirt, withdrawing a deck of cards that he held overhead. "An ordinary deck of playing cards," he said. He removed one from the deck and dropped all the rest to the floor. With the card held daintily between his teeth, he shook the cape from his shoulders. "Nothing up my sleeve," he said, extending an arm and pulling at the cuff. He inserted the card inside, wiggled his arm, and pried the cuff open again. "Voilà! Something up my sleeve!"

He bowed so low his turban almost touched the floor. The groaning crowd hissed and booed, threw napkins and coins at him.

"Still working on the details," he said. "Now, has my first volunteer been selected?"

Alan put his sunglasses back on, made himself small. This was no time to be drafted as a volunteer, to be exposed to the light and the flurry of excitement his recognition always brought. But not long ago he had enjoyed publicity, had lived for it, would die without it. Who cared if people loved him or hated him? At least the stupid fuckers knew his name and had an opinion, they knew that he was famous and that they were not famous, that his life mattered and theirs did not.

"Then since Rebecca has apparently retired as my assistant, I will select a volunteer myself." Perry tilted his head back, covered his eyes with his hands. "I see a name swirling out of the mist. I see . . . Jessica Petersen!"

The woman hesitantly stood, urged on by the others. "Don't you even *ask* if I'm a virgin," she snarled as she approached him.

Perry scanned the crowd, his eyes twinkling. "Say, John? Is the little lady still a virgin?"

John shrugged. "She's got this headache thing."

"Proof enough." Perry took her hand and guided her into the recliner, where she plopped down and nervously covered her knees with her skirt. "As all of you know, my hobby and my passion are the study of hypnotism and its value to psychology," Perry said. "Several of you disagree with this, but it's my party and I can try if I want to."

Alan found himself laughing heartily for the first time in many days.

"So this is the game," Perry said. "I am going to perform hypnotical magic on this poor, unsuspecting lady." Here she tried to rise but he put a hand on the crown of her head and gently pushed her back down. "In less than a minute, I will have complete and utter control of her mind." The recliner featured a wooden bar on the side, which he jerked upward with the toe of his shoe. The volunteer squawked as the backrest dropped behind her and the footrest popped up, then fiddled with her dress again.

Perry scanned faces. "My highly intuitive thought processes have detected a disturbance in the universal equilibrium. Rebecca?"

She raised her hand.

"There is supposed to be a chair here."

She jumped up.

"Meanwhile," he went on, "I was approached the other day by a starving man who told me he hadn't had a bite in ages. So I bit him."

Alan groaned, then chuckled. More coins were hurled, forcing Perry to cover his head momentarily with the cape.

"But seriously, folks," he said, peeking. "Seriously, I say. Once there were three traveling salesmen who ran out of gas on a country road. One was a priest, one was a rabbi, the other was a hairdresser. They drew straws to see who would—"

Rebecca appeared with a kitchen chair, dropped it, and scuttered away.

"Timing is everything," Perry said sourly. "Okay, kill all of the lights except the one beside me."

A switch was above Alan's head. He reached up and flipped it down; several lamps turned off.

"Good enough," Perry said. The room was now semidark save for a circle of light that encompassed Perry and Jessica. He seated himself and raised a hand. "Now give me complete silence, please. Are you comfy, Jessica?"

She nodded, but her face was full of apprehension.

"Okay then." He produced a gold ring that had tiny diamonds on it and seemed to float in the air below his hand as he showed it. Barring levitation, it was hanging on a loop of thread, Alan assumed. Probably his dead wife, Violet's, wedding ring, which was kind of a ghastly touch. Alan had known her those years ago: no woman on the planet could make cheesecake like Violet could.

Perry then dangled the ring close to Jessica's face. "Focus on this, please." He took hold of it and gave it a spin. Points of light winked wildly across the ceiling, danced on the rims of wineglasses, pierced Alan's eyes. "As you focus, open your mind to the light, let it enter you, let it become you. Concentrate with all your being, take the light inside you, let it fill your thoughts, let it become you. Let yourself relax, feel a relaxation that begins at the tips of your toes, wiggle your toes, now let them rest, sense them as they are, relaxed, all of you is relaxing."

After a minute he leaned close to her, his voice dropping down to a murmur. The spinning ring slowed, eased to a tiny halt, and began to gain speed in the other direction. Twinkles of light arced in different shapes, raked across the ceiling in prismatic beads that reminded Alan of the old trips on LSD he had given up not too damned far in the past, eight or nine years ago.

Finally Perry turned and pressed a finger to his lips. While he pocketed the ring, he gently used the wooden lever to pull the recliner upright in slow little bumps. "It is just you and I now, Jessica, you and I safe in my house. Will you please tell me your name?"

Her eyes were closed and she was breathing slowly. In a tired and warbling voice she replied: "Jessica Petersen."

"And what is your maiden name? Your name before you married John?"

Her upper lip twitched. "Jessica."

Perry smiled slightly and cast the audience a wink. "I want your maiden name, Jessica, the name you were born with."

Her facial muscles twitched. Alan could see her eyeballs roving back and forth under their lids. "My last name was O'Macklin."

"Good job," Perry said. "Now, Jessica O'Macklin, tell me how old you are."

"Nineteen," she said.

Perry thrust up a quick hand for continued silence. "So you were nineteen when your name got changed to Petersen, and so you are nineteen right now."

"Yes."

"Where did you and John go on your honeymoon?"

She twitched. "Upstairs at his mom's."

Perry turned. "John, you should be ashamed."

There was some laughter.

"Okay, Jessica O'Macklin. You were nineteen when you changed your name. Let's go before that, let's go ten years before that, when you were nine. Did you like boys?"

Her head jerked a bit from side to side. "Didn't matter."

"Were you good in school?"

"I did okay."

"Good. Now just relax for a minute, ignore everything you hear, you are asleep." He stood up and raised his voice to a normal level. "My friends, and John Petersen in particular, Jessica is now in a mild state of hypnosis and in no danger whatsoever. This is a stage in which she will answer questions freely, but in an oddly computeristic manner. Recall that when she spoke her maiden name and I asked her age, she said that she was nineteen. Since I asked her to *be* O'Macklin again, the only way her subconscious could deal with it was to regress to that age. She actually became nineteen again."

Behind the potted palm, Alan took another pull off the bottle of Absolut, grimaced, and thudded his chest lightly with his fist.

"So, Jessica O'Macklin," Perry said, "remind us of how old you are."

"Nine."

"Where are you right now?"

Her shoulders gave a twitch. "In my house."

Perry nodded. "Very good, Jessica. Do you remember being only five years old?"

"Yes."

"Where are you?"

"In my house."

"Is your mommy home with you?"

"Yes."

"Is your daddy home with you?"

"No."

"Where is your daddy?"

"At the bar getting drunk."

There was a small gust of laughter. Perry whirled and made angry gestures for quiet. "Jessica?" he crooned when he turned his attention back to her. "Do you remember being three years old? Do you remember having a birthday party?"

"Yes."

"Did you get a cake and some ice cream?"

"Yes."

"Good for you. So now we're going even farther back, you are only two years old, Jessica. Can you tell us about it?"

She was silent for a long moment, frowning, but all the facial tics seemed to be gone. "I didn't mean to spill it," she said at last. "It was too far from my plate."

"Is your mommy mad at you?"

"No."

"Is your daddy mad at you?"

"Yes."

"What are they doing?"

"He's hitting Mommy." At this point she became agitated, squirming in the chair.

"Then move away from that day, Jessica. It's all gone, everything is just perfect, and you are one year old."

Again she was silent, this time for about a minute. Alan had been taught that the human mind forgets nothing, that memories get swept aside but are never truly forgotten. If so, Perry was walking this lady clear back to the womb.

She spoke again. "Big people. One of them is warm and holds me and is always there."

Perry was drawing a breath for the next question when one of the ladies lucky enough to have a place on the sofa rose up quickly, waving a hand. Perry saw her and raised a finger, then bent back to Jessica. "Stay where you are, relax, you are asleep." He lifted his head. "A question, Lillian?"

"Yep. If she's one year old now, how can she talk? If you're only one your vocabulary is practically nonexistent. So why isn't she saying 'ga-ga' and 'goo-goo'?"

"Good point," Perry replied. "What you forget is that she is delving into ancient memory with her own adult brain. I am asking the adult Jessica to call up these memories and report them to me. 'Ga-ga' and 'goo-goo' don't exist in her vocabulary anymore." He turned his attention back to Jessica. "Listen to me now," he said. "I want to take you back even more. I want to take you back to the earliest memory you have. Do you remember the moment you were born?"

People began to murmur at this. Whether it was approval or dismay was hard for Alan to say. Perry had promised a good parlor game, and this was certainly one to be remembered.

"Tell me what you feel," he said. "Is it cold, is the light too bright, are you afraid?"

She made no response, not a movement. He waited until the time stretched on almost absurdly, then sighed. "Okay. You may wake up now, slowly and easily, remembering nothing." He stood up. "Regression is always a chancy thing, folks, and Jessica missed the ultimate chance tonight, to relive her own birth. That doesn't end the game, by any means, because the great Wilsoni has a wonderful surprise coming for us all." He put on a huge smile. "As many of you are aware, Associate Professor Hank Thorwald, Ph.D., has been my protégé and friend from the time he started on the staff of ISU. He has also been the biggest thorn in my side since the first time he beat me in chess. Hank, stand up and take a well-deserved bow."

Through the plastic palm leaves, Alan glanced over. Rebecca was prodding Hank; he erected himself with all the grace of a self-propelled Tinkertoy. Applause was meted out and he seemed to relax, started to smile.

"Enough, enough!" Perry said. "Does he have to steal *all* of my thunder?"

They clapped even harder, then braked to a quick halt when Jessica Petersen, last reported to be in a trance, suddenly sat bolt upright in the recliner. "Perry, I really don't want to do this hypnotism thing," she bleated. "Too scary."

"As the lady wishes," Perry said, and offered a hand. "It probably wouldn't have worked on somebody as tough as you are, anyway."

She got to her feet and faded from the light to rejoin her husband. "Well," Perry said, "since *that* didn't work, let's try it out on Hank."

Hank was about halfway back down to the floor and had to push himself up with his hands to stand again. "What?"

"You are tonight's guest of honor, Dr. Thorwald. Settle yourself upon my barber chair and I will clip away the rest of your doubts about hypnosis. Do you dare?"

Alan watched the off-kilter grin Hank was wearing, saw that it couldn't decide whether to stick to his face or fall off. Rebecca reached up and squeezed his hand, made indications of go ahead, it won't kill you. Hank nodded down at her and made his way to Perry, lifting his feet high over outstretched legs.

Perry motioned him into the recliner. "Does the doomed man have any last words?"

In the chair Hank looked about as comfortable as a hamster in the microwave. "No."

"Still don't believe I can hypnotize you back to the day you were born?"

He sat straighter and adjusted his shirt, squirmed a bit. "No, but I can play along."

"Still think I can't hypnotize you at all?"

His eyes grew sharper. "Not if I fight it."

Perry nodded and took the chair beside him, drew his cape higher on his shoulders. "If this is to be a battle of wills, let the best man win."

Hank nodded and clutched the fuzzy arms of the chair. "Agreed."

"Rook takes pawn," Perry said gently, and snapped his fingers in front of Hank's face. Instantly his eyes rolled up to show nothing but the whites. His head wobbled and fell sideways; his hands dropped from the chair to dangle a few inches above the floor. Alan's eyes widened and he rose involuntarily to his feet.

"Sometimes I play dirty," he heard Perry whisper just as he cranked the recliner down to lay Hank flat on his back.

II

L isten only to me. What's your name?"

Hank's head slowly lifted and straightened until it was in its normal position on his neck. "Hank."

"Not specific enough. What is your full name?"

"Harrison Wayne Thorwald."

"How old are you, Harrison?"

A slight pause. "Thirty-two."

"What is your mother's maiden name?"

"Roberts."

"Is she alive or dead?"

"Alive."

"And is your father alive still?"

"Yes."

Sitting cramped on the floor watching all this, Rebecca was becoming uneasy. Perry had said one or two words and snapped his fingers, and Hank had dropped like a sack of rocks. Was it to be a humorous act the two had concocted? That quit-smoking stuff at the Wabash Valley Inn had certainly grabbed him by the brain, perhaps prepped him for tonight.

Perry had sat down again. "Do you mind if I call you Hank?"

Hank's face was a stone. "No."

"All right then, Hank. Have you ever seen an ostrich on television, one of those nature shows?"

"Yes," he said in a dull monotone.

"Could you become an ostrich for me? Pretend you are that tall and mighty Australian bird?"

"Yes."

"Do it now."

Hank worked himself to his feet and poked his hands under his armpits. He puckered his lips as if to form a beak of sorts. He flapped his elbows, stretched his neck upward as high as it could go, looked around with bulging eyes. Perry's audience fell apart, howled with laughter. Rebecca grinned as hard as she could and sought other eyes to prove that she was enjoying this just as much as they were, everything was cool, Hank was making a fool of himself but we're friends here, this is just between you and me.

"Uh-oh," Perry said. "There's a pack of wild dingos chasing you now, ostrich. What will you do?"

Hank bobbled over to the recliner, bent, and tried to shove his head into the crease between the seat and backrest. He flapped his elbows, gobbled some weird clucking noises. A tiny swell of anger tried to take shape inside Rebecca but she shoved it away, this was a fun night and fun came in many forms, someone was always the goat, every party needed a clown, and for right now Hank was it.

"Enough of this, ostrich, the danger is gone and you are Harrison Wayne Thorwald again. Sit down."

He sat.

"Hank," Perry said, "let's go back in time a few years. You say you're thirty-two right now, but I say you are twenty-two years old. Tell me what's on your mind at that age."

He thought about it. "Rebecca's pregnant and we gotta get married *quick!*"

Rebecca died, simply keeled over dead on the spot—or so she wished. While people hooted and clapped, her head suffused with a rush of hot blood that made her face burn, even made her eyes water. She hung on to her smile by purely mechanical means, needing a cigarette now more than she needed air.

"Let's continue," Perry shouted, and made lowering motions with his hands. "Tone it down before the neighbors call in the troops."

Silence sputtered into being. Perry swiveled on the chair and addressed Hank again. "How about being twelve years old now, Harrison Wayne? Anything special happen when you were twelve?"

"Mom had a birthday party for me."

"I don't think we need to hear about that. Anything else?"

Hank paused. "That winter I was on a sled and I broke my collarbone when I hit a tree stump."

"I'm glad you healed so nicely. And now we're going to go farther back in your memory, we're going to see what interesting things you did when you were two years old."

Rebecca's blood pressure was dropping steadily along with the heat in her face. It was a relief to know that from this point on nothing embarrassing could crop up, Perry had made Hank two years old and the worst he might do would be to burp up some revelation about his parents and the way they treated each other, like Jessica Petersen had about her drunken father.

"Did you ever do anything really naughty?" Perry asked him, and if not for the people here Rebecca would stomp over and throttle his elderly ass. Why was he doing this, was he still pissed off about the confrontation at the Quad?

"I wet the bed."

"That's pretty naughty, Hank. Say, did your mom and dad call you Hank, or something special?"

"Sometimes they called me Hanky-Panky."

A chuckle as soft as a breeze swirled through the audience.

"That's cute, Hanky-Panky. Do you have any brothers or sisters?"

"I have—I *had* a sister."

"So you had a sister then? What happened to your sister, Hank?"

"She died."

Rebecca instinctively brought a hand up to her mouth. Neither Hank nor his parents had ever said a word about this sister.

"That's quite a surprise, Hank. What was her name?"

"Hannah."

"Do you know how she died?"

He was silent for a time. Again a twinge of anger plucked at Rebecca's mental strings. This was extremely private business here, so private that neither Hank nor his family had been able to mention it during their eleven years of marriage. She knew she should do something to stop all this but there were people here, people who were enjoying the show, and, anyway, she was frozen in place.

Hank stirred uncomfortably in the recliner, his first real physical action since the ostrich ordeal. "Yes."

"You know how she died, is that what you are saying?"

"Yes."

"How did she die?"

Hank squirmed again. "She smothered."

"Did *you* smother her, Hank?"

Rebecca was halfway up from the floor, moving on instinct, but before she could get fully to her feet and open her mouth one of the gentlemen sitting on the sofa had jumped up. "Perry, this is not funny," he said. Rebecca turned and saw that it was Rick Surmacz from the biology department.

Perry snapped his head around and found Rick with his eyes. "Are you afraid he will admit to killing his sister?"

"Of course not, Perry. I just think you're probing a little too hard. Can't we keep this spooky stuff as light-hearted as it *should* be?"

Perry stood, took hold of his cape with both hands and spread it in a good imitation of Batman, then bowed. "Though unafraid of the spooky stuff, the great Wilsoni begs a thousand pardons. But please allow me to continue as I take Harrison Wayne Thorwald through the portal of his own birth."

A timid bit of applause answered the question. Rebecca limbered herself back down to the floor, knowing that she would be forever grateful to Rick. But now lay before her the matter of broaching the subject of the dead sister with Hank, and she had to do it before any of the others here did.

"Let's leave the time when you were two, let's go backward in time beyond your second year, let's go all the way back to your first memory, Hank, let's go back to the moment you were born."

Hank lay in peace, a corpse.

"Do you remember being born?"

Time passed. Nothing.

"Remember the moment," Perry said with an edge of impatience sharpening his words.

Time. Nothing but ice cubes shifting in glasses as they melted. Perry stood up suddenly and began to pace where he could find room. His ridiculous earrings flashed as he strode back and forth into the light, out of it. Rebecca sensed that this freak show was coming to an end, that the party was over, and thank God for it.

Perry jerked to a halt suddenly, massaging his chin. "This is always the toughest part," he said as if to himself, and walked back into the lighted area. Without bothering to sit in his appointed place, he stood in front of Hank and folded his arms. "Hank!"

"Yes."

"Do you remember the moment of your birth?"

Hank seemed to choke slightly. His face twitched, his head jerked back and forth. "No."

"All right," Perry said, "I command you to remember the moment of your birth, there is too much light and you are cold and you are afraid and you are forced to *scream*, Harrison Thorwald, you are *screaming,* and in case you have forgotten, rook takes pawn and the king is ordering you to remember!"

He stepped back, breathing hard. "Tell me about your birth, Hank."

Hank twitched and jerked. Rebecca cut her gaze away long enough to glance at faces. She found wonder, apprehension. Back by the doorway Perry's former student had slid up from behind a forest of plastic palm leaves with his eyes huge and intent and visible to her for the first time. A chill of shock zipped through her body. Unshaven and gaunt, hardly recognizable, it was a TV personality, it was West something, he was famous all over Indiana.

She looked back at Hank, dumbfounded. Now a slow, growling snarl was percolating up through his throat. It widened, extended, pressure-cooked for a slip of time, and exploded in a scream so keen and awful that all the hair on her neck and arms stood on end.

"This is it!" Perry shouted as the echoes of the scream rebounded and died. "This is the primal scream, this is how life begins for newborns, they do not simply plug in their newly inflated lungs and cry, they take their first breath of air and shriek in terror at the bright and frightening place into which they have been propelled, cast out forever from the perfect world of the womb."

Rebecca turned her head for another survey of faces and saw that several people—several couples, actually—were in the process of standing up. Who could blame them? Life had been more fun on the patio, Perry's parlor game was a bad idea gone worse, and it was getting late. Rebecca stood up.

"Sit down!" Perry snapped. "This is just the beginning, now we get to the most amazing part of all!"

She hesitated. The standing people sat. She did too.

Perry spoke to Hank again. "Now that we have crossed the birth barrier, things will be easier. Are you feeling all right now?"

Hank was utterly composed again. "Yes."

"We're going to move beyond the moment of your birth now, you are in the before time, the time before you were born, the time before you were even conceived. I am sending you to one year before the day of your birth."

Murmurs, whispers, a set of disbelieving gasps: these rose from Perry's captive audience. Rebecca had heard about, maybe read about, this kind of hypnosis. The goal was to find out who you had been in a past lifetime. This, then, was the impetus behind Perry's determination to get Hank hypnotized, to take him back to a former life to find out why he was able to beat Perry in chess. And why not? Hank had said more than once that Perry was obsessed, obsessed almost to the point of insanity.

"Where are you now?" Perry asked softly.

"Nowhere."

"Is it light? Is it dark?"

"It is nothing."

"But you are still you, aren't you? Are you still Harrison Wayne Thorwald?"

"No."

"Then who are you? Do you have a name?"

"I am what I am. I am myself, I am me."

"Now go backward in time ten more years," he said. "Where are you?"

Hank was so heavily hypnotized that his lips hardly moved as he spoke: "I am nowhere."

"Then go back ten more years. Where are you?"

"I am nowhere."

Perry turned and stood up. "What we are witnessing now is one of the most mysterious and exciting things ever discovered in the history of mankind. I'm sure that no one here is ignorant of the fact that under hypnosis some people can be transported back to what seems to be a life previously lived. Now that I have broken the birth barrier with Hank, and with apologies to my friends here for the primal scream that I did not warn you of, I will continue. Hank is in no danger and will not remember any of this; I will awaken him with a suggestion that he feels better than he ever felt before."

He sat down. "Let's make a big jump," he said. "I want you to go back sixty years more, back to the year 1917. Where are you?"

Hank said nothing. Rebecca saw his eyebrows twitch once, but now she found Perry more interesting to watch. He had swiveled on his chair a bit and was looking at faces, his own drawn up in a tight little expression she couldn't quite define. He looked, in all honesty, like a little kid in school hiding an apple behind his back just before giving it to the teacher. Expectant, ready to beam out a smile, ready for lots of praise.

"*Frankreich,*" Hank said.

Perry's face drooped and his eyes widened. He spun to the side. "The year is 1917, Hank. Where are you?"

"*Frankreich.*"

"Rook takes pawn and the king speaks, Hank. Where are you in 1917? Aren't you somewhere else?"

"*Nein.*"

One of the ladies spoke up. Rebecca looked and it was Bob Govern's wife Debbie. "He's speaking in German," she said incredulously, and after a little thought Rebecca recalled that she was a high school teacher of both French and German, and coach of girls' volleyball.

Perry looked at her sourly. "'*Frankreich*' is the German word for France?"

Debbie was nodding. "I didn't know Hank could speak German, but he's doing pretty well so far."

"He took German in high school and practically flunked," Perry said. "Right, Rebecca?"

She threw up her hands. For all she knew little Hank and Hannah Thorwald had invented the fucking atomic bomb.

"Actually," Perry said, "it is common for those transported to another life to speak the language of the country where they lived. Documented cases abound." He turned his attention back to Hank. "I want to clear this up, Hank. You told me that in 1917, eighty-one years before this very day, you were in France. What are you doing in France in 1917?"

Hesitation. Then: "*Ich kämpfe.*"

"You're fighting? Who are you fighting?"

"*Die Franzosen.*"

"You're fighting the French?"

"*Ja.*"

Rebecca, already wide eyed with amazement at Hank's apparent fluency in German, wondered briefly how Perry was deciphering all this.

"Aren't you fighting another country too?"

Hank took a slow breath, seemed to sigh. "*Ja. England. Sogar die Amerikaner. Russland hat vor kurzem aufgegeben.*"

Perry rounded to look for Debbie Govern. "Too fast for me," he said.

She seemed to want to stand up, but did not. "He is fighting England and even the Americans. Russia recently gave up." She touched her lower lip. "Must be World War One, Perry. The Russians quit the war that year because of the Communist revolution. But right here I have to add that Hank's accent is marvelous, you could swear he was born in Germany."

Perry turned. "Hank, a lot of important things are happening in your lifetime in Germany, the whole world is in chaos. Am I right?"

"*Ja.*"

"But aren't you in France for a short time, aren't you there to tour the front and pin medals on the heroes of your country?"

"*Nein.*"

Perry seemed to be losing his patience again. "Then why are you there at all?"

"*Ich kämpfe.*"

Perry began to nod, up and down, up and down. Rebecca knew him well enough to see storm clouds brewing. But why? Hank had given him everything he wanted—the hypnosis, the horrible primal scream, a past lifetime and a new language that stunned her imagination and would be the talk of the university for years. She could imagine the surge in Perry's professional life, the inquisitive professors who would stop by, even the media if they got wind of this.

Of this.

Of *this*!

She lost the ability to breathe for a few seconds, clutched her throat until it was back, then hung her head to focus on the dark area of floor between her outstretched feet. Perry had invited his old student West-something here tonight, probably for the first time in years. Perry had invited staff people here for the first party since Violet died. Because of Hank's well-known scorn for Perry's hypnosis, Perry had consciously set out to humiliate him, had secretly hypnotized him once before. A couple of words, a snap of the finger, bam. Even managed to teach him some words in German, of all things, to make this phony-baloney past-life act as believable as it was. Yet that couldn't be the end of it, there had to be a *coup de grace* to all this.

"I know you are fighting," Perry said. "I know you are fighting the French and the English and the Americans. But I want you to tell me *how* you are fighting them. Are you in Berlin?"

"*Nein.*"

Perry wiped a hand over his mouth. As he did, his thumb dislodged one of his earrings and it thumped on the carpet.

"Tell you what," he said to Hank, pawing the other one off and slapping it away. "Go back one more year. The year should be 1916. Is it?"

"*Ja.*"

"Are you in Berlin?"

"*Nein.*"

"Then where are you?"

"*Frankreich.*"

"Are you in France to hand out medals to your heroic troops?"

"*Nein.*"

Perry made a fist and slammed it down on the armrest of the recliner. Under the solitary light dust jumped up in a small mushroom cloud. "Then why are you in France?"

"*Bin hier um zu kämpfen.*"

Perry whipped his head around. "Translation?"

Debbie Govern cleared her throat. "Am here in order to fight."

Perry turned without comment. "You are now going back another year, back one year. Is it 1915?"

Hank seemed to stumble a bit, then calmed. "*Ja.*"

"Tell these good folks where you are."

"*Ich bin in Frankreich.*"

Perry made his hands into fists, tapped them lightly on his thighs, then flexed his fingers apart. "You are in France to pin medals on your heroic soldiers, am I right? You have traveled from Berlin to the trenches in France, the war is still young and you are sure of victory."

Hank hesitated, then answered. "*Ja.*"

Perry seemed to slump back together to become his old self. "So you are in France to hand out medals to your troops. Is this correct?"

"*Nein.*"

Perry jumped out of his chair as if it had become electric. He got annoyed with his cape and ripped it from his throat, slung it over into the entrance of the hallway. Rebecca watched him in wonder, this angry old man who didn't seem to know he was still wearing a towel on his head.

Movement at the side of Rebecca's left eye caused her to turn. Richard Greiser from Hank's own earth sciences department had gotten to his knees. "Perry?"

Perry stopped. "What?"

"Excuse my ignorance in your field, and let me express my absolute awe in regard to what you have done tonight. But it strikes me that you're trying to get the entity that is Hank to say things he doesn't seem to want to say. You want him in Berlin, he keeps saying he's in France. You want him handing out medals, but he's busy fighting. Why are you—and don't get upset, Perry, you're the genius and not me—but why are you pushing him in a direction he can't seem to take?"

Perry drew himself together and stepped over to the kitchen chair beside the recliner. "I have my reasons," he growled as he sat. His turban tried to slip sideways off his head and he picked it away with two fingers, eyed it as if it had sprouted weeds, dropped it. "The year is 1915," he said. "Are you *always* in France?"

"*Hauptsächlich.*"

Perry looked at Debbie Govern with a shrug.

"Mostly," she said.

"Are you the kaiser?"

Hank took a large breath. "*Auf keinem Fall bin ich der Kaiser!*"

Debbie Govern translated. "No way am I the Kaiser!" She looked at faces. "'Kaiser' means king, so to speak. The king of Germany was called the kaiser. The Caesar, if you want to get technical."

"So then," Perry said to Hank, "you are not the kaiser. You are not Kaiser Wilhelm the Second, you are not the leader of Germany in the First World War. Is that correct?"

"*Ja.*"

"Then just who in the hell are you, Hank?"

"*Ich bin Gefreiter in den Gräbern des grossen Krieges.*"

Debbie stood up. "I am a corporal in the trenches of the Great War."

"And what is your name, Corporal?"

"*Mein Name ist Hitler. Gefreiter Adolf Hitler.*"

"Oh my God," Debbie Govern breathed, and sank back down. "He said his name is—no. It can't be. It can't."

A horrible, breathless kind of silence clutched the room. Rebecca's heart faltered in her chest.

Perry turned to face them. "That's not right," he said, his face full of alarm and his white popcorn hair sticking up in sweaty bunches. "I programmed him to be Kaiser Bill, you know, the comical kaiser of World War One." He spun around. "State your name!"

"Adolf Hitler."

Perry rose up, backed away from him. "That's not right, that's not how this is supposed to go! You're the kaiser, you're funny old Kaiser Bill, you're supposed to goose-step around the room because this is a great joke, this is a great gag!"

He stumbled over a pair of outstretched legs that were quickly drawn away, danced for balance, whirled around. "He's the kaiser! He's just supposed to be the kaiser!"

He turned again, jumped at Hank. "Say your name, goddamnit! Tell us who you really are in this past life, tell us the words I told you to say!"

"*Mein Name ist Adolf Hitler.*"

"It is not! Tell me the truth!"

Hank paused, then craned his head in a horrid sort of slow motion to look directly into Perry's eyes. "*Mein Name,*" he said, "*ist Adolf Hitler.*"

People were getting to their feet. Rebecca jumped up, somehow twisted her ankle, and dropped down again. Her teeth clicked together, nipping her tongue on both sides. The salty taste of blood drew warmly in her mouth.

"I didn't do this!" Perry began shouting at them. "This is a gag, this is supposed to be funny, I've been teaching him some German under hypnosis and telling him he's the Kaiser!" He plunged over to Hank and hauled him out of the chair with two hands stuffed full of shirt. "Be Kaiser Bill!" he snarled in his face. "*Be who I fucking told you to be!*"

Hank was standing very well on his own two feet now. "*Mein Name,*" he voiced in precise and very German little bursts, "*ist Adolf Hitler.*"

Rebecca struggled to get to her knees, worked at getting on her feet, but the room canted sideways and she felt herself falling, falling.

And then, for a long time, only darkness.

THE RISING STORM

12

Berlin in July, fifty-five years after the war that destroyed it, one decade after the demolition of the wall that cut it in half, six hours after dark on a nondescript Saturday night: the streets black and shiny from an evening soaked with rain, a drapery of steam drifting up from the pavement, streetlights as dim as candles. It was a city that had lapsed into its nightly ritual of calm, but the haunted land of Germany still breathed beneath it, was restless and brooding as it always has been since the Romans came bearing the gift of civilization, then left when their own collapsed. That was the birth of the Holy Roman Empire of the German Nations, the First Reich.

Karl-Luther von Wessenheim, who could trace his ancestry back to those times, tonight stood on the cement cobbles with his breath steaming out in billows of cigarette smoke, taking in the city scenery with his shoulders hunched up to his ears, his eyes slitted and small, wondering how Berlin must have looked the day Hitler died. For him this was becoming an obsession, this business of trying to envision Germany's dark, final days, but it eased a certain hunger. Since meeting with the two experts of the Hitler era, he had not slept much. Here in Berlin the war years were still etched into the fabric of time and space, he knew, and if only he could capture them in more than just his dreams he could make them come alive: the buildings here gutted by bombs and fire, the sky alive with enemy planes, antiaircraft guns pounding out shells while people huddled in their basements waiting to live, or to die.

But he had not been born soon enough to count himself

among the survivors. He was a *Nachkriegeskind* when he entered the world in 1946, a child of a generation that would never know the horrors of a war that left one out of every eight Germans dead. The drunken woman Frau Dietermunde and her clandestine group of elderly Hitlerjugend, they were all children of that war, but their only memory of the Führer was the propaganda they had been fed in school and could not abandon. At the auction in Frankfurt von Wessenheim had watched as a faded, hand-sewn banner traded hands for almost sixty thousand Deutschmarks. The crude stitching, the work of a zealous schoolgirl, bore a message: *"Aus der Ruinen kommt Rache!"*—"Out of the ruins comes revenge." Even as Germany crumbled into ashes the children vowed to be true to their Führer, and never give up the fight. Even, apparently, if the fight had been reduced to the trading of Nazi keepsakes.

Von Wessenheim dropped his latest cigarette to the sidewalk and crushed it under his shoe, then skinned the sleeve of his windbreaker back and turned his wristwatch to the light of the street lamp to his left. Three-fifteen. Three-fifteen in the morning and the man who was supposed to meet him here was late. Von Wessenheim dug inside his jacket for another Reemstma, growing vaguely angry at this. Nobody seemed to care about punctuality anymore, the Germans were getting as lax as the French and the Italians, who were notoriously unpunctual and quite unconcerned about it. It seemed to him that all of Europe was idling in neutral while the Americans bustled about trying to fix everything that went wrong with the world, but that was just fine, both the English and the German empires that had once controlled a third of the globe had shriveled and died, and the same decline would befall the Americans someday. A hundred years from now maybe Egypt would rise from its grave to rule the world, or maybe Iceland. Or maybe Hitler would return and rule side by side with Jesus when he showed up. The Hitler Youth bunch would love that.

Scowling, he applied a match to the tip of his cigarette, inhaled deeply, and flicked it away into the gutter. Even at this hour the streets of Berlin were not completely quiet, some cars and cabs still rumbled, the headlights sparkling on the wet pavement and reflecting wildly in the glass walls of the high-rises. Behind him stood a stone archway, and he stepped back into the darkness below it. Above him now rose the dead and blackened hulk of the Kaiser Wilhelm memorial church, Berlin's monument to the tragedy of war. Known to Berliners as the Rotten Tooth, its former magnificence and most of its tower had been blasted apart by bombs in 1943. Now supported from collapsing by an artificial skeleton of twisted steel and iron, its lighted clock proclaimed to the city that it had stopped at ten minutes before two and would never start again.

Von Wessenheim looked around himself uneasily. Had terrified Berliners huddled under here as the bombs rained down? Were they killed on this spot by flying shrapnel or the concussion of blockbuster bombs? He glanced at his feet and hurriedly stepped to the side, imagining that the patterns of light and dark there indicated blood that had flowed, but it was only a trick of the neon lights from the shops across the street.

This was bullshit, he decided, pulling an angry puff from his cigarette. You go to the trouble and risk to set up a secret meeting in the dead of night but the other party involved doesn't bother to show up. Inside von Wessenheim's windbreaker resided an envelope containing a sheaf of crisp new Deutschmarks paper-clipped together, forty thousand of them if one were to count. These were intended to encourage cooperation from the city bureaucracy that issued—or did not issue—permits allowing everything from the cutting down of a tree in one's own backyard to the digging up of an entire city block in search of fossils. In particular, the *Tiefbauamt,* the Office of Underground Construction, had to be consulted. The first requirement for a permit to dig, von Wessenheim had learned by telephone, was a very good reason for doing so. The second was the payment of an application fee. The third requirement was the submission of detailed printouts of the intended excavation, and an on-site survey by an official of the *Naturschutz- und Gründflächenamt,* who would assess the environmental impact of such excavation and remain on site during critical stages of the project. A lesser man, von Wessenheim knew, would have retreated from the tangle of such bureaucracy, but the royal house of von Wessenheim had not endured a thousand years by retreating.

Earlier today at the Berlinische Residenz he had dialed Franz Bohr's office number before he realized what he was doing, and had replaced the receiver with a frown. Without a right-hand man to handle his affairs he was suddenly off balance. Though Bohr suffered from a bad case of honesty he was surprisingly good at bribery. So how, von Wessenheim had wondered, does one approach a government agency in search of a weak link in the machinery?

It seemed simple enough: go there. And so he had gone. The *Tiefbauamt* was located farther from the Reich's Chancellery building than he had expected it to be, but the taxi ride from the Berlinische Residenz was an enjoyable one. Under glorious sunshine, as he motored along it had looked as if all of Berlin were undergoing massive reconstruction. Huge metal cranes fractured the horizon everywhere, swinging back and forth with seemingly no more speed than a clock as they erected skyscrapers of steel and glass. The streets were planted full of orange signs with arrows indicating detours, and pedestrians often had to cross on raised walkways made of plywood. The scent of a Berlin morning was in the air, a mixture of diesel exhaust and hot machine oil and bakery goods. If ever a city was poised for launch in the twenty-first century, von Wessenheim had thought with alarm, Berlin was aimed at the stars.

Yet it meant nothing to him. His sense of patriotism was a cool and indifferent one; in the summer he abandoned Germany for his house in southern France, usually spent the winter at his house on the toe of Italy's boot. And even walking here where not long ago German soldiers had fought to the last bullet, he felt no shame in that indifference. Patriots died for their country, while realists survived. The battlefield graves were stuffed with patriots.

Regretful that the taxi ride was coming to an end, he handed forty Marks to the driver and received a nod instead

of change, and a faceful of exhaust as the cab squealed its
way back into traffic. Squinting against the sun he smoothed
his clothes with his hands, turned and adjusted his tie in the
reflection of a window, and touched at the gray lines in his
hair. Here in Berlin he was glad to be as anonymous as the
tourists. He began to stroll, looking for street names and
building numbers; the *Tiefbauamt* was located at 10551
Turmstrasse, office number 35. In his career he had made
many questionable business transactions, always aided,
though, by his lawyer, Franz Bohr. Without Bohr this undertaking was unnerving; what he had in mind was in no uncertain terms illegal, could even earn him a prison sentence.
Perhaps he should not have fired the man in anger.

As he walked he shook his head, then cocked his jaw
higher. Bohr was a penny-ante type of lawyer not up to the
task at hand here. The discovery of Hitler's bones would do
more than put the Hitler Youth to shame, it would electrify
the world, stamp the name von Wessenheim in everyone's
mind. Then he could even *expose* the group, not just gain a
victory over them, *ruin* them one and all. Or maybe just that
alcoholic shrew Frau Dietermunde, show her a bit of what
happens when you try to publicly make a fool of Karl-Luther
von Wessenheim.

But when he rounded the corner onto Turmstrasse his
heart collapsed into his heels and the entire venture burst
apart inside him. 10551 Turmstrasse was an enormous building that sprawled magnificently to the left and right and
straight up. He had imagined the *Tiefbauamt* to be in a small
cinderblock office overcrowded with maps and plans, where
perhaps a listless and unhappy secretary could be bribed into
producing false documents. But this was huge, he could get
lost inside.

Someone bumped against him and von Wessenheim
lurched aside with a grunt. Cursing, he shook himself back
into order as other pedestrians lumbered past, then slicked
his palms over his hair and eyed 10551 Turmstrasse again.
How had Franz Bohr, he wondered, how had Franz Bohr
been able to accomplish these extremely delicate transactions
time after time during the years of his service? Bohr was gut-

less, Bohr was afraid of everything, but Bohr had laid results on the table.

So this much was obvious now: before he could start digging for Hitler's bones, he must dig for a new lawyer, a traditional German lawyer like Bohr who would handle not just his legal matters, but his day-to-day affairs. A new man, then, one with the capabilities of Franz Bohr but without the burdens Bohr carried, his squeaking nervousness and towering fears, his mother-hen traits that were so damned smothering. A true German *Rechtsanwalt* with guts, that's what was needed.

A taxi took him back to the Berlinische Residenz. The exciting scenery of a city being reborn flashed past but he did not see it, did not care. Again the fare was forty Marks but he paid it without noticing, strode past the Residenz's portly doorman in his absurd black-and-brass doorman's uniform, found the elevator, and went up. In his room he hurried to the phone and perched on the bed while he dialed.

Seconds elapsed while the connection sniffed its way westward, then locked in. Answering machines were not yet a European habit, so he allowed the phone eight rings, ten. With a curse he gave the phone's cradle a downward karate chop, froze his hand in that position for a few seconds, then lifted it and dialed again.

It was answered far away in Frankfurt by Franz Bohr's secretary, her voice full of professional dignity. "Offices of Bohr and Mittheim, attorneys at law. Your name, please?"

"I am Karl-Luther Von Wessenheim, calling for Herr Bohr."

"One moment," she said, and a tinny strain of music replaced her voice. Von Wessenheim touched his forehead and came away with his fingers wet. This was more excitement than he had experienced in years; the shirt under his jacket was sticky with sweat and his Italian shoes seemed to have caught fire.

"Bohr here."

"You must do me one last service," von Wessenheim grunted into the phone.

"Herr von . . . Herr von . . . is it you?"

Von Wessenheim could fairly hear him sit bolt upright in his chair. "Yes, Franz, it is me again. Forgive the intrusion, please."

"*Allerdings*," Bohr said, supremely polite as always.

"I need a favor from you, Franz, and will of course compensate you for your time."

Silence. A long breath. "Your termination of our relationship was very succinct," he said. "With help from American friends, I could translate your last words to me."

Von Wessenheim frowned. What last words?

"About the horse I rode in on. Immensely humorous."

Oh, that. "Inexcusably rude of me, Franz. I was overexcited. The sulfur fumes from the hedge in Bad Nauheim had a bad effect on me, and the day was hot."

Bohr breathed, in and out, in and out.

"Fine," von Wessenheim said. "I was a complete idiot. But this idiot is offering you a thousand Marks for doing nothing more than helping me, over the phone. Thirty seconds of your time. Hang up if disinterested."

For a couple of moments, it seemed as if he had indeed hung up. "All right," he said finally. "What?"

Von Wessenheim pressed the phone tighter to his ear. "I am in Berlin at a hotel. You know that I have never been to Berlin before, even since the reunification I have never traveled this far east. When business required it I always sent you to wade through the communists, and probably you have been here on other business, you have other clients, you must know the city."

"Not quite as intimately as you seem to hope, but well enough," Bohr said.

"Well enough might work, dear Franz. How have you been, anyway? The wife and children doing well?"

"My wife, Madja, is fine, and so is Tobias. He's our only child."

"Of course, of course. He must be up and walking by now, eh?"

"And doing well at school."

"Of course he is. Are you familiar with any lawyers who practice in Berlin? Exceptional lawyers of your own caliber, but more local to my current whereabouts?"

Bohr was silent, then said: "Quite a few, actually. I even lived in Berlin for several years when I was younger, as I've told you."

"Of course, *natürlich*, Franz. Can you recommend someone?"

"That will take some thought. Are you proceeding with your newest obsession?"

A sneer curled von Wessenheim's upper lip. "The project that you are familiar with, yes."

"The search for Hitler's skeleton, yes?"

Involuntarily, von Wessenheim slapped a hand over the receiver and hunkered down lower on the bed. "Please," he hissed into the phone, "we must keep this confidential."

There was a pause, and von Wessenheim imagined Bohr had covered the receiver to lean back and laugh at his continuing folly, but in a moment he returned sounding quite sober. "I know of a man who might do you well, and at last report he was practicing in Berlin. A worldly fellow, fluent in languages, quite comfortable at traveling the globe. No wife or children, like yourself, very dedicated. He's a bit of a mystery, though."

Von Wessenheim gave his shoulders a twitch. "What makes him mysterious?"

"His gloves."

Von Wessenheim blinked. "Gloves?"

"He wears black silk gloves at all times. Myself, I believe he suffered terrible burns as a child. Others say at least one of his hands is artificial. In either event, the man will not shake your hand if offered."

"An idiosyncrasy," von Wessenheim said immediately. "Fear of germs."

"Could be. But there is one other thing you should know."

"Yes?"

"That I am not recommending him to you, and that this is by no means a referral. I want no part of him, and for that matter I want no part of *you*. In my opinion, the course you are following is stupid and can only lead to trouble."

Von Wessenheim flinched. Stupid? Pretty blunt stuff. "Fine. Give me his name and number and I will never trouble you again." The urge to add "*Du Idiot*" was strong but he did not say it.

"I have no way of knowing his number. All I know is that his name is Ulgard, Rønna."

For a slight trace of time von Wessenheim thought Bohr was joking, but this was hardly the proper moment and Bohr seemed to be in no mood for it. "Sounds Czechoslovakian," von Wessenheim said doubtfully. "Transylvanian."

"He's just as German as we are," Bohr replied. "The war displaced a lot of Europeans."

"How does one spell that first name?"

"R-o-n-n-a. With a slash through the *o*."

"Scandinavian," von Wessenheim muttered.

"Whichever you choose to believe," Bohr said abruptly, and the telephone on his end gave out a decisive click. Von Wessenheim lowered the receiver onto its cradle, frowning. Rønna Ulgard. Had Bohr offered him this odd name as revenge, was the man hopelessly incompetent, a clown in his own field? Was Bohr at this moment feeling quite smug and clever?

The only way to find out was to phone his office. The top drawer of the nightstand slid open with ease for von Wessenheim and offered the sight of an enormous telephone directory. Berlin was the home of over three million people, or so he had learned. He flopped it open on the bed and turned to lie on his stomach, his hand already scooping up bundles of pages at a time in search of the business listings. In time he located a small and simple listing, just the name Ulgard, R., *Internationalerrechtsanwalt*, the number, and then nothing. Von Wessenheim crossed his ankles, his fingertips drumming as he frowned at it. Was the man too poor to afford a reasonable ad? Germans did not often blow their own horn with huge advertisements, but this was ridiculous.

He sat up, shrugged to himself, and dialed the number. A

look at his watch told him it was far from being noon, no chance that the man would be out to lunch. But the phone rang and rang; for all von Wessenheim knew Rønna Ulgard might be in China. He carefully replaced the receiver, deep in thought, frowning. To think that this exciting quest would die before it had a chance to bloom, and all for the lack of a silly permit! It occurred to him to simply take his case to the officials of the *Tiefbauamt,* perhaps convince them of its feasibility, and obtain his permit legally.

The notion suffered a quick death. Even the Hitlerjugend were laughing at him, and they were willing to kill each other for a chance to worship Hitler's bones. So at the *Tiefbauamt* the laughter would be even more boisterous as they shot down his idea as an idiot's dream. What, tear up the center of the city more than it already has been during all this reconstruction? Give the auto traffic even more headaches, force the pedestrians onto even more footbridges? *Nein, danke.*

Von Wessenheim slid his eyes shut and watched the floating shapes and shadows that resided on the insides of his eyelids. Actually, he had no intention of digging hundreds of holes around the Reich's Chancellery. Scientific techniques would replace random actions. Two able historians were already on his payroll, and expensive modern detection devices could peer through the ground without disturbing it. But eventually some actual digging would be necessary, possibly with a backhoe or a larger machine. That meant traffic interruptions, bystanders and police asking questions, public interest if the story got out. If the international press grabbed hold of it, it would become a media circus, others would start their own searches, hire their own scientists, and perhaps find the skeleton first. It would be a personal tragedy for the royal house of von Wessenheim.

He opened his eyes again, sure of at least one thing now: the mission needed a cover. Attention had to be diverted from its real nature. Street crews routinely chopped up perfectly good streets, pipe crews routinely dug deep holes for no apparent reason, so the operation must appear to be doing those unremarkable things as it worked to find Hitler's bones. But still, the matter of the permit—

The phone shrilled suddenly, making von Wessenheim jump. Probably either Dr. Rudiger, who wore his socks in his pocket, or the lady historian Dr. Friedl von Lütringen. He recovered and snatched up the receiver. "Yes?"

The voice that replied was low, not terribly audible. "Herr von Wessenheim?"

"Yes?"

"I am Rønna Ulgard. You called."

"I did?"

"What do you need me to do for you?"

"Oh." Von Wessenheim removed the receiver from his head, frowned at it, and stuck it to his ear again. "How did you . . . ?"

"I am accepting very few new clients, Herr von Wessenheim. What do you want from me?"

"Want?" Von Wessenheim swallowed. "I need a permit for excavation."

"Where are you going to excavate?"

"Reich's Chancellery area," von Wessenheim said. "But I don't think we should be talking of this on the telephone. Why don't we—"

"We will," Ulgard said. "Tonight at the Rotten Tooth, three o'clock."

Von Wessenheim took a breath. "This is awfully sudden."

"My fee is ten thousand Marks. I will need another thirty thousand for the permit."

"But you don't even know—"

"I know enough to get you the permit, so what else matters? Three o'clock, Herr von Wessenheim. Cash. And please be alone."

Now, though, standing in an archway under the ruins of the Kaiser Wilhelm Gedächtnißkirche in the middle of the night, von Wessenheim felt very much the fool. Most likely Bohr had played a nasty joke on him with one of his colleagues, the colleague pretending to be this mysterious Rønna fellow. What they might not realize was that they had put him in danger with this prank, he was out here alone with a small fortune in cash, easy prey for street toughs. Resignedly, he slipped his hands into the pockets of his windbreaker and stepped out into the light of the street.

"Herr von Wessenheim?"

Von Wessenheim lurched back with a grunt, pulling his pockets inside out as he maneuvered to keep his balance. "Ulgard?" he hissed, turning in a clumsy circle. "Is it you?"

The man stepped out of the shadows. "I have your permit. Do you have my money?"

Von Wessenheim unzipped his jacket and withdrew the envelope. "Forty thousand Marks."

Ulgard extended his own envelope. As von Wessenheim took it he saw that the man's hands were black; he remembered what Bohr had said about the gloves.

Ulgard accepted von Wessenheim's envelope and immediately stuck it inside his clothes. Von Wessenheim opened his and unfolded the permit, turning it to the light.

"You are now a corporation called *Grundwerk Deutsche Metalle*," Ulgard said. "I suggest you affix that name to any implements or machinery you use."

Von Wessenheim ran a fingertip over the embossed government seal. It felt quite real—or had he dumped forty thousand Marks into a forgery? He turned and opened his mouth to speak. "What if—?"

"It is genuine," Ulgard interjected. It seemed to be a specialty of his, a vastly annoying habit. "Good-bye, Herr von Wessenheim. Perhaps we will do business again someday."

With that he walked away. Before von Wessenheim could even fold the permit and put it back into the envelope, a dark Porsche with blackened windows slid to a noiseless stop at the curb and Ulgard lowered himself inside. The door thumped shut and the car zoomed off to the curve where Kurfürstendam became Tauentzien Street, veered right, and dwindled into two red dots in the mist.

Von Wessenheim stuck the envelope inside his windbreaker, shrugged, and hurried off to the nearest taxi stand just as it began to rain.

13

Hank drove into his reserved parking spot on campus two hours before his first class on Monday, feeling better than he had felt in a long time. For breakfast he had downed three eggs, a big pile of hash browns, and four good-size pancakes. Rebecca, the chef of this masterwork, had been a bit frumpy and a lot unhappy all weekend, since the party, but not Hank. Perry could stick his German mumbo-jumbo straight up his ass, schizophrenia was not on the menu of Hank's life after all, and he had been hypnotized perhaps hundreds of times over Perry's chessboard and was the victim of a bizarre practical joke. And to be honest, the German phrases were still strolling through his mind to pop up here and there and say "*Guten Tag.*" They should dwindle soon, he supposed.

Sheldon Hall was cool and quiet inside, smelling faintly of the new paint that had turned the walls from beige into light green in the last week. Painters' buckets and drop cloths had been shoved aside to make a passageway, and an electric scaffold dripping with a thousand dried colors looked like it might be fun to ride up and down on. Hank cut left at the stairway and hopped up to the second floor with his briefcase banging painlessly against his thigh, cut left again and almost ran head-on into his graduate assistant, MaryLou Hanscom. She fell back with a grunt and the top two books of a stack in her arms bounced to the floor and opened themselves.

"Sorry," Hank intoned at the same time she did, and bent to pick them up for her. "What's the hurry, MaryLou?"

MaryLou was about as homely as a woman could get, but behind the cat's-eye glasses and acne-pitted face resided a remarkable mind. "I guess I've got a case of the klutzies," she said as Hank placed the books back on top of the pile. "Dr. Morgan asked me to deliver these to him, and it took all morning just to round them up."

"Good work, soldier," Hank said with a smile. "Have you got the office open?"

"Yep. But no coffee on. Didn't expect you so quick." She put on a quizzical look. "Dr. Thorwald?"

He raised an eyebrow.

"The party Professor Wilson had? Is it true?"

"True? Yes, there was a party."

"And he hypnotized you?"

Hank's blood pressure edged upward a couple of strokes. "Word is getting around, I take it."

She nodded. "He hypnotized you to a past life, and you said you were, um, like the German kaiser or something?"

He was aware that his eyes were narrowing. "Or something? That's how the rumor goes?"

"Not really." Her cheeks reddened in an upward progression of blotches. "In my past life I was probably a spider or something. A bug. Maybe a kitchen chair."

He smiled, but only to put her at ease. "Perry's parlor game was exactly that, MaryLou—a parlor game. For your information, he also convinced me that I was an ostrich. Did you hear *that* part of the story?"

She lowered her head. "No."

"Or that he admitted he hypnotized me before, made me fluent in German while we played chess?"

"No."

He took a breath, then realized with a start that he was browbeating the poor girl and that she didn't deserve it. "Oh, hell," he said, and picked up his briefcase. He put his hand on her shoulder. "Me very sorry, me go make coffee and leave graduate assistant alone. Okay?"

Her red face softened into a grin. "Me sorry too, boss. Me shut up, go finish chore."

"See you in a few, then," he said, and they parted. He heard the rapid click of her heels on the stairway, much faster than usual, and kicked himself hard in the mental pants. The tale of

Perry's party would probably swirl hard and fast around here until it died of its own lack of wind. Thankfully, most of the faculty was vacationing for the summer or on sabbatical somewhere, the student population was a fifth of its norm, and there would be no more faculty parties until someone got that wild urge just before winter hit. Perry had probably created a subject for party talk from here to eternity the night Hank Thorwald got his unbelieving ass hypnotized and declared to the incredulous crowd that he used to be . . . used to be . . .

He aimed himself forward and leaned into a brisk walk, headed for his office at number 211. Rebecca had told him that the party fell apart after Perry pulled his prank, that no one there found it even vaguely funny, that they left in disarray and that Perry's oddball party had been a catastrophic flop. Throughout the weekend Hank had actually expected a lot of phone calls, expected some support or at least condolences for such an embarrassment, but the phone rang only twice for him and not Sharri, Bud Lewis from math and Jason Ayers from biology calling to express their disgust with Perry's idea of fun.

He veered into his office. It was the size of a respectable closet, but tenure would solve that. In the meantime the walls were layered with metal shelves bursting with books and sagging folders. His sole filing cabinet supported the telephone and the decrepit Sanyo coffee maker, and his desk was barely big enough to prop both elbows on when dumb students or dumb faculty forced him to hang his head in despair. A small television, also a Sanyo, was parked on a rolling table that was in the way no matter where he rolled it. He dumped his briefcase in its usual spot behind the door and went to work making coffee. As he poured distilled water from a jug into the back of the machine there was a rap on the door that was instantly followed by a surge in the air, a sweet wave of cologne rapidly pressing its way inside.

Hank turned. With no surprise at all, he saw Wally Lautermilch leaning inside with a stupid grin on his face. "*Sieg heil,* good buddy," he said, and blared out a couple lungfuls of laughter. "*Eins, zwei, eins, zwei.* Hup-hup, march!" He took a step inside. "Howya be, Adolf?"

Wally Lautermilch was Hank's private proof that anyone

and their dog could get a degree if they pestered people long enough. "Yo, Wally," he said without spirit. "Heard about the party, did you?"

"Who hasn't? Tell me, was his real name Hitler, or Schickelgruber like they used to say?"

"Very funny."

Wally waltzed on in. "Maybe not so funny, homeboy. Some people are getting scared of you."

Hank rolled his eyes. "I don't buy that for a second. It was a trick Perry dreamed up, revenge for me kicking his ass in chess and then quitting the team."

"Awful lot of revenge for such a minor crime."

"Perry's an awful lot weird."

"That goes without saying." He eyed the empty coffeepot. "What, Hitler didn't drink coffee?"

"Just making it," Hank replied, shaking the jug of water in Wally's face. "Machine's busted, goes real slow, takes half an hour to finish, so no sense in you waiting around."

Wally Lautermilch, also known on campus as the Prince of Polyester, did not get the hint. "So tell me what it was like, Hanky boy. Do you remember what you said while you were zonkered?"

He shook his head as he screwed the cap on the plastic jug. "I remember sitting down, and I remember waking up after everyone else had left. Except Rebecca, of course. She read Perry the riot act, then told me what had happened on the way home."

He grinned. "I'll bet you just about shit."

Hank nodded. "I shat."

"So what're you going to do back to him? Spray-paint his car or something?"

Hank stared at him. "Yes, Wally. That is what I am going to do. Might even toilet-paper his house."

"Wicked," Wally said, sounding quite amazed. "Count me in."

"I'll call you."

"Do that."

They looked at each other. Finally, Wally paid attention to his watch. "Oop, gotta run. Class in fifteen."

"'Bye," Hank said, and closed the door when he was gone.

He got up again and set about finishing the coffee, emitting a belated burp from breakfast that tasted like used pancakes. When the coffee maker was turned on and threatening to actually make coffee, he gathered up the pile of student papers that MaryLou had graded for him, giving each one a quick checkover to see if he agreed with her diagnosis, but after scanning a few shoved them away. This was no fun, his former good mood was growing more sour all the time—first there was MaryLou and then there was Wally—and his day had barely started.

The door drifted open and Hank turned: MaryLou again, lightly tapping the door with a knuckle. She had never done that before. Behind her two students he did not recognize ambled to a stop and looked over her head to stare at him. One of them whispered something; the other's eyes grew wider.

"Please close the door," Hank said. She hurried inside and pushed it shut just as another head popped in to ogle him. This was getting pretty damn stupid, he though angrily. By noon a hundred heads would be out there, kids would be hanging from the trees to take a look at him.

Idiotische Studenten . . .

"Dr. Morgan gave me this, asked if you'd seen it," she said, and handed him a videotape.

He looked it over. Old and battered, no label. "What's on it?"

She shrugged.

"He didn't say?"

"Actually he said not to rewind it, start right where it is. He was taping an old Jerry Lewis movie Saturday afternoon and then something else came on."

Hank moved to the rolling tray that held the TV perched on top of a vintage VCR. He squatted and slipped the tape inside. The screen flickered and filled with light, black-and-white light. Jerry Lewis and Dean Martin were clowning around on a golf course. Hank leaned and adjusted the volume so it was higher.

The screen changed. Now it showed a newsroom with the big black letters "WXRV" on the wall. The familiar torso and head of Alan Weston were facing the camera. Hank frowned, struck with a terrible premonition.

"I made a promise, and I keep my promises," Weston said soberly to the camera. "Just a few days ago, after being attacked and held hostage in my own house by a neo-Nazi motorcycle gang, I promised my uncle Max, and all of you watching the live coverage that terrible day, that I would begin the process of eradicating the hidden anti-Semitism that festers in the Midwest."

His eyes drilled the camera. The pause dragged on almost absurdly. Suddenly Weston dropped out of sight, as if he were standing on a trapdoor that had fallen open. A moment later he popped back up again. Now a little square of black paper or tape was stuck under his nose, a Hitler mustache. "I found out that Hitler is alive! I met him personally! This is no joke! He lives in Terre Haute! He teaches college there! Join me tonight on WXRV-TV at eleven when I present a very, very exciting story on *Alan Weston on Us*. See you then!"

Hank took small steps backward until the desk stopped him, almost unable to draw a breath. Alan Weston hadn't been at the party. So what was *this* bullshit?

Then a small groan eased through his lips. The former student . . . wearing a hat and sunglasses to disguise himself. But of all the people on the planet, what the hell had Alan Weston been doing at that party? He wasn't even faculty.

MaryLou was watching him. "Can he do that? Can he tell your name?"

"It doesn't matter. Morgan taped this Saturday. What's done is already done."

She rushed forward suddenly and ejected the tape. "Well, I won't ever believe it, Dr. Thorwald. I know you well enough to know that all this is very absurd. And there is no way I will ever, *ever* believe you were Hitler. No matter what everybody else believes."

He wondered if he should thank her. The phone twittered and he snatched it up. "Hello. Thorwald here."

"Hank?" It was Rebecca. "You'd better come home."

A bit of adrenaline touched his bloodstream. "What's wrong?"

"Somebody's thrown rocks through the windows."

He dropped his weight onto the edge of his desk. "Somebody's throwing rocks through the windows?"

"No, *thrown*. Past tense. Sharri and I were cleaning some clutter out of the garage like you wanted, we heard glass breaking, and came in to find three windows broken out and glass all over the front room."

MaryLou was mouthing something, questions. Hank ignored her. "Call the police," he said. "Don't clean up anything, leave it all the way it is. Vandals did it and the cops will never catch them, but if they see the cop cars out front it'll scare them for the next time."

"Ten-four," Rebecca said, and the phone went blank.

He lowered the receiver onto the cradle. Ten-four? Where did *that* come from?

MaryLou had pressed closer. "What's happening? Bad news on the home front?"

He turned. "I've got vandals chucking rocks through the windows in broad daylight."

"Oh my God," she said, and sank down onto his chair. It rolled backward a few inches while the wheels squeaked out a request for oil. "I pray to God it *is* vandals," she said, her voice labored and hollow. "I pray to God."

He leaned closer to her. "You think they're connected."

She looked up. "The news is spreading, Dr. Thorwald."

His heart gave a couple of big and unsteady beats that pulsed in his throat then were gone. "This Hitler stuff," he said softly. "Why did Perry do it?"

She stared at him mutely.

He raised himself to his full height. "Gotta go home, MaryLou."

"You know you have a class coming up." She looked at her wristwatch. "In an hour and forty-five minutes."

"I'll be back. If not, you'll have to stand in. Go over their tests, play some of the 101 videos, do what you have to."

She stood up. "Not a problem."

He offered her a quick and lackluster smile, looked around for an aimless moment, and left.

14

The policeman knocking on the door was red-faced from the July heat when Rebecca opened it. His partner, a shape in the black-and-white car on the driveway, appeared to have his head lowered, reading something. Rebecca swung the door wide open and Officer Tooley, according to the metal bar above his pocket, stepped inside. He removed his hat to fan himself with it. "Nice house."

"Thank you," Rebecca said, and pointed. "All the rocks came through the front windows. My daughter and I were in the garage when we heard the crashing."

"Kids," Officer Tooley said. He looked to where Sharri was kneeling over one of the stones, studying it intently. "Got any enemies, kid?"

She looked up at him. "Nope."

"Then we got random vandalism here, Miz . . ." He fumbled a pocket open and drew out a soggy-looking notepad.

"Thorwald," Rebecca said.

"Thorwald. Right. You got a husband who lives in the house?"

She nodded.

"Has the husband got any enemies, Mrs. Thorwald?"

She thought of Perry but dismissed it. "No enemies."

"Looking pretty hard like random vandalism." He eyeballed her. "You got any enemies?"

"No," she said.

"Random vandalism. Call us if it happens again." The notepad disappeared. He turned.

"You're done? That's it?"

Officer Tooley put his hat back on his head as he turned again. "No, I'll ask the neighbors if they saw anything."

"So what should I do?"

He eyed the sparkling field of ruined glass. Beads and triangles of reflected sunlight winked and flashed on his face. "Get on the horn with your insurance company, if you don't have a big deductible. Personally, I think you can replace all this for less than a hundred bucks."

"So there won't be any kind of investigation?"

"Nothing to investigate, really. But like I said, I'll talk to your neighbors."

She mustered a good attitude. "Okay then. Thanks."

He smiled. "Not a problem."

She opened the door and he went out into the heat. Rebecca watched him go, frowning. Not a problem? Not for him, anyway. She eased the door shut, uncomfortable inside her own skin, feeling as if she'd just bought a door-to-door vacuum cleaner she didn't need.

"So now what?" Sharri asked, rising.

Rebecca could only offer her a confused little shrug. "Wait until Dad gets here, maybe take pictures for the insurance company. Then we have to pull out the pieces of glass still stuck in the windows, and clean everything up."

"Fun," Sharri said glumly.

The doorbell gonged. Rebecca wheeled around and opened it. A young woman wearing two red pigtails on each side of her head stared in at her. The police car was just backing out of the drive. "I'm a student reporter with the ISU student newspaper, the *Sycamore*. Could I get an interview with Professor Thorwald?"

Rebecca shook her head. "Not at this moment, no. He's at the university."

"Specifically, please. This is very important."

"Then specifically, I would say he's at his office at number 211 in Sheldon Hall, or else somewhere on campus." She pressed the back of her hand to her forehead, aware now of the heat. "Why do you need him?"

The woman—just a red-headed teenager, really—took a step back. "At this point I can't divulge anything without involving freedom of the press issues. It would be best if I could simply talk to him, get to the basics of this whole story, and let the public decide."

"Meaning?"

The girl cocked herself forward. "Maybe I should pursue the story from your angle, the wife. You are the wife? Yes. Did you know that Professor Thorwald spoke German under hypnosis and revealed that he was Adolf Hitler in a past life?"

Rebecca found herself speechless.

"So you haven't been interviewed yet? Good. Eyewitness reports are always the most valuable, but the story gets fuzzy if repeated too often, so then *prior* to the hypnosis, did you know that your husband was Hitler, and how did you feel when you found out?"

Rebecca was aware of Sharri coming up behind her. "Dad was Hitler? Who says?"

"You are his daughter?" the reporter asked. "Good. When did you first learn of your father's past life as the Nazi madman?"

"The what?"

Rebecca folded her arms over her chest. "Get off my property."

The reporter looked at her blankly. "Property?"

"Off my property." Rebecca stepped back into the house and rested a hand on the edge of the door. "My husband was not Hitler, the whole thing was a sick practical joke staged by Dr. Perry Wilson of the psych department at ISU, and he's the one you should be interviewing." She pressed a hand flat to her chest; the extra serving of surprises today was just too much. "Humor me. Go away."

Her face fell. "A practical joke?"

"Talk to Perry Wilson. He'll explain it all."

Her shoulders slumped. "I came out here for nothing. Skipped a class, even. But that's what they teach us, anything for a story. 'Bye."

Rebecca slammed the door and leaned against it. A drop of sweat trickled from her hairline to the tip of her nose; she pursed her lips and blew it away.

"This is like Halloween or something," Sharri said. "Everybody's acting weird."

Rebecca heard the knob turn and whirled around to shout through the door: "I told you to get off my property!" But the door pushed her aside and Hank stumbled in looking scared.

"Are you two all right?" Relief registered on his face as he backed against the door to close it. His eyes strayed to the broken glass all over the carpet. "Perry's going to pay for this," he growled. "That twisted bastard is going to cover all this in full. Then I'm going straight to administration and demand a full inquiry. *Then* I am going to kick his ass, the dumb old bastard."

He stalked into the living room. Rebecca joined him in this new survey of the damage, crunching broken glass into the sparkling carpet despite tiptoeing in odd directions to avoid it. "The cop said it was random vandalism," she told him.

"The cop was wrong, Rebecca. The world has a lot of weird people in it and they know what happened at the party. Reincarnation is a crock of crap but even my own grad assistant has a tough time dealing with it."

Sharri piped up, "Is reincarnation where you get born again?"

Rebecca turned. "Supposedly you live many different lives."

Sharri shrugged and wandered off toward the kitchen. "We got any more Popsicles?"

"Might have," Rebecca said, and stepped to where Hank stood holding the drapes apart. "They survived okay," she told him.

"How about the rocks?" He let the drapes fall from his hands. "Any markings or messages on them?"

"Just rocks," she said, pointing. "They look like the river rocks Fred Harlan has around the trees on his lawn next door." She indicated the area outside the shattered window. "Somebody could have picked them up from there."

"Or," Hank said darkly, "Fred Harlan himself could have thrown them. Didn't he have a grandfather who fought in World War Two?"

"He's mentioned that, yeah. But you had one who did too."

"That's true, thank you very much. But nobody likes Hitler, and maybe he thinks his grandpa's war is still on."

She laid her hands gently on his arm. "First of all, Hank, Fred is not a nut. Second of all, Hank, Fred values his landscaping above his own life. You know how he is. Would he waste his decorator rocks on us?"

His fierce expression hung on for a bit, then faded. He took her in his arms. "Convince me that we'll get through this. All I need is your reassurance."

She hugged him, then drew back. "You have my firmest assurances that we will get through this, one way or another we will get through this intact." She kissed him. "Enough convincing, Hanky-Panky?"

He was smiling but managed to insert a frown in its place. "Have you been talking to Mom and Dad?"

She raised her eyebrows. "Which mom and dad?"

"Mine. Did they tell you they used to call me that?"

Her first instinct was to lie. The nickname Hanky-Panky, another party favor from Perry, led straight into Hank's childhood, and his childhood led straight into the subject of a vanished sister. Rebecca intended to reserve any broaching of that subject for the perfect time, the perfect moment, and here, today, right now, was about as far from perfect as a golf ball shot straight into the water. "Just popped into my head," she said sprightly. "I'll try to think up something else."

"No big deal. So you call our insurance company, let them take it from here, and I'll go back to work. I just had to see all this myself and make sure you two were all right."

"We're fine," she said. "So don't worry."

"Fat chance of that," he said, and left.

But someone was sitting in his car. The sight of this stopped him dead in his tracks on the little front porch, made him blink a few times. Though the sun was reflecting against the windshield in a big white slash, he could see easily enough that a dark figure was in the passenger seat, possibly wearing a wide-brimmed hat. He strode to the Lexus, jerked the door open, and leaned inside. "Okay, you," he started to say, but his voice squeezed down to nothing and his eyes grew larger.

It was a full-size inflatable woman with a head full of fake blonde hair, one of those sex toys sold at porno shops. It was tightly inflated and jammed rather uncomfortably into the passenger side, both feet poking against the floor, its midsection held in place by the seat belt. In the crotch area some kind of hair or lint was glued in a triangle to mimic pubic hair. Hank had seen one or two in his life, though he couldn't recall where.

On the oversized left breast a letter had been sketched with a black marking pen: *E*. On the other, an *A*. Hank lifted the part of the seat belt that separated the two breasts and found another letter: *V*.

"Eva," he muttered, and drew himself out of the car to scan the neighborhood. Nothing was unusual, the sky was blue and birds were busy in the trees and none of the parked cars in the driveways seemed unusual. Quite a nice day, actually.

He walked around the car and got inside. No sense showing this tasteless thing to Rebecca, no way in hell Sharri should see it. He fished his keys out and started the car, feeling an unsettled, betrayed kind of anger, wondering if some perverted bastard with a taste for rubber women was watching him through binoculars right now, maybe up in a tree with the birds, maybe rising up from a manhole just to watch and gloat at street level. How could people be so just plain rotten to other people? He dumped the gearshift into reverse and backed out of the drive, aware of the smell of the naked lady, brand-new vinyl or plastic straight from a factory in Taiwan, something that resembled the new-car smell he liked. It was in his mind to carry Eva up to his office and tape her to the outside of his door, ample warning that the joke was appreciated but growing stale, find somebody else to laugh about, this is an institution of learning and not horseplay.

It was when he stopped and was shifting out of reverse that a big white station wagon zoomed out of someplace to the right and screeched to a stop in front of him, blocking his way. What bounced out of it all full of smiles and laughter was Ben Jademan, professor of mathematics, currently wearing tennis whites and a pink terry cloth headband, and his wife, Gayleen, in the same uniform. As he approached, Ben jokingly pounded the hood of the Lexus with a fist, grinning so hard Hank knew his face must soon rip in half and spill his teeth and eyeballs to the asphalt.

"Did I getcha?" Ben shouted at the closed window. He pointed down and Hank lowered the window. "Wow, you love her so much that you're taking her out for a drive," Ben howled. "Honeybun, look! Hank's fallen in love with our precious little Eva!"

Gayleen Jademan giggled into both hands, her bright blue eyes bouncing from one direction to the next. She was known in faculty circles to be ditzy, Ben was known to be a manic-depressive not yet on medication. Inside the dark confines of Hank's body, a blunt object seemed to suddenly plunge from his head to his gut. This tasteless stunt had not been delivered by anonymous crackpots. It had been delivered by a coworker. He leaned to the side and unbuckled Eva, trying to appreciate that Ben and Gayleen had gone to a lot of trouble for this gag, probably intended to stick the thing in the car at his university parking slot, maybe even got chased off when Hank came storming out too early.

"Hell, Hank, you keep her," Ben managed to say between snorts. "She's one hundred percent made in Deutschland—just like you!"

Hank forged a smile that was all teeth, no lips. "You got me a good one," he said. "Boy howdy, by gosh."

Ben squatted to be at eye level, the few gray strands in his brown hair sparkling in the sunlight. "Some of them are saying they believe it," he whispered, "and this is my way of saying I don't. Okay? Do you understand that?"

Hank nodded. "Yes. I appreciate it, Ben."

"You spoke in German. That's an amazing thing, but hey, Debbie Govern was there, and she spoke German too. Translated what you said."

"Perry taught me," Hank said. "He hypnotized me earlier, made me fluent in the damn stuff."

"Right. That is right, he told us he had. He actually went pretty nuts. You scared the living poop out of him."

"I did?"

"Yeah." Ben squatted again and stared intently into Hank's eyes. "So you don't remember any of it? None?"

Hank's eyes slid down a degree. "None."

"You spoke in German. Pretty impressive German too. Too much even for Perry to follow. That's when Debbie had to translate."

"The practical joke of the century." Hank raised his left arm. "Uh-oh, got a class in twenty minutes, Ben. Sure you don't want Eva back?"

He grinned. "Hey, she was good enough for Hitler, she ought to be good enough for the likes of you."

Hank smiled genuinely. "You'll be getting paybacks for this, you know. No practical joke goes unpunished."

"Wouldn't expect any less," Ben said.

"Okey-doke." Hank touched the gearshift, expecting Ben to retreat to his car but Ben stayed, looking in at him with an expression that dwindled from a genial smile to an outright frown. "Hank?"

Hank took a breath. "Yes, Ben?"

"If Perry taught you all the German, how come he needed a translator?"

"I don't follow you, Ben."

Ben nodded slightly to himself. "That's the funny thing about the whole deal, the part I just can't figure out. How did you speak more German than he taught you?"

"Hypnotism is a funny thing," Hank offered.

"Yeah, I guess it is." He righted himself suddenly. "Off to the tennis wars, compadre. You have a good day."

"Will do," Hank said, and watched them go. When they were out of sight he got under way, forgetting for a while that an inflatable woman was seated in plain view beside him as he motored through town.

How did you speak more German than he taught you?

Good question.

15

The old man's last birthday on this earth wasn't as happy as it should have been, but Rønna Ulgard did not care if the man died unhappy or died laughing. He had mere weeks left to live so his son David had arranged a spectacular gift, the gift of a lifetime, the private showing of a video made especially for him. But during the screening of the special video Rønna had made for them, he seemed more excited about it than his dying father.

"Christ, Dad, you've waited a *lifetime* for this!" the son was hissing into the old man's ear, his gaze jumping from the ear to the television on the wall. Sweat stood out on his forehead: summertime in Coral Gables, Florida, can be a killer, even late at night. The old man's head was propped up on pillows so that he could better see from his nursing-home bed. The air-conditioning was never turned on in this room because Gerald L. Clarret suffered from a permanent chill. In World War Two he had been an infantryman in the Ardennes Forest who fought in the Battle of the Bulge, which occurred in the winter of 1944–45. Frostbite had claimed several of his toes and both earlobes. Since that winter he had been almost phobically averse to cold weather, a condition that worsened as he aged.

"Look at how he's bleeding," his son David whispered loudly. Rønna Ulgard watched him as he prodded his father, goaded him. David was a market analyst from New York who had made a lot of money. It was likely that this was his first visit to his father since the old man had entered the nursing home. Now that Gerald L. Clarret had received the final pronouncement of cancerous doom, David was gracing him with the best gift he could come up with—a video of revenge.

"Listen to him scream!" David dived for the television and cranked the volume a bit higher, but not too high. The home was full of nurses and their aides; they would not like what Gerald L. Clarret was watching. "Dad, *look!* That's the German bastard who *shot* you even though you had your hands up. Remember? Christ, it cost me a *fortune* to find him. *He's* the reason you had to limp in pain all your life. Look at him, Dad, *look* at him. *Listen* to him screaming. Hear that?"

Rønna Ulgard focused his attention on the television, contemptuous of this stupid little man. For a five-minute video, he had paid Rønna Ulgard an enormous sum of money in American dollars. The screen showed the death throes of a certain German war veteran named Hermann Schenke, also a soldier in the Battle of the Bulge. On the video he was hanging by his thumbs from a rafter in his own barn in upper Bavaria, suspended a few inches off the ground by piano wire. He had been dressed in an old German Wehrmacht uniform Rønna Ulgard had ordered from a costume shop in Frankfurt. Two of Ulgard's hired thugs, their backs to the camera, were beating the old soldier to death with clubs, changing the routine occasionally by whipping him with leather straps. His face was a welter of cuts and gashes. His thin gray hair poked out in spikes. He writhed and screamed as he twirled by his thumbs and in the background his cows answered his calls while chickens pecked at the hay underfoot.

"He's *dying*, Dad! I'm killing him for *you*, for the suffering he caused you all of your life!"

Gerald L. Clarret, old and gray-faced, stared wordlessly at the television. Perhaps, Rønna Ulgard thought, he did not believe that the man being tortured was really the same young German who had shot him with a bullet that shattered his hip that frozen December night, but he was, oh yes he was, old Hermann Schenke had been easily tracked to his Bavarian doorstep through army records and the small veteran's pension delivered to his rural mailbox. Rønna Ulgard did not deal in shoddy merchandise.

"Now they're spinning him in circles! How come his

thumbs don't just pop out?" He poked his father in the ribs with his elbow. "Stay *awake*, for God's sake! This is the Nazi bastard who shot you, I could go to prison for a billion *years* for getting this!"

Rønna Ulgard stood up. His customer was satisfied, it was unbearably hot in this small room, and there was no reason to remain. He should not have stayed for this viewing but the market analyst had said his dad would jump up and down on the bed when he saw this, might even be cured of his cancer out of pure joy. Instead, he lay in bed with his rheumy eyes all wet and his tongue bobbling in and out.

"Just an old man," Gerald L. Clarret wheezed, and turned his face away.

His son jumped up. "What the hell do you *mean*? I moved heaven and earth to get this!"

"I'm tired."

"Christ, Dad! You see that man there?" He pointed at Rønna Ulgard. "You see that man wearing the black gloves? I paid him thousands of dollars for this! *Hundreds* of thousands of dollars!"

Rønna Ulgard left the room. This was a family matter, one deserving privacy. And if the young fellow kept ranting, the nursing staff would be throwing him out soon. He strode down the hallway with its polished green floor and its pebbled green walls that stank of age and urine, his gloved hands pressed inside the pockets of the expensive black suit that was his trademark. He had a car sitting outside under the full moon, a rented Audi to get him down the road to Miami International, where a Lufthansa L1011 would whisk him from Florida to Frankfurt, if one could call an eight-hour flight a whisk.

He elbowed the door aside and stepped out of the building, pausing to lift sunglasses out of his pocket and settle them over his eyes. He slicked his hands over his hair, front to back. Despite his Nordic heritage he had been born with hair as black and shiny as bubbling tar. He did not know why.

Rønna Ulgard walked to his car. It was unlocked. There were ten thousand things in the world worth locking, but a rental car was not one of them. He got inside and drove away.

There was a lot of business to take care of in Berlin, a lot of clients wanting the special services no other lawyer in Germany had the courage to give them.

"It's almost closing time," Pat the bartender said.

Alan forced his eyelids upward, an act that required the effort of every muscle in his face. The room was heaving like a schooner. He had not been asleep but on a lower plane of existence, his thoughts a pleasant and meaningless buzz.

Reality hurt. "Kill me," he bleated. "Don't make me live through the hangover I've got coming."

"Hey now, look at the bright side," Pat said. "Chances are you won't survive it anyway. Your liver walked out with a beautiful blonde about four hours ago."

He groaned. "Hope it was packing a condom, Pat old buddy. I can't afford the paternity suit." This struck him as absurdly funny and he raised his head in a sudden move to bellow laughter at the ceiling. There was a grimy ceiling fan overhead but it did not seem to be turning; instead, it was the ceiling that was going in circles. "Wild ef-ex," he said, awestruck.

"You keep doing that and you'll puke and I'll have to clean it up," Pat said. "Save it for the cab."

"Cab?" Alan lowered his eyes and saw two perfect images of Pat the bartender standing side by side. "Why can't one of you drive me home?"

Pat did not crack a smile. Instead he moved closer to plant his hands on the bar, and hunkered down slightly to stare into Alan's face. "The best asset a bartender can have, besides being big enough to kick the crap out of unruly customers, is the ability to listen to tales of woe with professional sympathy, sort of like a psychiatrist but a lot cheaper. I commiserate while dumping alcohol down the throats of these poor bastards, a trick of the trade."

"Commiserate," Alan said dreamily.

"Amazing what the common man can pick up from Webster here and there, eh? I tended bar for a while at a country club in Massachusetts, learned how the snobs talk. And in my line I've seen a lot of fucked-up people. I don't mean *fucked-*

up on booze, I mean *fucked-up* in the head. *Loco* in the *cabeza*."

"Is that your diagnosis of me?"

Pat smiled. "Hardly. You just tell the truth too often. The only person you lie to is yourself, and it's fucking you up."

"Freud in a size-fifty apron."

"Careful. I might stretch you out on my couch." He made a fist and waved it under Alan's nose.

"Okay, so I'm a liar and you're anorexic. When's the wedding?"

"You use humor to sidetrack people who get too close to you. Myself, I fart."

"That would explain the stench here."

"And the hours you spend inhaling it here. Alan?"

"Just resting my eyes."

"The last guy who fell off a barstool here broke his neck."

"Mmm. Better than being lynched by your entire family and a rabbi."

"For?"

"Perjury, sedition, misanthropism, and malfeasance."

Pat snorted. "Even in Massachusetts they don't use words like that. Translate."

"One more drink, Jack and Coke."

"So rich, so famous, yet he can't even keep his eyes open. No booze for you, one year!"

Alan grinned. "Pat's a booze Nazi." He clucked out a wobbly laugh. "Why couldn't I have been one of Seinfeld's writers? Why couldn't I have *been* Seinfeld? Or even Kramer? Or even the poor bastard who sweeps up after the show? Why the fuck did I have to be me?"

"Because you play the role so well, Alan."

"Just my luck to be born with talent like this." He cracked open one eye, saw one Pat, closed it and tried the other eye. One Pat from a different perspective. With both eyes open the Pats finally merged into a single image. The beginning of a world-class headache immediately announced its presence throughout his brain. "Sobriety is returning, much to my chagrin," he said. "There are no longer two of you."

"I know people who would dispute that," Pat said. The

pudgy lines of his face seemed to squinch together as if he were performing some mental computations; he then seemed to reach a decision and squeezed himself out of the bar area into the grand showroom. Alan turned and watched him draw the shades down, smack the switch that turned off everything neon, and trundle back. He poured himself a beer and set it down beside Alan's empty whiskey glass.

Alan felt genuinely flattered. "Sir," he said, "I will gladly pay you Tuesday for a Jack and Coke today."

"Oh." Pat stood taller and turned to snatch the Jack Daniel's bottle off its shelf. A little ice, a dash of Coke, it was in Alan's hand. He lifted it to his lips, inhaled the smoky aroma of fine Tennessee whiskey, and downed half of it without pause. With luck, he supposed as he thunked it back down on the bar, it might chase his headache away.

"I have heard that it is possible to drink yourself sober," Alan said as he pounded his solar plexus with his fist. "I have also heard that sloe gin affects you slowly; that if you drink beer through a straw you get drunker; that if you suck on a penny, alcohol won't show up when the cops give you a Breathalyzer test; that if you drink a bottle of vinegar, marijuana won't register in a urine test; that if you get a woman drunk she will do anything you desire." He lifted his glass. "Lies, all of it. People lie all the time."

"Never fails," Pat said with a big smile. "Give a customer enough time and room to talk and he will eventually cut the crap and get down to the guts of the problem."

Alan frowned at him. "Be so kind as to elaborate, my son."

"I will, my father, and here is the elaboration. You have condemned yourself to death by alcohol for the crime of lying to the thousands of people who watch your TV show."

"My TV segments."

"Your TV segments. For the last three years you've snooped and pried and dug up liars in the city government, in the police department, in the average man on the street, and even in your own fucking media. Alan Weston strikes again, Asshole Weston nails these lying fuckers and makes the world safe for democracy."

Alan pressed the cold rim of the glass to his lower lip.

"My mission is indeed a holy one," he said, feeling vaguely uneasy.

"The only person you *won't* nail on TV is Alan Q. Weston. Instead, you nail Alan Q. in the privacy of your head, set up a private kangaroo court, and convict him, order him executed."

"The Q stands for Quasimodo, by the by. Or is it Queenie? I'll have to ask my mom."

"More humor," Pat said, as deadpan as a corpse. "Alan, and you can believe this or not, I happened to catch the afternoon news on WXRV before I came to work. They showed a tape of your Saturday segment."

Alan shrugged. "This is supposed to bother me?"

Pat lifted his glass and regarded it. "The condemned man, having been sentenced to die, commits suicide on live TV while simultaneously drinking himself to death." He put the glass to his lips, cast a wink at Alan, and downed the beer in four gigantic swallows. "Unga-bunga," he wheezed before wiping his mouth across one of his huge forearms. "Reminds me of my drinking days of yore."

"What in the fuck are you trying to tell me?"

Pat thunked his empty glass down on the bar and began to gently twirl it between his finger and thumb, letting its heavy base wobble in controlled circles. After a long moment spent staring at it, he said, "Do you by any chance remember Skylab?"

Alan frowned. "A space station we put up twenty or thirty years ago. Maybe thirty-five, I don't know."

"Yeah, that one. It was big news from NASA back then, the best thing they had going. I was a kid, maybe thirteen. All the cereal boxes had Skylab stuff on the back; in some I had to dump the cereal out into a giant bowl to get the plastic model. Other ones had Skylab stickers and stuff for kids, that kind of junk. I even bought the real glue-together model and painted it, hung it from a string in my bedroom."

He paused. Alan nodded, shrugging slightly.

"Skylab was up in space for years. Us kids got tired of it, we moved on to other fads. Eventually Skylab was abandoned and just drifted out there for years, forgotten. Suddenly, from out of the blue, it was big news again. Remember?"

Alan was just raising his glass to his mouth. "Not for sure."

"The trusty old son of a bitch was trying to come back home to Earth from an orbit that was decaying by the second. The word went out and people started watching the sky for it. Not to see it spinning around in all its glory, but to watch it burn up."

Alan set his glass on the bar. "The spiel you are presenting is called an allegory and it is nothing new. You are comparing my career to Skylab. We both rose up fast, worked hard and hot, and share the same fate: decay and burnout. Did you think this would surprise me, make me realize the error of my ways? Jesus, Pat, stick to bartending."

Pat stopped twirling the glass. "For a smart guy you sure are stupid."

Alan cocked his head. "Care to clarify that?"

"Yes. Despite your cynicism, my allegory ends like this: if there had been a man on board the old Skylab, a man sitting in the cockpit, he could have flipped a switch and fired the thrusters, saved the space station at the last minute. The damn thing would still be alive and circling the Earth."

Alan made motions of impatience with his hands. Pat reached out with remarkable speed and captured his wrists, both of them, squeezed them hard apart. "You're not Skylab, you guessed it wrong. You're the man sitting in the cockpit, the man who can fire the thrusters to save the whole fucking thing from decay and burnout. But you know what scares me, Alan, what really scares me about you?"

"Probably the size of the lawsuit you've got coming," Alan grunted, struggling.

"Funny man." He released him. "What scares me is that the time to fire the thrusters has come and gone, you're the man in the cockpit and your survival depended on you flipping that switch, but you didn't do it. Instead, you sat here drinking up all the rocket fuel, found some new biker pals, then made a total idiot out of yourself about that swastika on your door. Yes, Alan, I have been known to read newspapers, and I can watch TV like a pro. So then straight out of your ass you yanked a phony script about the bikers beating you, declared yourself Super-Jew of the Midwest instead of telling the simple truth, and now you have conveniently coughed up, of all the ridiculous fucking things in the world I have ever heard, a new Hitler who lives about seventy miles from here. And you actually wonder why nobody takes you seriously anymore."

Alan stared at him. His headache was thudding loudly to the beat of his heart; something inside him seemed to be slowly melting, like a block of plastic in a fire. Suddenly the roar of motorcycles ripped the night and the flashing white beams of headlights bristled from the mirror behind the bar.

"Looks like your pals are back," Pat said.

Something cold glanced across the top of Alan's stomach, as if he had swallowed a small sliver of ice. The cowbell over the door clanked and feet tromped across the floor. The smell of cigarettes and marijuana walked in with them. Pat stood taller. "Closing down in fifteen minutes, state law," he said loudly. "Order now and drink as fast as you can. You men want pitchers and glasses?"

One of them dropped an arm around Alan's shoulders, then slowly sank onto the stool beside him. "Three pitchers of Bud and one Jack and Coke."

Alan looked at him. "Hey, Commando. Many days no see."

Commando's arm slid away. "How have you been, Alan?"

He shrugged, already knowing that it would look more like a nervous twitch, and it did. "Just hanging in."

"I hear that." He sat up straight and flexed his hands. His sleeveless leather jacket creaked as he moved and the tattoos on his arms seemed to crawl underneath the hairs. Alan glanced at Pat. He was working at pouring beer into large plastic pitchers. The rest of the motorcycle crew, instead of heading off to play pool, were standing in a restless cluster off to the side. Pat swung around and glided a pitcher onto the bar, then another. When the third one was in place he opened a floor cooler and hauled out cold mugs, three in each hand.

Alan saw Commando match eyes with one of the others. With a start he saw that it was Shaver, the guy who had trounced him in pool time after time and believed that Jesus was coming back to rid the world of blacks and Jews. His eyes were dark, his face emotionless. As Pat turned and bent for another handful of mugs, Shaver stepped behind the bar. He swiftly inserted a hand between the cooler and the stand that supported the cash register; he whisked out the ax handle Pat kept there for rowdies and jerked it overhead.

"Pat!" Alan shouted, too late. The ax handle cracked across the top of his head and he dropped instantly. Glass broke on the floor.

Commando stood up. "He'll be okay, Alan. But I can't say that much for you."

He jerked him off the barstool as the others crowded in.

16

Hank Thorwald went to bed at the usual time that night but sleep would not come no matter how many times he demanded it or punched his pillow into new shapes. When he got back home from work, the insurance adjuster had already come and gone and two workers from a local glass company had a white van parked in the driveway and were almost done reinstalling everything that had been broken. Miraculously, the insurance policy contained a vandalism clause that covered broken glass one hundred percent with no deductible.

Rebecca was snoring softly beside him on the queen-size Serta Perfect Sleeper, her breath carrying whispers of the cigarettes she had smoked during the day and the sweet mouthwash she used to disguise it. In the uncertain light Hank lay on his back with his fingers interlaced behind his head, his eyebrows drawn down low, his thoughts circling in a lazy mental spiral, nothing concrete to deliberate here, just basking in a sense of unease. A sideways look at the clock and its blue numbers told him it was after three. His first Tuesday class wasn't until eleven and he could sleep in, but he knew he would not. Might never sleep again—

Glass broke downstairs. Hank surged upright in bed, his mind clear of everything but the knowledge that he had been expecting this, had been lying awake waiting for it. He rolled to his feet in one lithe motion, but at the top of the stairs he hesitated. The only light available down there was donated by the control panels of the stove and the microwave, a distant green tint that cut the living room furniture into blocky shapes and made the walls glow. He took a step down, his heart hammering in the middle of his chest, and then another, knowing that there were exactly eleven steps down from the top, calculating that he had nine more to go, thinking somehow that this would give him an edge over the vandals when they jumped him.

Aufsicht!

It was like a shout from the middle of his brain. His balance failed and he was forced to sit abruptly to keep from falling. Thanks for the German lesson, Perry, he muttered inwardly, and rose up again, shaking. He lowered himself another step, left hand trailing the wall, right hand creeping along the varnished surface of the banister. It came to him that he carried no weapon, nothing. He took another step, his eyes wide and searching, his throat as dry as bleached flour. At the bottom of the stairs his ears, finely attuned now, picked up only the slight hum of the refrigerator in the kitchen, to his left, and a jet passing overhead just at the rim of hearing. No new breaking glass, no cackling vandals sprinting across the lawn as he'd imagined, no car packed full of teenagers roaring down the street tossing beer bottles into the black air. Nothing. *Nichts.*

But the silence meant equally nothing. Hunkering down, he soft-shoed a path to the front windows that were so fresh and new, split the drapes, and peered out.

Nichts. The usual nighttime scene—his lawn, houses, trees, parked cars, a moon that painted the scene with silvery shadows. Hank let the drapes fall together and straightened.

So had he dreamed it? He stood for a moment rebuilding the memory, letting the tape play inside his head, listening for the crash that had jerked him out of bed. Real? Not real? Maybe something had fallen in the garage, could be that a neighbor's cat had gotten inside somehow. He cut down the hallway and hesitated at the door that opened on the garage, pressed his ear to it and held his breath. Nothing. He turned the knob, pushed the door open, and flipped the light switch.

The garage was warm, the smell of motor oil and half-empty paint cans heavy in the air. All the boxes belonging to Rebecca's parents were just as he had left them after finding G-pa's wartime stuff. Under the single brilliant light he could see that his Lexus was unharmed, as were the big pebbled-glass windows in the walls. He stepped down onto the cement and found the floor surprisingly cool under his feet. Crossing to the automatic door, he found that the four small windows decorating the upper section looked intact, and ran his fingers over them feeling for cracks.

Absolut nichts. Reassured now, he flipped the switch that opened the garage door. With its customary squeaks and groans it labored upward. Cool air surfed across his bare feet, his knees, his chest. In the spreading rectangle of light he saw that a brown beer bottle had been smashed to pieces on the driveway, some of the bigger shards being held gamely in place by the soggy red Budweiser label.

He shook his head wearily. All this drama because some teenager had launched a beer bottle from his car. Grumbling, he found the push broom and temporarily shoved the mess to the edge of the drive where the concrete became grass. Down the street, to his left, a pair of headlights swung around the corner and headed toward him on Quartermaine Avenue, probably some poor slob who either got home from work late or left home early for work. Hank hustled into the garage as the headlights grew brighter, leaned the broom against the nearest wall, and gave the switch another hit. The door rattled down, slowly. The courtesy light blinked out.

"Dumbass teenaged drunks," he grumbled, and went back into the house, headed for bed.

But a few seconds later, the driver of the car, a man named Jerry Bainbridge who was tired to death from twelve hours of a special IRS audit at the bank he managed, was surprised to see, in the glow of his headlights as they swung past house number 1225, that the garage door he had seen assembling itself now presented the finished mural of a giant swastika, bleeding red paint against the tender backdrop of beige.

Karl-Luther von Wessenheim, Frau Doktor Friedl von Lütringen, and Herr Doktor Konrad Rudiger were assembled at the Berlinische Residenz Wednesday morning. Frau Doktor von Lütringen had secured a room at the other end of the

Residenz but Konrad Rudiger, of lesser birth and concerned with economy, was quite satisfied with the *Fremdenzimmer* he had rented above a nearby pub. He had arrived this morning carrying a dozen cardboard tubes stuffed with newly printed sectional maps of central Berlin in May 1945. Frau von Lütringen had amassed a similar arsenal of current maps and a box full of books on the life of Adolf Hitler. Her own book, *The Secret Power of Eva Braun*, had been placed neatly on top. Rudiger's book bulged from his pocket in paperback form: *No Such Dignity in Death*. Von Lütringen's book was of course the airing of her idea that Eva Braun had controlled the Reich in the last days; Rudiger's questioned the indignity of Hitler's burial and Martin Bormann's involvement in it. Von Wessenheim had only two things to offer these scholars: the money to finance all this, and the digging permit that had cost him so much and had forced him to deal with that unpleasant and mysterious man, Rønna Ulgard.

"Coffee?" he asked them as they set down their wares. "I had a fresh pot brought up."

Frau von Lütringen eyed the silver tray on its perch on the little writing table. All the other furniture had been shoved to the walls. "Thank you, yes."

"Gives me heartburn," Rudiger grunted.

Von Wessenheim poured her coffee. "Today I hope to pinpoint at least three possible burial sites for excavation tonight," he said as he handed the cup to her. "I believe we're all agreed that this undertaking is not only feasible, it has a good chance of success and is mandated by the need for the ultimate closure of the war that destroyed all of Germany. When we finally present the remains of the Führer to the world, the old chapter will be closed and a new one will open. A Germany risen from the ashes, a Germany free from the taint of its past, free from the bones of the man who single-handedly destroyed her."

"Well put," Dr. Rudiger said, and slapped his hands together in a mimicry of applause. "I do my best work in the morning, though, so let's get on with this."

"The whole project just seems so grand," Frau von Lütringen said. "It's like unearthing the pharaohs of Egypt, even the tomb of Tutankhamen, but without all the gold and jewels and regal finery, all the riches of an ancient empire."

Von Wessenheim raised an eyebrow. "Hitler was no less a pharaoh than any of the Egyptians, Frau von Lütringen. He commanded an empire, had millions of soldiers at his command, had all of Europe at his feet." He took a quick breath, growing embarrassed. "But this is simply the history that I learned in school, and that was a long time ago."

"Yet correct on every point," she said, and set her coffee cup on the silver tray inscribed with the flowery script of the Berlinische Residenz logo. "But it is my belief that Adolf Hitler took very few treasures to his grave."

"Interesting," von Wessenheim said. "Not really our concern, though."

"I say this because he was not a man prone to pinning medals all over himself. In the First World War he was awarded the Iron Cross for bravery in battle. That was the only medal he ever wore on his uniform, even as Germany's Führer. His underlings, notably chief of the Luftwaffe, Hermann Göring, wore almost enough colorful medals on their chests to pull them to the ground."

"As I recall he was a tremendously fat man," von Wessenheim said. "A drug addict."

She nodded. "Addicted to morphine as a result of treatment of injuries sustained in World War One. In fact, almost all of the top Nazis were war veterans, which I believe contributed to their ruthlessness and peculiar lack of pity for their victims. In World War One, on all sides, pity was a thing left at home. The war was a ruthless slaughterer of seven million men who had no reason to be fighting each other, and its only outcome was another war that killed millions more, most of them civilians on all sides."

"Agreed, those were awful times," von Wessenheim said impatiently. "Shall we lay out the maps now?"

She eyed him, then dropped her gaze. "First I think we should assemble the Reich's Chancellery area as it was in 1945, and trace Hitler's and Eva Braun's every move in the last few days of their lives, which would be the middle of April to the thirtieth of that month, 1945."

"Wrong!" Herr Doktor Rudiger blared. Von Wessenheim and von Lütringen turned, startled. "Absolutely the wrong tactic, the wrong approach, the one taken by every historian to date. We must concentrate on the movement of people *outside* Hitler's bunker, those who came and went in the last days, who they were and what business they had. The war was lost, Hitler had no more orders to give to his vanished army, so most of the traffic had to consist of his burial crew."

Von Wessenheim looked back to Frau Doktor von Lütringen, not knowing what to expect, preparing a verbal fire hose to douse the flames that might erupt. Her blue eyes were flashing, but in seconds a dazed kind of frown settled itself over her face. "I believe you have a valid point," she said. "Very valid. We historians peer inside the famous bunker, yet ignore its most humble guests. Not once have I thought of it this way."

Rudiger already had his mouth open and a finger raised to rebut; instead he tipped his nose a few degrees upward and peered down its length at her. "Maybe you ought to read some of my earlier works, good Doctor von Lütringen. I even wrote a profile of the janitorial crew that kept the bunker clean. Eighteen women who swept up dust as soon as the bombs overhead shook it loose, all of this while Hitler was asleep in his soundproof bedroom."

Von Wessenheim stepped between them. "Why don't we review the principle events of the last few days of Hitler's life while the maps uncurl? I have only a little knowledge of that time in our history."

"Good idea," von Lütringen said. "That would put us at the latter part of April. Acceptable?"

"Sounds fine."

"So would you like to begin?" she asked Rudiger sweetly.

"Ladies before gentlemen," he said with a sour expression.

"Very well then." She pulled her skirt tightly around her knees. "Imagine this: World War Two has been grinding along for five and a half years, all of Germany's beautiful cities have been reduced to burning rubble and heaps of corpses. It is three days before Eva Braun drinks poison as the Führer fires a pistol into the back of his throat, eight days before the German army surrenders at Rheims, France. The atmosphere in the multitiered bunker varies between wild hopes that the Führer can perform a miracle at the last moment like he did in so many of the early battles of the war to a frightened acceptance of defeat. Everyone is issued a small glass capsule filled with cyanide to hide in their mouths. As the Russians advanced into Germany's eastern lands, they had proved to be as ruthless as the Nazis themselves, and suicide was often preferable to torture. Several instances from my studies stick in my mind: bundles of captured German soldiers roped to invading Russian tanks as a bizarre kind of armor plating, and a young soldier who was strung between two poles and skinned alive."

"The horrors of war," von Wessenheim said, touching his lips. "But please concentrate on the activities in and around the bunker."

Dr. Rudiger cleared his throat. "A historian should never get emotional over the details of war, Frau von Lütringen. War turns sane men into insane beasts. Apes with bombs, monkeys with rifles, chimps with knives. The story never changes."

Von Wessenheim stared at the man, then forced himself to create an inward shrug. Eccentric, not crazy. Eccentric, despite the burned-cornstalk hair, not crazy.

"Then pardon me," Frau von Lütringen said. "But I lost both my grandfathers in the Battle of Berlin, and at times they haunt me."

"Your feelings come through in your book, without being maudlin," von Wessenheim said. "Commendable."

"Thank you."

Rudiger sighed loudly. "Can we get on with this?"

She set her teeth together and glowered at him. "Fine. Hitler has been in his bunker without pause since January sixteenth, 1945, one hundred and two days. It is reported that at this time he has been suffering from hideous nightmares. His personal physician, Dr. Morell, is feeding Hitler dozens of mysterious pills every day, giving him injections of various drugs. In reality the pills are quackery and Hitler is quite insane, even his own generals refer to him as a 'mad dog' and try to assassinate him, without success."

"Common knowledge," Rudiger muttered.

"So common that I did not know it," von Wessenheim snapped, and Rudiger sank back in his chair, grumbling.

"Hitler's fifty-sixth birthday came on April twentieth. He and Eva Braun and a few friends attended a dismal little party of sorts. Everyone who saw Hitler in these last days was appalled by his condition. He shook and trembled, his speech was slurred, he smelled bad and even drooled. It was obvious that he had been stricken with Parkinson's disease."

Rudiger sat up straighter. "I have to interrupt here. The idea that Hitler had Parkinson's disease is absolutely preposterous. It is no wonder that he shook and trembled! The stresses on him were enough to drop other men dead. At worst, he suffered a severe case of nervous tremors."

"Your disagreement is noted," von Wessenheim said.

Von Lütringen shifted her weight, crossed her legs, drew a long breath, and pressed her skirt smooth again. "Regardless of his mental state, he was still the Führer of Germany, and in that capacity he often gave his last surviving generals—when they were able to make it to the bunker—the impression of a man in a state of utter collapse. He issued absurd orders. In one case he ordered that all Germans be handed weapons and herded to the center of the country to form a huge circle that would fight to the last bullet. In another order he commanded that all towns and villages, all farmland and all property, be burned to ashes so that the victors would have no spoils. The fact that all of the Germans would then starve to death was of no consequence."

"Obviously, those orders were not followed," von Wessenheim said.

She bobbed her head. "After these sessions with the generals, Eva Braun quickly hustled Hitler off to bed and returned to countermand his orders. It was becoming obvious that Eva herself had become the incapacitated Hitler's spokesperson, and more. Hitler was spending most of his time either sleeping or ranting or playing outside with his dog whenever there was a lull in the bombing. Due to his disease—excuse me, his nervous tremors—he had, in effect, become as helpless as a child. Eva Braun's child. And it was Eva Braun who directed the last days of the war."

Von Wessenheim glanced at Rudiger, who clenched his jaw and gripped the arms of his chair with white-knuckled hands.

"It was two days after his birthday when Hitler's mind finally collapsed forever. According to witnesses in the bunker, he was ranting as usual when it suddenly dawned on him that the war was lost. Becoming as pale as a ghost, he swore to kill himself."

"That is the moment," von Wessenheim said. "We must seize upon this. As soon as Hitler swore to kill himself, his burial wishes would become, naturally, the next order of business. What does history say about this?"

Rudiger piped up. "History says that he ordered the SS to go siphon an enormous amount of gasoline out of the wreckage of nearby cars. He then married Eva Braun, the wedding followed by a reception. After that he and Eva went into a room where Hitler wrote out his last will and testament. Then, while the party guests huddled at the door, Eva bit down on her poison capsule. Hitler shot himself while crunching down on his own capsule. The people at the door heard the shot, supposedly, and went in. There sat Eva on a couch in peaceful repose, and Adolf at the other end slumped over."

"Which is where the facts fall apart," von Lütringen said. "Some people there claimed they heard a shot. Some didn't. Some say the door was heavy and soundproof, others say it wasn't. The cyanide in Eva's capsule should have resulted in immediate convulsions—but they say she was sitting with her feet tucked comfortably underneath her. Some testified that Hitler shot himself through the mouth. Others say the right temple. There is rumored to be a photograph showing the dead Hitler with a hole in his forehead. Not one person who was there tells the same story."

"Which is the basis of my book, and the reason you hired me, Herr von Wessenheim," Rudiger said. "It is obvious that everyone present in the bunker that day has lied about it. These people adored Hitler. They had been hastily told a concocted story of burial by burning, but they had to come up with their own versions of the suicide. In reality, Hitler and Eva Braun, and very likely the mysterious Martin Bormann, left the bunker via one of many secret passageways, and vanished forever."

"But not to South America?"

"Unthinkable. The risk of capture was too great. They killed themselves, all right, but not in the bunker, and their bodies were laid to rest somewhere, not tossed into a bomb crater to be burned. I am sure of it." Rudiger looked at von Lütringen. "Can we at least agree on this?"

She pursed her lips and toyed with the hem of her skirt momentarily. "Agreed," she said quietly.

Von Wessenheim stood, his fists balled with determination. "We will find them, my colleagues. We will find them at last."

17

It was just before dawn when Rebecca Thorwald was lifted out of sleep by the sound of people talking. She let her eyes drift open and looked at the clock on the dresser: five in the A.M. The garbage haulers picking up the cans, she thought—but they didn't come until Thursday. Puzzled, she swung out of bed, careful not to wake Hank, and clumped down the steps barefoot.

The voices came from the front of the house. She hopped down the last step and veered toward the living room. A new picture window had been installed yesterday; getting the drapes back up had been a real chore, as was ferreting out every sliver of broken glass from the carpet on hands and knees with a flashlight and a magnifying glass. Now she slowed, admiring her handiwork, then crossed the room and pulled the door open.

Her front lawn had sprouted people. Six, maybe eight vague shapes in a variety of poses, maybe even ten or twelve. Instantly a camera flash seared her eyes with a burst of bluish light. She staggered back a step, blinded.

"Mrs. Thorwald?" a voice barked out. She was aware of a forward surge of the shapes, shadows closing in. "Rebecca? Did he paint it there himself as a warning to the world?"

"What?" she asked reflexively, blinking against the glare of the blue rectangle that had been imprinted on her eyes. Another flash exploded silently and she shielded her face with her hands. Belatedly it came to her that she was in her night-clothes; she scuttered backward, found the edge of the door, and whipped it shut. The ornamental brass knocker on the outer side of it clunked once, proof of a good, solid slam. "Hank!" she shouted, turning. "Hank!" She bumbled across the lightless obstacle course of her own living room, her shins thudding into chairs, her right kneecap receiving a direct hit from a corner of the coffee table that made her clutch her leg and howl.

"Becka? What's going on?" Hank thundered down the stairs. "Is somebody out there? Are they breaking windows again?"

"People," she groaned through her teeth, hopping on one foot, searching for the shape of anything that might be a chair she could collapse into.

"What? People? Where?"

"Front yard. Taking pictures."

"Taking pictures?"

"Yeah."

"What for?"

Rebecca's good knee cracked against the invisible coffee table. "Jesus fucking Christ, how should I know? Open the door and look for yourself!"

"Sorry," he muttered, and slipped past her close enough for his knuckles to graze her nose as he walked. She heard him scrabble for the doorknob and sensed the door being swiftly pulled opened. She wondered if Hank was in his underwear, but of course he probably was. She blurted out a warning: "Shut it, Hank! You're in your—"

The doorway was machine-gunned with light. Hank ducked back inside and repositioned himself so that only his head was sticking through the doorway. "Who are you people?" he shouted. "What do you want?"

A lot of strangers answered in a riot of voices that made Rebecca think of movie stars and the way they were always mobbed by fans. Hank drew back and pushed the door shut. "I can't believe it," he said wonderingly. "It's a bunch of reporters looking for Hitler."

She thought of the ISU reporter yesterday, the eager-beaver little lady who had needed a door slammed in her face. "I'm calling the police," she said. "We've got ten thousand people trespassing on our property, and that's against the law."

The doorbell gonged, a daytime sound that seemed weirdly out of place this early in the morning. "Okay," Hank said. "You call 911, I'll make sure they don't bust the door down until the cops get here."

She hurried toward the kitchen and the weak light provided by the stove and the microwave. The phone on the wall sported a lighted dial set and jumbo numbers, a gift from Hank's myopic parents several birthdays ago. Just as she reached for it, it chirped. She snatched it up. "Hello?"

"Hello! This is Doug McRainey with station WTHI in Terre Haute. I'm calling you from the white van outside your house, wanting to know if you or your husband would care to be interviewed. I have a cameraman ready and anxious to get his lights set up either out here or inside your home."

"What?"

He repeated his words, his voice professional and newsy, as if he were serving up the flawless, scrubbed-face and shiny-toothed evening news that graced WTHI in the evenings. "No," she said into the phone. "There's nothing here, we're just ordinary people."

"Of course you are. We'd like to talk to you just to get your side of this nonsense, leave the decision to our viewers."

She felt the small hairs at the back of her neck prickle. "What's with this decision thing?"

Doug McRainey chuckled. "Was he Hitler, or was he not?"

With a gasp of disbelief, she smacked the receiver against its cradle. It rang immediately, perhaps short-circuited by the blow. She pressed it to her ear. Nothing.

Then: "Is this the Thorwald residence?"

She nodded.

"Is anyone there?"

The doorbell gonged. She slid her eyes closed. "What do you want."

"Hello! This is Tige Branson, WTWO news team. We'd like to dispatch a cameraman and Melanie Wilks, our features reporter, to see if she could talk to you on camera. Would that be a problem?"

"It would," she said nastily, and hung up. For a second she

hesitated, wondering what she was doing, then remembered: dialing 911. But with her finger poised to stab the big green nine, she noticed Sharri wandering out of the dark wearing a long white T-shirt that bore the bug-eyed likeness of Darth Vader, much of which had flaked off in the wash.

"Mom, what's all the noise about?"

"Nothing. Go back to bed."

The doorbell bonged again. "Who keeps doing that?"

Rebecca pressed the phone to her chest and hissed: "Just go back to bed!" With those words, for the first time ever, she recognized the voice of her own mother. She took a breath and hooked the receiver back onto its base. "Wait, Sharri, you know most of it, so I guess you ought to know it all. There is a pack of people—reporters, I guess—out front who heard about that Hitler thing and your dad. Remember?"

"Uh-huh." She raised her arms overhead and yawned, stretched.

"It looks like word of this stupid thing is spreading."

Sharri ran a quick hand through the tangled expanse of her brown-blonde hair, tossed her head. "Was he?"

Rebecca leaned forward slightly. "What?"

"Was he that guy a long time ago?"

She straightened. The doorbell gonged. She heard Hank shout something, heard the door bang shut, heard the knocker clunk to prove it. "How can you ask that?" she demanded hotly. "Haven't you been going to Sunday school since you were a baby? Did anybody there ever mention past lives?"

"Reincarnation."

"Yes, smarty, reincarnation." She took in a quick breath. "You'd better get dressed 'cause this is going to be a long day."

Sharri turned and shambled off, mumbling.

"Don't strain yourself," Rebecca muttered, and punched 911 on the dial. It was answered on the first ring by a man who sounded tired but interested. "Emergency, 911. What is the nature of your emergency?"

Nature? "It's not really an emergency," she said. "It's just that a bunch of people—reporters, I guess—are out on my front lawn trying to get an interview with my husband. He's in his underwear and they keep ringing the doorbell." She felt herself redden. "It sounds silly but they might try to break into the house. They keep taking pictures of us and won't leave."

A pause ensued that was just long enough for her to wonder if he had hung up. "Your address?" he finally asked, seeming disappointed.

"1225 Quartermaine Avenue."

"That's in Bluewater Pointe?"

She wondered how he knew. "Yes."

"Your name?"

"Thorwald. Harrison Thorwald. Not me, I mean, I mean my husband. That's how we're listed in the phone book, if that helps."

"We'll send a car out that way."

Click. That was it. She had never dialed 911 in her life and right here and now, on her debut night, she had sounded like a complete, stark-raving idiot. The police would probably not bother to come at all.

Hank hurried in, breathless. "I gotta get dressed. I locked the door, so we're okay for now." He glanced down at the phone in her hand. "Cops on the way?"

Rebecca hung it up. "So they say."

"Good enough. I get dressed, then you get dressed. The doorbell rings again, ignore it. If windows start breaking they're gonna regret it." He zipped away and sprinted up the stairs. Rebecca felt a touch of pride in Hank's new take-charge attitude. In a way it was inspiring, maybe even romantic. The doorbell bonged again and Rebecca was quickly jolted by a spurt of anger. It was getting lighter outside and the hobgoblins of the night were beginning to pale a little. She flipped the kitchen light on, drew herself more erect at the familiar sight of the gleaming white appliances she used and kept clean every day, turned and went to the front doorway.

The door had a peephole. She rose slightly on tiptoe and pressed an eye to the little brass circle. In the pre-morning gloom outside, she saw only the distorted, curved shapes of people she did not know. Hank's feet pounded out a cadence down the stairway. She turned and saw that he had climbed into some raggedy jeans and a sweatshirt obviously yanked out of their bedroom closet in the dark and at high speed. His shoes were untied, the laces straggling behind.

"No sign of the cops yet?"

"It's only been a minute," she said.

"And is Sharri still in bed, with all this racket?"

"She came out and I told her to get ready for a rough day."

"Let's hope it's not." The phone chirped; she lifted it, dropped it. A stupidly simple idea struck her and she brightened. "Why don't you just go out there and talk to them, Hank? Hell, invite them all in and I'll make coffee, we can clear up this whole mess like civilized people. We can send them to Perry's house where the *real* story is."

Hank's eyes narrowed, shifted left and right. He let out a big breath, and grinned. "Baby, you're the greatest." He stepped over and snatched her toward himself by her waist, enfolded her tightly in his arms. "This is why we got married," he said. "To make two minds better than one."

She drew away. "I thought it was because I was pregnant."

"I'd completely forgotten."

The doorbell gonged just as the kitchen phone warbled again. Hank lifted his arm and looked at his watch. "We have never been so popular so early in the morning." When the phone repeated its plea, Hank stepped toward it, popped it off its base with two fingers, and caught it as it dropped. "Speak."

Rebecca watched Hank's face as he listened. Hank murmured a thank-you and hung up. When he turned his eyes were small, his face slack. "That was Ben Jademan in math, the guy with the inflatable woman. He said to read today's paper before I do anything else."

"Ben Jademan is a nut," Rebecca said. "Screw Ben Jademan. He's full of bullshit, thinks he's a tennis pro, him and his dingbat wife deserve each other."

"But he was awfully serious, no clowning around. Said he'd gotten a few calls, people wanting to know if he was at Perry's party, who the Hitler was."

"And he immediately steered them your way. I'll bet you a million dollars that he did, the rat."

"The paper's probably here by now." He struck off toward the living room. Rebecca scurried up the stairs, hit the bedroom light switch with her elbow, threw on a bra and some shorts and a shirt, and jumped into the bathroom just long enough to arrange her hair in a pattern that seemed familiar, then rub her front teeth with a finger.

Below her the front door thumped shut. She charged down the steps. The clamor of voices outside was louder, the doorbell gonged again. At the base of the stairs, Hank was striding past with a harried expression on his face and the *Terre Haute Tribune-Star* rolled in his fist. "Hyenas," he muttered as he worked the rubber band off. "The damn thing's been stomped half to death. And where are the cops?" With the paper flat on the countertop, he whisked through the crumpled pages. "Nothing about me in the national news, thank God." But in the area/regional section his hands slowed, and he bent lower to read, with Rebecca getting a side view:

ISU OFFICIAL DECRIES RUMORS
by Jeff Silver

ISU Dean of Faculty Albright Clereau met with student representatives late Monday to denounce the "winds of rumor" that he says are sweeping the campus. The meeting came in response to Indianapolis TV newsman Alan Weston's assertion Saturday that an ISU professor had been Adolf Hitler in a past lifetime.

"The concept of reincarnation springs from religion, and like all religions can be neither proved nor disproved," Dean Clereau told the group of students. "I am surprised by the number of persons alarmed by this, especially considering the source."

Alan Weston of station WXRV is renowned both for his investigative prowess and his shock-jock delivery. His Saturday evening segment exposed what he termed the "Hypno-Hitler of Terre Haute." Though he did not identify the professor by name, he stated that under hypnosis the professor unexpectedly revealed, in fluent German, that he had been Hitler in a past lifetime.

"I would vigorously prosecute any member of the faculty suspected of neo-Nazi activity," Clereau said. "That is simply not the case here."

Attempts by the *Terre Haute Tribune-Star* to contact Alan Weston have failed.

Hank straightened just as Rebecca snaked an arm over his shoulder. "Hey, it's not that bad," she said, and kissed the side of his face. "He didn't give out your name."

He turned his head just as the doorbell rang again. "This is what nails me, Rebecca." She drew back, not understanding, and saw that his face had been completely drained of its summer tan. "People are talking, rumors are spreading. I've already got a front yard full of snoops with cameras, and every man who was at the party is trying save his own ass at my expense."

"Which is why," she replied, "we have to invite these snoops in and give them a dose of the truth. It's the only way."

He straightened. "Then let's do it. We can end this nightmare right now and it'll be ended forever."

The phone trilled. Rebecca turned her head from the sound and breathed a hopeful sigh. "Amen to that."

Hank made for the door. Rebecca was instinctively crossing the living room to tidy things up, rearrange the sofa pillows, when Hank pulled the door open. "My wife makes great coffee," she heard him say jovially. "Care for some?"

Frau Dietermunde had just finished a sidewalk lunch at Cafe an der Hauptwache in downtown Frankfurt when she hailed a waiter and asked for a telephone. With her at the square glass table was a man named Jakob Fahrer. Thin and white-haired, he was older than Frau Dietermunde by five years, which made him a senior member of the surviving Hitler Youth. As if to prove his eminence, he carried a left arm that ended, at his wrist, in a stump; in 1944 the explosion of a British time-delay bomb had torn off his hand while his Hitlerjugend troop was digging survivors from the burning rubble of an air raid that had devastated Frankfurt fifteen hours earlier. Frau Dietermunde knew him well enough to know that the loss of his hand was a subject never to be brought up. Time-delay bombs were meant only to kill the rescuers of the people trapped beneath the demolished buildings, and by his reckoning were a war crime. Bring up the subject and skinny old Jakob could rant for hours. Privately, Frau Dietermunde thought he should count his blessings. The loss of his hand had saved him from service in the army late in the war, probably on the Russian front that winter of 1944 as the Soviets snowballed over eastern Europe, headed for Berlin.

The waiter, stiff in his white coat, reappeared shortly and handed her a remote, then plucked up its stubby antenna when she failed to do so. After a dismissing smile she held it at arm's length in the sunlight beyond the shade of the umbrella and studied the buttons.

"A wonder of technology," Jakob Fahrer observed as a vagrant breeze tugged at the napkins on the table. "With such things, fifty years ago we could have beaten the British."

She offered him a distracted smile. How portable telephones could have won the war she did not know, or care. By getting her reading glasses out of her purse and settling them on her nose, she was able to press the proper buttons, then hesitantly put the thing to her ear. "Hello? Is anyone there?"

The dial tone indicated the first ring. She folded her glasses away, embarrassed at herself and her age and the youth in her that was gone. After two more rings the phone was answered. "Office of Bohr and Mittheim, attorneys at law."

"This is Frau Dietermunde calling for Herr Bohr," she said.

"He is expecting your call. One moment please."

"That pasta was somehow bad," Jakob Fahrer grunted, pushing his plate toward her end of the table. He licked his lips. "Too much wheat."

"Bohr here."

"Franz! I hope all has gone well."

He snorted. "How do you define well, Frau Dietermunde?"

She smiled. "I know this is hard for you, dear Franz! How is your little family?"

"Safe for now from him and from you," he replied coldly.

"Good. Then you must tell me if it all happened as I said it would."

Bohr let out a breath that was branded with anger. "He did in fact call, and I did in fact steer him to Rønna Ulgard as you requested. With that done, I hope not to hear from you again."

He hung up. Frau Dietermunde spoke into the dead phone: "How wonderful of you! Thank you so much for your efforts on my behalf, my good man, and I look forward to our next meeting!"

She searched the face of the phone for a way to shut it off, squinted at it in the sunshine an arm's length offered, then was relieved of the duty by the waiter, who plucked it out of her hand. "Any more calls, *gnädige Frau*?"

She smiled up at him. "One more, actually, but it's long distance to Berlin and my lawyer there is probably busy with other things. He's *always* busy."

"Sorry to hear that. Care for a dessert, then? And for the gentleman something, perhaps more wine?"

"We must be going," Frau Dietermunde said.

"Bad pasta," Jakob Fahrer said. "Feed it to the British bastards, make *them* taste it."

18

It turned out that there were actually nine people crammed onto the Thorwalds' little porch outside, two women, seven men. In response to Hank's offer of coffee, some of them hustled in while others sprinted away to their news vans. Cameras were hauled in on the shoulders of more strangers, lighting equipment was noisily unfolded and erected while the floor got snaked over with electric cables. Questions were fired at Hank in a babble of voices coming as fast as buckshot; in the chaos he thought of movie stars dealing with this every day and pitied them and their public lives. Who could live like this?

"All of you please sit down," he said, extending his hands as if to push everyone away. Piercing lights snapped on from the left and he was blinded. There were two video cameras, one bearing the WBOW logo in big blue letters on its side; the other belonged to station WTWO. Hank squinted, wondering who the rest of these bozos might be, figured them to be local newspaper people. They were all chatting it up like old friends. When the aroma of fresh coffee drifted in from the kitchen, he stuck two fingers into his mouth to create his patented super-loud whistle-monster, an act he had perfected as a kid that could be heard six blocks away even in the rain.

The room was instantly silent. "You people are guests in my house," he told them. "Shall we all be polite, or do I have to send you back outside?"

"Mr. Thorwald," a shape in the dark said. "How long has that big red swastika been on your garage door, and who put it there?"

He frowned. "What in the world are you talking about?"

"The big red swastika painted on your garage door."

"Hold on," Hank said, raising a finger. "Nobody move, no-body move an inch."

Rebecca appeared from the kitchen, a can of Starbucks coffee in her hands. "A swastika on the garage door?"

They both bolted to the front door, took a hard right in the rising light of dawn, and skidded to a stop on the driveway to gape at it, Hank with his shoelaces straggling behind his heels and Rebecca with her hair trying to sag to her shoulders. "Middle of the night, I got up and smelled paint in the garage," Hank recited hollowly. "I figured it was our house paint."

"Kids," Rebecca grunted. "A joke on us."

Hank turned. Past the cars and vans he saw their neighbor across the street, Mrs. Gillmore, standing on the sidewalk in her shimmering blue robe with the morning paper at her feet, staring with her mouth open. A pair of early joggers had stopped to gawk, their forearms still held in the horizontal running position, mouths hanging just as open as Mrs. Gilmore's. Hank closed his eyes. Pretty soon all the inhabitants of Quartermaine Avenue would get in their cars to go to work, and they would drive by with their mouths hanging open. Half the local world would cruise by eventually, and all of them, with their mouths hanging open, would see this thing.

"Where are the fucking police?" Hank whispered savagely, his face a rictus of sudden anger. "I want to know where the fucking police are."

Rebecca ducked her head. "There are fourteen million people watching us," she said quietly. "All of the reporters are now on the front porch again, listening to us and probably taking pictures. May I suggest that you calm down and that we go back inside, let me finish making the coffee, play this thing lightly, get it over with."

Through the confused mists of his anger, he was able to realize that this was good advice. He exhaled the breath that was locked inside him, flexed his hands, and pulled in a chestful of new air that was cool and damp: no problems here

at all, my fellow Americans, everything is *wunderbar*.
"Okay, got it," he mumbled, and they locked arms. For this
deed cameras flashed, followed by reporters scrambling back
inside. Rebecca headed off to the kitchen and Hank placed
himself back in the fishbowl of light.

"Okay, we've seen it. We have no idea where it came from,
no idea who did it, some high school prank, I expect. I'll
paint it over and it will be gone. That ends that, so what else
do you want?"

Someone rose. Hank could make out white pants, maybe a
blue shirt, then heard a woman's voice. "Mr. Thorwald?"

He nodded, shielding his eyes, squinting. A microphone
on a pole began to hover over his head, turning itself this way
and that like a periscope.

"I have spoken with some of your friends who attended the
hypnotism party, and they all report that you confessed to being Hitler in a past life. Do you deny it?"

"I was the victim of an elaborate practical joke," he said.

"Yet you spoke German quite fluently under hypnosis."

"Which can be easily explained, and if all of you will just
listen and report exactly what I say, this whole farce will
blow over and we can all get back to reality."

A man's voice: "What did you say in German? Can you repeat it?"

"How would I know, *dummkopf?* I was in a trance."

A murmur arose. "You said '*dummkopf*,'" a different voice
informed him. "That's German for 'dumbhead.' Why did you
use that word?"

Hank swallowed. "Just . . . poking fun at myself." He felt
the skin of his face grow thin and hot. Why the hell *had* he
used a German word? Because the fuckers kept popping into
his mouth all by themselves, that's why. "A friend of mine
hypnotized me repeatedly and taught me some German
phrases. So at the party he hypnotized me again and I regur-
gitated it all back." He spread his hands. "It's that simple,
see? No magic in it, no past life."

The woman spoke again. "But according to my sources
you spoke far *more* than just some phrases. And that you had
been hypnotized to become the German kaiser, not Hitler."

He narrowed his eyes. "Did your sources mention that I was first hypnotized into becoming an ostrich? I spoke ostrich, I acted like one." He looked for understanding eyes, saw black holes in dim faces. "People, the answer to every bit of this lies in the mind of Mr. Perry Wilson, psychology professor at ISU. It all started with him. You got questions, go to the source. I can give you his office hours, give you his address, his telephone number. I'll even drive you there."

A man in khaki slacks stepped forward, his face assuming form. "I'm Ronald Dean, a reporter with WTHI. I've repeatedly tried to phone and visit Mr. Wilson, but so far without success. He wasn't seen at all at the university, is, in a sense, absent without leave. Any idea why?"

He whipped up a foam-padded microphone and poked it at Hank's chin; Hank was busy frowning. Perry missing? Perry missing his *classes*? "You must be mistaken," he said into the mike. "The man hasn't missed a day's work in years."

"Like in about five years?"

Hank shrugged. "I suppose. I've only been here three."

"Ever hear of his involvement in the Chaim Goldberg disappearance?"

"Who? No. What are you talking about? What's that stuff got to do with me?"

The reporter cocked his head. "I was hoping you could tell me."

Rebecca's voice rang out. "Come fill your cups!"

Hank got no sense of movement from anybody. "I'm not saying another word until those lights are out and I've got a cup of coffee in my hands, people. Either pack it up or join the party."

Lights died off, one by one. Inside his eyeballs they remained as floating blue cubes. He rubbed his face and drew his hand across his eyes. What a way to start the day. Now with the adrenaline leaching out of his system he felt weary and disjointed, a prime candidate for a dark room and a bed. But this was all worth it, he told himself doggedly, this was the beginning of the end to the whole fiasco.

Rebecca made her way to him and gave him a full cup, one sugar, one cream, as usual. "You are doing great," she said.

"Just knock it off with the German words, make yourself a little more relaxed-looking, and smile more. I wish you'd had a chance to shave. And your hair's a fright."

She walked away. Hank scowled into his coffee, aware in the drift of steam that big grains of sand were lodged in the corners of his eyes. Suddenly she was back, whispering fiercely in his ear. "Now I remember, Hank! You remember Alan Weston at the party? That he told us about an Israeli student who used to play chess with Perry? That's who the reporter was talking about. Weston wasn't putting us on, it really happened! The kid disappeared—and so did Perry, for a week! Just like now!"

He stepped back and fingered the spit out of his ear. "Okay, I remember, yeah. But who cares? It doesn't matter if Perry chopped him up into chess pieces or ate him on toast— what's it got to do with me?"

"Probably nothing. It's just . . . weird. I wonder where he went."

"Who, the kid?"

"No, Perry. Suppose he's holed up in his basement?"

Hank shook his head. "Perry is embarrassed and ashamed of what he did to me, and now he needs time alone to let things cool down and formulate an apology."

She thought it over, then let out a sigh. "You're probably right."

Later that morning MaryLou Hanscom was having a cup of coffee in Professor Thorwald's office while she graded papers. Someone pushed the door open and she looked up. It was Ben Jademan, dressed in his trademark double-breasted suit with a tennis-racket pin holding his tie to his shirt and a fog of Tommy Hilfiger's latest cologne swirling around him. "Just popping in to see how Adolf's weathering the storm," he said. "I got a phone call from a reporter but I kept mum, you know. Nothing to say, no comment, boom. Phone on the hook. Is he around?"

"He's not due in until his eleven o'clock class," she said. "He gets here around ten."

"Lucky bastard. I've got a nine o'clock that runs till noon

twice a week and it kills me." He craned his head to examine the room; one suntanned hand drifted across his chest into an interior pocket of his suit coat. "I've got a gag thing here, something I ran across yesterday and couldn't resist." He withdrew his hand. "Mrs. Jademan likes old stuff, she's reading up on antiques to see if she wants to get a mania about collecting it. We found this in a little shop and she decided it was the perfect gift for Adolf. Check it out."

He advanced and presented a small metal box to the front of her nose. MaryLou stepped back to focus on it. About half the size of a Rubik's Cube, it had at one time been painted red but most of that had flaked away to reveal the tin underneath. "Now watch this," Ben said. "It looks like there's no lid, just this little button here." He put it down on the desk and made a grand show of pushing the button, then pulled his hand away. "Don't know who made it or why, but it's a genuine antique."

MaryLou waited. Suddenly the lid of the tin box popped open. Up jumped a spring-loaded Adolf Hitler wearing a teepee of brown cloth as a Nazi uniform, his porcelain head pink and mustached, his right arm up in a fascist salute. "Isn't that great? Too perfect to pass up." He shifted his eyes to Hank's briefcase, in its usual spot behind the door. "Oh, yeah," he muttered, grinning. "The plot thickens."

He used a thumb to push down the comical Hitler and snapped the lid shut. "This will slay him." He brought the briefcase to the desk and plopped it flat on MaryLou's paperwork. He snapped the latches open and lifted the lid. With a gasp he immediately slammed it shut again. "Oh my God, please tell me I didn't really see that," he whispered.

MaryLou had not seen. She leaned to the side and slowly raised the lid, wondering if something might jump out. Instead she saw a big fancy knife. Both the hilt and the scabbard were embossed with silver swastikas.

"He's known it all along," Ben said softly. "That son of a bitch."

MaryLou and Ben studied the pretty knife as if it were alive, fascinated by the flickers of light that were bouncing off its stately contours. When someone rapped on the open door they whirled in unison to stand shoulder to shoulder. "Hello," Ben rasped out.

"Hi." It was a young woman with red hair pulled into pigtails. "I'm a student reporter with the ISU newspaper. Could I get an interview with Professor Thorwald?"

"Not here," MaryLou grunted.

"Of course not," the woman said. "He's never here, he's never there. Has he gone into hiding?"

MaryLou and Ben Jademan swiveled their heads to look at each other. Both of them shrugged, then Ben seemed to sag a little. "Hell, there's no reason I should protect him," he whispered. "My maternal grandfather was Jewish, died in Europe someplace during the war, probably in a concentration camp like all the others. So why should I?"

MaryLou was still too deep in shock to reply.

He raised his head. "A regular Lois Lane, huh? So are you ready to get famous?"

She cocked her head. "Meaning?"

"Meaning come on in and take a look at this."

She came on in.

19

Hank parked the Lexus in his allocated space across the street from Sheldon Hall only thirty minutes before his eleven o'clock class. Though his slot was unprotected from the sunshine—the more seasoned professors had a chance at getting shade from a building or a tree—he turned the motor off and waited in the dying cool of the air-conditioning with his head hanging. It had been an exhausting morning. Even after the reporters listened to his simple story, they drilled him with dozens of new questions until Rebecca had enough of it and gracefully shooed them out. He had trudged up the stairs and flopped gratefully onto the bed in his clothes but sleep was impossible, there were too many uncertainties. He had danced as fast as he could dance for the reporters but they had wanted more.

He raised his head, blinking in slow motion, aware of a vaguely sore throat that might signal an overworked voice or the onset of the flu. Blearily he watched a knot of summer students walking under the trees across the street, young men and women whose sun-dappled faces were not yet blemished by the worries and wrinkles meted out by time. Even when he was their age, Hank realized glumly, he already had a wife and a baby and a regimen of college years that would leave him no time for football or fraternities or beer parties or anything but classes and study, study and work to supplement Rebecca's meager paycheck by doing odd jobs on the weekends. But as lean as those years were, he and Rebecca had known they were working for a good cause. Not many people with a Ph.D. wound up needing food stamps.

He took in a large breath and turned the rearview mirror aside to look at himself. Nondescript guy with nondescript hair, nice teeth unless you're a perfectionist, a gray shirt with a black collar and no necktie, not in these hot summer days. He dropped his hand and popped open the door of the Lexus, limbered himself out, and took in a new breath of hot, muggy air, which was replaced by air-conditioning again as he entered Sheldon Hall. As he trudged up the steps, he realized that he had no idea what today's lecture was supposed to be about. Something to do with earth science, that was safe to assume. The second floor was deserted. He aimed himself toward the hallway his office branched from, and wondered briefly if MaryLou might be there.

He found the door to his office standing open. The smell of boiled coffee was bitter in the air. When he entered he saw that his briefcase was lying open, the Nazi ceremonial dagger his grandpa had saved from the war lying on top of his papers and folders. The two swastikas gleamed, one on the scabbard and one on the hilt. As he lifted it a cold gust of certainty swept through his mind, a certainty that on top of all his latest disasters this Nazi dagger in his innocent baggage would convince even the doubters of his guilt.

A burst of white light electrified the air around him. He whirled and saw a skinny young man in the doorway lowering a bulky camera from his face. In a quick jerk he brought it up again and snapped another photo. Hank recognized him from somewhere, had seen him before, then put it together. This was one of the students present at the Quad who had helped pick up the plastic chess pieces Perry had stiff-armed off the table during that miserable little confrontation there. Hank strode toward him. "May I ask what the hell you're doing?"

"Photo op," he replied.

"No photo op," Hank snarled at him, and went for the doorknob, shifting the dagger to his left hand. The camera popped again. Hank raised the dagger as if to strike him.

Pop. The photographer lowered his camera again. Hank smashed the door shut. From the other side came a triumphant cry: "Yes!"

Hank turned and spun the dagger across the room as if it

were a hot Frisbee. The scabbard separated from the blade as it whirled and smacked against the screen of his computer, cracking it with a dismal little crunch. The knife itself crashed against the blinds. No glass broke behind it but the slats burst instantly into a crazy and permanent new design. Hank stood panting, eyeing the products of his sudden anger, but no feeling of remorse arose, just an increase in the volume of the blood already pounding in his ears.

Growling deep in his throat, he advanced on the computer monitor. It was a goddamned piece of shit from a defunct company called Mentor-Com. He lifted it with both hands, grunting from its prehistoric bulk, and spun to launch the world's first Mentor-Com satellite. It arched through the air with its cables tearing free of the hard drive, then crashed to pieces against the office door. Some kind of white gas belched up as it hit the floor, the mysterious stuff inside a picture tube.

Now the hard drive teetered off the desk and fell, dragging the keyboard with it. New thumps and crashes. Hank whirled and stared down at them, the symbols of his servitude here. He had long wanted to kick the crap out of the temperamental bastard, and he aimed his kick at the slot of the floppy drive that spent more time unable to read itself than working. The plastic splintered and the face of the entire unit levered slowly open to expose the secret metal things inside and the remarkable amount of dust that coated them. His next kick sent the panel skittering across the floor to gouge a nick in the baseboard beside his filing cabinet.

"Oh, fine!" he shouted. "It's just the fucking paint!" With his hands clenched into strange claws he lurched to the filing cabinet. It had been hand-fashioned by Fred Flintstone out of wattle and pig iron. But what about the other teachers here, what about the Perry Wilsons here? No, that stupid bastard had a file cabinet made of polished Zebrawood with real brass trimmings.

Hank crouched, took it in a bear hug, and lifted it. Heavy didn't begin to describe the weight. With a growl he levered it out of balance and jumped back to let it fall, which it did with a metallic bang that shook the entire building. He turned in a shuffling circle, panting with his hair dangling in his eyes, no end in sight to the rage that was crackling inside him, no end to the need to smash them all.

Schadenfreude . . .

Yes, *sha-dun-froy-duh*, the joy of destruction, Hank Thorwald did not need a thirty-pound *Langenscheidt's Dictionary of the German Language* to interpret words for him, Perry had made him a linguist of the highest order with his repeated doses of hocus-pocus. Hank's jerking eyes lit upon the Sanyo coffee maker. Sanyo was a maker of radios and televisions and maybe computers, but Sanyo did not know coffee from sake. Their pathetic machine leaked and it dripped on the floor.

He swiped the glass pot from its stand; it shattered in a gush of shards across the floor. With both hands he jerked the plastic base back and forth to rip it from its moorings. As it tore free small blue and yellow explosions of electricity accompanied the extraction of the wiring, instantly filling the room with the acrid smell of freshly burned copper. He let the Sanyo fly. It smacked against the blinds; a heartbeat later they dropped to the floor in a jangling heap. A jumble of foreign words ricocheted inside the heated curves of his skull too fast to understand. He whirled and mashed his hands over his ears.

A small, flickering motion caught his eye. A couple of sheets of paper on his desk had caught fire. Hank watched them, insignificant little blackenings of paper with the barest hint of flame. One house in a French village could burn to the ground without touching others off, it was all a matter of luck and where the artillery happened to fall next.

All a matter of . . .

"Oh Holy Jesus," Hank whispered. His knees buckled but he rose and staggered to the desk. As he smothered the simple flames with his hands, the door opened behind him. It was a campus security officer, one of the old guys who dressed like a cop but wasn't one, doubtless one of the old guys who waved hello or good-bye at Hank sometimes as he drove past in the Lexus. He raised an eyebrow to look at Hank, lowered them both to take in the sight of the room.

"Bad day at the office, Doc?"

A cluster of students and staff were pressing close behind him. Hank saw familiar faces, strangers' faces. Behind them two skinny arms suddenly thrust up holding a wobbling but familiar camera. *Pop,* it went, a hiccup of light.

The officer stepped farther inside and turned to ease the door shut on the gawkers. Sharp pieces of plastic screeched across the floor. "Please tell me there ain't no dead bodies in here," he said as he crunched over the broken stuff. He stopped beside Hank and dropped a hand on his shoulder. The smell of a recent cigarette drifted from his breath and Hank stooped quickly to retch into his hand, his guts stopping just short of bringing up a glop of breakfast cereal.

"Sometimes you just got to let it go, let it clean you out," the officer said, and patted him on the back. "I've seen what the drink can do to a man." His hand slid up to Hank's shoulder again and forced him around to face him. "But now they got treatment programs, they put you in the toaster for twenty-eight days and out you pop, clean and sober and raring to go." He paused, tugging slightly on Hank's shoulder with his thumb just beneath his collarbone, a thumb that seemed likely to know a secret pressure point that could drop him to his knees if necessary.

"I have a class," Hank said in a voice that was cracked and whispery. "I'll be all right."

"You'll be doing more damage than you already have," the officer said kindly. "My name's Sam Archer and you can trust me to do what's right for you. Now come along."

Hank let himself be urged out. Past the door the murmuring people spread apart to let him wend his way through with the security officer guiding him. He looked for familiar faces, someone to explain this to, but Ben Jademan was wearing a strange mask and MaryLou Hanscom cringed away from him, when he tried to move toward her. All of the faces seemed familiar, all of the faces seemed strange. He understood now why the accused hid their faces during the perp walk. Not so much to elude recognition as to be free of the wondering eyes and the merciless cameras that documented every moment of indignity and shame.

His new friend Sam Archer drove him to the security office, parked him on a metal chair while making a lot of small talk, then had another officer guard him while he moseyed to the phone and made a couple of phone calls, keeping his voice just low enough that Hank could hear the lilt of his speech though he understood none of the words.

He didn't need to. In less than ten minutes, a THPD sergeant swung the door open and stepped inside in all his blue-and-silver finery; following him in full suit and tie was Albright Clereau, the elderly dean of faculty, the man who three years before had risked hiring a young graduate with good grades but no teaching credentials, believing that Harrison W. Thorwald was a man to put his trust in. Their eyes met. Clereau's moved up slightly before glancing away, and in that instant Hank realized that his hair was sticking up like a clump of wild grass. He was about to face the hardest job interview of his life looking like a madman.

Sam Archer locked the door.

The yellow backhoe had been digging for only forty minutes when it struck something hard. Under the intense glare of four halogen light trees, Karl-Luther von Wessenheim's excavating company, *Grundwerk Deutsche Metalle*, was busily unearthing a section of street near the site of the former Reich's Chancellery. Von Wessenheim himself had retreated from a drenching midnight rain to the only dry spot available, was standing under the wildly flapping parachute canopy his workers had stretched between poles. He was wringing his hands. This area of Berlin was in bed for the night, but the backhoe was roaring like a dragon as it broke the asphalt into chunks, and the light trees seemed brighter than the sun. The street was blocked with yellow sawhorses emblazoned with the international DO NOT ENTER signs; the crew he had hired believed they were digging for a valuable church bell blasted intact from the spire of a nearby church during the war. Everything here looked and seemed quite legitimate. Also, folded inside his black windbreaker was an excavation permit that made all of this legal. But still he was afraid.

It was when the backhoe hit something with a clunk that

shook its entire frame that excitement began to replace his anxiety. Out in the rain personally directing the dig was Dr. Konrad Rudiger, a strange man clad from neck to heels in an orange rain suit with a tweed hat on his head and shiny black Oxfords on his feet. Frau Dr. Friedl von Lütringen was back at the hotel working out future dig sites. But would they be necessary? Von Wessenheim hurried out from under the canopy, flipping the hood of his jacket up to protect his head from the downpour. Success so soon?

Rudiger was bent over the crater, holding a flashlight. Von Wessenheim peered down and saw only jagged earth being rapidly liquified into mud. "Something solid," Rudiger shouted over the noise of the diesel. "I'll check it."

He made his way to the bottom, his orange raincoat whipped into crazy shapes by the wind and the hammering rain. At the bottom he squatted and stuck a hand into the mud, worked it around, and shouted something. Von Wessenheim stooped and cupped his hands around his ears.

"Solid metal," Rudiger shouted. "Not a pipe, much bigger than that. Hold on." He worked his way back up, gouging handholds in the mud, and stood again, panting. "Seems to be a large, perhaps rounded metal object."

"A coffin?" von Wessenheim asked.

"If so, a very large one." Rudiger darted from von Wessenheim's side, shoved two curious workers aside as they approached, and clambered up the backhoe to shout at the operator. His words were lost to the diesel and the wind.

"Could be the bell you're after. Right, sir?"

Von Wessenheim lurched around: one of the hired crewmen was gawking down, his yellow hard hat dripping rain onto his boots. Before von Wessenheim could reply the man spit a streak of brown tobacco juice into the pit. "Could be the lost ding-a-ling, eh?"

Von Wessenheim grabbed the man by the lapels of his raincoat, stricken with a sudden and uncharacteristic anger. "You keep your spit and your comments to yourself!" he snarled in the man's face. "What's down there might make all of us look small, especially a misbegotten *Schweinhund* like you!"

He shoved him away as hard as he could shove. The worker was forced into a quick shuffle to stay erect. Without another glance he scrambled away and found busier work in the stark shadows cast by the dump truck idling behind the backhoe.

Von Wessenheim touched his throat. The stress here was enormous, he was unraveling like a ball of yarn being teased by a cat, and in this instance the cat went by the name Frau Dietermunde and her Hitlerjugend brigade. Though these labors in the dark were secret, they would not stay so. Failure here would make him look as stupid and insolent as the crewman here with his stupid mouth full of tobacco.

Dr. Rudiger splashed his way back. "We're going to gently scrape along the surface of the object, discover its horizontal length."

Von Wessenheim looked over at the backhoe's shovel, a large mouth rimmed on the lower jaw by metal incisors as big as a human hand. "How gentle can he be with that? He might tear the object open."

"It's a risk," Rudiger said, blinking against the rain that dripped on his face from the brim of his soggy tweed hat.

"Then we can't afford it, Herr Doktor. Order the men to dig with shovels."

"Shovels can't compete with the water, Herr von Wessenheim. It would be like trying to bail out a sinking boat with its own oars."

"Damn!" Von Wessenheim looked around at the dark bulk of the city, the blinding lights, down at the crater. Raindrops danced furiously inside it, causing chunks of the wall to curl and flop lazily down into the pool at the bottom. Rain on the light trees sizzled and steamed from the heat of the halogen bulbs. He jammed his fists angrily into the pockets of his jacket. "Then do it," he shouted.

Rudiger made motions to the backhoe operator. The engine roared and spat out a burst of black smoke. The shovel jerked upward, cocked itself, and slowly nosed into the hole. Von Wessenheim saw that the operator had stood to lean out of the machine for a clearer view. Good man. Two workers hoisted a light tree and trudged closer with it, set it at the rim where the asphalt was gouged and broken. Von Wessenheim edged closer. The business end of the backhoe slowly sank into the muddy water, filled, and was brought up. The crooked yellow arm and the thick black hoses that controlled it swooped to the side. The water was dumped in the street; von Wessenheim rose higher and saw it all go surfing down a curbside sewer drain.

The next mouthful contained a lot of mud. Several of the new employees of *Grundwerk Deutsche Metalle* scurried into the crater with shovels and began dredging up the remaining goop, flinging it up onto the street. Von Wessenheim heard the sound of metal grating across metal as he backpedaled out of the way; their shovels were verifying the find. Shielding the side of his face from the light, he moved forward again and peered down. In places the shovels were scoring shiny lines across the object; these were quickly erased by dirty water. The idea that this thing might be Hitler's coffin, maybe even the roof of Hitler's burial chamber, tantalized his mind, but with effort he was able to push it aside. Few great ventures were successful on the first try. It would be ironic indeed if this thing turned out to be a large church bell. It might even make excellent press for the estate of Wessenheim: here the last surviving son of Wessenheim unearths historically important church bells as a public service.

He shook his head, covered his eyes for a moment. The best publicity in an undertaking like this was no publicity at all.

The scoop of the backhoe was easing back inside the hole. Dr. Rudiger stumped over, his hat now completely collapsed atop his head. "He's a good man, an expert," he blared, indicating the operator. "Says he can peel a potato with it, so don't worry."

"If it were a potato, I would have the utmost confidence," von Wessenheim said sourly. He searched his pockets for his pack of cigarettes, found it, and was able to extract a Reemstma with his fingernails. A lit match followed. It was instantly smacked by a raindrop and extinguished. With a growl von Wessenheim lowered his face and tried again. A puff of smoke followed.

Rudiger had turned his head. "Uh-oh."

Von Wessenheim looked. A green and white BMW *Stadts-polizei* car had skirted the blockade and was drawing to a halt just outside the range of the halogen lights, its windshield wipers thumping back and forth. The door swung open and a policeman uniformed in the standard green-and-white colors got out. "*Guten Abend*," he said, approaching. "What are we digging for tonight?"

Von Wessenheim jabbed his hand inside his windbreaker. "A church bell," he called out. His voice seemed overly loud and a little too high-pitched. He cleared his throat. "Frightful night, Officer. Isn't it?"

The officer nodded as he peeked over the rim of the hole. "A bit wet for an excavation crew. Any luck?"

"Enough mud for all," Rudiger said.

The policeman nodded. "Church bell, you say?"

"Yes." Von Wessenheim produced the document. "It is of great historical value."

He took it, turned it to the light. "*Grundwerk Deutsche Metalle*. Didn't you men help dismantle the Wall?"

"Yes," Dr. Rudiger said just as the word no was about to exit von Wessenheim's lips.

"Yes. Yes, indeed," von Wessenheim coughed up. "We helped unearth the groundwork, the metal reinforcements beneath the soil."

The policeman folded the paper together and handed it back. "So you have a bell to find. From the war? Of course from the war. How else would a church bell wind up in the ground?"

"A strong wind or a strong choirboy on the rope," Rudiger said, and all three laughed. Von Wessenheim pulled a long drag from his soggy cigarette and forced his shoulders, which were hunched up painfully, to relax. The permit obtained from the mysterious Rønna Ulgard had proved itself genuine, or at least genuine enough for this fellow. A large and heavy burden lifted from his heart; finally, a lawyer who could be trusted to do what was needed—to do *whatever* was needed—to please his boss.

"Then I'll leave you men to your work," the officer said, and snapped an exaggerated salute. "Good luck."

"*Gott im Himmel, eine Bombe!*" someone cried, and von Wessenheim spun in time to see three of his crewmen scrambling up out of the hole on all fours as if chased by killer bees. The shovel end of the backhoe jerked up hard enough to bounce the machine on its big wheels; the man in charge of peeling the potato quickly killed the engine and leapt down from the cab.

"Oh my God," the policeman breathed. "You've found a bomb."

"Bomb? A bomb?" Von Wessenheim stood puzzling, his mind temporarily on pause and unable to process this sudden information. He was here to find a bell, not a bomb. Someone had made a mistake. Someone had mistaken a bell for a bomb.

"Everyone evacuate the area," the policeman shouted, not hesitating to take charge. "You men, pick up your barricades and put them farther down the streets, direct the cars away, divert all traffic as far from here as you can."

Two of von Wessenheim's crew were, unfortunately, half a block away and still running. The policeman dove for his car and began shouting things into the radio. Dr. Rudiger, in the meantime, had wandered to the edge of the pit and was aiming his flashlight down into it. He turned: "By God, it's an unexploded five-thousand-pound bomb. A blockbuster bomb. Must have lost its stabilizer fins to some shrapnel and landed on its belly, dug itself deep into the ground like a big fat worm. This is actually quite a find."

Von Wessenheim's brain unlocked and he tossed his cigarette aside. "Go to your car, get out of here. We want no part of this."

Beneath his waterlogged hat, his face sparkling with rain, Rudiger looked as if he might laugh. "Get involved? I have waited a lifetime to get involved in one of these! The story of the Third Reich lies here at my feet, here is one bomb out of the four hundred thousand bombs dropped on Berlin in those years; I stand at the portal of a time machine." He pulled his hat from his head and wrung it out like a rag, then wrenched it back down over his skull. For the first time von Wessenheim noticed that he had large gaps between his front teeth.

"Don't worry, I'll take command," he brayed. "Go ahead and run, I won't tell anyone, I'll claim this as my own archaeological find, I hired the digging crew, you had nothing to do with this."

Von Wessenheim snapped his head around. The policeman was still shouting into his radio, the darkness had not yet been broken by the flotilla of strobing lights that would sail in from the police stations and the fire departments. Not to mention the media people, the reporters, the cameras. Not long ago he had come across a story in the *Frankfurter Allgemeine*, while having breakfast in that city, that twenty-eight thousand Berliners had been evacuated from their homes and businesses because of an old bomb that had been unearthed. After being disturbed from their airless slumber, these rusting behemoths had a tendency to shrink and explode. Now it was taking place again right at his feet, national news was in the making, and here he stood atop it.

He took a sideways step to run. One mention of his name and the old guard, the Hitler Youth who were now so old and so smug, one mention of his involvement in this disaster would turn his reputation to mud, would reduce the glory of the house of Wessenheim to the status of a joke. He had not loved his father and his mother had not loved him, but he had been born to nobility and was duty-bound to protect it.

He took one last glance at Rudiger. A strong gust of wind was flapping his orange rain suit against his bones like a rubber flag and the air was alive with sparkling water. Von Wessenheim ducked his head deeper into the hood of his windbreaker, found the cords at his throat that would cinch it tightly around his face, and tugged them so hard that his eyebrows were mashed against his forehead. In this state of incognito he hurried past the yellow backhoe his money had rented, then passed between the poles supporting the parachute canopy that huffed up and down as if alive. His rental car tonight was a black Audi he had parked nearby. As soon as the door was unlocked and he was safely inside, he looked back. His secret digging area was a geyser of light in the blackness, the wild colors of the parachute canopy billowed up and down with all the power of strobing neon lights. Secrecy in this city of eight million was impossible, Rudiger was a madman, and Frau Dr. von Lütringen was a kook with her ideas of Eva Braun running the Reich. His quest to find the Führer's bones had already cost him a small fortune and the only thing to show for it was one bomb big enough to blow an entire city block to the moon, big enough to catch the attention of the press, maybe the world.

He turned his eyes to the dashboard, turned the key, and dropped the gearshift into place, his thoughts smoldering with anger and despair. The elderly Frau Dietermunde was probably right, entire nations had spent years searching for Hitler's bones and had found nothing; it was like traipsing across foreign mountaintops looking for an inch or two of Noah's ark sticking out of the snow. What he needed was people who were effective in what they undertook, not people who had written questionable books and thought themselves experts. He needed people who accepted a challenge knowing they could succeed. People along the lines of that man Rønna Ulgard, people who wasted no time debating the issue, simply said yes I can do it, or no I cannot.

Von Wessenheim nodded in the darkness, the muscles of his face relaxing. Yes. People like that, a man like that. Rønna Ulgard, who with the snap of his fingers had made an excavation permit appear out of nothing. A handful of money, of course, but no more incentive than that. And von Wessenheim had plenty of incentive.

He drove back to the hotel, marveling at the number of fire trucks and police cars that zipped past him with their lights flashing crazily in the dark.

The phone on the kitchen wall at 1225 Quartermaine Avenue rang for about the twentieth time. Sharri Thorwald had been sitting at the counter for an hour picking up the phone when it rang, listening briefly then saying "My daddy's not home," or "Go away," or whatever happened to pop into her head, then hanging up. Her mom wanted to rip the phone cord out of the wall but there were phones all through the house, so rip them all out? Fortunately, at ten Mom had to go to work at the department store, the MidwestBest downtown where she subbed whenever a worker called in sick or quit unexpectedly. In Sharri's view it was a good thing for her to be called in today. Between the jangling phones and the drifting tide of people floating around outside it was impossible to do anything but await the next call, the next set of gawkers. Sharri had gone out earlier to look at the garage door. A beehive of people had swarmed around her with microphones and cameras as soon as she'd stepped out, and she'd fled back inside. Back when it was still dark this morning she had stood in the shadows of her doorway watching her dad as he talked to everyone, admiring him for turning all those people into a respectful classroom. When he drove away in his new car, the TV vans were gone but some of them ambled back as soon as the Lexus was out of sight, the reporters no longer chiming the doorbell, staying politely on the outer sidewalk but acting ready for something to pop out of the ground nearby so they could stick a microphone at it. Then when her mother left in the Pontiac everybody vanished. The lawn looked sad and trampled and a fair number of cigarette butts were strewn around in various poses of death. The whole weird thing with the reporters seemed to be over at last.

Which was a good break for Sharri. Her mom had warned her not to leave the house, but her mom wasn't here anymore. There was business to take care of so she was most certainly going to leave the house. Not that she was up to anything bad; a couple of days ago she had committed a sin against the Ten Commandments. Today she was going to atone for that sin by undoing it.

Sitting at the counter with a bowl of soggy cereal between her elbows and the morning sun slanting through the kitchen windows, she allowed the telephone ten more rings, counting them off aloud. When the countdown ended she snatched the receiver off the wall and clamped it to her ear. "Hello, world."

A high, madcap voice clamored in her ear. "We stand ready to join our reborn leader in the building of the Fourth Reich! We stand ready to pledge our futures to the will of the leader whom God has promised will rise from the ashes to lead us out of the darkness and into the light! We stand ready to fight and die for—"

Sharri pinched her nose shut. "Pweas deposid tweddy-five ceds before gontinuig."

"We are willing and able to—"

"Thag you for using AD ad D."

She hung up. Even these tries at humor were losing their charm. Done with it all, she pushed the bowl away. Everything here in the house wanted her to leave, the glaring sunlight was silenced here and there by unexpected shadows and the air was flat and unfriendly. She peeled herself off the stool and pressed a hand against her chest.

It was still there, of course. She had worn the swastika necklace for two days and each time it poked her at a new angle or pressed coldly against her skin she was reminded of it, and how she had gotten it. She had not talked to her girlfriend Nandy since the incident in the basement—finding that briefcase stuffed full of black costumes to wear during sexual intercourse. She reached both hands behind her neck and felt for the clasp of the necklace. She wanted to take it back, put it back into the briefcase she had stolen it from, erase the sin from God's slate. Only . . . the desire was more than impossible, the desire was stupid. Though she had not talked to Nandy since their discovery, life at her house had probably taken a turn for the worse.

Unless Nandy had kept her mouth shut. Sharri hoisted the phone and was glad to hear nothing more than the dial tone in her ear. She poked the numbers.

"Hello?"

"Nandy?"

"Sharri? Hang on, I'll go upstairs."

Sharri waited. She lifted the stolen medallion from inside her shirt and thoughtfully fingered its many edges. The moment she'd stolen this thing, that was when the glass had started breaking and the world had begun to intrude. God was not horsing around here; you do not steal a Nazi cross and hang it around your neck, you do not steal anything and hang it around your neck without angering the Lord. "Thou shalt not steal" didn't leave any room for doubt.

Nandy came back. "Your house is famous!" she squealed. "I've been seeing it on TV and trying to call but your line is so busy!"

"Yeah," Sharri said glumly. "So busy."

"And your dad is totally famous! Was he really Hitler?"

Sharri scowled. "I don't know. Mom says he wasn't, and Dad says it's all a big practical joke. Can I come over?"

"Sure. Come on."

Sharri cleared her throat, not quite done with the conversation. "What about that black stuff, the hood and the whip? What did they say?"

Nandy laughed. "All that stuff was only Halloween costumes they wore to a party once."

"Really? That's all?" She shrugged to herself. "Okay, I'm on my way."

"See you in a minute then."

She limply planted the phone into its place and drew a dispirited breath. This news was the worst of the worst. The missing necklace would be noticed and had to be put back. Sharri wasn't stupid enough to imagine sneaking it into that old briefcase in Nandy's mom's bedroom closet; just handing it back to Nandy with instructions for its return was as close to absolution from sin as she cared to get. Maybe a confession, the first one of her life, would have to be made at church in that spooky little booth with the curtains.

She jogged to the front window and stuck her head between the drapes. All seemed clear outside, no more TV vans or people milling around, just a motorcycle with a white helmet upside down on its seat, parked over by the neighbor's shrubs and halfway hidden from sight. But despite the lack of activity out front she chose to exit through the patio door and take the back route to Nandy's; she had seen how quickly the storm could gather on the street. Her backyard was not large—scandalous for the price, Dad always grumbled—and just beyond its fence lay backwoods Indiana. As she went through the gate, bugs jumped up with alarm, big green grasshoppers and brown crickets whickered through the air in panic. Ahead lay the enormous mountain of hard-packed earth the Bluewater Pointe kids called "the Dirtpile." None of them knew how it had come to be. Rumor reported that it was a failed volcano. Sharri's dad told her it was piled there by the bulldozers when the houses were being built, that it turned out the property it was piled upon belonged to someone else, and that the whole mess would be stuck in court for the next five hundred years.

She was cutting a semicircle around it when the noise of a motorcycle touched her ears. She looked up to the peak of the Dirtpile, squinting and shielding her eyes against the sun with both hands. Any second now, if she were a judge of sound and distance, a big hairy dirt bike would zoom over the tip of the Dirtpile, swoop through the air and come down hard, maybe crash in a big ball of dust. But in this case the motorcycle pretty much limped over the crest and immediately keeled over on its side, then began to slide down the slope with the driver still stuck to it. Worst jump she had ever seen; the guy in the white helmet had chickened out at the last minute, managed to kill the motor, and was paying for it now. Finally man and machine rolled in a heap down to the base of the hill, where they skidded to a stop on a bed of dirt just a dozen yards from where she stood.

"Are you all right?" she called out, drawing closer.

He lay there like a discarded scarecrow with a white helmet for a head. She leaned over and hesitantly knocked on it. "Are you alive in there?"

The scarecrow sat up. It worked its helmet off with both hands and let it fall between its knees to reveal that it was really a young man with sweaty black hair and a face that needed a shave. "Dumb stunt, anyway," he muttered sullenly. "My bike's all bent now."

"All your gas is leaking out too," Sharri told him.

"Damn." He sprang up and lifted the bike, then swept the kickstand down with a foot. The kickstand punched into the dirt as he let go and the bike, a Suzuki by name, fell over onto its other side. With a snarl he lifted it and guided it by its bent handlebars to a spot where the dirt was hard-packed. This time the dirty Suzuki remained upright. Strapped tightly to the back of the seat by two red bungee cords was a rumpled canvas bag. He unhooked one of the cords and bent to look inside the bag, shoved his hands in and moved things around. Seeming satisfied, he left it alone and ambled back toward Sharri. "I've always wanted to try jumping a hill like that," he said with a rueful smile. "Better luck next time, huh?"

She twitched her shoulders. This guy was maybe nineteen or twenty, kind of skinny but awfully handsome in his dusty T-shirt and jeans. "You'll get better," she said, and reddened, forced to drop her gaze.

"No, I think one time's enough." In the awkward silence that followed he suddenly extended a hand. "Johnny Laine," he said. "And you would be?"

"Sharri." She slipped her hand into his for a few vigorous shakes that almost rattled her teeth. "Sharri Thorwald."

"And so what do you do for a living, Miss Sharri? Besides watching complete idiots roll down mountains of dirt?"

She could only sneak glances at his face. "Nothing. I just—I just walk around back here a lot, look at the flowers."

"Then you must be a nature lover, Sharri Thorwald."

She could only shrug. Whatever was stirring inside her was running all her thoughts through a blender.

"That's what I am," he said. His voice was deep and gentle. "I'm a nature photographer. I rode out here to take pictures of the flowers. I won a prize once for a picture I took of my niece holding a rose."

"Wow," she said to his chest.

"So I drove out here to shoot some of those yellow stalks, the ones that get yellow pollen all over your pants."

She looked down. Her jeans were quite golden. "It's goldenrod, and it comes out in the washer," she said guiltily.

"Cool. Hey, you know what? I want to get a shot of you standing in the goldenrod, maybe holding some of the stalks. If I win a prize for it, we'll go celebrate, we'll go out for dinner or something. Deal?"

While he went back to his motorcycle, she jerked some goldenrod out of the ground and twisted the roots off, getting her hands dirty and her chest and arms smeared with yellow. But he had no complaints when he returned. She saw that his camera was very expensive and professional-looking as he quickly screwed a large black lens onto the front, fiddled with some knobs and stuff. Finally he circled her halfway and dropped to one knee. "Okay, Sharri Thorwald," he said. "Pose for me."

She straightened and clutched the golden stalks to her chest.

"Lower them down a little, Sharri."

She slid them down.

"Big smile. Look right at me, look into the camera, big smile."

Click-click-click-click!

"Now put the flowers down, drop them there, put your hands on your hips and look above me, get mad at the sky. Snarl at it, Sharri, you're a tough kid, you're a punk!"

Click-click-click-click!

He stood up, grinning. "Good work, kiddo. I'll call you about that prize." He turned and jogged to his motorcycle, stuffed the camera into the bag and looped the bungee cords over it. With a couple of kicks, the engine blatted to life coughing out blue smoke. Sharri's new friend Johnny Laine swung in a big jagged circle then roared up the side of the Dirtpile, the engine screaming.

She saw that he had left his helmet behind. With a burst of panic she raced over to it and hoisted it up. "Johnny!" she shouted, flapping it overhead. "*Johnny!*"

He had reached the crest. With a mighty shout—"*Wahoo!*"—he launched himself out of sight. Sharri gasped. Now he was probably crashing down the other side of the Dirtpile. She set herself in motion, bent against the slope and touching at the dirt with her left hand while she climbed. She reached the top gasping for air. Too shaky to stand anymore she sank to the warm ground and searched the opposite side of the Dirtpile for Johnny's fallen motorcycle, his broken body.

Nothing. This side was as blank as the other. Grateful but disappointed, she let her head fall. Johnny was far better on two wheels than he thought. He had launched his bike over the crest as fast as any pro, had held on tight and hadn't wiped out. Good for him.

She raised her head. Something was stuck to the bottom of her chin. She lifted a hand and plucked it away, felt it. The necklace, the swastika necklace. It had been hanging out of her shirt. That meant Johnny Laine had seen it, Johnny Laine had photographed it hanging in plain sight from her neck.

Now put the flowers down. Drop them there . . .

A nature photographer with no need for nature. He was one of Them, he had spied on her, had even crashed all the way down the Dirtpile just to put her off guard, just to get a few pictures of the daughter of the man who used to be Hitler.

She got to her feet. Her throat was hot and tight, almost too tight to breathe through. A sob burst out as she hooked her fingers around the cheap little swastika, a necklace so pathetic that the chain popped apart with only a tug.

She turned, drew back, and threw it at the sun.

✠

THE TRAGÖDIE

20

Hank Thorwald raised his head from the countertop. Somebody was pounding on something, *thud-thud-thud*. In the midst of his stupor, the sound had rattled him enough to drag him back to awareness. He looked around blearily, smacking his lips. His mouth was dry, so dry his tongue was stuck to the roof of it. By his left elbow was a bottle of Absolut vodka, empty. On the counter in front of him was a glass with about an inch of water and a chewed-up slice of lime in it. With a groan he shoved them away. His eyes burned in their sockets and his face felt bent from having slept on his cheek. The clock on the microwave was holding steady at 2:14 A.M. but it meant little, he had been drinking since about 1:30 in the afternoon, the hours were all blurry. The house was dark but for the green glow of the appliance clocks and smelled heavily of old cigarette smoke. Hank swiveled his head in painful slow motion. At his right elbow was a glass ashtray jammed full of butts. He picked one up and strained to read the lettering just above the filter, wobbling back and forth on the stool. "Marlboro," it said in crumpled letters. Rebecca did not like Marlboros, she smoked Camel Lights. His own former brand had been Marlboro. He slapped at his breast pocket and jerked his eyebrows up: after all these years he was smoking again, had a pack in his pocket like in the olden days. The Wabash Valley Inn hypnotism of Roger Bevins-Clarke had finally worn off, had worn off a little too much. Time to sue the bastard.

He worked himself off the stool and staggered to the sink, dug a glass off its shelf and filled it with water. Blood pounded thickly in his head. His stomach was trying to achieve a slow boil and his lungs seemed full of ashes. The water was lukewarm but he gulped it down with a groan of gratitude, wolfed down three more before turning the water off. He scraped an arm across his mouth and aimed himself in the direction of the living room. As far as he knew, Rebecca was upstairs in bed and Sharri was downstairs in bed. Nothing was out of order. The noise he had heard could well have been his drunken brain cells screaming as they died.

The dean of faculty, Albright Clereau, had suspended him pending the next meeting of the board of deacons in September. Per university bylaws he could challenge this decision at a full faculty hearing in two weeks, if he requested that one be assembled. In either case he was banned from campus until the meeting and prohibited from any contact with the students. Faculty members would be advised to refrain from speaking with him about the matter until said hearing, said meeting. Said in plain English, he didn't have tenure, and he was fired.

Which was why he steered the Lexus not immediately homeward after that. Instead, he steered the Lexus into the parking lot of a lounge called the Stone Pelican on the eastern side of town where all the railroad shuntlines crossed, a place he used to visit while a student after a tough day of midterms or final exams. None of the other students back then seemed to have found it, which was ideal. Hank had been a family man with no time for the game of the sexes or the drunken brawls of rutting males.

He had sat quietly at the corner of the bar pretending to watch a basketball game on the little television on the wall there, slowly feeding himself Planter's peanuts out of a bag. How many beers he drank he did not know, but at some point he had begun purchasing shots of peppermint schnapps to grease his gullet. When he left the Stone Pelican, darkness had settled in for the night and he was blotto.

But not too blotto to dive into the Absolut as soon as his soles touched the kitchen linoleum. In bits and pieces he remembered talking to Rebecca, maybe even crying as he did, and also retained a distorted mental scene of some shouting between them while Sharri stood by watching, as gray and silent as a gravestone. And oh God, his drunken fingers had dialed his parents in Fort Wayne and he had blubbered his story out for them. Of their reaction he had no recollection at all. Knowing Dad, whose on-and-off union pipefitter's job had taught him patience over the years, he had probably said to just hang tight until the dust cleared. Mom still thought he was young enough to change careers if this one didn't pan out; she was an advocate of change.

Thud-thud-thud.

That was the sound, he remembered it now: it was the sound created when someone bapped their fist against the glass patio door. Hank turned and shambled out of the dining room, back into the kitchen. He slapped at the light switch and squinted through the sudden glare. Somebody was out there, no big surprise. Another son of a bitch looking for an interview? Hank narrowed his eyes. Somebody was due for a nasty surprise. He lurched to the stove, thudded against it with his hip, reached beside it to the wooden block of kitchen knives. He jerked one out of its slot and regarded the long blade. This knife was like the one Norman Bates had used in *Psycho,* this sucker could ruin somebody's day in a hurry. He thought of answering the door with this sucker clenched in his teeth like a pirate, then let the crazy idea die and slipped the knife back into its slot and went to the door. He slid it open.

It was his neighbor from the house to the left, the guy with all the teenage kids and jet skis and motorcycles cluttering his driveway. He looked like an average Joe, always had looked that way. A chiropractor by trade, so the story went, and right now his name was as unknown to Hank as the number of hairs on his aching head. "Well, hi," he said anyway, absurdly flattered by the visit. "Nice night."

The man had a look of dire seriousness on his chiropractical face. "My daughter's in college, she works part-time at a Circle K, wants to be independent, makes her own money and stuff. She heard about you, brought this by." He extended a fist. Protruding from both sides was a tube of newspaper rolled as tight as a stick. "Thought I'd let you get advance warning before this hits the grocery stores in the morning."

Hank took it, sobered by his expression. "Bad news for me, I guess."

"It's all bullshit, neighbor. It's like a malpractice suit with no witnesses, nothing but accusations and no defense except to deny it. I went through it once and I wish you well."

He turned and walked away. He was wearing yellow slacks, Hank saw before he moved out of the light. He had gotten up in the middle of the night to bring this gift and had pulled on yellow pants. Maybe it was the popular gear of chiropractors, maybe he just had lousy taste. "Thank you," Hank called out, heard no reply, and slid the door shut. He went to the dining room table, a big solid oak creation noted mostly for the Thanksgiving turkeys and Christmas hams that had been dismembered on it, and rolled the newspaper out, holding it flat with his palms.

It was a cheapo tabloid familiar to him from the racks at grocery checkouts, the *Weekly International News,* in black and white. There were two huge pictures beneath a banner headline. One of the black-and-white shots showed Hank Thorwald with a wild look on his face, a madman brandishing a Nazi knife with the swastika visible between his fingers. The other showed Sharri Thorwald grinning shyly into a camera with a tiny chain around her neck that held a swastika at her chest.

A surge of raw fear stole his breath. He fumbled a chair away from the table and dropped onto it.

The headline was tall and black:

REBORN HITLER LIVES IN INDIANA
Avowed "Son of Hitler" Recruits Children
for Master Race

With a jerk he flipped the entire paper over, hiding the page by instinct as if it were a dirty picture. Anger tried to take possession of his mind but he was too tired, too utterly spent from that mindless rage at his office to invest any emotion in it. The picture of Sharri was an obvious retouch job; probably some demented computer whiz who worked for this prestigious newspaper had added the necklace pixel by pixel.

The picture of himself with the knife was no mystery either. The only mystery was how a tabloid had gotten a picture of Sharri to doctor, and how the young photographer at ISU had sold the picture of Hank holding the Nazi dagger in such a short time. Could things like that be faxed? Hell, what *couldn't* be faxed?

He glanced guiltily at the stairway. No Rebecca. He folded the paper in half, in half again, folded it over and over until it could not take another fold, was the size maybe of a rich man's wallet, then went to the kitchen, glanced around, and on instinct jammed it into the garbage disposal. It seemed fitting. Garbage into garbage.

Dreck zum Dreck . . .

Hank's arms snapped up and he clutched his head with both hands while a moan of agony crept up his throat.

"Dad?"

He released his hair and quickly lowered his hands. Sharri had appeared out of nowhere, was standing just inside the kitchen wearing a long T-shirt with Scooby-Doo's brainless face printed on the front. With a jolt he saw that her eyes were swollen and red from crying. "Ah, jeez, Sharri," he groaned, and went to her. She looped her arms around his waist and hugged him fiercely. All along he had thought she was immune to this; tonight's drunken spectacle, featuring Dad Thorwald in a premiere gala performance, had obviously dragged her straight into it. "Whatever I said, I didn't mean. Things have just been tough lately and I let it get to me."

She drew back. "It's not that. Yesterday I—"

The front door gave a small thump. Hank turned his head in time to see that it had been pushed open about four inches, allowing in a slash of black night. Through that gap, launched by the fleeting image of a human hand, something was tossed into the foyer. A gray string of smoke trailed it as it arced through the air. When it bounced down on the living room carpet, a shower of sparks burst up. He clutched Sharri tighter and swiveled to shield her.

The door banged shut. Hank surged into action, moving on an instinct he didn't know existed. He snatched Sharri up and clamped her to his chest, already pistoning his legs to launch them both toward the short hallway that went to her room. Two more leaps put them in front of her door. It stood open. Hank dived toward the location of her bed in the darkness, wresting her around in midair so that he could land on his back to cushion her. On impact the bed frame cracked with all the noise of a tree struck by lightning and the entire bed crunched to the floor.

He wrapped her in his arms and shielded her with his body. With his eyes clenched shut, he waited for the bomb to explode, his mind roiling with possibilities: the wall would crash down, killing them, the entire upper floor would collapse, killing them and Rebecca too.

That was when the machine gun started firing. Hank tightened instinctively, then groaned in recognition and scrambled out of the ruined bed. He had been a patriotic American long enough to recognize a string of firecrackers left over from last year's Fourth of July. He emerged from the hallway just as Rebecca was stumbling down the stairs. The firecrackers on the carpet were doing the usual jumping jacks as the central fuse worked its way down the string, each explosion spraying out yellow sparks and gouts of blue smoke filled with shredded paper. The pale rose carpet they had spent two weeks shopping for was trying to catch fire in spots.

He looked back up at Rebecca. She had leaned against the wall, slumping listlessly on one shoulder. Her hair was a disaster and her face had lines and shadows he had never seen before. In her eyes he saw signs of the damage he had done tonight.

Du betrunkener Idiot . . .

At last his anger brimmed over. The firecrackers quit and in that expanse of silence he charged to the door, ready to track down the son of a bitch who had done this, chase him down in the dark and kick so much of the living shit out of him that he wouldn't have to buy Ex-Lax for the rest of his life. Hank wrenched the door open and jumped out onto the little porch with his teeth set together hard enough to make his gums bleed. Instantly he was blinded by a huge circular beam of light and heard, just at the edge of hearing where things tend to fade off to a murmur, a man say, "I *told* you that'd get his ass out of the house."

A camera flashed, as visible as a pop of blue light in the darkness surrounding the circle of light. Hank shielded his face with his arms, desperate to see. He ran to the left for a better look and only managed to crash into the knee-high hedges there. Flailing for balance he pitched face first into the stretch of geraniums Rebecca had planted in the spring. Despite the recent heat the ground was still soggy from all the rain; Hank executed a push-up and squirmed his feet free of the hedge. Smeared with dirt and polka dots of flower petals, he worked himself upright with a howl of rage, still blinded by the light that was now bristling with the flashes of popping cameras. He heard laughter. Someone hooted. Through slitted eyes he surveyed the street. The hulking images of cars, no vans. This wasn't the local press, he realized. This was a far meaner crowd.

"Get the fuck away from my house!" he screamed at them.

More lights: neighbors were clicking on their bedside lamps.

"Show us a seeg hile," someone called to him. "Sprecken-zee some Dutch."

Mud squelched between his fingers as he clenched his hands into fists. He plunged blindly into the dark, snarling out curses, aching to tackle one of these ghostly bastards, to leave muddy knuckle prints and stripes of blood across a face or two. He was aware of people scurrying out of the way and he snatched out at them wildly, his shoes carving loops in the grass. The ground under his feet was suddenly a cement sidewalk that snatched the remains of his balance. He pitched forward with a cry that was quickly edited by the fender of a black Buick Regal parked along the curb.

His only thought as everything else in his mind was smashed away was that if Rebecca came out to drag him inside, her messy hair would wind up in the newspaper photos.

MaryLou Hanscom owned a white Honda Civic she had purchased one year ago, brand new. On this hot Tuesday night, she was driving that Honda through downtown Terre Haute carrying a load of guilt that she could not bear anymore. Last year Professor Thorwald had co-signed for the car after the bank laughed in her face. Prior to that MaryLou had exhausted her undergraduate student grant and had not been able to work toward her master's until Dr. Thorwald hired her as his graduate assistant. There had been trouble with her parents and Professor Thorwald had talked to them on her behalf. There had been a boyfriend he warned her away from, and he had been right, the man was a complete jerk and was on parole. There had been nights she couldn't deal with homework and he had come over to her cubbyhole apartment to help.

And after all this, she had turned on him. Abandoned him. She was crying as she drove. Word of his suspension had rocked the university despite the summertime lull. The entire faculty and a handful of his students and former students were mad, they wanted to know more. As MaryLou sought to explain what had happened, she realized the absurdity of it all and that she had committed treason, had fed him to the wolves.

She placed a call to his house. After a lot of busy signals, little Sharri had answered. She had sounded toneless and dead. She said Dad's in bed. She said his face was all smashed in. She put Rebecca on the phone and Rebecca was a wreck. They beat him up, she'd said. He went outside to talk to them and they beat him up.

It was then that MaryLou started crying, and she still hadn't stopped. The evening paper had dedicated an entire lower front-page corner to the story. A small photo inset showed Professor Thorwald's street and driveway overpopulated with cars and people. The tone of the article was light: look at this craziness in Terre Haute's own backyard. No mention, though, of any beating. Just fun and games—Terre Haute is getting some national attention so let's all hitch up our britches and smile real big.

As she came within a dozen blocks of the Bluewater Pointe subdivision, she smeared her tears away with the heels of her hands and talked sternly to herself. Professor Thorwald needed a friend, not a blubbering pile of regret. She needed absolution, but the most she could expect was cordiality, or less. When the security officer had led him out of his office, Professor Thorwald had searched her face but she had turned away, almost literally turned her back on him. It would be nice to apply the allegory of Peter denying Christ, but Peter had gone on to become a saint while MaryLou Hanscom would remain a garden-variety fink until the day she died.

Three blocks from his house she encountered traffic. Quartermaine Avenue, "Q-main," as Professor Thorwald called it, had become Sunset Strip. Cars with out-of-state license plates were in front of her, behind her, the dark night was awash with gleaming headlights and brilliantly red taillights. MaryLou flicked her air-conditioning off and cranked the window down, poked her head out. Someone in the area had mowed grass during the day and the smell of it was sweet and nostalgic in the warm summer air. As her car inched along, an old VW bus already parked at the curb disgorged a band of what she could only describe as renegade hippies, lots of hair and scraggly beards and cans of beer in hand. They unloaded picket signs, squares of poster board mounted on tall wooden slats. MaryLou caught a clear glimpse of one as it was hoisted up, and gasped.

DEAD HITLER DIE AGAIN!

News groupies, she thought. A bunch of kooks hoping to show up on the news. They probably roamed the country looking for the chance. She wanted to shout something, opened her mouth in outrage but knew she couldn't, wouldn't.

And so she minded her own business. She saw a man wearing a camouflage uniform standing at attention on the sidewalk, watched with widening eyes as he lifted an arm in a *sieg heil* salute, then whisked a cell phone up to his ear. As traffic crept along and she realized there would be no parking spots, she saw that Professor Thorwald's house, his entire property, was surrounded by a dense moat of human beings. A group of Japanese tourists burdened heavily with cameras were photographing each other with the house in the background. On the sidewalk a young woman was speaking into a microphone, bathed with light and filmed by a guy with a large video camera on his shoulder. The call letters on it identified the crew as belonging to WXRV. Wow, she thought, all the way from Indianapolis. Then as the light pivoted she saw with a jolt the immense swastika gleaming like fresh blood on the garage door. A kernel of anger sprang to life inside her followed by a fresh burst of guilt. Instead of abandoning him to the wolves, she should have been here scraping that paint away for him.

The house itself was dark and deserted-looking. Professor Thorwald's prized Lexus was in the driveway. Its tires were flat. Rebecca's little blue Pontiac had a single small swastika gouged out of the paint on the lip of the trunk and the rear window had a starburst pattern of cracks centered on a hole that might have been made by a rock, or even a bullet. MaryLou gripped the steering wheel harder, stunned. How in the world could so much humanity descend so quickly? She snailed along in her white Honda all filled with righteous rage, picturing the things she should do to drive this circus away and hating herself, on top of all the other reasons, for not having the courage to do even the slightest thing but drive past the house and feel bad.

Eventually the spacing between the cars got longer, things speeded up. She pulled to the curb at the first available spot and jogged the four blocks back to Q-main, slowing toward the end to shoulder her way through all the people. The night was filled with the hum and squawk of conversation, there were arguments going on, shouting. Big drops of water swooped out of the sky and she ducked: one of Professor Thorwald's neighbors was using a water hose to keep people off his lawn, his face strangely intent under the porch light. MaryLou's feet faltered as she crossed Quartermaine. Could she afford to be identified as sympathetic to the Thorwalds?

Any sort of notoriety could jinx her plans of teaching at a major university. If she went inside she would be metamorphosed from the status of gawker to the status of gawkee, the cameras might flash, the reporter over there twirling her little microphone like a tassel on a pastie might jump at her for an interview.

MaryLou stopped, even took a backward step. From this distance she could now see that the house had windows whose glass had been reduced to long glittering spears sticking out from the frames. But hadn't Professor Thorwald already taken care of that? Had it happened again? The drapes had grown long vertical slits that made them hang lopsided. As she stared a bottle rocket whistled over the roof tracing a shimmering line of orange sparks. It exploded directly over the house—*crack!*—and was gone. Far behind her people hooted and clapped. Someone hammered out a rapid but disjointed beat on a drum, a tom-tom or the like, while a tambourine jangled; it seemed as if the renegade hippies had their sound system all set up. This seemed to be a world-class spectacle populated by both the serious and the crazy, people were here to either see a show or make one. While she stood locked in thought and hesitation, motion to the left snapped her eyes around: a dark figure was sprinting away from the driveway. It lunged under the police tape and shoved people away as it stood up. Apparently, the dark figure had gotten into Professor Thorwald's car and turned the dome light on. She frowned, squinting a little. It wasn't the dome light, no. It was flickering, it was . . .

Flame. His car was on fire inside. Her jaw slid open and a small sound came up through her throat. Her mind jumped to the news photos of Northern Ireland, of the Middle East. Streets in flames, cars burned into twisted figures like the blackened bones of a dinosaur. But not here, dear God, not here.

The WXRV news team leapt into action. Their lights kicked back on and swung in dazzling arcs while the crew repositioned everything toward the Lexus. The flames leaped up, becoming shadowed by the smoke trapped inside. With a sort of communal gasp, the front line of the crowd dissolved momentarily, then solidified and surged closer. MaryLou was pushed forward to the point that her waist pressed against the yellow tape, bulging it as she teetered at the edge of balance and forcing one of the thin wooden police stakes out of the ground. She gave a huge backward shove with her fanny and was able to recover.

The flames inside Professor Thorwald's Lexus grew huge and began to gout crazily up and down. Then the upper half of the Lexus ripped apart with a blast of light and sound she would never forget, a tremendous explosion of flame and a deafening *FOOMP!* that instantly clogged her ears with a high-pitched whine that would take hours to get rid of. A roiling black cloud of smoke blossomed skyward, erasing the stars. Howls and screams followed the explosion while a large chunk of the driveway audience fell back. MaryLou realized that the gas tank would explode next, and if the tank was full or even a quarter full, even if it had nothing left in it but a gallon or two, it would go off like a firebomb, would *be* a firebomb.

She pivoted to run. Her eyes grazed the Thorwalds' doorway as she whirled and there stood Rebecca with her hands clapped to her cheeks, the burning Lexus lighting her face a sickly orange. In that momentary shred of time, MaryLou knew that she did not want to be associated with her or Professor Thorwald or anyone else here, that the thing to do in this situation was to run and never come back.

A lot of people were turning, the scent of panic seemed to sprout in the air. The gas tank ignited with a terrific explosion that knocked MaryLou to her knees. The night was interrupted by day: in that flash of light, her eyes were imprinted with a burnt-orange photograph of people frozen in time, in terror. She heard them scream in a mélange of male and female voices, sensed the outer perimeters of the crowd falling back. She got to her feet and became dazedly aware of a sharp pain stabbing the top of her head. When she reached up and probed her scalp for the source of it her fingers came away warm and bloody. Some flying thing had skipped through her hair, grazed her skull. Shrapnel from the car, then. She hazarded a look at the Lexus. Despite being blasted apart the remains were burning ferociously, tires and all. The row of little windows in Professor Thorwald's garage door were now glittering blank slots and the door itself had buckled inward to distort the shape of the swastika. Burning chunks of upholstery littered the lawn and sparkled dirtily on the pebbles of glass that had been belched onto the grass by the first explosion.

A frightening new set of screams rocked the night. Mary-Lou's eyes widened: a human shape was running onto the lawn from her left, completely on fire and writhing inside a leaping yellow pyre of flame. As she watched with both fists pressed to her mouth, the figure dropped to the ground and rolled but it was soaked with gasoline and only created a burning swath in the grass. The acrid stench of burning hair—and an unfamiliar, sweeter odor—wafted hotly past her face. Just as she whirled around to run from this horror she saw a tall and thin man named Professor Hank Thorwald gallop out of his house carrying a large white blanket that flapped as he moved through the crazy firelight. He spread it apart and lunged at the burning figure who was still struggling on the incandescent ground.

She turned and fled, stepping all over people, whimpering as she clawed her way through the obstacles that separated her from her Honda. Police or fire truck sirens spoke up from far away, 911 had been dialed, she was relieved of any further duty on this sinking ship. Outside her car she rifled the circumference of her key ring without finding anything useful. A sob burst out as she pawed through them another time and she was crying again, the burning figure was burned into her brain and never again in her life would she see fire without seeing that figure and crying for it.

The Honda's key showed up between her fingers. She unlocked the door and fell inside. As soon as it clunked shut she covered her face with her hands and screamed into her palms until a sort of internal balance was reached and she no longer had to. Normalcy came back quickly in her familiar world of "My Honda," she knew every button and switch by heart, there were never any surprises here. She hugged the steering wheel and rested her cheekbone against it as the tears on her face slowly dried. Cars drifted past throwing spears of white light, arrows of red light. Then the sirens came close enough to rattle the windows and she jabbed the key into the ignition in a sort of low-grade panic, anxious to be away from here, away from here forever.

The Honda started on command. MaryLou aimed its snout into the bumbling traffic, laid on the horn until someone gave room, and drove away.

21

Karl Luther von Wessenheim sat alone in his suite at the Berlinische Residenz staring at a television that was not turned on. In his hands was a softcover copy of *Mein Kampf*, the book authored by Adolf Hitler in the 1920s while he was in prison for his famous *Putsch*, the failed attempt to seize power from the Weimar government that had ruled since the end of World War One. Von Wessenheim had spent the last eleven hours reading it from cover to cover and was now in a stupor from so much information crammed into his brain so fast. It had been an ordeal; despite modern Germany's successful democracy *Mein Kampf* was still banned, so the English version had been retranslated, in the 1960s, back into German by a neo-Nazi publisher in Nebraska, and was at times indecipherable. But von Wessenheim had done it, for eleven hours had delved deep into the mind of Hitler hoping that the insight gained would lay bare the inner man, reveal his deepest secrets.

It hadn't worked. When Hitler wrote the book, he was barely into his thirties and few men that age wonder aloud where they will be buried. In fact, the book had been startling in its lack of cohesion. The man was not a great writer, *Mein Kampf* was an exercise in confusion. Much like, von Wessenheim glumly realized, this attempt to find his bones.

He stared tiredly at the blank eye of the television. It was early afternoon outside and the sun was shining down on a Germany that no longer had an enemy in the world. He was a very rich and titled man who at this moment could be snorkeling the tidal pools of Tahiti or gambling away money by the bushelful at Monte Carlo, yet he was here in Berlin and would not leave. He had no love for Germany but he belonged to her by birth, his prehistoric ancestors had trod the ground here and were part of the soil. Maybe, a sly little part of his thoughts suggested, if he could hand the world the bones of Hitler the curse of being German would be lifted, and then he could love her.

He slapped the covers of the book together and sent *Mein Kampf* spinning across the floor. Another waste of time and money. This whole undertaking felt mismanaged, he had made poor choices and followed them with worse ones. The experts on the cutting edge of new Hitler research had turned out to be published buffoons. The media here in Berlin were still buzzing about the blockbuster bomb *Grundwerk Deutsche Metalle* had unearthed so dreadfully unexploded. Thousands of people had been evacuated while it was defused, even the international press had found it newsworthy enough to report throughout Europe, and most likely America and Australia. Though his phony excavating company was not an item of interest, he could no longer use the name, therefore that little transaction with the attorney Rønna Ulgard had been a monumental waste of money. Unless, von Wessenheim knew, he decided to risk another excavation. Hire new experts, spend more money, dig somewhere else, probably unearth Godzilla himself and *really* make the news.

He let himself slump back onto the soft cushions of the couch, feeling weary and old. In former times of trouble, he would call a prostitute service and spend an evening being pampered and amused, but it was too early and that did not interest him now. Since starting his collection of Hitler memorabilia, it had come to occupy him more and more, especially since he had learned that the secretive Hitlerjugend already owned the biggest prizes and would forever outbid him. Even a hat, a silly hat worn one time by their beloved Führer, was dangled beyond his reach. He hoped desperately that Frau Dietermunde and her associates would not connect the discovery of the unexploded bomb with him—but how could they? *Grundwerk Deutsche Metalle* was only one excavating company among hundreds in Berlin.

Aching with these thoughts he let his eyelids fall shut. Through closed windows the rush of the city outside the hotel came to him muffled, became a monotone that was soon pleasant. His thoughts were slowly peopled by figures who spoke, by images that came and drifted away. His head sagged and he drowsed into a gently floating kind of sleep, aware of the outside and aware of the inside but aloof from it all.

Until the phone rang. At the second ring he forced his eyelids up and found that the room had become dark. So few seconds of sleep, so many hours gone by. The phone rang again and he rocked to his feet, repossessing himself from the dream thread by thread. By stumbling toward the sound of the next ring he was able to locate the telephone, and grabbed the receiver from its cradle. "*Ja?*"

"Karl-Luther," a woman crooned. "How are things?"

Von Wessenheim pressed a hand across his forehead and squeezed his temples. "Good evening, Frau Dietermunde. How kind of you to find me."

"I know your taste in hotels, Karl-Luther. Only the finest will suit you. In fact, the *Residenz* is my preference as well. So very old world, yet so very modern."

Von Wessenheim turned, irritated, and looked through the windows. It was raining. It fit his melancholic mood quite well; his only wish now was to be left alone. "Is there something I can help you with?" he asked her. "Or did you call just to chat?"

"I never call anyone without a reason," she said cheerfully. "I wanted to make sure you were all right."

"All right?"

"Yes. Uninjured."

"Uninjured?"

"I have heard it was a very close call, knocking about on an old bomb that could have exploded at any second. I— *we*—are quite concerned, and hoping that you might give up your sad endeavor. The next bomb could kill you. Innocent people could be injured. Are you willing to take that risk?"

Von Wessenheim darkened, tired of her condescension. "You are afraid of me," he said. "Afraid that I will find what you and your Hitlerjugend cannot."

She tittered, a flowery laugh. "You cannot find a legend, dear Karl-Luther, and you cannot undo a myth. No one will ever find the bones of Jesus, and no one will ever find the bones of our Führer. Think about that."

"I have thought about it," von Wessenheim said coldly. "And my thoughts tell me that you are all insane."

She was silent for a moment. "Then let me leave you with this. The next bomb you uncover might not be as tame as your first."

Von Wessenheim pulled the receiver away from his ear, intending to hang up, then reconsidered and thrust it back to his ear. "This is too preposterous to endure. The chances of me finding another bomb are fantastically remote."

"But what were the chances of finding a bomb on your very first try?"

"Are you taking credit for that, Frau Dietermunde? That somehow you and your group arranged it?"

"Of course not, Karl-Luther. But as patrons of the arts we sometimes subsidize the research of historians interested in the National Socialist era. They are often grateful for the support, even years afterward."

Von Wessenheim's body froze, seizing him halfway down into a sitting position over the sofa. Good God, Rudiger had selected the site of the first dig. Rudiger had been ecstatic upon finding the bomb. But even if he was working for Frau Dietermunde and the Hitlerjugend, how could he or they have known exactly where to dig to find an antique bomb? "You must be so very afraid of me," he said, and lowered himself comfortably upon the sofa. "Are you afraid that his bones might prove to be human, Frau Dietermunde? Are *all* of you afraid of that?"

"End your search," she said.

"If my task here is as impossible as you say, why are you

so worried about it? I'll simply keep digging up bombs until one explodes and kills me."

"Blowing yourself to bits is your own business. Creating international interest in the archaeology of Berlin is not."

"Oh yes, now I see." He shifted to the side and retrieved his pack of Reemstma cigarettes from the arm of the sofa, shook one out and, smiling slightly, stuck it between his lips. "I will never find your Führer's bones, but if I dig up a bomb or two the rest of the world will take interest, and with their sonar and their satellites *they* will help find all the bombs, and unwittingly the Führer's bones as well."

She said nothing. Von Wessenheim lit his cigarette and inhaled deeply from it. "End of conversation, Frau Dietermunde?"

"Yes, Karl-Luther. The conversation is over, but the issue is not. Good night."

"A fond good night to you."

He hung up, smiling very widely now. First Frau Dietermunde and her cronies had laughed at him, and now they were afraid of him. There was great satisfaction in that. If again he asked for the top hat once worn by Hitler, she would probably give it to him for free, even have it dry cleaned at her own expense. Anything just to keep him from finding Hitler's bones. There was only one problem troubling him now: how in the hell to find them. Even his stately wealth paled before the cost of using the newest in high-tech devices, machines that could see below the surface of the earth, satellites that could spew exotic beams or super-cameras that could extract images of objects no bigger than a grain of sand. His best route this time might be his original idea, hiring someone to track down the survivors of Hitler's bunker, identifying those people and offering them huge sums of money for the truth. The simple truth.

Which would mean he had to hire a detective. A good one, a man who could deliver on his promises. Again his thoughts turned to Franz Bohr; whom might he recommend? Von Wessenheim reached to the coffee table and, frowning now, poked his cigarette into the ashtray, stubbed out its burning ember. There was a drawback to this: Franz Bohr was not his lawyer anymore. It was possible that Rønna Ulgard was his lawyer. Unfortunately, he had spoken barely a dozen words to Ulgard so far, and had received about as many in reply. Had the excavation permit been their first business matter of many more to come, or a one-time deal?

He turned on one of the lamps and stood, poking another Reemstma between his lips without being fully aware of it, then crossed the room to the open drapes and, looked out across the city, feeling very alone. He was facing tremendous odds, but if ever his life had meaning, it had meaning now. The Wessenheim bloodline ended with him; he could only immortalize that name by carving it into the pages of history books. Karl-Luther von Wessenheim, the man who solved the biggest mystery of all time.

Resolution rose in him. Rønna Ulgard's number was in the telephone book. The hour was late and he was surely at his home, protected by an unlisted number, but if he did not at least *try* to contact the man this very evening, von Wessenheim knew he would be up all night fretting about it.

The phone book was in a drawer of the nightstand beside the bed. Von Wessenheim hefted its bulk and carried it back to the sofa, turning on another lamp and, as he sat, touching at his pockets for his reading glasses. With them nestled on his nose, he flipped the pages of the huge book. A hesitant thought crept into his mental view: it had cost a fortune to get an excavation permit from the Berlin authorities. How much would Rønna Ulgard charge for recommending a private detective? Worse than that, how much might the private detective charge?

"*Macht nichts,*" he murmured aloud. It didn't matter, no longer would he let the expenses trouble him. In a few decades he would be buried forever along with the royal house of Wessenheim, and a pauper's grave was just as comfortable as the grave of a rich man. He dialed the phone and was not surprised to hear it ring and ring on the other end of the connection. Still it felt good to hear it, it meant he was taking action, his momentum was rebuilding.

After eight rings he hung up. As he pocketed his glasses, the quaint Hummel girl-and-boy clock on the wall above the television indicated ten-fifteen. On the floor below the television lay the bootleg version of *Mein Kampf* he had tossed there. His mind had cleared from its overdose and he considered leafing through it with a pencil to darken the lines that even hinted at Hitler's preferences or taste. He had survived the First World War as a young corporal, had been decorated for heroism. From that experience he could have developed a hatred of trenches and a fear of being buried, which would make it likely he would have wished to be cremated. Then again, his love of military life and his anger that the war was not fought to the last man could indicate that he had *enjoyed* life in the trenches, and would choose burial.

Von Wessenheim shook his head slowly back and forth. Psychiatry was best left to the psychiatrists. *Mein Kampf* was as mysterious as the man who had written it so many years ago. He mashed his cigarette into the ashtray and stretched his arms upward as he yawned.

The phone clanged its double *ring-ring* loudly in the silence. Von Wessenheim lurched halfway to his feet, startled. Frau Dietermunde again, ready this time to beg.

"Yes?"

"I am Rønna Ulgard. You called."

"I did. Yes, I did."

"What do you want from me this time?"

Von Wessenheim touched his throat. "To thank you, Herr Ulgard, for your excellent service."

"You are welcome, Herr von Wessenheim."

Silence appeared, inflated for long seconds as von Wessenheim tried to swallow while having forgotten how.

"Anything else?"

"Yes. I need a referral, if you don't mind. I need the name and number of a reputable private detective."

"There is no such thing," Rønna Ulgard said.

"Oh." Von Wessenheim's brain went blank. "I guess that was all, then, I was just wondering about it."

"What service do you need?"

"Service? Ah, let me see. Service. Service. Oh yes, I need to find several people."

"In which country?"

"Well, I suppose Germany. They are German people."

"Give me their names."

Von Wessenheim fumbled about himself for a fresh cigarette. "I don't really have any names to give you, Herr Ulgard. Sorry I bothered you for something so trivial."

"It is not a problem. I can always make time for my clients."

Von Wessenheim sat up higher. "Then I am your client, and we have a partnership. Is this so?"

Ulgard's voice was professional and busy. "From the moment money exchanged hands, by German custom, I became your representative in all legal matters until you formally terminate our relationship."

"That is good," von Wessenheim said. "Good that I have you on my side. The house of Wessenheim gladly welcomes you aboard, I am pleased to say."

He expected a *danke schön*, some trivial talk, but got none of it. "Who are these people you wish to find?"

Von Wessenheim hesitated. "I hope you won't think me insane, but the people I need are the persons who were in Adolf Hitler's underground bunker on the day he committed suicide." He stopped, awaiting a reaction that could easily be skepticism, even laughter after so many years and so many history books that had beaten the subject to death. When none came he continued: "Of course they would be quite old now, some of them already dead. You see, I believe that certain facts have been withheld by these witnesses, and I would like to interview them. Converse with them, I mean, more as a fellow German than an Allied interrogator."

"Is there any chance that your phone is tapped?" Ulgard asked.

Von Wessenheim sat up straight. "The thought has occurred to me."

"I will call you back on a secure line."

Gone. Dead air. He sat mutely staring at the unlit cigarette between his fingers, then hurriedly clapped the receiver down. This Rønna Ulgard with the line through the *o*, this man was prepared for things Franz Bohr would never have dreamed of, he instinctively knew that secrecy was necessary when dealing with the National Socialist past.

He was applying flame to his cigarette when the phone clanged. He leapt to his feet and brought the receiver to his ear. "Yes?"

He heard a series of beeps and boops. "This line is secure," Ulgard spoke into his ear, sounding somewhat tinny. "Let us continue."

"Right. I do not know the names of these people at this moment, but I can get back to you after some research."

"I will handle it all," Ulgard said.

"Oh, of course. Fine." The man was simply amazing. He probably had a staff of dozens, researchers and detectives and operatives all over the world. He was obviously the best in his field. "I thank you in advance, Herr Ulgard. This is of critical importance to me."

"I will call with a progress report in twenty-four hours, Herr von Wessenheim. Please carry your cellular phone if you happen to leave the *Residenz* for any significant amount of time. The number, please?"

Von Wessenheim puffed on his cigarette. Like many older Europeans, he was leery of all the newfangled *dingsbums* high-tech was producing nowadays, electronic toys to amuse the Japanese and the Americans. "I'm afraid my valet in Frankfurt failed to pack mine for this trip," he said. "He's new."

"Then please stay in your hotel, if at all possible. Things may start to move very quickly."

"I will do that," von Wessenheim promised.

Ulgard hung up without another word. "And a good evening to you too," Von Wessenheim murmured. He lowered the phone slowly, despite the abrupt ending unable to suppress a smile of pure joy. Franz Bohr had directed him not only to a new lawyer, but to a worker of miracles.

He dropped onto the sofa and dragged the phone book

onto his lap. There was nothing to do now but wait, but no
reason to wait alone. He phoned a prostitute agency and followed it up with a call for room service, one bottle of the
house's best wine for him and a couple of beers for the girl.

22

When it was finally light enough to be called daylight outside, Sharri eased out of her room, the gun held in both hands. She shuffled sideways down the hall to the kitchen and paused at the juncture there, the gun hanging heavily between the thighs of her cut-off jeans. To her left she could see a corner of the new picture window that was smashed to pieces again, could see the ruined drapes hanging in tatters to the floor. To her right, visible through the sliding glass door, were cars and vans and people milling around at the edge of the backyard, some of them carrying binoculars or cameras or signs. After the man burned to death on the lawn, the police had set up yellow sawhorses to keep everyone back.

She walked into the kitchen. Normally at this hour she would be asleep but Sharri could not adjust to the murmur of voices outside, the police radios that crackled so loudly whenever they spoke up. It was like trying to sleep on a table in the school cafeteria at lunchtime. Her bright green eyes were now burdened with purplish circles, in the mirror her face looked like a raccoon's, her hair like a haystack.

She dropped to her haunches and duck-walked to the living room. Her laborious movement brought her to the stairway where Dad lay upstairs in bed with his arms and parts of his face coated in aloe vera gel and wrapped with gauze. Where Mom was right now was a mystery, but hopefully she had gone to the grocery store: all the good breakfast cereal in the house was gone.

On her knees and elbows she crawled up the stairs, favoring the gun. She moved slowly across the short landing, not wanting her dad to hear. At the open doorway she cautiously eased her head inside and listened for breathing, for snores, picked up nothing yet. By stretching hard she poked the gun under the bed, out of view, then crept deeper into the room. At last she heard a light snarkeling, like someone who had just drifted off and was sliding into the land of real sleep. Sharri rose to her knees and looked.

Dad was flat out in his blue pajamas; his bandaged wrists and hands hung out of his sleeves and his face was shiny all over, lumped with gauze in places. His hair had been cooked short above his forehead and the burned smell of it lingered.

She dropped down again. After the incident with the fire-crackers, she had seen her mom gather up a stack of newspapers from the dining room table and hurry upstairs with it. One of the papers, Sharri had seen, sported a red headline, and in her life she had never seen a newspaper with a red headline. A look under the bed revealed nothing but darkness. She got down on her stomach and wormed her head under the bed, probing with her hands until she found them.

She dragged the stack out and immediately raked in a swift breath. Her own face in black-and-white was looking up at her from the first page of something called the *Nightly News Revue*.

DAUGHTER OF REINCARNATED HITLER
DEFIES COURT ORDER
She Threatens Judge: Don't Take My Swastika!

She could not believe it. It was not possible. There had to be a law that prohibited lying in newspapers, it might even be part of the Constitution. She set it aside and sat cross-legged on the floor.

The next one on the stack had the red headline. Beneath it was a picture of her father looking wild-eyed and crazy. He had a knife in his hand. Between his fingers, easy to see, was a swastika emblem on the knife's handle. But how had they caught him doing this? She read the name of the paper: *The National Scene*. The absolutely huge headline was this:

HYPNO-HITLER RAMPAGE ROCKS
INDIANA COLLEGE TOWN

She read the first few lines of the article, closed her eyes and shook her head, then tossed it aside.

NAZI COLLEGE PROFESSOR FIRED

At least in this one Dad's picture was at the bottom of the page, it was just his normal head and the writing was short. The big story above it in *America's News Now!* was about a dinosaur egg that hatched in a laboratory. The baby dinosaur, surrounded by surprised-looking scientists, looked more like an iguana. She slid it under the bed feeling both angry and afraid. The next one in the stack was just as bad.

HITLER RETURNS TO FIGHT JESUS
AT BATTLE OF ARMAGEDDON
Nazi Troops Will Rise from the Grave

It occurred to her that she had seen these kinds of newspapers before, they were usually right at the checkout counter at grocery stores and they often had on them either pictures of Jesus or pictures of aliens. And TV stars, a lot of those. With a flip of her wrist she propelled *The World Reporter* under the bed. Underneath it *The New Investigator* had been awaiting its turn. The front page wasn't much different than her dad's daily paper, photos and stories about real things, a decent-looking newspaper. She wafted it open and there was the same tired old picture of Dad with the knife.

HITLER RISES IN THE HEARTLAND?
"Reborn" Nazi Dictator Emerges in Rural Indiana

Sharri felt sickened enough to just open the window and throw all the crap back at the world but the window was blocked by a screen and there was still one paper left, maybe it had something good to say. Again the front page was harmless, it was concerned about the ghost of somebody named

Bluebeard terrorizing people in a hotel in France. Page two was cut into four sections with more stories about ghosts in France. But on page three was the reason the *Worldwide Weekly Messenger* belonged here:

NAZI DAD AND DAUGHTER SAY "WE ARE THE MASTER RACE!"
Reincarnated Hitler Promises World War Three

Both pictures stood in stark black-and-white under the headline, Dad with the knife, Sharri with the swastika necklace, as well as a small drawing of the United States with a big black swastika in the middle and littler ones around it like snowflakes.

And that was it. That was all of them. She shoved everything deep under the bed while hot tears gathered at the rims of her eyes. How could they do that to her, to her dad? Grown-up people writing lies for newspapers, reporters who faked their stories and made them sound true. Worst of all, everyone who read this stuff would believe it; if it were about someone else *she* would believe it. There was no reason not to.

The gun was cold to her hand when she retrieved it. When she rose she spent a moment looking at her dad in his collapsed blue pajamas. A mosquito had landed on one of the spots of his forehead that was not covered with cotton or gauze, a big Indiana mosquito with its loathsome hind legs curved upward in the act of stabbing its blood-sucker into his skin. She watched it but could do nothing, she was helpless to help him. Finally, she blinked and the waiting tears skittered down her cheeks without finding a hold on her skin.

She dropped to her hands and knees again. The gun was tight in one fist. With the other she knuckled her eyes back into shape before crawling out of the bedroom and headfirst down the stairs. Morning wind, smelling of rain and the things that had burned last night, flapped through the ruins of the drapes. At the base of the stairwell, Sharri rose to her knees, her face a blank with two hard green eyes. The world was out there, the world that had done this to them. It was time to show the world that the Thorwalds were going to fight back.

She jumped to her feet and raced to the front door, pivoted at the last second and slammed against the wall beside it. It hurt her shoulder blades and tailbone but she had learned the trick from the cop shows. She launched away from the wall, whipped the door open and jumped out onto the welcome mat, simultaneously jerking the gun up to eye level in preparation for firing.

Enough people to fill her school's auditorium to the rafters were held at bay behind the yellow sawhorses. The bright-green maple trees on the front lawn still wore tatters of pink and white moss under the rain, the rolls of toilet paper hurled into them. A blackened slash on the lawn showed where the man had burned. Police lights blipped and flashed endlessly and their radios squawked. As Sharri hunkered low in her cop imitation, her eyes wide from the fresh-air immensity of all this, a large portion of the crowd seemed to notice her at once and a discordant cry rose up as if sung by a choir of drunks. A host of pale faces turned in unison. One second of silence drifted past, two seconds. Like a corral full of wild horses the mob suddenly tried to scatter, the mass of them shifting in waves, colorful umbrellas bobbing, everyone shouting at once.

Except the people with all the electronic equipment bristling from their TV vans, the reporters and the cameramen. As Sharri shut one eye and put both fingers on the trigger, their cameras flashed with more brightness than the sun on a hot day; she seemed to feel the heat of them against her face and bare legs. She noticed without interest that the police officers were reaching for their guns as they dropped into slow-motion squats. She raked the trigger back with all the strength her fingers owned, letting a shout of her own burst out.

The gun popped with a small burst of smoke. She fired again and again, swiveling back and forth, *pop-pop,* watching half of the crowd scramble on top of each other while the other half dove to the ground. A red ribbon of paper caps curled out of her gun, jumping up a little each time she fired. Her dad had given her this cap gun for a birthday present long ago and it had taken her six months to shake the idea he wished he'd had a boy. She wasn't much into cowboys so it had laid at the bottom of her toy box all this time. It was a wonder the caps weren't all duds by now.

Pop-pop, she fired away, *pop-pop*, until one of the cops put a bullet through her chest just above her heart. She pitched backward and fell inside the house. Her legs stuck out over the welcome mat.

Just a fucking pop gun, the officer whispered after he ran to where she lay, and knelt in a puddle of her blood to feel for a pulse. When the ambulance arrived four minutes later he was sitting on the curb, weeping while his fellow officers pinned the girl's crazed father to the lawn.

By noon ABC, NBC, CBS, and CNN were in Terre Haute to cover the story for the evening news.

MASS HYSTERIE

23

Rebecca was too dazed to absorb the reality of what greeted her when she fumbled open the door of the police car and stepped out. She had been taken into custody the moment she drove within smelling distance of her house at 1225 Quartermaine. At Perry's her heat-blistered Pontiac had been reluctant to start. Chugging and popping, she had steered it through town in a state of both embarrassment and shock. Perry's face had been so deeply blue. How could he have endured the final moments of suffocation in that bag?

But as she was hurried out of her car and into a police cruiser she decided not to tell them about Perry just now; it would embroil her in yet another tragedy. The officer driving the car did not have much to say, perhaps because the police car scattering traffic in front of them had its siren shrieking its strange highs and lows. However, he did say that she had to prepare herself for some bad news. But she's not dead, he blurted out hastily, and Rebecca clapped both hands over her mouth. He hastily explained, as they tore up the streets between 1225 Q-main and Regency Hospital, that Sharri had jumped outside the house firing a cap gun. One of the rookie officers had returned fire and shot her through the chest.

Rebecca relieved him of the burden of further explanation by weeping noisily into her hands. But within sight of the alabaster walls of Regency Hospital she wove herself back together strand by strand, feeling as if she literally had been battered and unraveled like a flag, tattered to pieces in a hurricane, atop a lonely pole. When she stepped out of the car, she was still dazed, but not unaware. At the foot of the sidewalk that led to the entrance, she paused to brace herself for the people of the media who waited in an animated crowd at the doorway. An officer appeared at Rebecca's side and put a firm hand on her shoulder just as another officer popped up to do the same to her other side. They swiftly escorted her through the mob of utter strangers. The most remarkable thing, she realized as she neared them, was that as cameras clicked and flashed the people were all shouting, their community of voices blending into a hash of dislocated phrases. *Mrs. Thorwald, can you tell us . . . what you think about . . . do you believe . . . Rebecca, how do . . . what is your reaction to . . . if indeed it proves true . . . Mrs. Thorwald, can you explain how . . . really raised your daughter as . . . when did you first . . . Rebecca, at which point did you . . . any statement regarding your . . .*

Suddenly she liked these policemen very much; without their strength she would crumple. Yet they had shot Sharri, one of their number had shot Sharri through the chest and almost killed her. She would be scarred for life, perhaps a breast had been destroyed, she would need a mastectomy bra to replace the preteen bra she wore now with such pride and embarrassment. At the entrance, two sets of amber glass doors, the policemen eased her through and immediately veered to the right. She was ushered to a waiting area, started to squirm against their arms, then was released. She stood wobbling, at a loss, knowing only that Sharri was somewhere else.

A silver-haired policeman in a strangely decorated blue uniform strode toward her, smiling. He reached out both hands as he neared. "Mrs. Thorwald," he said. "How are you?"

She shifted her eyes nervously, wondering. "Fine."

"So brave. I've been told by the surgical force that Sharri is doing just fine."

"Where is she?" Rebecca said.

"Still in surgery, in good hands. In the *best* hands. You have my word on that. And your husband is A-okay too."

She edged her head a little to the side. "Hank is here?"

His eyes flickered, darted away and back. "And doing fine."

Her heart lurched. "You shot Hank too?"

He turned. "James? We have a communications matter here."

A man in a suit who had been lingering behind the officer in the fancy uniform jumped to his side and offered Rebecca a toothy smile. "Mrs. Thorwald," he said broadly as he shook her hand. "Glitch in transmission, my apologies. Sit with us?"

"Has my husband been shot?" she asked.

"No." He shook his head. "No, no. Your husband is fine. At the time of the accidental shooting, he suffered some stress-related symptoms that required a very mild medication. He's resting comfortably and doing super. Sit with us?"

"Take me to my daughter."

"Doing just fine in surgery, Mrs. Thorwald. Did anyone introduce you to Matt Windsor? You probably recognize him as Terre Haute's chief of police."

She looked at him but was unable to follow.

The chief cleared his throat. "Mrs. Thorwald, I express my deepest sympathy for the unfortunate accident that took place today. I have ordered a full investigation into the incident, and the officer suspected of being responsible has been relieved of duty until such time as his involvement can be proved. In the meantime I speak on behalf of every police officer in the city when I say I am deeply troubled by the incident, and wish you and your family well."

He stuck out his hand again. Rebecca looked down at it, at his blue sleeve with the gold circles braided around the cuff in gold thread, and poked her hand into his. He gave it a gentle squeeze. To the side of her left eye she was aware of a video camera bobbing around, and shied away from it. "Can you help me find my family?" she asked, hearing her voice crack, not wanting to be a crybaby in front of this important man but helpless to do any better.

The chief raised a hand and snapped his fingers. Her two uniformed ushers appeared beside her. "Take her wherever she needs to go," he told them. "Get her anything she needs here, I don't care what it is. Above all, keep those media bastards away. Until further notice she is our guest in this city."

The officer to her left lowered his head. "Where to, Mrs. Thorwald?"

Her vision blurred beyond salvation. This was all too much, she had been alone in this hell for so long and now, finally, someone cared. The whole city cared. She sucked in a great, hiccuping sob and let part of her weight fall against him. "To where it doesn't hurt anymore."

"Pardon me?"

"My husband's room."

"Not a problem."

They marched her along, coming to a halt at the face of an elevator door. The wood-veneer doors slid away from each other and she was propelled inside. All three of them executed a clumsy about-face to watch the doors shut again. One of the cops leaned over and poked button number 3. She stared at the number as the elevator rose, was still staring when the doors eased open. It came to her belatedly that she had not smoked a cigarette for a long time, hours. The need was there like a rising fever but wasn't important anymore, she would rather sit with Sharri and Hank for all eternity than go outside for a smoke and show the world the power of her addiction.

They took her to room number 314. The door was open and the light was on. Both policemen turned to stand guard after they released her to go inside.

She crossed to the bed. Hank was asleep with his mouth hanging open, not his usual style. Someone had worked on his burns, put new salve and bandages on areas of his face, bound his arms and hands loosely with gauze. The blue hospital blanket was tucked under his chin, but he couldn't stand any bedclothes that lay higher than his chest. And he always slept with one arm free of the covers. Idiosyncrasies, everybody had some. She bent and moved the blanket down. He snored, gobbling at the air. She pulled his favorite arm from under the cover and gasped.

Deep red welts encircled his wrist. She lifted the blanket. The other wrist bore the same thin rope marks. At the cuffs of his blue hospital pajamas his ankles were in the same shape. Somebody had tied him up. Her man Hank, one of the most gentle men she had ever known, had been hog-tied by the cops.

Anger started to rise, but fell quickly away. Hank wasn't quite the same person anymore. He had by his own account demolished his office at the university. And to top it off he had gotten shit-faced drunk the night before. He had said a lot of hurtful things, he had mumbled stuff in German, twice he had shouted the same phrase, something like veeduh guh-boren bin ish. Only God or a German tourist might know what it meant. Rebecca went upstairs to bed crying, then rationalized everything away. Her own father sometimes drank too much.

She eased the covers over the middle of Hank's chest, pulled his favorite arm free again and tucked it beside him. So obviously drugged-out he looked old and stupid. The mental bugs Perry had infected him with were working like a virus, eating him from the inside, changing everything about him. One brief session at the no-smoking affair had hit him like a bomb. Weeks or months or years of Perry's hypnosis were acting like a massive overdose of LSD, Hank was on what the hippies used to call a bad trip, a bad trip that just kept getting worse.

It looked as if Hank would be asleep for a long time. She turned and crossed back to the door. "I need a piece of paper," she said. "And a pen. Please?"

The cops looked at each other and shrugged. One of them produced a little notebook and tore out a sheet for her. He followed it with a pen.

"Thanks." She went back in scribbling a quick note, studied Hank for a bit, and tucked it beside his pillow. Eventually, he would see it. "I want to see my daughter," she said as she came out.

Instantly, the cop who had poked the elevator button made a walkie-talkie appear. "Is the daughter out of surgery yet?"

The voice of a woman said to hold on.

"They're checking," he told her.

She said thank you.

The radio spoke again: "They're wheeling her out of surgery right now, moving her to post-op."

"Take me there," she said.

He spoke her request into his radio. It remained silent for a long time. Rebecca watched an extremely old man hobble past pushing a metal hat rack perched on little wheels, from which dangled a plastic bag of cloudy liquid. A tube from it snaked down into the collar of his blue pajamas. His mouth drooped, his eyes were rheumy and gray. She wondered why he could not straighten his knees.

The radio made noise. "Tell her an ICU nurse is on the way to escort her."

He looked at Rebecca. "Guess we wait right here, but it might take a few minutes. Hospitals are just like airports, nothing happens on time." He smiled for her. "Can I get you something?"

Automatically, she shook her head no, then voiced a thought without meaning to. "Unless one of you guys smokes."

"I happen to smoke way too damn much," he said, and fetched a pack out of his back pocket. He handed her a crumpled Camel Light, her own brand. Just the feel of it was reassuring, this stupid paper tube with its pinch of tobacco and its sturdy filter that snugged so familiarly between her lips.

"Light," the officer was saying. He slapped at his pockets.

"Hold on," the other man said. "Nobody's allowed to smoke in this hospital."

Rebecca was offered a book of matches in the same crumply condition. "The chief said to get her anything she wants. She wants a cigarette." He smiled at her. "Go ahead, Mrs. Thorwald. Light up."

She took them gratefully, ripped a match out, and stroked its red tip across the striker. Yellow fire. She raised the flame and inhaled a mouthful of smoke. It hit her lungs like an old friend who dropped by to hand her a thousand-dollar bill.

Down the corridor the elevator bell dinged softly. A nurse in classic dress complete with folded paper hat bobby-pinned to her hair stepped out, looked both ways, then found Rebecca with her eyes. She raised a hand and strode toward her. "Mrs. Thorwald?"

"Oh shit." The cop who smoked reached and snatched the cigarette from her fingers. "Uh, this is her," he called out, and pawned it off to the other cop. He growled something nasty and hiked away trailing a tattered string of smoke.

The nurse walked up and squeezed her hand. "Your little daughter is doing quite well, the surgery went just as expected. She's a strong girl. Pretty too, like you. Shall we go see her now?"

"Can I talk to her?" she asked as they set into motion. "Can she talk?"

"She's still sedated from surgery." The elevator was waiting, open, and the nurse motioned her inside. "She won't be fully herself again, mentally speaking, for several days. A wound like that, and surgery following so closely afterward, are severe physiological traumas. Psychologically, you add the anesthetic, the pain meds, and it all totals a little girl who needs lots of time to heal in both her body and her mind." She pressed the button for floor 1. "I hope I'm not painting a grim picture, Rebecca. Is it Rebecca?"

She nodded.

"Sharri will be just fine. Time sees to that. In a few years having been shot so terribly, and having survived, will make her the envy of her classmates. I know it sounds horrid, but it's true."

The doors walked themselves slowly shut. "The scars," Rebecca said. "Will she be scarred?" The real question was *Did she lose a breast*, but Rebecca was unwilling to ask it. It might sound absurd, measured against the simple saving of her life, and the answer might be yes, which she could not bear to hear.

"Slightly. The entry wound was very small, as is usual in gunshot wounds, and the fact that the bullet struck her scapula prevented an exit wound, which might have been huge. I think that if I had to choose a chest wound, God forbid, I would choose hers. No lower, no higher. Perfect."

Those words brought a gush of relief to Rebecca that let

her know belatedly just how deep her fear had been. She covered her eyes with a hand and sobbed.

The elevator tried to open but the nurse poked a finger into the DOOR CLOSE button and kept it there. She dropped a warm hand on Rebecca's shoulder. "You've been brave for a long time, I'll bet," she said gently. "Go ahead and let it out. I can wait, and Sharri's in dreamland. Sweet dreamland, where nobody can hurt her."

Rebecca clenched her teeth and groaned as she pulled herself together again, strand by ragged strand, until she felt as whole as she could get. "Take me to her now," she said with a toss of her head. She dabbed at the ruins of her hair and wiped her eyes. Makeup was a memory, she looked like walking death and she knew it. "Please."

"Then walk this way," the nurse said cheerfully, and let the doors breeze open.

"*Ja?*" Karl-Luther von Wessenheim said into the phone. He was three-quarters asleep and not quite sure where he was, whether in Brussels to check his real estate holdings or in Frankfurt for another board meeting. "Hallo?"

"I have news for you," a man's voice said. "One of the three persons I contacted is willing to speak with you."

Von Wessenheim rocked on his feet as he looked for familiar things in the dark. The memory of a bottle of wine was cobwebbed into his brain, there had been a girl here who had brought her own bottle of very cheap wine, and he had drunk his own and a lot of hers, then the two beers. His only duty tonight had been to stand watch over the telephone. He had been faithful to that. And now here was the reason.

"Good job, Herr Ulgard." Von Wessenheim's voice was wheezy from too many Reemstmas chain-smoked between the time the girl left and the time he fell asleep beside the phone, whenever that was. He lifted his wrist to his face and consulted his watch. Too dark, every bulb in his room at the *Residenz* was turned off. Or broken. The girl had been one of those crazy redheads who jumped around a lot as she stripped for him, full of power and youth but giggly to the point of needing an oxygen bottle when she was finally naked. Von Wessenheim had been acutely aware of his age as he asked things of her, but she was a businesswoman in her own right, she was working for a living, and she was good. He vaguely recalled handing her a fifty-Mark bill as she kissed him good-bye. Now he bumbled to the door and slapped at the wall until he found a switch. Light roared into his bloodshot, sleepy eyes. "All right, we must arrange a meeting," he said belatedly into the phone.

"Already done. Hold on, let me switch us to a secure line."

Von Wessenheim waited, feeling his strength and his resolve return. Softly the phone said *beep-boop, boop-beep.* "Herr von Wessenheim, are you still there?

"Still here."

"The man was an ordinary Wehrmacht soldier during the Battle of Berlin in April of 1945. He was ordered by the SS to siphon gasoline out of cars near the Reich's Chancellery. He claims that was the gasoline used to burn Hitler's body. The man is now about seventy-five years old. Unfortunately, he is quite aware of his peculiar position and demands money for his testimony."

Von Wessenheim was gripping the receiver in his hand almost hard enough to shatter it. "Oh my dear God." He pulled in a breath just in time to keep himself from collapsing for lack of air. "I will give him whatever he asks. Tell him that."

Rønna Ulgard was silent for a time. "Very well. Stay by the phone."

He was gone. Von Wessenheim hung up and held out his hands for inspection. They were shaking with nervous tremors, comically so. He touched his face and found his lips bunched together to keep a shout of joy inside. That aged army soldier, actually alive and present during the last moments of the Third Reich—what a remarkable place to hold in history! And being a common soldier playing a small role he would have nothing to gain from hiding the truth of what had happened. In all the books von Wessenheim had read since undertaking this, no mention had been made—though he may have overlooked it—that the soldiers who siphoned the gasoline out of the cars were present at the burning. Perhaps he had read that they all had been killed later in the battle. In a brain overstuffed with data and hungry for sleep, he could not be sure.

He stuffed his hands into his pockets and ambled in a slow circle around the sofa, suddenly frowning. If the old soldier confirmed that Hitler's body had been burned in a bomb crater, this entire endeavor and the money he was prepared to give the man were Deutschemarks thrown into the wind, lots of them. A more prudent individual would assay his losses at this time, weigh the appropriateness of throwing good money after bad, and perhaps back out of the deal, lick his wounds, get on with life. But that individual would have to live the rest of his life not knowing what might have been, forever wondering if he had been sensible for quitting, or just too tight-fisted to keep going.

So there could be no backing out. But he would set a limit on the money he was prepared to pay the old man. Ten thousand Marks seemed reasonable, he was probably living on a veteran's pension, just getting by. Ten thousand would probably make him drool.

The phone clanged like a handful of steel bells, making his head thump. He leapt at it and whipped the receiver up. "Von Wessenheim here."

"He demands one hundred thousand Marks."

His knees folded and he was dumped on the sofa. "You're kidding," he gasped as he bounced. "That is preposterous."

"Very well. Call me if you need other services."

"No! Wait!" He rose up. "Are you there?"

"Yes."

"Bargain him down to half that amount."

"I already bargained him down. He is aware of his unique position."

"If he is indeed the person he claims to be, though."

"His name is Gerhard Brunner. I have seen his identification papers and his record of wartime service. He fought in Berlin, was captured by the Soviets, and spent the next four years as a slave laborer in Siberia."

"So has he ever been questioned about his role at the bunker?"

"By the Russians, only briefly. He verified that he helped

collect gasoline on the day in question. My research indicates that he has been largely ignored because of that small role."

"Then what can he possibly tell me?"

Rønna Ulgard breathed loudly into the phone. "Since I do not know what you want from him, I have no way of knowing what he can tell you."

Von Wessenheim placed a hand over his eyes. "Yes. Of course. Sorry for all the questions. You may tell the man that I accept his terms. I believe you said you have already arranged a meeting for us."

"Yes, for this evening. I'll meet you at the airport in an hour."

"Airport?"

"Berlin-Tegel airport, yes. I've taken care of the tickets. Can I assume your passport is up to date?"

Von Wessenheim shrugged to himself, unable to believe these things were happening so fast. But Rønna Ulgard had said they would, and he had not lied. "Yes, I sometimes do business in Austria and France. Where exactly does this man live?"

"Exactly?" Von Wessenheim heard papers rustle. "I believe it is pronounced Boy-see."

"Boy-see?"

"Boy-see, Idaho. It is a part of the United States of America. Are you fluent in English?"

Von Wessenheim realized his jaw had fallen open. He closed it with a snap. "Not fluent. Passable at best."

"No one forgets their native tongue, so the old man still speaks German. For all other circumstances—restaurants, hotels, car rentals—I can either handle them myself or translate for you." He paused, shuffling papers again. "Just as you enter the airport from the taxicab area go hard to the left. There is a small bistro with no chairs, the patrons stand at tall white tables. Meet me there in one hour."

"This is certainly as fast as you promised," von Wessenheim said. "You are a remarkable attorney, Herr Ulgard. I only wish I had found you—"

He realized he was talking into a dead phone. "Hello?"

Nobody. He put the receiver on its cradle. One hour. The

Berlin-Tegel airport was nearby, just a few miles north. A cab might need twenty minutes to drive there, maybe thirty depending on the morning traffic. That left just thirty minutes to get himself cleaned up and a bag or two packed. He started to stand but stopped halfway to his feet, his eyes captured by the copy of *Mein Kampf* on the floor. It had fallen off the sofa in all the excitement and lay there halfway open as if baring itself to the world, daring to be understood. But it was hopelessly outdated, the man who had written it was gone, his politics seemed absurd in these complex modern times, his theology of ultranationalism was extinct. But still he fascinated people. In death he continued to recruit followers, his swastika was recognized worldwide, he was one of the most famous people in the history of all mankind. Yet he had vanished without a trace.

Unless someone found that trace. Von Wessenheim tore his gaze from the book and hurried into the bathroom for a quick shower, wondering what he should pack for the trip, wondering what the weather was like in Boy-see, Idaho, wondering if he should purchase a cowboy hat.

24

Hank stirred in his sleep. Something clattered sharply to the floor. He rolled onto his side with a groan and looked down. It was a television remote attached to his bed frame by a beaded chain. The bed frame was made of chrome tubes. He eased over onto his back and ground his knuckles into his eyes. Pain stabbed his face and he jerked his hands away. His arms were wrapped in gauze, his fingers greasy with something that smelled funny. He sat up: somehow he had found his way to a hospital.

Mein Weg zum Spital . . .

"You just shut the fuck up!" he screamed. The television bolted to the wall stared down at him with its baleful solitary eye, reflecting his own image on the green glass. He clapped a hand over his mouth and his eyes jerked to the left. The door was, fortunately, shut. He eased himself down onto the mattress and pinched at the covers to tug them up to his chest. As he did he saw that he was wearing a plastic bracelet that slid loosely up and down on his forearm, one of the ID things like Rebecca had worn while in the hospital having Sharri. His wrist bore the impression of tight handcuffs. Fear seized him. He might have gone berserk again and this time hurt someone, maybe even Rebecca. He flattened a hand over both eyes, begging his memory to cast him a clue.

Blood. He saw blood glowing such a huge neon red that no artist's palette could ever match it. Sparkling, crimson blood splattered all over the door and the floor, the raw smell of it drifting into the house. People yammering outside, a mob pressing in hungrily for something that he was not willing to give them.

But he could only remember the edges of the scene. He released his eyes and rubbed his hands on the bed. There was a big clock on the wall to the right of the TV. The shortest hand was edging toward six o'clock. The room's only window contained sunlight: six in the afternoon, then, really six in the evening, though the summer sun would not set until ten. On the wall to the right was a pleated vinyl door that was stretched shut. He sat up and lowered his legs over the bed. His ankles wore indented pink circles where they had been cuffed; the rings were streaked with jagged scabs where his skin had torn and bled. A memory of treatment like that should be fresh and hot but it was utterly missing. Something about the blood.

The door of the room swooshed open fast enough to change the air pressure and Hank flattened himself back down on the bed. A nurse came in and assessed him as the door fell shut. In her white uniform she stood out as a big-boned woman with a fringe of gray above her ears, and eyes that had seen their share of surprises. "That was quite the verbal alarm clock," she said. "Are you in pain, Mr. Thorwald?"

"Had a nightmare," he said. He remembered one of the missing parts suddenly. His neighbor had brought an armful of tabloid newspapers to the back door and left them there in a stack. Afraid Sharri would see them, Rebecca had scooped up the pile and stuffed it under the bed upstairs. His memory of this day was a hash of images and faces; he clearly remembered trying to smother the flames on the man who was on fire, remembered that he had gotten burning gasoline on his arms and some of his face. His hands were tangled in the blanket but had survived the ordeal red and blistered. After that his memory was fractured.

"Burns and nightmares are never fun," the nurse said. "From what I've heard, you're lucky you got away with what you got, burnwise."

"Thank you," he said bitterly.

Suddenly she smiled. "That was a very brave thing you did, Mr. Thorwald. Very brave."

He raised an eyebrow. "What was?"

"Trying to save that man." She skirted the bed and lifted his arm, touched at the loose wrapping of gauze. "I saw it on TV."

Hank's spine stiffened. That whole fiasco on television, all of Terre Haute watching. He had explained to the reporters, over coffee, that there was no news to be found at his house. Then a man burned to death on the lawn.

"I want to tell you that I don't believe any of that stuff," the nurse said. She put his arm down. "Between you and me and the fence post, it's a pile of horseshit."

He looked into her eyes. Sympathy was there along with a kind of hopeful camaraderie. If sides were being drawn, he saw that he could count on her support.

"Thank you," he said, drawing his arm up to his chin.

She stepped back, surveying him, surveying the room. "Oh, here," she said, and dropped from sight as suddenly as if she had walked into an open manhole. Hank rose up slightly on his elbow but she popped back into view. "The remote," she said, extending it to him. "In this hospital we even let Hitler watch TV. Ha-ha."

"Ha-ha," he said as he ignored it.

She aimed it up at the television with both hands. "If you want cable the hospital adds it to your bill. If you don't want it you're stuck with the big four networks and only get static on all the rest. It's part of my duty here to explain this. Look at the television."

He looked. The picture crackled slowly alive and became a video snowstorm, a mad splatter of colored dots smashing against the screen. She flipped it to a channel showing a commercial for United Airlines. All the faces were orange and the sky was brown.

Her eyes were busy watching him. "It's fine," he said, unwilling to donate more time to her. "Thanks."

She plopped the remote onto his stomach and reached past his head. "This is the call button for nursing services." A thick white cord was brought into his view. She showed him the business end of it. "If you need help just take this in your fist and push the button down with your thumb. A nurse will respond."

"That's good," he said as she tucked it under his arm. "Thank you."

"Since you're ambulatory nobody's going to walk in and stick a frozen bedpan under your butt." A new smile changed the lines of her face. "Unless I put it on your chart, of course."

Hank regarded her with every intention of making his own smile, anything to get her out of here, but the machine that operated his expressions was out of service. The best he could put together was a wrinkling of his eyelids, an upward turn of the left edge of his mouth. "You'd better not," his voice warned in a stupid falsetto.

She opened the door and walked away leaving it standing wide open. Hank let himself relax fully onto the bed. His first idea was that he must get out of here. His burns weren't bad enough to warrant anything other than a few more applications of salve now and then; even the gauze was optional. But going back home was an impossibility, it was a war zone. Maybe just staying right here was the most advisable route, lie down and watch television until Perry resurfaced and ended this.

Just then a policeman in a blue THPD uniform leaned in, glanced at him, and pulled the door shut.

Hank lay motionless, thinking, his eyes jumping as he inspected various locations on the ceiling. He appreciated having an armed guard because there were a lot of angry people out there; it was a very thoughtful gesture from the city of Terre Haute. But one nagging question needed to be answered before Hank could fully express his gratitude: was the cop outside the door put there to guard him? Or was he put there to keep him from leaving?

By chance Hank glanced at the television and saw his own face on the screen. After a moment of shock, he fumbled for the remote and found the volume button.

. . . ison Wayne Thorwald, a thirty-two-year-old associate professor at Indiana State University here in Terre Haute, Indiana. Despite his insistence that the entire hypnosis was merely a practical joke, word has

*spread far beyond the boundaries of this ordinary Mid-
western town . . .*

The shot of his face cut to an aerial view showing the
white roof of his house and the sea of people gathered around
it. He jerked to a sitting position and studied it, trying to
guess when it was filmed. That scene then cut to a choppy
nighttime view of his car exploding.

*. . . firebombed, resulting in the death by burning of a
twenty-eight-year-old protester. The supposed reborn
Hitler attempted to smother the flames with a blanket
and received minor burns to his arms and face . . .*

Hank watched himself sprint from his house, a bounding
shadow against the flames, his blanket flapping. The screen
exchanged it for the orange face of the reporter, a blonde
woman holding a tall black microphone. She was nobody
he'd ever seen on the local stations.

*. . . stage for another tragedy early this morning, when
eleven-year-old Sharri Lynn Thorwald, the couple's
only child, burst from the house with a cap pistol and
began firing it . . .*

Hank's heart gave a lurch. On the screen, filmed by an unsteady camera, Sharri was shooting a cap pistol. The camera
swung to show the crowd falling back while people
screamed. Just as it turned to find Sharri again, one of the
kneeling policemen fired. The camera hesitated on him.
Screams and shouts followed immediately. It was like watching an old film of John F. Kennedy being shot in Dallas. With
his thoughts thick with dread, he watched the scene rotate
back to the front door of his house.

*. . . struck the girl just above her heart, wounding her,
but not fatally. Matthew Windsor, the Terre Haute chief
of police, held a press conference shortly afterward in
which he defended the department. He did state, how-*

ever, that the officer who admittedly shot the girl was relieved of his duty pending an investigation. Meanwhile, Sharri Thorwald is in stable condition following surgery . . .

A gray-haired man in a fancy blue uniform was being buried under a barrage of camera flashes as the reporter spoke. The next cut showed an ambulance trying to wend its way through the crowd.

. . . the girl's distraught father attacked the officers and had to be restrained. Heavily sedated, he was taken to the same hospital as his daughter . . .

Cut to the face of the reporter.

. . . the people gathered here, some who have journeyed from as far away as California and New York, expressed a wide range of reasons for coming. Though few seem certain that Hank Thorwald was really Adolf Hitler in a past life, those who believe it are united by a common theme: to stop him before he rises to power.

Things are certainly getting strange—and deadly—here in Terre Haute, Indiana. This is Susan MacWirth for CBS News.

He swung himself out of bed, sick with the knowledge that he had lain here hoping for a reprieve from reality when his own daughter was in the same damn hospital with a bullet in her fragile little chest. Why hadn't the nurse said anything? Why hadn't the cop bothered to mention it when he'd poked his head in instead of wordlessly pulling the door shut?

Verdammter Schweinhund . . .

Hank snatched up the pillow and wrapped it around his face, pulling it so tight his fingernails hurt, burying whatever he thought he might scream into it. The maddening voice sounded like his own, but it was Perry's. He would give everything he owned, except for the lives of his wife and daughter, to be rid of it. To his knowledge there was only one sure way, but it was too permanent.

He lowered the pillow and lurched to the folding door, shoved it to the side. His clothes were neatly folded on the metal shelves. The thin blue gown he was wearing seemed to be tied together in the back somehow; while the burned skin of his arms crackled with pain he ripped it apart. The hospital's ID bracelet was surprisingly hard to tear apart. When he was dressed—his underwear and everything else had been laundered, were stiff and smelled strongly of hospital-strength detergent—he stood at the door pushing his hair into a semblance of neatness. It would do him no good to emerge looking like a lunatic. It would do him better to emerge looking so damned good that the cop would mistake him for a visitor. He slowly turned the big aluminum knob and let the door drift open an inch.

A wedge of empty hallway. Nothing but. He pulled the door toward himself a cautious handful of inches and stuck his head through. To the left was more hallway, deserted. He looked to the right and saw the blue fabric of the policeman's sleeve, was close enough to his armpit to smell the deodorant he favored. The cop noticed him and stepped away from the wall. "Mr. Thorwald?"

"I need to see my daughter."

"I'll relay that request to my superiors," he said with a freckled smile. "Excuse me."

Hank watched as he stepped briskly away. His black belt had a big leather holder for his radio, which he snatched out and raised to his face. He rotated and saw Hank watching him. He rotated again to present his back. From the other direction of the hallway a trio of white-haired ladies made their way along wearing the strange black shoes of the elderly. The woman in the middle was in tears and the other two were simply forging ahead with her. Hank wondered what had happened.

The young officer was done, and came back. "You need to hang tight, Mr. Thorwald. The chief of the Terre Haute Police Department wants to meet with you. He's downtown but will be here within the hour."

Hang tight? It was an option full of loopholes. Hank put himself fully in the hallway. "My daughter is in this hospital with a gunshot wound you guys gave her. I want to see her."

"Oh. Hold on." He scuttered away pulling his radio out again. The words that followed were half whispers that echoed along the corridor, indecipherable. Then he was there again, smiling. "The chief is rounding up some media people, so you and I have to wait here. And here's the good news: your daughter is in the ICU and doing fine; the surgery was flawless and she'll be back on her feet in a matter of a week, so I've been told. She's heavily sedated right now and wouldn't respond to your presence anyway." He lowered his eyebrows while maintaining the smile, a strange effect. "You really should be in bed, Mr. Thorwald. Look at you."

Hank stared at him. Media people? "I think I'll just mosey to the lobby and buy a newspaper. Hopefully I won't scare anyone."

The policeman shifted his weight and scratched the side of his head. "The chief's on the way. You have to be here when he gets here."

"I'll be right back." Hank jingled the coins in his pocket. "Got exact change, it won't take long."

"I'll have somebody else get you a paper, sir. You really should stay right here."

"Nonsense," Hank said. "I've been cooped up in there forever, it's way too stuffy and I'm allergic to something." He took a couple of steps to the right. "A box of Kleenex wouldn't hurt, either. I'll ask the nurses."

"Okay, stop right there," the young man finally said. "Get back in your room."

Hank turned. "What are the charges?"

"Assault on an officer times three."

"So you guys tied me up."

"Not me personally."

"So now your chief is on the way to pardon me face to face. Oops, we put a bullet through your daughter's chest, but we will make up for it by dropping the charges against you. And he's bringing TV and radio and newspapers and a couple of satellite feeds to record the ceremony."

"I don't make policy, I follow orders." His expression darkened so drastically that Hank thought it must be a subject taught at the police academy. "You either get back in your room or I propel you there. End of discussion."

Hank had no energy to invest in a battle of wills. He turned and bumped the door open with his shoulder, his eyes catching sight of the stark black number 314 stenciled on the wood. It might as well be the words "County Jail"; he was incarcerated here and the only other way out was the window, but if this was room number 314 it was located on the third floor and a long way up from the ground. Hank crossed to it, and with a clattering snap hauled the venetian blinds as high as they would go. He pressed his forehead to the rain-spattered glass. The sky was dismal and low over the rear of the hospital grounds, fog made the hedges gray, the trees looked miserable as they stood there sifting the rain into bigger drops. He flipped a latch on the aluminum window frame and was surprised by how easily the two big panes slid apart. Warm air gusted in, smelling of the paper mill over on the western side of town. He stuck his head out and looked down. Grass growing all the way to the foundation of the building, the healthiest and greenest grass he had seen in years. Maybe a man could hang from the window and let himself drop down onto that grass, he supposed. Question was, how far did that man have to crawl to get his broken ankles repaired?

Probably just to the other side of the hospital. Hank slapped the window shut and turned around. There was no need to escape, the chief would come here to do whatever he had in mind, Hank would be released with official apologies for their having almost killed his daughter. Maybe even be driven home in the chief's own police cruiser. So better, then, just to lie low and wait. He was grumpily ambling to the bed when he noticed two things: one, the gauze that enclosed parts of him had grown blots of blood where his skin had cracked open. Two, there was a folded piece of paper on the bed where the pillow had been. Neither event brought much joy, event number one telling him he would soon be hurting pretty badly when the scabs started to form, event number two piquing his interest only slightly. He opened the paper and was shocked to see Rebecca's handwriting. Automatically, he crushed it in his fist and glanced at the room door. Still closed. He jogged into the little bathroom and locked the door. Utter darkness. The switch was easy enough to find and he read what she had written. It was short, but it ripped the breath from his lungs.

Hank—
    Sharri is alive. Perry killed himself. I'll be back if they let me.

While he fought to draw a breath, his hand wadded up the pathetic little note, squeezed it hard, and threw it into the toilet. His breathing returned in a croaking wheeze that was almost a sob. That stupid old geezer, that lonely chess-obsessed son of a bitch, had taken his own life, but why? This had all been a monstrous practical joke. You don't kill yourself over a practical joke. Nobody would. Unless . . .

Unless?

Unless it hadn't been a joke after all. Unless it was real, unless he had ruined a man's life with a parlor game that stopped being a game and instead became a horror. Unless Harrison Wayne Thorwald really had been the Führer of Nazi Germany not so very long ago. Even if it were not true, the only man who could disprove it had killed himself.

He pulled the door open. For the sake of his wife and daughter he had to disappear. A new identity in a new town, a new state. At the foot of the bed he jerked up a corner of the mattress. Covering it were two sheets, a woven thermal blanket, one standard hospital-blue blanket thin enough to see through, with a wetness barrier on the reverse side. He ripped them all free of the bed, tossed the pee protector away, then got busy twisting everything into ropes and tying the ends together. The knots he constructed were probably not in the Cub Scout manual, but when he pinned one of the sheets to the floor with his foot and jerked on the other one as hard as he could, a few inches raveled through but the knot tightened steadily to plug up the leak. When the thing was finished, he dragged it to the window like the tail of an enormous kite, constantly twisting it in his hands to keep it wound up, and coiled it in a pile. The hospital was too modern to have exposed pipes or a radiator nearby so, beginning to sweat, his eyes bright and his jaw set, he quietly rolled the bed to the window. He knotted one end of his creation around a leg of the bed, rose, and slid the window panes apart. With a grunt he heaved the remainder out and poked his head through the window to watch it fall. Better than nothing, maybe a ten-foot drop at the end. Without hesitating he stuffed himself out into the hot, damp air. Some dim future day the world might forget about him. Until then he would run.

With a mental good-bye to everyone he knew and loved, he started down.

25

Karl-Luther von Wessenheim had never in his life seen such desolation. His mental images of Berlin blasted to pieces by the war paled before what he saw from the starboard window seat of United Airlines Flight 922 as it descended for landing at the Boise International Airport. Everything he could see below was lifeless and brown. After flying five miles high over the Midwest, he had watched as the trees and farmlands suddenly ended at the Rocky Mountains to become naked, lifeless prairie that rolled on forever. Thin lines of green sketched the course of an occasional creek in the endless hills. How the displaced Europeans—the early Americans—had spread this far in wagons pulled by oxen he could not imagine. And he honestly could not imagine why they had bothered.

He shifted irritably in his seat. It had taken ten hours to reach New York, five more to Denver, and three more to Boise. How the people traveling in coach could stand it he could not imagine. Even the first-class seats seemed to shrink as the hours and jet engines droned on; the air lacked oxygen and was hot. Normally he needed three full days to recover from jet lag, but this time there was no time at all. He and Rønna Ulgard were scheduled to board again this evening for the trip back to Berlin. How he would survive another eighteen hours in the air von Wessenheim did not know. Not to mention the stopovers, the reboarding, the dark and dirty shuttle buses at JFK in New York where you could get robbed at gunpoint, the standing in line for customs with his heavy suitcase in one hand and his briefcase in the other—he was getting too old for this.

Under a fierce white sun, as the aircraft banked, Boise slid into view. The city looked like a handful of broken glass thrown against the base of a mountain range, the last outpost of western civilization. He looked at his watch. They should have landed five minutes ago.

"Here at last," he said, leaning slightly to speak to Rønna Ulgard in the next seat. "Quite a trip."

Ulgard did not reply. For the last three hours he had been reclined in his seat with his eyes masked behind dark glasses, a tiny headphone stuck in each ear. Thin black wires disappeared under his jacket and into, von Wessenheim supposed, a small cassette machine that played his favorite music. His hands in their tight black gloves lay solemnly on his lap. Irritated, von Wessenheim prodded his shoulder with a couple of fingers.

Ulgard turned his head. "What is it?"

"We're landing."

He pulled his seat upright and plucked the tiny speakers from his ears. Von Wessenheim caught a few strange words that sounded like Russian buzz from them before they were stuffed away. Maybe, he thought, maybe this was how he learned his languages, with tapes from Berlitz or Langenscheidt. Never a wasted moment, always busy. Von Wessenheim felt a twitch of envy pluck at his self-confidence. Ulgard was visibly twenty years his junior, not one gray strand in the mane of inky black hair that swept back from his hairline and down to the nape of his neck. So much younger, a man without a drop of royal Germanic blood in any of his veins, but a man who knew what had to be done in order to succeed.

The United Airlines first-class steward ambled by inspecting laps. "Fasten your seat belt, please," he stopped to say. In that moment von Wessenheim lost all grasp of the English language and sat open-mouthed, on the verge of a reply that didn't seem likely to come.

"*Sicherheitsgurt,*" Rønna Ulgard said. "*Zuschliessen.*"

"Yes, thank you," von Wessenheim said to the steward, and fished under his buttocks for the seat belt while his face grew hot. In England he could make his way, but these Americans spoke too fast and blurred every word into the next one, they barely moved their lips when they talked and were often mystified when confronted by a foreigner. He clicked the seat belt together and turned his attention back to the window. . The landing gear gave an alarming clunk underneath as it fell into place and the jet suddenly sank faster than his stomach could. He pressed a fist to his chest, holding the day's intake of airline food down, and watched Boise rise up. The roofs of the houses were white whereas the roofs in Germany were red. He had been in America before but most of his dealings had been in New York, a few times in Chicago, once in Philadelphia, and once in Baton Rouge, where the humidity was so terrible that the wallpaper in his hotel room was peeling off the walls and cockroaches the size of bratwursts prowled the corners.

Below the aircraft, trees were evident now. The center of the city featured a few skyscrapers and streets that marched sensibly in orderly squares out to the suburbs, where even in such vastness the houses crowded each other for room. He leaned back and endured the fright of landing with his eyes closed. When he received a nudge from Rønna Ulgard he bumbled to his feet, aware that he had dozed for a few precious seconds, and groggily stumped along behind him into the airport. While the other people from the flight straggled to the escalators, Ulgard found a stairway to the street-level exit as surely as if he had been here before. As they stepped outside, von Wessenheim was blinded by the sun bouncing off the cars in the parking areas, and nearly felled by the shimmering heat. "My God," he groaned, chasing after Ulgard while gasping from the thin air.

A stretch of six taxis waited outside, several an ugly yellow color no European would dare paint his cab. The driver sat unmoving while they got inside, snapping gum between his teeth. The car smelled strongly of spearmint.

Ulgard leaned forward. "We have two bags bearing the name von Wessenheim. Please get them from the luggage carousel for us."

Von Wessenheim concentrated on understanding the English. "I drive a cab," the man said to the windshield. "You need a skycap."

Ulgard reached an arm over the seat. "One suitcase and a leather briefcase. We will wait here."

The driver got out and was gone. Von Wessenheim wondered how big the tip was, probably an American ten- or twenty-dollar note. Now Ulgard brought out a notepad and began leafing through the pages. Von Wessenheim leaned his head back against the seat and slowly felt his breast pocket for his Reemstmas. There was nearly a whole pack left because one could no longer enjoy a smoke on flights in the USA, as if flying itself wasn't sufficient punishment.

There was a "No Smoking" sticker in the cab. Von Wessenheim lit up anyway and stuck the cigarette out the window. "This day will kill me," he muttered.

"And it will be over soon enough," Ulgard replied. Von Wessenheim could not see behind the sunglasses, but he suspected they disguised the man's contempt. In his life Ulgard had probably endured worse things than an eighteen-hour flight, but he was not as old, did not suffer from allergies and chronic infections that sapped one's strength. And he didn't smoke two packs of Reemstmas a day.

The cabbie was back just as von Wessenheim dropped his cigarette to the curb. When the bags were in the trunk, he jumped back in. Though he sniffed the air and gave von Wessenheim a disapproving eye, he seemed eager to please. "Where to, men?"

Rønna Ulgard had torn a page from his notepad. "Here is the address."

He took it. "You got it, pal."

"I am not your pal. Just get us there."

Von Wessenheim glanced at Ulgard. James Bond, he found himself thinking. James Bond with a bad attitude.

"Very well, sir."

Off they went. Von Wessenheim blinked against the coarse grains of sleep in his eyes, rubbed them with the backs of his hands and wished to God he had brought sunglasses. It was no wonder that the land here was brown and dead; it got incinerated daily. Hot air was blasting through his open window so he rolled it up and let his head fall against the glass. For one hour of solid sleep he would give half his fortune. For eight hours he would give it all.

Ulgard jabbed him with a finger. Von Wessenheim turned. Ulgard wordlessly passed him a tiny plastic packet with some brown-orange crystals in it. He made motions of inserting a pinch of them into his nostrils, then inhaling. Von Wessenheim balked, but gave in after some thought. He sniffed a pinch of the stuff into each nostril. Pain explored the recesses of his sinus cavities and slowly faded away, leaving him with eyes full of tears.

Ulgard smiled at him. "You'll be feeling better soon."

He was right. By the time the cab pulled to a stop in the middle of a neighborhood of small, neat houses, von Wessenheim had been recharged as neatly as if he had been opened up and had gotten fresh batteries installed. He stood outside the cab seeing things with bright and eager eyes. As Rønna Ulgard paid the driver and collected the luggage, he walked up the sidewalk that led to the front stoop of a white clapboard house. His heart, already galloping, gave a lurch. Inside, a former German soldier waited, one of the last to fight in Berlin, one of three young men sent to collect gasoline with which to burn the Führer's corpse. If anyone knew the truth, he did. But would he tell it?

Ulgard caught up as von Wessenheim rapped on the door. The curtains were swept back to reveal a wizened old face topped with a curl of white hair that rose from the old man's scalp like a plume of steam. "What do you want?" he demanded. "Who are you?"

"I am Karl-Luther von Wessenheim, and this is the man you spoke with on the telephone," von Wessenheim said in English. "You are expecting us."

"What's that?"

Von Wessenheim tried the answer in German: "*Ich bin Karl-Luther von Wessenheim aus Deutschland! Sie erwarten uns!*"

"Germans? Are you Germans?"

Rønna Ulgard put the luggage down and nudged von Wessenheim aside. He tried the doorknob but found it locked. With quick sleight-of-hand, he had a thin piece of plastic slightly larger than a credit card between his gloved fingers. With a simple click the door wafted open. "Calm down," he shouted to the old man as he pushed inside. "We're here with your money."

Von Wessenheim's eyes took in the house of a man who had fought for his country and then left it forever. Small and quaint and hot, framed pictures of children and infants on the walls, sensible furniture and a wooden cuckoo clock hanging on a decorative chain. An indefinable smell was present, the scent of an old house housing an old man whose bladder control was questionable. Almost as an afterthought he retrieved the bags from the doorstep. There had been no way to smuggle a briefcase full of money through customs, but a cashier's check drawn at the EuroBank Zentral was no problem. Hopefully, the old man still had enough wits about him to recognize it as money.

This Gerhard Brunner had lost his fright and was beginning to understand as the memory visibly bubbled from the depths of his elderly brain. Dressed in baggy jeans and a T-shirt with a cartoon cat on the chest, he did not look the slightest like a former soldier of the feared German army. "Show it to me," he said in English as he dropped himself onto the room's little sofa. Von Wessenheim went to a chair with the briefcase and twirled the locks to the proper combination, opened it, and withdrew the small manila envelope. "In here," he said in English. "Your money."

"One hundred thousand dollars, is it?"

"One hundred thousand Deutschmarks."

He looked over to Rønna Ulgard. "Which one of you was on the phone?"

While von Wessenheim sought to understand the language, Ulgard spoke up. "Can you still speak any German, old man?"

He sat up straighter. "*Ja. Natürlich.*"

"Then let's stick with it." He glanced at von Wessenheim, then away. "My client would like to hear your recollections of the day when you and two others were ordered by the SS to collect gasoline to bring to the Reich's Chancellery in

April of 1945. You have told me that you remember that day clearly."

"And I do." He stood and tottered to the open door, shut it. "You get as old as I am and you forget what you did two minutes before, but the old memories are cast in stone. I was there on that day."

"Fine." Ulgard nodded to von Wessenheim. "He is yours."

"Please sit down again," von Wessenheim said. The crazy stuff he had inhaled was making him jittery. Sweat was trying to break free of his hairline. It was win or lose now, his money was on the table, he would either leave this house elated or leave it in despair, but in either event leave it one hundred thousand Deutschmarks poorer. He closed the briefcase and slid it off his lap to the floor. "Tell me what happened the day Hitler died."

"Coffee first?" Gerhard Brunner asked. His cuckoo clock suddenly began to squawk as the cuckoo flipped in and out bearing its message ten miserable times. Hanging on its chains, the entire clock swayed back and forth. The drug was acting strangely on von Wessenheim, or else the heat and the thin air; the noise was magnified and his heart was pounding at a furious clip.

"No coffee," Rønna Ulgard said. "Continue."

"I was one of the last survivors of my unit. We had all been either killed or separated by the crazy nature of the fighting—from street to street, jumping this way and that to close the leaks as the Russians advanced into the city, trying to kill as many of them as we could. We were outnumbered twenty-five to one, the war was lost and utterly hopeless, but if you admitted it aloud the military police would either shoot you or hang you. The city was demolished, much of it was on fire. There was no food or water, the dead lay where they fell, it was a warm day and the flies buzzed over them in clouds. Dead horses were in the streets, the civilians were carving them up for food. It was the end of civilization, the end of the world. We had no fear of dying because everyone else was dead, and with Germany erased from the map we had no reason to live. Or so we felt."

"Terrible," von Wessenheim said, trying to imagine it but unable to.

"Then in the early afternoon came an SS lieutenant. He gave three of us two jerry cans each and told us to fill them with gasoline from the cars. He waited, hiding in the rubble while we ducked and dodged the artillery fire. Shrapnel nicked my ankle and the bottom of my boot filled up with blood."

He began removing his shoe. When the sock was peeled off, von Wessenheim observed a flat area that replaced the jut of the man's left outer anklebone. "Hurt like hell. Didn't heal for months because the Russians made me walk from Berlin all the way up to Siberia. A thousand miles with this thing infected. If I had lagged behind the other prisoners, the Russians would have shot me. So I did not lag."

He lapsed into silence as he pulled his sock and shoe back on. When he relaxed again his eyes tried to drift shut.

"Herr Brunner!" Rønna Ulgard snapped. "Please tell Herr von Wessenheim about the day the Führer was cremated."

"Yes, indeed. When we had filled our cans, the lieutenant led us to an enormous building that had been heavily damaged by artillery and rocket fire. I was a boy from a backward village in Bavaria, I did not know that it was the *Reichskanzlei* and if I had known, I still would not have known what its function was. We were told to stand by."

Von Wessenheim raised a finger. "Herr Brunner, I have read that the gasoline was brought to the Reich's Chancellery the day *before* that, under Hitler's orders as preparation for his death."

Gerhard Brunner stared into his eyes. "That is not true. I remember it clearly."

"So you say you collected the gasoline on the very *day* that the Führer killed himself."

Brunner nodded his white head. "That is what I am saying. Where in that area would you store six big cans of gasoline overnight? They would cause a terrible fire if hit by shrapnel or a bullet."

Von Wessenheim swallowed. Here was a fact no one else

had ever bothered with; people had told the Allied interrogators that the gas had been collected the previous day. From his research, and with the grudging help of Konrad Rudiger and that silly woman Friedl von Lütringen, von Wessenheim knew that the idea had never been contested in the history books. A single jerry can held perhaps ten liters, and six of them held sixty. A hot bit of shrapnel would ignite one and then the heat would explode them all; the area above Hitler's bunker would have been a firestorm. The air vents would have sucked it in, fumes and panic would have emptied the bunker.

"I choose to believe you," he said to Brunner. "But have you ever disclosed this to anyone else?"

"I have."

He felt an emotion as heavy as a stone form in his brain and drop into his guts. "So I guess it is common knowledge and nothing new."

The old man leaned forward, licking his lips, his eyes blue and bright. "The SS lieutenant identified me and one other who was still alive, and we were quickly interrogated by the Russians. We said that we drained the gasoline, that we delivered it and went back to the fighting until we were captured, and knew nothing further."

"So then you lied to them," von Wessenheim said, relieved. "You said you brought the gasoline the day before."

"No. The *Russians* said I brought the gasoline the day before. In a very short time, I decided they were right."

Von Wessenheim pressed his shaking hands together. "So the Russians set up a conspiracy of lies. Stalin wanted proof that Hitler was dead, and they made up a story to provide it. You were forced to take part."

Gerhard Brunner focused his eyes on him, his tongue dabbing at his lips. "Are you a reporter?"

"Absolutely not," von Wessenheim answered.

"A writer, then? A historian? I have spoken to them before. They ask me if I did more than collect the gasoline, and I tell them, truthfully, I am only Gerhard Brunner and no, I did not do anything but that. Soon they lose interest in me because the role I played was insignificant. They always look for important people and I am not important, they will not pay me for answers because they have no questions. You, sir, are the first person willing to pay for my testimony. Give me the money."

Von Wessenheim still had the envelope in his hands, but he hesitated. "Herr Brunner, am I buying the truth, or am I buying lies?"

He smiled slightly. "I have been interrogated by the Russians and the British and the Americans and even the Israeli Secret Service. Never once have I been interrogated by a German."

Von Wessenheim tapped the envelope nervously on the wooden arm of the chair. "Patriotism from a German who became an American?"

"The Germany I fought for died in the war. It is still dead." He pointed at the envelope. "Give me the money."

Rønna Ulgard gave a small nod: go ahead. Von Wessenheim stood and put it in the man's trembling hand. "You drive a hard bargain, my friend."

"In this country, if you are old and have no health insurance, you are a dead duck. *This* is my insurance now."

"Very well." Von Wessenheim sat again. "Tell me what you have told no one else."

Brunner took a breath and coughed into his fist. "Ahem. On the thirtieth of April, 1945, I arrived at the Reich's Chancellery at about three in the afternoon. With two others I stood by, not knowing what was going on. Mortar fire from the Russians occasionally burst nearby, so many times we had to flatten ourselves on the ground. I still remember the sour smell of the rotting leaves under my face—they had all been blown from the trees by bombings. All at once a Wehrmacht colonel came and ordered us to open our cans, so we did. About a minute later two SS soldiers in black uniforms came out carrying a corpse. It was wrapped in a cloth, but a fancy woman's dress was hanging out. They put her on a concrete slab that had a door in it, one of the entrances, I figured out, to the Führer's underground bunker. Then, immediately, two others came out with another body wrapped in a blanket. It was heavily soaked with blood. When they set it beside the woman, another man in civilian dress knelt and lifted the blanket momentarily. I saw two remarkable things at that moment."

"Two things?" Von Wessenheim's breathing was becoming labored. "What two things?"

"I saw the man insert a wire with several teeth on it into the mouth of the corpse."

Von Wessenheim sat bolt upright. "What was that? What was that?"

"I saw the man open the jaw of the corpse and place a wire, with several teeth attached to it, into the dead man's mouth."

"My God," von Wessenheim wheezed. "To skew the dental records!"

"And in that moment," Brunner went on, "I saw the dead man's face and some of his clothing. Then, abruptly, one of the SS officers shouted at us to leave, even pulled his pistol out and waved it. And that was it. By the time I looked back, they were dumping all that gasoline onto the bodies."

Von Wessenheim tried to speak but could not, every trace of saliva in his mouth and throat had turned to dust. "You . . . ," he croaked. "You saw . . ."

"I'll get you some water," Rønna Ulgard said, rising. Von Wessenheim jumped to his feet and advanced on the old man with his hands outstretched and shaking. "Whose face?" he rasped, rocking on his feet. "Whose?"

"The face was bloody, but I know what I saw. I knew our Führer's face from the newsreels; with his little mustache he had a very distinctive look."

Von Wessenheim dropped to his knees, his vision blurring while the room spun in wild circles. "Who was it?" he screamed. *"Tell me!"*

"It was— Are you all right?" Brunner turned. "Hurry with that water!"

Von Wessenheim got two fists full of Brunner's cartoon-cat T-shirt and dragged him closer. *"Tell me! Tell me!"*

Brunner tore free of his hands. "It was a dead German soldier, damn you! Not Adolf Hitler at all, just a dead German soldier!"

Von Wessenheim fainted.

26

Something nudged Rebecca. She smiled and rolled slightly in her sleep. A dream had crafted a new world for her, a soft and pastel world no bigger than the backyard of her home, in which Sharri had butterfly wings that flashed and sparkled under the sunlight. Rise up, Rebecca was telling her. You can fly!

"Mrs. Thorwald?"

Another nudge. It was then that she realized she was asleep, and knew she was about to wake up to a world as loveless and cold as the touch of a dinosaur's claw. When the dream fragmented she woke up with a scream.

"I'm so *sorry!*" a voice told her. She struggled to sit up. The bench under her was hard despite its orange padding and was hopelessly small; how she had slept at all was a miracle called exhaustion. When she was finally upright, something felt cold on her face and she jerked an arm to swipe away some drool from the side of her mouth.

It was the nice and very sympathetic nurse who had accompanied her into intensive care to see Sharri. "There is a policeman here who says he needs to talk to you," she said.

"They found Hank?"

"Oh now, honey, I don't know. But it does seem to be important."

She stood up. Every muscle involved groaned while she swayed on her feet. A groggy run of her tongue across her teeth told her that their unfamiliar coating was getting thicker.

"He was going to wake you up, but I said you needed a

gentler touch. Are you in any shape to talk to him now?"

She wiped her eyes and nodded. An attempt to comb her fingers through her hair was cut short by snarls as dense as wool. "I'll do my best," she croaked. The nurse waved a hand overhead. Rebecca turned to watch as a man stepped out of the corridor into the ICU waiting room, waving an arm as well. Through the film of sleep over her eyes, Rebecca at first thought the approaching shape and color was the chief of police, and her hackles rose. Something about that man was creepy. But when she blinked again it was just a guy in regular clothes, jeans and a gray sweatshirt with the sleeves torn off. "Sorry for the late hour," he said when he was close enough. "Your message got relayed to me, and I'm here with the results. And a couple of questions."

Rebecca was not aware of any message she'd left. "Did you find Hank?"

"Not yet. But I'm sure he's okay. Shall we sit down?" He glanced at the nurse, who got the message and went away. "The way I see it, if Hank was able to climb down a three-story building, he can handle himself in the world. Sit?"

She sat on the bench across from him and folded her arms. "As far as I know, he might not have any money on him, nothing but credit cards to live on. No clothes but what's on his back, no pain medicine for his burns, no—"

"We cancelled his credit cards, Mrs. Thorwald. May I call you Rebecca?"

She eyed him flatly. "No you may not. And there's no way you could cancel them since you don't even know what he's carrying." She offered him a tight little smile. "And why would you do that, anyway?"

He raised his eyebrows. "There was an unlocked fireproof strongbox in your den that contained all the credit card names and numbers to call in case of a lost card."

She stood up. "I hope to God you had a search warrant, Mister."

"Steven Gleeworth, actually. Detective Steven Gleeworth. And yes, I did."

She sat down again. "But why? Do you want him to starve out there?"

"Absolutely not. We want him in custody for his own safety." He raised his head and sniffed the air. "Do you ever get used to that smell? It's like rubbing alcohol and bales of cotton."

She offered him a shrug. Who cared how the place smelled?

"There are a lot of weird people arriving in Terre Haute by the minute, Mrs. Thorwald. There's a huge crowd outside the hospital as we speak, an army of oddballs. A third of them want to hang him, another third want to put him on trial first and *then* hang him, and the rest either want to gun him down or take him back to Idaho to be their Führer. We've got neo-Nazi thugs and Jewish Defense League heavies fighting in the streets, and television crews from as far away as Israel and Russia filming everything that moves."

"Do they know he's not here anymore?"

"They do not, which keeps *them* occupied and Mr. Thorwald safer. As soon as he tries to use a credit card, we'll instantly get the location from the FBI computers."

Rebecca's spine tightened and she tipped forward a few inches. "The FBI? When did this become a federal case?"

"It's not. We're just accessing their computer." He clasped his hands together between his knees. "Mrs. Thorwald, I don't think you understand the scope of this thing. A lot of people want to know who they were in a past life, even if they don't believe in such stuff. Most of the time they like to think they were Cleopatra or George Washington, important historical figures. Then along comes a man who out of the blue tells the world he used to be Hitler, then speaks fluent German that he has no knowledge of and recites some historical details most people don't know, such as Hitler having been an ordinary foot soldier in World War One. I personally think reincarnation is bullshit, but this is powerful evidence, powerful enough to sway me if I had to decide yes or no, yes, reincarnation is real or no, it is not."

"So which is it?" she asked bitterly.

He took a long breath. "I honestly don't know anymore."

She lowered her head. Tears filled her eyes with stinging warmth and she dropped her face into her hands. A gush of sobbing bent her over until her chin was at her knees. Everyone was deserting Hank; people who had known him for years, friends and relatives, were remaining as distant and unspeaking as the Mars rover that had fascinated Hank until it was frozen into silence by the cruelties of that world. She was aware of the detective moving to sit beside her as she wept, and felt his hand on her shoulder. She tried to shrug it away but could not.

"Listen to me," he said. "Maybe I used to be Vlad the Impaler in a past life. It's an interesting idea, but it speaks nothing about who I am now."

She jerked her head up. "Listen to yourself!" she hissed at him. "Did Jesus say anything about living many lives? Aren't we all Christians, practicing or not? And Jews, practicing or not? Where does it say in the Old Testament or the Torah or whatever they read at their church that Abraham or Isaac or King David was reincarnated? It doesn't. All those people out there are junking their beliefs in the hope that Hank *was* Adolf Hitler. They want it to be true because it proves that when we die we don't stay dead."

"Good point." He moved back to where he had been sitting before. "The ultimate proof that we live forever. Even Hitler gets a second chance at life."

The nurse had given Rebecca a handful of tissues, which she had jammed into a pocket of her jeans. Now she tugged them out and unfolded one. "My faith in my church alone is strong enough to let me believe in eternal life." She blew her nose and mashed the tissue into a ball. "Did you know that Hank was an ostrich a couple of minutes before he became a Nazi?"

The detective's face was becoming tinged with a reddish color and his eyes seemed to favor his knees. "I just work the logistical angle, really, I study crime scenes and construct scenarios, try to figure out the criminal's next move, if there is one." He looked up. "Please accept my apology, Mrs. Thorwald. I didn't know about the ostrich stuff."

"So I guess your crime scene here is a hospital room where a former ostrich flew out the window."

Steven Gleeworth tapped a couple of fingers against his

forehead. "I still have questions, Mrs. Thorwald. Questions whose answers might help us find Hank, help us protect him. If you don't mind?"

"I do," she said sourly.

He repositioned himself. "Seriously here."

She took a breath. "Okay, sorry."

"Fine. Where do you think he might be headed? Any idea?"

She shook her head. "No idea. Just running."

"No favorite hiding places? A log cabin in the mountains?"

"There are no mountains in Indiana."

"Figuratively speaking."

"To my knowledge Hank doesn't have any safe havens, which I think is what you mean."

He bounced his head up and down a few times. "Does he have any relatives living nearby?"

"Nearby? Some. Aunts and uncles, cousins."

"A close-knit family?"

"The most he could expect from them at this point would be a sack lunch handed through a crack in the door on a stick."

The detective smiled. "Sounds like my own clan. Does Hank have any really close friends, even old high school buddies, who would take him in on a moment's notice?"

She deliberated. "Maybe one, a friend he had in college, but he lives out west now."

"Do you know where?"

"Colorado, I'm pretty sure. Someplace close to Denver. Loveland, I think."

"His name?"

Rebecca slapped her hands down onto her knees. "If I can recall from our Christmas cards, his name is Hector Romero, he married a coed named Gwen who's already popped out four kids while Hank has only the single fruit of my womb, the girl in ICU who is fighting for her life right now because of a bullet you cops shot into her chest."

"Even though I wasn't there, you've got my apologies. Where did Hank grow up?"

"Right here in Terrible Hole, Indiana."

"What about his mother and father? Still alive?"

She nodded.

"Live nearby?"

"Fort Wayne, which isn't exactly nearby. We hardly ever see them."

"And your parents?"

"Gone. Our garage was full of their stuff before it all burned up. They're roaming America in an RV as big as Moby Dick, looking for a place to retire."

"Have they tried to contact you about this?"

"They don't know anything about it, unless they read cheap tabloid newspapers, which they don't."

He looked at her sharply. "You haven't seen TV?"

She cocked her head quizzically. "Local stuff. Or?"

"It went national," he told her. "As soon as Sharri got shot."

Her shoulders slumped. This was bad news, but she found she could bear it because the *worst* news in the world could only be delivered by a doctor coming out of the ICU to inform her that Sharri had died. So the news that the Thorwald family saga had gone nationwide was just another lash from the same whip that had lashed them before. "Big fucking deal," she coughed out from the bottom of her throat.

"I'm sorry. But it emphasizes why I need to know all these details about Hank's life. He's in grave danger no matter where he runs, because if somebody recognizes him it won't be long before a lynch mob gets together. I don't have to tell you how unpopular Hitler is."

She raised her head. "Hank is not Hitler, Mr. Detective. He's an intelligent and gentle man, and as far from an evil dictator as you can get. This whole thing is not only preposterous, but an obvious setup."

"By Perry Wilson."

"Yes."

"I hope you realize that it's not part of my job to find out if Hank was really Hitler or not. My job is simply to find out where he went, and bring him back."

Rebecca let out a sigh. "Then I guess I should wish you luck."

He frowned. She saw that he had begun twisting his hands. "Maybe you shouldn't, Mrs. Thorwald."

"Rebecca is fine," she said. A frown to match his own was sculpting her face. "What do you mean?"

He pulled his hands apart. "I'm treating your husband as a suspect in the disappearance of Perry Wilson, Rebecca. The only suspect, actually. No one else has the remotest motive for doing him harm, as things stand right now. He hasn't been seen or heard from since the night of the party, so the conclusion is obvious."

She stared at him. Strange little pricks were prodding the bottom of her stomach, an unusual case of stinging butterflies.

"I've talked to his neighbors and relatives, and all they know is that he's gone. I've checked the bus lines and the airlines, wandered the university, I've been inside his house twice." He lifted a hand and snapped his fingers in front of his face. "Nothing. But I think your husband knows exactly where Perry Wilson went."

After a blank moment she finally understood the butterflies and the stinging: she was going to laugh. She was going to sit right here while this vile bastard accused Hank Thorwald of murder, and scream a good long foghorn blast of laughter into his face. But her more sober side reminded her that this was the ICU waiting room, people like her had sat here over the years wondering if loved ones were going to live or die; it was sacrosanct, in its own way.

"When were you there?" she asked him, one hand cupped around her throat. "Today?"

He lowered his eyebrows into a straight brown line. "No, yesterday."

She clapped her other hand over her mouth. Tears wanted to stream from her eyes and her stomach muscles were tightening in and out: laughter without sound. It had only been this very morning when she'd found the secret entrance to Perry's dismal, hole-in-the-wall basement. The memory of his tortured blue face was branded eternally into her mind but this cop, this local Terre Haute detective who had probably learned his trade through a correspondence course that did not even offer Ostrich 101, he had failed to look under the

Persian rug that hung over the basement door. And he dared to think that Hank had killed Perry.

She uncovered her mouth. The insanely inappropriate urge to laugh was rapidly being replaced by the urge to see this fool gone. "I have a hot tip for you," she said. "Go back to Perry's house one more time. Enter the den, which looks like a library with all the books falling off the shelves, and then turn your head to the left. You will see the door to the basement that I left open earlier this morning. Walk carefully down the stairs, which are steep. Prepare yourself for a big surprise." She flashed him a broad and ugly smile full of unbrushed teeth. "You might even get a promotion."

He lowered his eyes, then quickly raised them. "We're not enemies here," he said softly.

She bent toward him. "Oh yes we are. Ten zillion people think Hank was Hitler, and one detective-cop thinks he's a murderer. I'm his wife of twelve years and I am officially declaring war on you." She reached out and took hold of his shoulders. Haltingly, he rose up as she did. "You say there's an army of people down there, right? Then you go down and tell them that Rebecca Thorwald declares war on them. If they want World War Three, they've got it."

His face was a solid block. "What will I find at Perry Wilson's house?"

Motion tugged her eyes to the right. A nurse was jogging up the hallway with the stethoscope that was draped around her neck bouncing rapidly in time to her steps. She cut hard to the left and banged through the ICU's double doors. Sudden fear made Rebecca weightless as she dumped everything from her mind and bounded into the corridor. The doors were still swinging when she plowed through them.

The light was so dim compared to the waiting room that she could see only the shapes of the patients under the green-and-blue glow of the machines that were working to keep them alive, could faintly hear the clicks and beepings that indicated success. She saw that the nurse was bent over the bed Sharri had been placed in. A small monitor was displaying a straight green line where Rebecca assumed the pointy peaks of a healthy heartbeat should show, *beep beep beep*. Her only knowledge of these machines was from doctor shows on TV but it was safe to assume that they had no reason to lie.

Sharri was dying. Rebecca mashed her hands over her mouth to stifle a scream; at the same moment she was struck from behind and knocked off her feet. On her hands and knees, she watched as people in white lab coats poured into the ICU. "Get her out of here!" someone shouted. Hands were instantly in her armpits and she was jerked erect, then dragged out of the room. She struggled, desperate to see over the heads of these doctors and nurses.

"You're better off out here," Steven Gleeworth said in her ear as he pulled her along.

"You let me go!" she screamed, thrashing. From the sides of her eyes she was aware of other people, other visitors to this house of horrors. They were shrinking back from her with their eyes large and frightened. Detective Gleeworth clamped a hand over her mouth and dragged her into an elevator. With the toe of one sneaker, he punched the button that closed the doors.

"Now cut loose," he said, and released her.

Briefly she went at the doors, slapping them with her open hands and screaming Sharri's name, but hysteria was not her style and it soon wore thin. She reassembled her dignity and turned to face the detective. "I'm done."

"Fine." He poked the button with the big *L* on it. "You and I are going to the cafeteria to wait this out. You probably haven't eaten in days so I'm going to at least jam a doughnut and a glass of milk down your throat before we go back upstairs. Agreed?"

Rebecca clasped her hands under her chin. "What if she dies?"

"That's never an easy question to answer. All we can do while the doctors work on her is hope. Just hope."

"And pray," she said. "I have to pray."

"There's a chapel on the same floor. We can take care of both."

"Pray first," she said. "Prayers are more from the heart when you're fasting."

He took her elbow and escorted her toward the chapel. The

corridor was surprisingly busy, and a good 10 percent of the people were uniformed police. "Mrs. Thorwald? Rebecca?"

"Mmm?" She was distracted, wondering when the last time had been that she had used her rosary, and where it might be.

"Since we're coming from the heart here, would you like to tell me what I'm going to find at Perry Wilson's house? Maybe save me a trip?"

"It won't save you a trip," she said as they walked, "but I will tell you. This morning I found Perry in his basement with a plastic bag over his head."

"Suicide?"

"Yes. His hands weren't tied and he could have yanked the thing off at any time."

Detective Gleeworth's stride faltered, then quit. "Tough way to go. Lots of willpower needed to do that."

She stopped. "He was a tough old guy."

"Of course, I guess somebody could pin his hands behind his back after they got the bag over his head. He'd pass out in thirty seconds, less if he'd been fighting for his life and was out of breath."

She faced him. "Hank is no killer. Not in a million years."

"I guess we'll see." He turned and walked away, leaving Rebecca to find the chapel on her own. Instead, she waited until his head was no longer bobbing among all the others, then backtracked to the elevator. After a handful of unbearable seconds ticked past and the doors remained closed, she chugged along the hallway looking for a stairwell, found one, and took the stairs three at a time. At the third floor she slammed against the heavy metal door and burst into the hallway, then stopped. The wallpaper around the ICU was pink stripes on white, these painted walls were a monotone of beige. With her shoes squeaking rapidly on the waxed linoleum, she sprinted to her left.

She began to weep as she ran, alone and abandoned and reduced to this crazy search for her dying daughter. She skidded around a corner and saw only more corridor, not a human being in sight; there were huge and somehow frightening pipes running overhead that were painted the same color as the walls. Near the middle of the abandoned corridor a little electric arrow showed the way to an exit and she took its advice, banging through the metal door just to find herself on another stairway. She hesitated, looking up and looking down through a blur of tears while the door clanged shut behind her. This was crazy, she knew, she was lost in a building full of people on the inside and an army of people on the outside. No air-conditioning had been reserved for the stairwells and a line of sweat trickled down her forehead as she loped down the steps. At the next landing she armed it away and peered through the little rectangle of glass set in the door. Pink-and-white wallpaper—there was the waiting room from which she had just been hauled away by a well-meaning detective; it had been the wrong floor after all.

She pushed the door open with forced slowness. In the next few seconds, she was going to learn if Sharri was alive or dead or still halfway between with that flat green line indicating the missing beats of her heart. She walked to the ICU with a keen and awful dread building so heavily in her chest that she had to mash both hands to the crevice between her breasts to keep her heart from stopping. At the ICU door she pushed her face to the glass. Instantly the door banged against her forehead and she leapt back instinctively. The same lab-coated crew that had knocked her to her knees was walking out in a tight bunch. She stayed back as they cruised past her, her heart leaping with fantastic hopes as she took in the sight of their faces. When they were gone she gently pressed the double doors apart and stepped inside.

All the lights had been turned up. The monitor at Sharri's bed still showed a single green line as flat and uninterrupted as a bar of freshly cast steel. As she watched, the display broke apart into twisted bolts of green lightning that faded into utter blackness. With her face as blank as that empty screen, Rebecca staggered to the bed on legs that no longer worked right. A nurse was bent over Sharri, lifting the blanket to either tuck it under her chin or drape it over her dead face.

The voice that came out of Rebecca was a frightened squeak. "Is she dead?"

The nurse jerked and spun around with the blanket still in her fists. It was the woman who had been so kind. "My God, but you scared me!"

"Dead, or not?"

The nurse smiled. "You would not believe the heart attacks we suffered around here. There might have been a power surge or lapse, but anyway, the machine reset itself. First thing in the morning, the hospital administrator is going to get on the horn to the manufacturer. We'd already greased the de-fib paddles to shock her. Thank God for good old-fashioned stethoscopes, huh?"

Rebecca's eyes rolled up into her head and she wilted to the floor, fainting for the second time in her life, the second time this week.

27

Detective Gleeworth drove his own car to the house on Applewild where Perry Wilson lived. During the twenty-minute drive, Gleeworth had tried to imagine a man killing himself by putting his head in a plastic bag. The instinct to breathe was one of the most powerful forces in human physiology, and no human being in all of history had yet been able to commit suicide by simply holding his breath. But along comes Mr. Wilson, a distinguished college professor. In despair over the mistakes in his life, he forgoes pills or razor blades or guns or a rope with which to hang himself. Instead, he decides to end it all by pulling a plastic bag over his head. Then he sits down to watch his last TV show, maybe browses through the family photo albums until the need for air is so great that he, that he . . .

That he rips the fucking bag off his head and thanks God for the sweet, cool air. Nope. Suicide, Gleeworth decided, could not be committed that way. Hell, even guys who hanged themselves probably spent the last few seconds trying to pull themselves up the rope.

So.

His car was a decade away from new and the shocks were bad, it bounced up and down as if the Wilson driveway were a trampoline. He brought it to a stop behind a vintage yellow Chrysler with a serious sprinkling of rust on its big chrome bumper, then got out. He had been here yesterday and had found nothing, but now as he walked to the house he found at least one thing that had changed. A dog had left an enormous turd in the overgrown grass and it was now part of his right shoe. Cursing under his breath, he dragged his foot as he went. He was not a fan of dogs in general and actively hated dogs that shat outdoors. The Gleeworth home was, though, the residence of nine cats who sometimes used the bathtub as a litter box. But they were loving little furballs and the Mrs. didn't mind cleaning up after them.

He hopped up on the stoop and scraped his shoe on the edge of the concrete. Yesterday he had gotten into this house twice by using the key hidden to the left of the stoop under a small red flowerpot that featured a fossilized plant. Now, though, the door hung ajar, the knob area crushed and splintered. Mrs. Thorwald was a very determined lady. With a gentle push of his hand, the broken door swung open.

He went inside. There was the faintest hint of something rotten or moldy in the air now, which he had not smelled yesterday. Rebecca had said go to the den, take a left or a right, look for a Persian rug crumpled on the floor, find a basement. She didn't appear to be any crazier than most women, at least not until her kid flatlined. What the heck, anybody could go bugaboo under stress like that. He had no kids because they weren't all that far removed from having dogs in the house, but someday, yeah. The Mrs. was starting to sweat it pretty bad, had taken to knitting booties and marking off the calendar in chunks of twenty-eight days.

He made his way through the house, pausing once to sniff the air again. Definitely something rotten. He tried to calculate the time necessary, in this heat, for a body to decompose enough to emit a recognizable odor. The party that had taken place here last Friday evening was the start of the Thorwalds' trouble. If Harrison Wayne Thorwald had come back later that same night and killed Perry Wilson, the old bugger would be a hive of maggots by now, as hot as it was. But in the mystery basement, of course, it would be much cooler, fewer flies.

Inside the den he saw that Hitler's wife had ransacked the room. Things that had been on the bookshelves now lay in heaps on the floor and on the furniture, tidal waves of books hung suspended in the act of trying to leave their shelves, braced by the piles below. While standing in the doorway, according to Eva Braun, he was supposed to look to his left, which was handy because a look to his right resulted only in a darkly paneled wall. He stepped inside and picked his way to the room's most obvious feature, two ratty chairs facing each other at a thick table topped by a chessboard. Today, along with all the other changes, one of the chairs had been shoved out of place.

He turned around. His attention dropped to the Persian rug that lay in a heap at the foot of a door that had not been there yesterday. He remembered the rug and its red and purple and yellow colors hanging there, and it had honestly not occurred to him to expect anything hiding behind it. Now that the door stood so easily ajar, it was asking him how come his very own self had not discovered it and he could offer no excuse except lack of precedent. Not since his hippie days had he encountered a rug hanging on a wall.

So Hitler's main squeeze had been here, all right. It would be to her everlasting regret having reported the body, because the body had been murdered by her husband and the Führer of her child, Harrison Wayne Thorwald. That was kind of a Germanic name anyway, come to think of it. Thorwald. *Eins, zwei,* hup, hup.

When he pulled the door open with his elbow, there was a sudden ballooning of the aroma of rotting meat. Bad sign, but it fit the scenario. A light was on down at the foot of the crude wooden stairway. Gleeworth tromped down, readying his mind for what he would see. Festering corpses tended to come alive in one's dreams—they were too ghastly to ever forget—but it helped to have an almost cynical detachment: oh, look at this sorry fucker, the dumb bastard's got maggots in his eyes.

At the bottom he stood in hard-packed dirt. A cricket chirped a brief hello. There was a workbench against a wall with a high-back wicker chair parked in front of it, its back to him. Breathing through his open mouth to avoid the smell, crouched slightly to keep from hitting his head on the heavy wooden joists overhead, Detective Gleeworth shuffled around the chair to take a look at the sorry bastard.

But the sorry bastard wasn't there. Nothing was. Gleeworth used a foot to work the chair back a few feet. Under it, shadowy in the uncertain light, was an enormous mouse trap. He bent closer. Rat trap, it was, and a good one. The pinch bar had mashed the rat straight through the middle and some of its guts had squirted out its mouth. Glistening maggots performed their sluggish dance.

Gleeworth stumbled up the stairs, retching into his hands.

It did not bother him one bit to wake up Rebecca Thorwald again. The clock on the waiting room wall indicated nine-thirty and a wasted day's worth of twilight was painted on the windows in dismal tones of gray and orange. The smell of hospital hung in the air like poison gas. He found her asleep on the same bench, all curled up like a fetus. Someone had found a blanket for her. Her ratty hair and careworn face made her look like she'd spent an hour or two banging around inside a clothes dryer, but he poked her shoulder hard and rudely, enough to bring her awake in a flash.

"Sharri?" she asked, struggling to sit up. "What?"

"Rise and shine," Gleeworth said. "Tell me that basement story again."

Recognition dulled her eyes. "What basement story?"

"How you went down and found Perry Wilson dead."

She tugged the blanket up over her shoulders. "I told you," she said. "I found a door behind a Persian rug, I opened it and went down into the basement. Perry was dead."

"Lying on the floor."

"Sitting in a chair."

"Regular old chair, like a dining room chair?"

"Huh-uh. A big tall wicker chair."

"And he stank? Did he stink real bad?"

She executed a slow and weary shrug. "I don't know. The whole basement smelled funny."

"Like a decomposing human body?"

"I've never smelled a decomposing human body."

"But you've smelled rotten meat."

"Yes, who hasn't? But it wasn't like that, more like moldy."

He took in a breath thoughtfully. "Where was the chair, exactly?"

"There was a workbench or something. The chair was right up against it."

"So you had to turn it around to find the body?"

"I just walked beside it and looked."

"Okay." He slid a hand down his face. She obviously hadn't invented the story, there was no doubt she had discovered the damned basement just as she'd said she had, so either she had hallucinated the dead body with a plastic bag over its head or somebody had gone down there and removed the dead body with a plastic bag over its head. That would mean Mr. Thorwald had done his Spiderman act and immediately made his way to the old professor's house to pick up the body and dispose of it. But on foot?

"How many cars do you and your husband own?" he asked her.

She had let her head fall. "Two. One burned to death at home, the other one burned almost to death and is a few blocks down the street from my house, probably still smoking."

"Would any of your husband's friends loan him a car?"

She craned her head to look up at him with the weirdest expression he had seen in some time. "They won't even open their doors for him, so now you've got them handing him car keys?"

It was a lapse of memory. His face began to redden. "For your information, I was just now at Perry Wilson's house, Mrs. Thorwald. I went down in the basement like you said to but there was nothing in it but an empty chair. Looks like your husband decided to get rid of the body. Did you know he was going to do that?"

She began studying his face, up and down, up and down. After a bit she said, "My daughter is still alive."

Gleeworth's eyes locked somewhere about the level of her chin. When a long chain of seconds had stumbled past, he felt strange, and realized that he was not breathing. "Ah Christ," he said on the exhale, knowing that his face was now red enough to paint a barn with. He dropped down to sit beside her. "I get so fired up about things. Is she going to be all right?"

"It was a glitch in the heart monitor machine," she said. "She's doing fine."

"So the whole thing was bogus?"

She took hold of the edges of the blanket and curled them tightly to her chest. "It probably had a purpose. I think God was shaking me up, slapping me around, reminding me of how easily life comes and goes."

A touch of his embarrassment returned, but it was inward. From the look of things, if God had in mind to shake her up, he had done an outstanding job. "The body you found is no longer there," he said softly. "I know you were tired, exhausted like you are now, and I know you must have been frightened in that spooky old house."

She chuckled, a sound that made him look hard at her and smile. "I've spent a billion years in that spooky old house," she said. "And when I went down in the basement I was mad, not frightened." She lifted both hands and rubbed her eyes, then glanced up at the clock. "But I was jumpy. I was very jumpy."

"What were you expecting to find?"

She tightened into herself, frowning. "I was expecting to find Perry down there wearing a cape and silver earrings like he did at the party, I was expecting him to jump out and say 'Gotcha!' so that the whole thing would be over."

"But he was dead. With his hands untied and a bag over his head."

She drew in a breath. "That is how I found him."

Gleeworth stalled in place, going over things, then felt the internal click that let him know he had gotten all the truth out of someone and there was no more reason to go on. He stood up, sorry now for browbeating the poor woman. "Hey, look," he said, "you're not doing anybody any good hanging around here. Let me drive you home."

She looked up at him. "Home is too dangerous. And for all I know it's been demolished by now."

"Then a motel. You can sleep on a real bed."

She shook her head and offered him a smile. "I need to be here when she wakes up. She's going to be awfully scared."

"What about your job? Do you have a job?"

"I'm on call," she said. "But lately they haven't called."

"Food, then. Did you ever get that doughnut?"

"I'll be fine."

He checked his watch. "Cafeteria's closed. How about Burger Doodle?"

"What's that?"

"You know. Every burger place is pretty much the same, so I call them all Burger Doodle. How about a doodle double cheeseburger and a Coke? French fries? My treat?"

She lowered her eyes. "All I really need is to be with my daughter."

"But if you don't eat something, your little girl won't have a mother left, and nothing is scarier than finding a skeleton in a hospital waiting room."

He was relieved to see her smile. "Worse if it's in a restaurant."

He laughed. "I'll be back before you know it."

He got another smile as acknowledgment. In reality, he wasn't quite the angel of mercy here: food from Burger Doodle would sit a lot better in his stomach than the TV dinner he had planned. "Don't go away," he said.

"Not a chance," she replied.

28

I figure you for a good guy," the truck driver had said. "Glad I picked you up. I don't often take in hikers, not at the rate they hijack you and kill you for the change in your pocket, but I could tell you were needing a ride in a serious way." He pulled a hand from the big steering wheel and offered it. "The name's Bob Manning. Who might you be?"

Hank's brain had popped up a name for him to grab. "Harry Thompson." He shook the man's hand. "Glad you didn't pass me by, Bob."

"Hell." Bob Manning shrugged his shoulders as he bounced on the seat of the big eighteen-wheeler, an open beer between his thighs. His diesel was roaring steadily and in the big rearview mirror Hank could see the exhaust pouring out as black as bat shit and tattering in the wind. The remains of Terre Haute were flashing past, the little town of Brazil and then the big town of Indianapolis were scheduled next. "I figured nobody as banged-up and bandaged as you could be a threat. Looky here."

Hank looked. Bob was digging at his backside, trying to get his wallet out. When he did he flipped it open and used his teeth to separate the credit cards and pictures. "There she is." He passed it over. "My baby girl. She was born with spina bifida so those lumps under her scalp are the shunt tubes that drain the fluid buildup. You see that smile? She's only three and could be on the cover of *Cosmo*, if anybody saw her. She'll walk someday too. I promised her that."

"Cute girl," Hank said. "Adorable."

"That's why I picked you up. You got more bandages on than she does after an operation."

Hank handed the picture back. "Got some burns. Industrial accident."

"Do tell." Bob was a smaller man than Hank supposed truckers should be, he had a thatch of red hair on his head that was seriously trying to fall out and green eyes as bright as emeralds. "Chemical?"

"Huh?"

"Chemical burns. Acid burns."

"Oh. No, just gasoline."

Bob Manning lifted the beer can for a drink, then dumped the transmission into another gear and gave the speed limit on Interstate 70 a good reason to mistrust him. "Burns hurt," he said. "I don't care if you burn your finger on a match or stick it in a red-hot toaster till it smokes, the result is the same. The pain is the same. The worst pain there is, being burned."

Hank nodded agreement. With the warm morning air blasting through the open windows the decorations on his face, the cotton and the gauze, were flapping him to death. He watched himself in the jittering mirror as he plucked everything off and fed it to the wind. Hairs of cotton stuck to his face and had to be pulled off one by one. This huge semi was a wonder—he had never been inside one—it was like the locomotive of a train. Bob Manning was steering but the hammering diesel under the white snout of the truck was in command here. And the noise of it—you had to shout to be heard, the secret voices inside your head were reduced to mumbles, reduced to nothing.

"So how far east are you headed, Harry?"

"What?"

"Your destination east."

Hank had honestly thought they had exchanged enough conversation to allow for an hour or two of silence. But truckers drove mostly solo, he guessed, and the loneliness was what led them to pick up hitchhikers despite the danger. "Bayonne, New Jersey," he said. Two years ago he had ordered an exercise bike from a catalog as a Christmas present for Rebecca. It didn't come and it didn't come, Christmas drew too close for comfort, he called the company in Bayonne and they swore it was on the way. Christmas Eve came and he wrote a card and stuck it in the tree, promising a belated gift. At that point Rebecca blurted out how thankful she was that he had not bought her that stupid exercise bike she used to want. So he called Bayonne and canceled the order. Instead, he got her an eight-hundred-dollar jewelry chest. She loved it.

"You call that home, do you?"

"Home is wherever I hang my hat," he said, and immediately felt stupid.

"King of the road, eh?" He laughed. "If you want to make money traveling, you need to get yourself a job behind the wheel of a big rig, Harry. You're practically your own boss, you never pay for your own gas—diesel or whatever—and you get to sit down on the job. Drink beer all day long if you want, just don't get caught. And women. Women love truckers. You married?"

Hank nodded.

"Kiss that idea good-bye." He grinned. "Unless you like getting some strange stuff now and then."

"True blue," Hank said, tired of this. He rubbed his wrists, which were starting to itch. He must have gone completely crazy, but he might never remember. Blood, blood splashed on the sidewalk, on the welcome mat, Sharri pitching backward with a bullet in her chest—people everywhere, an ocean of screaming people, flashbulbs in his eyes, hands grappling at him, pinning him—

"Getting nigh on to chow time," Bob said. "I usually stop around eight or nine, unless I'm drinking more beer than I should. Then I stop between midnight and never." He laughed. "There's a diner in a little town up ahead that serves up the best shit on a shingle you'll ever eat. Little place called Mike's Bait and Plate. It's ten minutes out of the way but worth every mile. You in a hurry?"

Hank snorted to himself. In a hurry? For what? The general idea was to locate Rebecca's mom and dad on their travels and room with them in the Country Coach. Their last phone call had come from the eastern seaboard, they were traveling from upper Maine down to the tip of Florida to check out retirement villages. Rebecca could field their next call, he'd call her from a phone booth, he'd meet up and cruise with the folks until all of this became second-page news. In the meantime he could live off his credit cards. As of now Rebecca was going to have to make her department store job a full-time one just to make the house payments.

"No hurry at all," he said to Bob Manning.

"Good, then." He popped a cassette into the dash player. Instead of the country music Hank expected to hear, Beethoven blasted out. "I lead the band while I drive," he shouted, jerking an invisible baton up and down with his right hand. "Call it a hobby. And it keeps me awake too."

Hank eyed him, then grinned for the first time in days. "Go for it," he shouted back.

They roared down Interstate 70 East bellowing diesel smoke and classical music.

That had been an encouraging prelude to Hitchhiking 101: a kind-hearted trucker with a comical quirk, a Hank released from life's troubles by merely sticking out his thumb and declaring himself—just like Bob Manning had said—king of the road. But in the end Bob drank too much beer and skipped the town and supper entirely, then as he drove and got smashingly drunk he began to unload the details of his life. The ex got custody of the daughter because the ex's rich father bribed the judge. The child support payments were too big. Whenever his visitation time came, the ex always stuck the baby back in the hospital because her shunts had supposedly gotten pushed out of place. And more . . .

Bouncing in the dark with the engine roaring at a steady pace and the highs and lows of Bob Manning's complaints blending into the community of noise, Hank began to seriously nod off just before midnight. Interstate 70 was a glowing cement path under the moonlight that the white snout of the truck lapped up mile after mile; he had not slept in years and the two beers he had drunk just to be sociable might as well have been roped to his eyelashes to serve as twelve-ounce weights for his eyelids. Time after time the soft hands of sleep lowered his chin all the way down to his chest only to let him jerk his head up again, startled into wakefulness by a distant shout in a foreign language, and then as it faded he would nod off again. Twice Bob Manning jabbed a finger into his shoulder as he made a point, drunk enough to believe he had an audience. To avoid it Hank sank low in the seat and crossed his arms over his chest. Finally he slept.

Then lights. Reds and blues. Whites, all twirling. Hank shoved himself up higher in the seat. A heavy downfall of rain was drilling the windshield while the truck idled without a driver. A glance into the mirror on his side showed only the reflection of the cop lights, but when he leaned toward it the view widened and he could see that Bob Manning was in the midst of a roadside sobriety test, trying hard to count something on his fingers as he stood swaying. Three state troopers shined flashlights at him while rain dripped off their hats and thunder walked overhead.

Hank's burning eyes widened and he held up his wrist, cocking it to find some light. It was a little after two. He wondered if he was still in Indiana or if the truck had made it across the state line into Ohio. But now that the story had jumped from backwoods Indiana into the national news, it didn't matter where he went, he would always be wanted.

The driver's door swung open and a flashlight found his face. "You co-driving this rig?"

Hank's mind sparked and twitched and could not come up with an answer. Sleep was more real than this.

"We've got to take your friend in for driving drunk. Were you asleep just then or passed out?"

"Asleep," Hank mumbled.

"Get down here and do some tricks for me."

Hank slid across the expanse of the seat. When he had clambered down and was on his feet, the cop, instead of making him walk the traditional straight line, lifted a ballpoint pen up to his face. "Keep your eyes on this without moving your head." A flashlight came blindingly into play. Hank followed the moving pen without problem, blinking against the glare.

"You're sober," the trooper said. A dollop of rainwater slid from his hat as he ducked his head to pocket the pen. It splashed down on Hank's shoes, which were not exactly the traditional garb of truckers. Again his flashlight strobed across Hank's eyes, lingered on his face. "Better let me see your CDL, just so I can say I did my job."

Fear kindled a fire that burned the last dregs of sleep from his head. He dug for his wallet, not quite certain what a CDL was but very certain that he did not have one. He had never actually said he was the co-driver, but to confess that he was just bumming rides might mean—*probably* meant— the routine insertion of his name into a nationwide police computer.

"Where the heck do I keep that thing?" he mumbled as he leafed through all the forgotten store receipts and bank deposit slips that populated his wallet. "Did I leave it at home?"

"Nasty burns on your arms, guy. Looks like you're flat broke too, huh?"

"Credit cards," Hank said. "Safer than cash."

"Mind showing me your regular operator's license?"

"I think I have that," Hank bleated. "The picture's terrible." Thoughts churned through his head: he hadn't been driving so the license issue was pointless. It might be better to cough up the phony name he had adopted, and there had to be a billion Harry Thompsons in the country. But what about a social security number? He gave up the search. "I lost my license last year," he said. "Drinking and driving."

"Just like this guy, eh?"

"Right. I was only along for the ride with him, no intention of driving. He's my brother-in-law, see, and I was heading back home. Bayonne. New Jersey. I'm Harry Thompson, and that's where I call home."

"That's odd. He told me he picked you up out of the blue over by Terre Haute and you drank all his beer."

"He's crazy when he's drunk. Blames everybody else. Forgets his own relatives."

The cop stroked Hank's face with the light again. "I'd like to take a look at all those credit cards you've got, Mr. Thompson. Just so I can say I did my job."

Hank smiled. He smiled and thought and smiled some

more while rain pattered down on his hair and his brain packed its bags and stomped off in a huff.

"Come over here with me," the officer said. He used the flashlight to indicate the way toward the flashing cars. "No weapons on you, I trust."

Hank spun on the toe of his left shoe without quite being aware that it was going to happen. He had not been born with the talents of a ballerina and had not made any lunging moves since tennis sprained his ankle three years before. He fell heavily to his knees on the wet pavement. With a grunt he pushed himself up with his hands and scrambled on all fours under the trailer of Manning's idling truck. By rolling himself through the wet grit he was able to pop up on the other side. The cop was shouting things. Hank scanned the road bed with eyes full of green and purple circles left over from the flashlight. There seemed to be a gully that dropped into blackness, then some skinny metal fence posts high on the far side. With all the colorful lights pulsing through the night, the face of the landscape chattered in and out of reality, solidly lit one moment and blurred into red-and-blue haze the next. He hurried forward with his arms out for balance and jumped for the bottom of the gully, dimly hoping for a soft landing.

He got cool water instead. It closed over his head but panic reflexively surged him back up into the air; the water was only chest high. Gasping, he grabbed handfuls of weeds to pull himself up the embankment while the toes of his sneakers trenched out scoops of mud. When he was erect and the lights were printing his shadow in triplets, he ran for the dark country bordered by the fence posts.

A burst of white light illuminated him from behind. He threw himself flat on the ground expecting to hear a bullhorn speak: give up or we will shoot. Instead the light lingered for a while on the tall weeds overhead, swept back and forth, then came to rest overhead again; his world became green. He waited while rain drummed down on his back, trying to hold his breath, hoping that no cop in his right mind would dive into a black and watery ditch just to chase a guy who hadn't even broken the law.

Flucht vor der Polizei . . .

Unlawful flight. There's your crime. He grabbed a breath and righted himself just as thunder broke the sky in the east. A backward look through the intense light offered the sight of Bob Manning, handcuffed, being inserted into one of the three police vehicles busy there. What they were going to do with his truck, Hank could not guess. Now one of the state troopers, a lurching frame against the spotlight, splashed into the ditch holding a flashlight that jittered and pointed skyward as he slogged through the water and crawled up the other side. Hank prodded himself into a shambling run to break out of the cone of light but it swiveled effortlessly to pin him down again. The officer running full tilt behind him shouted words that a fresh clap of thunder obliterated. Bent low at the waist, sliding and skating on the weeds underfoot and falling to his elbows twice, Hank forged a zigzag path while the beam of the trooper's flashlight bounced through the rain and he shouted other things. At the farthest edge of his sight, as the spotlight moved to follow him, Hank glimpsed one of the fence posts and caught a hint of barbed wire. A wild plan braced his hopes: drop down and watch the cop run smack against that fence. It might even be electric, which would stun him long enough for a quick escape. At the same time that his thoughts hatched this plan, his thighs jammed against the upper strand of the barbed wire. His knees and shins brunted into the other two strands below. The entire fence contracted to flip him fully over while carving out chunks of his jeans and the meat underneath. He slammed down on his back. A long moment of uncertainty captured him: he was at home asleep and had fallen out of bed, the force of this wretched dream had knocked him to the floor. Now he would crawl back up and draw himself tight against his wife's warm body and drink in the smell of bedroom sleep that came from her; he would adjust the covers so that they were not touching his throat and take care to stick one arm out in the fresh bedroom air so that he didn't feel mummified.

The cop was getting closer. His footfalls were a combination of slather through the weeds and squelch-pop in the mud. The beam of his flashlight swung up and down as he ran, each stroke of it cutting the rain. Hank rolled groggily onto his side just as lightning arced through the clouds and turned the world white. The picture stamped inside his eyeballs showed that this cop was really a sheriff's deputy who looked to be all of twenty years old, a big fellow with a big chrome star flashing on his chest. Perhaps confused by the light, possibly blinded by a sudden blurt of rain in his face, he barreled into the barbed wire running far faster than Hank had been. The impact ejected his flashlight from his hand; whirling end for end it traced a rainbow across the sky. The barbed wire pulled taut, creaking against the posts, then let out a twang that sounded as if a thousand volts of pure electricity were coursing through it.

Hank lay still for several seconds, then pushed himself up. Silence now but for the rain. He hazarded a look over the bobbing tips of the weeds back to the freeway: rotating lights that sliced the rain, public servants who never tired. There was a strange knot in his stomach that he belatedly realized was hunger: the last thing he had put inside himself in the last few days was two beers.

The deputy uttered a grunt. Hank crawled over to him and rose to his haunches. The deputy moaned words that were too round at the edges to catch. Hank reached out and touched him. A frown settled onto his face as he did. Something was really screwy. The deputy was all knotted up, some of him was missing, and his arms and legs seemed to be poking out in impossible directions. Barbed wire stabbed at Hank's hands from equally mysterious directions. He thought of the flashlight, wondering if it could be found, but was relieved of the task when long forks of lightning traveled overhead to meet the horizon at both sides. In that long moment he sank back to see what was what here.

The light winked out just as one of his hands swung up to clap itself over his mouth. The deputy was hanging off the ground, twisted and tangled in a crazy spiderweb of barbed wire. His throat had been torn open on one side and was pulsing blood in big drops.

Blood. *Blut*, in German. Barbed wire. *Barbed wire*, in German?

Stachel . . . Stacheldraht? *Stacheldraht!*

The boy from Wiesbaden was a slight little slip of a soldier. He was fifteen years old and his name was Frederik. He was wearing a tattered uniform much too big for him and a helmet that almost covered his eyes. His boots had been pulled off the feet of a dead soldier because the German Reich, the Second Reich, was out of boots and men and materiel and was starving to death. But the war went on year after year, World War One went on, and during a ferocious night assault Frederik became tangled in the huge hoops of razor wire that protected the French trenches. He tore himself to pieces as, in his terror in the thundering darkness, he panicked and tried to claw his way out. His uniform was sliced to rags, his skin flayed from his muscles, and even his eyes were gouged out by the three-inch barbs. He was killed when morning broke, by a Frenchman who saw that he was still moving among all the dead bodies suspended there, and mercifully shot him through the head. It happened on March 11, 1917.

Hank drew away from the deputy and hung his head. There was no doubt now, he was even recalling names and dates from over eighty years ago; he knew details of Hitler's early life no one in the world could know. He lunged forward and clawed at the deputy's shape in the dark, tearing his hands on the rusty prongs knitted into the wires but feeling nothing. He slapped at the soggy uniform, then turned the deputy like a pig on a spit until he found his holster. A leather strap held the gun in place. It opened with a snap and he jerked the gun out. Police revolver, .38 caliber. It was as heavy as a gallon of water.

The deputy squirmed. Hank raised the gun and fired twice, *kapow-kapow,* as fast as he could pull the trigger. The barrel sprouted a big orange flower each time and the kick the thing carried was amazing. The doors of the police cars popped open and people piled out in a hurry. Hank rose to his feet through the drifting haze of gunsmoke. They would find their deputy and they would rescue him. It might be that they would realize their fugitive had alerted them, and give Hank some good press. But hell, they didn't even know who he was, just a drifter.

Rain beat down on his head. The pistol was feeling comfortable in his hand; with it he was not as naked, not as scared. He had no plans to kill anyone, but there were a lot of people out there interested in killing him. Now the other cops were vanishing from his sight one by one as they jumped into the ditch. He turned and eyed the darkness that awaited him. No way could he dare hitchhike on the freeway anymore, which meant sticking to the back roads and making his way east in little segments. He scrubbed the water from his eyes with a forearm, hoping to spot the deputy's flashlight glowing in the distant weeds. Tonight, owning a gun and a flashlight would be the equivalent of driving a Cadillac. Could be he would get even luckier by finding a barn or a shed to sleep in, free of the rain. Or find a chicken coop, where raw eggs were the breakfast specialty.

To a starving man they actually sounded pretty good. He leaned into a loping trot, hunched slightly, scanning the ground for signs of the flashlight, thinking about trench warfare and the flares that were shot into the sky to light the battlefield, the blinding ones that floated down on little silk parachutes spitting white fire.

29

We must get back to Germany," Rønna Ulgard said as he bent over the bed. "I have other business."

Karl-Luther von Wessenheim heard the voice and came groggily awake. His head was thudding with pain. "Oh my God," he moaned, and turned his face into the pillow. Hot Boise sunlight was slashing through the gaps at both sides of the drapes, too raw to endure. If not for the air conditioner, he would have been baked and served by now.

"I rescheduled our flight and we depart in an hour. I've already checked out of my room. We must get to the airport."

"You go alone," von Wessenheim said into the pillow. "I'm too sick to fly."

Ulgard became quiet just long enough for von Wessenheim to hook into the fringes of the last dream and haul himself back aboard. But the next moment, grappling at him like meat hooks, Ulgard's gloved hands found enough flesh and skin on his arms to hoist him high in the bed. His eyes popped open. His hangover had stitched them with bright threads of scarlet. "What are you doing?" he cried.

"Waking you up, sir." Ulgard dropped him. With amazement von Wessenheim saw that a naked girl was lying atop the sheets. The bouncing mattress shed her like a drop of water and she plopped onto the pale blue carpet, still asleep. Or dead. His memory of the night did not exist. "The airport is only two minutes away, but you'll want to take a bath and eat breakfast. Or?"

Neither one seemed worth getting out of bed for, but Ulgard did not seem likely to leave him alone, so von Wessenheim swiveled around grudgingly and put his feet on the floor, snugging them between the girl's legs. Something was nagging at him from the back of his mind, something either tragic or wonderful that he should remember. Something about the war. Hitler. A German soldier lying dead on the ground.

"Yes!" he shouted, springing up. With embarrassment he realized that he was nude, and snatched up a blanket. No wonder he had gotten so fabulously drunk last night, no wonder he had refused to spend the night in an airplane! A party had been in order. A grand party that should have included thousands of guests and a hundred kegs of champagne. Hitler had not been incinerated by his most loyal. He had been taken to a mighty temple, a pyramid in the ground, and interred like a pharaoh. Or else slipped away to Argentina with the SS soldiers, and died there of old age.

Despair seized him. What if that were true? But no, both Rudiger and von Lütringen—and all the books written by experts since that fateful day in April of 1945—agreed that Hitler had committed suicide. In a perspective mindful of his sense of mission, he had most certainly killed himself. Mussolini had been hung by the heels and defiled as he dangled upside down from a wire like a dead pig. That fact had stunned Hitler. In no way would he let himself be humiliated, even after death. And of course his troops were standing by, ready to die for him after he was already dead. To risk capture would have been unthinkable. So he *was* there in Berlin. Somewhere.

He stumbled around picking up his clothing. Wine and beer bottles littered the floor. Some clever wag had stubbed out cigarettes on the carpet. He wondered if he had impressed her with his masterful command of the English language. It was to be hoped, anyway, because he doubted that he had impressed her much in bed. But now he was sober, his hangover was fading, it was being suppressed by the sheer joy of *knowing* that he was not a fool, that he had outsmarted Frau Dietermunde and her geriatric Hitler Youth cohorts, who should now be called the Hitler Elderly and soon the Hitler Dead. Von Wessenheim had been born too late for the war, but he would outlive the secretive bastards and the world would know his name.

A constant and annoying noise drilled into his recognition: water was splashing in the bathroom. He decided that bathing could go to hell and went in to tell Ulgard, blinded by the white glare of the walls under the hot bulbs, but he was not there. Drawing a bath for a client was a little more than a respectable lawyer would usually do, von Wessenheim knew, but he was in a hurry to get back in the air and had probably slipped out to fetch one of those abominable hamburger-joint breakfasts for von Wessenheim to gag down. He fiddled with the strange plastic bathtub knob while steam burned his lungs and finally got the water turned off. Back in the bedroom he found a crumpled pack of Marlboros on the TV table and snatched one out. The girl stirred in her sleep, smacked her lips, then dropped her head and began to snore gently. He had chosen a blonde this time. Her clothes, he saw, had been pitched into a corner, a drift of slinky red cloth tossed atop a pair of red stiletto-heel shoes. How he had found a decent prostitute in this last outpost of humanity he did not know. At some point in the near future, when his face appeared on the news as the solver of earth's greatest mystery, she might turn to her friends and say with pride that she had worked for him one night.

He scoured the room for matches, finally locating a book of them under the desk. The cover informed him that he was at the "Holiday Inn at the Airport." His hands were trembling as he lit up, either from excitement or too much alcohol, or even the lack of nicotine, he supposed. The first drag seared his chest and induced a fit of coughing that doubled him over. The damned Marlboros were eating his lungs alive, they needed their usual Reemstmas. He stuck it in his mouth again anyway and dressed himself, still slightly off balance from the overdose of wine, enough so that when his foot snagged in his trousers he hopped in a staggering circle until finally collapsing on the bed. It was so silly that he giggled, but abruptly stopped when he noticed that the ceiling was beginning to rock back and forth like the keel of a boat on the high seas. His stomach gave a lurch and he sat up. The cigarette stung his eyes and he jerked it from his lips.

The room began to turn. Von Wessenheim put a hand over his mouth, which was suddenly full of saliva. He rose and tottered into the steamy bathroom, lifted the toilet seat, and dropped to his knees.

The wine was still red.

Rønna Ulgard was at the outdoor telephone stand at the front of the Holiday Inn building, sweating in the heat as he punched in a long series of numbers. Calling collect to Germany from a public phone in the USA required almost two dozen pokes at the little blue keys and lots of waiting. But when the connection went through, he could hear Frau Dietermunde's voice quite clearly.

"It went just as expected," he spoke into the phone. A young woman wearing only a yellow bikini and sneakers strolled past; he lowered his sunglasses slightly and watched her. His tongue dabbed at his upper lip as he did.

"Oh, the old man was brilliant. Quite a performance. Von Wessenheim nearly had a stroke."

The young woman turned and looked at him curiously. The black gloves did it every time.

"Probably passed out again. Von Wessenheim drinks wine as if it were water."

He stripped his glasses from his face. His eyes were cold brown beads that glittered in the light.

"Twelve hours if the flights are on time. Yes, I'll call you when I arrive."

Her eyes were soft and blue. He lifted a finger and made come-here motions. The woman became visibly frightened and hurried away.

"Thank you, Frau Dietermunde. Good-bye." He hung up and settled his sunglasses on his face again. Back in the room he stood waiting for his eyes to adjust to the dimness. Von Wessenheim was being noisily ill in the bathroom. Rønna Ulgard snorted and strode to where the woman lay between the two big beds. He roused her by tapping the sole of her foot with his pointy shoe until her head wafted up.

"The party is over," he said. He went to the wall and tossed her dress at her. "Rise up and shine."

She groaned, tried to perform a push-up on wobbling elbows and collapsed. Shaking his head, Ulgard crossed to where she lay and grabbed her elbows to hoist her up. She complained and tried to wriggle free. With a grunt he pinned them together at the middle of her back. She screeched, then found her balance and whirled around to face him. "You hurt me, you bastard!" she shrieked. He ripped the glove from his right hand and raised it to slap her. Her eyes shifted over as she cringed against the blow, and she let out a gasp. When he hesitated she said, "Jeez, Mister, what the hell is all that?"

He slapped her. She spun in a complete circle and fell on the bed. "Nothing you will ever understand," he hissed. When his glove was back in place, he reached into a pocket of his suit jacket and brought out a handful of American money, fives and tens. He crunched them into a ball and dropped them on the bed beside her. "Be out of here in thirty seconds and that money is yours."

She was out in fifteen, money in hand. "Fuck you too," she informed him before the door whomped shut. Ulgard dismissed her from his thoughts and went into the bathroom, stepping over a rumpled pair of pants that had gotten turned inside out. The stink inside was cigarette smoke and alcohol; von Wessenheim had one side of his face resting on the ceramic toilet bowl while a thick yellow fluid drained from a corner of his mouth. It was gall, Ulgard knew, the hideously bitter fluid that came up straight from the deepest reaches of the stomach during intense vomiting. Probably von Wessenheim would sleep like a dead man through most of the upcoming travel. He would be easier to handle that way.

"You're ill," he said, and hauled a handful of toilet paper off the roll beside the toilet. He balled it up and worked it into von Wessenheim's hand. "Can you stand?"

"Stand." He made a grimace of disgust and rose enough to spit into the toilet. "I can try," he said in English, dabbing at his mouth.

Ulgard helped him to his feet. "Usually a person feels better shortly after this kind of episode." He released him and lifted his wristwatch into view while von Wessenheim stood swaying. The flight to New York via Denver left in about forty-five minutes. If any passengers were flying standby, one or both seats could be lost. Ulgard was no more a fan of this sweltering outpost in the desert than von Wessenheim and Germany was cool and truly beautiful this time of year. "I'll pack your luggage," he said. "You might finish dressing."

"Finish dressing. I will finish dressing."

Ulgard went out. Von Wessenheim's leather suitcase was keeled over beside the lamp table, black and expensive and unopened. His matching briefcase, which he had cracked open at the old man's house only long enough to withdraw a check for one hundred thousand Marks, had gotten shoved under the bed. Rønna Ulgard dragged it out and knelt on the floor. After a glance at the bathroom, he fingered through its papers and receipts, then shut it and toted it to the door.

Presently von Wessenheim himself stumbled into view. He had splashed water on his face and not dried it, but looked better. He picked up his fallen slacks from the floor and was able to pull them on, found his shirt draped over a lampshade and guided his arms into it. Ulgard watched wordlessly as he came across one sock and stuck a foot into it, found one shoe and became befuddled because it did not belong to the foot wearing the sock. Exasperated, Ulgard collected the rest of his clothing and handed it to him piece by piece with instructions for its usage. When the ordeal seemed close to an end, he phoned for a cab and propped the door open with the suitcase, waiting impatiently in the sunlight for one to appear.

"I have my briefcase," von Wessenheim said, wandering again. "But my suitcase is missing."

"By me," Ulgard said, and watched as von Wessenheim fastened bleary eyes on him. "Here at my feet."

"Good man, Herr Ulgard. If only I had employed you before, I would now own a hat with flakes of Hitler's DNA in it. That, as of yesterday, is no longer relevant."

"Quite," Ulgard muttered. The man was still half drunk and babbling.

"Then off we go, I expect." He tilted toward the door and set himself in motion, his eyes squinting tighter and tighter as he neared the sunshine. At the door his eyes were fully closed. "My dear God," he wheezed.

Ulgard lifted sunglasses out of the inner pocket of his suit coat. "I bought them for you last night. In anticipation of this moment."

He took them with trembling fingers. "Good man, Herr Ulgard." The little price tag still dangled from the bridge, but he set them on his face regardless. "Such heat. Incredible. Makes one wonder why the Europeans ever migrated this far."

"Perhaps in search of water," Ulgard replied, and von Wessenheim cackled like a chicken, was still cackling when the taxi drove up. Ulgard got him into the rear seat and paid the driver to handle the bags, then settled back. But at the gates of the airport von Wessenheim was visibly fading, last night having slept the sleep of a drunkard, which Ulgard knew was sleep that merely imitated the real thing. He would soon be nodding off. Von Wessenheim was a pleasant man but Ulgard agreed with Frau Dietermunde that he was not worthy of great things and would amount to nothing more than the sad and utter end of the royal House of Wessenheim, which had survived the war but would not survive von Wessenheim himself.

When the bags were checked in and assurances given that the flight was still theirs, Ulgard was patiently leading him toward the security checkpoint when von Wessenheim suddenly balked. Ulgard turned to signal him but rather than falling into one of the chairs, which Ulgard expected, he had come to a stop in front of a row of bulky newspaper vending machines. Losing patience, Ulgard backtracked. "They have newspapers on the airplane," he said to him, then followed the line of his open-mouthed stare, frowning.

HEWLETT-PACKARD ANNOUNCES CUTS

It was the local Boise paper, the *Idaho Statesman*. Ulgard was aware that the computer company was headquartered here, but why that should stop von Wessenheim in his weary tracks was a mystery. Perhaps he owned a large portion of the company's stock and was afraid the layoffs were going to cause a tumble in the value of his shares.

"We can get a paper on the plane, you know."

Von Wessenheim jammed a hand into his pants pocket and withdrew a couple of Pfennigs. With a growl he dropped them to wander across the airport's red carpeting, and held out his hand. "Give me fifty cents. I want this newspaper."

Grumbling inside, Ulgard handed over two quarters and watched as von Wessenheim bent over and dumped them into the slot. He pulled the face of the machine open to the squeal of startled hinges and captured a paper. Looking very sober, he scanned the front page, then folded the newspaper over and brought it closer to his eyes. Ulgard waited without patience as other passengers went past at the same determined and worried pace he had found in airports all over the world. "Something of interest?" he asked tiredly.

"Damn this language and its spelling. Here." He extended it. "Read this for me."

Rønna Ulgard took it. Several smaller headlines flanked the top story. "Right here," von Wessenheim said, moving to jab at it with a finger. Ulgard backed away slightly from the smell of his breath, and read.

HISTORIAN SAYS REINCARNATED HITLER HAS HIS FACTS STRAIGHT HYPNOTIZED PROFESSOR RECALLS PAST LIFE

"Rine-car-notted," von Wessenheim said, pressing closer. "Translate."

"*Wiedergeboren*," Ulgard said.

"Strah-igt?"

"*Korrect*."

Von Wessenheim frowned as he puzzled. As if it suddenly occurred to him that he was wearing sunglasses with a price tag stuck to his nose, he peeled them from his face and dragged Ulgard by the elbow to a row of red plastic chairs that lined a section of the wall. "You must read me the entire report," he said as they stood with the Idaho sun burning on their backs through the big tinted windows. His hands were trembling even worse than before. "First in English, then translate."

Ulgard consulted his watch. "Our gate is a long walk from here. There will be plenty of time on the airplane."

"Just read the damned thing for me!"

Ulgard looked at him sharply and was surprised to see that von Wessenheim was growing. Inside his wrinkled gray suit he was visibly becoming larger, was inflating to fill it out. His spine straightened to make him tall, and when he spoke again every trace of his bumbling hangover was gone. "We will sit right here and you will read it to me slowly. I apologize for my ignorance of the language, but there is nothing more important in my life than this single thing that I ask of you now."

Ulgard nodded. "Very well."

They sat and he adjusted the paper.

Terre Haute, IN—Professor Robert McClaren, head of the department of history at Indiana State University, told reporters today that after reviewing statements made by the so-called Hypno-Hitler, Harrison W. Thorwald, he could find no fault with his grasp of history. Thorwald, 32, who has received increasing media coverage since a man burned to death on the front lawn of his home in this city of 60,000, last week revealed under hypnosis that in a past life he had been none other than Adolf Hitler, the Führer of Nazi Germany from 1933–1945.

Thorwald, who was fired from his teaching post after an unrelated incident, has apparently gone into hiding since the shooting of his young daughter by Terre Haute police two days ago. Police spokesman James Bellows termed the shooting "regrettable but understandable" after the girl emerged from the besieged house firing a realistic-looking cap pistol into the crowd of gawkers.

"My God," von Wessenheim muttered. "This is incredible." Ulgard merely grunted, and read on.

In another twist of this bizarre story, the hypnotist, Perry G. Wilson, also a professor at ISU, reportedly committed suicide by asphyxiating himself with a plastic grocery bag in the basement of his Terre Haute home. The body was discovered yesterday by Thorwald's wife, Rebecca, but police now say it has vanished.

Meanwhile, hundreds continue to flock to Terre Haute from around the nation, as well as from other countries, sometimes bringing violence with them. Street battles between neo-Nazi groups and radical Jewish organizations have erupted, as well as clashes between the Ku Klux Klan and African-American activists.

National religious leaders, both Christian and Jewish, have united to denounce the debacle as a "deadly farce," pointing out that both Christians and Jews have never included reincarnation as part of their belief systems.

For local reaction, see **Hitler**, *page 2C.*

"My English must be getting better, because I understand almost all of it. Read me the next section."

Ulgard slapped the paper together and tossed it aside, uneasily aware of what was beginning to cook in von Wessenheim's sodden brain and by no means willing to let it get that far. He rose and pulled his sleeve back to show von Wessenheim his wristwatch. "If we miss the Denver flight, we miss our connection to New York. If we miss New York, it will be hours before we can get a flight to Berlin because most Lufthansa flights terminate at Frankfurt. Do you grasp that? Do you want an eight-hour train ride on top of all that time in the air?"

Von Wessenheim stood and eyed him steadily. "Do you believe in fate, Herr Ulgard?"

"I believe in nothing. Especially not reincarnation."

"But *I* believe in fate. And I am open to new ideas. I am the man who invested a fortune to find nothing but a rusty bomb. I am prepared to spend another fortune to dig up every square kilometer of Berlin. But if this man was Hitler in a past life, he can simply *tell* me where he arranged to be buried. No more experts to hire, no more machinery to rent. German efficiency at its finest."

Ulgard took a forward step and jabbed a gloved finger against his bony chest. "Listen to yourself, the heir to the Wessenheim line speaking soberly of such a preposterous thing as this. What would German royalty think?"

"Royalty can lick my ass. Fate has selected me to deliver the Führer to the world."

"Just as fate selected the Führer to lead Germany to greatness? Just as fate selected the international Jewish conspiracy to defeat us?"

Von Wessenheim drew back slightly while several emotions crossed his face in rapid progression. Ulgard glanced around and noticed people steering clear of this shouting match, saw far to his right that a uniformed airport security guard was watching with careful eyes.

"That is certainly a strange thing to hear you say, Herr Ulgard. If not for your age, I could believe you were once in the Hitler Youth."

"Nonsense." Ulgard touched at the knot of his tie as he cleared his throat. "I'm trying to stress the absurdity of your idea that fate is calling you."

"Then we won't call it fate, if you are uncomfortable with the term. We'll call it luck. Yesterday I learned from an old soldier that the body burned at the Reich's Chancellery was not Hitler's, it was a German soldier with some of Hitler's bridgework stuck in his mouth. There is the real conspiracy, the most monumental deception ever attempted, but even *it* failed because the soldier's body was destroyed by a bomb and never found. But it is my luck, thanks to you, Herr Ulgard, that I talked to the old soldier before he could take his secret to the grave. And it is *my* luck that I have a lawyer of your caliber." He smiled. "This kind of luck doesn't happen often, Herr Rønna Ulgard with your Norwegian slash through the *o*."

Ulgard turned his head away. Von Wessenheim's breath was bad enough to melt paint and he was still rocking on his feet from the night's festivities; now he was brazenly trying to become chums. Ulgard stepped back, his face set in a

sneer of disdain. He could not afford to miss another day of
work in Berlin. He was scheduled to be in court late tomorrow afternoon to plead the case of a client so guilty of fraud
and embezzlement that he should be hanged, but Ulgard was
confident he could make him walk free. But without his
lawyer in court tomorrow, the man was sure to get ten years
in prison.

"I consider our relationship terminated as of this moment,"
he said to von Wessenheim. "Good-bye and good luck." He
turned and walked away, grumbling under his breath.

"Wait," von Wessenheim said. "Please."

Ulgard quickened his pace. Why Frau Dietermunde was
afraid that this misguided man might really find Hitler's
bones he could not guess.

Von Wessenheim caught up with him. "Herr Ulgard,
please," he said, taking long, irregular strides to keep pace.
"You're walking away from a great mystery that you and I together can solve."

"I already wished you good luck," he snapped.

"Listen! Please! Don't you realize the enormity of this
undertaking?"

People were watching again, Americans trying to guess
which language this might be. "I only realize the enormity of
my losses if I am not in Berlin by tomorrow," Ulgard said
quietly.

"Money, then? Is it money?"

"Business is money. You should know that."

Von Wessenheim seemed to drop back a little. Suddenly he
hooked a hand around Ulgard's elbow and spun him quite
neatly. Before Ulgard could haul in a breath to complain, von
Wessenheim had taken hold of the lapels of his suit jacket
and jerked him to stand face to face. "Five hundred thousand
German marks," he hissed with his horrible drunkard's
breath. "Five hundred thousand marks for locating and delivering that man to me."

"You've lost your mind," Ulgard said, and pushed him
away. Von Wessenheim tripped over the pile of the carpet and
plopped down on his ass. A quick glance showed that the security guard was more than interested, that he was now en

route and speaking into his radio, so Ulgard turned and got himself going, not willing to get dragged into a security office to explain this ridiculous confrontation.

Incredibly, von Wessenheim leapt up and spun him around again. In an unintended reflex Ulgard raised a gloved hand to strike him.

"One million American dollars per day!" von Wessenheim shouted, shying back. "Do you hear that? One *million* American dollars that can be earned in a single day!"

Ulgard quickly lowered his hand, stunned. His tongue darted out and dabbed at his upper lip. "I must have it in writing."

"Then I will write it," von Wessenheim panted.

"With the signature of a reliable witness."

"The security agent running toward us will make a very good witness." He extended a hand for shaking. "Be my attorney again, Herr Ulgard, and be a millionaire as well. All for simply finding a young college professor and making him talk to me."

Ulgard took his hand without hesitation and shook it. To assuage the security guard he hooked an arm around von Wessenheim's shoulders and hugged him close, patting his back like a close friend. They had had a spat, he would explain, but now everything was just fine between the two. Better than fine, and would you mind witnessing an oral contract?

It turned out, after Ulgard pressed a twenty-dollar bill into his hand, that the guard was quite pleased to be of service to these two nice foreign gentlemen.

RISKING ALLES

30

A light snapped on, and no wonder. Hank froze in place with a squawking, flapping chicken snared in one fist, his stolen pistol in the other. The entire barnyard population had gone mad when he began looking for eggs in the dark, his stomach a twisted knot of hunger with no aversion to sucking raw eggs in the middle of the night. He had walked for miles after the bout with the deputy and the fence, probably in zigzags or circles, until stumbling upon this little farm in a pouring Ohio rain that seemed likely to drown the world. Lightning had been his only guide.

But now, this. The farmer had a shotgun and a flashlight and the powerful fact that he was protecting his home and family, two good reasons to shoot.

"You'll be wanting to let the chicken go," he said, gesturing with the barrel of the shotgun. "My wife's already called the sheriff."

Hank let his fist relax. The chicken hit the dirt running.

"Now how's about discarding that revolver?"

Hank stood motionless, able only to think that having this pistol would keep him alive, that without it he was easy prey for the people who wanted him, the people who hunted him.

In the backglow of the flashlight, the farmer was looking impatient: "Is the answer no, or are you still thinking it over?"

Hank hesitated a bit, then lowered his hand but did not drop the gun. The farmer stroked him up and down with the flashlight. "Who are you, anyway?" he asked gruffly. "I know I've seen you someplace."

Hank simply stared at him. This was the way it would be forever, people would look at him and scratch their heads, would lean to the side and ask others: Who is that guy? And invariably, someone would figure it out, and Hank would have to run.

"Christ sake, you must have a name. When I tell my grand-kids about this I don't want to call you Mr. X through the whole story, and my grandkids like long stories." He seemed to relax, letting the barrel of the shotgun droop. Hank deliberated: should he take a leap and confess to being himself, hoping the farmer had already judged the media stories about him absurd?

"Fine, then," the farmer said. "When the sheriff gets here, he'll solve the mystery, and we'll just see."

Hank took the leap. "Hank Thorwald." And that pretty much said it all.

The farmer drew back, frowning. "Oh my God," he breathed. "You."

In his tone, in his reaction, Hank sensed the urge to kill. Quickly he swung the pistol up with both hands and aimed it at the farmer's face. "Don't make me waste a bullet on you. I've only got four left."

"I could blow you in half with this shotgun, and you know it."

Hank used his thumb to pull the hammer back. It clicked into place, ready to snap forward at the touch of the trigger. "A man tends to spasm when he's shot. You'll die with me."

To his surprise the farmer lost his nerve. "Then I guess you'd better be on your way, Mr. Thorwald." He put the shot-gun on the floor and took a backward step, holding the flash-light's beam on Hank's pistol. "You know how to get out."

Hank frowned, wary. "Kick it toward me."

He did. "Won't do you much good," he said as Hank bent to pick it up. "No ammo."

Hank gathered up the shotgun anyway, unable to tell if it was loaded or not, unsure how to handle the heavy thing at all. As he fumbled with it, the faraway wail of a siren pierced the walls of the barn, rising and falling with the patterns of the wind. "Which way is the best to go?" he asked the farmer, sick at the idea of another chase in the dark through the open fields. "Any dense woods around here?"

"Any way off my property is the best way for you to go."

Hank swooped the gun up and fired. A tin bucket hanging from a nail in the wall jumped away and bonged hollowly on the floor. A couple of the cows in their stalls kicked against the boards. "You'd better get more helpful than that," he snarled at him.

He pointed the flashlight. "Head north. Go out the same damn door you came in, and keep going. The woods up that way are thick and full of brambles, if that's what you want."

Hank nodded. "Hand over the flashlight."

To his surprise the man shined the light on his own face. "I won't do that, not for you or anybody else. It's a Snoopy flashlight from my granddaughter on Christmas. She saved her pennies."

The beam found Hank again. When she was little, Sharri had relied on her Snoopy Nite-Lite to keep her safe in the dark. "Maybe you'd better keep it, then," he said ruefully, wondering how much lower he could fall before the fall ended forever. He shifted his eyes to the farmer. "Could I ask you not to tell the cops which way I headed?"

His eyes gleamed, as hard and as cold as diamonds. "You can ask."

Hank turned away. The Snoopy flashlight illuminated his way to the back of the barn as chickens darted between his feet. At the door at the back of the barn he shuffled around. "Hey there."

"Still here," the farmer said.

"Do you believe?"

"Believe what they're saying?" He drew in a slow breath. "I'm thinking that I do, Mr. Thorwald. Seeing you in this shape, I'm thinking I do. And you?"

Hank bent and leaned the shotgun against the wall. The siren was close now, there was not much time. "I've got three bullets left," he said. "I'm thinking about saving the last one for myself."

The farmer's reply was swift: "That's what Hitler did."

Hank pushed the door open and went out into the rain, abandoning the shotgun. A gust of wind blew the door shut behind him.

31

Detective Steven Gleeworth stumped down the rickety basement stairs at the Wilson house. The lightbulb was still burning and the wicker chair was still pushed to the side. He clicked his flashlight on. The rat trap and the rat pinned to it were still there. He looked away quickly and concentrated on examining the parts of the basement not revealed by the tired old bulb. Spiderwebs loomed. Spiderwebs every damn where. Gleeworth loved spiders about as much as he loved dead rats. The walls were interesting, carved by the blade of a handheld shovel shortly before the last Ice Age. Overhead, the thick, hand-hewn beams spoke of carpenters long dead. Why anyone had bothered to dig out this huge hole in the ground and call it a basement he could not guess. Maybe the workbench was the goal, the owner of the house made birdhouses for a hobby. Whatever the reason, it was as dismal as a mausoleum and downright spooky.

Gleeworth turned in a slow circle, holding the flashlight at the level of his eyes. The unexcavated portion under the house was an average crawl space, about two feet of room between the ground and the thick floor joists. More spiderwebs dwelt in that expanse but they were old and frayed, the spiders long gone for lack of flying bugs to snare. There were a few things to see, as his light probed the dark, besides just the dirt and the dust. In the distance a small stack of yellowed newspapers; over there a brown water hose sloppily coiled like a dead snake; over that way a bicycle wheel with rusty, broken spokes poking up. Other junk, as he turned, none of it remarkable.

Which meant that he was going to have to crawl around. By clambering onto the workbench and then getting on his knees he got himself into the crawl space and used his elbows to hitch forward on his stomach. A sweep of the area found no rats, not a rat in sight. He came to the newspapers and applied light to the top one. *Terre Haute Tribune,* January 12, 1928, a rail workers' strike had shut down delivery of coal to Terre Haute. He pushed it aside and the top page crackled apart into yellow confetti. Below it: January 13, 1928, the mayor vows to import coal from Kentucky despite the risk of union violence. Gleeworth shook his head, unable to figure out why anyone would go to the trouble of sticking this stuff in the crawl space.

He crawled on, using the flashlight to scout for rats and shred the cobwebs before they could become part of his hair. It came to him that maybe this was a dumb idea, that the forensics crew should come here to look for subtle clues before he flattened them all. His detective instincts, which were often wrong but so far had never led to disaster, insisted that Thorwald had buried the body of Perry Wilson down here, very likely dismembered him and buried the pieces in shallow holes. Filled them up, patted the ground down smooth again, no more Perry Wilson.

He came to a wall of the foundation. It was made of red bricks, he noticed. Back in those days Terre Haute was a big producer of bricks; something about Indiana clay was special. He aimed his flashlight along it and slowly swept the beam across the surface, noticing the hillocks and depressions. None seemed unusual. By his reckoning the kitchen lay above him. Following this wall would bring him under the bedrooms. But the light only showed more of the same lumpy terrain. Still he crawled on, willing to circumnavigate this big expanse of nothing under this big empty house, inch by inch if necessary.

Something snagged itself under the tongue of his left shoe and he jerked. It then stabbed his skin through his sock like a rat sinking all its teeth through his flesh at once. Squirming over onto his side in a panic reaction, he swooped the light down to see if the rat was small enough to defeat.

There was no rat. There was about six inches of electrical wire sprouting up from the ground and wearing a coat of knitted-cloth insulation that had not been manufactured since the 1940s. He curled himself tighter and got hold of it in his fist. Yanking on it unearthed an ancient light switch, the push-button kind that could be found in the remains of old houses that had burned to the ground due to faulty switches. Gleeworth disconnected it from his shoe and tossed it aside, amazed again at the crazy crap one could find in places like this. Easing over onto his stomach again, he dragged himself forward. A bicycle wheel was coming up next, and he refused to wonder why or how it had gotten here.

His flashlight went out. From life to death in the space of a millisecond. He banged it against his other hand and it functioned again. He twisted the end cap to make sure the batteries were in tight. Instead, the bulb winked on and off again. He tightened the plastic ring that held the lens in place and succeeded only in creating another light show. Grumbling under his breath at the manufacturer in faraway Taiwan, he continued to crawl.

Ahead he could see an approaching corner. A once-over with the stuttering flashlight didn't rouse any clues. So far he had this chore about halfway done. Far to his left was the mushroom of light that capped the basement. To his right the red bricks formed an angle that forced an adjustment in his steering. The flashlight quit about then, and no amount of physical torture made it seem likely to work.

Fine, he decided unhappily, this was bullshit anyway, forensics should be down here doing this in a scientific manner, and without something to light his way the house seemed to be pressing down on him, making it hard to breathe. It would be bad to get stuck down here with all these tons of house resting above. What if—and this was remote but it scared him anyway—just what if this old house collapsed before he could get out? Or an earthquake, there had been a mild one a few years ago, Terre Haute lay atop the Madras Fault and was due for a big one.

Panting, he abandoned the effort and headed back toward the basement. His elbows were getting sore and the front of his pants was steadily funneling dirt into his underwear. As he crawled his right hand closed over something hard and hairy. With a stifled scream he jerked away, his skin crawling, his hackles bristling: he had gotten a handful of rat. The need to escape was there, he had to stand up or go mad, this god-forsaken crawl space was shrinking. He rolled over and reached forward again. His other hand found the rat. It was moving with him. This time he screamed.

Panic seized him fully. He tried to climb to his feet, once, twice, in the dark battering his head and shoulders on the beams. Finally, on hands and knees, moaning with a terror he knew was groundless but could not overcome, he scrambled furiously toward the light of the basement, butting headfirst into the beams if he rose too high. When he finally slid, belly first, into the wide-open basement, he lay on the workbench, shaking and drooling, sweat cascading from his hair. Inhaling large gulps of air, he got himself to his feet, then pummeled his clothing both to rid it of dirt and to brush the filth of the rat away from his hands. That done, he sank onto the wicker chair to gather himself together. He had suffered episodes of mild claustrophobia all his adult life, but never like this. He was thankful that no one else had been here to watch, he was horribly embarrassed as it was. But that thing with the rat, that was crazy. It had felt hairy and hard, and in his panic he had managed to put a hand over it twice. Not a soft, squishy rat, though—more like a smooth rock covered with hair. Or a bone covered with hair.

Gleeworth sat more erect. The top of Perry Wilson's sev-ered head buried—and not very well—under his own house? Hank Thorwald not just a gawky young college teacher, Hank Thorwald a murderer? There was only one quick way to find out: crawl back under the house and unearth the hairy thing.

A tremor shook him from head to toe. No. No way could he go back under there again. Besides, this was a job for the forensics team. If they busted ass on this all morning, he might get a formidable warrant for Thorwald's arrest by af-ternoon, and then some solid FBI help as soon as he crossed the Indiana state line. And in reality it was fortunate that

Gleeworth had left the crawl space when he did. No sense tainting the evidence.

He was just standing up when sudden noise overhead froze him in position. Footsteps, the floor of the house creaking, over here, over there. Gleeworth frowned, thinking hard. Thorwald? No way, why come back? Perhaps a thief who'd seen all the newspapers unread on the porch?

Standard police issue was a Smith & Wesson 9-millimeter semiauto, but there weren't many places you could stick that big gun without leaving a telltale bulge. Instead, Gleeworth used a .380-caliber AMT Backup. It wouldn't drop a man dead in his tracks and it only held five rounds, but it was as flat as a slice of bread and made one hell of a scary noise. He had drawn blood with it twice in four years without a fatality.

Gleeworth drew the pistol and scaled the stairway quietly, mindful of the squeaks lurking in the old boards. At the open door he cautiously poked his head into the den, then pulled back to listen. He cocked a glance toward his watch. It was edging toward six and seriously trying to get light outside. All the windows were covered over by wall hangings, but sunlight of a sort was framing the edges. He picked his way over the books and stopped at the doorway, heard nothing, and moved out into the hall.

The refrigerator slammed shut. To hell with police training, all you had to do was grow up in an average American family to recognize the unmistakable breezy thump of the common refrigerator. Gleeworth made his way past the front door. The light in the house was dismal, not much better than total darkness. As if to prove this, he drove his left shin against a low coffee table. Something slid noisily across it to clump on the carpet. Ashtray full of cigar ashes, it smelled like. Gleeworth bit back the string of curses he reserved for moments like this. Off in the kitchen the sliding patio doors rolled immediately open and shut. He lifted a foot to get going and stuck it into the fallen ashtray, which zipped across the rug like the flat chunk of glass that it was, and took his foot with it. With a whoop he performed a backward somersault that he knew, even as he was airborne, was going to end badly. He crashed down on his ass and his teeth snapped shut, *clack!* The little pistol flew from his hand.

Pow! Across the room a lamp exploded. He was up in a second, embarrassed enough to glow in the dark, thanking God the bullet had found a lamp and not his balls. Back aching, he lumbered into the kitchen and through the patio door, ready to give chase and hoping he was up to the task.

No one was out there. Gleeworth used police procedure to duck and dodge around the outdoor grill, the only edifice in an otherwise empty yard, then relaxed with a scowl on his face. The person was gone.

As he walked back to the house, he was forced to admire Perry Wilson's patio. Beautiful polished rock sparkling with gems of long-ago rain, that magnificent barbecue grill made of the same stuff, cement holes in the ground where torches on tall poles stood to light up everything. With Wilson dead, he wondered, would the property go on the market? The house might be older than the pyramids but it was built as sturdily as a fortress and worth a fortune. Which took Gleeworth out of the bidding pretty fast.

A slice of sunshine rose up to tinge the clouds pink and orange. Gleeworth looked at his watch again as he entered the kitchen, and slid the door shut. Sleep was getting scarce lately, this Thorwald thing was nagging at him more and more. Fuck Hank Thorwald, he was the bad guy in all this, his time was almost up. The chickenshit bastard had run away leaving his daughter near death and his wife in charge of everything. In Gleeworth's opinion she was doing a damned fine job of surviving. Some people grow during hard times, and some people shrink. Rebecca was growing just fine, she was a survivor and she would make it.

In the hallway he noticed a small scatter of some sort of gray material on the floor. He dropped to one knee and pinched some between his thumb and forefinger, felt it, smelled it, tried to make sense of it. He made a mental note to tell forensics about it, then locked the house and went to his car. Under the front seat was a roll of yellow police tape and a handful of long wire stakes to string it around the house.

When that chore was done, he radioed the station to request a forensics crew, was promised one as soon as possible.

So far, so good. Gleeworth didn't know who had been prowling inside Perry Wilson's house, but if somebody was truly buried in the crawl space he knew damn sure who it was, and he damn sure knew who had killed him.

32

It was shortly after eleven in the morning when Rebecca arrived at her house at 1225 Quartermaine in the Bluewater Pointe subdivision south of Terre Haute, Indiana, driven there by a very courteous young policeman who nosed his blue-and-white copmobile between the cars and crowds of people with a hesitation that seemed almost apologetic. A couple of blocks from home she saw that her little Pontiac was still where she had left it but the windows had all been smashed and the paint was etched down to the metal with wild slashes and carved graffiti, and of course the spray-paint artists had been at work.

The THPD cruiser passed through the police corridor and pulled up to the curb in front of her house. With horror she surveyed it while her heart tumbled. 1225 reminded her of a road sign out in the country that had been shot full of holes just for sport. All the windows were history and the powder-blue vinyl siding had enough cracks and bullet holes to be used as a cheese grater. Sharri's blood on the front door was still a brutal splash that had faded from red to brown. Hank's beloved Lexus was a black skeleton with melted tires. Rebecca turned, dismayed mostly by the bullet holes.

"I thought you guys were protecting my house."

"So far we've arrested more than thirty people carrying guns," he replied. "We've got our hands full just trying to keep the arsonists at bay. But I can assure you that not one individual has entered your house for very long."

Her eyebrows jumped up. "For very long?"

He became nervous. "In the dark it's hard to spot slow

movement. Some of the people were in Vietnam, they learned how to be invisible."

"So is it safe to sleep in my own house tonight?"

He shook his head. "Hardly. But I do have the chief of police's invitation to lodge you in a hotel or a motel at our expense." For a moment he eyed her without speaking. Then: "To be honest, we have been swamped by this ordeal. We even had three guys pulled out of retirement to perform necessary traffic control. It's that bad."

"Sorry for their inconvenience," she said sullenly, and got out. As she walked to the house, she became aware of a growing swell of noise, a thousand voices being raised. When she turned she could see them, the strange and ugly crowd pressing forward against the yellow sawhorses while the police spread into a human chain to hold them back. They were alien to her, these hungry people, they had left their lives behind to come here and ruin hers. It occurred to her to raise both hands and flip them all the bird, but the gesture would show up in the media and the mainspring that powered this circus would be wound nice and tight again. She thought of asking the police for a bullhorn so that she could state her case, but the crowd wasn't here to listen. It was here to speak.

She was turning away when something dark flitted toward her vision. She snapped her eyes shut at the same moment she recognized a rock being thrown. It clunked against the socket of her right eye. She staggered back and plopped down on the grass, ripped with a pain sharper than any she had ever experienced. With one hand cupped over her eye she screamed into the palm of the other. The entire right side of her head was afire with hot, molten pain, she could feel the skin around her eye inflating to close it shut.

Another rock thunked on her skull, another in the grass beside her. Half-blinded, she got unsteadily to her feet and walked in a small circle looking for the door of her home. There was commotion, she was aware of that, she knew that the police were trying to protect her. A thrown object jabbed her shoulder blade like a dull arrow and made her squawk. When she turned slightly she saw a colorful Rubik's Cube bumble to a stop in the grass.

Somebody had thrown a Rubik's Cube. Some demented bastard had assaulted her with a goddamned Rubik's Cube. Of the ten billion things to throw at a riot, he or she had chosen this. She snatched it up and wheeled around to face her accusers. The cops were using batons to jab at the people. One of the yellow sawhorses keeled over and some people fell across it. Her personal driver had hopped out of the car and was jogging toward her. Rebecca jumped up on tiptoe.

"You sorry bastards!" she screamed while a thin line of blood ran from her eye like a teardrop. "You want Hitler? You got him!" She threw the cube back at them. It hit a cop on the shoulder and he jumped as if shot from behind. "This is total war, us and you!" she screamed, prancing on her toes, waving both fists. "Anybody hear me? Total war. Come and get it. You watch what happens."

A gun fired. Glass nearby shattered instantly and she twisted her head to look. The beveled glass porch light she had always liked was dribbling shards down onto the concrete; the whole frame of it was twisted out of shape, as if punched one good time with a boxing glove. Bullets were the most amazing things.

She turned her head again. Another sawhorse crashed over as a man broke out of the crowd. He hopped the curb and raced up the walk, leaping over the young cop, who had gone into a crouch. If he had a gun it wasn't visible in either hand; Rebecca clenched her lower lip in her teeth and raised her fists. No fear, none, it was now or never, this maniac was the beginning of the end.

He leapt at her like a big flying squirrel. She had time to duck her head and then he crashed down on her, ten thousand pounds of weirdo crunching her flesh and bones into the grass of her own lawn. Her breath whoofed out in a solid clump that might never return, but still she drew up her hands to claw at his face, knowing that he couldn't rape her with all these cops around but anxious to brand him as her own.

"Ow! Dammit! Mrs. Thorwald!"

He was trying to stand and shield his face at the same time. She used her fingernails to go for his eyes. Suddenly a pair of cops popped up and hauled him off her. "I am a police officer!" he shouted as they jerked him upright just long enough to get a new hold, and then he was shoved face first into the grass.

Another shot was fired. She was hoisted up, carried at high speed, and thrown into her house. As she drew in her first real breath, the maniac, looking a lot like Detective Gleeworth, was thrown in next, followed by the two cops using their own locomotion. Rebecca's young driver, currently as white as an egg, charged in last. He hurled the door shut. Something clunked against it three times; she assumed the rock thrower was not done with her yet but no, wood chips were exploding as bullet holes appeared. Another bullet blew the ornate brass knob to pieces and the door drifted open. More shots were fired outside, guns that sounded different. Louder.

"Deeper into the house," one of the policemen shouted. Rebecca was halfway erect; Detective Gleeworth, shiny badge in hand, caught her in a bear hug and danced her all the way to the base of the stairs, then pushed her to the floor and crouched down. When he finally released her Rebecca sat up, still mad, mad at the world and mad at these cops. Gleeworth pocketed his badge; the next thing she saw in his hand was a pistol that was absurdly small. He smelled lousy too.

"She's in a safe zone," he shouted.

One by one the other cops, pistols drawn, glanced cautiously outside and seemed to get a signal. One by one they ducked and ran out, the last man leaving the door to flap open and closed, open and closed.

"Stay down," Gleeworth snapped at her. He put his hand on her head but she knocked his arm away.

"Screw you, flatfoot. I refuse to be a victim anymore."

"You've been watching too much TV." He forced her down and straddled her to pin her to the carpet. "Better to be a victim than dead over all this silly shit."

She twisted against his weight. The vision in her blackening eye was squeezed off as the eyelid puffed fully shut. "Ever heard of a police brutality charge?"

"Ever heard of resisting arrest?"

She glared up at him. "So now I'm under arrest? This is why you came here?"

"No. I came to tell you that I found Perry Wilson's body."

Her struggles ceased. "So I was right. He *is* dead."

"Yes." He released her tentatively. "Hank Thorwald buried him in the crawl space under the house. On my belly I searched every inch and finally found the top of his . . ."

He got off her but stayed on his knees, hovering slightly over her. "You don't want the details. Suffice it to say that his disappearance is no longer a mystery. Forensics is unearthing him as we speak."

"Beautiful way to put it," she said, still lying on her back, her voice poisoned with sarcasm.

"You don't seem too upset by this, if I might point that out."

She lifted an arm and swept it to indicate the entire house. "Perry Wilson destroyed my family and our home. Hank was fired, I'm as good as fired, my daughter was almost killed, and now I've got a black eye and what will probably be a scar." She sat up. Outside, the shooting went on as occasional pop-pops. "You want me to start boo-hooing about Perry? Wrong person, wrong place."

"I meant upset about the fact that your husband killed him and buried him under his own house." There was a long break in the gunfire and he used his thumb to flip a lever on the side of his pistol. "I think you finally understand that nobody else in the world had a better motive for doing it."

"I know of one," she said, and sat up.

Gleeworth was reaching behind his back; his hand reappeared without the gun. "Who might that be?"

"Thorwald, Rebecca, maiden name Willden, white female, age twenty-nine. Would prop him up and kill him again if given the chance."

"You be funny." Just the breath of a smile swept across his face. "And you look funny with that shiner of an eye." The expression dissolved and he cocked his head. "Sounds like our gunman's been neutralized, Becka."

She raised both hands and pushed him away. Off balance, arms pinwheeling, he crashed over onto his back. "Don't you dare call me that." She got up. "I came here to take a shower and change clothes. Can I do that without police supervision?"

He stood too, massaging an elbow. "Be my guest, Mrs. Thorwald. I'll just stay right here and guard your life."

She had barely aimed a foot at the bottom stair when a uniformed cop hustled in, banging the door against the wall. "Are you Detective Gleeworth?"

He glanced at Rebecca and shrugged. "I keep a low profile."

"Sir? Telephone." He was extending a cell phone. Words etched onto the side of it let the world know it was the property of the THPD. "It's forensics."

Gleeworth snatched it out of his hand and thumped it to his ear. He made a motion that Rebecca understood as don't go yet. "Gleeworth here."

Rebecca sighed, not interested, knowing that there was a shower to be had upstairs and a really nice bed to sleep in, unless it was full of bullet holes.

"No shit? Let me know if you find out." He lowered the phone and seemed to be searching for a way to turn it off. Finally he handed it back to the other officer. "Anybody dead or wounded out there?"

"Nope."

"Thanks for the phone."

The officer left. Gleeworth looked at Rebecca. "That was forensics."

"So I gathered."

"They dug up the body parts."

"Good for them."

"It's not Perry Wilson, though."

She gasped. More bodies in Perry's basement? Lots of bodies?

"It's a male between the ages of eighteen and twenty-five who's been in the ground for a long, long time. Years."

Years? She pivoted and sank down onto a stair before her knees could fold and drop her in a heap. Gleeworth looked at her sharply. "You know something here that I don't?"

"Chaim Goldberg," she whispered, then raised her head. "How long have you been on the force here?"

"Pushing four years. Why?"

"So you probably don't know. An Israeli student at ISU

disappeared more than ten years ago. He played a lot of chess with Perry."

Gleeworth shut his eyes and rattled his head back and forth. "Perry killed his chess partner? Talk about a sore loser."

"But don't you see what that means?"

"It means I'm going to reopen the case."

"And it means that Perry intentionally set out to destroy Hank."

"Sore loser again?"

"Fuck you."

"Okay, fine, so Perry set out to destroy Hank's life, and then killed himself when it worked. Killed himself in a highly impossible way."

"I don't care if he hanged himself by the balls and twirled to death, Detective. It was suicide and not murder."

"Sorry. Hank's motive in killing the old guy is still intact."

"You don't even know Hank," she said bitterly.

"I will soon."

He eyed her.

33

Karl-Luther von Wessenheim, on the verge of collapse, climbed back into the long black Chrysler where Rønna Ulgard sat. The air conditioner was working quite well: after von Wessenheim slammed the door he aimed one of the vents to blow on his face and fell back against the seat, utterly spent. A good liar he was not, but he had done his best.

Ulgard looked him up and down. "Did it go well?"

"Water," von Wessenheim gasped. "I need water, I can no longer speak."

Ulgard dropped the shift into gear and set the Chrysler in motion. "There are little stores in this country that sell an amazing variety of items, including bottled spring water. *Kreiss-Ka und Sieben-Elf*, they're called."

Von Wessenheim was wiping sweat from his eyes, still panting. "What's that? That makes no sense."

Ulgard said it in English: "Circle K and Seven-Eleven."

"Oh, those. Yes. Cold spring water out of a plastic bottle."

They drove on through the bright summer afternoon. Terre Haute, it had turned out, was a pleasant old college town but the air in places smelled horribly of creosote, and was so thick with humidity that von Wessenheim's clothes stuck to his skin. They had arrived late yesterday after a murderous night of trying to fly from Denver to either Indianapolis or Chicago. Their original flight was Denver to New York and then on to Berlin; because of the change they were forced to be on stand-by status and spent the night watching plane after plane depart from Denver going to Chicago or Denver to Indianapolis, no extra seats in sight, not even in coach. Finally, at the O'Hare airport in Chicago, they had endured a three-hour layover because one of the old propeller shuttles between O'Hare and Terre Haute had developed a problem that grounded the whole fleet until they could be certified airworthy.

Thus, no sleep for him and definitely no sleep for Ulgard. He was paying him a million dollars a day and had no wish to watch him sleep through it. His rapidly dwindling fortune could take three days of this abuse before he called it to a halt and walked away with his dignity and enough money left to last him into his dotage. But if they were hot on the trail by then, if Hitler's bones were close enough to smell, he would give it all, would live in rags and starve if it became necessary. He was not unaware that great men often led lives of deprivation and despair. Famous artists, writers, men of ideals like Martin Luther and Germany's greatest writer, Schiller. Hitler himself had come out of the army highly decorated for bravery, but penniless, a misfit in society, and in those years of poverty his obsessive hatreds had taken root. The world was still reeling from his catastrophic impact on history.

Von Wessenheim noticed that Ulgard kept glancing at him through his ubiquitous sunglasses as he drove, so finally he sat up straight to report his findings. "When I said I was a reporter from Switzerland, the woman immediately got hostile. Apparently the police department is tired of reporters."

"Understandable," Ulgard said. "Go on."

"She said that Thorwald has not been seen for several days and has probably fled Terre Haute. She suggested I take the quickest flight back to Europe and she would call me if the situation changes."

Rønna Ulgard's lips curled upward in a sneer. "Americans don't know what to make of Europeans, Herr von Wessenheim. That policewoman probably expects you to be just that stupid."

"Whatever." Von Wessenheim loosened the knot of his tie. "I am no good at impersonation. She knew I was no reporter."

Ulgard shook his head. "Don't give the woman more

credit than she deserves. You found out what we needed to know before moving on."

Von Wessenheim thought it over, and nodded. "More than we learned by wading through the crowd at the Thorwalds' home, at least. I have never seen so much human energy wasted on hating an empty house. Even the neighbors looked to be guarding theirs with guns."

"Guns are easy to get in this country," Ulgard said. He lifted a gloved hand from the wheel in a gesture. "Some states have no waiting period whatsoever, one can purchase a gun and walk out of the store with it. Idaho comes to mind."

Von Wessenheim's gaze swept over to the profile of Ulgard's face against the city. "As in Boise? Don't tell me you purchased a gun there."

"I wouldn't dream of telling you."

"And you smuggled it through three airport security checks? That's impossible."

Ulgard looked at him. "Not many things are impossible, Herr von Wessenheim, but thousands of things are slightly possible. It's a matter of choosing correctly between the two. Hup, here's your store now." He quickly steered the car between the yellow parking lines in front of a Circle K, bouncing the front end up and down hugely as he miscalculated and went up onto the walkway. "American cars like this should be called arks," he growled. Von Wessenheim saw, as Ulgard fought the wheel, that the black leather cuff of his right glove had gotten jerked down a bit, exposing some of the skin of his upper hand. Thin blue slashes like the scars of stitches circled his wrist.

Ulgard killed the motor and took in a measured breath. "You are here." He pulled his gloves tighter.

"Water," von Wessenheim said. "Water and cigarettes. Have we eaten?"

"Get what you need. I'll be fine."

Von Wessenheim heaved the massive door open and clambered out. The raw, dry heat of Boise was a pleasant memory compared to this. He trudged into the store digging at the back of his pants, wondering if he had any American dollars left in his wallet. When he came to the row of coolers where beer and soft drinks hibernated behind frosted glass, the store's air-conditioning finally enveloped him and he stood transfixed, washed with pure pleasure. But a young fellow wearing his hat backward barged past him and the moment was over. Von Wessenheim reached out and hauled one of the glass doors open. He saw a medium-size bottle of a very dark wine. MOGEN-DAVID 20/20, the label said it was. It reminded him of the new age of the year 2000, facing the millennium with twenty-twenty vision. With a shrug he hauled it out. It wasn't quite pocket size but it wasn't big enough to cause him to get drunk. At the checkout counter he set it down. The clerk, a young man with bushy orange hair and wearing a nose ring, picked it up and grinned at him. "Mad dog," he said knowingly. "Woof."

"A pack of Marlboro cigarettes," von Wessenheim said. "Unless you have something better."

"Oh, we got that. We got that." He reached overhead and a pack of cigarettes fell from its hidden rack to land flat on the counter. "Camel Wides, Jack. Stout smoke. Put hair back on your chest."

Von Wessenheim turned the pack in his hands. It was an odd size, big and bulky. "Fine."

"You got an accent," the clerk said. "I notice things like that. Ten bucks even." Ignoring his cash register, he watched von Wessenheim dig through the confusion of international cash in his wallet. "You're from England, right?"

"Yes." He found a twenty-dollar bill and handed it over.

"Come here to interview Hitler, am I right?"

The wallet went back into his pocket. "Do you know where he is?"

"This store here is kind of like rumor control," the clerk with orange hair said. "People from all walks of life come here and they tell me things, they keep me informed. Right now I know more than most of the Terre Haute reporters, and all I do is just stand here all day with my ears open." He tapped a finger at his temple. "And I get paid too, Doc."

Von Wessenheim nudged his tie aside and put the cigarettes into his breast pocket. "Can you tell me where he is?"

He glared at him. "Instant replay." He tapped his temple again. "And I get paid too, Doctor Dumbass."

All this strange English was too much. "One moment," he said. "You must talk to my associate."

The other customer in the store came up behind him. Von Wessenheim turned and hurried out to the car to tap on the window. Ulgard made it slide down. "The clerk in there knows where our man is."

"Oh? Where?"

"No." Von Wessenheim gathered himself together. "The clerk wants money for the information. Handle it for me."

Ulgard twisted his face into a sour expression. "A clerk in a convenience store has no way of knowing anything that concerns us. Get in."

"But he might," von Wessenheim insisted. "At this point we don't dare pass up any opportunity."

Ulgard pushed his door open. "As you wish. I'll talk to him."

"No more than one thousand American dollars," von Wessenheim called as Ulgard marched inside. He skirted the car and stood by the door of the Chrysler nervously tearing open his new pack of cigarettes and trying to remember the words his limited knowledge of English could not translate. The other customer came out opening a little bag of potato chips with a plastic bottle of Coca-Cola tucked under his arm. On his arms and chest and bare legs sprouted enough hair to fill a pillow. Von Wessenheim dropped inside the car as he ambled past, feeling very prudish and foreign.

The car was still running, the air conditioner blasting. Von Wessenheim aimed another vent at his face and blinked against the cool wind as he watched Ulgard talk to the young man inside. As the conversation went on, he began to fear that Ulgard had not heard him and might start promising the clerk multiple thousands of dollars, dreading the idea that another fortune might be traded away today.

Ulgard suddenly reached with both hands and took fistfuls of the young man's orange hair. Using those handholds he smashed his face down on the counter, then hoisted him up again. Blood was suddenly evident. He shook him like a dusty suit of clothes. More words followed as von Wessenheim looked on in horror. Ulgard bounced the clerk's face off the counter again and heaved him backward; he caromed off the wall, spun in a staggering circle, and keeled head first into the overhead cigarette display before plunging out of sight. An avalanche of colorful cigarette packages sluiced out as if to bury him. The noise of it was enough that von Wessenheim could hear it in the car.

"Cheap little con man," Ulgard said when he was back. "All he had for sale was rumors." He handed over the bottle of wine that, in his zeal, von Wessenheim had forgotten. His twenty-dollar bill was pasted around it, stuck in place by the moisture hazing the bottle.

"We can't leave without paying," he said.

Ulgard stopped halfway in the act of buckling his seat belt to stare at him. "Swear to me that you did not say what I think you just said."

Von Wessenheim shrank back. "I swear it."

"Good. Buckle up. It's a good habit to get into."

Von Wessenheim did it with shaking hands. Stress was everywhere, stress lurked in the smallest of deeds, the simple purchase of a bottle of wine might now entail a high-speed escape from the police. And so much more lay ahead. He raised the bottle and sniffed it. Grape juice. Simply grape juice. Unhappy, he tipped it back and took six huge swallows just to slake his thirst.

"Don't worry," Ulgard said reassuringly. "Those convenience store clerks are routinely gunned down in this country. For *that* little headache he won't even bother to call the police. And besides, we're gone."

Gone they were. Ulgard shot the Chrysler out onto the street while von Wessenheim held on tight. These jumbo cars were imposing, and were equipped with imposing engines as well. Despite the tons of steel resting on the wheels they howled out a scream of pure power and belched blue smoke while the rear end fishtailed. But again von Wessenheim's heart fluttered. What was Ulgard doing, did he *want* the cops' attention? Panicked, he craned his head this way and that, his eyes guilty and fearful, scouting for the police cars that he envisioned as following.

"Rumors are strange things," Ulgard said conversationally. "Usually they are worthless, sometimes they are helpful, and once in a while they are exact. Here is what the grocery man wanted to sell me before I knocked sense into him: he has heard that Thorwald has been kidnapped by the CIA. That information is so patently stupid that I was obliged to knock even more sense into him. It led me to the solution of our problem, though. However . . ."

Von Wessenheim waited with his eyebrows raised, leaning slowly closer to Ulgard as he drove. "Well?" he blurted out when he could stand it no longer.

Ulgard spun the wheel suddenly to perform such an amazing about-face that in a wink of time it was over and von Wessenheim found himself inside a car headed in the opposite direction. Even though it was still plenty full, not a drop of wine had sloshed from his bottle of Mogen-David grape juice. Surely the man had taken a high-skill driving course where he had learned tactics like this. "So," von Wessenheim said, "where to now?"

"Back to the Ramada Inn. Sleep is in order."

Von Wessenheim stared for a bit while his hopes slowly dwindled and his eyelids drooped, then plugged the bottle between his lips and tilted his head back, sucking furiously. The moment had finally arrived. His brash promise of one million dollars per day was now going to create the most expensive nap ever taken on the planet by a human being. "We should plunge ahead," he said carefully. "Keep our momentum."

"Sleep first, Herr von Wessenheim. You look exhausted."

"Nonsense. And look at you, you're quite lively."

"That I am. That's why I'm leaving you at the Ramada while I go about doing what has to be done, finishing what has to be finished."

Simply that. Dear God, simply that. Von Wessenheim slouched with relief, every bone and muscle beseeching him loudly for a bed as if having heard and understood it all. A dozen questions came to mind but he forcibly boxed them up

and set them aside. Not many days ago he had gotten an excavating permit from this same man simply by asking and
paying. This situation was no different. It was clear that
Rønna Ulgard did his best work alone.

The Ramada was only a few miles south of Wabash Avenue. Ulgard drove under the awning in front of the reception
area and stopped. "I will report back to you by ten tomorrow,
Herr von Wessenheim. I estimate that this whole thing will be
wrapped up within forty-eight hours."

Von Wessenheim took another couple of swallows from
the flat bottle of Mogen-David. It seemed as if the stuff might
contain alcohol after all. "I hope you understand the importance of swiftness in this matter."

"Ten o'clock tomorrow," Rønna Ulgard said. "Good-bye."

Von Wessenheim worked himself out and stood clutching
his wine bottle to his chest as Ulgard squealed the Chrysler
across the cement, leaving black tracks. He thought about his
new cigarettes again, wanting to try one before going to
sleep. They were in his breast pocket, but no amount of
pounding on his clothes produced a book of matches. Disappointed, aware that he was tottering on his feet while a hot
gust of wind blew his hair to tatters, he headed inside with
one of the Camels stuck between his fingers. His eyelids had
grown too heavy to bother with the act of blinking; just maintaining them at half-mast required all the upward strength his
forehead muscles could exert. At the edge of the front desk
he stopped for another drink, guzzling as he rocked back and
forth, wishing it were a Coca-Cola or a Pepsi to quench the
thirst brought on by too much air travel and too much heat.
Or, even, the damned spring water he had intended to buy in
the first place.

With a fumbling hand he searched himself for the room
key. A bit of shadow fell over him and he looked up. To his
right a young lady in a white shirt and red vest had glided to
the desk. "Sir?" she said.

The sector of his mind that dealt with the English language
closed down for the second time in as many days. "*Kein
Problem,*" he said in his most hasty German, realizing that, as
scattered as he was, he probably looked a fright. He grinned

like an idiot with absolutely nothing intelligent to say that
was not German.

"Areyouregisteredhere?"

Von Wessenheim put on an expression of utter bewilder-
ment.

"IfnotI'llhavetoaskyoutoleave."

It was all gibberish. An idea struck him. He clapped the
bottle onto the desk and began another search of his pockets.
Nothing but a handful of change. Had Rønna Ulgard pocketed the electronic key when they'd left this morning? What
room number did they have, anyway? As he patted himself
down, the cigarette in his hand broke apart. Growing both
desperate and angry, he hooked the remaining stub between
his lips. As he did, his right elbow clipped the bottle, knocking it over. Sweet purple wine surfed across the red desktop
where just yesterday evening he had filled out a registration
form and slid American cash into a different girl's hands.
Meanwhile the woman lifted a telephone receiver to her ear
and punched some numbers while eyeing von Wessenheim as
warily as a cat.

"ThisistheRamadaInnIhaveanintoxicatedmaninthelobb-
whowon'tleave."

She babbled on for a few seconds, then hung up. Von
Wessenheim remembered that as a child he would sometimes
keep his house key in his shoe. But had he done that with the
flat plastic room key? Wouldn't he be able to *feel* it there?

Flushed with embarrassment, he walked to one of the
stuffed chairs that adorned the lobby, then sat with the idea of
removing his shoes. His book of Holiday Inn matches, he
discovered, was tucked under the upper rim of one of his
socks. He plucked it out and lit the remains of his broken cigarette, inhaled deeply, and sank back with his eyes drifting
shut from the sheer pleasure and comfort of it. There didn't
seem to be an ashtray nearby, when he opened his eyes again,
so he performed the properly German act of tapping the
ashes into his cupped hand. Presently, the big glass doors
swept open and two policemen walked in. After a brief conference at the desk, they came at him.

"Howarewedoingtodaysir?" one of them said, and carefully removed the cigarette from von Wessenheim's fingers. "YougotanyIDonyousir?"

It was like watching a foreign movie without subtitles. He spread his hands and shook his head slightly back and forth to indicate that he had not understood.

"Doyoulivenearby?"

Von Wessenheim could only smile.

"Areyouspeechimpairedsir? Canyouhearme?"

The girl at the desk leaned over it. "Hetalkedaminuteago."

He was urged to stand up. "Isthereanyonewecancallforyousir?"

Von Wessenheim shook his head, weak with embarrassment. To his eternal shock they took hold of his wrists, forced them behind his back, and handcuffed them together. A trace of his language ability returned and he was able to speak at last.

"What do you do? What do you do?"

They escorted him to their car.

34

Detective Steven Gleeworth steered his car to a stop at the Soldiers Bend police station and killed the motor. He climbed out and took in a breath of warm Ohio air. Sunset was gone and the dark air smelled like sweet honeysuckle, calling up childhood memories he was too tired to pursue. The engine clicked as it cooled in the breeze and he wondered for a strange wisp of time how many times the pistons had gone up and down in the last four hours, was it thousands or millions? Odd how one's mind could fracture when deprived of sleep for long periods. He clunked the door shut and wove a path to the station, still wearing the blue jeans and sleeveless sweatshirt he had put on days ago, but his badge was in his pocket and this small-town prisoner pickup wasn't likely to attract a crowd. Extradition papers were not even necessary, Ohio was glad to get rid of him and the meals the taxpayers had to dish out.

Gleeworth went inside to find most everything buttoned down for the night, a couple of empty desks doing nothing while a light burned inside a small room off to the right. "Yo," he called out. "Terre Haute here for a prisoner."

A door squeaked open and a wedge of light grew from it. A large man lumbered into view wearing the local uniform with the name "Grubbs" pinned to it. "You Gleeworth?"

"Yup. Here for Thorwald."

"You can have him."

Gleeworth hauled in a breath. "Troublemaker?"

"Nah, he's just half out of his head. Babbling on in German, or at least it sounds like the Dootch my grandma used to holler at me." He stuck a key into a box on the wall and hauled a ring of keys out. "Gotta see your badge and ID."

Gleeworth laid them out on the edge of a desk. A passing glance satisfied Grubbs. "We only got a four-man lockup," he said as he led the way deeper into the building. "Not like the big city."

"Be glad," Gleeworth said.

"I'm tickled shitless all day long. Here he is."

Gleeworth stopped. The light was dimmed for sleeping but Hank Thorwald was up on his feet and pacing the length of the cell. His clothes were torn and muddy, and he had lost a shoe. He tossed a glance at Gleeworth. "Okay, Adolf," the big man blared as he wielded the keys on the lock. "You got a new baby-sitter, and he's taking you out for a walk."

He turned to Gleeworth and spoke loudly: "He started walking back and forth and talking to himself right after we got him, and it's been getting worse, he's pacing like a tiger I seen in a zoo. Word to the wise: he's gonna blow. You got a cage in your rig?"

Gleeworth nodded.

"Put him in it."

"We'll see."

"Up to you." He turned again. "Einz zwy dry! You sprecken zee dootchy, ya?"

Hank Thorwald stopped and shook his head back and forth. As Gleeworth watched he put both hands to the sides of his head and squeezed his skull, his face wrenched with some kind of pain, his lips working as he whispered to himself. "Hank?" Gleeworth said, and Hank dropped his hands. "I'm taking you back to Terre Haute, Hank. Are you going to be trouble?"

He just cocked his head and stared.

"Come on out of there," Gleeworth said. "Let's get you back home."

He nodded. With a cautious glance at Grubbs he ducked out of the cell. Gleeworth could easily imagine the big man harassing him back here with no one around, rattling the bars and poking things at him as if he were a chimp. Sometimes people became cops just for the pleasure of its power. As

Gleeworth was about to turn, Grubbs suddenly grabbed Thorwald from behind and pinned his arms together. A set of handcuffs flashed as he swung them like a chrome hatchet.

"That'll keep your hands off your pecker," he said, and grimaced with the effort of snapping them tight; Thorwald's face twisted with pain. Grubbs offered Gleeworth a wink. "Old Adolf don't get no slack from me, not after thinking he could conquer America."

Gleeworth kept his face blank. Old Grubbs would have made a good concentration camp guard. He shoved Thorwald forward and Gleeworth hung back, trying to assess the man from these first impressions. "Unpredictable" just about summed him up. He had unwittingly walked the plank from his leisurely suburban life to a sudden plunge into the cold, black water of life on the run. He was no good at it, obviously. Almost nobody was.

Grubbs opened the door and shoved Thorwald out into the night. At the car he stood by while Gleeworth located a set of handcuffs that he wasn't sure he had. When the cuffs had been exchanged, Grubbs pushed his prisoner into the back of the car and slammed the door. "You watch out for old Hitler there," he advised Gleeworth. "He might try to conquer the world again."

"Thanks," Gleeworth replied. Once inside he switched on the dome light and looked back through the wires of the cage at Rebecca's husband. He was sitting upright in the middle of the seat with his bony legs cocked at cramped angles, staring forward with his head upright, his hair pointing in unusual directions and his clothes randomly buttoned to his skin by a couple of dozen scabs. "You're better off with me," Gleeworth said, and Thorwald flicked his eyes over but said nothing. Gleeworth started the car and drove out of Soldiers Bend the same way he had come in, but just before the ramp to I-70 West he pulled to the side of the road and got out.

"Turn so I can get those cuffs off you," he said when the back door was open. "I want you to know that I have been in close personal contact with Rebecca, and that Sharri survived the gunshot and is doing just fine."

Thorwald scooted over and bent so that Gleeworth could

get at the cuffs. When they were off he sat up again. "Thanks," he said, rubbing his wrists. "Thanks for the news. You don't know how much it means to me."

"I actually think I do, Hank," Gleeworth said. "Can I trust you to sit up front with me?"

Hank looked at him. The light was dim and his face was mostly a patchwork of shadows but his eyes gleamed. "I don't know," he said quietly. "I think I'd rather just stay back here."

"That works too," Gleeworth said. He got back inside, aware of the honeysuckle again, and pulled down on the gear shift. A telephone let out a shrill and sudden *tweet*. He fumbled around in the dark, cursing. Cell phones were just the latest in his list of gripes with electronics, the first being the indecipherable VCR he had bought ten years ago and still couldn't figure out. His fingers hooked around a coiled wire that could be traced to the cigarette lighter. Tracing it in the other direction resulted in the phone. He poked at its greenish numbers and put it to his ear. "Hello? Hello?"

"Detective Gleeworth?" The sound was bad, full of crackling and whooshing.

"Right here."

"We got a positive ID on the remains you found under that house."

He put the bulky little phone in front of his face and blew through the tiny holes where the sound came out. "Huh?"

"ID on the skeleton. Young guy named Goldberg."

Gleeworth sat back, amazed. "What, did he have his name engraved on his skull?"

"Dental records on file from a ten-year-old missing persons case. Any idea who he was?"

"Yeah, I do. That all?"

"That's it. Where the hell are you, anyway?"

"Headed home." Gleeworth poked at the buttons but they stayed green. He jerked the cord out of the lighter and stuffed the whole mess under the seat.

A great clanging bell sounded and Karl-Luther von Wessenheim yanked his head up from his pillow, for a dazed moment feeling like the six-year-old boy he'd been, sleeping at home in the quiet village of Wessenheim a handful of years after the war. Because Wessenheim was a small German town with no factories, World War Two had passed it by; it was untouched by the bombers that had flown overhead with their cargo of destruction and death. Nevertheless, the great bell rang each time just before the bombers appeared on the skyline, sending people scurrying to their basements, he and his pregnant mother included. Over five dozen of the town's men and teenagers had been shipped off to the army and most of them had not returned. When he was six years old, the survivors of Germany were almost done rebuilding, but the little town of Wessenheim had not suffered the slightest crack in its foundation and needed nothing. Now when the great bell clanged it was either time for church, which little Karl-Luther hated, or time to be at his desk in school, which he hated more. Any deviation from that schedule invited the anger of his mother, who did not love him.

These images bled away from his eyes as he fully awakened. He was on his stomach. In front of his face was a blank cinder-block wall. Slightly to each side was a vertical bed post made of tubular steel. Each of his hands was wrapped around one of these, one pole in each fist as if he were determined to pilot the bed to a safe landing. He did not know much about any of this but he knew he had money and he knew he had Rønna Ulgard. And, too, he knew he was still in America.

The great bell sounded again; this time he recognized it for what it was: the door to his cell clanging shut. Exhausted, he pushed himself up on his hands and swiveled to swing his legs out of bed. The cell was abominably hot and he was drenched in sweat from the effort of sleeping away his drunkenness in it. That single bottle of Mogen-David 20/20 had hijacked his senses and transformed him into a stumbling moron as if by magic. These Americans did not fool around when it came to fermenting wine. Perhaps someday he would import a case or two to Germany, throw a party for the Hitler Youth, and watch them rumble.

A policeman wearing casual clothing and a badge sloppily pinned to his sweatshirt brought a new prisoner to join von Wessenheim in the tiny cell. He stood stoop-shouldered, listening to what the policeman had to say. English was a monotonous language spoken with only a slight moving of the lips, and the sentences were heavy with the deep-in-the-throat *rrr* sound that was the sole property of American English. *Rrr-rrr-rrr.* Americans sounded like an old motor that wouldn't start.

But he did understand a bit of this: the policeman was promising to find the man's wife and bring her here as soon as possible. Then they discussed money for a thing called "bael." Posting "bael" to get out of the holding cell.

The policeman went away. The man looked like a hobo and gave von Wessenheim only the slightest glance before settling onto the other bed. The weight of the world was on him, von Wessenheim could see, and he was missing a shoe. He untied his single shoelace and muttered a phrase that made von Wessenheim sit up straighter.

"Zum Teufel mit der ganzen Sache."

To the devil with the whole mess. Von Wessenheim could not imagine he had heard it right. He cleared his throat and queried the man in German: *"Sind Sie deutsch?"*

He glanced at von Wessenheim. "What?"

Von Wessenheim reddened. "Please excuse me. I have not been hearing correct."

The man offered a confused but genial smile. He got his shoe off and fell backward on the bed. A bit later he hauled his legs up and flopped out straight on the thin mattress. By the time von Wessenheim drew another breath, he was snoring. Lying down again as well, von Wessenheim studied his quarters with sober eyes. The bars that held him captive had received many coats of paint over the years, were blistered and pocked and currently a greasy white. Fluorescent light shone from a long box in the ceiling protected by a heavy wire mesh. The walls were a ghastly pink color and the floor was cold, hard cement. Separating the two beds, bolted to the outside wall, was a steel toilet that had, despite its solid construction, been kicked and hammered into dents and dimples. The smell hanging in the hot air was composed mostly of a minty disinfectant.

He had never been in a worse place. But, oddly, he was beginning to view his trials and tribulations with the eye of an historian. Once the body of Adolf Hitler was presented to the world, there would be keen interest in the man who had found it, much like the case of the man who had discovered King Tut's tomb, Howard Carter. Von Wessenheim would likely be approached with a book deal. Now that his fortunes in this endeavor were going from bad to worse to hopeless, a real tale was developing. It would not be long before this very jail cell was described in detail on the printed page. It was important, then, to absorb every bit of it. The fact that he had been cast in here for public drunkenness would have to be altered, of course, but he imagined it to be a small matter in the business of publishing. Besides, that's what ghostwriters were for.

Sleep was a million miles away but it felt good to lie here and imagine success. Gradually, his new cellmate's snores went from the nasal exhalations of early sleep into the deep, bearlike roar of someone completely unconscious. He began to toss and turn, mumbling as he snored. After only a few minutes of it von Wessenheim opened his eyes, frowning. There was no pillow to wrap around his ears. He sat up. He was dehydrated by the alcohol, his body was clamoring for water. But it was the snoring, that was the primary thing that was impossible to endure. Von Wessenheim turned his head to stare at the other man hatefully. Unshaven, filthy, his clothes bloody and in tatters—a common street bum tossed in here with German royalty.

Disgusted, he probed for his cigarettes and found them missing. Alarmed, he replayed the mental tape of his arrest. It was cloudy, but sharp in places. Upon arrival here they had taken his belt and his wallet, he remembered that. They had asked that he remove his shoes and socks and turn the socks inside out. Very odd. He got his socks back, and when he bent to pull them on his feet, his pack of Camel Wides slid out of his shirt pocket and slapped on the floor, scattering a couple.

So they had confiscated them. His matches too. He had been stripped of everything but his dignity. Angry, he stood and went to the bars. Nothing to see, the place seemed shut down for the night. Surely a city the size of Terre Haute had a bigger jail, but this seemed to be it, he and the snoring man were alone. A holding cell, the policeman had said. *Eine Haltungszelle.* What other kind could there be? A non-holding cell? The fabled Land of the Free was too full of mysteries to ever make another visit worthwhile.

He shuffled around. Now the man on the bed looked like a corpse thrown from the window of an automobile moving at high speed. His limbs were tossed in every direction and his mouth gaped wide enough to display every inch of his dental work, which wasn't extensive. Von Wessenheim wondered very briefly what had brought such a young man to this deplorable place. Probably the illegal drugs that made him sleep so deeply that he could not even hear his own death rattle.

It was frivolous but von Wessenheim clapped his hands over his ears, his last chance to keep his sanity. The noise drilled through and he knew there could be no respite from this unless he acted. He went to stand at the side of the bed where his cellmate lay in such disarray. With a knee he prodded the bed frame, once, twice. It was obviously useless. He bent over the man and reviewed his lackluster knowledge of English again. *Aufwachen* was the German command, but what was the English version? Another snore rattled his ears and he hauled in a breath to scream.

"Um Gottes Willen, aufwachen!"

For God's sake, yes. For God's sake at least.

The man squirmed. His eyelids bumbled open and shut and he slurred a few nonsensical words: "Rook takes pawn." To coax him into turning over onto his stomach, the only sure cure for snoring of this magnitude, von Wessenheim gently prodded him. But his consciousness drifted away and he snored again, lightly this time as his whisker-stubbled jaw relaxed. Von Wessenheim rose upright and lurched back to his bed. His ghostwriter would be hard-pressed to convey such feelings of intense fatigue and maddening frustration.

Resigned, von Wessenheim sat on the bed and dropped his

face into his hands. To punctuate his snores the young fellow now began coughing out grunts and half-formed words, jerking around on his bed enough to make it squeak back and forth.

"*Ich bin Gefreiter* . . ."

Von Wessenheim's head jerked up. *Ich bin Gefreiter?* I am a corporal? No, fatigue was making him hear things again. The man was simply muttering nonsense.

"*Auf keinem Fall bin ich der Kaiser* . . ."

What?

"*Verdammte Juden* . . ."

Von Wessenheim clapped both hands to his chest, one on top of the other. Damned Jews. He had said it quite clearly. Why would an American street tramp curse the Jews in his sleep?

"*Ich bin Soldat . . . ich kämpfe . . . ich bin* . . ."

Von Wessenheim rose up, morbidly fascinated, the solution to this mystery close enough to reach and snatch from the air like a drifting soap bubble. It had been exciting to imagine that somehow Fate was directing him, but in reality he was an agnostic, he did not know if there was a God and he did not care if there was a God. But Hitler had been a firm believer in fate, had felt himself guided by her until the last minute, when he had realized that she had betrayed him from the start.

"*Schadenfreude* . . ."

He drove himself to his feet. This German word indicating pleasure in the misfortune of others was probably nothing most Americans would know or ever have a use for, which meant that this young man who snored so loudly while squirming like an octopus was either a fellow German in the throes of a nightmare, or the man who had told the world he had been Adolf Hitler. Von Wessenheim had taken only one step toward him when suddenly a case of nervous trembling besieged him. His mouth became as dry as ashes and he felt heavy with the weight of his age and the importance of his mission. It far surpassed the venue of Frau Dietermunde's group of former Hitler Youth, it surpassed his own petty insistence that he purchase a top hat that might have been worn by the Führer.

With his shaking fingers clenched into fists and held stiffly along the outer seam of his trousers, he marched to the other bed and looked down at the man. He was a common bum. He was an unwashed bum. He was a raggedy bum who spoke German in his sleep and was—or was not—the bum who would help immortalize the name of the royal house of Wessenheim.

But first he had to wake up. Again von Wessenheim hesitated to do it. Only when the bum inhaled a larger breath than usual and blew it out with all the volume of a tuba could he act. He bent and took the man by the shoulders and began shaking him. "*Aufwachen, mein Freund,*" he crooned. "From the bed stand up and talk with me."

At first he flopped this way and that but after a few seconds began to fight against it. His eyes slid open but were rolled up too high in their sockets to indicate consciousness. Von Wessenheim shook him a little harder, then released him and wiped his hands on his shirt, waiting for him to cast off his slumber and come awake. Instead, he slowly rolled over to face the wall and brought his knees up in a fetal position. A gentle snore drifted out of him.

Enough was enough. Von Wessenheim lifted him off the bed by the front of his shirt, manhandled him around to sit upright, and clutched a handful of his hair to keep him that way. "*Aufwachen!*" he hissed in his face, then rose higher for a moment to scan the area for listeners before ducking down again. "*Bist du Adolf Hitler? Bist du der Führer?*"

His eyes blinked open and shut again. "*Also wurde ich anti-Semit.*"

Von Wessenheim gulped in a quick breath. It was a famous line from *Mein Kampf*, the book Hitler had written in prison. "*Bist du Adolf Hitler?*"

He stiffened and his eyes stayed open but were glassed over, as if he were in a trance. After a slow breath he replied: "*Ich bin Führer des Deutschen Reiches.*"

Von Wessenheim released his hair in awe and staggered back a couple of steps with his skin pimpling into gooseflesh and his heart pulsing in his throat nearly hard enough to burst it. The goddess Fate was in this cell with him, he could feel the weight of her presence and it almost drove him to his knees in prayer. When his vision clouded and became full of sparkling stars he realized that he was forgetting to breathe and sank to his knees, but not to pray. The world might never believe that this simple man was Adolf Hitler, but it would not scoff when the tomb was uncovered.

After a few deep breaths, he shuffled forward. "My Führer," he said in German, "did you make arrangements to be buried in a secret place?"

Something about the man's eyes changed, as if a lamp behind von Wessenheim had glowed alive. His pupils shrank and lost their waxy stare. "Did you?" von Wessenheim said, alarmed.

"I made . . . I made . . ."

His head was sinking. Von Wessenheim clutched it between his hands, digging furrows through his greasy hair. The Führer was falling asleep again, he was becoming the American again. "Did you?" von Wessenheim pleaded. "In the name of God, tell me yes or no."

He sank back on the bed despite von Wessenheim's efforts to hold him up. Von Wessenheim rose and hovered over him, needing an answer to his question before his sanity left him forever. "Please tell me," he moaned. The Führer's eyelids were closing, so he held them open with his thumbs. "Were you buried in a secret place?"

He snored. Von Wessenheim made a mewling noise. The answer to the biggest mystery of the century lay in this man's mind and von Wessenheim was losing him. Again he took hold of his shirt and jerked the man up off the bed. "Answer me!" he shouted in his face. "Give me an answer!"

His eyes came open with infuriating slowness.

Von Wessenheim was panting from the effort of keeping his mind from cracking in half. He raked in a breath and shook the Führer as if battling an attack dog with his bare hands. "Were you buried in a secret place? *Ja oder nein!*"

He could not help himself: he hauled back and slapped the American hard enough to eject a spray of saliva from his mouth. Von Wessenheim's next words were bellowed from the depths of his lungs. "*Ja oder nein ja oder nein ja oder nein!*"

A door clanked open somewhere. He heard the slap of shoes against the cement floor and froze in place while the American's shirt slid through his fingers. He flopped down. A whisper drifted out of his mouth and von Wessenheim dropped to his knees again. He pressed an ear to those moving lips but heard only one fading word distinctly.

"*Ja.*"

Yes. Yes, the real Führer was buried in a secret place. Yes, the search for his tomb was a valid endeavor. And yes, von Wessenheim was the man chosen by Fate to find it.

By the time the jail keeper came to the cell von Wessenheim was covered up on his bed pretending to sleep. In reality he was both laughing and crying into his pillow, and would keep doing so until he fell asleep an hour later.

35

Frau Ilsabeth Dietermunde was not in a good mood when her telephone jangled in the middle of the night. At seventy years of age she was not yet feeble enough to require a night butler, so she slept with a telephone in the grand bedroom of her family's historic mansion overlooking Bad Nauheim, the town whose mineral waters were legendary. Normally no one with any sensibilities at all would dare call so late. But when she opened her eyes and looked at the numbers on the clock she realized that this offense was even more serious. The caller had surpassed all the bounds of civility by dialing her number at 3:58 in the *morning*. No one in all of Germany was up yet.

She lifted the ivory receiver reminding herself that it was broad daylight in America, and perhaps some young businessman needing her direction had not yet learned that the whole world does not run on New York time. "Hallo," she said grumpily, then heard the voice and immediately sat up in bed. She snapped on the bedside lamp. "Rønna?"

"Calling you from a steaming hothouse called Indianapolis, Indiana."

"In America still? Is von Wessenheim with you? Tell me what's happening."

"I hope you are sitting down, Frau Dietermunde."

"I'm in bed, for God's sake, have you forgotten that the world is round?"

"Is your line secure?"

"Of course it is. I have it screened twice a day."

"Good. Herr Karl-Luther von Wessenheim has retained me

for new services, and is in a motel room in a nearby town waiting for me to kidnap a man who believes he was our Führer in a past life."

She frowned, her newest facelift causing the skin of her face to crease and wrinkle in odd ways. "You are to kidnap a man? Do you dare?"

He drew in a quick breath. "You miss the point. The kidnapping is not a problem, it is the fact that von Wessenheim has thrown all his logic and research out the window in favor of talking to a man who says he was once Adolf Hitler. And he is paying me a large sum."

"How large?"

"One hundred thousand American dollars per day. Two hundred twenty thousand Deutschemarks, roughly."

"My God, the man is desperate. Will you pledge ten percent?"

"As usual."

"You are a good son. So what is your next move?"

"To extend this farce until the man is penniless."

Frau Dietermunde stroked a hand through her blonde-tinted hair as she thought about it. "You must continue to demand more and more money. Tantalize him with small successes in locating the . . what is he again?"

"The reincarnation of our Führer."

"Could there be any truth to that?"

She thought for a confusing moment that the connection had failed. "Listen to me," Rønna Ulgard said evenly. "If the Führer's soul has been reborn in another man, why do we keep the flame burning, why risk our professions and our lives?"

Frau Dietermunde nodded, embarrassed and slightly angry at being chastised by her own son, but it was evidence that she had raised him in the faith. Yet the idea of the Führer reborn was huge in all its possibilities. "You're right, Rønna, my age makes me stupid sometimes."

"People in America have gotten even stupider. The man was driven from his home by angry mobs, fired from his university professorship, and his young daughter was shot by police."

Frau Dietermunde drew herself upright. She had hoped to see the faith rise from its underground existence in her own lifetime, but with so much hate against the Führer in the world, it would not happen until her generation passed away. And maybe even her son's generation, and the one following. But it *would* happen, inevitably. A rebirth from the ashes.

"So sad to hear," she said.

"And that is all for now. I'll keep you informed. Good-bye."

She slowly levered an arm and pressed the receiver onto its resting place. Von Wessenheim had excited her when he was first invited to participate in an auction. He was royalty, and he was bitter about the ruination of Germany's peerage by the war. But as he dabbled in the wartime baubles and memorabilia it became evident that his concern was only for the investment value of the baubles and memorabilia, nothing else. Despite the delicate hints laid before him by herself and other members, he had been too cloddish to see them, he had never expressed an admiration for the Führer and was concerned only with the money to be made. Those actions rendered him unwelcome, but he maddeningly came back again and again with no comprehension of the reality behind the bartering. Most people, she and the others had learned over the years, do not collect National Socialist pistols and badges and uniforms unless they are sympathetic to—or at least fascinated by—its principles. That included hundreds of Americans and British and Australians and the whole melting pot of Europe who doted on these things. And to understand its principles was to realize that it was not over, that it had risen above its earthly boundaries after being purged by the fires of war. National Socialism was now reduced to a primitive underground church, Frau Dietermunde acknowledged, but its roots were spreading worldwide. Like ancient Christianity, it would flourish in secret.

They were grand thoughts. She extinguished the light and lay back down in bed. Sleep chased her like a bright ghost in the dark but never quite caught up.

Rønna Ulgard got back to the Ramada Inn just after eight in the morning, having spent the night scouring the planet for a

Mr. Harrison Thorwald. In truth, he had driven straight to Indianapolis to add mileage to the rental car so that when von Wessenheim returned it, the receipt would prove Ulgard had been logging many miles on his search. He had lodged himself at the Marriot Hotel and watched television to scrape some of the rust off his skill with English until falling asleep. The call to his mother early this morning had left him with a bad taste, though: even *she* had paused to wonder if Thorwald was the Führer reborn. If that were true, the Hitlerjugend would have more to dabble in than Nazi artifacts.

But back in Terre Haute the room at the Ramada was empty. It appeared to have been that way all night. The air conditioner was off and the beds had not been touched. The sink and bathtub were dry, the television cold, the water inside the toilet tank warm and not recently flushed. Mystified, he clopped down the stairs and asked at the desk, but the crew had changed shifts and the youngsters currently running the show knew nothing. Ulgard wandered over to the restaurant and ate a breakfast of ham and poached eggs, puzzling as he glanced through the *Terre Haute Tribune-Star*. He asked the waitress if she or any of the staff had seen a silver-haired gentleman yesterday afternoon who was slightly tipsy.

No. But the waitress *did* recall a police car having been out front around two or two-thirty yesterday afternoon. This news filled Ulgard with foreboding. He leafed hastily through the pages of the newspaper and found the section that listed births, deaths, fire department activity, and arrests for the previous day. The print was tiny but Ulgard was not yet old enough to need reading glasses. The elderly von Wessenheim, however, would need a pair to find his own name, and find it he would, because there it sat misspelled in black and white, Wessenheim, Carl L., public intoxication and public nuisance.

He peeled off his sunglasses and let his forehead drop onto one of his gloved hands, staring down at the crumbs of toast and yellow traces of egg yolk on his plate without seeing any of it. The drunken old fool had gotten himself thrown in jail. It probably involved a prostitute, or the search for one. And this was the man Rønna Ulgard's own mother regarded as a threat to the survivors of the Hitler Youth. It was absurd. But still the mission was important; above all else, Mother wanted von Wessenheim to fritter away all his time and money on this preposterous reincarnation thing and that was what he would do, that was what would happen. But, in fact, it would be easier to simply arrange for him to die. Ulgard had investigated him thoroughly and knew he had no relatives and no heirs, no one who cared, not even a loyal butler or maid. He could easily be strangled and stuffed into the rest room at some gas station near here. Already he was known to the police as a drunk. They would not waste much time with him. Off to the crematorium and then the pauper's cemetery, here lie the ashes of Johann Doe.

The idea was funny but not funny enough to laugh about. Ulgard dropped a twenty-dollar bill on the table and struck out across the Ramada's parking lot. The day's heat was beginning to get serious and the big black Chrysler was as hot as a toaster inside. The air conditioner labored well as he drove toward the heart of Terre Haute.

As he neared Wabash Avenue, a stately old building emerged on the left, a nineteenth-century structure of limestone that was capped with the tapering dome American architects favored in those years, possibly trying to copy the capitol building in Washington. From its peak a flagpole thrust up bearing a huge Stars and Stripes that was hanging motionless in the absence of wind. At the intersection he stopped for the red light, lifting his sunglasses to examine the courthouse. Just to the right of it was a flat-roofed, redbrick building undergoing construction of some sort. The entire area was a sea of automobiles. He saw several police and sheriff's cars parked in the spaces at the front of the red building. That would be police headquarters. Whether Terre Haute's jails were housed inside it, or in the basement of the courthouse, was simply a matter of asking someone.

The red light became a green arrow. Ulgard made the Chrysler leap forward, very much liking its power, and cranked the steering wheel with one finger hooked around a padded spoke, very much liking its power steering. But he was gentle as he brought it to a stop in front of the station. Getting out into the staggering heat simply reminded him again of the money he was earning, and as he walked to the door he adjusted his necktie and his lapels, and tugged his gloves up tighter. Terre Haute did not seem to be a hotbed of crime, considering the lack of activity he saw as he went inside, but it was still mid-morning and crime was more a creature of the dark.

The lobby was empty. On the wall to the right was a directory complete with room numbers and arrows that indicated the direction one should walk. Ulgard ignored it and strode deeper inside the building, brushing past uniformed officers and civilians as he penetrated the hallways. Things always got more serious as one gained distance from the area available to the public, and it was inevitable that someone would protest.

"You can't be back here."

Ulgard stopped, took his sunglasses off, and turned around. A man had jumped through the doorway of an office wearing a wrinkled white shirt and an orange necktie.

"This area is not open to the public," he said, stepping closer. "You'll have to go back the way you came."

Ulgard draped an expression on his face that indicated serious confusion. "I come to get my friend," he said. "To pay bail monics for he."

The man smiled immediately. "Come with me," he blared loudly in Ulgard's face as if he were deaf. People worldwide tended to believe that a foreigner had a better chance of understanding if the words were shouted. "I'll get you straightened out."

"Thanks to you," Ulgard said humbly.

"So," the man asked as they walked, "you from Italy?"

"Tyrol."

"That's a country?"

"The German-speaking part to Italy."

"I recognized the accent." In the lobby he grabbed an officer cruising past. "Nate, this guy's here to bail out a friend. Could you walk him through it?"

Nate took a quick peek at his wristwatch. "Guess I got time. Yeah." He put on a big smile. "You speak English?"

"Little bit," Ulgard replied, using his thumb and forefinger to indicate a small gap. "But I like USA big much."

"Nice gloves," the policeman observed. "A little too hot though, isn't it?"

"Thank you," Ulgard replied.

"Mmm. What's his name?"

"Karl Wessenheim."

"Okay, let's see if we can't get your friend out on bail."

Ulgard followed him. Sometimes dumb was the smartest play a body could make. When they realized that von Wessenheim had jumped bail and would never be seen again—at least not in *this* city and state—they would wish they had not been so accommodating.

The bail was only two hundred dollars, and the release procedure took less than twenty minutes. Karl-Luther von Wessenheim, German royalty, was trundled out in handcuffs. His silver hair looked as if it had been struck by lightning and his unbuttoned clothing rearranged in a storm. He seemed intensely worried and his eyes were darting until they paused on Rønna Ulgard. Something about him seemed explosive: the man was ticking like a bomb. Ulgard had been glancing through a magazine; he set it aside and stood.

"He's here!" von Wessenheim called out to him as the officer struggled to unlock the cuffs. "I've found him, I found the man who was the Führer! He is here!"

"Calm down," Ulgard said evenly. "If you act like a madman, they will take you right back inside."

Von Wessenheim continued to struggle. "Did you hear me, man? Did you? The Führer is here!"

Ulgard thanked the heavens that he was not shouting the Führer's name out loud. A couple of gleeful Adolf Hitlers would draw suspicion. "Shut up, shut up," he said with a smile and a pleasant tone.

Von Wessenheim relaxed and let the officer do his work, but the fever in his eyes gleamed madly. When the cuffs were off, von Wessenheim sprang forward and hugged Ulgard. *"He is here,"* he whispered over Ulgard's shoulder as he clenched him tight. *"We must get him out!"*

Ulgard untangled himself from his arms, embarrassed.

"We must walk out of here like sane men," he said as he pushed von Wessenheim gently away.

"My God, no! Our man is here, we were in the same cell. He spoke German to me in his sleep!"

"The door is just behind you," Ulgard said without motioning. "Turn around and march out before they drop a net over us both."

"Net? Why?"

Ulgard gently took hold of his shoulders and turned him around, offering an apologetic smile to Nate. He got a wink in return. Nate looked at his watch, winked again, and walked away. His good deed for the day was done.

"Don't make me push you," Ulgard growled against the back of von Wessenheim's neck. "Get to the car so we can talk."

Von Wessenheim spun around. "Don't forget who's paying your wages, Herr Ulgard."

Ulgard bristled. "Don't forget *why* you are paying my wages, Herr von Wessenheim."

"To find the man who used to be Hitler. Instead *I* have found him. Through the intervention of divine fate he has been delivered to me, and I no longer question the mission that destiny has chosen for me. I will deliver Adolf Hitler to the world."

Ulgard glanced around. Von Wessenheim's loud jabbering in German had already attracted some ears, but at the mention of Hitler heads were turning. He hunkered lower. "All right. I will get your man before you get us arrested. Harrison Thorwald, is that correct?"

"It is burned into my memory."

Ulgard dug the keys to the Chrysler out of a pocket of his slacks and pressed them into von Wessenheim's hand. "Go sit in the car. Stay there. I will get this man for you, Herr von Wessenheim. And together we will find the Führer."

Von Wessenheim stood taller. "That's the spirit."

36

The car was an inferno inside but von Wessenheim sat primly on the passenger's seat with his knees together and his hands folded in his lap. Sweat shone on his unmoving face and tracked down his forehead in big drops that soaked into his eyebrows. The breaths that left his body were cooler than the breaths he drew in; the car was black and the interior was black and the sun was so hot that the asphalt of the parking area had warmed his soles through his shoes. In such heat the poisons of yesterday's wine were sweating out through his pores, but more important, this event was being branded into his memory: the killing temperature, the agonizing wait, the hunger and the thirst. Add to that the injustice of his false arrest, his unkind treatment by the guards, the humiliation of being handcuffed, and the confiscation of his cigarettes. In the hands of a skilled filmmaker, this scene could be a very powerful one.

He had doubts but still he sat with his knees together and his hands folded in his lap while the heat sank deeper into his flesh. In his lifetime he had enjoyed the privileges of wealth but was not a stranger to suffering; he supposed no one was, really. His mother had died while she was away in France and had specified her wish to be cremated there without a funeral. Karl-Luther had been seventeen years old when a special-delivery postman arrived at the mansion to hand him a small cardboard box tied up with string and double-wrapped in waxed paper. Removing the waxed paper revealed the sticker on the box: it contained Madame Katherina von Wessenheim. In shock and surprise he had dropped it and a corner of it had split to release a small white gush of Mother onto the floor. How she must have hated him.

Vaguely unhappy now, von Wessenheim opened the door and let some air inside. He had good reason to be unhappy, he realized, because he had not slept for about ten years and had been served jailhouse slop for breakfast. In order to eat he had been marched to a cafeteria and been forced to sit with jailbirds. Never in his life had he seen so many tattoos. Amazingly, a lot of those tattooed men had been emblazoned with swastikas and other Nazi items. One man's skinny arms were wound with blue and red snakes and the words "Aryan Pride" were tattooed all over the snakes. The breakfast crew had consisted mostly of white men with long ratty beards and hair, and some angry-eyed black men segregating themselves at another table. His frazzled nerves were popping and crackling like a live wire dangling from a pole; he had not known which group presented the most danger to him. When he finally realized no one cared if he was sitting there alive or dead, the allotted time was almost gone and he was forced to gobble.

As he was about to stand outside in hopes of catching a gust of air, he remembered that Ulgard had offered him the car keys and that he had put them in his pocket. Cursing himself and his lapse of memory, he fished them out and lay across the seat to stab one of the keys into the slot on the steering column. The car shook itself alive. A computerized bell with a clapper as soft as a marshmallow gently pealed to remind the driver to buckle the seat belt. Happier, he propped himself up on an elbow to study the dials in the center console, easily locating a snowflake and the emblem of a fan. He twisted them both and sat up, then fiddled with the radio. It was alive with knobs and buttons and sliding switches but none of them made it produce sound. Irritated, he poked and pulled at the knob of the glove compartment, needing something to do to help stay awake. When it finally dropped open, not even a map or an owner's manual was inside to make the effort worthwhile. Scrunching backward, he straightened his legs and arched his back in a huge yawn. His spinal cord made pleasant little crackling sounds. But when he pulled his foot back, something tugged at the toe of his shoe. Thinking it was snagged on the carpet, he jerked back harder. There was a small tearing sound.

He sat up. Growing from the end of his shoe was a strip of heavy gray tape all twined together and stuck to itself. Ignoring it, he rocked himself forward and probed under the dashboard with his hands. Something was there in the dark and mysterious space auto manufacturers left under the dash, some thin and bumpy thing. More tape plucked at his fingertips. He hooked them into the whole nest and grunted as he peeled it all away and out into the light.

A gun. A pistol, to put it more precisely. A funny little flat thing made mostly of black plastic with a comically short blue metal barrel sticking out. The thing was hardly more than a peashooter. It probably fired those little .22-caliber bullets marksmen used for inexpensive practice. In Boise Ulgard had mentioned having a gun he could slip through airport security. With only that small metal barrel to show up on the X-rays it might be either ignored or camouflaged inside a smoker's pipe or camera or other piece of mundane equipment.

He suddenly realized that he was holding property not meant for his eyes. He hurriedly jammed it back under the dash and mashed the snarl of tape upward, hoping it would hold. When he let it go, it stayed. Then sudden noise jerked him more erect. Cars and motorcycles were roaring into the parking lot at high speed, chased by two vans with miniature dish antennas anchored to their roofs. Von Wessenheim realized with an audible groan that the media had discovered his prize. He whipped his head around, trying to see them all at once as they descended on the station. The vehicles came to a stop wherever they pleased and people scrambled out to crowd around the entrance, where an officer, looking every bit as astonished as von Wessenheim himself, blocked the door with outstretched arms.

Someone had leaked the news, a policeman, perhaps, or a civilian employee, somebody who had learned of the famous prisoner and had collected thousands of dollars from the paparazzi. Possibly even the plainclothes cop who had put

Thorwald in the cell last night; he had looked both over-worked and impoverished. It did not take a lot of money, von Wessenheim knew from experience, to bribe a member of the working class.

Photographers were still arriving, several even on bicycles, laden with cameras and lenses. One good photo of Thorwald might be worth a fortune to a hungry tabloid. The ones on bi-cycles, he saw with surprise as they dumped their bikes with-out ceremony and joined the squirming horde, were teenaged kids. Just one lucky picture of Thorwald in a menacing pose and they would secure their futures as professional photogra-phers. How odd that they should ignore the man in the rented black Chrysler; in a day or two they would be jostling each other for a shot of *him*.

Something was happening, the crowd was falling back. Von Wessenheim craned his head higher and saw, above the bobbing heads, that the door had opened. At least two police-men were clearing a path. Cameras began to flash, hesitantly at first, then in a barrage. He opened his door and stood, squinting in the heat: Thorwald, with Rønna Ulgard at his side, was trying to make his way out. Von Wessenheim's spir-its soared: Thorwald was free. In the motel they would hyp-notize him, get the information, and dump him somewhere, then back to Germany.

More vehicles arrived in a sudden wave. Von Wessen-heim's eyes widened as people piled out. It was the gawkers and the protesters; the lunatic fringe had abandoned the house and had followed the media circus here. Their angry voices and shouts as they joined the melee rose steadily. More policemen exited the building to form a protective ring around Thorwald and Ulgard. The flash of cameras was now a sparkling cascade of light, a glow like the stuttering of a fluorescent tube. He realized belatedly that he could be of as-sistance here and hurriedly put himself back in the car. Slid-ing behind the wheel, he dropped the gear shift into reverse and backed out of the slot hard enough to spin the rear tires. Something crunched underneath but he ignored it. With the gear shift in drive, he made the car leap forward and glanced in the mirror. Broken spokes and bent wheels, somebody's bicycle was ruined. By maneuvering between the randomly parked cars, he came to the outer circumference of the mob and hammered the horn. Grudgingly, the people gave way, some shouting at him and beating on the top of the car with their fists, annoyed at his passage. Several others sat on the hood for a ride, and a huge bearded man jumped onto the rear bumper of the Chrysler and bounced himself, and it, up and down while shouting anti-Nazi epithets at the top of his lungs. Two men in camouflage clothing dragged him off and began beating him to the ground.

And then was the ring of uniformed policemen, which did not give way. One cop fought his way to the window and von Wessenheim quickly rolled it down. "What the hell are you doing?" he bellowed in his face.

"I am pick up car," von Wessenheim shouted back. "For Thorwald to pick up."

"Good. Stay right here, don't move." He clawed a route through the bodies and shouted things at the other cops, gesturing. Several turned, looked back at him, and nodded.

The circle of police became an oval, part of it bulging out to clear a path to the backseat of the car. Suddenly Thorwald was there, being pushed forward by Rønna Ulgard. A policewoman raked the door open and Thorwald plunged inside. Ulgard wrestled his own way in and she slammed the door shut. "Get us out of here," Ulgard growled as he used a fist to hammer each door lock down, front and back.

The car had become the focus now. People pressed in, the cameras machine-gunned von Wessenheim's eyes with light, hands that were mashed against the windows looked bloated and weird. The car began to rock from side to side. The first police batons made an appearance. He watched, aghast, as the cops began clubbing people. The female officer had an aerosol can in hand and was spraying it directly into a man's face. He pitched away, screaming and clawing at his eyes. The air conditioner sucked a drift of it in and von Wessenheim's own eyes began to burn. With a huge and sudden crunch, a brick lodged itself halfway through the windshield, spraying von Wessenheim's chest with a buckshot of glass pebbles. He uttered a short scream of surprise.

"Try going backward," Rønna Ulgard said over his shoulder. "Slowly, though; if you kill somebody we'll be tied up for months."

Von Wessenheim lifted the gear shift with a hand that was palsied. He looked over his shoulder but there was nothing new to see, the car was encased in bodies. Overhead the roof made boinging noises as someone walked on it, danced on it, then plopped down heavily to sit on it. A pair of hairy legs ending in hiking boots thudded down on the windshield, then began kicking it in with its heels. A policeman used a single stroke of a baton across the shins to quickly abort the act; the man fell howling to his knees on the hood and rolled off.

But the car was making progress. Nursing the brake, von Wessenheim finally idled into clearer territory. The police were performing miracles, by his reckoning. Could they prevent the crowd from following? He doubted it. Which meant trying to hypnotize a man in a motel room when the motel itself is surrounded by a screaming mob.

Ulgard spoke over his shoulder again. "You have your man, Herr von Wessenheim. Now what?"

He dropped the gear shift a couple of notches, spun the wheel, and found he had an uncluttered route to the street. The Chrysler surged forward with unexpected power. The brick in the windshield slid free of its moorings in the shattered glass and scraped across the dash, then thumped heavily on the floor. "I had in mind to hypnotize him at the motel," von Wessenheim answered.

"You can do that?"

The car bottomed out as he left the parking lot and squealed into a right turn. In the rearview mirror he saw a quick spray of orange sparks. Thorwald's face rose into view, dazed. And behind his head, closing fast, a pack of cars and motorcycles.

"Who are you guys?" he asked.

Ulgard put both gloved hands atop Thorwald's head and pushed him down. "You must stay out of sight."

He hunkered down. In the side mirror von Wessenheim watched as a motorcycle approached, one of those low-slung machines where the driver's knee almost touches the pavement during high-speed turns. It was green and white and built purely for speed, he saw as it drew beside the Chrysler. The helmeted man on it lifted a camera and began snapping shots with one hand extended, no aiming, flash-flash. Another photographer on a similar motorcycle—this one orange and black—came up behind him to wield his own camera, concentrating on the backseat area. A look at the speedometer showed sixty miles per hour. Von Wessenheim looked back at Ulgard. "Should I go as fast as possible?"

"The limit here is forty and you're doing sixty. My advice is to slow down."

"To the speed limit?"

Ulgard shook his head. "To a crawl."

Von Wessenheim found his face in the mirror. "Did I hear you correctly?"

"The police force in this town just suffered an attack on its own headquarters, Herr von Wessenheim, and they are not happy about it. In just a few minutes, every available car, and every state policeman within radio distance, is going to converge on this area and make sure we get safe passage."

"So then I should drive to the motel?"

Ulgard shook his head. "We saw what happened outside this man's house. The motel will become a circus and we'll be under armed guard."

Von Wessenheim lifted his hands from the wheel, exasperated. More of the paparazzi massed around the car, their cameras winking and flashing under the sunlight. "Where to, then?"

"The airport. They can't outrun us in the air."

He thought about it as the speedometer dwindled. "But there will be a new pack of them waiting wherever we land. This entire country is obsessed."

"But Europe is not. England maybe, their press is notorious for sensationalism, but not the nations of the Continent. And especially not Germany herself. Who would want to dredge up the Hitler stuff again? If we fly to Frankfurt or Berlin, we can walk away unnoticed. And since my work for you has ended, I need desperately to get to Berlin anyway."

Von Wessenheim frowned. It was his very intention to

dredge up the Hitler stuff again. It had never occurred to him that he might anger people.

Mr. Thorwald rose up again, cautiously this time. "Who are you guys?" he asked again. "Where are you taking me?"

"We are Amnesty International," von Wessenheim replied, very much to his own surprise.

He sat up taller. "No kidding?"

"We're taking you to safety. But please stay low. A maniac may try to shoot you."

He ducked down. Around the car, as the speed slipped below twenty, the motorcycle riders had drawn ahead to photograph from the front, weaving crazily as they swung around to aim their cameras.

"There is a problem with that," von Wessenheim said. "This man must have a passport when we land in Europe."

"At the airport I can call an associate of mine," Ulgard said. "When we touch down in Berlin, he will be waiting with it."

"But there has to be a photograph."

"Don't doubt me on this one, Herr von Wessenheim. Just drive."

He drove. At ten miles per hour his nerves began to fray badly. At this point the motorcyclists felt free to stare inside the car, one matching the pace with a hand resting on the edge of the roof. His helmet clunked against the glass as he peered inside. "Oh good God," von Wessenheim groaned. "Look at these idiots."

"Patience," Ulgard said soothingly.

Thorwald surfaced with another question. "You went to *jail* just to contact me?"

"I did," von Wessenheim said to the windshield.

Thorwald dropped a firm hand on his shoulder. "Thank you. Thank you both. I don't even know your names, but thank you. This is just the greatest thing."

Von Wessenheim turned. Thorwald had tears shining wetly in his eyes. He knuckled them away but more welled up. Despite his noisy sleep in the cell he was visibly on the verge of a mental collapse brought on by more than fatigue. Fifteen or twenty hours in the air would at least give him time to recuperate.

"Amnesty International is what we like to do," von Wessenheim said blithely, feeling better about his command of English. "We like helping people. My friend here will say the same." He turned. "Am I speaking the reality now, Mr. Ulgard?"

Ulgard cast him a glance. "In your own strange way."

Von Wessenheim smiled uncertainly. "Then we agree."

Thorwald seemed suddenly alarmed. "So where are you taking me?"

"Sweden. It's a neutral country, your safety can be found there."

"Sweden?" He sank back and wormed himself low on the seat. "*Sweden?* For how long?"

"Until our experts have cleared you, and our lawyers have won the cases."

"What about my wife and my daughter? Can they join me there?"

"Yes, very shortly." Von Wessenheim swallowed but it got stuck halfway down his throat. Why was he spouting all these mad things? He chanced a look back at Rønna Ulgard and found that he had lifted his sunglasses just to marvel at him with his little brown eyes—probably for his stupidity. But these kinds of lies were justified, Thorwald could not be stuffed into an airplane against his will. He needed to go voluntarily or the whole mission would collapse, and most certainly the announcement that the reincarnated Führer was headed for Germany would not sit well with him. So maybe Ulgard's naked eyes were expressing admiration instead.

Flashing lights appeared distantly behind the Chrysler. Von Wessenheim took in a breath of relief. Within seconds more sparkling colors strobed into view ahead. At the sight of them, the cavalcade of cars and vans began to ease back but the motorcycles kept in a bunch surrounding the Chrysler, the riders knowing, he assumed, that no police car in the world could catch up with their slick little machines. His urge was to floor the gas pedal and break free, but with effort he fought it off.

A new sound, a big and throaty rumbling, caught his ear just as a gleaming chrome giant of a motorcycle slid into view to the left of his eyes. He jerked his head to see it fully and saw that it was manned by a big, scruffy-bearded man who was wearing black leather gloves with the fingers cut off. He made motions that indicated von Wessenheim's window should be rolled down. He didn't have a camera or any visible weapons except his frightening looks.

"He wants to tell us something," Ulgard said. "Crack your window."

Von Wessenheim did. The chrome motorcycle swung close as the driver leaned down to shout, "You got Hank Thorwald in there, right?"

Von Wessenheim experienced a moment of confusion, then nodded.

"Where you headed?"

Ulgard leaned forward. "He asked where we are going. Tell him."

Von Wessenheim snapped his head around. "Have you gone mad? We're trying to outrun this crowd."

Ulgard took his shoulder in one gloved hand and squeezed it hard, pushing him back and forth. "Will you ever stop questioning me! *Verdammte scheisse,* do what I say for once!"

Von Wessenheim hastily fingered the button that made his window slide down, opening it all the way. "Yes, we have him!" he shouted into the hot and blustery air. "We do have him in this car!"

"Where's he going?"

"We drive to the airport with him!"

The man lifted a hairy arm and made motions with it. Von Wessenheim sat, dumbfounded, as he pulled in front of the Chrysler on his huge machine, gunning it noisily as he veered back and forth to force the smaller machines away. The green-and-white motorcycle took a direct hit and wobbled irretrievably hard to the right; it bounced over the curb and ejected the driver skyward before skating into a row of hedges. Another one followed behind it, skidding on its side until its crotch engaged a metal pole that twirled it in circles, also ejecting the driver.

More noises of power: the slow-moving Chrysler was

quickly engulfed by thrumming motorcycles manned by persons von Wessenheim could only describe as hippies. Long hair, tattoos, beards split in half by the wind, black leather pants and glistening machines. Several of them offered him a thumbs-up. He smiled with genial confusion, lifting a hand in return. But the largest part of his mind was occupied with Ulgard. With Thorwald in hand, his million dollars a day was over and all he wanted now was a good excuse to get back to Germany. And all this hoopla, it seemed, was proving him right. Once in Berlin, Thorwald could be hypnotized not only to reveal the location of Hitler's tomb, but to show von Wessenheim the way in person. So, fine, Rønna Ulgard wanted to go back to Germany, and go they would.

The greatest discovery of the century was only hours away.

A MATTER OF LEBEN
UND TODT

37

Later that morning Rebecca did herself a favor and ate an entire meal in the hospital cafeteria. Sharri had awakened just before daylight but was utterly uninterested in visitors. As Rebecca clutched her hand, she had stayed in a zone between in and out, never once showing any interest in her mother or anything at all. One of the ICU nurses explained that after getting shot, then undergoing the additional trauma of lengthy surgery, her mind right then was reduced to its most basic function, that of keeping the body alive and the brain in a minimal-reception mode so that time could work its miracles and let her walk out of here healed, the ordeal mostly forgotten.

So Rebecca allowed herself some free time. Yesterday at the house, right after Gleeworth left, she had showered but not slept despite the sweet nothings the mattress kept whispering. It was crucial to her that she be at the hospital for the awakening. It was no lie to say that she was disappointed by Sharri's low-grade reaction, but just seeing those green eyes crack open again thrilled her. Twelve years ago no Sharri had existed, yet now Rebecca could not imagine having existed without her, could scarcely believe there had been a world at all before she arrived in the middle of a summer night howling and kicking. Without insurance at the time, it took the young Thorwald family more than two years to pay the hospital bill, month by month, payment by torturous payment.

And then Hank had graduated. And then Hank had gotten his miraculous professorship. And then this ... this ... *thing*.

"You think too much," she mumbled to herself, and poked her fork into her mouth. The cafeteria at this after-breakfast hour consisted of a few knots of people, most of them either dressed as hospital workers or wearing ID tags, the rest of them people like her, displaced by some sort of medical disaster. Besides scrambled eggs and hash browns she had secured a plate of pancakes, a doughnut, a tall glass of milk, and a slice of collapsed-looking apple pie.

A duo of hospital workers noisily got themselves in place at the free-standing table beside her booth. She looked, and was cast the usual glances. Noncommittal, she began picking the pie apart with slow jabs of her fork to free the apples from the crust and assess their age.

"I think it's bullshit," the man said flatly. "I have since it started, even before I saw him. It's all a big push by the weirdo press, those papers you women buy in the checkout section. I'm telling you, this guy was hired by them to pretend this shit, and between him and them the whole crew is getting rich."

"Beg to disagree."

Rebecca glanced over again, her heartbeat prodded into a higher cycle when she realized that Hank was the subject. The woman at the next table was trying to transplant her dishes from a tray onto the little table, jamming bowls and plates against each other. "I popped up there to see him an hour before he vanished. Some people say he crawled down the wall like a spider, some people say he jumped out and walked away because the ground here is so wet and soft." She collected the other tray and dumped them both onto an empty table. "I tell you, there was no way out of that room except by helicopter. A lot of people heard a loud noise about then. A lot of people. And you know what that means?"

Rebecca jabbed at her disappointing pie while the man spoke up quickly: "Hitler farted?"

They both laughed. They both sat there and laughed and then started eating and had not a care in the world as they talked and poked fun at Hank. Rebecca studied them with glances as she played with her pie, her eyes stealing from face to face, envious of their simple good humor and the easy lives they must lead.

"A lie detector could solve this whole thing," the woman said. "Park his ass in a chair and fire questions at him. The lie detector would prove it either way."

"So why haven't they done it?" the man said through a mouthful of food. He wagged the piece of toast he was busy with. "You want to know why they haven't done it? I'll *tell* you why they haven't done it. They haven't done it because the whole crew is getting rich."

"You think so, eh? Fine. In a past life I was the bride of Dracula. Give me and my crew money."

"First you find a crew. Then you take a lie detector test. Then we'll talk money."

They laughed uproariously, drawing glances. Rebecca granted herself clemency and gave up on the pie, already anticipating a cigarette as the true dessert.

"Seriously speaking, though, the whole thing was a setup. I mean, what the hell was Alan Weston doing at a college faculty party?"

In the act of drinking the last of her milk, Rebecca choked.

The woman frowned at him. "Who?"

"Alan Weston. You know, the TV muckraker. *Alan Weston on Us*."

"I think I've heard of him."

Rebecca hunched forward and let the milk drool back into the glass, then crushed her napkin to her mouth, coughing while milk ran out her nose.

"What planet do you live on, woman? Alan Weston is famous for faking news stories. So here he shows up in Terre Haute at a college teachers' party, and the next day he spills the beans on live TV. We've got a billion tourists in town, which helps the economy. The mayor is so grateful that he hands Weston twenty-five percent, probably a million dollars or more. With that much dough he doesn't need to work anymore. And I might add that he hasn't been on TV all week."

Rebecca could breathe again. The stuff about the mayor was crap, but Alan Weston *had been,* except for the usual spouses, the only nonfaculty member at the party. He had been specially invited by Perry. So either Alan and Perry had concocted this whole thing or Perry had been using unsuspecting Alan to spread the word on television.

"I wish I was like you," the woman said to the man. "Superbrain, knows everything, but washes dishes for a living to keep his identity secret."

And maybe Alan killed Perry. Alan found out he'd been set up, that he had been used in a con game, got enraged and killed him and was on the run, hence not on TV anymore. That, or Perry killed himself when Alan threatened to expose him. The new murder suspect would, at least, make Gleeworth gleeful. The suicide route fit her perception of justice better, that his misdeeds so tortured Perry that he could no longer live with himself.

"Shut up and eat."

This revelation had Rebecca shaking. In her haste to get going she rose too quickly and snagged her thighs on the underside of the table. The glass of half-finished milk clunked over to pour out a starfish shape on the tabletop. Unrepentant but anxious to be gone before the starfish got big enough to start dripping on the floor, she left the cafeteria at a trot. Since Hank's disappearance the police presence at the hospital had all but vanished, which was actually a relief to her. Along with the cops had gone most of the media. With Hank officially missing and nothing new to report they had gone off in search of other prey, in search of new headlines. But oh dear God, if the media found out that Gleeworth was bringing Hank from Ohio this morning to lodge him in the city jail the festival would kick into high gear again. At least—and this was given very grudgingly—Hank would be safe in jail. Safer than at home.

In the hallway she slowed, passing a uniformed cop who didn't even glance at her. The paging system uttered the muted *bong-bong* that indicated a message was coming up. She had been in the hospital long enough to give it no notice; only when she heard her name spoken did she stop to listen, hoping it would be repeated. It was: a calm female voice was asking her to pick up the nearest red telephone for a phone call. She looked around but couldn't find one. Again at a trot she headed for the main entrance, but just around the corner was a niche in the wall that housed a red phone. "Incoming Calls Only," a sticker beside it said.

She put the receiver to her ear. "Rebecca Thorwald."

"This is Detective Gleeworth. How's Sharri?"

"She woke up for a minute." She lowered her voice to a whisper. "Did you get Hank?"

"I got him, yeah."

"Is he okay?"

"Not injured, if that's what you mean. Scrapes and bruises."

"Pick me up," she said. "I want to see him."

Gleeworth hesitated. "See, I was exhausted after the drive, and it was way early in the morning, so I went home and got some shut-eye."

She shrugged. "So?"

"So I just now got to the station again. Hank was bailed out of jail about an hour ago."

"Bailed out? Who bailed him out?"

Gleeworth cleared his throat. "The paperwork was signed by a man named Alfred Histler."

"Who in the hell is that?"

"A guy from Tyrol."

"Where's that?"

"Italy."

The phone slipped down as her hand involuntarily relaxed. She brought it up again, speaking measuredly. "A total stranger from a foreign country paid the bail money, and off they went? Poof?"

"Not really poof. Somehow the media got wind that Hank was in jail. A mob of them showed up just as he was walking out the door. It was total chaos, I guess."

"Where'd they go?"

"To the local airport."

"Airport? *Airport!* And flew away?"

"And flew away."

She pulled the phone away and frowned at it, then put it back to her ear. "And nobody stopped him? He can't fly away if he's out on bail, can he?"

"Actually, he's free to go anywhere he wants. He's not charged with murder yet."

"Maybe he was being kidnapped. Did anybody ask him? Where were you cops?"

He sighed. "Guarding the airport. The whole thing was just crazy."

Rebecca let herself slump against the wall. "Where did they fly to?"

"O'Hare."

"Did they stay there or catch another flight?"

"We're not really sure. The Chicago police are en route to O'Hare right now. Looks like the news traveled faster than the shuttle plane. The airport called them with a plea for crowd control."

Her memory of the O'Hare airport was one of huge crowds anyway; toss the media and the crazies in and the place would explode. "So what's the bottom line here?" she demanded. "Good-bye forever, Hank? Enjoy the spaghetti in Italy, send me a card now and then?"

"No. Wherever he winds up, Italy or not, crowds are going to gather. The media is going to come in full steam. Just watch TV for the next couple of days."

"This is your advice?" she shouted into the phone. "Watch TV? Wave if I see him?"

"Calm down, it's possible that Hank is in good hands," he said. "This might be the best thing."

People were walking past. She whirled to face the wall and cupped a hand over the mouthpiece. "Who did you say bailed him out?"

Papers shuffled. "Alfred Histler."

"Jesus fucking Christ, Gleeworth, go back to cop school. Hank's been kidnapped by the crazies." She smashed the receiver onto its hook and turned, panting, seeing everything as if through a red sparkle of rage. The cops in this town had done nothing but bungle time after time, her house was demolished and Sharri was half dead and Hank had slipped through their fingers—they had even guarded the fucking airport while he was being skyjacked. What she had overheard in the cafeteria was now the soundest advice she had ever gotten: find Alan Weston, the only participant in this catastrophe who had walked away unhurt.

She stalked to the entrance and lit a cigarette on the way. An employee pushing a trash can on wheels veered over to confront her. "Ma'am, I'm afraid you can't smoke in here."

She eyed him without breaking stride, the cigarette hanging from a corner of her mouth. "You just try and stop me, Bozo. Just try."

He let her pass. When the automatic doors swung inward the heat of the day smacked her full in the face. She shielded her eyes from the withering sun as she searched the parking lot. If she guessed right, there would be a THPD vehicle pulling up real soon, the same one that had brought her here yesterday. So far the chief of police had made good on his promise to ferry her anywhere she wanted to go, and with Sharri certifiably alive Rebecca had intended to camp at the best hotel in town, the Wabash Valley Inn, where once upon a time she had tried hypnosis so she could quit smoking. But all that had changed in an instant.

As she dragged in another mouthful of smoke a flash of reflected light grabbed her eyes. A blue-and-white car with cherries on top was moving her way. It had been waiting under the lot's only scrap of shade, three tall sycamore trees standing at the farthest corner. She hurried to the curb to meet it as it stopped, then levered herself inside and slammed the door, taking a look at him. Yet another chauffeur, this time an older man. Really old. "Where to?" he asked.

"To station WXRV in Indianapolis. Will you do that?"

He lifted a hand and slowly stroked a gnarled finger up and down the length of his nose. This was one of the retired cops who had gotten called to active duty because of the crowds, she realized. Had to be, or else the retirement age was up to sixty-five. "Well," he said in a deep and raspy voice that spoke loudly of being a smoker most of his life, "I was told to take you anywhere you want to go. Since we're in Terre Haute, I can assume that means I can take you anywhere in

Terre Haute. However, we are also in Indiana and I assume that means I can take you anywhere in the state of Indiana. But that raises the ugly prospect of going nationwide, and if you get nitpicky we could be talking about a journey to the moon."

Rebecca tried to smile but the adrenaline was rushing through her veins too fast to let it stick. "Do you know how to get to the station? In Indianapolis? Can you ask somebody?"

He lifted his foot from the brake and let the car idle forward, then spun the wheel around. "At my retired age I don't need permission anymore. If I screw up they can't fire me. You might notice that I'm not even wearing the traditional uniform."

She gave him a better look. The retired cop had on the usual uniform from the waist up, but below that were cream-colored corduroy pants, bare ankles, and high-top black basketball shoes. "You see," he said as the big car bounced onto the street, "because of the stir created by your husband, I was called back into the force. Yesterday I was radaring traffic on Ohio Street and forgot what the posted limit was. Didn't issue one ticket. Slept most of the time, actually. So I thought, why the hell wear pants and shoes that are both too tight? That is why I am now your driver."

"Good to know that," Rebecca said, bouncing impatiently on the seat.

"Do I sense a certain agitation?"

"I need to get there fast."

"Then I'm the right guy for you." He flipped a switch on the dashboard. Rebecca looked at him quizzically when nothing happened.

"The overheads are on," he explained. "Lights. Flashing lights. Now I can go fast. With the siren, even faster."

She smiled at him as he applied gas. "What's your name, guy?"

"I've learned at the old folks home that my name is Dutch. That's what my balloon-toss team calls me, anyway. Dutch."

"Dutch." Rebecca weighed the information, bobbing her head up and down. "I've heard the name a million times but never truly met a man named Dutch."

"We keep a low profile."

She smiled again. "So will you take me to Indy?"

He turned his head and offered her a smile graced with perfect white teeth that had *Made in China* sparkling all over them. Her cigarette was suddenly glowing hotly on her fingers so she flipped it out the open window.

"Littering. Flaming debris. Five-hunnert-dollar fine." He wagged a finger at her. "Don't make me go back and make you pick up that butt."

A wavering smile clung to her face as she watched for his expression to soften.

"Well?" he demanded.

She spread her hands with no idea what was under way.

"Do we have to go back and get that butt, or will you make it easier and give me a whole cigarette? I've been out of smokes for an hour waiting for you, I'm dying here."

She grinned and handed him a Camel Light.

38

I'm afraid that's all I know," the pretty young woman said to Rebecca as she put the phone down. "Alan Weston is no longer employed by station WXRV."

It was not the first time she had made an unproductive call in the last few minutes. For a television station protected by the rights of free speech, the station was awfully close-mouthed when it came to the disappearance of its most famous employee. "And no one knows where he went?" Rebecca asked in disbelief. "He didn't report for work and was fired? Does he even know he was fired?"

The young woman's eyes were wide and blue and so full of innocence you could jump in and swim to Hawaii. Rebecca's, however, were green and laced with bright wisps of red from lack of sleep, and one of them was nested in a purple bruise. Around her the lobby of WXRV was a *trés chic* mixture of curves and glass blocks and mirrored walls, heavily decorated with potted trees. "Honestly," the woman said, "I don't know if he was fired or if he just quit. I don't get invited to executive meetings here, I'm just the receptionist."

"Isn't there *somebody* I can talk to here besides you? Is there a personnel department where they keep employment records?"

"Of course, but they can't be handed out to everybody who walks through the door."

It made more sense than Rebecca wanted to admit. Now that she had cleaned up and was well-dressed, she felt more in control of events. No more huddling on hospital seats, no more being swept along by the wild currents of fate. If there was even the slightest smell of Alan Weston, she would sniff it in the air and track him down. "Who's the boss here?"

"The station manager, Mr. Danberry."

"So can I talk to Mr. Danberry?"

"Yes."

Rebecca had already lifted a finger to start wagging it as she demanded things; in light of this sudden news she made a small interior sound and dropped her hand. Waiting in the heat of the parking lot outside was her new friend Dutch, who had stopped to buy cigarettes so as not to smoke up all of her Camel Lights. But dressed in his half-cop, half-civilian clothes, it was Rebecca who had to go into the 7-Eleven to buy them, which was no big deal. During the drive they had talked a lot. He had wanted to know what business she had at WXRV but she'd told him a lie: applying for a job.

The woman lifted the telephone and punched a couple of numbers. "Mr. Danberry? I have a woman here who would like to talk to you."

She looked up at Rebecca, then clapped a hand over the mouthpiece. "What's your business, he wants to know," she whispered.

Rebecca bent over and whispered back: "Trying to locate Alan Weston."

Her hand slid away. "Trying to locate Alan Weston."

Rebecca straightened and smoothed her clothes, touched at her hair.

"Okay. I understand." She hung up and looked at Rebecca. "Mr. Weston is no longer employed by station WXRV."

Rebecca glowered at her. "That does it. Where's Mr. Danberry's office?"

"He said there's no reason for him to see you because that's all he knows."

Rebecca stepped back and examined the area. Between two potted palms to her right was a corridor. To her left was a short corridor that seemed to branch off in two directions. The carpeting was a flat and sturdy royal purple. She stared hard into the blue eyes. "Which way is Mr. Danberry's office?"

She immediately flicked her gaze to indicate Rebecca's right. "It moves around a lot," she said uneasily.

"Thank you for your help." Rebecca took a breath and struck out on a course between the potted palms. Behind her she heard the receptionist punching at the phone. Lock your door, Mr. Danberry, bad news is about to knock.

But Mr. Danberry—or somebody dressed in a suit and looking as important as Mr. Danberry—glided out into the hallway to block her just before the carpet turned to linoleum and led off in new directions. "Please stop," he said, spreading both arms. "We have programs under way."

She stopped. He was a tall man and she had to look up. "Are you the station manager?"

He stepped closer. "Yes."

"Mr. Danberry?"

"That would be me. Are you the one asking about Alan?"

"That would be me."

He was frowning as he peered at her. "I'm afraid Mr. Weston is no longer employed at this station."

"So I gather. Do you know where he went? To a different station?"

"Let's walk back to the lobby," he said, moving as if to take her arm but simply showing the way instead. "Noise has to be kept to a minimum this time of afternoon. Local news under way."

She led the way while he tagged along. In the lobby she turned. Before she could speak, he was talking. "Actually that's all I'm at liberty to tell you, unless it is in the best interests of station WXRV."

"It is critical that I contact him," she said. "I *must* get his phone number or address."

He was shaking his head. "Due to his celebrity, if you understand me, Mr. Weston maintained an unlisted number, and his address is just as private."

"But you have them on file here."

"Are you a family member?"

"My name is Rebecca Thorwald."

"Oh." His face paled visibly. "How are you, ah, how are you and your husband doing?"

"Bad. He has been kidnapped and my daughter is in intensive care with a bullet hole in her chest."

"I see."

"Alan Weston gave out everything but my husband's hat size."

He touched his chin. "If it's any consolation, that is one of the reasons he is no longer employed here. That, and the fact that he hasn't bothered to show up for almost a week."

"And so you understand why I have to find him."

He stood motionless, assessing her. "First off, I sympathize, and I can assure you that many others have been, we'll say, smeared by Alan. And second, I can tell you that this station has been taken to court because of him more times than I can count. Fortunately, we have very capable attorneys."

She narrowed her eyes. "So don't bother suing you?"

"I did not say that."

"Okay, you did not say that. So let me say that I will promise not to sue WXRV if you give me Alan's phone number or his address. Deal?"

He sighed as he lifted his wrist for a time check. Nice Bulova, lots of gold and sparkles. "I can't make deals with company policy."

"Last chance," she said as her anger and frustration combined to produce a brain chemical as hot as orange lava. "Cooperate, or pay the price."

He stooped slightly to be at her height, widening his eyes as he pressed uncomfortably close. "What was that?"

She couldn't help it: she shoved him away with both hands. Unfortunately he lurched backward into a potted palm, lost all balance, and fell against one of the big windows that formed a large part of the outside wall. It cracked from top to bottom in the shape of a zigzag. Rebecca sucked in a breath, glad that he had not plunged all the way through it.

Mr. Danberry straightened. Behind him the glass collapsed with a sudden jangling blurt, dropping instantly into a sparkling heap that sluiced across the sidewalk outside and the floor of the lobby inside. Two potted trees crashed over. Safety glass, Rebecca noted. Nice greenish crumbles.

"That's it, call the police!" Mr. Danberry shouted. He slogged through the ankle-deep glass, pointing a finger at Rebecca. "And you just stay right there!"

"The police are already here!" the receptionist cried. Rebecca looked. Dutch had just pulled up to the curb and was leaning to push the passenger door open. She wasn't a lawyer but she wasn't stupid, either: she ran out as if the building were caving in behind her.

"This is what you do at job interviews?" Dutch asked as she threw herself inside the THPD cruiser.

"Go," she said, and hammered on the dash.

He applied gas. "I hear they're always hiring at McDonald's. Wanna drop by and burn one of them to the ground?"

"Okay, so I lied."

He spun the wheel and maneuvered out of the parking lot. "You didn't have to, Rebecca. Now you've gone and hurt old Dutch's feelings."

She put a hand on his arm, surprised to see how badly her fingers were trembling. Never in her twenty-nine years had she caused such a scene. "I'm actually trying to locate Alan Weston."

"Oh, great," he groaned. "What do you want with *that* bastard?"

She raised an eyebrow. "I see you're familiar with his work."

He took off his blue cop hat and slapped it on the seat between them. "He's a crook and a gutter rat." He cleared his throat and glanced at her, ran a hand over his thin gray hair. "Now please tell me you're not a relative or I will be forced to cut out my own tongue."

"Not a relative."

"Friend of his?"

"Nope."

He grinned. "Why are you trying to find his worthless ass?"

"You know who I am, don't you?"

"Do I know who you are? Sure. Rebecca Thorwald."

"You know what's going on with my husband, right?"

"Yep. When you're old, you get to the point where you think you've seen and heard everything stupid that there is. Then along comes something stupider."

She lit a cigarette. "Where are we going?"

"You still need to find Alan Weston, right? I'll bet I can find him pretty fast."

"Really?"

"Here's a guy." Dutch jerked the wheel hard to the left. He slid to a quick halt and Rebecca saw that he had pulled up beside an Indianapolis cop in a white car. She craned around and saw that they were in a grocery store parking lot somewhere smack downtown. Unfortunately, Dutch had parked in a way that stuck her in the middle of the conversation. He leaned over and she sucked her chest in, held her head high. "How do!"

"What's up, partner?" the Indy cop said loudly to the side of her face.

"Trying to find Alan Weston for this nice lady."

"She a relative?"

She shook her head.

"Good. What do you want to find *that* bastard for?"

"I've got some questions I hope he can answer," Dutch said. "Do you know his address or phone number?"

"No, but I could sure get them for you, considering what went on a few days ago."

Rebecca drew a perfect blank and stared dumbly at her oblong reflection in his sunglasses while heat waves shimmered up from the asphalt.

"Some bikers ambushed him at a tavern," he said. "Creamed him."

Dutch leaned over again. Somewhere along the line he had put his hat back on. "You mean he's dead?"

Rebecca felt the last bits of her hopes begin to vanish.

"We couldn't get that lucky. Ambulance took him and the bartender up to Northeast General and put them back together."

"So that's where he is?"

"Nah, he's back at home. The mayor's got us patroling his house twenty-four seven. Hold on."

Rebecca watched as he lifted the mike of his police radio and spoke into it, and caught the address from the dispatcher. 16674 Grand View Northeast. "I got it," she told Dutch, then turned to the Indianapolis cop. "I got it."

Dutch offered him an exaggerated salute. "Many thanks!"

"You take care."

Rebecca took the last draw on her cigarette and snuffed it out in the ashtray as he drove away. "Any idea where Grand View Northeast is?"

"It's bound to be up by Northeast General Hospital. My daughter popped me out my first grandchild there on the snowiest day on record since 1916, middle of the coldest night on record since 1954. We almost named her Frosty."

Rebecca smiled. "So what did you name her?"

"June. No one wanted to be reminded of the ordeal."

She laughed, and so did he. His developed into a coughing fit bad enough for her to have to reach over and remind the steering wheel of which way to go. When Dutch resurfaced he was as red as a cut of raw lamb. "Mercy," he exclaimed, pounding his breastbone.

"Light up another one," she said dourly.

Alan Weston's house stood at the end of a circular cul-de-sac populated by upscale houses with four-car garages. It was the only house that had a sheet of plywood for a front door and an Indianapolis police car parked in its driveway. Dutch idled up beside it and Rebecca got out, sweating in the heat. While he made small talk between the cars, Rebecca went to the ersatz front door and knocked on it. There was no reply, but she didn't really expect one. When she pulled on the sheet of plywood, it held fast. She noticed nails that had been sloppily pounded and bent. It seemed Alan Weston was no carpenter.

She skirted the house, prowling in its shade for another door. Houses like these could guarantee you at least two more. In the back she found a swimming pool with a lot of debris—grass, leaves, bugs—floating on top of the water. The lawn needed mowing. The cement surrounding the pool narrowed to become a sidewalk to the glass patio door. She clopped up the two steps and tried to slide it apart. Locked. Around the other side of the house was another door set beside a large window that allowed a good look at closed drapes. The place was dead. Was Alan dead? Had the Indianapolis cops kept vigil on a house with only a corpse inside?

She backtracked to the pool. A metal shed that had not yet acquired the dents and dings of age stood past the pool, at the corner of the lawn. She tromped through the high grass and saw a padlock securing the latch, but that was okay, there was no need to get impatient. She returned to the patio door and studied it: the standard sliding-glass type, secured from the inside by a small latch. She stood sideways and pressed her hip into the glass, leaning weight onto it to test its strength when it wouldn't budge. Pretty strong, actually, not ordinary glass by any means. She pounded on it with her fist. No reply.

There was a deck chair by the pool. She folded it together and smashed it down on the cement, again and again, until a good, solid piece of wood separated from the rest. The remains of the chair went into the pool. The solid piece went into her right hand.

She hiked around the house to a low window, took the stick of wood in both hands, and smashed the glass. If Alan was asleep he was probably awake by now. The thought curled her lips into a smile as she worked to clean out the entire frame, expecting him to appear, but he did not. "Rebecca Thorwald is coming in," she shouted into the house. "Remember me?"

No reply. Dead? Not a chance. With a leap she was already halfway inside, teetering on the fulcrum of her stomach. With her hands she dragged herself fully inside and sprawled on the floor, then scrambled upright. It was a spacious den or unused bedroom that contained a desk with a blank computer atop it. Wadded balls of typing paper were strewn all over the floor. She bent and snatched one up, then spread it out. Even to her it was recognizable as a page from a movie script.

The door was closed. She jerked it open. Still no Alan. His house smelled a little like Perry's, too much unused space for one person. She wandered through the gloom, finding the kitchen, a bathroom, a room that was anybody's guess, and another bathroom. Wherever she went the air was flat and dead, the sense of someone living here absent. At the end of a hallway she came upon the remains of the former front door and pressed her fingers over her mouth as she examined it. The swastika was huge and purple.

She sensed someone behind her and spun around. What she saw made her stagger back and turn her head away.

"What the fuck do you want?" Alan Weston growled at her.

Rebecca drew her head slowly around, remembering her anger and the strength it gave her. "I want you," she said, meeting his eyes. He had been beaten to hell and back. His entire face was a bloated lump, his nose smashed into a crooked smear. Between his scabbed and swollen lips the gaps of missing teeth showed, and both hands wore metal splints to hold broken fingers in place. Even his hair was missing in slashes where it had been shaved away to stitch up his scalp.

"Get the hell out of here," he rasped, and turned. He was barefoot and in his bathrobe this late in the day, she saw. The bikers had done more than rearrange his face, they had broken him somehow. Nevertheless she spun him around and pushed him against the door, pinned him there by his shoulders.

"You know what the fuck I want?" she shouted in his face. "I want you to go back on TV and tell all the people that you and Perry set Hank up for this crazy bullshit." He struggled but she held him fast. "And when you're done doing that, I want you to write a letter to all the newspapers in the country explaining why you took part in the conspiracy to destroy our lives."

"You're out of your mind," he said, and jerked free of her. "There's no conspiracy, I just report the news. Now get the fuck out of here."

He turned and shambled away. "Did you kill Perry Wilson?" she called after him, and he paused but did not turn.

"Perry's dead?"

"Either suicide or murder. I say it was murder."

Now he did turn. "Must have been, because the Perry I know would never kill himself. Are you sure of all this?"

"I found him dead in his own basement a couple of days ago."

He dropped his head, then quickly raised it. "Then you're right, it had to be murder. But I didn't do it. I haven't left this house in days. The cops are outside, they know that."

"So you're denying it. And you're denying it was a conspiracy."

He studied her silently, then: "Get the hell out of here."

He turned. She followed. "Why were you at that faculty party? Who better to spread the word but you, a TV reporter? Are you going to tell me it was coincidence?"

"Perry invited me."

"How utterly convenient."

He spun around. "I was trying to back out but you dragged my ass in, bent over backward to make sure I stayed. Remember that detail?"

She did now, and with the memory came the collapse of the conspiracy. Alan Weston had been surprised that it was a faculty affair that evening and had tried to leave. She wouldn't let him. "Perry set you up," she said wonderingly. "He knew exactly what Hank was going to do. And he knew that you would spill it all."

"Bravo, Sherlock." He turned his back again. "Now get out of here."

This time she took two giant strides and spun him around. The urge to slap him was there, but there were no places left on his face that weren't already painful. "Listen to me," she said in a dark voice. "You are going to dump the smart-guy routine right now. I met you at the party and you had a soul, you were a normal guy. Be that way again."

He pushed away from her. "Fuck you. Get out."

"Why are you hiding the real Alan from me?"

"You've lost your fucking mind, lady. Get out before I—"

She cut him off. "Before you what? Before you give me a black eye to match the one I've already got? Before you call the cops? Hell, there's two of them in your driveway and they don't give the slightest shit if I kill you dead. Before you go on TV and ruin my life?" She scooped in a breath. "Well, here's a news flash for you: *you already fucking DID!*"

She couldn't help it: on the last word she swung out and hit him. Her fist thumped against his left ear and he reeled to one side clutching it. The arms of his bathrobe slipped to his elbows and she saw that his left forearm and wrist were encased in a fresh plaster cast. The bikers had been ruthless.

But so was she. "My daughter's in the hospital with a bullet wound. My husband was kidnapped this morning. Perry killed himself in the basement where he chopped up your friend Chaim Goldberg and buried him, and you want me to leave. Here's another news flash, Alan: you're coming with me even if I have to drag you kicking and screaming."

He slumped against the wall with a groan and slid down to his haunches, his face screwed up with pain. Finally he cracked one eye open and said, "Perry killed Chaim Goldberg?" He worked himself upright, one hand still cupped over his ear. "That son of a bitch. That crazy old son of a bitch." He peered at her with both eyes open. "What do you want with me? What do you think I can do?"

"I want you to do what you do best, Alan. I want you to investigate Perry Wilson, just like you might do to a Mafia gangster. Start with his birth and follow his whole life. Lay it all out. Find out why he murdered the Goldberg kid, why he did this to Hank, and maybe even why he killed himself."

He let go of his ear; Rebecca was glad to see no blood trickling out of it. "I can't go out in public looking like this," he said. "I'll need two weeks to heal up, then another week in a dentist's chair just to replace my teeth. And then I've got to come up with a batch of new television segments to fill the gap."

Rebecca deliberated, but only for a moment. "I was just at WXRV. I talked to Mr. Danberry. You've been fired."

His eyes wandered to the side. She thought she saw the breath of a smile drift across his face. "And so it ends." He looked at her sharply. "Chaim was a good friend of mine back then. I watched him fall apart and blamed it on homesickness. Then he was gone. Even the police didn't suspect Perry. He was absolutely distraught."

"Might be nice to know why he killed your friend. Might be nice if you came back to Terre Haute with me."

He leaned his back against the wall, looking at the ceiling as he made mental calculations. "My relatives are about one day away from having the house bulldozed to find me. I don't even know what they think about the hypno-Hitler segment, if they want to praise me or condemn me for it."

Rebecca clamped her teeth over the words she wanted to say about his stupid segment; no sense blowing the progress she had made with him. "Nobody here will know you're in Terre Haute, Alan. I've got a retired cop in a marked Terre Haute car sitting outside with a cage in the back. You can lay low until we hit the open highway."

"No need to hide." He used his hands to frame his face. "Would you recognize me with a mug like this?"

"I see your point."

"You got a computer there?"

Her heart fell. "Yeah, but we can't get near it. The house is a no-man's-land."

"Then we'll take mine. Give me a minute to get dressed."

She went into the kitchen for a glass of water and a silent prayer.

39

"Have you ever been to Europe?"
Hank turned from the window. "First time."

They were traveling second class, jammed shoulder to shoulder in a wide-body Lufthansa jet: Mr. von Wessenheim, the elder of the Amnesty International men, and Mr. Ulgard, who sat throughout the flight with his eyes closed, listening to something through little earphones. They had spent sixteen hours in airports and in airplanes since flying out of O'Hare. Now, with Berlin approaching and one final hop to Sweden remaining, Hank had never felt so lost, had never felt homesickness as despairingly as he felt it now.

"Do we have a long layover in Berlin?" he asked.

"Layover?" Von Wessenheim did not seem to understand.

"Waiting for the next flight to Sweden."

He cleared his throat. "First we must spend time in Berlin."

"Oh." Hank frowned. "Why?"

He matched Hank's frown. "For secrecy. We may have been followed."

Hank craned around, realized how futile it was, and turned his attention back to the window. His fate was no longer in his control, that was obvious, but Amnesty International was a respected outfit with lots of clout. At least from what he knew of it. Rising up below the plane now were the red roofs of Berlin, everything neat and square and tidy. In a strange way he was surprised to see color at all; the only pictures he had ever seen of Berlin were war photos of smoking black-and-white ruins. Now, glistening skyscrapers thrust up in

bunches; he saw lots of trees and greenery and moving lines
of cars that sparkled under the morning sunshine.

Aus der Ruinen kommt Rache . . .

The Lufthansa wide-body swayed silently from side to
side as it drifted over the runway, then bottomed out with a
jolt. Mr. Ulgard finally removed his earphones and yawned
into his fist. Hank had long since stopped wondering about
the tight black gloves, thinking they must be a Swedish fashion like the English with their umbrellas, the French with
their berets. His own fashion statement was a missing shoe,
but at least von Wessenheim had loaned him a sock.

"Home at last," von Wessenheim murmured as the huge
plane taxied toward the terminal, its long wings bobbing.

Hank turned. "You live in Germany?"

"No." He offered Hank a quick smile. "Home at last in Europe. That is what I meant."

"Will the circus be waiting for us?"

"Der Zircus?" He smiled. "That is a good way to say it,
Herr Thorwald, but no, there will be no *Zircus* here."

Hank hoped he was right. At the terminal, after marching
through the mobile ramp, he expected a strict inspection of
all passports, but the people were filtering through the velvet
theater ropes, past uniformed customs agents seated at tables,
often simply being waved through. Ulgard put a hand around
Hank's elbow and gently tugged him to the wall. Von
Wessenheim followed, looking nervous.

"We've had a passport made for you," Ulgard said softly.
"Remain here."

He strolled away. Immediately, a man wearing shorts and a
blazingly colorful Hawaiian shirt, two cameras slung around
his neck, wandered into the area looking confused. He
bumped into Ulgard and stepped away, apologizing loudly.
Ulgard pointed a direction for him to go.

"My God, the man is brilliant," von Wessenheim whispered.

Ulgard came back and slipped the passport into Hank's
hands. "Shall we?"

They merged into an aisle. The agent requested Ulgard's
passport, and was very interested in Hank's new one, glanc-

ing from his face to the photo and back. "Automobile accident," Hank ventured, touching his battered face.

"Proceed to the baggage area."

They took an escalator down one flight to the baggage carousels. Von Wessenheim's suitcase was the only piece of luggage; after fetching it they stood in another line, waiting. Hank watched an agent open a woman's purse and briefly rifle through the contents. Von Wessenheim offered his suitcase. The agent put a hand on it. *"Behält Ihr Koffer ausländische Frucht, Gemüsse, oder Fleisch?"*

Hank's brain pushed out an easy translation: Does your luggage contain any foreign fruit, vegetables, or meat?

"Nein," von Wessenheim answered.

"Alles gut."

"Everything in order," Ulgard said to Hank, and they walked away. To von Wessenheim he said, "I must get back to my office. Good day."

He veered away. After a bit of hesitation von Wessenheim dropped his suitcase and hurried after him, his briefcase flapping; they conferred in whispers. "Herr Ulgard is a lawyer working for us at Amnesty International," von Wessenheim said when he returned. "He has offices in many countries."

"When do we leave for Sweden?" Hank asked him as he lifted the suitcase for the old guy; von Wessenheim was visibly crumbling with exhaustion.

"First we lie low," he said. "Is that correct? Lie low?"

Hank nodded.

They joined the flow of people, matching their pace. "I have a suite at a hotel here in Berlin, the Berlinische Residenz. We will lie low there until the time is right."

"And your people are working to bring my wife and daughter to join me?"

"Very shortly."

"Can Sharri be transported already?"

Von Wessenheim smiled. "Of course."

Hank's stride faltered. "You've talked with her doctors?"

"Doctors?" He slowed and his smile faded. "Who did you say again?"

"Sharri."

"That's an English word I do not know."

They drifted to a complete halt and as Hank looked into the other man's pale blue eyes the rapid-fire events of the past twenty-four hours lost their individual focus to become one solid event: whatever the reasons, yesterday he had been in Terre Haute, Indiana, and today he was in Berlin, Germany. Of all the places on the globe, Berlin. Maybe it truly was a stopover on the way to Sweden; maybe von Wessenheim and the other man truly belonged to Amnesty International; and it could be that other activists were handling Rebecca and Sharri's escape. But new doubts insisted it was not so.

"It's my daughter's name," he said quietly. "Sharri."

Von Wessenheim was glancing around. "I believe the doctors said she can come in three days."

He walked on. Hank followed, lugging the suitcase, more afraid now than when the Ohio police had caught up with him in the woods north of the farm where he'd tried to steal a chicken. The airport was bright and strange, night and day had been reversed, policemen wearing unfamiliar green uniforms and carrying machine guns patrolled the corridors. Without doubt he could outrun the old man, but he had no place to run to. He had no cash for a return ticket. Gleeworth had already informed him, on the drive from Ohio to Terre Haute in the back of the police car, that his credit cards were worthless. All he had left, Hank knew, was a man named von Wessenheim to follow, for better or for worse.

There were plenty of taxis waiting outside, all of them cream-colored Mercedes. Despite the sunshine it was a cool day. Von Wessenheim relieved him of the suitcase and stuffed it in the trunk while Hank stood on tiptoe, amazed: beyond the taxis and parking areas lay a huge city fanning out in all directions, a glimmering Oz full of mysteries. He did not recognize anything. Even the rapid-fire German spoken between the cabbie and von Wessenheim came too fast to follow. So much for Perry Wilson's language lessons.

Hank settled himself in the rear after Von Wessenheim took the front seat. "*Zur Residenz,*" he said to the driver, who promptly tore away from the parking slot. The ride that followed was twenty minutes of high-intensity stunt driving, veering from lane to lane without apparent reason, slinging around corners with the tires squealing. Von Wessenheim turned and offered Hank a smile as he banged around in the back. "The German drivers are legendary for their speed," he said. "And the Autobahn has no speed limit."

Hank thanked God that this was not the Autobahn, just ordinary city streets. When the cab came to a brisk halt he climbed out to look around in awe. The buildings were beautiful, fantastically ornate, everything was as clean as if newly scrubbed from top to bottom. He had imagined Paris might be like this with its shops and boutiques and outdoor restaurants, but never Berlin.

Von Wessenheim drew up beside him and offered the suitcase. "Isn't this city *wundervoll,* Herr Thorwald?"

"Phantastisch," Hank muttered, still drinking in the sights.

"You just spoke German," von Wessenheim said, his eyes widening. "How interesting."

Hank felt himself redden. "Learned some from television. Where did *you* learn German?"

Von Wessenheim blinked. "In school. Swedish is a Germanic tongue, which made it easier."

They walked into the Residenz. Hank stood waiting on the plush red carpet while von Wessenheim talked with the clerk. The hotel with its white statuettes and polished wood, ornaments and chandeliers, was too fancy to be comfortable. It was obvious that his benefactor was a man of wealth, even of stature. It was also obvious that he had planned to bring Hank to this overblown hotel all along; at the airport he had admitted booking the room in advance. And besides, wasn't Amnesty International headquartered in London?

He did not know for sure. Von Wessenheim turned and gestured to the stairway with his eyes. Surprised that there was no elevator, Hank hiked up the steps carrying the bag. In the hallway von Wessenheim unlocked the door and Hank went in hesitantly, hoping not to be surprised by a media horde, but the room was mercifully unoccupied. He craned his head back and forth, taking in the sight of a suite that in its luxury could rival anything offered on the *Titanic* so long ago. But that was ominous in itself.

"Please make yourself to home," von Wessenheim said. *"Haben Sie Hunger?"*

Hank lowered the suitcase and rose with a shrug, his face as blank as a fresh fall of snow.

"Food," von Wessenheim said. "I will call room service if you like."

Hank thought. The two Lufthansa meals had been palatable but meager, so to be honest he was hungry. Very. "I'd like to discuss things with you first, Mr. von Wessenheim. The details about Amnesty International, and what happens next to me and my family."

Von Wessenheim raised an open hand. "Mr. Thorwald, you have nothing to worry about anymore. All things are taken care of."

"So what am I supposed to be doing?"

"Enjoying your freedom. Here you can have any food you want, fine wines and liquors, you can watch videotaped movies all day long in either German or English, you can sleep away your jet lag." He lit a cigarette. "Camel Wide? Care for one?"

"No."

"I can get you any book you want to read. I can get *anything* you desire."

"And in return?"

He smiled. "Nothing. I want to show you the city, let you get to know Berlin."

"What about Sweden? When does that happen?"

"As soon as my companions arrive in Stockholm with your wife and child. Perhaps a week."

Hank scrubbed his face with the palm of a hand. "Why so long?"

"These are delicate undertakings, Mr. Thorwald. You saw the uproar that followed your departure. We would like to avoid that with your family."

It made lots of sense. Amnesty International might really be the engine driving this after all. Torn, Hank shoved his hands in his pockets and ambled to one of the open windows. A bright European sun was pouring its white beams into the room and the air carried the freshness of morning. His eyes burned and his head ached, night and day were up-side-down and the resulting jet lag was lending everything a cast of unreality.

He turned in time to see von Wessenheim leaving the room. A door clicked shut and water began to run. Hank strode to the entry and pulled the door open. A glance in both directions revealed an empty hallway. No guards to keep him here, apparently he could walk out. But he was a prisoner of Berlin; even if he hitchhiked his way out he would still be penniless in a foreign country. So he gently pulled the door closed and wandered the room with his hands in his pockets. Von Wessenheim had left his cigarettes and matches on an ornate little table; he shook one out and lit it. The matchbook bore the Holiday Inn logo. The other side gave the location: 3300 S. Vista Avenue, Boise, Idaho.

Boise. Hank put it back, frowning. Why in the world had von Wessenheim been in Boise? Idaho housed a couple of high-profile white-supremacist garrisons in the backwoods. A few of their representatives had noisily joined the crowd at 1225 Q-main. Any connection?

He wandered again. Everything was neat and tidy except for the briefcase tossed on the sofa, the suitcase left by the door, and a cardboard box shoved in a corner with things sticking up from it. Hank crouched before it and found them to be cardboard tubes with tin caps plugged into the ends. He hooked his cigarette in a corner of his lips, pried one open, and partially shook out the contents: detailed maps. Baffled, he replaced the cap, then lifted out a handful of books. The topmost one grabbed his eyes and made him clap a hand to his chest in surprise. It was a dog-eared paperback copy of *Mein Kampf*. He rummaged further while his heart picked up speed. More books, all of them imprinted with either a swastika or the name Hitler or his face, most of them with all three.

A toilet flushed. He quickly put things back in order and jumped up. By the time von Wessenheim reappeared, he had assumed a casual sitting position on the sofa, cigarette dangling easily from his fingers. "I must take a bath," von Wessenheim said to him. "For you there is a bath in your bedroom." He pointed. "I trust you will wash for our meal, *ja?*"

"Yes."

He picked up his suitcase and carried it away. Hank let out the breath that had been idling in his lungs and rose as soon as he heard a door close. Beside the sofa sat a white telephone with gold accents atop a Victorian-era wooden stand. A single drawer beneath it seemed likely to house a telephone book. Hank slid it open and saw only a pamphlet embossed with the hotel's name. A quick leaf through its pages was an excursion through confusion. There had to be a telephone book somewhere in the suite—unless Germany simply didn't *use* phone books, had some kind of master computer with all the numbers inside it. He replaced the pamphlet and slid the drawer shut, then gently lifted the phone to his ear.

Nothing. He pressed the nine on the base unit, the standard number in American hotels for reaching an open line.

Nothing. He hung up, biting at his lower lip, took a drag off the cigarette, then lifted the receiver again. This time he pressed zero.

Clicking noises. "*Bedienung.*"

He hooded the receiver with a hand and whispered into it. "Do you speak English?"

"Yes."

"Are you able to connect me to the American consulate?"

"Yes. Please hold while I search for the number."

He swept the receiver from his ear and hung up. An American consulate existed in Berlin. He had only the vaguest idea what kind of duties a consulate performed but occasionally one made the news by sheltering Americans from foreign trouble. It was good to know, as a last resort.

In his bedroom he found more museum pieces, things that would make an antique collector drool. The huge bed was draped with a satin spread that sparkled with gold and silver trim. He ignored the finery and undressed, dropping his clothes in the middle of the floor. While the claw-footed tub was filling with steamy water he noticed a little box of bath bubbles with directions in three languages. What the hell, he dumped it in; he liked showers but hated baths so it couldn't hurt. When the tub was finally full he lowered himself into the sudsy water slowly, his breath catching in hitches. The hint of a smile played at the corners of his lips when he bottomed out: he had not bathed like this in years. No wonder Rebecca liked lounging in the tub with all her fancy oils. He ducked his head under the water and rose back up wiping the suds from his eyes.

He had not shut the bathroom door. A young man stood where it would have been. He was wearing a snappy blue suit and looked like an FBI agent at about ten in the morning on an easy day. "Mr. Harrison Thorwald?"

Hank gaped at him, wondering if it were so.

"You come with us."

The German accent was mild but obvious. He extended a hand to lift Hank out of the tub. When Hank refused he showed the other hand, this one busy with a pistol. "Come out fast," he said. "Now."

Hank stood up. A young woman popped into view and eyed him in his suit of suds. Ducking quickly out of sight, she returned with the satin bedspread bundled in her arms. "Wrap him in this." She shoved the bundle to the man standing in the bathroom doorway, who forwarded it to Hank.

"Wrap yourself in this."

He stepped out of the tub and swung the blanket over his shoulders, eyeing the gun, wondering which end of hell he was about to be thrown into this time.

40

When Rebecca arrived at her house at 1225 Q-main she saw that it had burned to the ground. Dutch pulled to a slow stop at the curb, his mouth hanging open, staring. In the backseat Alan Weston rose up wordlessly. A fire truck was parked on the muddy ruins of the lawn but the last few firemen were packing their gear.

In a trance, Rebecca pushed her door open. The wreckage maintained the shape of the house, the garage had collapsed without fully burning, and Hank's Lexus still sat on its melted tires. Strings of smoke drifted up from the ashes. She saw the familiar shapes of the washer and dryer, and the charred skeletons of the kitchen chairs sticking up from puddles of black water. Even the sides of the nearby trees had burned. A wave of despair rose and stuck in her throat like an extra heart, pulsing as she fought back tears. Dutch got out and put an arm around her shoulders but mercifully said nothing.

Somewhere behind her a camera flashed, the light sparkling on the fire truck. She whirled, lunged, and jerked the camera from its owner. "You leave us the fuck *alone!*" she screamed at the man. The camera had an unused neck strap hanging from it; she used it to whirl the camera overhead in a blurring circle. Another move swooped it down to explode on the asphalt. The little yellow canister of film rolled away trailing its negatives like an active tail.

"You smashed my camera!" he shouted, and Rebecca went for him. Suddenly Dutch's arms encircled her waist and he lifted her kicking and shrieking.

"Killing him won't do you any good," he said as he planted her back on the sidewalk. In fact, all but a handful of gawkers had gone, along with all traces of the police. "You don't want to be in jail when Sharri needs you most."

She pushed away from him and sobbed into the palm of one hand as she gave the burned house, the graveyard of the Thorwalds' dreams, another look. A fireman carrying an ax was poking at things. God, all the baby pictures of Sharri, her baby book, the handful of photographs from their tiny wedding, all of Hank's diplomas and stuff—gone. Forever. It was a hurt so deep she thought it must kill her.

Dutch touched her elbow. "Let's go someplace else, girl. There's nothing you can do here."

She stepped away from him, wanting to stay, but in another moment she was desperate to leave. In the police car they drove slowly past her little Pontiac; beaten and scarred, someone had finally burned it too. Now there was nothing left, no reason ever to return. If she had seen this before confronting Alan, she might have killed him, literally ended his life in anger. Now she felt only a dull distaste for his work, a dull distaste for him, and an unwillingness to dwell on the fact that he was probably the only man alive who could save Hank, save them.

"I'm going to have to take this cruiser back soon," Dutch said after a long silence. "Grand theft auto might get my pension cut off forever, so decide where you go next." He winked at Rebecca. "Sorry. The little woman is going to start wondering where I am, at which point she usually starts calling old boyfriends."

Rebecca smiled for his benefit but in truth was thunderstruck. Without a car she was homeless and on foot. Now that Hank was gone and the crowds had dispersed, the chief of police's offer of a free hotel room had probably expired. That left her in the care of Alan Weston, who probably had a lot of cash in the bank and a lot of credit cards, and who could get the upper hand with her pretty quickly. And if he rented a car, he could be gone tomorrow.

"Do you know that apartment complex out on Dixie Bee Road?"

"Which one?"

"The cheap one. I know a girl out there, whatever it's called. Dixie Bee Flats? Take me there."

"Can do. Alan?"

He was fiddling with his disassembled computer. "Yeah?"

"He's with me," Rebecca said. "Whether he likes it or not."

Alan pushed himself forward and looked at her appraisingly, his lumpy face neutral, then attached a slight, one-sided smile to it. One of the stitches holding his lower lip together split and he ducked away with a squawk.

"He seems okay with it," she told Dutch soberly.

MaryLou Hanscom opened the door. Rebecca saw a scream trying to get out of her and shoved her backward with a hand pushed between her breasts, then turned and ushered Alan in. At the door, before closing it, she waved to Dutch. He waved back, squinting in the afternoon sunlight, and drove away. All of Alan's computer stuff was piled beside the welcome mat, but it was daylight so it would probably be safe for a while.

"Where's the bathroom?" Alan asked MaryLou.

"Uh?" She had wrapped both hands around her throat. "Over there." She pointed. "Through that door."

He hurried off. "Listen," Rebecca said. "I need your help, and I need it bad."

MaryLou's eyes behind her old-fashioned cat's-eye glasses were big and unblinking. She dropped her hands. "Jesus, Mrs. Thorwald, what *happened* to you? And that *guy* with you, who *is* he? And how come the *police* brought you?"

"We came here to borrow your car for a few days, MaryLou."

"My car?" She clutched her throat again. "The Honda?"

"Please don't tell me no, MaryLou. Remember, Hank cosigned for it."

"But I've made the payments on time!"

"That's not the point. You've heard of Alan Weston, right?"

"Uh-huh."

"Well, that's who's in your bathroom right now. We're preparing his next television segment."

She appeared to be strangling herself. "Alan Weston? Ohmygod. *Ohmygod!*"

"Professor Thorwald was kidnapped by Italian terrorists early this morning while our entire house burned to ashes. Did you know Sharri got shot by the police?"

"Oh no, that's *horrible*," she said. "I've been so busy with school since Professor Thorwald left, I didn't know. I got there that day, and he was gone. It really shook me up, made me mad. And a lot of other people too."

"So you understand. Alan Weston is going to help me, but we have *got* to have a car for the next day or two." She searched for words. "Do you have any other transportation? Friends who could drive you? Your mom or dad?"

MaryLou took a few steps to the side and began wringing her hands. "God, I don't know. I've been busy like crazy, I'm fielding all of your husband's classes, he left me without a clue of what to do."

"Not on purpose," Rebecca said.

"No, but my dad isn't feeling good, and even the car is running bad. Sometimes it won't start at all."

Rebecca drew back. "Your car is less than a year old."

"It has a *lot* of problems," MaryLou said with her eyes jumping.

Alan walked back into view. "I'd forgotten how small studio apartments were. Lived in a couple myself, back in the hungry days."

Rebecca gave the area a quick glance, making cognitive note for the first time that she was in MaryLou's tiny kitchenette. "So your answer is no? After the things Hank did for you?"

She held her head up with her eyes closed and her lower lip quivering. "I'm sorry. This is too sudden. You should have called."

Rebecca looked at Alan, angry and embarrassed. He brought a hand up and touched his swollen lips with a finger, at the same time poking his thumb out to indicate the room he had just come out of. A couple of nods sealed the message.

"Then let me at least use your bathroom," Rebecca said sourly.

"Of course, Mrs. Thorwald. Please don't hate me."

Rebecca walked past Alan into a box-size room with barely enough space for the television and the timeworn easy chair that was aimed at it. On the floor beside the chair a neat little stack of newspapers had accumulated. Rebecca lifted them one at a time: the Terre Haute paper mixed among tabloids with screaming headlines, Hank's face, Sharri's face, some of the photographs retouched to show a Hitler mustache on Hank, one with a preposterously fake dagger clamped between Sharri's teeth. It just never ended. She carried the stack back into the kitchen and smacked it down on the countertop beside the little sink. MaryLou saw and put a hand over her mouth.

"Why have you turned your back on him?" Rebecca shouted at her.

MaryLou backed herself against the wall. "Because my— because if I—"

Alan wagged a hand. "Who is this, anyway?"

Rebecca turned. "Hank's graduate assistant."

"Simple," he said. "Hank's poison. The association will ruin her future."

Rebecca eyed her. "Is that it, MaryLou?"

She nodded while tears sprang to her eyes. "I can't afford to be known as Hitler's grad assist. I want to be a university teacher but I have to keep my record clean."

Rebecca's face hardened. "You lied about fielding his classes, didn't you?"

The tears spilled out. "Dr. Greiser took them all."

Richard Greiser had been at the party, Rebecca remembered, and she wondered if he believed or did not believe. "Give me your keys, MaryLou. Hank just repossessed your car."

Her purse was hanging from a hook on the wall. She rummaged through it, sobbing, and dragged her keys out. "Can you do that?" she asked as she freed a single key from it. She looked at Alan. "Can she do that?"

"Not legally," he replied.

She raised her chin. "Then forget it."

Rebecca was glaring hate at Alan. "However," he said to MaryLou, "I'm thinking of doing an entire show on Professor Thorwald's former grad assistant, her dirty dabblings in neo-Naziism with the mad professor. The networks might even pick it up, NBC and all the rest. National news."

"You wouldn't."

He eyed her steadily. "You're talking to Asshole Weston."

She swallowed with an audible click. "Fine, then." Wearing a little-girl pouty face, she passed the key to Rebecca. "You can have the payments too. And I'm canceling the insurance."

"Let's go," Rebecca said to Alan. MaryLou slammed the door behind them hard enough to knock something off the walls inside; there was a crash followed by a scream. Carrying Alan's computer and a paper bag stuffed full of wires and cables, they came to the little white Honda. Rebecca put the bag down and paused before unlocking the door. "You threatened her with doing a show," she said. "I thought you called them segments."

"I'm done with segments," he said. "My next TV project is going to be a *show*. A *network* show. Even if it kills me."

"And the first show will exonerate Hank completely. Even if it kills you."

He merely smiled, which made his lip bleed again.

41

Yᴏᴜ have certainly captured the imagination of the western world," the woman said. "Not so much in Germany, but elsewhere."

Hank sat motionless on a knobby wooden chair that had been shoved under him, clutching the satin bedspread around his shoulders. A black velvet bag was over his head, had been for the last hour. Wherever he was, he had made the trip in the trunk of a car.

"My name is Ilsabeth, Mr. Thorwald. Welcome to Germany."

Hank waited, tensed, blind. Fingers fumbled at the back of his neck, untying the drawstring. The bag was whisked up and he was forced to squint his eyes. In time he saw that he was sitting in front of a spacious wooden desk in a large office suite. Slats of sunlight cut through the vertical blinds to his left; to his right stood the man and woman who had hijacked him from the bathtub. Behind them a wet bar gleamed with dozens of liquor bottles.

"I want to know if it is true, Mr. Thorwald. Will you be honest with me?"

He looked at her. The blonde hair was a bleach job and a couple of face-lifts had tightened her skin, but by the pink rheuminess of her eyes and the size of her ears she was old. "Honest about what?"

"Were you Adolf Hitler in a past life?"

He glared at her. "You kidnapped me for this?"

"You have not been kidnapped, Mr. Thorwald. You have been rescued."

"By Amnesty International, I suppose."

She shook her head. "That was Herr von Wessenheim's game. Here I will tell you no lies."

"Good. When do I get to go home?"

She smiled. "I will tell you no lies, but I cannot predict the future. Do you know why Herr von Wessenheim brought you to Berlin?"

"No."

She bent forward and plucked a cigarette out of a silver box. "Smoke?"

Instantly he was reminded of the old war movies, the evil Nazi offering a smoke to the American hero just before the torture started. The American always refused. "Fine."

She rolled one across the uncluttered desk and followed it by shoving a book of matches his way. He poked his arms out of the bedspread, lit the cigarette and pushed the matches back, then covered up as best he could.

"Would you like to know why von Wessenheim brought you to Berlin?" she asked casually.

He choked on the first puff: menthol. An examination of the cigarette showed that he was smoking an American brand, a Salem. Ick. "I suppose."

"Here is the answer: Herr von Wessenheim believes you were Adolf Hitler. It is his wish that you tell him where the dead body of the Führer lies."

Hank's face went blank. "Why? Who cares?"

"Herr von Wessenheim cares, very deeply. He believes it will make him rich and famous."

"He's already rich, isn't he?"

"And getting poorer all the time."

He puffed nervously on the cigarette, hating it but glad to have something to do besides sit in fear.

"So again," the woman named Ilsabeth said, leaning forward while tapping her Salem into a glass ashtray, "were you Adolf Hitler?"

He shifted his weight. "I was not Hitler. I was hypnotized by a fellow professor—as a joke—to speak a few words in German, and to claim to be Hitler."

"So you did speak German?"

"Only what he taught me."

"Then tell me—*braucht man Versicherungsdeckungskarte bei einer Straßenbahnhaltestelle?*"

He popped out an involuntary answer: *"Das ist Blödsinn."*

"Marvelous," Ilsabeth said as Hank constructed a mental gallows and hanged himself from it. "A senseless question full of big words answered with a very sensible reply, as if you'd lived in Germany all your life."

Hank felt his face flush a shade toward red. "My teacher was an amazing man."

"And so are you, Mr. Thorwald." She directed her attention to the other two. "Ask the doctor in," she said in English. "Stay at the door, we cannot be bothered."

Hank rose halfway up as they left the office, an awful certainty taking shape in his mind, but she jumped to her feet. "Sit down, Mr. Thorwald, you have no place to go. The doctor is a registered hypnotherapist and presents no danger to you."

He sat down again and clutched the bedspread tighter with one hand, toying with the cigarette with the other. The door behind him opened as she took a sideways step to close the vertical blinds; gloom spread through the room. Hank was aware of a smell in the air, flowery perfume. Then the doctor stood in front of him, a dark-haired woman of about forty wearing a white lab coat. Her scent reminded him of the last funeral he'd been to: G-pa's, his grandfather who had brought a Nazi dagger home from the war.

"Hello, Mr. Thorwald," she said with a thick accent. "May I call you Hank?"

He simply shrugged. She bent and plucked the Salem from his fingers, then crushed it in the ashtray.

"Okay, Hank. Are you comfortable?"

He gave her an unhappy look. "Not at all."

She turned to Ilsabeth, who had resumed her position behind the desk. "His chair is too hard," she said in German. "You must switch."

Ilsabeth jumped up and wheeled her chair beside Hank's. He stood, hating his helplessness. Without clothes he felt like a child in front of these women. When the chair had been replaced behind him, he lowered himself into it gingerly. Very soft. He wondered how Sharri was faring.

"Better?"

The doctor was back to English again. He twitched his shoulders in reply.

"Look up at me, Hank, concentrate on me. You see my finger? I touch you between your eyes, and now I slowly bring my finger away, I stop right here and I go left, I go to your left, and now I go right, I go to your right. Follow it with your eyes, my moving finger. Now I touch between your eyes again and draw my finger away, I go left, I go to your left, and now I go right, I go to your right. Follow it with your eyes, follow my moving finger. You feel yourself relaxing, maybe just a little bit, maybe just a little bit. You let your stiff shoulders relax but still you watch my finger, my moving finger, I go down, I go to your left, and now I go up, I go to your right, you concentrate on my finger . . ."

As an exaggerated, numbing drowsiness began to overcome him, he realized that her finger was tracing a swastika in the air.

Karl-Luther von Wessenheim woke up cold and miserable. Groaning, unable to open his eyes, he rolled to his left and plunged underwater. With a gasping whoop he sat up.

Bathtub. The suds had become an oily stain on the cold water. He needed a moment to think, then surged to his feet. Many towels hung from ivory rods; he clawed at a fat one and draped it over his shoulders, then stepped out of the tub, shaking as he dried off. The slant of the sun through the single bathroom window was alarmingly low, as if he had slept away a lot of the afternoon. Cursing himself, he wrapped the towel around his waist and strode out of the bathroom. Thorwald was in no better shape than he was, both had gone for days with only fragments of sleep. But Thorwald was a young man, he had more stamina. Would he have fled wearing only one shoe?

He came to the other bedroom and leaned against the door frame. Thorwald's clothes were a pile on the floor with one shoe sticking out. He wasn't in bed, but the bathroom door was closed. Von Wessenheim breathed again, tempted to peek into the bathroom, but what the hell. Thorwald was probably asleep in the tub. He pushed away from the door frame with his heart slowing to a more normal rhythm, then with a jolt focused on the bed again.

The spread was missing. The thick quilt beneath was rumpled and twisted, as if the bedspread had been pulled away in one fast motion by a magician. He jerked himself up taller and the towel slithered down his legs to puddle at his ankles. His breath was trying to leave him; he pressed a fist to his mouth to keep it in. Why would the man take the bedspread into the bathroom? There could be no reason. Naked but for the graying hair on his body, von Wessenheim lurched on shaking knees to the closed door and rapped a couple of knuckles against it. "Mr. Thorwald? Mr. Thorwald?"

No reply came. Already knowing its outcome, von Wessenheim gently pushed the door open and took a look at the tub. No suds, the water even looked cold. Thorwald had simply walked away while his benefactor slept in a tub of cold water. He had simply walked away.

He turned and shambled out of the bedroom, his bare feet dragging across the carpet. Berlin was an enormous city. Finding one man among its multitudes was impossible. Unless one considered the fact that the man was wearing a bedspread.

Wearing a bedspread?

The phone rang just as he walked past it. He snagged the receiver and lifted it to his ear. "*Ja?*"

"You are awake. Meet me at the Stadtsbank Berlin main lobby in one-half hour."

"Ulgard?"

"You are going to transfer funds from your bank in Frankfurt into mine here in Berlin. It is an electronic transaction that needs only minor paperwork, which will be handled here."

"Transfer funds? What funds?"

A pause followed. "Do not joke about this. It is our agreed-upon fee for my endeavors in finding your man. Two million American dollars for two days' work."

"Oh, that." Von Wessenheim plopped bonelessly onto the sofa, crumbling under the simple weight of gravity. It was getting hard to think. "Can't you handle it yourself?"

"They will hardly transfer two million dollars from your account without seeing you in person, Herr von Wessenheim. Be sure to bring your driver's license and passport, and I'm sure you'll have to call Frankfurt in the presence of the board."

Von Wessenheim noticed that one of his fingernails had gotten chipped somehow. He stuck it between his teeth and slowly gnawed the imperfection away, wondering how it had happened.

"Hallo?"

"Mmm?"

"The Stadtsbank Berlin in one-half hour."

"Can't make it," von Wessenheim said, examining the nail. Now the others looked ragged in comparison.

"When, then, can you appear?"

"I've had no lunch at all, not one bite. I intended to call room service but fell asleep in the bathtub."

"It's after three in the afternoon," Ulgard snapped. "Save your appetite for your supper."

"Call again later." Von Wessenheim hung up and went studiously back to his fingernails. A few drops of water fell from his hair onto his fingers and he licked them away. They tasted like soap. He drew his legs up and collapsed sideways, remembering the wisps of a former dream.

The phone shrilled again. With a groan he sat up and got it to his ear. "*Ja?*"

"What game are you playing?" Ulgard asked nastily. "Are you unwilling to pay me?"

"I will pay you soon. Perhaps later tonight." He hung up.

Clang-clang. Von Wessenheim lifted the receiver. "*Ja?*"

"The banks are closed at night. Are you all right, Herr von Wessenheim? Are you fully awake?"

"I don't think so."

He hung up. In seconds he was asleep, sprawled naked on the sofa.

Ulgard entered the suite eighteen minutes later. The door was not locked. He stopped abruptly and regarded von Wessenheim as he dozed. Circling the sofa, he saw that the old man did not seem injured, as would be the case if Thorwald had overpowered him or knocked him silly. Neither man had been in any shape for battle, really. A quick check of the suite revealed two bathtubs with cold water in them. In one of the bathrooms von Wessenheim's clothes were on the floor. Thorwald's clothes were on the bedroom floor in front of the other bathroom. There was no evidence of violence.

But Thorwald was missing, along with one of the bedspreads. Not a good way to kidnap a man, wrapped up in a bedspread, unless you are a bumbling amateur or in a really big hurry. Or both.

He paused at the door to the hallway with his hand on the knob. "Stupid old bitch," he muttered, and left.

42

Heat was the key factor in trying to live in a mobile home—a trailer house, as Rebecca had always called them. The roofs of the older models tended to be corrugated aluminum, the walls no thicker than a small-town phone book. Room for insulation there was not much. But Alan Weston was enthusiastic. It reminded him of his early days, he had explained, reminded him of the starving years when he had rejected the good jobs his journalism degree would bring for the impossible dream of going straight to television at age twenty-five.

They had posed as newlyweds for the manager of Dixie Acres. A car wreck had caused their injuries—too much shaving cream on the windshield, Alan explained. Trailer number 12 already had a phone line installed, so all that had to be done was to call the phone company from the manager's trailer, which was kept bearable via the wind blasting through a swamp cooler that dripped rusty water all over his kitchen floor.

"It's awfully hot," Rebecca said now, her lower back aching from staying on her feet too long. This trailer featured shredded furniture but she was afraid to sit on any of it; a trip to the bathroom found that the toilet looked halfway clean, but a couple of wasps were walking on the plastic window. Alan did not reply: the phone line was plugged into the back of his computer and he was busy with the keyboard. The splints on his broken fingers were causing problems and his language was getting darker each time he had to pound on the backspace key with his thumb.

"I'm going to the hospital to see Sharri," she said, unable to bear the heat or watch him anymore.

He stopped typing and looked up at her. "How hard will it be for you to get into Perry's house?"

"I've *been* in Perry's house. I found him dead there."

"Okay, how hard will it be for you to get into Perry's house again?"

"Considering the fact that the cops are digging up the whole crawl space as a crime scene, it should be extremely hard."

"Do you know the names of Perry's children, maybe where they live? Phone numbers?"

She shook her head. "They're estranged from Perry, never write or call."

"He must have pissed them off royally."

"But rarely talked about it."

"Okay. You need to get in there and box up every bit of family history you can find. Everything."

"What am I looking for?"

"Anything that tells us who Perry was before we knew him. When and where he was born, who his parents were, the names of his children so we can contact them, former places he worked. Stuff like that." He lifted his wrist to see his watch. "And pick up some light beer and a bucket of Kentucky Fried on the way back. Original recipe."

"You want I should wash and wax the car while I'm out?"

He frowned at her. "Don't complain. You hired me for this gig and I expect room and board, at least. So far I've gassed up your cop friend's car and laid out eighty bucks for this sty."

"I thought you liked it! You said it reminded you of the hungry days!"

He nodded. "Exactly. And every time I was hungry, I sent my wife out for a bucket of Kentucky Fried."

"Who paid for it?"

"Actually, she did. Her folks had money."

"Well, my folks is broke." She stuck out a hand. "I told you what they did to my credit cards, Alan. The day will come when I can pay you back. Believe me."

"Why not go to your bank and unload some savings?"

"Savings? We're still paying off Hank's student loans."

He stood and unlimbered his wallet. "Yank out all of it, I can't handle it with these finger splints anyway."

It was an impressive bundle. Rebecca plucked it out and saw that it was mostly ones with a couple of twenties mixed in. She folded them tight and stuffed them into a pocket. "You have any coins?"

He stood up again. "Wanna hold me by the ankles and shake? Jesus." Grumbling, he fished out a respectable handful of change. "Need a Coke or something?"

"Phone call," she said, snatched out a quarter and a dime, and handed everything else back. Outside, as she hopped down the three wobbly steps to the ground, she got out the key to MaryLou's Honda. She was struck by the smell pervading the heat of the afternoon here in Dixie Acres, the sour stench of garbage and baby diapers. Her new neighbors, hunkering outside in patches of shade while dirty toddlers sat blank-faced in the dust, watched her with appraising eyes. MaryLou's car was the newest one here by about fifteen years, so it obviously did not fit. With relief she got into it, and with relief she roared away.

The nearest pay phone she spotted was outside the Texaco station just before the Honey Creek Square shopping mall. The phone book was intact, saving her from dialing 911 for a nonemergency. Instead, she phoned the Terre Haute Police Department direct and asked for Detective Gleeworth.

It took a few tries to get transferred. Finally: "Gleeworth."

He still sounded tired. "This is Rebecca Thorwald."

"Oh. Hi. I got a report that Hank flew from Chicago to New York, JFK airport. Make any sense to you?"

"No. I need a favor from you."

He hesitated, then said, "What kind of favor?"

"I need to get back into Perry Wilson's house."

"His body is not there. Believe me, I looked."

"I don't want his body. I left some things there on the night of the party that I never got back."

He exhaled a quick breath into the phone. "We've still got people working over there. Tell me what it is and I'll go get it."

"It's a bunch of things you wouldn't be able to find."

"Try me."

She closed her eyes. Why did everything have to be so hard with this guy? "Plates, serving dishes, several bottles of liquor, silverware, plasticware, long-stemmed glasses, tumblers, beer glasses, extra ashtrays, cooking utensils, barbecue spits and a bag of charcoal, tablecloths and napkins . . ."

"Never mind, I'll meet you there."

She smiled. Her list of fantasy party supplies was growing thin. "Twenty minutes?"

"Thirty minutes. I've got to finish up something here."

"Thirty is fine. 'Bye."

It turned out to be more like an hour. Alan's mention of a bucket of chicken had finally piqued the interest of her stomach and now it was demanding just that. Breakfast had been at the hospital this morning and, since then, nothing but a glass of water at Alan's house. She wondered, as she waited in the car, if Hank was hungry right now, even alive right now. Probably so, because if the crazies went to the trouble of flying him to New York, they wanted him there alive. She tried to remember the last time she had been with him before this catastrophe struck and found herself reaching all the way back to the hypnotism at the Wabash Valley Inn. Life had been so uncomplicated then. Her biggest problem had been her smoking, but now that seemed like a silly thing to bother oneself with.

She was almost done with her tenth Camel Light when Gleeworth finally showed up. Together they ducked under the police tape and hiked through the overgrown grass to the front stoop. A plain white van was parked behind Perry's old yellow Chrysler, the police forensic team, she assumed, still busy unearthing things in the basement. She wondered if more bodies would be found.

There was a big ugly hasp holding the front door shut now, coupled with a huge round padlock. Gleeworth produced a key and got it open after a few false tries. "All that stuff to pick up and you didn't bring any bags?" he said.

She went inside. "The Dumpster I live in was fresh out, Detective." The aroma gathering here was smelling more of age and neglect; this was becoming a haunted house. She struck off toward the kitchen. Gleeworth followed. She went through the motions of searching for things, hoping he would wander away. Below the floor she could hear an occasional ghostly voice, and began to hope he would go down there to chitchat with the boys. But he was more interested in being her shadow.

"Maybe you could rustle up a box for me?"

"I can't leave you unguarded. This entire house is a crime scene and you might taint the evidence. Basic police rules."

She turned to face him with her hands on her hips. "After all we've been through, you don't trust me?"

"Not that." He raised his hands. "You might inadvertently walk off with evidence."

She sucked in a breath and held it long enough to gather the right words together. "You didn't know squat about this until I called, you didn't know Perry was dead and you didn't know a body was buried underneath this house until I got you started. Without me you'd still be investigating jaywalkers and stolen bicycles. Or guarding airports so kidnappers can fly away unharmed."

He crossed his arms. "You know what?"

She crossed hers too. "Don't even bother me with it."

"You know what?"

She moved through the kitchen opening and slamming cabinet doors, looking for her stuff that did not exist, ignoring him, losing hope that he would go away.

"You know what?"

Rebecca walked to the patio door and took a look through the glass. The patio was a geometric study in polished rock slabs, the torches that had burned so brightly that night were still erect, the wind had blown a couple of party napkins and a drift of cigarette butts deep into the safety of a corner. If she had known what would happen here that night, she would have incinerated the house to prevent it. But that was then, and this was Friday. Or Thursday. She didn't know which.

"Having spent time with your husband," Gleeworth said loudly, "I thought I'd let you know that I do not believe he was—"

Rebecca spun around. "Shove it up your ass, Gleeworth, you're too late. The only thing you can do for Hank now is to get the fuck out of here."

His eyes sharpened. "What are you really looking for?"

"The same thing I asked you for in the first place—the reason Perry did this to Hank."

"More specific, please."

"I want his past, from the day he was born up until the day he died."

"And it's here in the kitchen?"

"It's somewhere."

"You're right. It's all in a shoe box at police HQ."

She took a step toward him. "You already ransacked the place?"

"Not me. Detective Dale Harding is handling this case now. He spent half the night here and came up with almost nothing."

"A birth certificate?"

"Nope."

"Personal records? Bank statements? Insurance policies?"

He shook his head. "Whoever killed Mr. Wilson and hauled his body away made sure all of his private papers were hauled away too."

"Then what's in the shoe box?"

"Photographs. Pictures. Postcards."

"That's all?"

"Yep. Nothing useful."

Disappointed, she went to one of the kitchen stools and sank onto it. In front of her were enough liquor bottles to pave the way to nirvana if she chose, but she did not; Hank had tried that route and it had been a disaster. Now something was nagging at the back of her mind, an important memory that refused to surface fully. "What about the den?" she said. "Nobody could flip through every book and magazine in one night."

"You'll have to ask Harding. Besides, what would he stick

in a book? His birth certificate? College diploma? Lousy filing system, Rebecca, and you know it."

"Hold on," she said, lifting a hand. "There's something I can't quite remember, something I saw here the other day."

He remained silent while she frowned at the liquor bottles without seeing them. Something in the hallway, maybe in one of the bedrooms. Something on the floor? Something on the ceiling? *Something*.

"Done yet?"

She moved her gaze to capture him. "It'll pop up. Always does, eventually."

Gleeworth shrugged. "Happens to everybody. Can we go yet?"

She stood up. "Surely your detective missed a thing or two, Gleeworth. Did you ever run Perry Wilson through your Nintendo crime computer?"

"Funny. Killer comedy. In fact I did. Two traffic tickets in the last seven years. Nothing else."

"So he's clean."

"The Nintendo tells no lies."

"I want to walk through the whole house until I remember this damn thing. May I please?"

"Who's stopping you?"

She took one step and the memory was there like a surfacing bubble. "The attic," she blurted. "The hallway coat closet has the entrance in the ceiling to the attic. Maybe Perry's important papers are up there."

He raised his shoulders and let them drop. "Couldn't hurt to look, I guess."

She turned and lifted the stool, carried it into the hallway and whisked one of the sliding closet doors to the side. With a shove she raked the hangers, most of them empty, to the side as well. The wooden hanger rod came out with just an upward push; she handed it off to Gleeworth. "Okay, I need the stool," she said, and shuffled backward as Gleeworth set it inside.

"You're going to need a flashlight up there," he said. "I've got a brand-new one out in my car. Hang tight."

"Okay." She plopped herself onto the stool and dug out a mashed and bent cigarette, almost the last one. When it was alight she let herself relax. Her hopes of finding something in the attic were absurdly high and she knew it, but it beat the hell out of that gnawing disappointment. From the basement she again heard voices from the crew under the house. How could they stand digging up dead bodies, what kind of person wanted a job like that? Frowning, she took a long drag off the Camel Light, then frowned more deeply. Something was wrong, she was smoking air. An inspection of the cigarette showed that it was torn almost in half just past the filter.

"Great," she muttered, and tried to pinch it together. Instead it broke and the lighted part tumbled to the carpet. It bounced a couple of times in a spray of orange sparks. "Oh, *dammit!*" she hissed, and scooted the stool back into the hallway. Dropping to her knees inside the closet, she used the filter to mash out the ember. It left a small black circle in the pale blue rug but hell, this was the closet, it was no big deal—and it was Perry's house so the rug deserved it. She was backing out when a little white card stuck halfway down behind the baseboard caught her eye. With two fingers she plucked it out. On her feet again she stood in the hallway and turned it over: an old black-and-white photograph of a baby in a frilly white dress and bonnet. The baby was being displayed to the camera in the arms of a large-breasted woman in a dowdy dress, but the shot did not include her head or anything below her waist. Not the world's cutest baby, Rebecca decided, and not the world's greatest photographer. Probably an early photo of Perry Wilson.

She turned it over again, losing interest, then noticed that several words had been written faintly on the back in pencil. Turning it to catch the light made the words readable.

Hannah Wilson
Geb. 4.11.47

An electric shock exploded from the crown of her head down to the soles of her feet and rebounded, unlocking her knees. She dropped down and almost fell forward on her face. Suddenly Gleeworth was standing over her. "Rebecca?" His hands moved around her, never touching. "What's wrong? What is it?"

She raised the picture with a shaking hand. Gleeworth took it and looked it over. After a few seconds she was able to rise to her feet again; his face, when she looked, was blank. "So? It's little Hannah Wilson."

"It *is* little Hannah Wilson," she squeaked out. "Not Hannah Thorwald, Hannah *Wilson*."

Gleeworth hunched his shoulders up. "I think I missed the first half of the movie."

She snatched the picture back. "Listen. While Hank was hypnotized he confessed that he had a baby sister named Hannah, that she died in infancy. But it wasn't his own memory, somehow Perry slipped it into his mind, maybe even by accident!" She clutched the picture to her chest and spun in a circle, squealing with delight. When she saw that Gleeworth looked like the only kid in the theater not wearing 3-D glasses, she stopped. "Don't you see? This means that everything Hank said was programmed into him! Somehow Perry got his own dead sister into the act, or it was a key word that showed Perry that Hank was completely under his spell and ready to spout the bullshit about being Hitler, Perry's lame bullshit about Hank's supposing to be the Kaiser—Perry did it all. He did it *all!*"

She fell against Gleeworth and hugged him hard enough to squeeze a groan out of him. "I knew it, Mr. Bigshot Gleeworth, I knew all along that it was a lie!" She began to cry on his shoulder, not caring that in his line of work this clue might seem lame. "I kept the faith," she whispered fiercely. "It was the hardest thing I've ever done in my life."

He made no move to disengage himself from her arms. She held him and wept until it was all gone, the anxiety and the dread and the fear, and then she was done.

"Flashlight," she croaked, pulling away. "Let's do it."

"Aren't you going to blow your nose on my sleeve?"

She coughed out a laugh. "Sometimes you can be so sweet."

His flashlight was on the floor, near the closet. Rebecca replaced the stool and got on it. "These trapdoor things just push straight up, right?"

"Yeah."

"Okay, let's see what happens when I do this." She flattened both hands and pushed. The lid went up easily, it was more like a shallow box. While gray bits of insulation floated down she pushed it fully up and maneuvered it to the side. "So far so good. Flashlight, please. It's as dark as night up there."

He clicked it on and handed it to her. Slowly she rose, not anxious to have a spider jump at her, but as she stood fully into it the heat was so dry and intense that she knew nothing could survive here. Ghostly light was supplied by a few little vents in the roof. She brought the flashlight into play and saw an undulating sea of gray insulation stretching into darkness. She slowly turned, frowning as she looked at the absence of things. A huge brick chimney came into view, its sides frosted with dust. She completed a 360-degree turn and her hopeful face fell, there was nothing here at all. She rotated around one more time, faster, but the scenery stayed the same. Except—

She bent slightly at the knees. Directly in front of her was a rectangular depression in the powdery insulation. She lowered the flashlight enough to create shadows around it: a box had rested here, not a very big one, but bigger than a shoe box by far. The image was crumbled along the closest edge, as if the box had been dragged a few inches before being lifted.

And something else: a little triangle poking up from the flattened insulation. She gave it an intense flashlight treatment and believed, for a time, that it was another photograph embedded there. When she lifted it out, she saw that she was wrong, that it was an envelope. With her heart thudding faster, she lifted the unsealed flap and saw canceled checks, maybe twenty of them, all signed by Perry Wilson.

"Any luck?" Gleeworth asked from below.

She reassembled the envelope and its contents. These were

the only clues left. With God's help Alan might find what he needed.

"Well?"

She stuffed the envelope inside her shirt, tucking most of it inside the left cup of her bra. A quick check of herself with the flashlight showed no telltale sharp edges. Gleeworth shouldn't be looking there anyway. "Nothing but a million tons of insulation," she called out. "Coming down."

As an afterthought she used a hand to smooth away the indentation, erasing it. When she lowered the flashlight Gleeworth took it. "I've got the stool, it won't wobble this time," he said. She put both arms overhead and did a deep-knee bend.

He helped her to the floor. "If it's any consolation, Dale Harding probably checked up there and took whatever he found."

"I just had to try," she replied. "At least I know for sure now. Have him call me if he finds something."

"Sure. Are you living back at home now?"

She looked at him, hoping that this was not an unfunny joke, but his expression was earnest. "Yeah," she said. "Home sweet home. And Sharri is doing fine."

"Good to hear," he said. "Good to hear."

43

The five o'clock train from Berlin to Frankfurt was jammed with college students heading home for the weekend, but this was only a simple annoyance for Frau Ilsabeth Dietermunde and the people traveling with her in one of the first-class cars. The doors of their cabin were pressed shut but the noise of the drinking students leaked through louder than the *clack-clack* of the rails underneath, lots of stomping and singing and laughter. In the olden days it would have reminded her of the exhilarating Hitler Youth meetings, stirring her blood, but too many years had passed; those memories had lost their soundtrack. Yet she was full of exhilaration now as the train rolled on toward Frankfurt: across from her sat the hypnotherapist, and beside her, the ghost of Adolf Hitler.

She was sure of it. Under hypnosis Mr. Thorwald had recited a speech given by the Führer in Nuremburg when she was eight years old, the year her father had taken her to that beautiful city to see the savior of their nation. His diction, the message as she remembered it, even the Austrian accent were precise. Listening to him speak almost made her weep despite the brainless sheen of his eyes. Such a wonderful man Hitler had been, such a wonderful empire Germany, such a disastrous end.

She spoke to the doctor. "Is he aware of what's happening?"

"In the sense that a sleepwalker is aware," the doctor replied with a nod. She passed a hand over his slack, inanimate face. "He won't suddenly collapse or cry out. He's quite manageable."

"Marvelous. Can we get him to shave?"

"It's a possibility, Frau Dietermunde, but you saw how clumsily he dressed in the new clothes, bumbling about. In his mind it is as if he is swimming in a world of dim molasses, with no past and no future."

"Interesting turn of phrase. Will he remember this?"

"Only as one might remember a dream."

Frau Dietermunde sat back, thinking. She had not asked the doctor to inquire about the location of the Führer's physical remains because she did not want the doctor to know. She found it possible that Hitler had not known his own burial site, or even planned for it ahead of time. He believed, until the very last moment, that Germany would still win the war through divine intervention. But like Jesus, it was his fate to die before his mission on earth was complete. Today no one wanted to find Jesus's body—it would destroy the notion of his physical ascension into heaven. Hitler's body laid bare would do the same. She did believe, firmly, at the core of her being, that Adolf Hitler was divine, the second incarnation of Jesus, sent by God to punish the Jews who had killed Christ and to establish the New Order. Now, like Jesus, only his disciples were left to finish his work.

In this sense there was no alternative: Mr. Thorwald needed to vanish forever just as Jesus had, and vanish he would. But first the others of the group had to hear him, to know that the spirit of the Führer was eternal, that he would live forever. It might even prod more young people to join.

The train slowed and she looked out the window. It had been a glorious day, and the evening was no less pleasant. A sign on a pole slid past announcing that the next stop was *Bahnhof* Potsdam. To her relief many of the college students headed out of the train as it slid to a shuddering halt, taking their enthusiasm and their beer with them. The doors to her first-class cabin featured small windows, to aid privacy, and she watched their heads as they filed past, the lost generation who knew nothing of patriotism. Soon the outer doors levered shut with a hiss of compressed air, thumping securely closed, and immediately the train lurched, smoothly building speed. In Frau Dietermunde's life she had seen rail cars and locomotives blown over on their sides from the concussion of bombs, had huddled with her mother and sisters in Frankfurt's subway tunnels while giants walked overhead on thundering feet. They had been terrifying times, but as she aged she looked back upon them as her best times, those years when her life was a grand adventure.

A head stopped at one of the small windows, two dim eyeballs peering rudely inside. Frau Dietermunde nudged the young man sitting with her, and pointed. But before he could rise to give the voyeur a piece of her mind the doors were raked apart unexpectedly. Her son, Oskar Adolf Dietermunde—a name he hated and had legally changed to Rønna Ulgard—stood there looking sour.

"Hello, Mother," he said flatly, and indicated Mr. Thorwald with his chin. "What are you doing with *him*?"

She stood up quickly. "Everyone out, this is private. You too, Frau Doktor. It will take only a moment."

They rose and filed out without comment. Rønna Ulgard stepped inside and slid the doors together behind him. His face, normally balanced and professional, was taut with anger. "May I sit?"

"It depends on what is bothering you," Frau Dietermunde snapped. "Thank you for embarrassing me in front of colleagues."

"Colleagues? Barbie and Ken?"

"What is that?"

He swiped a hand through the air. "A useful Americanism. Those children kidnapped Hank Thorwald in the most bungling manner I have ever seen."

She narrowed her eyes. "He's sitting here, isn't he? There are no police around, are there?"

"By sheer luck."

Frau Dietermunde sat down. "So what are you here to do? Escort me to Frankfurt?" She patted the seat beside her. "Stop looking so fussy, sit with me."

He took a step forward and sat beside Mr. Thorwald. "Drugged?"

"Hypnotized."

He frowned as he examined one side of him. "What has he told you? That he was the Führer?"

"Yes."

"And you believe him?"

She drew in a slow breath. "I do."

Her son stood up. His father was an American soldier who had raped fifteen-year-old Ilsabeth Dietermunde in the smoldering rubble of Frankfurt shortly after the war. He did not know that, and she hoped he never would.

"So what are your plans for him?"

"To let him speak before the group."

"And then?"

"Kill him."

Rønna Ulgard smiled bitterly as he tugged his gloves higher. "So all my work has been for nothing. Von Wessenheim keeps his millions and I keep handing ten percent of my miserable earnings to a church that doesn't even own a building yet."

"Hardly miserable. And don't forget the churches of the heart."

"I'm too old for your propaganda, Mother. Give me Thorwald. Business is business."

Now she stood up as well. "So that von Wessenheim can find the moldering bones of the greatest man who ever lived? So that von Wessenheim can extinguish the light of our church? For God's sake, Oskar, that man can destroy us!"

He strode forward and in an instant had a gloved hand around her throat. "There is no Oskar, Mother."

She tried to shove him away, sure that he would never hurt her, familiar with his tantrums since he had been a little boy and did not want to wear his gloves. But he pressed her down to the seat again, squeezing her neck with a shaking hand, his face hard and shiny. His breath smelled of beer, unusual for him. "I am taking this man, good Frau Dietermunde, and you'd better get used to the idea, because he was not Hitler and he does not know where his former bones are."

"Let go of me," she gasped, wrestling with his arm. She saw that this scene was being watched through the windows of the door and held out a flat hand to signal her colleagues to stay out of this.

"To me he is worth a fortune, Mother. To you he is a sideshow freak."

He released her, finally. She coughed into her fist, then raised her head. "Why are you allied with von Wessenheim?" she cried. "Why do his interests mean more to you than mine?"

He adjusted his clothing. "Von Wessenheim will make me rich. All you have done for me is to curse me with *these*." He offered his gloved hands.

She jumped up to shout in his face, "And they have served you well, up to now. Maybe you should spend a day without the gloves to remind you of your duty!"

He placed his hand on top of Mr. Thorwald's head. "Tell him to get up."

She smiled. "He does not listen to me, *Rønna*, he listens only to the doctor."

"Damn. Tell her she is coming with me."

Frau Dietermunde motioned overhead. The thin doors rolled quickly apart. "Werner," she said mildly, "could you take care of this matter?"

The young man stepped forward and poked a large black pistol against the back of Ulgard's neck. He froze instantly, knowing. "Everybody sit," she commanded. "Oskar Adolf Dietermunde, you behave yourself until the next stop or we will stuff you through a window. *Verstehst Du?*"

He turned and slowly settled onto the seat, understanding quite well. "And what is the next stop?" he asked bitterly.

"Magdeburg. Will you need money for a car or a hotel? For the next train back to Berlin? I have some cash with me."

"No thank you," he said.

44

"This is good stuff," Alan said to Rebecca between mouthfuls. "This one is *really* what I was hoping for."

She was sitting on the trailer's excuse for a living room couch, an expanse of dirty fabric and exposed stuffing. "The chicken?"

Alan was on the folding chair in front of his computer, leafing through the envelope she had found in the attic. "No, these checks you got at Perry's. They represent his entire household outlay for the month of August, last year. You couldn't have done better."

She was grateful for the encouragement and the food but not grateful for the heat. The day's light was failing fast but the temperature refused to budge inside the aluminum toaster she now had to call home. Just before stopping at the KFC she had popped into the hospital for a quick visit, but again Sharri was out cold, still in ICU and well cared for. A few minutes of holding her hand and speaking to her blank face had probably done Rebecca more good than it had done Sharri, and she had left the hospital feeling confident. "Which check?"

He was busy gnawing the meat off a leg. "This one." He dabbed his fingers on the napkin on his lap and picked up the check, flapped it. "Paid to the order of Midwestern Specialty Properties. I know that outfit, I've tried to tag them before."

"Tag them?"

"Catch them in the act."

"Of . . . ?"

"How should I know? They're big and they make a lot of

money and they're mysterious about it. For me, that makes segments appear before my eyes."

She picked up her Coke from the toadstool of foam rubber sticking up between her thighs. "So why did Perry write a check to them? Investing in property? A lot of people do that, you know."

"Midwestern Specialty Properties is not a developer, Rebecca. It owns commercial property, mostly nursing homes."

"Then explain Perry's check."

"He's paying for somebody in a nursing home. You said he has a sister."

"A dead sister. He probably smothered her in her crib."

"Or left her brain-damaged, if any of that is true." He tossed the bone at the KFC bucket in the middle of the floor. It missed. "Hell, maybe his mother or father is still alive."

Rebecca considered it possible. "Around ninety years old, but that's not unusual, especially for a woman." She brightened. "Go on the Internet and see if anybody named Mrs. Wilson is in one of those nursing homes."

Alan got up and went to the bucket, squatted there searching for his next piece. "I take it Hank was the one who used the Web."

"Hank and Sharri. Why?"

"Because what you just asked me to do is almost impossible, Rebecca." He lifted out a breast and gave it a nod. "I'd have to hack into their system and that would take days, weeks, might never work." A twelve-pack of Miller Lite was beside the chicken; he tore it open and pulled one out, then went back to his chair.

"Then why did you bring your computer?"

"Because I have a network of journalists in big cities who do minor legwork for me as a favor that I repay in kind. None of us ever really works alone, not at the major network level anyway. And I still have some friends at WXRV."

"So there's nothing we can do by ourselves?"

He shook his head, then changed the motion into a nod. "Plenty we can do by ourselves." He leaned back and jammed a hand into a pocket of his jeans. "You take this pile of coins and drive to the nearest phone booth. Call every nursing home in Terre Haute and pretend to be a family member. Midwestern Specialty Properties is headquartered in Indianapolis but owns nursing homes in two or three nearby counties, I know that much."

"And if that parent is not in any of the Terre Haute nursing homes?"

"While you're gone I'll message my compadres at the station."

She stood up and let her chicken bone fall into the bucket as she passed. "Please don't hog it all, Alan, at least save me a breast."

He had his teeth sunk into his newest piece; his eyes swiveled up to look at her. "Damn." He pulled it from his mouth. "Where the hell are you going so fast? There's plenty of time to eat. You can do all that shit later."

She hesitated, thinking. He was right. There seemed to be no rush with any of this, she could even put it off until tomorrow. But Hank was out there lost in the world, and if she let the momentum flag she might lose him, lose him forever, and spend the rest of her life regretting it. She had loved him at first sight and had lost her virginity on the second date with him; as trite as that might sound, it was important to both of them. As long as he was alive, she had to keep up the momentum.

She formed both hands into a cup in front of Alan's face. "Dump."

Alan put his fist above it and let the coins fall.

But she came back empty-handed. In the heat and the darkness she walked from the car through currents of unfriendly smells and stumped up the rickety steps. The trailer's door was open. Alan had turned off all the lights. Rebecca groped the wall beside the door until finding a set of switches, and flipped them all up. Only the living room light glowed to life.

Alan was asleep on the couch. Seven empty beer cans stood sentry around it. The bucket had been knocked over and hundreds of small black ants were prowling the original-recipe surfaces of the chicken; things had changed quite a bit in the last hour and a half. She had been gone longer than she had expected because at the Texaco station, using the phone to dial every nursing home in the city, she had watched from the shadows as a pregnant girl lumbered her way from an old Camaro into the rest room. Her thoughts leapt back to the only pregnancy of her life and the emotional drawbridge of it, at times glorifying in the new life inside her and at times hating it. Suddenly now, the need to be with Sharri stabbed at her. In the hospital she had sat brushing Sharri's hair with a palm, so engorged with love for the girl that her heart had physically ached. Sharri's lips had been cracked and dry as the small puffs of her breath passed between them, and Rebecca had used her own saliva to moisten them.

And now coming home to this. She kicked the nearest beer can. It whisked over Alan's face and pinged against the window above the couch. His eyes split open, saw her, and widened. "Hey," he croaked. "Where'd you go?"

"How can you do this?" she shouted at him.

He rolled up to a sitting position looking worried. "Do what?"

"How can you sit back and relax? Hank's life is hanging in the balance and you go and get *drunk!*"

He rocked to his feet. "Forgive my lack of memory, but did we get married recently?"

"You're supposed to be e-mailing your pals in Indy, or whatever you do. I called every nursing home in town but the only Wilson I found was one of the janitors." She paused to kick the bucket away. Pieces bounded across the floor losing ants. "You might think this is a vacation, Mr. TV, but it's a race against time."

The muscles in his temples began to flex in and out. "Don't make me mad, Rebecca. When I get mad I stay mad for a long time. Think about where you'll be without me in this, think about how much you stand to lose if I go. And I will go. So stop."

Her eyes were as sharp as shattered emeralds, her emotions just as jagged. With a huge effort she shoved all of her anger aside and stepped back from him. "Could you at least please uphold your part of the bargain?"

He took a breath. "I already did. My guy found a Mrs.

Anna Wilson residing in one of Midwestern Specialty's nursing homes over in the north end of Indy. Place called Autumn Leaves. The address is over there on top of my hard drive."

She walked backward another step, wilting inside while small and shameful bits of her soul turned to instant scars. "Sorry I flipped out," she said.

He shrugged the subject away. "So I figured we'd sleep it off, head there tomorrow, see what happens."

She pinned a faint semblance of a smile to her face, the best she could come up with. "Okay, sure. Great. Thank you." At the door she turned the light off and silently lifted the scrap of paper off the machine. "I'm going to catch a smoke. Feel free to crash out, I won't bother you again."

"Already there," Alan said.

She stepped outside and shut the door. A cool breeze was winding between the hot ones that played across her face. A glance at the hazy sky offered only a scattering of the stars that so fascinated Hank. She wondered if he was looking up at the sky in New York right now, maybe beaming mental messages off his favorite one, but she did not know which one that might be. For her there could be no sleep tonight, not when a woman named Anna Wilson was close by at a place called Autumn Leaves. Alan would probably pull more tricks out of his sleeve tomorrow, but for tonight she had to know for sure.

The Honda still had plenty of gas. She started it and clicked her seat belt together, turned on the headlights, and slowly crawled out of Dixie Acres hoping Alan would not hear . . .

. . . and two hours later steered her car to a stop in the parking lot of the Autumn Leaves nursing facility, exhausted. The drive from Terre Haute had been hell: as she had driven in the darkness the nymphs of sleep coiled their warm shapes around her, each of them whispering with voices that spoke of feathers and pillows. So she had slapped herself repeatedly. She rolled all the windows down. She drove hanging on to the steering wheel, loudly beseeching God to keep her awake.

Now she killed the motor and slumped over the wheel, dazed and groggy; in a few seconds she was able to push the door open. Forcing herself erect, she took a look at Autumn Leaves. Only one story tall, brown brick facade in the front, a small lawn interrupted by a handful of flowers. After a march to the single glass door, she found it unlocked so she went right in, expecting to find a nurse or a receptionist at a nearby desk, maybe a bad smell in the air. There was, in fact, a desk but it was manned by an empty chair and a blank computer, and the air smelled just fine. Autumn Leaves was as quiet as a tomb.

She walked down the corridor that lay ahead. The doors were numbered but she found, with a sinking heart, that there were no names listed, and turned back the way she had come. But after waiting a large block of minutes in the absolute quiet, she leaned over the desk hoping to spot a roster. When none jumped into view, she glanced around again, then made a loop to get around the desk. Aware that she was starting to sweat, she pulled open drawers and gently leafed through the contents, but found only the papers and files of a typical office.

She resumed her position by the door just before footsteps thumping across the carpet announced an arrival. The woman who sauntered into view was heavy and short and not dressed in a uniform of any sort, just sweatpants and a tank top with her yellowed bra straps ribboned around her shoulders. "Can I help you?"

Rebecca smiled. "I'm looking for Anna Wilson's room number. It's urgent."

She squinted one eye as she walked. "Why's that?"

"Her son has died and she doesn't know it yet."

The woman took up her post behind the desk. "And you want to wake the lady up with *that* news? Do you know what condition she's in? Are you a relative? A friend?"

"Not really a relative. No, actually."

"Visitation is denied, then, that's the policy, especially this late at night. You might go in there and have her sign away her life savings, make her buy phony insurance, alter her will."

"I give you my word I would not do that."

"Sorry. Come back during the daytime when we have enough staff."

Rebecca tried to envision leaving without results: there was no way she could survive a drive back to Terre Haute, and that left her sleeping in the car or getting a motel room, if enough of Alan's money was left. She worked the roll of bills from her pocket and held it low as she counted through it. Unexpectedly, the woman leaned over her desk to get a glance. Right then Rebecca knew what had to be done; she reeled out a twenty and a scattering of ones, folding them together in her hand. "What room number was that?" she asked as she extended her arm over the desk.

"About twice that number."

She jerked her hand back to put more into it, mostly ones this time, wondering if a security camera might be watching and wondering why she should care; she let the bills fall. "This is ridiculous, take the money and give me the damn number."

"Number one." The heavy woman pointed. "First one on the right."

Rebecca clenched her teeth in anger. Jamming the rest of Alan's money into her pocket, she stalked to room number one and turned the big aluminum doorknob. When the over-head light stuttered on she took her first look at Anna Wilson, who may or may not have been Perry Wilson's mother. She was asleep. Age had done her no good at all, her white hair was sparse and her shrunken mouth was toothless; she lay like a skeleton under a thin blanket of skin. Rebecca stepped slowly to the bed and bent over her.

"Mrs. Wilson?"

Wrinkles wrapped in wrinkles. "Can you wake up, Mrs. Wilson?"

Her eyes snapped open, as colorless as eggs. Rebecca jerked up with a gasp. It took a moment to arrange her thoughts: "Mrs. Wilson? Can I talk to you?"

Anna Wilson's eyes were roving. "What's that? Martin?"

Rebecca bent low again. "Do you have a son named Perry?"

"Perry? Is that you?"

"Is Perry your son?"

The blank orbs of her eyes moved ceaselessly. "Martin?"

"Perry is here," Rebecca said. "Perry wants to talk to you."

"Perry? You come here now."

Rebecca straightened; the old woman's breath was ghastly. She sucked in a fresh breath and bent low again. "Who is Perry?"

"My boy. Perry?"

There was motion by the door. "She had a disease that destroyed her eyes," the heavy woman said. "I think her brain went first."

Rebecca's heart was pounding: this was indeed Perry's mother, she had said "my boy." "What else do you know about her?"

"I know she got here about three years ago, acting just like she does now. So old she doesn't even have the sense to die."

"Anything else? Family history?"

"I'd have to look at her data sheet."

"Will you do that? It's extremely important."

She smiled, all teeth and no humor. "Talk me into it."

Rebecca left town flat broke, but she left with what she wanted.

45

The train slid into the long dreary expanse of the Frankfurt *Bahnhof*, slotting itself between the dozens of others that rested there. When Frau Dietermunde stepped out the air was heavy with the hot-metal smell of the electric engines, the huge station alive with people and thundering machines. She turned as the doctor coaxed Mr. Thorwald down the steps onto the concrete apron. He was indeed walking in his sleep, but it was becoming a handicap. The next train to Bad Nauheim was scheduled to leave in a few minutes, and if they missed it there was a twenty-eight-minute wait for the next one. Her nerves frazzled easily and the Turkish workers here always smelled bad to her. After the war there had not been enough men left alive to rebuild Germany, so hundreds of thousands of Turks had emigrated. Now they would not go away.

"For God's sake, pull him out of his trance," she snapped. "He has nowhere to run, not while he's penniless in a foreign country."

The doctor leaned close and said several words into his ear, then passed a hand over his face. Frau Dietermunde saw awareness come into his eyes, replaced instantly by fear. And no wonder. The last thing he probably recalled was sitting in an office in Berlin being hypnotized, and—*hoopla!*—suddenly he is standing in a train station. It was a miracle that he did not cry out.

"We must hurry ourselves," she said to him over the noise, and took his hand. Her two young friends and the doctor followed as she tugged him along the apron to the main platform, where they took a quick turn to the right, muscling through the crowd. Train number nineteen was in its slot being rapidly boarded. With the precise timing that the Germans were famous for, train number nineteen would pull out at the prescribed hour and minute even if the doors swung shut in the very faces of the last to board. She glanced back at Mr. Thorwald and was amazed to see a pair of tears slip from his eyes, as if he were a child lost in this horde of foreigners. He quickly wiped them away with his other hand, becoming a man again.

The conductor made sweeping motions as they neared: hurry it along or be left behind. Frau Dietermunde stepped up into the train, panting, and pulled Mr. Thorwald in. The other three clambered aboard, then the conductor. He leaned out and waved his arm to the engineer; the doors shut themselves. Instantly, the train lurched into motion.

She looked for seats: plenty. On this local shuttle there were no first-class accommodations, an annoyance but not a dire one. Frau Dietermunde seated herself and had Mr. Thorwald sit across from her, their knees almost touching. "What is the term for that in America?" she said quietly, leaning toward him. "A rude awakening?"

He blinked slowly and nodded. If not for his new pants and shirt and shoes, he would appear to be a *Säufer,* a common drunk. Before appearing before the group tomorrow she would have her butler, Heinz, tend to all his personal cleanliness. Perhaps, for the presentation, she might even put a swastika armband around his bicep just like the one the Führer used to wear. But no, she was becoming silly. It was not the man they were invited to see, it was the eternal spirit of their childhood idol.

"So did you hear from me what you wanted to hear?" he asked her. "Did I tell you where my former bones were?"

"Heavens, no." She smiled for him. "What you told me is exactly what I knew you would tell me. I am very proud to be your friend."

"So, friend, where are we now, and where are we going?"

"We are leaving Frankfurt. In twenty-eight minutes we

will be in Bad Nauheim, and as my guest you will stay in my home, a castle on a hillside overlooking the famous city."

He did not look impressed. She went on: "One of your American presidents came to Bad Nauheim looking for a cure in its natural hot springs. Theodore Roosevelt, leader of the Rough Riders."

"Oh." Deadpan.

She decided she did not like this man much. The greatness inside him had been muted by poor genetics, and though he appeared Aryan there was no way to be certain, America was a racial melting pot and more than half of its Jews intermarried. She settled back to watch night fall as the northern outskirts of the city zipped past. In her youth the dying light had brought fear, because while the Americans carried out precision bombing by day, at night the British simply dumped their bombs in the dark.

"Sure is a big city."

Her thoughts were German. "Hmm?"

"Out there." He gestured. "Big city."

She cocked her head, puzzled. "Can't you simply say that in German?"

He folded his arms over his chest. "Sorry I said anything." Frau Dietermunde studied his face as he turned his attention back to the scenery, wondering again what the mobs in America had done to him, why he was so bruised, why his skin was flaking off. Beaten him? Burned him with fire? He should be happy to be away from all that, but he did not look happy.

"Do you have a family?" she asked him.

His jaw tightened and he did not look at her. "Yes."

"A wife? Children?"

"Yes."

"And where are they? Where do they live?"

He snapped his eyes to her face. "I don't know where they are, lady. I'm just the trained seal here, I balance the beach ball on my nose whenever you snap your fingers." He lunged forward and snapped his fingers in front of her face, startling her.

"You're getting loud, Mr. Thorwald."

He seemed about to stand up. The young man who had so diligently kept his pistol trained on Rønna Ulgard all the way from Potsdam to Magdeburg now hurried over to sit beside Mr. Thorwald. The tip of the gun made a brief appearance for his benefit, and Frau Dietermunde graced him with a flat, unloving stare. "If you become a problem, Mr. Thorwald, my doctor will inject you with enough Thorazine to make you *believe* you are a trained seal."

He matched her stare, but his was full of bitterness as well. "You people are never going to let me go," he said. "No matter what I do."

"On that you are completely wrong," she said with a trace of triumph in her voice. "We are going to let you go sooner than you think." She smiled. "So try to enjoy your last days in Germany."

When the first whip hit him, Karl-Luther von Wessenheim screamed. Instantly a soft fuzzy ball was jammed deep into his mouth, blocking it. Lashes whipped across his face, his chest, his arms, he was helpless to ward them off. Naked, he was, naked in the desert while a tribe of natives flogged him.

"Wake up!" one of them cried in German. The tribe made it a chorus: *"Aufwachen! Aufwachen! Aufwachen!"*

He woke up. Standing over him, gently slapping him awake with a pair of his own expensive slacks, stood Rønna Ulgard. Von Wessenheim sat up and expelled a rolled sock from his mouth.

"Quit howling and get dressed," Ulgard said and dropped the pants across von Wessenheim's bony knees. He walked away, turning on more lights than the single one already burning. "I hope your nap has brought you back to the world of the sane. Do you know where you are?"

Von Wessenheim pulled the pants on and began an immediate hunt for his cigarettes. "Berlin."

"Do you recall our conversation earlier on the phone?"

Memory struck, but not of that. "Oh my God. Thorwald is gone. He walked away. I let him go."

"Pretty stupid of you to leave him unguarded while you soaked in the bathtub."

He found the Camels, and suffered a coughing fit while trying to get one lit. At length he was able to speak again: "How could I have known he would simply walk away, turning his back on Amnesty International in favor of a starving existence in the streets of Berlin?"

Ulgard was looking out the window. "So are you ready to pay me now?"

Von Wessenheim sat and pulled his socks on. The urge to negotiate the price was strong, but he knew it would be useless against a man like Ulgard. Yet, in legal terms, his enormous fee had been an oral contract with no witnesses, the case could be in court for years. But he had watched Ulgard convince an American convenience store cashier of the error of his ways, and that treatment could become his own, only much worse. "I will pay you what I promised," he said truthfully. "But I would ask one more thing."

Ulgard spoke to the darkness outside. He seemed fidgety. "Ask it."

"If you can somehow bring Thorwald back to me, I will pay you an additional ten thousand Deutschmarks. They are not dollars but they spend well, and they are probably my last."

Ulgard turned from the window. Von Wessenheim saw now that he was finally looking weary from the last few days; his white collar was stained yellow with sweat and his face had acquired beard stubble. Even his slick black hair looked tired. Strangely, he began to chuckle. "So now you offer me ten thousand Deutschmarks. Mr. Thorwald is lost in the vastness of all Berlin, and to find him again you will pay me enough to buy a used car."

"Do you want to see me begging in the streets? Any more than that and I will have to sell my estate at auction."

Ulgard spread his hands as if to push von Wessenheim away. "I accept, do not embarrass yourself further. Now get ready to go, we have a train to catch."

His face fell. "Train? More travel? I cannot stand any more of it, you go alone."

"Your bank is in Frankfurt, Herr von Wessenheim. As soon

as we have custody of your Thorwald again, we are proceeding directly to it. So get ready."

"You believe Thorwald may be in Frankfurt?"

"Nearby. A small town to the north called Bad Nauheim, in the state of Hessen."

Von Wessenheim blanched. He staggered backward and was blocked by the back of the sofa. "Frau Dietermunde!" He slapped both hands over his face and howled between his fingers. "She haunts me, the woman came straight from the bowels of hell." He let his hands fall. "My God, that drunken bitch has my Thorwald!"

"Then I suggest," Ulgard said coolly, "that you get ready. A train departs within the half hour."

"A train. A train. Of course, a train. Why not a plane?"

"There is nothing there to be done tonight. Tomorrow, in broad daylight, we will strike."

"Strike. I like that. Strike."

He scrambled about looking for more clothes.

46

Rebecca made it back to Terre Haute; she did not know how. A miracle from God, maybe, or a miracle of the adrenaline coursing through her veins. The patient-data sheet she had purchased from the woman at Autumn Leaves had been filled out three years previously by hand, Perry's hand; she recognized his pointy scrawls instantly. It contained mountains of information, not much about Perry but a lot about Anna Wilson. Her maiden name was Oakley. In 1946 she had married a man named Martin Wilson. They had two children, Perry, the eldest, and Hannah, who died in infancy. That, and much more. In her hands the information was interesting but hardly useful; in Alan's hands it would be a Rosetta stone. Hopefully.

It was around three, pitch dark and hot, when she stumbled up the steps and into the trailer, thirsty and hungry. She made no attempt to close the door softly and felt no remorse when she turned on the light. The smell of fried chicken was in the air; she looked over and saw that each piece of chicken had become an ant colony of thousands. Her hunger fled instantly. Alan had squinched his eyes shut, not a big job since they were just a pair of narrow slits on a ruined face. He finally sat up and looked at his watch. "What's going on?"

"This," she said, and dangled the paper in front of his face. "I couldn't wait, I drove to Indy and bribed a woman at the nursing home. This is what she gave me."

He plucked it from her fingers, his eyes moving rapidly. "Lived almost her whole life in—Brazil?"

Rebecca snatched it back, frowning, then let out a sigh of

relief. She turned the paper and tapped the area. "Brazil, Indiana, Mr. Investigative Reporter. It's a town between here and Indianapolis."

"Oh. I never go to towns where my presence doubles the population."

"Five or six thousand people," she said. "Just take Wabash Avenue and head east."

"I'll make it a point to visit someday. Now let's think about what all this means. Anna Wilson, born Anna Oakley . . ." He looked up at her. "Anna Oakley?"

"Don't blame the messenger."

"Okay, Anna Oakley marries a guy named Martin Wilson in Brazil, Indiana, in 1946. She immediately pops out Perry—is there a hospital there?"

Rebecca nodded.

"Pops out Perry and later a girl, who dies in infancy. Anna has worked in brick factories and grocery stores, and her hobbies include crochet, macramé, and quilting." He lowered the page. "Why do they have all this crap?"

"So the staff at the home knows something about her when she first gets there. Something to talk about."

"Makes sense." He studied the paper again. "Looks like Martin Wilson died in 1977. Nothing happened between then and the day she was put in the nursing home by her son, Perry Wilson, of 1620 Applewild, Terre Haute." He read silently for a bit, then looked at her. "This is good stuff, Becky."

She sat beside him. "So you can use it?"

He nodded. "First I want to interview the mother, drag out of her what I can."

She was shaking her head back and forth. "Alzheimer's. Really bad. Just keeps hollering for Martin."

"Scratch that idea." Alan stood up and stretched. "Christ, look at all the fucking ants."

Rebecca erected herself. "So with that data sheet we've got exactly what you wanted to know."

He turned, cradling the cast on his arm with his other hand. "It's great stuff, Rebecca, up to a certain point."

Her heart fell. "A certain point?"

"There's a lot left to be done. I want to get a work history on him, get the name of every college and university he worked for before coming to Indiana State. I want to interview the people who worked with him and knew him, and then I want to dig deep between what they say and what they feel. I'd even be interested in talking to Chaim's parents in Israel, ask how he sounded in his letters while he was Perry's chess partner."

"How long will all that take?"

He bent over and got a beer out of the box on the floor. "Three or four days, if things go well."

"No," she said. The word was a reflex rising from the quietest part of her being, and she wondered if she had said it aloud. "Alan, *no!* I'm not going to let you sit here and chitchat with Goldberg's parents on the phone, and we certainly don't have three or four days. Get on your computer and do that investigative stuff right now!"

He popped the beer open. "*You're* not going to let me sit here and chitchat? I'm paying for every fucking thing here, I'm working for free, and *you're* not going to let me?"

She dropped onto the dilapidated couch with all the heaviness and grace of a bag of mulch. "It just won't do," she said, her eyes wandering, then fixing on the nearest piece of crawling black chicken on the carpet. She was silent for a long time, watching it, trying to find a way she could help Hank and not waste the whole night. "It just won't do," she said at length. "It won't do, it has to be faster. Hank's out there getting lynched, so it has to be faster."

Alan looked at her strangely, grudgingly trading his anger for concern. "I can't rouse any of my contacts in the middle of the night, Rebecca. There's nothing I can do right now. Nothing *we* can do. So let's get some sleep."

"But I *can* do something," she said, whining the words. "I can go to Brazil and I can talk to people. In a small town like that, people know each other." She wobbled to her feet. "You can stay here waiting for Israel to call, buster, but not me. I'm gone."

"You're dead on your feet," Alan said. "Let me put you to bed, we can't do anything tonight."

A vision was stuck in her mind now: Hank was sitting on a swaybacked horse with a rope around his neck. The tree was a sturdy one, it was a German oak. People crowded in, blank faces. The sun in the sky was a spinning swastika.

Alan put his hands on her shoulders as she tried to move past, and turned her to face him. "You're going to bed right now, girl," he said squarely in her face. Her eyes were open wider than normal; she was somehow vibrating under his hands. "Come on," he said gently, "off to bed. Before you have a nervous breakdown."

She wilted slightly, then stiffened and pulled away from him. An empty Miller Lite can got crushed squarely under the heel of her shoe and molded itself there. "Come with me," she croaked, walking backward with the can mutedly clanking on the rug. "They're killing Hank."

He stepped forward and reached for her hands, grabbed them both. The broken bone inside his cast shot out a surge of pain but he held on and drew her close. When she was within range he clutched her in his arms and held her tight. She resisted, groaning and batting at him with her fists, but he knew it would not last long. Suddenly she was crushing him in her own embrace and then the tears came, they wracked her in giant spasms that heaved and heaved and heaved, and then slowly ebbed while he held her.

He carried her, asleep, to the trailer's single bedroom.

But sleep would not come for Alan: he lay on the couch in the dark, heading into his second hour of waiting for it. It was abominably hot, that was one thing, and the other was the mosquitos. Finally he lunged to his feet and hit the light switch, intent on killing them, but they had become invisible against the battered paneling of the walls and the motley colors of the rug.

He plopped down on the folding chair and stared blearily into the blank face of his oversize Toshiba monitor. Saved on the hard drive was the screenplay he had been writing for over a year; he could work on it, but his guts had been telling him for months that it was a loser. One of its faults was the blatantly autobiographical lead character, a Jewish man stuck in a rural state—Arkansas, in the script—who aspires to greatness but is thwarted again and again by the local yokels. Another fault was that it was mean-spirited. Worst of all, it was uninteresting.

He was taking the computer out of suspend mode for a game of solitaire when he heard Rebecca cry out in her sleep. He waited, expecting her to come shambling out, but she soon punctuated the cry with a snore. He felt guilty about sitting here doing nothing, but there was nothing he could do at four in the morning. Since Perry's mother was in no shape to reveal anything that would point the way, he would have to track down living family members, probably by interviewing the old lady's neighbors in Brazil. They might know of brothers and sisters who were not dead yet, maybe living in the same town.

The Autumn Leaves data sheet had wound up on the floor with a shoe print and a couple of mashed ants dead center. Alan shook it off and took another look. Anna Wilson's address, before coming to the facility, had been 540 Grove Street. He wondered what had been done with the house there—by default it should have become Perry's. So had he sold it? Rented it out? Or simply let it stand there abandoned? Not once had he ever mentioned it, but Alan had been a student, not his realtor. He wondered if Rebecca knew, but hell, if she did she would have made a big deal out of it.

He sat at his computer as the monitor filled with light that he regarded glumly. The stumps of his broken front teeth ached and his arm was pulsing. Irritated, he stood and went for another beer, wishing he had stuck the box in the refrigerator. The Miller Lite was lukewarm so he downed it fast, trying not to taste it, thinking of other things. Roasting in this trailer did not remind him of the good old days with the ex he used to love, it reminded him that he was getting too old and too spoiled to live with this kind of discomfort. He walked to the door and yanked it open.

Outside seemed better, not nearly as hot. A breeze kicked up that cooled the sweat on his face. He looked at the little white Honda glowing under the moon and smiled, remembering the way Becky had commandeered it from the renegade grad assistant, its rightful owner. At first sight he had deemed Mrs. Thorwald a fawning socialite, the perfect faculty-wife-in-training. All that had changed now. If his ex had had half the balls Rebecca did, she might still be Mrs. Weston. Or at least wearing Mr. Weston's balls.

The silliness of it brought a little smile to his face. He dawdled for a while, and soon went back in for another beer. There were only two left; in twenty seconds there was one. Now the alcohol was starting to course through his veins, blunting the nasty edge of reality that this trailer offered too much of. His thoughts pounced on the Chaim Goldberg issue again as he opened the last can. Chaim had gotten very buddy-buddy with Professor Wilson. They started playing chess, more and more and more, then Chaim had begun to deteriorate. He became quiet and sullen, his skin got pasty and his eyes got hollow. Soon he vanished—and wound up dismembered in Perry's basement.

None of this was news. Alan sucked down the beer and dumped himself in front of the computer again, but rose just as quickly. A computer game could be entertaining for hours but it was a dead end, you walked away from it with nothing. He needed to go to Brazil to interview the neighbors of 540 Grove Street; worse than that, he needed to spend some time thinking about his next career move. WXRV had shit-canned him but his notoriety might spark a bidding war among the other Indianapolis stations; he could wind up accepting a huge salary.

A gentle rumble shook the sky to the west—another storm on the way; how he hated the Midwest. Maybe this was the time to fire off a salvo of resumés and sample tapes to the East and West Coast cities, escape Indiana forever. But he doubted his qualifications just as much as he doubted his abilities as a screenwriter. Here in the Bible Belt he was famous and hated and loved and feared, but in the New York scene he would be a rube straight from the cornfields. The New York media establishment would respond with a yawn. And Alan would wind up back here in Cow Pie, Indiana, his dreams in ashes.

The storm was rolling closer. Alan shut down his computer

and yanked all the plugs out. He scouted around for the Honda's key, even went into the bedroom to press on Rebecca's pockets for a keylike shape. When he found one in a front pocket of her slacks, he flattened his hand and gently probed inside. His finger splints made it harder than it had to be; she suddenly moaned and opened her eyes. Alan froze while heat rose in his cheeks, but luckily she was not really awake. Her eyes slid gently shut.

He pulled his hand free with a jerk. "Bastard," he whispered to the key, then headed outside.

47

Frau Dietermunde had not been this excited, this nervous, since her last wedding. She trotted ceaselessly from kitchen to grand ballroom to the grounds outside, where a crew of gardeners and floral consultants was trimming the trees and bushes, arranging the flowers in the huge stone flowerpots and the smaller stylized ones, making sure all the water fountains ran steadily and without foam. The weather was partly sunny, partly cloudy, a perfect mixture for her guests to enjoy as they drank cocktails under the portico or wandered the botanical gardens that were her pride.

Inside, the kitchen workers were red-faced and puffing as they labored in the heat and steam of preparing gourmet meals for seventy-four people, the first course to be served promptly at three o'clock. In the ballroom her young protégés were arranging seventy-four rented, overstuffed chairs in a large semicircle around the platform where Mr. Thorwald would be seated on a tall stool. The best part of the setup had been her own flash of inspiration: the platform was round and would rotate slowly by means of a concealed electric motor. This way everyone would be given a good look during the hypnotism.

But even more inspired was her decoration of the rotating platform. It rested only a few centimeters above the floor and was three meters in diameter, made of plywood mounted on a simple round frame that her maintenance worker had crafted early this morning. Her first impulse had been to lay plush carpet on it, but then the brainstorm had struck: why not decorate the naked wooden disk with an enormous *Reichsflagge* that would lie flat and overhang the edges of the platform, concealing the mechanisms underneath? Perched on his stool in the center of the giant rotating swastika would be Mr. Thorwald. Frau Dietermunde had paid a fortune for the rare flag at an auction years ago; it had flown at an outdoor National Socialist rally in 1935 and had immediately been packed away. Now it would be shown again as a tribute to the eternal spirit of the Führer.

All this called for unparalleled security, though; the interior decorators left the house uninformed, and the grand ballroom was today off-limits to the eyes and ears of the household staff. Any infringement meant immediate termination. Their unemployment compensation would remain tangled up in litigation for years. They would be blacklisted. To ensure that none of the staff penetrated the ballroom, all the doors would be bolted from the inside.

She found herself standing in the hot kitchen looking at her wristwatch: fifteen minutes until one o'clock. The guests would be here at one and would be served beer and other alcohol outdoors. For this she had to be there to greet them. Alarmed, she rushed up to her chambers and rang for the maid to help her dress. When that was taken care of, she forced herself to slow down to a more graceful speed; otherwise she would look damp and anxious to her guests. She made her way to Mr. Thorwald's room and rapped softly on the door. The day butler, Heinz, opened it a crack.

"How is he doing?" she asked furtively.

His face was stony, but that was nothing new. "He refuses to do anything I tell him."

"Will he be ready by two o'clock?"

"If nothing changes, no."

She frowned, shaking her head. "Remind him of two important facts, Heinz. One, I will not fly him back to America until he does what I ask. Two, the doctor will be here soon with a full medical bag."

Heinz looked puzzled.

"He'll understand what it means. And one more thing."

"Yes?"

"Tell him you'll break his stupid neck."

His face relaxed. "Very well."

She jerked the door shut. Heinz barked angrily and she was satisfied. Mr. Thorwald already happened to look beat-up. A few thumps here and there would blend in nicely.

At one o'clock she was out in the sunshine just beyond the shade of the portico receiving her guests. A tuxedoed string quartet lent gentle music to the air, the happy melodies of Strauss. The parking valet was a young recruit from the state employment service, which had made her nervous, but he was doing a good job finding spaces. As the last of the guests arrived a stray glance showed her that the tennis court now looked like the domain of a Mercedes dealership, which made her smile. The world's finest cars were built in Germany. The best of *everything* came from Germany.

She strolled over to one of the portable wet bars and let the young bartender make her a White Russian. In fact she would rather drink the admirable beer of the nearby Licher brewery, but in high society a woman should not drink the working-man's brew, especially when proposing a toast. Raising the cocktail high overhead, she called loudly for attention. "Ladies and gentlemen! Please!"

The conversations dwindled to nothing, and she smiled, turning back and forth. "A toast to all of my special friends on this very special day! *Ein Prosit zur Gemütlichkeit!*"

"Ein Prosit!" some of them called out, just a few at first, then more than seventy voices quickly expanded it to a battle cry: *"Ein Prosit zur Gemütlichkeit!"*

Frau Dietermunde sipped her drink. This was more than a toast to happy times, she knew, and so did they. It was a toast to the brave survivors of a war that had not defeated them, and was by no means over.

She downed the drink, disliking its syrupy taste, and ambled back to the bar. "Did you bring Licher beer?"

"Jawohl, gnädige Frau."

"Pour me some in a fancy little cup, as if I were drinking tea."

He smiled, looking directly into her eyes.

"Is something funny?" Someone dropped a hand on her

shoulder from behind. She put her party face back together
and turned, hooking a genial smile to it.

"Having trouble, Mother?"

Her party face dissolved. She pushed him away from the
bar. "If you make trouble I will have you arrested."

Ulgard stripped off his sunglasses. "I've come back to
apologize, Frau Dietermunde. I was exhausted from the trip
to America, I had not slept for days. I want you to know how
sorry I am."

She pushed him farther from the bar and studied his face.
Never in his adult life had she seen him so disheveled and
worn-out. "Did von Wessenheim ever pay you the fortune he
promised?"

"He did. Three hundred thousand American dollars for
three days' work."

"Incredible. Almost a million Marks. And how is he taking
the sudden loss of Mr. Thorwald after so much effort?"

"I believe he is headed for a nervous breakdown. At times
he is incoherent, and he often weeps without provocation."

Her smile was so huge that the skin of her face stretched
uncomfortably. The current facelift was only a year old and
still tight. "I hope the bastard spends his last days and the last
of his money at an asylum."

Seconds of silence plodded past; it seemed they were done
talking. Glad for her son's apology but anxious to start her
social rounds, she invited him to walk along, knowing that he
would refuse. He did. "So then," she said, "can you stay?"

"Not long. I don't doubt, though, that you have promised
the group a very exciting afternoon. Where is Thorwald?"

"Heinz is trying to get him bathed and dressed by two so
that we can suitably present him to the others in the grand
ballroom."

"And after that?"

"A seven-course dinner at three o'clock."

"No, I mean with Thorwald, where and how are you going
to dispose of him?"

She drew back slightly. "How could that possibly concern
you now? Your master has paid you a million marks for your

services, and your clients in Berlin are screaming for your return, you said so yourself. So go back where you belong.
Make me proud of you again."

His neck seemed to get thicker, crowding his sweat-
stained collar. "I think I'll have a drink and visit with some of
my old friends before I go, Mother. Maybe you should videotape the séance and send me a copy so that I too believe Hank
Thorwald was Hitler."

"*Adolf* Hitler," she said, reddening with anger. "Show
some respect." Several people ambled to a stop nearby and
were admiring a triangular plot of her new hybrid black
roses. She lifted a hand and smiled as if they had beckoned.
"Must do my duties as hostess," she said, and walked away
with her teacup full of beer.

Rønna Ulgard placed his sunglasses back on his face and
watched her go, his upper lip curling slightly. When she was
deeply busy with the conversation he turned and ambled into
the rectangle of shadow under the portico, pretending to admire the Greek columns he had climbed as a child. Casually,
he entered the building and looked at the many paintings that
were on the walls of the grand entryway. Nothing here at
Schloss Bad Nauheim ever changed except the seasons, he
could navigate the entire castle blindfolded. During his
lonely, secluded upbringing he had explored and reexplored
every corner and crack of this sixteenth-century relic. Like
all German castles built in the era of the Peasants' War, it had
secret passageways and an extensive network of tunnels so
that the inhabitants could escape capture if the castle fell. It
never did, and the tunnels were still there, old and damp and
frightening, some of them long since collapsed. His mother
had flogged him more than once for going into the tunnels.
She was afraid of them, but he was not.

He turned quickly and stepped out of sight. The nearby reception room was uninhabited. An enormous fireplace appeared to be built into a solid wall of wooden panels, but in
reality the farthest panel to the right, if pushed hard enough at
the proper place, would swing inward. Ulgard leaned a
shoulder against it and pressed his knee hard—painfully
hard—against the wood. Inside, a latch clicked. Hinges

formed on a blacksmith's anvil three hundred years before screeched and jabbered; cold, moldy air welled up. An oak ladder, still sturdy after all these years, leaned against bare earth. Ulgard reached out with a foot and put his weight on the ladder, then turned and slowly shoved the heavy panel shut. It gave a satisfying click. The twilight became absolute darkness.

He clambered down. After a full minute of it his feet struck dirt. Releasing the ladder, he pulled von Wessenheim's matches out and struck one. Now he had the choice of three tunnels: without hesitation he crouched and strode into the left-most one. All were buttressed with massive beams but some of these beams had long ago become soggy and unstable. When the match died he lit another, not wanting to walk face first into a damp earthen wall. Filthy clothes were what had gotten him into trouble as a boy.

Another wall of tunnels appeared, branching off toward destinations that were no mystery to him. Again he selected the left-most. Burning match after match he went on, moving uphill now, aware that things were getting drier. Presently he came upon another ladder that he had not seen for almost four decades. He smiled as he dropped the burning match, remembering the wonder and fear he had felt as a child alone down here in this otherwordly place.

He pocketed the matches and started up.

48

Alan parked in the abrupt little driveway at 540 Grove Street in Brazil. It was still plenty dark and raining steadily. Occasionally the sky lit up, offering him a better look at the town with the odd name, followed by tremendous wallops of thunder. He killed the headlights and motor and sat waiting and wondering for several minutes while rain hammered on the roof of the Honda. With no car of its own in the driveway, Perry's inherited house looked abandoned. But all the windows visible from here were covered with either curtains or blankets; it was hard to tell in the brief flashes of lightning. The house itself sat in disrepair, a few planks of its clapboard siding missing, shingles from the roof poking up in the overgrown lawn. Instinct told him the place was vacant.

But it had to be checked. He got out and hurried to the front door, then pounded his fist against it, grimacing at the pain in his fingers. A twist of the doorknob proved it to be locked. He quickly splashed his way back to the car. This was no fun at all. It was getting close to five o'clock, the time when a lot of people had to get up in the morning. If one of the neighbors turned on a light, bingo: answer some questions, please.

But it didn't happen, even after fifteen minutes it hadn't happened. He started the car and drove toward the downtown area, looking for the police station. To his left the fire department appeared, all the lights burning through the windows of the huge garage where the fire truck was parked. Alan discovered what he had hoped for: three police cars sitting unattended. The fire department and the police station were in the same building.

He parked, then went inside. After a few steps a tall countertop blocked his way and he propped an elbow on it, favoring his cast. A big red button was built into the wall. Alan pressed it.

Nothing happened. This was a fine night to be a crook in Brazil, the cops had all gone home.

"Anybody?" he called out.

Now a cop wandered out rubbing his eyes, yawning. "Sorry to bother you," Alan said.

He lifted a hand and wagged it. "No problem." His eyes widened as he neared. "Jesus, what happened to you? Car wreck?"

Alan touched his face. "Motorcycle. Listen, I need some information about a house here in town, need to know if anybody lives there."

"How come?"

"I'm an attorney with the Indiana probate court. I need to know who the house belongs to, and who's living in it."

"I don't know if I can help, but I'll try. You need to visit city hall, really. What's the address?"

"540 Grove Street."

"That's up over the railroad tracks, past the bait shop. Second house on the left."

"Anybody living there now?"

He shook his head. "The last people moved out and nobody else ever moved in."

"Know who owns it?"

"It's been a rental ever since Mrs. Wilson's son packed her off to a nursing home. Must have been three, maybe four years ago. Then about two months ago he—Mrs. Wilson's son, his name fails me—more than tripled the rent, jacked it beyond a grand, and the family had to move out. Ever since then it's been empty, and at that price it's sure to *stay* empty."

"You seem to know a lot about it."

"Wish I didn't. I went with the sheriff to evict them. Crying kids, crying wife, all their stuff sitting out on the grass. And Mrs. Wilson's son just standing there watching."

"So it belongs to the son now?"

He shrugged. "Don't know. Did Mrs. Wilson die?"

"No. The son did."

"You just made me believe in God."

Alan smiled, then went outside. The rain had suddenly dwindled to almost nothing and the sky was gaining colors in the east. He got into the Honda and stuck the key in the ignition but did not start it. It seemed his mission here was over. When Mrs. Wilson had gotten bad, Perry had taken over the house and rented it out. Nothing odd there. Two months ago he jacked up the price to force the renters out. That was not an unheard-of thing for a landlord to do. But in this ramshackle town a thousand bucks was a fortune, nobody could afford it, especially not for such a dump of a house. That left a couple of hard questions. What had turned our pal Perry, Perry who made very good money at ISU, into such a heartless miser? And why did he want the house, a source of small but steady income, suddenly vacant?

Alan started the car. He drove back to 540 Grove and pulled up at the curb, intending to talk to the neighbors. As he glanced at the house one of the curtains was lifted slightly, then quickly dropped. He blinked, not sure he had seen anything more than a rivulet of water slipping down the car's window. He got out and skirted the house, hiking through tall weeds. Around back was a small wooden porch; a porch swing hung askew from one remaining chain. The rusty tin roof of the cinder-block garage had been rearranged by the wind. The place was a shit pile, yet every window in the entire house was carefully guarded from view.

Alan stood out front again, frowning. It was highly possible that a transient had broken in and set up camp inside. Or even the family that had been forced out could have come back—but no, not with a handful of noisy kids. He called up the memory of the curtain being lifted. Had he seen it? Should he get a police officer to kick his way in and check it out?

He snorted, amazed at himself. Despite being beaten almost to death, he was Alan Weston. Alan Weston performed his own investigations. The cops only showed up *after* Alan Weston was done. By the time they got there, Alan Weston was already on TV with the facts.

It was still dark enough. None of the neighboring houses showed signs of life. He stood in front of the door sizing it up, noting the falling-apart condition of the knob and the fact that there was no deadbolt, then backed away a few measured steps. A mental X marked the spot. Two strides were followed by a sideways leap; both feet crashed against the X. As he dropped to the wet ground, he knew instinctively that he had succeeded. He got up, his arm under the cast clanging with pain, every part of his upper body feeling broken and somehow loose.

It was dark inside the house. He walked in cautiously but without the fear that had dogged him lately. The house smelled of bygone tobacco smoke. When he was able to make out shapes, he went to the nearest window and pulled the curtains aside. The other curtain rod in the room supported a thick blanket; he jerked it down. The feeble light of morning was better than the nothing he'd had before. He walked farther into the house. "Anybody?" he called out as he spread apart the heavy kitchen curtains. A refrigerator and stove became visible. "Anybody here?"

He moved into another room that contained a dresser and a bed frame, no box springs, no mattress, but obviously a bedroom. "I'm here as a friend," Alan said loudly as he uncovered the window. "Don't be afraid."

He moved on to the bathroom. Even its tiny little window was covered, not by a curtain but by a square of filmy black plastic taped in place. "Hello? Anybody here?"

He turned to walk out but stopped short of the door, brought to a halt by the strangest thing. An electric razor was lying on the sink just beside the hot water faucet, in the little depression where a bar of soap was supposed to be kept. Alan shuffled slowly around and pulled open the mirror above the sink to reveal the medicine cabinet.

Its shelves were bare but for two brown plastic prescription bottles. Alan lifted one of them and strained to read the label, but it was too dark. He sidled to the window and cocked the container to the best available light. It was enough to read by.

A moment later the bottle dropped from his fingers. The

air in his lungs squeezed out with a low, almost soundless moan as he turned for the door. Something came out of the dark, a pale streak that blurred toward his face. He blinked and raised his arms, but not quickly enough. An enormous smashing *crack!* flung him backward. He dropped onto the toilet as if to use it, then slumped forward and fell facedown on the floor.

IN THE TUNNEL

49

At ten minutes before two, the man named Heinz lashed Hank's hands together behind his back with a length of electrical cord and pushed him out of the room. With an arm hooked around his neck he was forced down the stairway. He struggled against the man's choking grip anyway, determined to make such a commotion that the old lady would quickly tire of him and send him packing. What she had in mind for him now he did not know, but Heinz had dressed him in a brown suit and black necktie, put glossy black shoes on his feet, and combed his hair to the side. Probably the old lady wanted him to look like Hitler. She was insane. They all were. And now he saw that she was waiting on the ground floor by the stairwell.

He fought harder for her benefit, actually giving Heinz a tough time. Instead of being scared she got mad: "Mr. Thorwald! We have warned you that if you cannot behave we will *make* you behave."

She looked away from him and made motions. The doctor who had been on the train walked into view, still wearing her white lab coat. A medical bag hung from one hand. She balanced it on the newel post and opened it to withdraw a large syringe.

He went slightly limp upon seeing it. Heinz seized the moment and manhandled him down to the landing. He stood him up in front of the old lady with the difficult name, Frau Deetersomething. "I don't understand you," she said into his face. The output of her breath was spiked with alcohol. "I saved you from a terrible fate and still you struggle against me."

"You are holding me against my will."

"Just cooperate for one more hour," she said. "And then you can join us for a wonderful dinner."

She seemed earnest, even charming, but Hank had learned a lot of dismal things about the human race lately. "Okay," he said, relaxing. "Tell Heinz to let me go."

She smiled. "You're quite safe in his hands, Mr. Thorwald. Bear with us for an hour."

He tensed up again, struggling against the man's muscular arm. Her face hardened and she turned quickly to the doctor. "Do it."

"Wait!" Hank croaked out. "*Gnädige Frau!*"

Her face became smooth again. "Do you see, Mr. Thorwald? The secret man buried inside you wants a voice, and will become a wonderful voice if only you would step aside!"

"Then take him," Hank said bitterly. "Take him, and let me go."

She examined his eyes. "That's what I've been asking all along, dear Mr. Thorwald. Let us, my friends and I, enjoy his company for just a short while, and then both of you may go."

"Swear to it," he said, remembering the oath carved into G-pa's wartime dagger. German soldiers had died to uphold that oath, perhaps thousands of them. "Swear to it on your honor."

She put a hand on his shoulder. "I swear to it on my honor."

Karl-Luther von Wessenheim was chain-smoking, his hands trembling slightly as he brought the latest cigarette to his mouth, sucked on it, inhaled, and blew the smoke out the car's window. Half an hour before he had dropped Rønna Ulgard off just out of sight of *Schloss* Bad Nauheim, and had quickly driven back to the spot Ulgard had shown him. Dense summer forest surrounded the rented Volkswagen here as it cooled in the shade. This was a seldom-used country road, just a couple of ruts dug out by the passage of tractor tires when the ground was wet. Directly to the left, somewhere among the dense trees, was supposed to be a false culvert, one of the forgotten exits of the castle's ancient tunnel system. It was from there that Ulgard and Thorwald were going to emerge sometime soon.

He looked at his watch, shook his wrist, looked again. Time seemed to have ceased. Little yellow butterflies were spinning in mad circles inside a bar of sunlight in front of the car, but he only found them irritating, found all the scenery irritating. After impatiently mashing the cigarette in the ashtray, he pushed his door open and sprang out, restless with both excitement and exhaustion. Rather than go mad he started off into the forest, careful of his footing on the slick carpet of dead leaves and pine needles. Fortunately the lack of penetrating sunlight had killed all the lower branches of the trees and he could walk erect.

As he penetrated deeper into the forest he glanced back at the car again, not willing to get lost and ruin it all. At that moment the ground sloped away and his footing was gone. With a whoop he was dumped onto his back to skid down an embankment. The bottom held a few tiny puddles between the gathered stones and he smacked down in the water.

"Zum Teufel!" he cried out, jumping up. After pummeling his clothing with both hands and lighting a fresh cigarette, he lost his anger and went looking for the tunnel exit, motivated by curiosity and a need to reassure himself that Ulgard knew what he was talking about. But the reassurance didn't seem necessary. Rønna Ulgard was a wizard, a magician who could make the impossible happen: von Wessenheim had seen it for himself. But to know the tunnel system of this modest castle among all the thousands in Germany?

The culvert deepened gradually. He followed it to a sudden end at a sloping embankment. Doubt made him shake his head. Hundreds of years of shifting dirt had closed this exit, ten thousand rainfalls and ten thousand snowfalls had packed it shut tighter than a cork—but so far Ulgard had not failed him. He plucked away a small clearing among all the ferns and greenery that grew on the sloping earth and pawed out a clump of dirt. It got under his fingernails but he did not care. When he went for another handful, he nearly sprained his fingers. Frowning, he stuck his cigarette between his lips and used both hands to dig. Something hard was blocking the exit, but not just a random stone. As he worked it became obvious that he had encountered a wall or door of some sort. He thunked it with a fist and realized that it was a plank. He flipped the cigarette away and began digging faster, until he had uncovered it all: the opening was covered by seven or eight thick wooden boards stacked horizontally. They were termite-eaten in spots, mushy in others, all of them slick with green-black mold.

He hesitated, wondering, then hooked both hands over the topmost plank. The ends of it were still dug into the dirt. After some tugging it loosened, and he gave it one last great pull.

The entire wall started disassembling itself from the top down. He jumped back as everything clattered in a heap to expose a dark hole in the side of the earth. Absurdly tall toadstools rimmed it, all of them thrusting upward. The smell pushing out was dank and filthy. Von Wessenheim edged close and took a look inside, his nose wrinkling. The castle was far, far away; this was incredible.

He walked away a bit and sat down on the slope of the culvert. While smoking another cigarette he pondered his next move. Simply waiting here was too nerve-racking. Ulgard's plan to steal away with Thorwald was far too vague; if even the slightest thing went wrong, von Wessenheim might sit here all day and all night, waiting, afraid to leave. All day and all night tomorrow as well.

When the cigarette was finished he tossed the butt away and stood. He was tempted to go inside. If Ulgard or Thorwald was injured in the escape, his presence could be vital. He was only vaguely familiar with castle tunnels: his own in Wessenheim had never been extensive and had filled with water and collapsed ages ago. The Peasants' War, just like World War Two, had left the town unharmed while hordes of Germans died elsewhere. He *did* know that the tunnels could be deceptive. But he also knew that a tunnel this long was a main shaft that should run straight into the belly of *Schloss* Bad Nauheim. If he did not veer off the course, he could be under the castle in less than an hour. And perhaps be of assistance to Rønna Ulgard.

Standing before the heap of rotting lumber at the entry, he debated, agonized. He checked his cigarette package, patted the new one in the inner breast pocket of his suit, and counted his remaining matches. Ten or fifteen, plenty for the next couple of hours. After lighting another cigarette he pulled in a resolute breath and stepped over the fallen boards. He was forced to duck to enter, but once inside the ceiling was higher and he could stand erect. Somewhere, distantly, water was dripping.

He appraised the darkness ahead. It was dark but only children were afraid of the dark. There was no reason to hesitate. He started off.

Hank sat atop a tall wooden stool with the heels of his shoes hooked over one of the rungs, watching sullenly as the enormous room filled with elderly people. They were talking gaily among themselves as they filtered through the rows of plush chairs seeking one to their liking. Gnarled fingers pointed at him, discussions were held, old men with rheumy eyes stood with their arms crossed over their chests, glancing at him as they made private conversation. He knew the question on everyone's mind, it was a question he asked himself a thousand times a day, a question that was often and unpredictably answered in simple German: *ja*. Never *nein*, always *ja*. Yes, you were.

Music began to play from a large speaker, the drums and fifes of wartime marching music, probably the tunes played for the crowds at Nazi parades when these old people were kids. His next thought was of the Hitler Youth, and as soon as he thought it, he knew. The Hitler Youth were reassembled here, today, and after all these years, to hear their Führer speak from the grave.

He tipped his head back and closed his eyes. Everyone, every single person on planet earth, wanted something from Hitler. To revile him or to admire him, to kill him or to raise him from the dead. The young man with the promising future, Mr. Hank Thorwald, had ceased to exist.

The music banged and crashed, several of the audience had started to clap in unison; the circus was beginning. And Hank was in the center ring, planted in the biggest swastika he had ever seen. Suddenly the floor beneath him lurched and he jerked his arms out for balance, alarmed. But in seconds it was obvious: the platform was turning. Shame burned inside him and put color in his cheeks. He hung his head, weeping without sound or tears, watching the ghosts of his wife and daughter fade inside the darkness of his closed eyes. It would be better to die than to endure a life of this.

A hand wormed under his chin and jerked his head upright. He looked: Frau Dietermunde. "Keep your chin up, you, these people want to see confidence! Sit tall and proud!"

"Kill me," Hank said.

"I will if you don't act properly." She turned and offered the room a broad smile, then made a motion. In seconds the doctor was at her side. "He needs a stimulant," she said in German. Hank understood every word.

"Impossible, Frau Dietermunde. The object here is to take advantage of drowsiness to put him into the deepest hypnosis possible."

Frau Dietermunde turned to him. "Are you determined to ruin this for me? Sit tall and proud!"

Hank narrowed his eyes. "You want tall and proud?" He stood up. "You want me to be tall and proud, you crazy old hag?" He jerked the stool off the floor and hoisted it overhead, saw her horrified reaction, then turned to the crowd. "You're all a bunch of fucking lunatics!" he screamed over the music. "I wasn't Hitler, I'm an American college teacher with a great wife and a wonderful daughter and a life to live! And that's *all that I am*!" He spun around and smashed the stool down on the center of the swastika. All four legs snapped noisily in half while the seat rolled away, wobbling like a lost tire. Hank bent to snatch up what was left at his feet but then someone jumped him from behind, clawing at his face, raking deep scratches from his chin up to his hairline. Just as he realized that it was Frau Dietermunde herself, she clamped a skinny arm around his neck and squeezed.

The doctor appeared with her syringe. Hank twisted and kicked, his face purpling, unable to believe that an old woman could do this to him. But she had been in the Hitler Youth and had been well trained. Even as the doctor jabbed the needle into his right shoulder he was in the process of passing out from lack of air. He saw flashing yellow twinkles as his vision dimmed, he continued kicking and writhing as they turned to green, then went slack as the color changed to a thick and bloody red.

Black was the only color left.

50

Rebecca staggered out of the trailer's miniature bedroom and into the short hallway, needing to use the bathroom, needing to know what day it was, what time. Sunlight was shooting through every window and crack; the heat was unbearable. She found the bathroom doorway and stumbled through it. Wasps were still walking on the plastic window. It no longer seemed important. When she was done she stood and pulled herself wearily back together. Pushing the shower curtain aside, aching to get clean, she saw that the tub contained no dead insects or animals. She thankfully cranked both knobs but got a bare trickle of water. Pipes under the trailer buzzed and thumped.

"Son of a bitch," she whispered, and turned them off with both anger and regret. Out in the living room she saw that the box of Miller Lite was empty on the floor, and that Alan's computer screen was blank. She moved to the door and pulled it open to lean outside. The Honda was gone. Maybe Alan had gone out for doughnuts and coffee—but no, the sun was shining down from directly overhead, it was noon or better.

At a loss for what to do, she went to the TV and turned it on. The local midday news was recapping today's events in Terre Haute: thirteen injured in last night's street fights between neo-Nazi thugs and Jewish Defense League heavies. Immediately she shut it off and got a glass of water from the kitchen sink. It was warm and tasted horrible.

She sat alone for two hours, frazzled and growing steadily angrier. No phone, no car, no telling when Alan would be back. Unable to take it anymore, she marched to the door and whipped it open, ready to flee the trailer. The data sheet from the nursing home levitated off Alan's computer and seesawed to the floor. She picked it up, frowned at it, then folded it small enough to fit into a back pocket. Braving the killing sunshine, she walked to the lot manager's trailer. His big rusty swamp cooler was going full blast. She clumped up the steps and beat on his hot door with a fist until it opened.

He looked at her, rolling a cigar from one corner of his mouth to the other. "Yeah?"

She backed down a step. "I have to make a phone call," she said. "Can I use your phone?"

He closed one eye and squinted through the other, aiming a finger. "Out there on the highway is a Texaco station. Pay phone there. Works, too. Try it out."

She frowned. Now that he was her landlord, his friendliness had taken a quick hike. "That's miles away," she said.

"Almost two miles, matter of fact."

"Anybody else here got a phone?"

He plucked the cigar out of his mouth and regarded it. "The trailers are all wired for it, but by the time people wind up living here, Ma Bell shoots on sight. Me, I pay my phone bill."

"I'll give you a dollar. How's that?"

"Can't do it," he said breezily. "Then I'll have people *promising* to give me a dollar, and next thing you know I'm a bill collector."

"Five dollars," she said.

His eyes shifted left and right. "Hurry up."

The difference in temperature inside almost dropped her to the floor with gratitude. She let out a sigh of relief and stood in front of the howling cooler. He brought her a cordless receiver and she eyed the buttons, but hesitated before dialing 911. This was no emergency. But what the heck.

A man answered: "Emergency 911."

"This is a critical call to Detective Steven Gleeworth. Can you patch him through?"

"I can transfer the call."

"Do it."

The line went dead and she smiled lopsidedly. You just had to sound confident.

It came alive again. "Yeah, Gleeworth here, who is this?" He sounded impatient.

"This is Rebecca Thorwald."

"What can I do for you?"

She cocked her head, wondering. She had hung up on his incompetent ass yesterday. Now his tone was simply—impatient.

"I'm in a trailer park just outside town without a car. I'm immobilized and I need to move."

"Are you asking to borrow my car?"

It wasn't a bad idea. "No, I just need a ride here and there."

"Can't do it. I have to be at a conference in Indianapolis in two hours. I'm out the door, actually."

"Miss the conference," she said flatly. "This is more important."

"Really? You have something new? Something I can work on? The whereabouts of Perry Wilson?"

Her temper ignited. "Just give me a yes or a no."

"Okay. No."

"You are such an asshole!" she shouted, then controlled herself. Five bucks for a phone call shouldn't end up wasted. "What about Dutch? Dutch the retired cop—give me his number."

"I can't do that. I can't hand out somebody else's number."

Her jaw clenched so hard she heard her teeth noisily crunch against each other. "Then tell me his full name so I can look it up."

"Retired cops usually have unlisted numbers. Too many prank calls."

She let her eyes slide shut. "Jesus Christ, Gleeworth, why don't you just come out here and kill me?"

"Let's do it this way," he said after a pause. "Tell me where you're at and I'll call Dutch myself. He'll come and get you."

She opened her eyes. To her surprise a couple of tears had been waiting to fall. "Thank you. I'm at Dixie Acres Mobile—"

"Been there. What number?"

"Trailer twelve."

"Blue-and-white job. Used to be a meth lab. I'll send Dutch."

"What if he can't come?"

The line was dead. She brushed the tears off her face and handed the phone back to the manager. "You tight with the cops?" he asked her warily.

She straightened, and tossed her head. "Hate 'em. Absolutely hate 'em."

But she didn't hate retired cops. Dutch showed up within half an hour, piloting an old black Chevy S-10 pickup. Rebecca had been waiting in the shade on the front steps of the trailer with her chin on her hands, hoping none of the neighbor ladies wanted to get chummy. She was just about to give up on Dutch when he nosed the little pickup onto the long gravel drive that was her new main street. For a fantastic moment she thought it was her own father: the truck was a carbon copy of his, down to the chips in the paint and the rust around the doors. But he had sold the truck years ago, back when Sharri was still a kid. Still, seeing Dutch again was like seeing an old friend.

She climbed in and scooted over to plant a kiss on his cheek. "Thank you, Dutch," she whispered in his hairy old ear.

He smiled at her, reddening a bit. "Where to today, Miz Becky?"

"Alan ran out on me," she said, and got the data sheet out of her pocket. "There are only two addresses on here and one of them is Perry's own house, so I think Alan went to this one here." She tapped the page. "He wanted to interview the neighbors. Probably got a hot lead there and took off like a rocket."

Dutch looked it over while she held it under his face. "Over in Brazil, huh? That isn't far." He cocked his head and glanced at the trailer sitting there, blue and white and sizzling under the sun. "This is where the police chief set you up?"

"It's a bit rustic, but I call it home."

"Indiana condo." Layers of heat shimmered above the

Chevy's hood as he jockeyed the old truck back and forth until it was aimed the other way. "Five-forty Grove Street, eh?" he said as they started off. "You sure that's where Alan went?"

"If I assume the best of him, yes. If I assume the worst, he's joyriding in a borrowed car with a fresh batch of Miller Lite."

"So which assumption do you choose?"

She considered it. "I assume the best."

"Any reason?"

"Because probably for the first time in his career, he's trying to put something back together that his TV show destroyed."

Dutch regarded her with suspicious eyes. "Despite his scumbag reputation you truly do believe that?"

She put her hand on his shoulder. "Right now I've got only two friends left in the world, Dutch. Only two friends who aren't afraid to help me." She tightened her hand. "Alan Weston is the other one."

51

"Where and when were you born?"

"I was born in Braunau am Inn, Austria, in the year 1889," Hank said in German, exhibiting a pronounced Austrian accent.

"Who was your mother?"

"Klara Hitler," he said.

"Your father?"

"Alois Hitler."

"Did you fight in the First World War?"

"Yes."

"Your unit?"

"The Sixteenth Bavarian Infantry Regiment."

"Were you ever wounded in battle?"

"I was shot in the leg in 1916, and I was blinded by poison gas just before the end of the war."

"Did you receive any awards for heroism?"

"The Iron Cross."

"And what did you do after the war?"

"I stayed in the army."

"Which career, afterward, did you pursue?"

"Architecture."

"So you became an architect?"

"No."

"And the reason?"

"I failed the entrance examination."

"Were you then a wallpaper hanger or house painter?"

"No."

Frau Dietermunde turned to the audience. "The myth fostered and sustained by the Allied propaganda machine is disproved at last."

A subdued chuckle coursed through the ballroom. The chandeliers were dimmed to an eerie orange glow. An overhead spotlight cast a circle of dazzling white around Hank; one of the Hitlerjugend had donated his comfortable chair and stood offstage with his arms folded, frowning. Suddenly he raised a hand, wagged it. "Frau Dietermunde?"

She looked over at him, annoyed. "Yes?"

"All of this raw data can easily be gotten from a book."

"I'm just starting, Herr Knecht. Have patience."

He bowed slightly. Frau Dietermunde turned her attention back to Mr. Thorwald. "Herr Hitler, there is a photograph of you dated 1932 in which you are seated beside an elderly man. Can you tell me who that is?"

"Yes. Field Marshal Paul von Hindenburg."

"Are you wearing a hat in that picture?"

"Yes."

"Describe it."

"A short black top hat that did not fit."

She smiled, wishing that von Wessenheim were here to learn that the hat was indeed genuine. But Herr Knecht, standing there in the dimness, was looking anything but impressed. Despite enjoying this very much she knew that he, and all the others, would not begin to believe until they heard the Führer speak more than just brief answers to questions. She leaned over Mr. Thorwald.

"Stand up."

He rose slowly and stood, rocking slightly back and forth.

"My Führer," she said loudly, "please repeat the speech you gave in Nuremburg in May of 1937." She turned and nodded to her young associate. He made a motion and the platform, with a shudder, began slowly to rotate. The stark black shadows onstage swung strangely in and out as it did.

Mr. Thorwald raised his chin higher. "My German ladies, my German gentlemen, my beloved German children, I have come to your beautiful old city of Nuremburg as the leader of a Germany built upon the strength and determination of the First World War, forged now into a new Germany refined by the indomitable will of her people and made pure by the blood of the martyrs . . ."

Von Wessenheim's last match went out to leave him in utter, pitch-black darkness, but he was not afraid. After fifteen minutes of walking, and with only two matches remaining, he had decided that penetrating the tunnel system was a dereliction of his true duty—staying in the car—and simply turned around. By his calculation, now that the matches were used up, the tunnel's exit should be only a few hundred meters away, but as he walked on it refused to appear. More minutes hurried past as he picked up the pace. He thought of scuba divers lost in underwater tunnels, their air supply dwindling as they searched in vain for an escape.

He walked face first into a solid earthen wall. Thinking he had misjudged his aim, he felt his way along, chiding himself, but wherever his probing hands were thrust they encountered more wall. In time it came to him that he had found a dead end. But that was not possible. He had walked straight into the tunnel and was walking straight out. But the tunnel ended there nevertheless.

In the dark he fumbled a cigarette from the pack and set it between his lips. As he patted himself down for a book of matches, he realized that they were all gone, of course they were all gone, he had burned the last one fifteen—maybe twenty—minutes ago. There could be no smoking until the exit was reached.

He backtracked, walking with one hand tracing along the moist side of the tunnel wall. Suddenly the wall ended. He shuffled along, probing the area with both hands paddling slowly up and down in front of him. After some time it became clear that this was a juncture, a Y shape that required a choice. His heart began to beat faster as the realization set in: he had gotten himself seriously lost. But either way he chose, he concluded, the left or the right, must eventually take him *somewhere*.

He decided that one's natural instinct would prefer the right, and that the constructors of the tunnel system, even in antiquity, had been aware of that. He walked slowly into the

left-most one, finding it narrower, both sides of its wall able
to be touched with outstretched arms. This might mean, he
supposed, that it led specifically to a small room of the castle,
perhaps a child's room. As such, it could be a short one. Perhaps he was already close to the underside of the castle.

But the tunnel narrowed without warning, and ended. Von
Wessenheim cursed his luck; he had come upon a collapse.
By this time he was sure he was filthy; his hands were slick
with mud and cold as well. One single warm line of sweat
was coursing down his forehead, which he wiped away angrily. The cigarette, forgotten between his lips, broke as his
hand passed through it. He spit the remains out and turned
back.

At the juncture again he had two choices and tried desperately to remember which was the tunnel he had already
walked through. In such total darkness everything had became strange, to turn in one direction was to lose the meaning of the others. He fought against a sense of suffocation
that was trying to rise into raw panic. His eyes ached for light
as he decided again which way to go, but his confidence was
gone and he knew that from this point on it would be a matter
of pure luck to get out of here before Ulgard and Thorwald
emerged expecting a fast car to Frankfurt. Ulgard would not
be happy, would probably be enraged, because the only key
to the rented Volkswagen was in von Wessenheim's pocket.

Rønna Ulgard watched the unfolding scene in the grand ballroom with growing amazement. With the secret panel free of
its ancient latch and pulled open just slightly, there was a
good, close view of Thorwald as he rotated. Ulgard could
emerge from behind, and in the space of two steps capture
him and drag him down into the tunnel. It would take days
for anyone to locate the exit among all the dead ends waiting
below.

But right now that did not matter. Nothing did—nothing
but Hank Thorwald, an average American Joe giving the
most brilliant and persuasive speech Ulgard had ever heard.
He spoke angrily of Germany's suffering in the First World
War, her unexpected defeat, the humiliating treaty of Ver-

sailles, the German Jews who had given Germany the fatal stab in the back—the *Dolchstoss*. Impassioned, he presented the disabled veterans of the war begging on street corners, attempts by Communists to seize power, rich Jews living in luxury while the German masses starved. And then, in words ringing of heroism, he told the tale of a handful of war-hero patriots, the fledgling National Socialist party, rising to power through blood and sweat, and then undoing, point by point, the evil that had been done by Germany's enemies.

And then he was finished. The rotating platform rounded to face the audience, then stopped. Ulgard was stunned. Standing cramped and twisted behind the hinged panel, one knee in the dirt and one foot on the ladder, he had forgotten time and place, had forgotten everything but listening to the words of the Führer. In the ballroom the remnants of the Hitler Youth staggered to their feet, mesmerized, then slowly began to clap. Through the crack of the panel Ulgard saw women in tears, old men smacking their palms together in a blur, smiles of hope and gratitude shining on every face.

It was time to pull the heavy panel open and grab Thorwald from behind. Even if the whole crowd rose up to batter it down, they would not succeed in opening it without knowing the pressure points that Oscar Adolf Dietermunde had spent years finding. So yes, it was time. He gathered himself. With the speech over, Thorwald stood there like a post.

Frau Dietermunde stepped into the light and signaled for silence. "I ask you now," she said solemnly, "can anyone among you doubt it?" She cast a scornful look at the man standing at the side. "Herr Knecht?"

He had a hand wrapped around his chin. "Sell me this man."

"I will do no such thing." She smiled at the Hitler Youth as they took their seats. "We may have time for another speech before dinner. Are there any favorites?"

Herr Knecht stepped up onto the platform and walked quickly under the spotlight to Frau Dietermunde. Ulgard recognized him at last and pressed the panel deeper into the wall, then put his eye to the slight crack. Knecht was one of the youngest of the group. The source of his money was a mystery, but he was generous with it when it came to buying Third Reich artifacts, and he was a solid member of the underground church. He drew Frau Dietermunde aside, putting them both so close to Ulgard that he could thrust a hand out and jerk Knecht off his feet.

"Sell me this man," Knecht said again, quietly. "I will write a check this very moment."

"Please bear with me," she said. "I have worked hard for this moment. Business can come later."

"Do not sell him out from under me," he said, his tone of voice slightly pleading. "I will top any reasonable offer by five percent."

"I will keep that in mind, Herr Knecht. Now leave."

He walked away and Frau Dietermunde strode to Thorwald's side again. "Give me a city and the date," she called out. "Frau Lange?"

Ulgard could not hear the reply. Frau Dietermunde spoke softly to Thorwald, and once again he began to speak. Ulgard settled himself into a less painful position and pulled the panel dangerously wide, wanting to hear every word that the ghost of Adolf Hitler had to say, willing to take the chance.

52

"Five-forty Grove," Dutch said as he pulled his little pickup to the curb. "No white Honda, no Alan. All this way for nothing."

"Drive around back," Rebecca said, frowning as she examined the house. Its windows, most of them without curtains, denoted to her a house abandoned, and the grass had not been cut for weeks. The view from the alley offered only a cinder-block garage with shards of tin for a roof and a brief wooden porch graced by a fallen swing.

"Back door's standing open," Dutch said, lifting a finger to quickly point. "Either Alan looked around and left or never got here at all."

"So why's the door open?"

"Busted doorknob, most likely. Where to next?"

"Hold on."

He put the truck in neutral. Hot exhaust drifted up past Rebecca's nose and she wrinkled it as she studied the back of the house. "Let's say Alan did get here. Let's say he found something important, and left to pursue it."

Dutch hardly sounded convinced. "Interesting angle."

"So let's go in and see what he found. Then we'll know where he went."

"And if we find nothing?"

"Then he's working the case a different way."

Dutch mashed the emergency brake down and killed the motor. "I admire your faith in humanity."

She got out, squinting under the sun. Despite the heat the overgrown grass was still wet underneath from the early morning rain. On the porch she peeked through the open door. The distinctive musky aroma of an abandoned house greeted her. She eased the door fully open and went inside. Hot. The first room, the kitchen, contained a stove and a refrigerator. The refrigerator was buzzing quietly.

She turned to call for Dutch but he was already behind her. "Who would leave the refrigerator on?" she asked quietly.

"Easy thing to forget," he said.

A short hallway branched immediately to the left. She veered through it and came upon the bathroom. At one time a square of plastic, probably a trash bag, had been taped over the window. Now it hung in tatters. "That's weird," she said softly, and turned around to leave. But Dutch had dropped to one knee and was probing the floor. He lifted his first two fingers and smelled them.

"I can't see up close without my reading glasses," he said, rising. "What does this look like?"

She examined them. "Pink stuff. What did you find?"

He smelled his fingers again. "Smells like seawater. Salty." He looked at her sharply. "Don't blame an old cop for jumping to conclusions, but there used to be a puddle of blood on the floor right here, and somebody wiped it away. Somebody in a hurry."

"Could it be real old?" Rebecca asked with her eyebrows rising. "Some kid who lived here had a nosebleed?"

Dutch shook his head. "It's dry but hasn't fully decomposed yet. Whoever bled here did it recently."

She clapped a hand over her mouth. "Alan? Could he have hurt himself?"

"Hold on." He spun around and went back outside. Rebecca stared down at the reddish patch on the floor, now so very apparent: it had visibly been scrubbed in circles. She sidled away from it until the back of her calves were blocked by the rim of the toilet.

Dutch was back with a flashlight and a pair of granny glasses perched on his nose. He got to his hands and knees and scanned the stain under the light. "We've got a dragging pattern going this way off the linoleum and onto the wooden floor," he said, and slowly crept out into the hallway. "All of this has been wiped around in circles, there's radiation at the edges, which indicates the marks of a terry-cloth towel. Even some fibers. *Lots* of fibers."

Rebecca was inching along behind him. "Wow, Dutch." She followed him through the kitchen and into another room.

"Now we go left here, and—" He repositioned the flashlight, hunkered down lower, then got to his feet. "The trail ends."

"Ends?"

"Meaning I can't follow it. The blood here's been wiped very clean. The towel might have been rinsed out, or else a fresh one was used."

"Give me that." She took the flashlight and dropped to her hands and knees. Close inspection revealed that the floor needed either a carpet or some new varnish. Frustrated, she lay down flat on her stomach and closed one eye to see at floor level. By illuminating the floor with long, wide sweeps of the flashlight, she was able to make out the layer of dust on it.

"There's a lot of fresh footprints down here," she said, and maneuvered into a different vantage point, sweeping the flashlight. "And here's where something was dragged, a clean sweep. It aims over that way."

Dutch helped her up. "The closet door over there, if you're right. Maybe you'd better let me check it out first."

She looked the door up and down. "Surely you don't think Alan's in there."

"Of course not, he's over in Indy with a blonde under one arm and a keg of beer under the other."

"Then let's do it and get back to Terre Haute. Alan might be waiting there in the trailer." She walked to the door and hauled it open. Darkness and a downward stairway lay before her, no light switch in sight. "Dutch, this is the basement door," she said loudly. "Can you come here?"

Again he was right behind her. Easing the flashlight from her hand, he went cautiously down the steps. She watched the beam swoop around in the dark.

"We've got a bloody towel down here," he called out.

She hurried down the steps. The air was cool, heavy with

dampness. It reminded her of finding Perry with the bag over his head, and at the bottom she crossed her arms to clutch her shoulders with her hands. Please, not another dead body.

Dutch was pushing things aside with his foot. The basement was home to stacks of old paint cans and empty jars with petrified paintbrushes stuck inside, broken furniture, rusty old shovels and lawn tools, and coffee cans full of old bolts, nuts, and screws. Another can contained plumbing parts, an old faucet; another nothing but bent nails and rubber washers. "Looks like somebody used to be a handyman," Dutch remarked. "A handyman who hated to throw anything away."

She coaxed the light from his hand and examined the upper walls, thinking again of Perry and his odd combination of basement and crawl space, but the walls here were cement and covered with shelves and Peg-Board, the Peg-Board heavy with tools and junk. "So I don't get it," she said. "A blood trail leads from the bathroom all the way down here, and just ends. Where's the body?"

"We don't *want* to find a body," Dutch said.

"But we want to find *something*. The blood isn't very old, all of this happened just a short while ago—and just coincidentally in the time frame when Alan would have been here."

"You build a good case."

"So someone *is* down here."

"That's where the case breaks down."

She handed the flashlight back and grabbed one of the shovels. "No, this is where everything *else* breaks down."

He jumped back as she went at the stacks of paint and junk, sloughing it across the floor, and at the things hanging on the Peg-Board, banging them aside. Rebecca saw Dutch stick a finger in one ear as he tried to work the flashlight in unison with the shovel. When a section of the Peg-Board had been cleared she wedged the blade of the shovel under it from the bottom, and forced it outward until it split in half. When the two pieces dropped away she went at another, slashing and hacking at it, but when it fell away, it, like the other, had solid concrete behind it. She stepped to the left and went at the next one until she realized that this was stupid, that she was trashing someone else's property, that there was no place down here to stash a body without it being obvious.

She let the shovel fall and slapped the hair away from her face, breathing hard. Dutch dropped a hand on her shoulder. "Not bad for one minute's work."

She looked at him. "Let's get the fuck out of here, Dutch. I'm tired of being in the dark."

He handed her the flashlight. "Light the way."

She lifted a foot and put it straight back down. "Is that paint up there?"

"Paint? Up where?"

"There." Stepping over obstacles, she zeroed the beam of the light onto the section of Peg-Board she had cleared. A line of thick red liquid had seeped through several of the holes where the hooks had gotten knocked away. She put a paint can against the wall and stood on it, went up on tiptoe. To the touch it was mildly sticky. When she brought it to her nose there was no smell—certainly not paint.

"Pry this one off, Dutch," she said hurriedly, aiming the light at him. "I think I found blood."

He scooped up the shovel and went to work. This time the sheet of Peg-Board let loose and fell away easily to reveal a dark, empty space behind it: a crawl space. Rebecca went on tiptoe again to shine the light inside.

A dirty bare arm crisscrossed with lines of blood flopped out of the darkness. She screamed and fell backward. Dutch caught her just in time. He stood her up and picked up the fallen flashlight, aimed it.

Rebecca gasped. The hand attached to the dangling arm had plastic splints taped to two of the fingers. Blood dripped from all of them.

"Alan," she whispered.

They hauled him out while clods of dirt rained down. When he was on the floor Dutch pressed an ear to his chest, then rose.

"He's dead."

53

Rønna Ulgard realized that he had let his physical condition slip over the last few years. A simple high-speed slide down the ladder and a full-tilt run back through the tunnel had winded him so badly that at the bottom of the ladder that would take him back up to the reception room, he had to pause for breath. His hands were shaking as he stood gasping, and sweat was gathering on his forehead despite the coolness of the air. But his face was set with determination and his eyes were sharp with intent.

Thorwald had really been Hitler. It was undeniable, it was fact, and he was not a man to accept far-fetched ideas. The speeches, the accent, the very *voice*, belonged to Adolf Hitler. A thirty-year old Bible Belt American could not pull off a hoax of this magnitude. In his past life he had been, unquestionably, the Führer of the Third Reich.

Breathing a little easier, Ulgard climbed the ladder, his soles skidding on the mossy rungs, but never too far. At the top he merely jerked the latch that kept the hinged panel closed, and clambered out into the room. If people saw him he no longer cared, there were hugely important matters to be taken care of. After slapping his hands against each other and adjusting his tie, he forced the panel slowly shut by pushing on the hinged side, then hurried into the hallway.

Everything was deserted, the staff was segregated and everyone else was still in the grand ballroom. He strode toward it, mopping his forehead with his sleeve. The nearest set of Renaissance doors, one of several that opened on the ballroom, was locked. With his plastic card it did not take long to gain entry. He was immediately blocked when one of the group's officers jumped up from his chair; he recognized Ulgard and offered a whispered apology before sitting down.

Thorwald was reaching the crescendo of his speech, his voice hoarse and shouting and at times unintelligible. For reasons related to the hypnosis, Ulgard assumed, he did not wave his arms or make gestures of any kind while his voice thundered through the crowd. As a boy Oskar Adolf Dietermunde, with his mother, had watched, endlessly, old black-and-white films of Hitler speaking at various rallies and functions. In fact, Frau Dietermunde had a sizable cache of films and audiotapes and LP records, which she treasured and would not sell at any price. Her favorite showed her, as an eleven-year-old schoolgirl in Nuremburg, handing a notepad up to the Führer after a daylight speech, watching unbelievingly as he signed it, and then clasping the notepad to her heart in an ecstasy caught on a reporter's film.

Now Thorwald had finished; the stage stopped turning. He stood like a robot while his audience applauded, not moving his head, not even shifting his eyes toward the loudest demonstrations of approval. Ulgard wended his way through the lines of chairs and knots of people huddling together as they clapped and exchanged words of amazement. Again he saw that Herr Knecht had crossed the stage to speak face-to-face with Frau Dietermunde. Without warning a prune-faced old man suddenly stepped into Ulgard's path, grinning toothlessly at him; with both gloved hands Ulgard heaved him and his happiness aside. A cry from that area rose up; he did not care. The old generation of Hitlerjugend was rapidly withering, growing senile; most of them were skeletons wearing their last growth of skin and would be dead soon. The next generation—and the next—could recapture the spirit of National Socialism directly from the soul of the man who had created it.

He stomped across the platform. "Frau Dietermunde, we need to talk."

She glared at him. "I am in the middle of important business."

Ulgard cast an unfriendly eye on Knecht. "You will pardon us."

Knecht turned away, angry. She frowned at Ulgard. "He just made an incredible offer, which he will probably now withdraw. What do you want?"

"You cannot sell Thorwald. We must keep him."

An expression of contempt transformed her face. "'We'?"

"The next generation. The Hitlerjugend will die without him."

"That is a lie. It is thriving. The church is expanding."

"With Thorwald, the group and the church will explode."

"Explosions incite media interest. Your master learned that when he unearthed a bomb."

Ulgard slapped her. She merely rocked slightly on her heels, smiling, her face taut and shiny. "I have always hated you," she whispered.

He ripped away the glove from his hand and held that hand in front of her face. "Imagine how long I have hated *you*!"

She eyed her needlework: two thousand tiny, interlaced swastikas, blue tattoos that covered every bit of skin, palms included, all the way to the wristline. To tattoo both hands, it had taken her eight weeks with a needle and a jar of ink. How little Oskar Adolf had howled. "But they made you remember where your duty lies," she said.

As he drew in a breath to blurt out an angry reply Ulgard noticed that everyone had grown silent, and swallowed what he had intended to say. A look showed him that seventy-four faces were watching intently.

Frau Dietermunde stepped past him and hastily went under the spotlight. "Herr Knecht," she called out, "I accept your offer. Please accompany me to my office."

The spotlight went off and the music came back on, thundering military marches. Ulgard jerked his glove back onto his hand. People seemed to have forgotten Thorwald, who stood, unmoving, in the dimness. Ulgard walked over to him and glanced around at the crowd: it was fragmenting, people were heading for the doors. He stood in front of Thorwald. "Come with me," he said softly.

The cool barrel of a familiar pistol poked the back of his neck. "Thorwald can hear only Frau Dietermunde or the doctor," the young man said. "I think it's time for you to leave, anyway. Yes?"

Ulgard nodded.

Frau Dietermunde closed the door and urged Herr Knecht to sit down. When she was seated behind her desk, she placed her hands together to form a steeple and smiled at him. "You have bought yourself quite a prize," she said.

He had placed a briefcase on his knees; as he opened it he returned her smile. A handsome man with a full head of silver hair, he struck her as the type who enjoyed yachting or golf, which would account for his deep suntan.

"I'm actually surprised that you would sell him at all," he replied. "I know people who would pay thousands to hear one of the old speeches so brilliantly performed. Tens of thousands. Not just our group but many outsiders."

"So you intend to display Mr. Thorwald in public?"

"Heavens no. The Jews would have him assassinated within days."

"Then what are your intentions?"

From the briefcase he withdrew a thick rectangle of paper and a EuroBank checkbook; after clicking it shut he set the briefcase beside his chair. "I have here a standard purchase agreement that I use in my business dealings. You probably want to look it over first."

"I do indeed." Frau Dietermunde got her reading glasses out of a drawer and propped them on her nose, then took the material he was extending to her.

"My intention is this," Herr Knecht said then. "Since Thorwald, when not hypnotized, appears to be a simple but excitable man, I believe that he should be kept on a regimen of tranquilizers until the time to perform arrives. Better yet a lobotomy, if that does not interfere with the hypnotism. I'll have to contact a surgeon first, of course."

"Whom do you intend to invite to the performances?"

"Trusted friends and associates only, Frau Dietermunde."

"Let me ask you something else, Herr Knecht."

"Ask me."

"What do you think ever became of the Führer's dead body?"

He lifted his eyebrows. "Burned in a bomb crater, blasted to pieces by a Russian artillery shell. It's common knowledge."

"And you don't doubt it?"

He frowned, cocking his head down. "Should I?"

"Absolutely not." She stretched across the desk and gave him the purchase agreement. "Fill it out and I will sign. Make the check payable to Frau Ilsabeth Dietermunde."

He put his briefcase back on his lap and scribbled furiously on the papers he had placed upon it. In thirty seconds it was done. Frau Dietermunde signed the agreement, then accepted the check. "I believe we have struck a deal that is beneficial to both of us, Herr Knecht." She rose and offered her hand. He stood and accepted it, shook it vigorously.

"I only wish I could tell the whole world about him," Knecht said.

"The whole world already knows."

"Bah." He waved a dismissing hand. "They merely suspect. We know for sure." He indicated her telephone. "May I? I must arrange transportation for Mr. Thorwald."

"Certainly."

When he was done they left the office arm in arm, just in time for a quick cocktail and then dinner.

"This should be far enough," the young man holding the pistol to the back of Rønna Ulgard's neck said. "Walk away and don't come back until your mother calls for you."

Ulgard shuffled slowly around. "I hate you," he said. "Take that."

He placed a half-hearted kick against the young man's shin.

"Ow! I have a gun to your head, are you crazy?"

"How do you like this?" He kicked his other shin.

"Ow! Shit!" He dropped down a bit and rubbed it. "Get away from me, I could kill you!"

"Stompie toes!" Ulgard squealed like a child and stomped on the other man's toes.

"Are you nuts?" The young man jerked his foot up, hopping a little. "Get going before I shoot!"

"Other stompie toes!"

The young man looked down in alarm and hopped backward. Ulgard casually took the pistol from his bobbing hand and drilled a bullet through the center of his forehead. The young man pitched to the ground. Ulgard examined the pistol. Heckler and Koch VP70Z, double-stack magazine that put eighteen more nine-millimeter rounds at his disposal. Not his weapon of choice, but it would do. Especially with so many guests in the castle.

He stuck it under his belt and went to work covering the body with branches and rocks.

54

After a moment of despair, Rebecca placed two fingers under the side of Alan's jawbone to feel for a pulse. From the eyebrows down his face was sheeted with a dry crust of blood; it had formed thin rivulets that crisscrossed his neck in weird patterns and had soaked into his shirt with enough left to trickle down his left arm. Something had smacked across the prominences of his eyebrows and split the skin in one long gash. She knew that upper facial cuts bled horribly: Sharri had provided her with at least two heart attacks from cuts on her forehead that appeared to spurt gallons down her face.

A pulse was there; she did not know if it was strong or weak. "He *is* alive," she said to Dutch. "It's your hearing that's dead."

"Sorry."

"Where's the hospital in this town? I know it has one."

"East on the main drag. Eight, ten blocks."

"We have to get him there."

He placed the flashlight under his chin and clamped down on it with his jaw, then stooped and put his hands around Alan's ankles. Rebecca got her forearms under his armpits and straightened. He seemed incredibly heavy and she was only able to shuffle a few steps.

"Wrong ends," Dutch said, taking the flashlight in hand. "When they're floppy like this it's twice as hard, but at least the feet are always lighter. Trade."

They were exchanging places when something crashed in the darkness behind them. Rebecca squealed. With a grunt Dutch spun around and slashed the area with light.

A cardboard box lay on its side where Alan had lain, its contents dumped across the floor. In the glaring light Rebecca saw folders and binders, a scatter of envelopes, two or three LP records in faded paper sleeves. One of them had rolled out and was leaning casually against a can of paint.

"Hell, just more junk," Dutch said. "Scared me half to death." He shined the light just below her eyes. "Ready?"

She shook her head, puzzled, then went to him and slipped the flashlight out of his hand. "That box didn't fall out until we got Alan out of the way, Dutch. It must be pretty damned important to be put there for safekeeping behind a dead man."

He moved his shoulders up and down. "Go, girl."

Rebecca picked her way to the box and squatted beside it, examining it intently under the light. At one time it had been a home for twenty pounds of GEORGIA CLING PEACHES, according to the logo on its side. She set it upright and picked through the remaining contents. A number of cassettes with their labels peeled to pieces, a dozen or so old hardback books and paperbacks, a stack of maps pinched together with a rubber band, and more LPs in blank white sleeves.

She duck-walked to the objects that had fallen out: an atlas of the world and a folded map of Europe, other books that she tossed back into the box, more cassettes with destroyed labels. She tossed the two LPs in and had to lean far to the side for the one that had come to rest against the paint can. With a grunt she got it and glanced at it under the light.

This one had a round white label at its center. She frowned at it.

HE STILL SPEAKS

Below that was a line of tiny print, words directing all inquiries to a post office box in Lincoln, Nebraska. Rebecca stood, thinking of keeping it, but it was too big to stick in a pocket so she dropped it into the box, not disappointed because she had not known what to expect in the first place. As an afterthought she jammed one of the cassettes into a pocket. "Done," she said to Dutch.

"Grab on." When she had Alan's feet in the crooks of her elbows Dutch stuck the flashlight under his chin again. "One, two, three."

They made it to the steps, hobbling over the debris or kicking it to the side, and lurched up the narrow stairway. After a rest in the middle of the house, they got him out on the lawn, and then managed to scoot him into the bed of the pickup. Rebecca sat with him, one hand cradling his head in lieu of a pillow, the other shielding the sun from his eyes in case they opened.

Dutch stuck his head out. "Ready to go?"

"Just don't kill us."

"Wouldn't dream of it."

They sat in a waiting room for more than an hour after surrendering Alan to the doctor who had met them at the door of the ER. Dutch had some small bills that the vending machines gobbled eagerly, providing Rebecca with a lunch of chocolate chip cookies and a Mountain Dew. When the doctor finally sought them out he seemed chipper.

"The protruding brow ridge is a remnant from our caveman past. Fortunately, Mr. Weston was hit there with what was probably a piece of two-by-four lumber, maybe something a little bigger. If the point of impact had been any higher, it would have crushed his forehead to the depth of an inch or more. If the object had been round, like the baseball bat I first suspected, the force of impact would have been concentrated in a smaller area that would have quickly broadened as the bat drove inward."

Dutch stood up. "You mean he got lucky, then."

"If a two-by-four across the eyebrows can be called lucky, yes."

Rebecca stood as well. "No brain damage?"

"A concussion." He adopted a puzzled look. "Where did all the older trauma come from? I heard last week that he was held hostage in his house by some bikers, but this stuff is fresher."

Rebecca and Dutch exchanged looks. "We just met up with him yesterday," Rebecca said.

"I suppose I'll hear all about it on TV soon."

"So when will he wake up?" she asked.

"I gave him a huge whiff of ammonium nitrate until he came around. Quite a vocabulary. But he has to be monitored for the next twenty-four hours to watch for peripheral symptoms such as amnesia or blindness."

"Ick," Dutch said.

"So you have to keep him that long?"

"With his permission. I assume he's insured through station WXRV."

Rebecca frowned uneasily. "He's not employed there anymore."

"Oh. Then you should make arrangements at the billing office. It's out front, the main entrance and to your right."

"What room is he in now?"

"Still in the ER, actually. "

"Thank you, Doctor."

The doctor touched his head in a parody of a salute. "Take care."

Rebecca let out the breath she had been saving if another question were necessary. "Dutch?" she asked tiredly.

"Mmm?"

"Who almost killed Alan and then stuck him in the basement?"

He pushed both hands into the pockets of his pants and hiked up his shoulders in slow degrees. "Only Alan can tell us, if he knows, but that two-by-four might have sailed out of nowhere and caught him unawares, hard as it hit him."

Absently, she touched the cassette that was stiff in her pocket. Possibilities rose to mind, but none of them made sense. "Does your truck have a cassette player in it?"

"Used to. Ate them regularly, then got full and quit forever."

"Great."

They stood in silence. "Are we supposed to wait here for Alan?" Dutch finally asked.

Rebecca had assumed it. "Heck if I know, he might have passed out again." She looked at the large clock on the wall:

1:45. "Whoever attacked Alan stole the Honda. Can we assume he'll return to the house?"

Dutch thought about it. "Why go back to the house? As far as he knows, Alan's dead and buried. And why drive a stolen car around? My guess is that it'll be found at the bottom of a strip mine under about thirty feet of water."

She clutched her head with both hands. "I wonder if Hank's doing any better than I am."

Dutch narrowed his eyes. "Are you going to start crying?"

She turned to him with glistening eyes. "So far I've made it thirty miles out of Terre Haute and only managed to get Alan halfway dead and MaryLou's car stolen. And the whole time Sharri's alone in the hospital."

Dutch moved quickly to her and took her arm. "Walk with me, girl. As long as you're walking, you know you're going somewhere."

She walked with him, fighting back useless tears of frustration. This hospital was different than Regency, smaller, older. The hallway smelled of too much floor wax applied too many times and the green walls were warty from a thousand coats of paint. Dutch steered her to the front entrance where yellow sunlight streamed through the big windows and caromed off the shiny floor. A few people were sitting on the plastic benches there, talking softly, and several others were studying the things pinned to the huge bulletin board on the wall.

"Feel like a cruise outside?" Dutch asked. "I can see the flower beds from here."

She shrugged. Why the hell not? Alan might be delayed for hours. "Sure."

Dutch opened the door for her. Coming up the shallow steps was an elderly lady escorted by a teenaged girl who wore little earphones fastened to a metal bow over her head. A purple plastic cassette player was clipped to her belt.

"Excuse me," Rebecca said, digging the tape out of her pocket. "Ma'am, could I borrow your sister for a second?"

From the old lady she got the smile she had hoped for. The teenager looked at her with a confused frown, then hung the earphones around her neck. "Could you listen to this for a second?" Rebecca asked her, offering the tape. "Tell me what kind of music it is?"

The girl took the machine from her belt, popped it open, and took out the cassette. When the other one was playing she put the earphones back on, making studious faces. "Just a lot of talking," she said a bit too loudly. "You listen."

Rebecca positioned the little foam speakers over her ears, holding them in place with both hands, listening intently. Dutch looked on, awaiting his turn, but after just a few seconds Rebecca peeled the headset away and extended it to the girl. He saw with alarm that all the color had drained out of her face; she was having trouble getting a breath. "Rebecca?" he said, moving to support her. "Girl?"

"Holy Jesus Christ," she whispered. "We've been—"

The door behind Dutch's back swung open. He spun and saw Alan Weston, decked out in new bandages, totter out. "Rebecca!" he called out, and lurched against Dutch. Dutch grappled at him to keep him from falling.

"God, I know!" she shouted at him, then aimed sharp and glittering eyes at Dutch. "The tapes are a language course, Dutch. They're the tapes Perry used to teach Hank how to speak fluent German."

"I guess that means he wasn't Hitler, right?"

Alan found his balance and pulled himself up higher. "Perry's been living in that house ever since the party. He tossed the renters out two months ago. He prepared everything in advance."

Dutch looked from face to face. "That's all fine and good, except for one thing: why?"

Rebecca straightened. "I guess we'll just have to ask Perry."

They hurried along the sidewalk to the ER side of the hospital and piled into the pickup Dutch had parked there.

55

Karl-Luther von Wessenheim came across something un-usual in the dark as he entered his second hour lost in the maze of tunnels. The way became suddenly choppy, and lots of dirt clods broke underfoot. As he picked his way along his head abruptly met the ceiling of the tunnel and he realized that yet again he had blundered into one that had collapsed. When he turned and was picking his way back he stepped on a thick branch or stick, and immediately froze. This was the first foreign object he had encountered. He squatted and felt it: cool and smooth, with knobby ends where other sticks were attached. When it finally came to him that he had dis-covered a partially buried skeleton he was gripped by a wave of superstitious panic that sent him on a mad scramble to es-cape this tunnel of the lost and the dead.

Which left him, when he tired of running and smashing face first into cold dank walls, just as lost. There were no di-rections anymore, just the impenetrable darkness; even up and down were suspect. For the hundredth time he reached for a cigarette and for the hundredth time remembered that he had no matches. He cursed aloud and the walls swallowed the shouted words; no echo, rapid silence. He could scream for help but the tunnels would absorb his voice, render him mute. His only hope was either finding his way outside or finding a way into the castle. But in such inky darkness he could not plot a course. He would have to walk until he either got out or dropped from exhaustion.

And so he walked, one hand held in front of him, the other hand tracing across the wall. Soon something crunched underfoot and he dropped into a squat to probe the earth. After a tick of time he closed his eyes and let his head fall.

It was his own discarded book of matches, empty. A wasted hour of probing tunnels that went nowhere. He raised his face in the dark and screamed out a curse. *"Verdammtes Unglück!"*

The earth inhaled the words. Von Wessenheim rocked to his feet, wondering which direction he had faced when he'd last stood on this spot. He probed the area and found the familiar three tunnel openings. Which had he chosen the last time? He recalled that one of them had ended in a cave-in but could not remember which.

He walked into the middle one. It went straight for a long while, though he could not shake the feeling that it was angling gently to the left. After five or six minutes he dared to believe he had chosen correctly. The air seemed fresher and he believed the smell of pine trees was in the air. It was with great surprise that he sensed a blockage, a coming together, and slowed.

Not another cave-in, he moaned internally. He bumbled around in the dark, reaching and probing. His hand fastened around the rung of a ladder and he clutched it tight, wondering. When he looked up he could see, very dimly but visible to his hungry eyes, an L-shaped crack of light far above.

He was under the castle. For several seconds he clutched the soggy wooden ladder in a grateful embrace, panting, then recovered his composure. That he would eventually find this ladder was a mathematical certainty he had simply surrendered to the stresses that had dogged him throughout the pursuit, the capture, and the losing of Mr. Thorwald.

His mind clear again, smiling with a bit of confidence, he started up the ladder wondering where it ended so far overhead.

Rønna Ulgard walked back into the *Schloss* Bad Nauheim with the pistol snug under his belt and hidden from view by his suit coat. Everyone was at dinner by now, probably tying their bibs around their scrawny necks while waiting for the round of appetizers. It did not matter to Ulgard that they had crawled under their school desks while the bombs of World War Two rained down. Their experiences, so often retold, had dwindled to the point of being anecdotes. The young people—and there were precious few of them—were anxious to haul the church into the twenty-first century. The original Hitlerjugend were becoming a detriment to the cause. In their shriveled bodies and wrinkled faces one saw only weakness. That would soon stop. They knew what euthanasia was.

But that did not yet apply to Herr Knecht, who was amazingly spry and physically quite strong. He would probably live to a healthy and robust eighty. Unfortunately, he had not been blessed with the intelligence to match his handsome looks and would like to have the front third of Thorwald's brain vacuumed out of his forehead, a lobotomy that would keep him as docile as a neutered house cat. But what if the reincarnated soul *resided* in the frontal lobe? Knecht was too dim to consider such possibilities. And so was Frau Dietermunde.

A look into the grand ballroom proved it to be deserted except for the seventy-four empty chairs. Ulgard did not know what had become of Thorwald but assumed he had been sedated half to death for transport to Knecht's estate, wherever that might be. He knew one sure way to find out: his mother's butler, Heinz. Though he was not a member of the group and might never have enough money to participate, he was smart enough to see what was happening around him, smart enough to play dumb when he had to.

Ulgard took the steps up to Heinz's room on the second floor. After a crisp knocking on his door it was pulled open slightly. "*Ja?*"

"*Hallo,* Heinz," Ulgard said. "*Wie geht's?*"

"Everything is going fine, Herr Ulgard." His tone was guarded and unsure.

"Well, let me in," Ulgard said, pushing on the door. "Let's talk of the old times."

"Maybe another day. I'm not feeling well."

"On such a beautiful day? You should get outside."

"It's one of those viruses."

"Open the fucking door and let me in, you little faggot."

Heinz scuttered away just as Ulgard smashed his weight against the door, bursting it open. Fragments of painted wood whickered through the room to clunk against the wall, then drop lightly to the carpet. Ulgard pushed the ruined door all the way open and searched the area with his eyes. Heinz had a friend over to visit, he saw, a pasty young man lounging on the couch wearing nothing but a disposable diaper between his skinny, hairy shanks.

"Where's Mr. Thorwald?" Ulgard demanded.

Heinz came closer, fastening his pants, and put on a sneering expression. "Since I'm not allowed to know anything here, I know nothing."

Ulgard grabbed him by the shirt and spun to smack him against the nearest wall, then pressed an elbow against his throat. "Frau Dietermunde may believe that, but I don't. What have they done with Thorwald?"

Heinz's nose flared with fear and hatred. "They sedated him and stuck him in a box in the service entrance. Some of Knecht's men are on the way to crate him up for travel."

"Travel to where?"

"I don't know."

Ulgard crushed his throat. Heinz twisted and thumped until the pressure was released. "That's all I know," he coughed out. "Why would I lie?"

Ulgard stepped away from him. "Good point, you've got nothing to gain. If you start spitting up blood, gargle with salt water."

"You told me that the last time."

"Well, it worked, didn't it?"

He left. The door crashed shut behind him. Avoiding either of the banquet rooms, he made his way to the long stone corridor that led to the service entrance at the rear of the castle, where a large wooden shed had been erected to house storage bins for non-refrigerated goods. In the dimness and warmth he lifted the hinged lids until he found Thorwald curled up among a pile of turnips. For a bit he looked down at him, this battered young man whose body housed the spirit of the Führer, then softly lowered the lid. The nearest escape tunnel

was back down the corridor and past the kitchen, to the fifth
room beyond, the old armory where broken swords and cast-
off sections of medieval armor now rusted in the dark. It
would be a long run and the chances of being seen were
great. With Thorwald sedated he would have to be carried
down the long slick ladder, if it had not disintegrated in the
last few decades, and then backpacked all the way to the exit
where von Wessenheim waited. It would certainly be a trial
of endurance.

Ulgard shifted his eyes left and right, thinking hard and
fast. This was dangerously new to him; his success in life had
come from methodical planning that minimized risks, not
dashing about helter-skelter hoping for the best. He needed
time. But there was only one way to get it.

By waiting. He sauntered into the open just as the sun
ducked behind some heavy gray clouds. Instantly, a mist of
rain filled the air and a rainbow popped into existence in the
valley below that straddled Bad Nauheim and its satellite village to the east, Nieder Mörlen. Ducking under a stand of
maple trees he peeled his gloves off and flexed his blue hands
with their profusion of tiny interlinked swastikas. On hot
days his hands could stink worse than his feet, the lifelong
gift from Mother. The rumble of a truck made itself known as
it chugged up the winding castle road and he pulled his
gloves back on.

It was a small white Toyota flatbed loaded with a wooden
crate that was strapped to it with canvas belts. The license
plate indicated Frankfurt. The passenger hurried out while
the driver waited, idling.

Ulgard ambled over. "Pickup for Knecht?"

He was a short, blocky man in a pinstriped suit. "That's
right."

"He's at dinner right now, but sent me to show you where
the package is."

The man followed him into the shed. "So," Ulgard said
amiably as he lifted the lid of the turnip bin, "where does our
sleepyhead go today?"

He got a sharp look. "Who are you?"

"I share this estate with my mother."

"Go eat dinner with your mother. Tell Knecht we've made the pickup."

"One more thing," Ulgard said while the man looked down at Thorwald.

The short man faced him again. "You just don't get it, do you?"

With one lithe move Ulgard jerked the pistol from his belt and jammed it hard and deep into the man's soft belly, then pulled the trigger. With his body as a natural silencer, the report was muffled to the sound of a small firecracker. Ulgard caught him as he dropped, opened a neighboring bin, and rolled him into it. The lid banged down. The gun went back under his belt. Three seconds had passed since Knecht's man said his last words.

Now Ulgard lifted Thorwald out; he was as boneless as a water balloon. He heaved him up over one shoulder and carried him to the truck. The driver leaned over and pushed the door open for him.

"Your friend got called in by Herr Knecht," Ulgard told him. "What do we do with this guy?"

"What is wrong with him?"

Ulgard thought fast. This was a simple truck driver, maybe even Knecht's hired gardener or maintenance man, obviously not in on the plan. "He drank too much. Where does that crate go?"

The driver fished under the seat and withdrew a clipboard. "Bahnhof Frankfurt. I'm to ship it to Herr Knecht's winter estate in France."

Ulgard manhandled Thorwald into the cab of the truck, frowning. At some point the dead man had been going to put Thorwald in the crate, probably bind him and gag him as well, then nail it shut. The truck driver would take care of the shipping with no idea of what the cargo was.

"Where is Herr Knecht's French estate?" he asked him.

Again to the clipboard. "Vicinity of Avignon."

Ulgard got in and swung the door shut. At any moment Knecht could come out to do exactly what Ulgard had done:

point out Thorwald in the turnip bin. But a regal dinner at *Schloss* Bad Nauheim came in many courses, and it was difficult to find a good time to slip away. Especially when the wine flowed to consummate a business deal.

"Let's go," he said, and thumped a fist on the dashboard. Thorwald keeled over onto the gear shift; Ulgard grabbed a handful of his hair and lifted him out of the way.

"Must have been good liquor," the driver said as they got under way, moving slowly down the steep road. He indicated Thorwald with a couple of jerks of his head. "Friend of yours?"

The need for chitchat was gone; it was now annoying. Ulgard yanked the pistol out and poked it against the driver's right temple. "Down there where the road angles sharply to the right is a smaller road to the left. Take it."

Without a word the driver heaved his door open and leapt out. Astonished, Ulgard pivoted fast enough to catch sight of him tumbling in the grass. The truck gained speed and wandered toward the drainage ditch on the left. Ulgard grabbed for the vacant wheel, then worked to heave Thorwald aside to get behind it. In the meantime the truck picked up more speed; with one hand Ulgard steered it around the curve to the sound of worried tires while the dial of the speedometer edged up. Finally in position, Ulgard pressed his foot on the brake. It went down but nothing happened. A quick glance below showed that the driver's clipboard had slid forward and gotten wedged underneath the pedal. With a snarl Ulgard crushed the pedal down hard enough to break the clipboard, but the truck had arrived at the next corner too fast. As he madly spun the wheel the Toyota overbalanced and crashed over onto the driver's side. Squalling and scraping, it slid off the road and settled in the dry ditch. Finally, with excruciating slowness, it turned itself upside down and rocked back and forth as if to get comfortable.

Ulgard crawled out, spidered around, and reached back inside to drag Thorwald out. With difficulty he hoisted him onto both shoulders and stood, then bounced up and down several times to position the weight evenly. It was a long run back to von Wessenheim's post at the rental car, but it was the only means left to escape the sprawling estate of *Schloss* Bad Nauheim unseen.

He set off at a trot, grunting under the load, already sweating in the intermittent sunshine.

Near the top of the ladder, von Wessenheim's upward pace had slowed to a crawl. In addition to being slick it was horribly wobbly, and the higher he got the more it began making cracking noises far below. In the dark he estimated he had climbed one or two stories high; if a light were suddenly switched on here he would take one downward look and faint. But just a few more meters above him the L-shaped crack of light gleamed as bright as neon to his starving eyes. Clutching the sides of the ladder hard enough to gouge crescents in the soggy wood with his fingernails, he forced his feet to push him upward another step. The ladder creaked and groaned while a moan formed behind his clenched teeth. With all the courage he could dredge up he willed his body to climb farther, assuring himself that if the ladder broke and he fell, these last few meters would not make his death any more certain.

With both feet on the third rung and his shins pressing against the second, shaking and breathless, he stretched his left arm toward the bottom seam of light. His fingers encountered damp wood. As he groped at it a cold metal hook snagged under his index finger. He clutched it tighter and pulled, hoping to cause a door to spring open, but the hook would not move, had probably rusted in place. For better leverage he climbed up one more step. The ladder shuddered beneath him and seemed to slip to the side. Beside the vertical slash of light he found dirt and mapped the entire area with his hand: the soil had been cut away around the door, framing it. To get the necessary leverage he would have to plant his left knee there, leaving only his right foot on the slimy ladder. And if it slipped?

It was worth the effort, he decided without a trace of bravado. A few more hours lost in the escape tunnels would drive him mad. Even if he burst through this doorway into

Frau Dietermunde's own bedroom, the embarrassment would pale in comparison to the horror of death in the dark. Resolved, he leaned to the left and shoved his knee out to catch the earthen frame of the door.

His knee found purchase in the clammy dirt. Again he groped for the rusty hook and found it easily. His balance was intact. He slid his eyes shut and let out the breath he had been holding.

Voices touched his ears. He brought himself back to awareness and pressed an eye to the vertical slit where light shone through so brightly. The first thing he saw, dead center in the narrow field of vision, was Frau Dietermunde. She was seated at a banquet table, flanked on one side by a fat, gray-haired matron and on the other by a man whom he recognized from the auctions in Frankfurt. Obviously, Frau Dietermunde and her Hitler Youth cohorts were enjoying a fine dinner, possibly celebrating their capture of Thorwald, which meant Ulgard had been correct, Thorwald was here. But this was also terrible news: by now Ulgard should have spirited Thorwald down into the tunnels. Hours ago he should have done that. Hours. But these were happy people.

So something had gone wrong. Von Wessenheim let his head fall, breathing in the sour musk of all the dirt below him, reeling from this newest blow after all the others. This time even the extraordinary powers of Rønna Ulgard had failed.

He looked through the crack again. Frau Dietermunde was smiling coyly as she brought a wine goblet to her lips, her eyes twinkling. Why, he wondered, would fate bring him so close to victory only to end his quest within sight of this? Through one eye he watched in helpless anger while she delicately sliced a portion of game hen. Where was Thorwald while these fools dined? In a cage? A dungeon?

"So tell me about your estate in France," she said blithely. "Will Mr. Thorwald be comfortable there?"

"The weather is mild," the man seated beside her replied, "though I doubt that he'll be aware of it."

Von Wessenheim's eyes flared in alarm. Frau Dietermunde had given Thorwald to this man, or at least loaned him. So now he was to be taken to France—but unaware?

"It's located not far from the Rhône River where it curves southward on its final journey to Avignon, and the Mediterranean after that. You must visit me sometime."

She batted her eyes so fast and overtly that von Wessenheim would have laughed had it not been so disgusting.

"Speaking of that," the man said, wiping his mouth with a napkin as he stood, "I need to see if the transport has arrived."

"Oh, sit down," Frau Dietermunde said. "I'll have someone tend to it."

He shook his head. "If you will all excuse me? Please continue, I will be but a minute."

A general murmur of assent rose. The man—von Wessenheim knew his name but could not dredge it up yet—Knavitch? Knabel?—walked out of sight while Frau Dietermunde again stabbed a fork into her game hen. In just these few seconds von Wessenheim had learned all he needed to know; after nightfall he would come up again to somehow get out. With a grunt he swung himself back onto the ladder and began slowly to climb down, muttering under his breath with his fear forgotten, his face cramped in a sneer of revulsion. The bleached-blonde bitch had struck again, and struck hard. Yet incredibly, now that she had Thorwald, she was instantly sending him off to France. And the man with the full mane of silver hair—Knieboldt? Knecht?—had said that Thorwald would not be aware of the weather.

Von Wessenheim froze in place, finally knowing. Rather than risk having Thorwald pinpoint the location of Hitler's body, they were going to keep him drugged for the rest of his life, wasting away in the bowels of a French castle. Unsure if he really was their Führer or not, they did not have the heart to kill him. This, then, was the form of leniency they practiced.

Again he continued to scale down the ladder, wracked with thoughts that assailed him from a host of directions, when again he suddenly stopped. That man, Knecht—yes, it was Knecht—had left the table to see if the transport had arrived. But it was Thorwald's transport, not his own. Thus at this very moment Thorwald was being put into a vehicle headed for France. Von Wessenheim reversed direction and hurried back up again, needing to hear more details about this matter of transportation. By car or rail? By air?

He had climbed almost all the way to the top when the ladder cracked apart, unzipping itself from bottom to top. With a gasp he threw his weight onto the left upright while rungs snapped apart under his pedaling feet. The upright yawed back and forth as if mounted on a spring before thumping solidly into dirt somewhere above. For half a minute he remained wrapped around it while it groaned and creaked. Rungs and chips of wood fell away to plunge soundlessly into the blackness below.

When the blood throbbing in his eardrums lessened he could hear conversation taking place above in the banquet room. With more courage than he had ever before summoned he inched upward, every muscle taut and shaking, his breath whistling as his lungs tried to squeeze oxygen from the air. It was a torture test usually reserved for military trainees on an obstacle course, but he fought his way back up to the L-shaped slit of light and dug his already soggy knee back into the impression it had left in the dirt. When a semblance of balance had been achieved, he pressed his eye to the vertical crack and saw Frau Dietermunde again. She had a spear of asparagus impaled on her fork and was dipping the tip into a little ceramic bowl. Suddenly she looked up to her left; Herr Knecht strode into the line of sight and took hold of the back of her chair with one hand before bowing down to speak into her ear. The fork dropped from her fingers and thumped on the thick tablecloth.

"Oh my dear God," she said aloud, and shot to her feet.

56

They crept up on Perry's house like a SWAT team, which Rebecca found strange but was unable to avoid doing: hunkering low to the ground, eyes and ears keen, all senses heightened. While Alan went around to the front she climbed up the steps to the porch with Dutch at her side, their footfalls careful and intent. She did not expect Perry to come out blasting a gun, but she had not expected Perry to try to kill Alan with a two-by-four and bury him in the basement, either. At the back door she flattened herself against the house and looked to Dutch for guidance.

His signals indicated that she should wait. They had already scouted the area for the Honda but had not found it; Dutch had left his pickup a block away from the house. At first he had insisted on getting the local police involved but Rebecca knew that if Perry saw cops around he would just keep going and the world would just keep thinking Hank was Hitler. The language tapes and the old records labeled in no uncertain terms HE STILL SPEAKS were fascinating but not proof enough of Hank's innocence. It had to come from Perry's own confession. And then, God willing, they could rebuild the house, get Hank's job back, and resume their old lives.

Yes indeed.

Dutch stepped through the open door. Rebecca peeked around the door frame to watch him go deeper inside. By the force-of-habit movements of his hands as he dodged from place to place she could see that they ached for a police revolver; the closest thing to a weapon he had was the flashlight sticking up out of his back pocket. After he disappeared entirely she finally followed, spooked by the late-afternoon shadows in the house, knowing that anything sudden right now would make her jump out of her skin. In the kitchen she paused to gently swing a few cupboards open. Canned food, mostly; Perry had purchased wisely. In the living room she met up with Dutch and Alan.

"We're going to scout the basement next," Dutch said. "I don't think Perry's here but we have to make sure."

"Then what?" she asked.

It was Alan who answered: "Then we lie in wait for the sorry bastard."

Dutch aimed a finger at Rebecca. "Keep in mind there's a good chance he'll never be back. He's not stupid, he knows that if Alan found him, others will probably follow. It's a good bet he's moved on."

She let out a groan. "Don't say that, Dutch, I need to keep hoping or I'll die."

"Then keep on hoping." He put on a smile for her. "Perry Wilson isn't a career criminal and he's going to make mistakes. The proof of that is Alan. The fact that Alan found Perry so easily, and the fact that Perry thought he'd killed him so easily. His hearing must be about as bad as mine, not able to pick up a heartbeat. Those are both huge mistakes, and he's going to make more of them."

She smiled. "Thank you very much."

"My pleasure." He raised his bushy eyebrows and glanced at Alan. "Let's check the basement, Mr. Weston. Rebecca, you keep an eye on things outside. He drives up, you let out a holler. If by any chance he just walks through the door, run. Scream while you run. Run as fast as you can to the back porch. We'll be right on his tail."

She moved to a window that offered a view of the little driveway. "Okay, I'm set."

They started off, but as Dutch pulled out his flashlight he hesitated, then turned. "To your knowledge, did Perry know anything about guns? Did he have any around?"

She shook her head. "Never saw him with one, ever."

"Did he have animal trophies on his walls? Deer he'd killed, bears, ducks, whatever?"

"None at all. He was a scholar, a bookworm. If not for Hank and the chess games, he would have been a recluse."

"Good. That, and the fact he nailed Alan with a plank instead of a bullet, suggests to me that he hasn't armed himself."

Alan stuck an arm out toward Dutch. At first Rebecca thought he was going to grasp his shoulder, maybe make a come-on motion. Instead he wobbled and dropped awkwardly to both knees. A sudden bright line of crimson blood slid out of one nostril. He jerked his extended arm inward to thump at his nose with his wrist. "Weird," he said, and easily got up again.

Rebecca went to him. "You are going back to the hospital," she said.

He drew away from her. "Not for a fucking nosebleed I'm not. Come on, Dutch."

He walked away. Dutch only offered her a shrug before he followed. Uneasy and frowning, she moved back to the window, thinking about what the doctor had said to look out for in Alan, amnesia and blindness. Preoccupied, it came to her only gradually that something outside the window had changed; even when she realized that a black motorcycle with knobby tires was now sitting peacefully in the driveway, it took time to process the fact. When everything finally clicked it was her body that reacted first, tearing her away from the window and beating a path to the open basement door. She flung herself through it and whirled to slam it shut.

"Somebody's here!" she shouted as she spun around again. *"Then get down here fast!"*

She hammered down the steps as fast as her feet would allow. Dutch's flashlight illuminated her way until the bottom, then winked out. She took a few slogging steps through the paint cans and junk on the floor before stopping in place to let it all clunk and rattle into silence. In the darkness she waited to hear the front door thump shut, waited for the opening wedge of light from the basement door to expose her. But neither of those things happened.

She whispered into the dark: *"Dutch? Alan?"*

"Be quiet!"

"But I'm standing here smack in the middle of the fricking basement!"

"Hold on."

The flashlight popped alive to guide her way through the obstacles and the lumpy shadows they cast. "Stay here with Alan," Dutch said softly. "I'll be over there."

She tried to find his face in the darkness. "Over where?"

He stepped away without answering, shining the light at his feet. At the side of the stairway he melded into the shadows and turned the flashlight off. Rebecca waited, as taut as a spring, gripping Alan's forearm with one hand, the other balled into a fist against her chest.

Something creaked above, a very muted sound, maybe door hinges, maybe not. Her senses picked up the pressure of slow and measured steps, then the hint of a floorboard squeaking. The ghosts of the movement overhead continued to roam, they seemed to be in the kitchen and she seemed to hear the refrigerator open and shut; they seemed to be in the bathroom and she seemed to hear the patter of urine in the toilet. All the while she wondered if whoever it was had even come into the house yet, if she had actually seen a motorcycle leaning over on its kickstand, or seen nothing.

Like a sudden explosion of white-hot phosphorous three overhead bulbs burst into being and laid bare the entire basement. Rebecca snapped up both hands to form shields above her eyes, thinking that Dutch had backed into a switch. But the door at the top of the stairs banged instantly open and a pair of feet started tromping down. Rebecca shrank back into the corner. Alan pried her frozen hand from his forearm and picked his way forward, stepping between the cans and other junk. She waited for Perry's face to bob down into view, two weeks' worth of rage sizzling inside her like a lighted fuse. Alan stooped and fetched up an unsplattered, full can of paint by its thin wire handle.

The face came into view. It wasn't Perry's. At the foot of the stairs the man—he looked more like a teenager—finally saw Alan and recoiled with a look of total surprise on his face.

Alan swung the can. The bottom rim of it cut a crease in front of the kid's ear and knocked him off the last step to crash down on the littered floor. Alan danced for position and hauled the can over his shoulder, this time with both hands. "Talk fast," he shouted. "Tell me how you didn't nail me with a two-by-four."

The kid rolled over when Alan moved as if to swing the can again. The gun in his hand was just a quick twinkle of blue steel until a flower of yellow fire popped out of the barrel, accompanied by a tremendous explosion. The can in Alan's fists gushed blue paint from holes in both sides. He heaved it away. The teenager—who to Rebecca seemed all of eighteen or nineteen—got to his feet, wrapping both hands fully around the butt of the pistol.

"You are Jesus, Mr. Weston," he said with a grin. "You really are the incarnation of the Jew named Jesus. I nail you with a beam of wood that should have killed you, and you rise from the grave." He looked around the basement with little jerks of his head while a line of blood traced a slow path down the side of his jaw. From where he stood, she saw, Dutch was still out of sight unless the kid stepped closer to her. Immediately she moved forward; he swiveled the gun to make sure she stopped.

"You'd be Rebecca. Sharri looks a lot like you. Nice kid."

She examined him, this unfamiliar biker with a full head of blond hair that had been creased and tattered by the wind, some acne scars on his cheeks, and a smirk firmly on his face. But even disregarding the smirk and the blood slipping down his jaw he looked vaguely familiar. "You know Sharri?"

"Oh yeah. She's got a crush on Johnny Laine." He swiveled the gun again, looking sly now, seeming to enjoy this. "I made her famous, Becky. Front-page photos in three tabloids on the same day. Like taking money from a baby."

Her stomach rolled with a quick and bitter wave of disgust. "You're one of them."

"The paparazzi? That's in Europe, Rebecca. Here I'm just a freelance nature photographer."

"You're the bastard who hung a swastika around her neck and took her picture."

"I'm the bastard, but the swastika was all her own."

"Liar."

Alan made a motion of some sort. Johnny Laine quickly pivoted and targeted him. "Problems?"

"It's my shoes," Alan said, looking down. He lifted a foot. The blue paint had formed rivers across the floor and was pooling around his feet. "You expect I should stand here and let my shoes get ruined?"

"A true Jewish stand-up comic to the end," Johnny said. "Notice I'm not laughing."

Alan put on a flat, broken-toothed smile for him. "What the fuck are you, junior? Local neo-Nazi wanna-be? Winner of today's Eva Braun look-alike contest? Squeak up, you little fuck, squeak up and talk like a man."

Johnny jerked the pistol overhead and fired it. Rebecca involuntarily clapped her hands over her ears. Gunsmoke billowed across the ceiling, glowing faintly blue around the hot lightbulbs. "You shut up!" he shouted.

Alan had flinched back. "Christ, boy," he said as he straightened, "won't the neighbors hear?"

"Good point." He looked across the basement. For a frightening second Rebecca thought he had become aware of Dutch. Then he motioned with the pistol. "Bring me that towel," he told her. "It's right over there, the wet one with the blood on it."

She moved away, searching, then saw it. Tweezing it up between her finger and thumb she lugged it over to him, then backed away.

"If you wrap the barrel in a big wad," he said importantly as he began working with it, "you can get most of the sound to bury itself in the overlapping fabric. The bullet simply punches through it. A homemade silencer, as you'll see."

Alan spoke with a voice that was losing its bravado. "Who taught you all this? Uncle Perry?"

Johnny Laine twisted the towel around the barrel until it was comically huge, his sharp blue eyes jumping from his

work to Alan and to Rebecca. "I don't have an Uncle Perry."
He formed a crude, one-handed knot to hold the wad in
place, looked it over, and nodded. "Mr. Weston," he said, "I
never thought I'd have to kill you twice, but the Jew has always been a survivor." He glanced at Rebecca. "You're a
Christian, I'll only kill you once."

Disbelief shuttered her eyes wide open. "I *am* a Christian.
What the hell are *you?*"

"My church worships the chosen one, the man who died
for the rest of us." He fiddled with the huge wad of watery,
blood-soaked towel that wrapped the end of the barrel.
"Clear enough?"

At that moment Dutch made his move, sprinting out of his
hiding place with something—it looked like a hammer—
raised in his fist. Johnny Laine sucked in a gasp of air and
slued around but Dutch crashed into him before he could fire.
Both of them hit the floor and skidded to the wall together.
She saw Dutch hoist the hammer up, saw him swing it down.
The kid jerked his head aside in time: the hammer drew
sparks from the rough cement floor. Alan galloped over and
tried to capture the gun as it flailed, grappling with Johnny
Laine's wrist. He beat his hand against the floor, grunting
from the effort, but his fingers would not unlock.

"Let it *go*, goddammit!" Alan grunted. He took hold of the
pistol with his least injured hand and wrenched it back and
forth.

Rebecca leapt over Dutch and Johnny Laine as they struggled. Dropping quickly to her knees, she leaned in to help
Alan as he fought for the gun. With both hands around the
barrel she twisted it back and forth; it was strangely warm
from the single shot that had been fired, slippery in her
sweating hands.

The pistol exploded with noise and fire. Rebecca flinched
at the enormous *boom!* and jumped to her feet with the bright
after image of yellow flame imprinted on her eyes. She became aware of a burning heaviness in her right side and
pressed a hand to it, the same area where she had gotten side
aches as a kid when she played too hard. When she lifted her

hand it was wet and dripping with a gorgeous coating of crimson.

The world of the basement slowed down. In a jerking form of slow motion she saw Alan leap up, she watched Dutch roll to the side, she looked on helplessly as Sharri's friend Johnny Laine staggered to his feet with the big pistol still firmly in his possession. Even as the strange new basement world faded out of existence she lunged at him, both hands out-stretched for the gun.

Then nothing. She crashed down painlessly on the littered floor knowing only blackness. Nothing but that.

57

Rønna Ulgard had taken only a few jogging steps carrying
Thorwald on his shoulders when a tremendous explosion blasted him to the ground. Thorwald tumbled away, arms
and legs flopping. Ulgard raised himself up on his elbows and
looked back: the gas tank of the Toyota flatbed truck had
blown apart in a delayed reaction. Orange and yellow flames
billowed upward, topped by a roiling black mushroom cloud.
The noise of the explosion, he supposed, could be heard all
the way down to the city. Which meant that the occupants of
Schloss Bad Nauheim, barely a stone's throw away, could
hear it too. And would soon come running.

He went to Thorwald and hoisted him over one shoulder,
then broke into a shambling run, smashing through the tall
hedges that bordered the orchard, dodging among the apple
trees. Like a soldier carrying a wounded comrade he charged
full tilt across an open field. Ground-nesting birds burst up
into the sky, squawking angrily. To his right a groundhog
poked its head up through its hole, gave him a quick look,
and instantly vanished.

The next obstacle was a copse of evergreen trees that had
been transplanted from the Black Forest so that Frau Dietermunde would have something green to look at in the winter-
time. After ducking and dodging through its expanse, his
lungs on fire and rivers of sweat stinging his eyes, he
splashed through the knee-high waters of the enormous goldfish pond that she never visited. In the middle of it the lily
pads entangled his feet and he fell forward; spluttering and
gasping, he got back on his feet and lifted Thorwald to his

shoulder again. Water sluiced out of their clothes while Ulgard slogged to the end of the pond, then jogged along a dirt
path flanked by tall weeds.

Frau Dietermunde's property ended at a paved road. Ulgard veered to the left and made his way along the shoulder,
limping a little from a ten-year-old gunshot wound to his
right ankle, his breath hitching up and down in grunts of
agony. Bright spots of light aviated in front of his vision like
a horde of white gnats. He knew enough about the human
body to realize that he was suffering from oxygen deprivation. And he knew enough about Frau Dietermunde to realize
that she would make it permanent if she wanted to.

From this point, Ulgard decided, it wasn't a whole lot farther to where von Wessenheim waited in the rented Volkswagen, perhaps another five minutes at a steady pace. He kept
running, his back and shoulders vised with pain and his legs
as heavy as logs. He paused long enough to look back: the
black cloud of the explosion had become a thin chimney of
smoke that rose to the top of the sky. So what were the Hitlerjugend up to now? Running around in circles? Hiding under
desks? Or using their remaining wits to mount a search party?

He turned away and leaned into motion again, never fond
of questions that could not be answered. Able to hear little
more than the distress of his own breathing, he was suddenly
rocked by the blast of a horn just behind him. He spun awkwardly and saw that a black Mercedes had stopped a few meters away. Two men were in it, both of them old and gray,
familiar faces from the Hitlerjugend crowd. They made no
move to get out; the driver simply kept a heavy hand on the
horn, signaling the others. Ulgard turned to run again but
slued back around instead. Why should these two old fucks
have a car when he had none?

He dumped Thorwald in the weeds beside the road and advanced on the car. The music of the horn switched from full
blast to an alarmed staccato. Ulgard made it to the driver's
door on legs that trembled and scissored. He went for the
door handle, but as he did the lock button sank out of sight. A
pair of watery, cloudy blue eyes watched him with a contempt usually reserved for wartime traitors. Ulgard turned his

back and drove an elbow against the glass, usually a sure guarantee that it would break, but he was utterly spent. Two more tries against the tinted window did nothing. He scanned the area for large rocks, knowing since childhood that such things were not available here.

Disgusted and angry, he backed away from the car while reaching down for the pistol stuck under the waistband of his pants. Shooting the old men was a last-gasp effort; however, it was better than no effort at all. But the pistol wasn't there. He flattened his hands and slapped them along his entire waistband, front and back. The memory of the goldfish pond bobbed up: he had tripped over the crap growing in the water and had fallen. The pistol, heavy by itself and heavier when stuffed full of bullets like it was, must have fallen out to sink like a stone.

For the first time in his adult life Rønna Ulgard experienced panic. The blaring horn and these two old men all needed to be silenced in a hurry but the Mercedes was built like a tank; the men were safe and so was their horn. A crazy idea sprang to his mind. Without weighing its consequences Ulgard bent at the waist and charged at the car. The crown of his head punched through the safety glass; he was suddenly nose to nose with the driver. He drove both fists through the remains of the window and hauled the old man out along with a cascade of glass pebbles. The horn finally quit.

Ulgard punched the old man in the stomach. The blow lifted his feet off the pavement. He fell to the ground in a discordant heap; Rønna Ulgard thought it possible he had died. The other old fellow did not hesitate when a friend was in trouble: he clawed his way out of the Mercedes and took off on foot, heading back the way he had come, stumping along as fast as his spindly old legs would allow.

Ulgard opened a rear door, went back to scoop up Thorwald and heaved him in, then slotted himself behind the steering wheel. He banged the shift into gear and stomped on the accelerator. The rear tires screamed on the hot pavement. The sun glittered on the hood ornament, flashing in his eyes. The car gave a huge lurch and he looked in the mirror in time to see the gut-punched old man spinning on the road like a Chinese firework. Apparently, some part of his body had had the misfortune of being under one of the wheels as it clawed for traction. If he wasn't already dead, Ulgard observed without caring, he certainly was now.

The road went into a series of sharp twists as it descended slightly. He took the turns with all four tires smoking. In the back Thorwald was banging back and forth, hopefully avoiding serious injuries. A scan of the mirror showed no one visibly on his tail yet, but there would be soon. At the last turn he slowed and cut left onto the little dirt road that ended in the trees, praying for a gust of wind to blow his incriminating trail of dust away. In just a few seconds he and Thorwald would be hiding inside the Volkswagen, motoring away while Karl-Luther von Wessenheim—hiding behind oversize sunglasses—cheerfully cruised them along to Frankfurt.

The twin ruts of dirt petered out completely. Ulgard drove the Mercedes deeper into the woods while briars and branches scraped the paint off, forcing the car to plow its way forward until it was hidden from plain view. Then he abandoned it. With Thorwald in his arms he jogged to the sedate brown VW, grinning inside as he panted for air.

But he froze in his tracks. Von Wessenheim was gone. Ulgard put Thorwald on the backseat and straightened, unwilling to realize what he already knew to be true: the unpredictable bastard had wandered away. It occurred to him briefly that without von Wessenheim there were no millions to collect. But that wasn't the most pressing matter now. Most important was the task of getting Thorwald the hell away from *Schloss* Bad Nauheim.

He dropped onto the driver's seat. No signs of violence, so maybe von Wessenheim had gone off to relieve his bladder. He reached for the keys, mentally on the road already, formulating his route, his next move. But something was wrong; he frowned and leaned aside to look at the steering column.

The receptacle for the key was black, and showed some scratches where other drivers had missed the keyhole. Of actual keys there was no trace. In a burst of frantic activity Ulgard probed every possible hiding place. Nothing. Nothing. Von Wessenheim had wandered off with the keys in his pocket.

It was enough to make a man weep. Ulgard jumped out,

seething. As he did he heard car engines racing down the winding road, a convoy of them. Run for the Mercedes, engage these people in a high-speed chase? Or hope the convoy would shoot past, then hot-wire the VW? Again he felt crushed by the unpredictability of the last few days, his inability to gain command. With a silent curse he knelt and began breaking away all the plastic parts under the steering column, his gloves saving him from cuts. It was necessary to locate the heaviest red wire in all the colorful bundles of wire that fed upward. When he had it in his hands he pulled on it, jerking it back and forth, his teeth clenched. After a long struggle it broke free and he reeled it out of the steering column, pausing only to remove his gloves, his hands trembling maddeningly.

He rose for a look. Now the individual cars were visible as they sped along the road. In far less than a minute they would be upon him. He turned back to his work. Two of the wires in the bundles were thinner than the red one but fatter than the others. He fed them between his thumb and forefinger while the tender skin of his hands complained. To test for a battery connection he raked each of the wires across the exposed steel mounts that supported the dash from beneath. The fat red one gave birth to a blinding shower of sparks.

Presently a horn blared. He ignored it, it was just the Hitlerjugend speeding past; there was nothing to see here in this country lane but tangles of brush and a few innocent trees. Finally he peeled the insulation from all three wires by zipping them through his clenched teeth. A gush of dust swirled across his backside and he stood up, blinking against it, wondering.

Cars just coming to a halt. Trapped, then. Something strange caught his eye and he turned his head a bit to the right: one of the Mercedes' big round taillights was merrily flashing a left turn. He had left the key on.

Frau Dietermunde rose from her little runabout car. Behind the steering wheel he saw her favorite butler, Heinz, who was wearing a smirk as big as France itself. Six more carloads of Hitlerjugend disgorged their elderly occupants, several of them toting pistols in their gnarled hands. Behind them the paved road too was clogged with cars.

Frau Dietermunde marched up to Ulgard. She swung a

hand to slap him but this time he caught her wrist. "You think he's a relic," he hissed in her face. "I think he's our savior."

"Which car?" she asked without emotion.

Ulgard let out a tired breath and released her. "The VW."

She lifted her arm and pointed. The others rushed to it. When they opened the rear door, Thorwald fell out on his head.

"You go, and you never come back," she said. "Come back and I'll have you charged with the murder you just committed on the road."

"Listen to reason," he said quictly, hiding his naked hands in the pockets of his suit jacket. "Thorwald isn't a nostalgia machine, he's the next step forward. Knecht is taking him to France to bury him alive."

She narrowed her eyes. "The entire western world is in an uproar about him. His return is too quick, this is not the time for his second coming. So he must vanish, maybe for a hundred years, two hundred years, or even three hundred." She stepped closer. "Look at the Christians now, Jesus has been absent for two thousand years and still they wait for him. We Hitlerjugend are not building the church for ourselves. We are building it for the future."

"And it will have no future until your club of the walking dead releases it."

Ulgard tensed for another slap in the face, but it did not come. Instead Frau Dietermunde stabbed a hand between the lapels of his suit coat and moved to snatch any weapon he might have. "Unarmed?" she said with surprise as she frisked him. "You're getting unreliable in your old age." She turned to watch Thorwald being toted away. He was put into Knecht's car, a red BMW with a black convertible top. "One minute ago that man wanted to kill you for stealing Thorwald," Frau Dietermunde said. "Unless I had intervened he would have done it."

Ulgard snorted. "He *is* a frightening old shit, isn't he?"

"You just stay here," she said through lips that were thin and bloodless. "When we are gone you hop into your little VW and drive away, and don't ever look back."

"May I attend your funeral?"

She ached to hit him, he could smell the desire in the air.

"You have been an embarrassment to me since the moment you were conceived in the rubble of Frankfurt, Oskar Adolf Dietermunde. Would you like to know why?"

He examined the unspoken secrets in her eyes. "No. Never."

The remnants of the Hitler Youth got themselves back into their cars. It took some time for the whole traffic jam to disassemble itself, but soon everyone was headed back up the hill to *Schloss* Bad Nauheim. With them went Thorwald to start his new life in France.

Rønna Ulgard found that he was alone again. The Mercedes was still busy flashing a left-turn signal. He had been betrayed by his own haste and Karl-Luther von Wessenheim's unreliability. The only bright spot in this dismal defeat was that Frau Dietermunde had not discovered the little .22-caliber peashooter he had purchased in Idaho, taped in small pieces to his shaved armpits.

He circled the Volkswagen to fetch his gloves and shut the passenger doors, then dropped wearily inside. This entire venture had been a catastrophe from the moment Frau Dietermunde enlisted him to be the replacement for von Wessenheim's fired lawyer. He had traversed the globe and brought to her the ghost of the only man she had ever loved, and in a twinkling she handed this man to some liver-spotted old shit who spent his winters in France, Germany's mortal enemy in the last two wars.

Ulgard set his teeth together while his eyes narrowed. There was no pleasing the bitch. He wondered how many tears she would shed after Thorwald's lobotomy reduced him to a zombie. Or how long she would weep if he had a fatal accident.

An accident. Yes.

He picked up the wires and wound the copper ends of the smaller ones together. When he touched the red wire to them, a few sparks jumped and the starter kicked the motor alive. Raking the gearshift into reverse and with a heavy foot on the gas, Ulgard dug trenches with the tires. Blinded by the ensuing cloud of dust, he fishtailed the VW out onto the paved road, where the unhindered wind snatched everything away.

58

Donald D. Dutchenreimer—Dutch to everyone but his enemies—rolled away from Johnny Laine while the echo of the pistol shot was still young enough to bounce one last time off the concrete walls. Rebecca had leapt for him but lost consciousness in mid-stride; she had dropped to the cluttered floor like a corpse. One of her hands was gleaming with blood, he saw, and knew then that the shot had not gone wild.

He lifted his eyes from her with a snarl welling up in his throat. The kid had frozen in place, was staring down at her as she lay broken on the floor with her right cheek flat against the gritty cement, her eyes closed. Both of his hands held the pistol in a white-knuckled embrace. As if sensing new trouble, he swung about and popped a shot over Dutch's head. A bit of sawdust sifted down.

Alan Weston was poised at Laine's other side. To tackle him they would have to work in unison. Dutch made motions with his eyes but Alan frowned, not understanding.

Johnny Laine spoke to Dutch: "Who the hell are you?"

"For the last couple of days her best friend," he answered, then shoveled his feelings aside and made his voice professionally bland. "I'm going over to Rebecca now, I need to see how badly she's hurt. I won't make a move toward you, so please do not shoot while I do this harmless little thing. You have nothing to fear from me, I do not have a gun."

He took a step. Johnny Laine stiffened.

Dutch turned on the chatter again. "Nothing is going to go wrong here, young man, it's just us three and Rebecca on the floor, we are unarmed and are not going to hurt you." He took another step, another, then slowly knelt beside her. A puddle of blood was forming around her midsection. He probed her spine with his fingers, felt gently at her rib cage. Nothing poking through; the skeleton on this side was intact. He turned her over, slapping debris out of the way, and laid her flat. What he saw made him release the breath he had been holding.

The bullet had bored through the waist of her shirt, leaving a scatter of burned particles around the edges. Blood had soaked the fabric, but not in the amount that would indicate a ruined artery. The kid, it seemed, had shot her through the appendix. All she needed was a couple of hours on a surgeon's table.

He stood up slowly, his eyes locking with Laine's and his hands spread wide apart to show their continued emptiness. "She's gut shot and needs emergency transport to the nearest hospital," he said. "And it has to happen right now."

"Go back to where you were," Laine commanded. His face, to Dutch's eyes, indicated nothing more than angry impatience. No qualms, no remorse.

Again Dutch let his training take over. "I'm doing exactly what you want, I'm going back, everything is fine." He began picking his way back to where he had stood before, moving slowly but with purpose. "You're safe here, I'm not going anywhere, Alan's not going anywhere, you don't have to—"

Alan turned and plunged noisily up the stairway, tripping to all fours, a blur of hands and feet that propelled him to the top. Johnny Laine swung around to fire at him. The pistol thundered out flame and smoke. Dutch poised himself to tackle the kid at about knee level when Johnny suddenly turned, bringing the gun to bear. Alan's footsteps thudded across the floor overhead and were gone out the back door.

Johnny fired. The bullet sizzled past Dutch's ear. He clapped both hands to his chest and crashed over like a sack of bricks, his chin slamming down on the claw of the rusty hammer lying discarded on the floor. A thick needle of pain stabbed up between his eyes, but it was a small sacrifice. As soon as Laine clattered up the stairs Dutch was on his feet, stumbling over to Rebecca for a check of her wound. She wasn't bleeding fast enough to die soon but she wasn't getting any better. Overhead all was quiet now; it seemed the kid had left the house just as Alan had, a dead run through the back door.

Rebecca muttered and rocked her head back and forth. He gathered her up in his arms, having to strain against the aches and twinges that the years had awarded him, and labored up the stairs. Steady drops of bright red blood leaked from his chin onto her shirt, dismal polka dots. Outside the heat at least carried a breeze. A car was parked at the curb in front of the neighbor's house to the left; Dutch hurried across the little yard. As he chugged past the property line where the weeds became a real lawn the driver's door of the car popped open and a man got out, giving Dutch a long, gape-mouthed stare.

"What in the world is going on?" he asked incredulously. "You're bleeding, both of you." As if his own words had finally sunk in, he hurried around his car to open the back door. "Is she unconscious?" he asked as Dutch laid her across the seat. "She looks dead."

"Not dead, but she needs a hospital *bad*. You live in town, you know where it is, right?"

"You bet I do. Get in."

Dutch pushed Rebecca's feet out of the way and pressed the door shut. He lowered himself onto the passenger seat and sat there all squashed in; miniature Toyotas had never been kind to him. The neighbor dropped inside and fired up the engine. "It's not far, but hang on."

Something touched Dutch's elbow. He looked down and saw Rebecca's hand between the seats. Turning farther he looked at her face. She mouthed something silently while her eyes drifted open and shut. Dutch squeezed her hand, giving her his best expression of reassurance. It occurred to him that this nice new car was going to be thick with bloodstains that no cleaner in the world could take out, but the neighbor seemed unconcerned.

Rebecca touched him again. He squinted at her as she moved her lips. Perry, she seemed to be saying without a voice. Her bloody thumb cocked up and aimed itself at the driver. *Perry*, she mouthed again.

Perry got the car in motion, finally. Before Dutch could re-act to Rebecca's warning, Alan Weston was suddenly stand-ing on the street with a three-foot length of two-by-four in both hands, the late afternoon sun shining down in dapples through the trees, his splinted fingers poking out, the cast on his arm forcing him into an awkward stance. His face was a perfect picture of determination. Perry diverted the car slightly to run him down. Dutch grabbed for the steering wheel and wrenched it in the other direction. Suddenly a passing car was there. Tires squealed. A horn blared. He saw Alan jump backward to keep from being hit, then recover and swing the board as the Toyota passed. The windshield crunched instantly into utter ruin. The car became a gut-twisting carnival ride as it spun in a swift and complete circle on the street.

Perry had his door open and was out before Dutch could drag in a breath. Moving pretty well for his age, he cut across the street and scrambled toward the motorcycle. Finally, Dutch was able to get his bulk out of the little white Toyota and started off at a lumbering trot while the tendons in his legs protested the unusual activity. He noticed that some of the neighbors were venturing out of their houses. "Call the police!" he shouted. Alan sprinted past him with various bandages flapping, holding the two-by-four over his head like a knight wielding a broadsword.

Perry was hammering the motorcycle's kick starter up and down with a foot. Alan skidded to a halt behind him. Dutch waited for him to swing the board down, hoping he remem-bered that a man could get killed by that simple weapon, but a pistol shot pierced the heavy air and Dutch ceased worrying about it: a spray of bloody mist burst from Alan's knee and he crumpled. Dutch swiveled his head and saw a bluish puff of gunsmoke drift up from the weeds beside the house. In-stantly he performed a U-turn, hunched down, and scurried back to the car. Another shot boomed: the asphalt directly in front of his feet grew a foot-long, sloping crater.

Then he was at the white Toyota, the passenger side. He

crawled inside and tried to squirm himself over the gear shift. Another bullet thunked against the car. Perry had left it running, which meant nothing because Dutch could not get himself into the driver's seat. Exasperated, he sat straight up in the passenger seat. The window at his right elbow blew apart to shower him with glass.

Rebecca's face rose up, pale and gaunt and smeared with blood. She crawled between the seats and laboriously pushed her head under the steering wheel. Dutch looked on, his heart thudding. He saw her push the little clutch pedal down with her left hand; with the other she mashed the gas pedal to the floor. The engine rose to a scream, and Dutch understood.

He jammed the gear shifter into first. "Let go of it!" he shouted, leaning sideways to take the wheel, and Rebecca released the clutch. Instantly the front tires went from silence to a scream. Dutch hauled the steering wheel around, his hands rapidly exchanging places as he spun it, trying to aim the nose of the car to the spot where Johnny Laine's pistol was sending out smoke.

"Hold on!" Dutch barked over the screaming engine. The Toyota bounced hugely over the curb and into the weeds. The front tires chewed ruts in a frenzy, kicking up clots of greenery; Dutch saw the kid rise up on his elbows with his eyes growing larger. He jumped to his feet and lifted the pistol to eye level. Though it had been fired maybe ten times, Dutch did not know how close it was to being empty, or if it had been reloaded. He ducked as shots punctuated the complaints of the overworked motor. The shattered windshield took a few direct hits and then dropped entirely from its moorings and onto the dash in a big, pebbly sheet.

Dutch heard a brief scream. Something big thumped under the floorboards. The car crunched against the side of the house. He recovered and dropped a hand on Rebecca's back. "We did it," he shouted, jostling her. "Let off the gas."

She just lay there. The spinning wheels dug holes while the front of the Toyota pitched up and down as if on a trampoline, grinding away its grille. Dutch leaned down and pushed her hand from the gas pedal. When the motor quit the silence was huge. After a moment of wonder he put his arms under her and gently maneuvered her out from under the steering wheel. When he was able to turn her over, he pressed an ear to her chest and heard nothing.

"Christ," he whispered. He clutched her in a tight embrace while his throat tightened. "Sorry, girl."

Rebecca pushed away from him weakly. "Get a fucking hearing aid," she groaned.

He heard a shout. It sounded like Alan in trouble. He worked himself out and trotted around front expecting to find Perry Wilson gone and Alan Weston lying on the lawn with his knee between his hands, howling with pain. Instead, he saw Perry flat on his back beside the fallen motorcycle with Alan straddling him. Alan had the two-by-four in one hand and was threatening Perry with it; his other hand gripped his bleeding knee. As Dutch approached Alan swung the board, his face contorted and his lower lip clamped in his broken teeth. Perry covered his face with his arms and howled while Alan swung it again, and again, shouting things. Dutch finally rushed over to stop him before Perry was dead.

Alan staggered away, his eyes gleaming with hate. "We're going on TV tonight," he shouted down at Perry. "You and me, me and you. TV tonight, Asshole Weston is back in the saddle and you are the first guest on my new show. You hear me, you pile of shit? Just me and you!"

Dutch knelt beside Perry. He was easily still alive, just knocked senseless for a while. Dutch reached for the pouch on his police belt that held his set of handcuffs, then realized he was not a cop anymore. Just seconds later he was relieved to see three police cars crunch to a halt at the curb, two of them local blue and whites, one the car of an Indiana state trooper.

The first thing they did for Dutch was ram him facedown in the weeds and cuff his hands behind his back.

59

Karl-Luther von Wessenheim entered the banquet room of *Schloss* Bad Nauheim by falling to the floor when the swinging panel finally allowed him inside, one-half hour after he had watched the entire cadre of Hitlerjugend storm away from the banquet table as if the castle walls had been breached. Fate was again influencing others to meet its needs, that was obvious; Fate had graced him with more facts in one minute than a squad of private detectives could have uncovered in a year: Thorwald was destined for France, vicinity Avignon, by rail.

He got exhaustedly to his feet, falling to the side before capturing a grip on the tabletop, leaving a dirty handprint there. As he stumbled between the chairs that had been shoved hastily aside, he glanced at the food and realized that he had been starving all these days, too many days to count. As he walked along its length he wiped his hands on his trousers and snatched up tidbits from the plates, one time stopping to shovel a forkful of beef and noodles into his mouth, another to lift a glass of red wine and drain it in three glorious swallows. Time was unpredictable now, the need for haste was uppermost. But as he ruefully fled the room his eyes registered some tiny thing that needed a moment to have an impact on his brain, and when it did he slued around with a different kind of hunger crowding to the forefront.

On the banquet table at the far end of its gigantic length lay a black-and-yellow pack of Reemstmas. A green plastic lighter rested atop it. The mere thought of smoking elicited a thundering demand from his lungs that he do so; his nicotine-starved body ordered him to grab the lighter. He pushed his way to the end and picked up the cigarettes. He heard, or imagined that he heard, the sound of several car doors slamming. He jammed the cigarettes into the inner breast pocket of his suit and clutched the lighter tightly in his fist. He did not know the layout of the castle any better than he knew the layout of the tunnel system. In the castle he could not get irrevocably lost but might be captured; with a lighter in the tunnels he could avoid dead ends and find his way out with no fear of being seen.

It was not an easy decision. He shook the lighter to gauge its remaining fuel by weight, held it to the light. Half full. Whether it would last thirty minutes or an hour was impossible to know. He put it in his pocket.

He heard voices. Lots of them. Approaching. Panic tried to seize him, so he ran for the hinged panel before the fear could freeze him in place. As he clambered through it, he remembered belatedly that the ladder had broken in half.

Doors banged open. The voices had arrived. He turned on his knees to sweep the groaning old panel shut. On the carpet, he saw, were the dirty footprints he had left on his travels in the banquet room. They led from the panel, circled the table, and dead-ended at the panel again. And he recalled having left a filthy handprint on the white tablecloth.

The latch clicked shut. Von Wessenheim got himself around the remaining upright part of the ladder and slid down it like a fireman, shattering the remaining rungs with his shoes, his teeth squeezed tightly together to hold in a scream while the wood sizzled through his hands.

TO THE HIGHEST EXTREM

60

"For God's sake pull over and loosen these," Perry said. "There's no feeling left in my hands."

At the wheel of the smashed-up Honda, headed for Indianapolis on Interstate 70 East, Alan offered him a glance in the rain-soaked evening light. "Fuck you."

Perry's arms were looped around the back of his seat, his wrists tied together with twine. His ankles were bound against each other and lashed to the mysterious rods and springs under the seat. "I'm supposed to get my hands amputated when you're done with me?"

Alan thought it over. "Yes."

Perry lapsed into silence, and Alan concentrated on ignoring him. After the cops sorted things out Dutch had stayed with Rebecca in Brazil. The fact that he was a retired police officer had helped enormously: despite crushing the kid under the car he was released on his own recognizance, especially since the uncovered corpse still held the pistol. There were five bullets left in it.

But Rebecca had needed transport to Regency Hospital in Terre Haute; the little hospital in Brazil wasn't able to do much with a serious gunshot victim other than simply stabilize her. In the ER Dutch had promised to stay by her side. The area just above Alan's left knee had suffered a bullet that had torn a chunk out of the meat there but missed all the bone. Some stitches, some wads of cotton, an injection of an antibiotic, and a compression bandage had put him back on his feet. Painfully.

Perry, though, had done nothing criminal and was simply

released. The Chaim Goldberg case showed up on the computer as reopened but the only charge filed had been against Harrison W. Thorwald. Immediately, Dutch had formed an emergency powwow with his compatriots on the small-town force, and they had thought enough of him to do what he requested. Later, Alan said his good-byes and left for Indianapolis. On the way out of Brazil he stopped at a convenience store, hoping to buy some rope, but wound up with a roll of packing twine. Later, when it was dark enough to get away with it, he left I-70 for a country road, stopped, and let Perry out of the trunk for the rest of the drive to Indy. He was nice enough, even, to remove the rag the cops had stuffed down his gullet to keep him quiet.

Another blue sign flashed past: REST AREA NEXT EXIT. Alan glanced at Perry again, who replied by cocking his head and widening his eyes at him: urgent. Alan lifted his foot from the accelerator, then after some hesitation pressed it down again. Why have mercy on the old shit? What kind of mercy had he offered Chaim, or Hank?

"Tell me why you did it," Alan said, "and I'll stop."

No reply. He squirmed in the seat with his face indicating distress. Despite the pounding Alan had given him and the time he spent in the trunk, he looked pretty good. Better than his victims, anyway.

"Last chance. Indianapolis is still a half hour away."

Perry jerked at his bonds, grunting while making no progress against them. "Okay, fine," he growled. "Turn off."

Alan hit the turn signal and slowed, then pulled onto the shoulder and brought the car to a stop with the exit still a quarter of a mile ahead. He clicked the emergency flashers on; the windshield wipers pulsed steadily back and forth. "Let's hear it."

Perry eyed him, and drew in a breath. "My hands are reaching critical, they're going to rot off if I don't get some circulation to them *now*."

"We both know that, Perry. Tell me why."

"Because since the blood supply is cut off, the tissues are dying."

Alan floored the gas. "That's it, screw you, I hope they make prosthetic hands."

"No, wait!" He let his head fall, then bobbed it back up. "I'm sorry, Alan. Loosen these things; I'll tell you everything."

"First you tell." Alan veered onto the shoulder again. "I'm listening."

"I always wanted to be famous," Perry said haltingly. "I knew that if I could pull off the greatest stunt of hypnosis ever done, I'd be on television. I'd be in the Guinness records. I would start the most monumental stir in hypnotism since the saga of Bridey Murphy, and be immortalized. And maybe even my children would come to respect me and we could become a family again."

Alan released the steering wheel. He lifted a hand and extended his index finger. "I'm actually in tears," he said, and made motions of sticking it down his own throat. "I'm so moved I must puke."

Perry glared at him. "I bare my soul and you make fun of me?"

"That horseshit would earn a flat F in English Comp 101. Try coming up with something a Ph.D. would be proud of. Perhaps the actual truth, even."

"The truth isn't always complicated, Alan. You asked, I answered."

Alan clicked the left turn signal on, examining the rain-pocked outside mirror. "I asked, you lied. End of story."

The rest area went past while rain pelted the windshield in choppy, gusting assaults. Alan nudged the wipers faster and turned the defrosters on to get rid of the steam. A green sign loomed: INDIANAPOLIS 28 MILES.

"I can't wait that long," Perry said. "My hands are probably black by now."

Alan bristled. "Rebecca Thorwald had to wait, and she had a bullet in her guts."

"If memory serves me, I was not there when she was shot."

"Who was the kid?"

"I didn't know him. I told the police that."

"Why were you living in your mother's house?"

"I already explained it. When the lunatic fringe got done with Hank, they'd come for me. 'Is it true? Is it true? Will you hypnotize me to a past life too?' And then comes the TV cameras, the reporters, the destruction of my privacy."

Alan snorted. "An easy answer for everything. Chaim Goldberg probably tripped and fell down your basement stairs, unfortunately landing in the giant blender you'd just invented. You had the language tapes and Hitler speeches because Uncle Hermann was visiting from Berlin. Christ, Perry, a first-year journalism student could see through your lies in a heartbeat."

"Sometimes the truth hurts," Perry grumbled. "Deal with it."

Again Alan swerved to the shoulder of the road, this time taking hold of Perry by his shirt when the car stopped, and jerking him as close as his bonds would allow. "Who the fuck do you think you are?" he shouted in his face, shaking him. "I used to *admire* you, I *respected* you, and all you do now is lie!"

Perry's eyes were tired but unyielding when Alan pushed him away. "Who do you expect me to be, Alan? You're going to put me on TV to confess my sins, but I have not sinned."

"You don't have to confess a damn thing, Perry. I'll do all the talking. You just stand there looking innocent while the wire services and the tabloids pick up your face. Then stand back while every inch of your life is exposed."

"Fiendishly clever," Perry muttered as the Honda found its way back onto the highway. "But it doesn't change the fact that I am in a really bad way here."

Alan looked over at him. His face was strained. Warily, he put his hand through the passage between the seats and slid his fingers across the vinyl backside of Perry's, searching low for his captive hands. When he found them they were cold, but what did that mean? He had pulled the twine as tight as he could after hauling Perry's ass out of the trunk, and at the time Perry had winced but not complained. Alan switched the dome light on and craned to see if Perry's hands had really turned black, but the angle and the shadows ruined it.

A sign winked past. GAS AHEAD, NEXT EXIT. He split off from the freeway and took the ramp. A green-and-white Sinclair station lay just to the right.

"Thank you," Perry breathed as they drove in. Alan slid the car against the sidewalk that bordered the station. He got out in the rain and limped under the harsh light to Perry's door, wondering how he could untie all the hasty knots in the tangles of twine, and then tie Perry's hands loosely enough to give him his circulation back without botching the intent. He swung the door open and bent over Perry's lap.

Perry screamed. Alan recoiled with a jump that clipped the back of his head against the rain gutter of the car, hard enough to see brief stars. Perry screamed as if his foot was mashed under a tire, as if both of his hands had been crushed in a slamming door. Recovering, awash with sudden adrenaline, Alan levered himself back inside, keeping his balance by hooking his left arm over the roof, and swung his fist into Perry's face. He screamed and bellowed. Alan hit him again. The shock of every blow sent searing pain up his arm but he hit him, hit him again, hit him until Perry's nose was bleeding and both of his eyes were swelling shut.

A hand clapped onto Alan's left shoulder. It tightened and pulled him backward. With a snarl he spun around. His knee shot pain up his entire leg; the Novocain was wearing off.

It was a large young man in a green uniform with raindrops bursting apart on his shoulders. "What the hell is going on here?"

Perry was still screaming, bawling now for help. The Sinclair man stiff-armed Alan aside and looked inside the car. In an instant he drew himself out again. "Why is this man tied up?"

Alan pushed him away. "Get lost, this is something personal."

Another employee hurried around the station. "What's going on, Jerry? Sound's like somebody's being killed."

"Call 911," Jerry said. His voice swelled with importance. "Tell them I've intercepted a kidnapping."

Fuming, Alan smashed the door shut and and got back in behind the wheel. The motor was still idling. Jerry the Sinclair worker bent back inside with something yellow in his hand. As Alan watched in disbelief he severed the layers of twine around Perry's ankles with one slice; it was a carpenter's utility knife with a shiny new blade sticking out. Crushing Perry with his body, the man hooked an arm around the seat and worked himself lower to cut his wrists free.

Perry pivoted and swung his legs out of the car. With a grunt of sudden exertion he rocked himself onto the sidewalk with a few inches of twine dangling from each wrist. His hands were as pink as his ruddy face. Alan jumped up in time to watch him scramble crazily away. Behind the station was a short stretch of manicured grass that Perry hesitantly navigated with both arms outstretched for balance. Below that was a surging creek, full of rain. The worst news was the unhindered woods that stretched beyond, a typical Indiana forest dense with scrawny trees. Inside there he could stay hidden for days.

Alan jumped out. "Thanks for nothing!" he barked at the Sinclair man. "You just let a murderer loose."

He made a face indicating lots of befuddlement. "You're a cop?"

"No. I'm Alan Weston."

"Wow. Sorry, Alan. Didn't recognize you with your face all smashed up."

Alan swung the door shut, pulled in a breath, and was about to set himself in motion when his uninjured leg buckled underneath him. Inside his head there was a painless feeling of his brain being squeezed to the side. His ears drilled out a high, electric squeal that ended, along with everything else, after four or five seconds. When he came back to himself he was surprised to find that he was lying in a puddle with rain beating down on his upturned face. The Sinclair man was bent over him with big, worried eyes.

"Did you trip on something, Alan?"

Alan hobbled to his feet. "Guess so." The sudden affliction was gone, he felt as good as before. It was the same thing that had happened a couple of hours ago; he did not require a neurosurgeon to deliver the verdict: you do not walk away from a shattering blow to the forehead, especially when it is delivered by a length of two-by-four lumber.

"Hey, your nose is bleeding something fierce," the Sinclair man said. He hauled out a stuck-together handkerchief that Alan waved away.

"Just keep an eye on my car," he said, turned, and loped after Perry.

61

Hank's eyes jumped open. The drug injected into his system did not have any gradients, no buffer zone where he rose to consciousness in a gently sleepy way, like a bubble drowsing to the surface from a depth of water. He had been out and now, bang, he was not.

It was dark. He was on a train, he could hear the rails clacking steadily below him. By the sound and feel, it was rolling along at a rapid clip. His last memory was of being at the center of a gigantic swastika, of being strangled to death by a man named Heinz. It had been a stage, the woman with the long name had wanted him to play Hitler on her stage, but instead he had starting smashing things. Then an arm was around his neck.

Afterward, nothing. No lapse of time—ten seconds ago he had been on a stage and now he was on a train in the middle of the night.

Or was it? He wanted to touch his eyelids to see if they were open but his hands were tied behind his back. He was sitting on his tailbone. When he shifted position a rope cut into his ankles: hog-tied again. Something soft was across his eyes and knotted at the back of his head. By leaning cautiously, probing with his head, he discovered the boundaries of this world: he had been stuffed—probably nailed—inside a wooden crate.

Fear swelled up but he pushed it away. He had not been put in here to die. Eventually someone would untie him and pull off the blindfold, lead him to the next venue of his life as a circus freak on the German circuit, Hank the Hitler snarling through the bars of a cage. Now he tested his ability to speak and found tape across his mouth. Nothing had been left to chance. He had become cargo.

Again he explored his world. The pain in his tailbone was growing, his buns were asleep and his legs had died. For relief he canted to one side, letting the blood flow, then the other. The crate rocked slightly. Curious, Hank wobbled himself back and forth, hearing its base clop to the left and to the right. An idea formed. He slung his weight from one side to the other, getting gradually into a rhythm, aware of hunger and thirst but ignoring them. The pain in his tailbone became a sharp agony so he focused on the steady clack of the rails below. He imagined the crate falling and shattering: he would find himself alone in an open boxcar, would leap out the door and tumble to a painless stop in the grass.

The crate rocked, the bottom of it banging violently now. With each lurch he got better at it, giving more of himself, aware that the laws of motion and inertia were immutable throughout the universe, and that eventually the crate would have to obey.

The crate teetered. Hank threw himself against the faltering side. Gravity held its breath, unable to decide.

"Do it!" Hank screamed through his nose.

It did. The crate smashed over onto its side. Wood broke and snapped as he fell heavily onto his shoulder. When things were quiet he lay unmoving, testing these new waters, getting used to the angle, arranging his next move.

He heard clumping sounds. Footsteps, maybe. Time ticked past with no meaning. Suddenly his stomach lurched as the fallen crate was hoisted back into position and set upright again.

He let his chin fall to his chest in the darkness behind the blindfold. He was not alone.

But Rønna Ulgard was. Alone in his small but very plush first-class business cabin he had drawn all the shades and locked the door. With his shirt off he jerked at the duct tape that was wrapped around his shoulders and crossed beneath his armpits. It hurt, but his mind was elsewhere.

Done with that, he disengaged the pieces of the mini-pistol from the tape: a two-inch gunmetal tube with a steel plunger that served as a firing pin, two small plastic blocks that clapped together to form a pistol grip at one end, and a cocking mechanism. He snapped the cocking mechanism onto the tube. It was a lever that could be drawn back with a thumb. No trigger was necessary, the lever would snap forward when released, striking the plunger. Pulling the plunger open now, he delved into the pants pocket that usually contained his keys and drew out a small bullet. It was standard .22 caliber, the ultimate in puny ammunition, but at close range it could pierce a human skull, shatter a human heart. He dropped it into the exposed slot and carefully let the spring in the plunger force the little bullet forward.

He stuck the little contraption under his belt and put his shirt and coat back on. Now he was armed. Reloading would be slow, but at most Herr Knecht might have two, perhaps three aides guarding Thorwald's crate in the baggage car at the tail end of the train. Abruptly he remembered Frau Dietermunde's assertion that he had grown predictable; now the gun went into the breast pocket of his pale blue shirt.

He tugged his gloves tight and sat down. At the *Bahnhof* he had purchased a rail map of France. Now he spread it across the facing seat and leaned over it, following the lines with a finger, his eyes stitched with bright seams of crimson and his brain fighting a deeper exhaustion than he had ever known. The methamphetamine he had shared with von Wessenheim after the flight to Boise was long since gone; he was now fueled only by determination. When it became necessary, as he pored over the map, he slapped his own face to stay alert. This was not going to be another haphazard, impromptu operation. No longer was he burdened by the unpredictable Karl-Luther von Wessenheim, his only focus now was on getting this job done. After roaring out of Bad Nauheim in the rented Volkswagen, he had blazed a high-speed trail to the main station in Frankfurt, where all trains from the outlying areas converged. Inside, disguised with a hat snatched from an old man's head and sunglasses plucked from the hair of a passing beauty queen, he had checked the timetables posted on the walls and waited in the shadows of the massive *Bahnhof*. Herr Knecht had disembarked and headed immediately to the freight processing office. Ticket already in hand, Ulgard sprinted to the waiting train bound south toward France, its first destination Mannheim, then Basel in Switzerland, and eventually Avignon and the Mediterranean coastal resorts that followed.

He folded the map and stuck it under the seat, the necessary areas of it memorized, and let himself lean back. Von Wessenheim owed him millions but he did not care anymore. Frau Dietermunde wanted Thorwald to be sedated for the rest of his life. The eternal soul of the Führer had survived the war but she did not care, she cared only about amusement for herself, and for her octogenarian cronies. The Hitler Youth, born out of a noble cause and tempered by the fires of war, had become pathetic. It was time, now, to get serious again.

He looked through the window at the greenery flashing past ever faster, waiting.

62

Alan surged through the knee-high water of the stream behind the Sinclair station. Rain splattered down on his head and shoulders in big warm drops. As he labored he could still see Perry. He had floated with the surging water and only now clambered out of it, laboriously grappling his way up the slick grass of the embankment. His pants were a darker black and his shirt bulged comically with water that had bunched around his waist. Alan laid himself on top of the stream and let it carry him, watching like an alligator as Perry gained the crest and stood wobbling for a moment, his hands on his knees, blowing and puffing. Then he started off toward the woods.

Alan hauled himself out of the water and climbed the sodden grass on all fours. The scooped-out bullet wound of his knee sang with the sharps and flats of serious pain. Then he was up and hobbling, breathing heavily through his nose because the inrush of air made his broken teeth ache. He shielded his face with his forearms as he lurched into the scruffy trees. Ahead, Perry was slowly forging a path.

The ground suddenly dropped. Large rocks jolted Alan's feet. With a cry he skidded to an uncertain halt, then dropped down on his butt. Blood was mingling with the water at the knee of his jeans now; the whole area thumped like a big, extra heart. Several hundred rugged feet below was an actual river, no temporary little stream created by the rain, a river just as big as the one Asshole Weston once dumped hate mail into as a media gag, the segment where he called them "love letters." In fact, almost all of them were just empty envelopes purchased at an office supply store. He had created a story where no story had existed.

After a time he stood up. Perry was long gone. Alan turned and saw the thighbone of a dinosaur zoom toward his face. He dropped to his knees. The bone whirred over his head with a low swooshing sound and smacked against a tree. Birds squawked and took flight. He jumped backward down the incline, his shoes skating on the slurry of rocks.

"You are fucking unbelievable," he said.

Perry went back into a batter's stance. The bone was a thick, deformed stick that had been stripped of its bark and crudely sharpened on one end. In his whole life Alan had never seen a log after a beaver was done with it, and here was one in Perry's hands. But Perry was fading, red-faced and gasping, visibly at the end of his endurance. He swooped it out toward Alan but Alan easily drew back.

"Just hold still," Perry croaked. He advanced, threatening with the stick.

"You're looking pretty bad," Alan said. "Give up this bullshit before you have a heart attack."

Perry swung it again, and missed. The weight of the stick kept him going; he whirled in a meandering circle and fell down, then used it to push himself upright again.

He coughed, the deep and liquid kind of cough usually heard from old men who had smoked since childhood, like Alan's own uncle Max. To Alan's disgust he spit a glob of phlegm between his muddy shoes. Strings of saliva depended from his lower lip as he again assumed a batter's stance.

"In the name of God," Alan groaned, "why are you doing this? Why did you do *any* of this? You've destroyed your friends and now you're destroying *you*!"

"Historical imperative," he panted.

"You got Sharri and Rebecca Thorwald and me shot, you got Hank Thorwald killed—all for a—*a what?*"

"Historical imperative, Alan. Do you think I *enjoyed* ruining them? Christ, I watched my own grandson get crushed under a car today, so do you think I'm doing any of this for my own gain? Hank and Rebecca were my *friends*! Hank was simply the most wonderful hypnosis subject I ever encountered. Better even than Chaim Goldberg, may he rest in peace."

Alan bristled. "Don't you mean rest in pieces?"

"Chaim killed himself, Alan. Killed himself in my basement with a plastic grocery bag over his head. I didn't know what to do with his body, where to take it, where to put it. So in the end I used a power saw. It was a horrible mess."

"You convinced him he was Hitler," Alan said softly.

"Yes. I could snap my fingers and he was under, like Hank. My only mistake was underestimating the power of his religious background, his Judaism. As soon as I had his subconscious mind believing he had been Hitler, his conscious mind began to erode."

"So he killed himself because a Jew would rather be dead than believe he was the ghost of Hitler."

Perry nodded gravely. "It still amazes me. In the meantime I have paraded dozens of students and faculty through my den, testing them over long and boring games of chess. All I was looking for was the best possible subject."

"But that doesn't answer *why*."

"Historical imperative. The tides of history dwarf the average man and render his life meaningless."

"In English."

"Fine. I made a promise to a man on his deathbed."

"And . . ."

"And now I'm dying. The same promise that killed my father."

Alan took a hobbling step closer to him, nodding, hoping to either get the stick or win Perry's confidence, but Perry, with a grunt of effort, suddenly swung it. Alan threw himself backward. Again Perry lost his footing and this time his grip: the stick sailed away, whipping round and round like a boomerang. Perry smacked down on his face with a yelp and began a slow but unstoppable tumble down the rocky embankment, clawing at the sharp gravel as he picked up speed. At the bottom of the gully, swollen with rain, the river had formed an energetic rapids complete with whitecaps and madly rushing water. It welcomed him with a splash of foam but was obviously not deep enough to drown in; all Perry had to do was stand up and it would be not much higher than his knees.

But Perry did not stand up. Instead he floated facedown and was carried away.

Alan stood at the rim of the embankment, breathing hard through his open mouth, his teeth protesting, but he waved the pain away with a mental hand. Perry was either dead or in the process of drowning. Alan did not much care anymore if he died, but his secret was dying with him. It would haunt the former starry-eyed reporter Alan Weston for the rest of his life if he could not find the answer to the secret.

He turned sideways and started down the side of the gully, his shoes carving elongated craters in the mud and gravel, his knee bleeding freely now. Perry's floating body was still in sight, caught in an eddy that twisted him in a slow spiral, then spit him out into the rapids again. At the bottom Alan had no choice but to fling himself into the water. He rose up, whipping his head back and forth to clear his eyes. The current wielded an awesome power, sweeping him along, banging his knees against the rocky bottom when he tried to stand. Perry's white shirt was a beacon; Alan swam toward him, each stroke surprisingly increasing his speed. He got to Perry and labored to flip him over, then struggled against the current to shove him toward the riverbank. Finally, gasping and coughing and at the end of his endurance, he was able to push Perry into calm waters. Clumping up on shore again, he dragged him out and collapsed, his chest heaving.

Something changed, he did not know what. He opened his eyes. A rock the size of a soccer ball was zooming toward his face like the moon falling from the sky. With a squawk he rolled to the side and staggered upright.

Perry was struggling to lift the rock out of the shallow hole it had created in the mud where Alan's head had been. Alan did not need to think before acting, he had played this scene before and knew the price of hesitation. He took a step and kicked out, on the upswing his foot catching Perry's chest.

The power of it flipped Perry over onto his back. Alan lifted the rock, swooped it overhead, then sat on Perry's stomach and brought it down on his face. Once was not enough, the old bastard had nine lives. He lifted the rock and smashed it down, raised it, smashed it, raised it again. Perry's face was pulverized, his nose mashed out of existence, both cheekbones crushed, his mouth an empty, bleeding hole.

"Tell me the rest!" Alan screamed, holding the rock overhead.

Perry twisted his head back and forth. The rain washed blood through his white hair, streaking it pink.

"Tell me!"

His eyes were sunk under two pools of crimson blood. When he opened them the effect was ghastly. "Ask Hank," he gurgled. "Hank knows."

"Tell me!"

Perry's hands rose up, weaving, and eventually locked coldly around Alan's throat. He strangled him without strength. With a groaning whimper Alan swung the rock down again. Bones crunched; he knew he was killing him but it wasn't really Perry anymore. He lifted the rock up and brought it down one more time, unaware that he was weeping as he did. "In the name of God," he moaned, "Hank is dead, so just tell me."

Enough was enough. Perry's forehead was crushed. His eyes had closed. Sickened, Alan heaved the bloody rock aside and wobbled upright. Perry's secrets had stayed his own until the end. Whether or not that was admirable he would need years to decide.

"Alaah?"

Shock paralyzed him in mid-thought. No one could talk through that face, no one could survive the damage. He had taken a few steps away but forced himself to turn now. "What?"

"Hak iss dead?"

Alan moved closer. "Yes."

"Theh cuh here. I ill tell you."

Crouching beside him, Alan leaned closer. There could be

no tricks, Perry was ruined, Perry was dying fast. Despite himself Alan took one of his hands and squeezed it. "Tell me, Perry," he said softly, and bent low.

Perry told him.

63

Rønna Ulgard left his private cabin at noon. He slid the door gently shut and walked carefully down the narrow aisle. At this point probably everyone was in the dining cars save for the train crew, but he had not chosen this moment because of that. According to the map they would soon cross the most uninhabited area of the journey. After killing the men guarding Thorwald in his crate Ulgard intended to simply push the bodies out the door. It would be days, maybe even a week before they were found.

He passed silently through two sleeping cars, where every berth was hidden behind drawstring curtains. The cars were all joined by walkways encased in pleated rubber walls where the noise of the wind murmured and whistled and the tracks clacked unnervingly loudly. He then traversed eleven standard cars with their huge upward-curving windows where the passengers spent the daylight hours enjoying the scenery. Finally, bringing up the tail end, was the baggage car. Ulgard carefully lifted the aluminum bar that allowed entry, and slowly pushed the door open with his gloved fingertips. Nothing was fancy inside, it was a colorful Eurorail on the outside but an ordinary boxcar on the inside.

He stepped in and eased the door shut. The boxcar smelled faintly of excrement. Ulgard stood motionless for two full minutes, swaying with the motion of the train while his eyes adjusted to the gloom cast by a couple of tiny vents in the ceiling, trying to get used to the smell. Suitcases and cardboard boxes came slowly into view, stacked against the walls and up to the ceiling, held in place by rubber netting. He saw the humped outline of mailbags, several bicycles lashed to the wall, a stack of surfboards, and two sets of scuba-diving tanks. But no wooden crates, not right here. He ventured deeper inside, one hand pressed to his chest to snatch out the unglamorous pistol if the need arose.

The smell got stronger. Ulgard saw that six or seven animal cages were secured to the wall at the rim of the huge sliding door, one of them big enough to house a Shetland pony. A growl drifted out of it as he moved closer. So did the smell. When he skirted past the cage the animal shrieked and threw itself against the wire. Fingers jabbed through it. With a flare of surprise he realized that it was a monkey of some kind, a chimpanzee or maybe even a gorilla.

Instantly, voices came alive. Ulgard dropped into a crouch, frowning, listening, his hand inside his breast pocket.

"Was für ein Lärm!"

"Bloss ein Schimpanse."

"So laut?"

He waited, unmoving. It appeared that Thorwald was being guarded by two of Knecht's men. He had expected it: he brought the tiny gun out and touched his thumb to the hammer. As they continued talking he got down onto his stomach to drag himself around the obstacles with his elbows. By the sound he knew the men were within touching distance of each other— the only problem in killing them was the time it would take to reload. He paused long enough to pluck another bullet out of his pocket and place it under his tongue for safekeeping.

The train leaned into a curve. Baggage and boxes shifted slightly against their restrainers. Ulgard managed to find a path behind Knecht's two goons, understanding now that they were sitting haphazardly on a couple of loose boxes. He turned to silently rise up on his knees behind one of the men, his pistol firmly in his hand, so close now to the man's head that he could smell the fragrant oil he used on his hair.

He snapped the hammer back, restructured his aim in the gloomy dark, and released it.

The noise of the pistol was no more than a balloon popping. Knecht's man spasmed into a reflexive spread-eagle be-

fore gravity pulled him down to the floor in a crumpled heap.
The other man stood up, looking wildly around. Ulgard
shook out the spent bullet casing and held the plunger back
long enough to insert the next one in with his tongue. For a
bare touch of time the other man sat down again as if to relive
the episode; Ulgard poked the tiny barrel against his head
and snapped the hammer again.

Pop! The owner of the gun store in Boise swore that he
would be satisfied with this preposterous little pistol or get
his money back; Ulgard was satisfied. Knecht's other man
slumped from his perch and spilled across the floor.

Ulgard stood up. "Mr. Thorwald?" he called softly into the
gloom. "I am here to save you. Where are you?"

Something thumped softly. Thorwald signaling his location? Or an animal restless in its cage?

"Can you speak, Mr. Thorwald? Or have you been bound
and gagged?"

Thump. Thump-thump. It sounded like a board rocking
back and forth, maybe Thorwald's crate as he tried to signal.
Ulgard shuffled in a circle as he loaded the pistol with a
fresh bullet. It was also possible—probable—that Thorwald
was still drugged out of his mind and the noise was just the
chimpanzee.

"I am Herr Ulgard, an official with Amnesty International.
Do you remember me?"

The thumping stopped. Ulgard rolled his eyes at his mistake. Frau Dietermunde had surely told him that von Wessenheim was not even remotely connected to Amnesty
International, and by default Rønna Ulgard. Now Thorwald
was afraid of him. That, or the monkey had gotten tired.

He dropped the pistol into a pocket. Without more light
this could take forever. He stalked through the maze of boxes
and baggage, following thin slits of light that hinted at the
boxcar's door. It wasn't difficult to find. With a grunt he lifted
the big steel lever that held it shut and spread the panels apart
a few feet on well-oiled rollers. Warm wind and fresh afternoon sunlight rushed in, the wind tugging at his jet-black hair
and the light burning into his sleepless eyes. Examining the
car from this newly visible perspective revealed that things

were stacked more neatly than he had believed. All items bore a standardized label revealing their contents, though he doubted very much that Thorwald's crate indicated a human being inside. The animals were sequestered from the other baggage, and the suspected monkey turned out to be a chimp indeed, blinking drearily against the sharp light with its lips inverted to reveal its teeth.

Ulgard forged his way back to the two dead men. Point-blank head shots rarely bled more than a few drops because the brain swelled quickly upon injury and stayed swollen after death, plugging the bullet hole. He dragged the bodies one at a time to the door and rolled them out with a foot, then went back to smear the blood into meaningless, quick-drying slashes with his shoes.

"Mr. Thorwald," he said as he pulled out the pistol and began reloading it, "I'm sorry for my deception in regard to Amnesty International, but I am truly here to free you. Herr von Wessenheim and Herr Knecht want something from you—it must seem to you that the whole world wants something from you—but I want nothing. Nothing except your freedom."

Seconds droned on. If he was awake it was possible that he had seen, or at least heard, the execution of Knecht's men. "My name is Inspector Schmidt," Ulgard said. "I am an agent with Interpol, the European police agency you may have heard of. Please be assured that you have nothing to fear from me. It was unfortunate, but I had to kill Knecht's men before they killed you."

With a shriek the monkey smashed against the wires of its cage. Ulgard lurched backward, startled, and instinctively raised the pistol, firing it. The bullet broke a chunk from the wooden part of the cage; it flapped through the air. The monkey screeched and capered. For one of the few times in his career, Ulgard was unnerved. But rage replaced this feeling. He stormed over to the cage and jockeyed it out of position. *"Verdammte Schimpanse!"* he bellowed, trying to push it across the floor. When it moved annoyingly slowly he spun and pressed his back against it, going into a squat, determined to shove it out the door.

But at this low level motion caught his eye. He relaxed, trying to find it again, staying quietly in place.

Again, motion. It came from inside a squat little crate that had small ventilation holes drilled in two rows around its circumference. A thin chain was wrapped around it like the ribbon of a birthday gift and it had a large padlock on top. He dropped to his knees and shuffled toward it until he was close enough to peer through one of the holes.

Blackness. Then a motion. Another animal cage? He approached it. "Mr. Thorwald?" he asked gently.

Thorwald's head bobbed up, visible through the pencil-thin shafts of light. He was indeed gagged and blindfolded.

Ulgard rose higher on his knees and got the pistol out. As he dumped the empty shell, Hank Thorwald let out a low moan through his nose.

"You have been nailed shut inside this miserable crate," Ulgard said. "I'll have to shoot the lock, then I will be able to lever it open to get you out. Hang on."

He got another bullet out and put it between his teeth, and again used his tongue to insert it. When that was done he let the plunger draw itself in. Holding the pistol like a dainty set of tweezers, he pressed the tiny barrel against the padlock.

"Can you move to the left side?" he asked politely. "I don't wish to shoot you."

Hank Thorwald nodded his head slowly, and shifted position. The crate rocked. Ulgard drew the plunger back with his left hand.

"*Oskar!*"

The shout jerked Ulgard upright at the moment the hammer mechanism of the pistol snapped forward. It fired with its customary little *pop!* Wood chips burst up and Thorwald immediately slumped inside the crate, if not dead at least seriously wounded.

Ulgard rose and whirled, baring his teeth. Frau Dietermunde, dressed uncharacteristically in pants, stepped from behind a stack of latticed crates, where she had been watching him through the gaps in the boards, for how long he did not know. His voice, when he spoke, bristled with rage. "What in the hell are you doing on this train?"

She ignored the question and strode toward him. "What have you done this time?" she demanded. "Have you killed him?" She bent over the crate, then straightened. "You are a bastard child," she hissed in his face. "Your father was just as dark and swarthy as you are, Oskar-Adolf, he had the same black hair and olive skin. And do you want to know why?"

Ulgard was trying to reload the pistol. "Shut up, Mother," he said as he worked. The muscles of his jaw tightened and released, tightened and released.

"He was an American soldier. He raped me in a burned-out building on Kaiserstrasse near the Hauptwache, in Frankfurt."

Ulgard drew the plunger back. "Shut up, you old hag, do not speak of this."

He was positioning a fresh bullet inside, difficult to do with gloves on, when Frau Dietermunde reached out abruptly and slapped the pistol from his grasp. When it spun to the floor of the car the plastic grip broke into its two original pieces while the barrel continued on to jump between the sunlit gap between the doors, lost forever.

Ulgard's face twisted with hate. His hands ached to strangle her but instead fastened on Thorwald's crate. With a guttural roar he pulled it out of position and skidded it closer to the doors. A broad sheen of blood described a curving slash on the floor as the crate moved. He hurled himself at the doors and forced them farther apart; a French afternoon swirled in on a tornado of wind. In the scathing light he dropped to his haunches and peered inside the holes of the crate. Thorwald lay motionless. Blood drained from his skull.

"You killed him!" Ulgard shouted over the noise. The rails clacked rapidly underneath. "You killed the only man you ever loved!"

She approached him, her bleached-blonde hair corkscrewing in the wind. "You expected me to love *you*, Oskar?" she shouted. "I could not, I cannot, I *will* not. Would you like to hear why?"

He rose to his feet, stricken instantly with the terror that had dogged him since boyhood. "No," he said.

A small and peculiar smile touched her lips. "I will tell you anyway. Your father was a Jew, Oskar."

He mashed both gloved hands over his ears with his eyes crunched shut, grimacing as if in pain.

"He was a degenerate Jew in the United States Army, a dark and swarthy Mediterranean Jew, he was your father, Oskar-Adolf Dietermunde, and I could have killed you at birth, but I did not."

Ulgard lowered his hands but kept his eyes closed.

"And I have spent every moment since then wishing I had wrapped your umbilical cord around your newborn neck and strangled you dead."

His eyelids lifted slowly. He took a deep breath. "So you punished me with these." He pulled his gloves from his hands. The marching rows of blue swastikas were sheened with sweat, flashing in the sunlight.

"To remind your German half of your lifelong duty to the Führer."

"You lie! Here sits your Führer in a wooden crate, he returned from the dead and you instantly sold him as if he were a horse."

Frau Dietermunde advanced on him, her old bravado intact. "The Hitlerjugend worships only one Führer, and his name is Adolf Hitler. Hank Thorwald is a pathetic shadow of that man, a curiosity, a freak."

"A bit of memorabilia to be traded at auction."

"That and nothing more."

"And when he is dead you will have him stuffed."

She stepped close. "Now leave me," she spat in his face. "Forget that you have a mother, and I can at last forget that I have a bastard Jew for a son."

Ulgard dropped his gloves and grinned at her. "I have read that after the war German girls traded sex for chocolate bars," he said. "Chocolate bars and nylons."

She swung out to slap him. He snagged her arm in one fist. "Good-bye, Mother."

He dragged her to the open doorway. She began to scream. She kept screaming as he took her by her shoulders, lifted her, and heaved her out into the sunlight. The Eurorail was moving fast and the roadbed was black gravel. He looked back to watch her touch down; crimson blood burst up in a long, misting cloud as she tumbled like a race car smashing itself to pieces. Sudden tears formed in his eyes. It would take days to find all of her.

As he turned he saw that he was standing in Thorwald's blood, and wondered what he, as a Jew, should do with Hitler's corpse.

64

Dutch got off the phone deciding that he was tired of the old bitch anyway. Forty-eight years with the same woman defied logic. Before he had retired from the police force, Mildred hadn't minded his long and often odd working hours, but now that he had nothing but time to kill she wanted him to kill all of it with her.

So he hung up on her. A couple of hours ago he had been dodging bullets, then had to kill a man by running him over with a car. Mildred was mad because his TV dinner had gotten cold. She began to shout. Dutch walked away from the row of blue pay phones in the lobby of Regency Hospital trying to recall the name of a good divorce lawyer. But hell, it would never happen.

Rebecca had been in surgery for almost two hours. Dutch went back into the elevator at the end of the corridor, punched the number two, and rose up alone and in silence. In his years on the force he had gotten to know a few of the doctors here, had helped out in the ER when needed after he brought in a minor stabbing or shooting victim, and in the years since he'd retired those ER docs had risen to higher rank. Best of all, they remembered him.

A soft, invisible bell dinged and the doors whisked apart. Dutch stepped out, wondering—not for the first time—if his diagnosis of Rebecca's bullet wound, and the diagnosis of the hospital medics in Brazil, had been correct. Maybe one of her kidneys had gotten blown to pieces instead of her appendix, maybe her lower spine was shattered, maybe she was hanging on to life by a thread.

He walked to the intensive care section. The lights inside were dimmed for the night. Some of the machines flashed glowing green messages in the secret code only nurses and doctors could read, while others pulsed and hissed, the sounds audible even through the pebbled glass. Dutch shoved his hands in his pockets, wondering if his presence here was necessary at all, and turned around.

He gasped and fell back against the glass: a pretty young doctor dressed in a white lab coat stood an inch from his nose. "Is that you, Dutch?" she asked as she took a backward step.

"Dutch? Uh, yeah, I'm him."

She offered her hand. "Long time no see."

Dutch eyed the golden name tag on her chest. "Vance?" he said wonderingly, then shook her hand with enthusiasm. "Dr. Diane Vance! Last time I saw you, you were in pigtails!"

She grinned. "I was a twenty-five-year-old intern. Remember how you pinned that guy down when he went ballistic in the ER, that guy on PCP? It was at that moment that I fell in love with you."

He looked her up and down. "I wish like hell you'd have told me, girl. I might have gotten more that night than a black eye and a dislocated shoulder."

They laughed. Dutch figured she had something in mind and the more time she spent dodging the subject, the worse the news would be.

Her face changed. "Dutch," she said, "I'm not a surgeon, but I did pop in to ask Dr. Kinney how your friend Rebecca Thorwald was faring, and talked to him while he worked."

He nodded. "So she's still in surgery."

"She is still in surgery. It turns out that the bullet she took was a nine-millimeter hollow point."

"Oh my God," Dutch whispered, raising a finger to his lips.

"It fractured into eight distinct pieces after it entered her body. Several of the fragments were stopped by her hip and pelvic bones, doing only minor damage. Bone is pretty tough stuff."

"Yeah," he said.

"A couple of other fragments destroyed her right kidney."

Dutch rubbed his forehead. "I was afraid of that."

"She suffered some intestinal damage as well. Dr. Kinney's confident he can restructure everything, but we'll have to wait and see."

"Good enough," he said. "And how's her daughter doing?"

"She's been running a 102-degree fever for the last twenty hours and is unresponsive."

"Meaning?"

"Infection. We're gorging her with antibiotics."

Dutch dropped his head. "Looks like they're both in for a long haul."

She used her fingers to smooth an eyebrow, frowning. "Rebecca Thorwald will most likely survive," she said. "We'll keep working on the daughter."

"Nothing to do but wait, then? Wait for good news?"

Dr. Diane Vance smiled. "I'd sure like to have a cup of coffee with you down in the cafeteria, if you call that good news."

Returning her smile, he shook his head. "It is, but I think I'll just stay right here till the lady's out of surgery."

The doctor stepped back. "Sure, Dutch. But I could bring a cup back for you. Black?"

"Black would be just fine."

She offered him a wink and walked away.

Dutch found a seat and settled in for a long wait.

65

Rønna Ulgard leaned out into the blasting hurricane of wind. The Eurorail train was hitting its maximum speed of 120 miles per hour as it sizzled over the railway toward Lyon in the south of France; his normally placid hair kicked up wildly while his eyes narrowed to black slots. The countryside was unremarkable here, but a deep river gorge lay ahead where a tributary river joined the Rhône. But it would be best to heave Thorwald overboard here in the open country—boaters and sunbathers tended to occupy the river and its banks—simply heave him overboard just as he had done for the whore who had been his mother.

It was all so devilishly clear now. In the ruins of war, young Frau Dietermunde had sold herself for food or clothing, probably dozens or even hundreds of times. She had even prostituted herself to a dark-skinned Jew. He wondered what she got in exchange, then let the thought disintegrate in the face of the wind.

Drawing back inside the car, he set his mouth in a firm line and worked Thorwald's crate to the edge of the door, grunting with effort while the wind drove tears from his eyes. Now one more shove would send it to the roadbed. He leaned out again. His own naked hands caught his attention. He was a Jew branded with the mark of Hitler. Worse than that, he hated Jews. He had been trained to hate them since birth for the destruction of the Third Reich. He had become perhaps the world's only Jewish Nazi.

He knelt in front of the crate and looked inside. If Thorwald wasn't dead, he was nearly so. In the depths of his being resided Adolf Hitler. Frau Dietermunde had been right in one respect: he had come back too early. Too early to revitalize the National Socialist movement, and too early to wreak vengeance on the Jews. He was of no help to the Nazis, and presented no threat to the Jews. Either way, he was of no consequence to the two sides of Rønna Ulgard, National Socialist patriot and Jew.

Ulgard placed his hands against the crate and strained to shove it out the door. It hung up against the track that supported the rolling doors. Standing, he lifted it slightly.

"Herr Ulgard!"

He spun around, his face drawn with alarm, then going slack with disbelief. By all reasoning the man who had shouted his name should be Herr Knecht on the trail of the missing Frau Dietermunde, or perhaps the trainman in charge of baggage investigating the open cargo door, but it was neither. Instead, filthy and disheveled and framed in a halo of angelic sunlight, stood Karl-Luther von Wessenheim.

"Jesus fucking Christ," Ulgard breathed in English.

"Isn't that Thorwald inside?" von Wessenheim blared over the roaring wind. "Have you lost your mind?"

"Stay back," Ulgard shouted. "Back, or I'll throw you out too!"

Von Wessenheim advanced a step. The floor was slightly discolored in a long, wet smear. "Stay calm, you must stay calm. Tell me what has happened."

"My mother was a whore," Ulgard groaned into the wind. "And my father was a Jew."

Von Wessenheim stared at him. How could it matter at this point what his mother and father had been? If his father was a Jew, it might explain his lack of Nordic features, but not why his eyes had taken on a madman's gleam. "You must be exhausted," von Wessenheim said carefully. "We both are. Let's shut the door and release Thorwald from his cage, then relax for a moment."

Ulgard silently shook his head as the wind flattened his shiny black hair against his skull, then burst it apart again.

"Remember the money," von Wessenheim said carefully.

"Give me Thorwald and we will go to the bank in Frankfurt for your money."

"Jews worship money," he said mechanically, "Jews sell their souls to the devil for money, Jews control the money while the Aryans toil in the fields." Suddenly he smiled. "You do not owe me money, Herr von Wessenheim. Not a Pfennig, no money at all. In fact, I owe *you* money." He stuck a hand inside his jacket and pulled out a handful of stray bills and coins. Von Wessenheim noticed his hands then: blue. A strange and faded sort of blue.

Ulgard threw the money at him. The wind kicked it in wild directions before sucking it out of the car completely; the coins were content to twirl on the floor. "If I were a Jew I could not have done that," he said. His eyes seemed to be bulging, the muscles of his jaw pulsing at his temples. "If I were, in fact, a Jew, I *would* not have done that. Any idiot can see the truth." He went into a sudden squat and pushed the crate farther out the door. The thundering wind pulled it out of his hands and spun it in a squealing half circle deeper into the dimness of the car; von Wessenheim's intended scream of horror left his mouth as a toneless blurt of relief. Ulgard dropped to his hands and knees to save himself from plunging headfirst through the cargo door.

"Have you gone *insane?*" von Wessenheim roared, advancing. "We moved heaven and earth to find this man!"

Ulgard tottered to his feet in the wedge of sunlight. Below him the wheels squealed into a curve of the tracks, metal zinging hotly against metal while the wedge slowly broadened as the train turned to the south. "I believe he is dead," he said.

Von Wessenheim gasped. A fresh smear across the floor had been painted there by the blood-soaked bottom of the crate. "My God," he said. "What happened?"

Ulgard's face grew overcast. "Frau Dietermunde made me do it."

"*What?* Where is she?"

The big man laughed. It was such an unexpected reaction that von Wessenheim took a quick backward step and nearly fell when the train lurched suddenly. He thrust out both hands and caught a tall wooden crate for balance.

"Straight out the door," Ulgard said, jerking a thumb toward the rectangle of blurring scenery. "Splat."

Von Wessenheim lost his ability to breathe for a period of time. Then: "You *killed* the woman?"

Ulgard nodded. "She was my mother, and a whore."

Von Wessenheim swayed on his feet, but not from the motion of the train. If Frau Dietermunde were truly Ulgard's mother, the implications were staggering. "Tell me it is not true," he said, already sick inside. "Please."

"She directed the entire scene, the entire time, through me. I am telling you this because I am not a Jew and no longer want your money."

Von Wessenheim clung to the crate to keep from falling to the floor. "The old soldier? In Boise? Was he a lie as well?"

"And a fine actor, for someone so elderly."

Von Wessenheim pressed his forehead against the grainy wooden side of the crate that supported him. His soul, his very being, was swirling inside him as fast as the wind, rushing down a mental drain. He had been Frau Dictermunde's puppet all along. How she and her fellows must have laughed at him.

"What about Thorwald, to make my shame complete," he asked dully. "An actor? The blood is red water, and the Hitler Youth are secretly watching this final scene?"

"No. Hank Thorwald is real. He was the only real thing in the entire charade. And now he has been shot and killed."

Von Wessenheim closed his eyes and crushed his face against the crate. If he were not so utterly drained and exhausted from the ordeal of the last few days, he knew he would weep. The final heir to the royal house of Wessenheim had become a pathetic court jester in a castle of ghosts. It had survived seven centuries and the ruin of Germany in the war, but would not survive him; upon his death everything would be sold at auction.

When he raised his head, Ulgard was again trying to shove Thorwald's crate out the door. His movements were somehow clumsy and off-kilter, as if he could not concentrate on the task long enough to finish it. Through its airholes Thorwald was a dark figure thumping back and forth as the crate jerked about. Suddenly, despite the roaring wind and the clattering tracks below, he heard Thorwald groan. Or perhaps he screamed through a mouth that was bound shut, a scream of agony through his nose.

Ulgard heard it and stepped back. Von Wessenheim could almost see the hair on the back of his neck bristle. "Yet the Führer lives," he said wonderingly. "Am I a Jew, or am I not?"

Von Wessenheim hurled himself at the crate and slid to his knees beside it. Thorwald was alive inside, twisting and rocking, screaming a strange scream. Madly von Wessenheim went at the big padlock that joined the chains together on top, wrenching it back and forth, rising to hammer it with a fist. If, despite Frau Dietermunde, the goddess of Fate had truly brought him together with Thorwald in a jail cell, if Fate had kept the man alive after losing so much blood, then Fate would see the drama played out to its end.

With a sudden bang the crate almost jumped out of his grasp. Von Wessenheim turned with a shout: Ulgard had rammed Thorwald's crate with a smaller one he had propelled across the bloody metal floor. The distance was too short for any kind of speed and Thorwald's crate had only moved a few inches, but a few more blows would send it out the door. With his heart pounding threadily in his throat and his hands shaking, von Wessenheim dragged it back, then rounded on Ulgard.

"You get the hell out of here!"

Ulgard stalked over and retrieved the crate, then grunted and strained as he dragged it back. Beneath his wild hair his face was dark and expressionless. He hunkered over and drove the crate forward again. Von Wessenheim leapt sideways before they crashed together. On its bloody lubrication Thorwald's crate squealed almost to the edge of the doorway this time; Ulgard was putting more energy into it. Enraged, von Wessenheim bent over the unwelcome crate, vised it in his arms, and propelled it back into the shadows while his shoes slipped and caught on the wet floor. Whirling around he faced Ulgard again.

"Your services are terminated!" he bellowed with all the power his lungs could gather, then pulled in another breath. "I will pay you every dollar I promised, or I will swear to God never to pay you. Just tell me which it will be, and go."

Ulgard breathed in von Wessenheim's face. His dark eyes were small, his eyelids heavy but restless. "No one must ever know of this. If I am a Jew, I am a dead man, the Hitler Youth will think I'm an informer, they will kill me. No one can know this."

Alarm trickled through von Wessenheim's blood. "I will never tell," he said. "You have my word on that."

"Not good enough," Ulgard said dreamily. Then the focus came back to his eyes. In a sudden, swift motion he snatched von Wessenheim in a bear hug and toted him to the doorway. Von Wessenheim jerked and fought, his alarm now a full-blown panic. The hot morning sun struck the back of his head and neck; the wind tore at his clothes. With his arms pinned to his sides he could only pedal his feet in a useless blur.

"*I will never tell!*" he screamed in Ulgard's face, writhing. "Please, *please!*"

Ulgard stopped at the edge of the doorway. Von Wessenheim's right foot struck something that imprisoned it.

"Good-bye, Herr von Wessenheim," Ulgard said, and flung him out.

66

Von Wessenheim screamed. For a crazy moment he was hanging suspended in the sunlit air; then gravity seized him and he dropped like a stone. His right foot, snared under one of the chains around the sides of Thorwald's crate, was jerked into an excruciating angle as his weight bottomed out. He felt the bones of his ankle snap, and screamed again.

In front of his face as he dangled upside down was a shiny steel wheel the size of a manhole cover, spinning at a mad pace and occasionally zinging out a spray of hot white sparks. The wind was trying to suck him under the baggage car, so he clawed wildly at the car's dirty underside, trying to push himself away from the wheel, aware that the black gravel roadbed, smelling of hot tar and burned diesel, was just a hand's breadth below his head.

He twisted around to look up and got a faceful of blinding sunshine and a roar of pain from his fractured ankle. But he was able to see—on and off—Ulgard leaning out the open doorway of the baggage car, his clothes whipping against his body. Once it seemed as if their eyes made contact, then Ulgard drew suddenly back. Von Wessenheim's muscles could not keep up the strain and he tumbled downward again to swing like a pendulum powered by the gusting wind, his broken ankle crunching back and forth, his face stretched in a grin of agony. Again he twisted himself as high as he could get, clawing at the Eurorail's aluminum skin, splintering his fingernails when they encountered rivets. Now he saw that Ulgard had a shoulder pressed to the crate and was straining to push it out, but it had become wedged in the lower corner of the doorway, stuck in the track the doors rolled on. Shards of bloody wood split from the base as he manhandled it. Again von Wessenheim was forced to drop down from exhaustion. His ankle was entering a kind of catatonic state; the pain had electrified him with its worst and now was backing down to a level that was dwindling toward numbness.

He tensed every muscle and rose again. His fingertips caught hold of the bottom of the doorway. Ulgard appeared beside the crate, his mouth moving with words that were impossible to hear. Von Wessenheim saw his gloveless hands clearly for the first time but was in no position to waste energy in wonderment. Ulgard bent and began to pluck von Wessenheim's fingers away but he was able to lunge upward. His hand snapped tight around Ulgard's wrist.

"Help me!" von Wessenheim screamed. "In the name of God, pull me up!"

Ulgard eyed him, trying absently to tug away from his grip. When realization returned to his lackluster eyes, he fixed them on von Wessenheim's hand and began pawing at it with his strange blue ones.

"*No!*" von Wessenheim screamed at him. "*Noooooo!*"

"Let go of me!" Ulgard snarled.

Von Wessenheim's hand was clenched in a death grip. When Ulgard set to the task of prying his fingers away from his captured wrist von Wessenheim, in desperation, gave Ulgard's wrist a fierce jerk, hoping to pull himself high enough to transfer his grip to the crate. It worked, but nothing like he had expected. Ulgard, off balance and in danger of falling out, reflexively caught hold of the crate.

The crate jumped. It teetered at the edge. Ulgard released his hold, arms pinwheeling briefly, before falling from the train. Von Wessenheim whipped his head around to watch him being torn to pieces on the hot black gravel. But what he saw instead ripped the breath from his lungs.

The train was on a trestle spanning a river. Ulgard was performing lazy somersaults in the naked air as he plunged toward the river a hundred feet below. He smashed against an outcropping of stone and bounced from it as if made of rubber, fell farther, and slammed down on another. His body, tumbling bonelessly now as it progressed down the gorge, finally arrived at the bottom, rolling to a stop on a thin strand of beach. Small figures below scurried around, people enjoying the river on a hot day.

Von Wessenheim held on to the crate in terror. He turned his head from the scene below and pressed his face to the rough wood of the crate. By swiveling an eye he was able to peer inside one of the airholes. Thorwald was silent now, slumped as if dead.

Suddenly he sat up. Inside the crate he began to slam back and forth.

"God, no!" von Wessenheim shouted, and braced himself tighter against the crate.

Thorwald kept it up. The crate shifted and groaned. Von Wessenheim hazarded another glance below. The trestle was just wide enough to allow the train passage, there was no danger of being smashed to pieces on huge black railroad ties. Instead there would be a clean drop into the canyon. Thorwald rocked back and forth, faster, harder.

"*Halt!*" von Wessenheim screamed. "*Aufhören damit!*"

Thorwald pumped himself back and forth, working with the determination of a bodybuilder. Von Wessenheim remembered a bit of English and shouted it: "*STOP TO BE DOING THAT!*"

Thorwald stopped. There was a distinct cracking sound and the crate fell out the door. Wood crunched as it caught the edge of the trestle. The wind velocity changed and von Wessenheim found himself clinging to a satellite plunging suddenly out of orbit, rotating gently while the bright circle of the sun turned around it, brightness exchanging itself for shadow, shadow for brightness. In a move not requiring thought he pushed himself away from the tumbling crate, in the deepest corner of his mind aware that if he were free of it and could hit the water feetfirst, he might survive.

His fractured ankle coughed out a new blast of pain from its tangled place in the chains; it was still held fast, there could be no feetfirst entry into the water. With a groan he crossed his arms over his head as the scenery rushed up to kill him.

67

The crate slammed into the river. Water belched up in a sparkling geyser. The Sunday beachgoers who had not been aware of Rønna Ulgard's long fall snapped their heads around at the sudden explosion in the middle of the river. People sat up in their beach chairs and lifted their sunglasses. A trio of teenagers turned their eyes from a mini-television and rose wonderingly to their feet in the sand. When the geyser collapsed the cloud of mist created by the impact drifted across the sun, staining the air with the colors of the rainbow, a tapestry of red and blue and yellow.

On the tossing water the crate had burst apart to become a raft. Von Wessenheim bobbed facedown while Hank lay on his back on the scatter of wood, dazed and broken but alive. His shoes had been torn from his feet. His blindfold had separated from his head and his hands were free of their bonds, but at a price: midway between his left elbow and wrist his forearm had a new and painful joint in it. For a time he stared at the fracture, then looked up to the brilliant sky. The underside of the train trestle was of interest, but the sun on his face was too bright, so he rolled on his side.

The raft was spreading, it would soon be nothing but planks. He had lost enough blood to be unconscious, but the water was cold and he was finally out of the crate and in his wandering mind he thought that he might live just a little bit longer, perhaps long enough to make it to shore. If he passed out in the water he would drown.

With his unbroken arm he began to paddle his disintegrating craft toward the people on the beach. A herd of them was gathering together but no one was swimming out to help. He did not know why. Maybe they thought a movie was being filmed here, maybe they thought it was a stunt. Or maybe they knew who he was and hoped he would die.

Von Wessenheim floated slowly past. Hank reached out and turned him over in the water. His eyelids and lips were blue. Grunting with pain and exhaustion, Hank tried to drag him up onto the boards of the shattered crate but they simply separated, some of them drifting away. The old man was not breathing, so Hank released him.

Von Wessenheim coughed. Water surged out of his nose. He turned his head and vomited a cloudy liquid into the river's green water. Hank reached out, his fingers surprisingly bluish and translucent from the loss of blood, and tried to haul him aboard again. With a weary groan the remaining boards of the crate spread away and Hank was dropped into the water. He kicked his feet to rise up and realized they were still tied together at his ankles. At the surface, trying to ignore the excruciating angles his left arm made as the water funneled over it, he turned himself in the water and looked at the unpopulated side of the river: the steep walls of the canyon dropped down to meet the water without even a hint of interruption.

He struck off for the shore where the people were gathered, feebly kicking his bound legs like a dolphin's tail and scooping erratically at the water with his right hand. Behind him von Wessenheim began to thrash. Hank turned again: the old man had taken hold of a single thin board and was gobbling panicky nonsense because its meager buoyancy would not support his weight. As Hank watched he lost hold of the board and frantically began to claw at the water. He sank out of sight, then regained the surface with a burst of froth and bubbles, gasping. He sank again, burst up again. His eyes were huge and rolling as he sank out of sight.

He could not swim. Hank gave a huge kick of his captured legs and reached out to snag the old man when he next popped up. The effort was too much: his vision dimmed to gray and then black; his next conscious moment he was at the river's surface coughing out water. A swift turn of his body showed that von Wessenheim had not resurfaced, was, in fact, probably headed for the bottom. But Hank waited, aware that bright red blood was dripping off his chin to stain the water. In better times he could hold his breath for eighty seconds, plenty of time to dive deep. Right now he would be lucky to make it to five.

Von Wessenheim finally clawed his way into view again, gagging on water and air and with mindless terror on his face like a rubber fright mask. Hank noosed his right arm around the old man's neck and stretched him out on his back. Pumping with his shackled feet he moved toward the shore, each stroke a slow-motion expenditure of an energy that no longer seemed to have a source, yet came again and again.

Finally—he would never know how many minutes or chunks of hours later—his heels scrubbed through mud, then sand. Shadows bobbed across the glistening water and were replaced by real people. As he was dragged to shore amid a jumble of sights and sounds and the brutal sun flashing in his eyes, it came to him that the woman carefully cradling his broken arm was topless. It was then that he knew he could not be in Germany anymore, that these were the deliciously decadent French or Italians who were dragging him ashore. They stretched him out on the beach, talking and shouting words that had no resemblance to Germany's no-nonsense Deutsch. Von Wessenheim got a similar treatment and was soon sitting up, his teeth chattering while a towel was draped around his pale shoulders.

The bare-breasted woman set about wrapping Hank's arm with an orange towel. Just inches from his face a man on his hands and knees was studiously examining the leaking wound in his head. Cell phones made an appearance and were jabbered into.

A gray old man wearing a ridiculous white bikini-bottom swimsuit below his hairy, fat stomach stood gazing down at him, his bushy black brows drawn together. With a sudden shout he drowned out the babbling voices: *"Regardez, tout le monde! Vous ne le reconnaissez pas?"*

Everyone turned to stare down at Hank. He lay motionless,

frozen while once again he watched potential friends turn into implacable enemies.

"C'est Thorwald, l'ancien Hitler!"

"Non," someone replied. *"Ce n'est pas possible!"*

"C'est possible! Regardez son visage!"

"Mais le nouveau Hitler, il est americain!"

The topless woman leaned closer. "Are you an American?"

Hank nodded, unaware of its implication, and she stood. She dragged up a handful of sand as she did. Without warning she hurled it down sharply into his face, stinging his eyes. *"T Salopard,"* she said, and spat on him.

The old man stomped righteously closer and kicked Hank in the ear with his bare heel. Golden sparkles burst to life inside Hank's closed eyes and he rubbed them with his single usable hand. Another kick caught him in the side and for a tiny pace of time he could not breathe. He rolled over. Despite the blows that came faster and harder he was able to rise and tried to run, but his ankles were still bound together, hobbling him. He tried to hop, blinking away the sand, but a big hairy fist sailed at him like a wrecking ball swooping out of the sky. The crunch of his nose breaking was like the snap of a wet Popsicle stick. Pain roared up his forehead and spread to his eyes, blinding him with tears. He sagged to his knees. A kick to the back of his head planted his face in the sand. When he tried to push himself up his arm was knocked out from under him. Someone took hold of his broken forearm and wrenched it back and forth; his groan of pain rose to a scream.

But he got to his knees again. One of the crowd jumped on his back to force him down. The growing crowd shouted and jostled. The person on his back was bellowing French words but not at him, was being kicked and hit in Hank's defense. He realized that he had acquired a protector but knew by experience that protectors didn't last long.

He was right. The body atop him was dragged away shrieking. He would never know who it was. Yet under the hail of blows he was still able to get to his feet again. Blood dripped from his nose to mingle with the line of blood seeping from his head. A teenaged boy jumped in front of him to caper and shout and make faces, ending the skit with a thundering punch to Hank's belly. His breath left him but he stayed on his feet, executed a kangaroo hop, executed another while his broken arm dangled lifelessly at his side. The kid skipped away waving his fist in victory and exchanging a high five with another boy.

A shadow on the sand leapt at him, blocking his way. It was another protector jabbering in French, a large woman in a uniform of some kind. After an angry round of words she was hauled aside. Hands and feet hacked at him, a pair of fists drummed on the top of his head as if to hammer him into the ground. Hank struck out blindly with his arm and connected with something soft. For his trouble he received a fist rammed straight up under his chin that kicked his head back against his upper spine; if his tongue had been hanging out it would have been amputated. He wobbled from the blow but shuffled his weight and remained upright. Ahead the narrow beach sloped up to become a hard canyon wall. If he could climb that, he knew, if he could make his way to that wall and claw his way up to the top, he might be forgiven. He had no conscious memory of having been the most hated man who had ever lived; he had no memory of having ordered millions to their deaths. But if he could crawl inch by inch up the canyon wall to the top, the world might be done with him, and it might let him be Hank Thorwald again.

A big black inner tube was dropped neatly over his head. It hula-hooped around his body and rotated to a halt around his feet, stopping him. Fists pounded his face. The gray old man shoved his bulbous nose against Hank's flat one and shouted indecipherable things. With a slap across Hank's face he turned and stormed off. Hank blinked as a colorful green swim fin smacked across his face, rocking him backward to sit down on the inner tube. It flipped up vertically and spilled him over. He laboriously disentangled himself from it. He rose again, weaving from side to side.

The canyon wall was simmering under the sun, radiating waves of colorful heat. Between the jutting layers of shale he recognized the broken black layers of hardened lava from a volcano that had lived and died so long ago that erosion had erased its height from the map; he saw a thin expanse of limestone that proved an inland sea had lapped at its banks here millions of years before this river existed. He had achieved his Ph.D. only three years ago. He had begun teaching earth science just a few months later, and had forgotten nothing of what he had been taught. None of it helped him now.

He crouched slightly and hopped forward in the sand. Laughter trilled up, snorted up. His eyes still burned from the sand that had been thrown in them but he could see well enough to hop again, one arm broken and bent, the other clenched to his chest. A spinning beach ball made of bright colors bounced off his head just as a darting shape appeared before him, a skinny young man dancing on his toes like a boxer. His scrawny fist smashed against Hank's nose, then pistoned back, rapid-fire, to split his lips against his teeth. Hank rocked on his feet but kept his eyes on the beauty revealed in the canyon wall ahead, a sculpted, sunlit gash in the earth that laid bare the evidence of its history, messages waiting all these years for an earth sciences teacher who could see and understand, and explain.

The crowd was swelling, four or five dozen feet scooping purposefully through the hot sand, angry voices yammering at each other, shouting at Hank. A sudden flapping thing swooped from the right like a bat. He blinked. It crashed into him and drove him to the ground on his ruined arm but he did not cry out. The time for that was gone. The figure sprang up. It was a kid about Sharri's age, prancing around holding an ice cream cone up high like a trophy. It was flecked with sand. He bent over Hank and stabbed the ice cream between his eyes. With his other hand spread flat, he mashed the soggy cone down until the crispy part split apart.

"*Hitler a un nouveau nez!*" he crowed when he sprang up.

Laughter. In that moment the last dregs of hesitant respect any of them might have had for Hank dissolved. Daylight darkened as legs encircled him. He scraped the cone and the warm ice cream off his face and mashed it into the sand.

When he looked up heads began blocking his view of the sky.

They closed in for the kill.

Karl-Luther von Wessenheim awakened as if from a long sleep, prodded into awareness by shouting voices. He opened his eyes and found himself staring at his crotch. Just as he lifted his head a little girl clipped his broken ankle with her foot as she darted past and he bit down on a scream, clutching his leg. His ankle was swollen to the size of his thigh, bulging grotesquely over his shoe. When the pulsing vise of pain abated enough to draw a breath, he looked himself over. His white shirt and sensible black slacks hung from his bones in rags, blasted apart by the force of his impact on the water. Peeking through the tatters was skin cooked strawberry red by the same impact. That he had not broken his neck was surprising; the fact that his foot was still attached to his body was a miracle. If the chains had not released him when the crate smashed into the river, they would have dragged him to the bottom.

He saw that the long thin beach was nearly deserted but for a handful of children splashing in the water. Swiveling himself around with his ruined ankle held high off the sand he saw that the beachgoers had packed themselves together to form a dense mob, shouting and bellowing in French. Von Wessenheim's ability with the language was respectable, but he did not need it. The word "Hitler" was unmistakable.

"*Mein Gott*," he breathed, and instantly forgot the pain. He jumped up but fell again, writhing on his back in the burning sand with his lower shin clamped in his hands and his face contorted, small tears leaking from the corners of his eyes. The immediate future looked bleak: he needed surgery and probably traction and probably a cast and a set of crutches and about two years to recuperate from this. But if Thorwald got beaten to death here at the last minute that recovery would be made in a home for the insane.

He rolled over and crawled, keeping his foot high, but when he reached the melee the people were packed together like Vienna sausages, a jostling wall of bare legs. He rose to stand on one foot, got his balance, and used his arms as a wedge to lean into the mob. A few angry faces turned, words snapped, and he was quickly elbowed away. With his balance gone he dropped butt first onto the sand like a toddler, but it saved him from using his ankle. Again, carefully, he got himself upright on one foot. Even though his pants were blown to tatters, his wallet was still where it belonged; he hauled it out and plucked it clean of money. Waving the bills overhead he tried again to break through, made a bit of progress, but his wrist was suddenly seized.

"Argent allemand!" a voice cried. A handful of people took interest, turning their eyes to follow the route from von Wessenheim's money, down his arm, and back up to his face. It was then that he realized he was flashing German money to these patriotic French. Before he could withdraw the offer his wrist was wrenched painfully until his fingers opened. He was relieved of the money; it was all tossed overhead like worthless confetti. The sunny day rained fluttering bills of green and brown. It brought more recognition to von Wessenheim than he wanted. Now several of the crowd turned to size him up, to bray anger at him. A red-faced old man stepped up, executed the open-handed French military salute, then spit in his face.

Von Wessenheim stepped back. His body weight shifted to his broken ankle and he dropped as the fires of hell seared his broken bones, but he was able to distance himself from the crowd by scurrying away on his hands and knees, moving blindly with his eyes squeezed shut against the pain. He did not know if the old Frenchman was following; he did not know how far he crawled. Something banged against his forearm and he stopped, afraid to look up and see the red-faced man, but when nothing happened he opened his eyes.

A tiny television was lying faceup in the sand. Stretched out before it were three abandoned beach towels. A trace of sound drifted out of it, a sonorous voice haltingly working through the intricacies of French pronunciation. It meant nothing. He swatted the TV away and began to turn.

"L'homme, qui etait Hitler."

He stopped. *The man who used to be Hitler?* He shuffled

back around and tilted the small screen, cupped a hand over his eyes against the glare of the sun. A man with a battered face, perhaps a professional boxer, was on the screen mouthing things. On the bottom of it, scrolling white words informed the viewers that this was a special message being broadcast live from the United States with a short translation delay. Von Wessenheim fumbled with the black box, seeking a volume control, but in the end simply mashed the whole thing to his ear.

And listened. His brows joined together and his lips moved silently as he mentally translated. What he understood struck him with the force of an executioner's ax. He got awkwardly to his feet and was unaware when the little television tumbled from his grasp. His eyes had become lifeless, as dull and emotionless as balls of waxed paper. Moments passed. Suddenly he dropped to his knees again and hauled the television to his face. Shaking, moaning, he found the volume knob and cranked it to its limit, praying that the batteries would not die before he could hear it all.

The man was still speaking. One of his arms was encased in a plaster cast. Ragged surgical tape flapped from his fingers. His words were being dutifully translated to form a horror story in French. Von Wessenheim listened in disbelief, slowly feeling his flesh sag against his own bones as he kneeled in the sand under the broiling sun, too stunned to do anything but breathe. The American man on the TV was explaining everything about Thorwald in merciless detail, details von Wessenheim would rather die than hear.

Suddenly the American television reporter looked away from the camera, frowning, and spoke to someone off camera. He rose to his feet and shouted. The camera swiveled. The picture went blank, then winked suddenly into the newsroom of a French station. Caught off guard, a man with carefully manicured red hair swiveled in his chair and looked at the camera in surprise. He nervously assembled some papers on his desk, looked above the camera, to the left of it, to the right of it. Finally, he was handed a slip of paper and announced that the American broadcast had been interrupted but would continue in a moment, then be rebroadcast in its entirety.

Von Wessenheim turned in a shambling circle, able now to use the tip of his shoe to support his weight between hops. He approached the crowd with the television tucked under one arm, pressed two fingers into the corners of his lips, and emitted an ear-splitting whistle. It was ignored. He whistled again but let it dwindle to an off-scale whine. Inspiration struck and he shifted the television to the other side, then raised his arm in a rigid Nazi salute.

"*SIEG HEIL!*" he bellowed. "*HEIL HITLER!*"

It took only seconds. They turned, almost in perfect unison, gawking at him with disbelieving eyes. Von Wessenheim lowered his arm and lifted the television overhead with both hands. He shouted at them in French: "Now I have your attention, no? This is a live broadcast from America. Mr. Thorwald was the victim of a terrible conspiracy. There is proof beyond doubt that he was not the German Führer in a past life. Proof that he was purposefully hypnotized and is the victim of a hoax."

They were sweaty and breathless, each face a picture of distrust.

"Just listen," von Wessenheim said, and set the mini-TV in the burning sand.

68

"... attended a social gathering of teachers and their wives and husbands approximately two weeks ago. It was there that I witnessed Hank Thorwald being hypnotized by a senior member of the faculty at Indiana State University. The hypnotist, professor of psychology Perry Wilson, was able to put Dr. Thorwald into a trance by merely snapping his fingers in front of Dr. Thorwald's face. I overheard a remark from Professor Wilson at that moment: *Sometimes I play dirty.* At the time I assumed this to be a part of the act."

Alan took a breath. The overhead lights were spearing his eyes and his head ached like a large rotten tooth. Just beyond the lights stood Mr. Danberry, holding a bloody Kleenex to his purpling lips. His teethprints were still on Alan's knuckles.

"First, Hank Thorwald was ordered to believe he was an ostrich and should act like one, which he did very well and without hesitation. After that he was taken back to his childhood, then to his birth. Professor Wilson then appeared to guide him to a past lifetime. When Hank revealed that he had been Adolf Hitler, Professor Wilson seemed distraught. The party ended on that sour note."

Something weird was happening, Alan's brain was playing tricks on him. For one or two fabulous seconds beautiful golden sparkles sifted through his vision, gently tumbling, several of them zipping away at high speed. But still his head, and his knee, thundered with a steady beat.

"So I revealed this on television. I had no idea of the horrors that would follow."

Danberry raised his wristwatch and tapped it. Alan had asked for one minute on air; this was the second run-through of a lengthy report.

"Let me get to the heart of this matter. Professor Wilson then faked his own death. Hank Thorwald's wife, Rebecca, came to me for assistance. Within two days we found Professor Wilson. I was transporting him to this station but he escaped. This was less than an hour ago. When I finally captured Professor Wilson again, I forced him to talk. He revealed to me that he had been born in Berlin, Germany, in 1938. His real first name was Paulus. At the end of World War Two, Paulus and his father made their way to the United States and took on new names. Paulus became Perry. His father kept his first name but changed his last name to Wilson. In reality, Perry's father was Martin Bormann, Adolf Hitler's closest confidant. In the Nuremburg trials after the war, Martin Bormann was sentenced to death for crimes against humanity. His whereabouts—his fate—were never known. Until now."

Alan took in a breath. His ears were ringing and his head pounded, the lights were becoming too bright to endure. He hoped that his family, at least his uncle Max, understood that a story like this had not come easily. "The Nazi war criminal Martin Bormann died in 1977 in a small Indiana town," he went on. "On his deathbed he asked his son, Perry, to take an oath, which he did. Perry found himself sworn to fulfill Adolf Hitler's last request of his friend Bormann, who had died too early to complete it himself. Hitler believed that within fifty years of his death Nazism would have risen naturally from the ashes because of the superiority of the Aryan race. By 1995 the new Nazi Germany would be anxious to enshrine its original founder, but wouldn't be able to find his remains. So Hitler entrusted Bormann not only with the construction of a secret burial place, but with the responsibility of revealing its location after fifty years.

"Jump to the present. In the pursuit of that duty, Perry Wilson drove a friend of mine to suicide, destroyed the Thorwald family, and got his own grandson killed. Rather than reveal himself and his family as the offspring of Hitler's right-hand man, he chose to make Hank Thorwald the enemy of all mankind, the keeper of the secret of where the Führer's bones lie. I'm sure it was a great disappointment to him that no one even bothered to ask.

"So I'm telling you now—and I think I'm being viewed in many countries via satellite—if you are holding Dr. Thorwald captive, or if you know where he is, this is the final truth: he was not Hitler in a past life. I know because I was at Professor Wilson's side when he made his dying confession. And I can prove that by showing the police where his body is. And if anyone out there needs *more* proof, here it is."

He raised his arms into view. "His blood is coagulated under my fingernails, it has soaked into this cast on my arm. And that's because about thirty minutes ago I murdered the evil son of a bitch with my own two hands."

Alan stood and extended a finger, then drew it across his throat: cut to a commercial. When the little red light above the camera's lens winked out, he took a step into the darkness. A horn as piercing as the siren of a fire truck screamed suddenly in his head. It drove him to his knees. He tried to lift his arms to cover his ears but one of them stayed dangling at his side while the other rose up trembling. Blood slipped out of both his nostrils, staining his jeans as he wobbled.

Then a tissue brushed against his mouth and was pushed up under his leaking nose. He cracked his eyes open and through a fresh burst of sparkles saw that it was Mr. Danberry.

The horn quit blowing. The silence was wonderful. Alan felt himself slip forward and fall, as if into a pool of warm water. His cheek bounced slightly on the sensible gray carpet. In a short time an ambulance was there, but by then he had drifted too far away to ever come back.

✠

NINE DAYS SPÄTER

The photojournalist's name was Rex DeCamp and he was fairly good at what he did but he had not encountered much success. His byline had appeared in over thirty newspapers and magazines but none of his writing was top-drawer stuff and the photos he took were rarely published. He had driven halfway across the country to cash in on the Thorwald-Hitler story but had wound up being a faceless reporter surrounded by half a hundred others on the Thorwald's front lawn. His only claim to fame now was that he had stayed on in Terre Haute while the others left, but only because his car was in the shop for the next three days. Some big deal about the transmission again.

Rex was hiking nervously down a corridor on the third floor of Regency Hospital with a notebook in his pocket and an expensive Minolta camera in his hand, hoping to find Hank Thorwald or his wife, even his daughter. The police protection for the Thorwalds had finally ended because now that the world knew he had been duped, interest in him had evaporated. All that Rex DeCamp wanted this warm afternoon was a postscript to the Hitler story, some thoughts now that it was all over. And perhaps a picture of Thorwald. Rex had *Life* magazine and about four grand in mind but would settle for *Esquire* and two thousand.

The third floor seemed strangely unpopulated. It appeared that construction was under way; the ceiling tiles had been removed and some of the pipes were shiny and new. Rex had scoured the first two floors without luck, but instinct told him—bolstered by the nursing staff's insistence that no

Thorwald was here anywhere—that a Thorwald was here someplace. He began opening each door he came to to peek inside. Some rooms had been stripped down to the plaster, others were repositories for stacks of mattresses and hospital gear. The police had been clever to house Thorwald up here. No hospital would bed patients in a construction zone. And no average photojournalist would expect it.

But Rex DeCamp did—until he had circled the third floor three times, eventually leaving every door open, and had found nothing. The elevator door was ruled off-limits by three wide ribbons of yellow contractor's tape. Signs indicated that the stairwell could be found nearby. For a while he stood motionless, probing his own instincts, wondering if he had any at all.

The elevator doors slid open. Rex ducked out of sight. A tall man with pleasantly graying hair took a step out. He had a Dr Pepper in each hand and three Cokes pressed to his chest. Rex watched him duck artfully through the three strands of tape, then stride away. After several cautious seconds Rex rose and followed. The man stopped at a long pleated wall that Rex assumed held the nurses' lounge or the like. He juggled the sodas to get a hand free. A latch clicked and the wall, made of shiny white vinyl slats, accordioned together. As soon as it was shut again, Rex hurried over and pressed an ear to it. He heard voices. Someone laughed.

He clutched his camera tighter and popped the latch, wanting to peek inside. The pleated door opened about three feet before relaxing to a stop. He stood exposed with his mouth hanging open.

"Who the hell are you?" Donald D. Dutchenreimer demanded. Rex looked at him, then at the other people: some guy with dark hair was sitting cross-legged on a chair with a Coke in his hand. He rose.

"No reporters!" Detective Steven Gleeworth shouted.

Rex blinked. There were three hospital beds jammed side by side in the big room. A little girl—she was Sharri Thorwald, he knew at a glance. And in the next bed, Rebecca Thorwald with a cigarette in her mouth. Beside her, lying on his own bed, was Hank Thorwald himself. Without wasting a second Rex swept his camera up and set about focusing it.

An arm encircled his neck from behind and jerked him a couple of inches off the floor. His Minolta left his hands and smacked on the linoleum. A voice growled in his ear: "You tell anybody who you found here and I'll have a warrant out for you so fast you won't make it out of the building."

"Grrk," Rex replied.

"Now get the hell out of here!"

When he was dropped Rex DeCamp bent to snatch up his camera, but froze in place. It had broken into three large pieces and a bunch of smaller ones. He had red-lined his only credit card to get it and was still trying to pay for it. With a groan he sank to his knees and began to gather it all up. He was sticking the pieces into various pockets when Rebecca Thorwald spoke. Her tone was not kind.

"Which tabloid do *you* work for?"

He rocked back on his heels. "Strictly freelance, Mrs. Thorwald. I sold a couple of pieces to *The Saturday Evening Post* last year."

"So what do you want here? The story's supposed to be old and dead."

He finished picking up the pieces and got tiredly to his feet. Detective Gleeworth took hold of the back of Rex's collar and snapped him upright; Rex answered. "I thought I'd do an article on your family now that everything is over, kind of like a P.S. on a letter, something upbeat. I was hoping *Life* magazine might run it."

Hank Thorwald, swathed in bandages and flat on his back, raised the arm that was not in a cast. "Rebecca? Maybe this is the guy for us."

Gleeworth walked away and sat again, sucking furiously at his Dr Pepper.

Rebecca glanced sharply at Rex. "Look at us, Mr. Reporter. Look at how we've ended up. Think you could be the first reporter with enough guts to put some of the blame on your own media? To hear what *we* went through as a family? Think you could sell it to a magazine?"

"I'd sure try," Rex said eagerly. "Maybe even write a book about it."

Rebecca looked at Sharri. She was sitting cross-legged in bed holding a small video game in both hands. She tore her attention from it long enough to perform a shrug.

"Hank?"

He closed his purpled eyes. "Stress the fact that I'm unemployed," he said through his teeth and the wires that held his jaw in place. "We'll split the royalties fifty-fifty."

"Actually," Rebecca told Rex, "he's been offered positions in almost twenty universities. Book publishers and movie producers have started calling. Everything's getting crazy. Good crazy, this time."

Rex swallowed. "Guess I just happen to be in the right place at the right time." With trembling hands he dug his notebook and pen out of his shirt pocket. Gleeworth jumped up and stalked out of the room, muttering. Rex maneuvered his vacant chair to the bedside. "Okay," he said, "where would you like to begin?"

Rebecca looked at the blank wall above him, her eyes growing hazy as she remembered. "I couldn't quit smoking. It started with that, that I couldn't quit smoking. So we went to a hypnotist . . ."

THE SECRETS BURIED
UNTERGRUND

The crew of *Grundwerk Deutsche Metalle* worked late into the night, digging immense buckets of dirt that had hidden under the pavement of Berlin for half a century. The glare of halogen light trees cut the streets and sidewalks into long strips of black and white and there was no rain.

The crew boss strode to the middle of the operation and raised a hand. The rattle of heavy machinery sank to an idle. He made hand signals followed by two thumbs down. The idling machines rumbled for another moment, then quit.

"Alles fertig, nach Hause gehen," he cried, waving his arms, and when the men were gone walked back to the shallowest slope of the huge crater that his crew had dug. The loose earth gave way partially under his feet as he descended, sending a small cascade of gravel and mud to the bottom, where Karl-Luther von Wessenheim stood with a powerful flashlight in one hand and a crowbar in the other. The beam jittered in the dark: nerves. He had been to hell and back for this moment, had needed eleven stainless steel pins to hold his shattered ankle together while it healed. Even now, and probably for the rest of his life, he walked with a pronounced limp.

The crew chief stood beside him. "It's definitely a man-made object," he said, and reached out to rap it with his knuckles. "Strikes me as being made of titanium or the like. No rust."

Von Wessenheim was closely examining every inch of the huge vertical slab, wondering if this were the side or the front of the tomb. There did not seem to be a doorway. He set about gouging out the soil that framed it, marking its perimeter, then set the crowbar aside and began digging with his fingers, hoping for signs that it could be opened from this side. Loons were nearby, calling into the night in their strange highs and lows; an elephant trumpeted. Berlin's huge *Tiergarten*, the famous zoo, was only a block away. The area had been one of the last strongholds of German resistance at the end of the war.

He felt something, an indentation. When he curled his fingers into the niche and pulled, the entire structure let out a groan. His heartbeat doubled its pace.

"What a strange sound," the crew boss said. "What is this thing, exactly?"

Von Wessenheim whirled around. "You may go now. Thank you for a job well done."

"Some kind of bunker, it looks like. Maybe left over from the war."

"It's late, you'd best get going. I'll take care of the halogen lights."

He frowned and stepped forward. "Hey, shine a light on this," he said, brushing a layer of grit from the metal with a hand. "Marks of some sort."

Von Wessenheim complied, wondering only how to get rid of the man. But what he was exposing almost dropped von Wessenheim into a dead faint.

"A swastika," the crew boss said. "I was right."

"Go away!" von Wessenheim brayed. "Go home, you've finished your work, send me a bill and I will pay it!"

"The government should know about this," he said as if having heard nothing. "This could be of historical value."

Von Wessenheim cast the flashlight aside and took the man by the shoulders. *"You're fired, do you hear me? Fired!"*

Recognition dawned in his eyes. "Fired? But what have I done?"

"Your services are simply terminated. Here." Von Wessenheim dug out his wallet and offered handfuls of cash. "Take it all. Sue me if you like. But for the love of God, *leave me alone!"*

He left grumbling but with both hands stuffed full of money. Von Wessenheim picked up the flashlight, then looked up with fearful eyes. The halogen lights above shone brighter than the lights of a circus. He clawed his way out of the crater, favoring his ankle, and hurried to kill the generators. The light died and he scrambled back down. He scrubbed at the exposed swastika on the metal door of the tomb, then aimed the flashlight at it:

Hier Wartet der Führer des Deutschen Reiches

Here waits the Führer of the German Empire. Von Wessenheim collapsed to his knees and crossed an arm over his eyes. Two small hot tears seeped out. On the French riverbank he had nearly died of despair when the television said that the Thorwald affair had been a hoax—but he had not heard the entire broadcast. When the crowd on the beach was settled in utter silence to hear the broadcast, von Wessenheim had tended to Thorwald, but had still listened.

Hank Thorwald had been given the ghost of Martin Bormann. Lying there smashed and broken in the sand, von Wessenheim was certain that Thorwald was dying. As he had done in the jail cell, he begged Thorwald's subconscious mind for one last dispensation.

So here he was. He stood up now with the weight of history on his stooped shoulders, and found the niche in the door. He pulled. Air hissed. If not for the uneven piles of earth it had to scrape across, the door would have been weightless. He took a shaking breath when it was open and shined the flashlight inside the utterly black cavern.

Gold gleamed. The walls were dressed with flags. Von Wessenheim took a faltering step inside, his heart thundering in his chest, his mouth as dry as hot desert sand. The air was thick and musky, dead. Two golden sarcophaguses sat side by side on two exquisitely carved wooden biers. He went to the smaller one and swept his light over it. The youthful face and body of Eva Braun rose from the gold in the fashion of King Tutankhamen. Von Wessenheim turned in a stumbling circle to inspect the walls. Swastika flags of red and white and black, maps of Europe dotted with swastikas, crossed swords with SS adornments and black tassels.

He used a hand to test the lid. It rose with ease, counter-balanced somehow. A dank, moldy smell bloomed up and he stared down at the earthly remains of Hitler's wife, a skeleton with patches of skin curled like confetti and a dark clump of hair still clinging to her skull. He swung the lid back down, shaking so violently that the flashlight nearly fell from his hand. Forcing his lungs to suck in gulps of the dead air, he steadied himself against her coffin until a form of calmness intervened. It would make no sense to drop dead at the pinnacle of his success.

In time he was able to move to the other sarcophagus. Never much one to adorn himself with baubles, this one bore no likeness of Hitler's face but had a swastika imprinted in the gold, the insignia that had guided Hitler and the German nation from early victory into total ruin. Von Wessenheim extended a trembling hand and touched it. The lid wafted open. He shut his eyes, nearly weeping again, aware that this moment would be emblazoned forever in the history books, that it was the crowning glory of the House of Wessenheim. He opened his eyes and aimed the jittering flashlight inside.

Empty.

His scream awakened Berliners three blocks away.